Praise for *Lord of the Isles*

'Unlike most modern fantasy, David Drake's *Lord of the Isles* is an epic with the texture of the legends of yore, with rousing action and characters to cheer for' Terry Goodkind

'*Lord of the Isles* has it all – treacherous queens, faithful and faithless courtiers, peasants and shepherds who are more than they seem, wizardry fair and most foul, quests, love beyond the grave, and all manner of despicable plotting and unabashed heroics . . . A fast-reading and complex fantasy adventure.' L. E. Modesitt, Jr.

'True brilliance is as rare as a perfect diamond or supernova. *Lord of the Isles* is truly brilliant. Plot, pace, excitement, characterization, but most of all the finely honed and superb use of language mark this as one of those exceptional books you will want to have bound in leather and pass on to your grandchildren.' Morgan Llywelyn

'Some authors are powerful storytellers. Others evoke images that we did not believe existed. When the two are combined you have a powerful writer. *Lord of the Isles* is a magnificent example.' Gordon R. Dickson

'A genre fantasy with more suspense, action, and horror than most . . . Drake's magic is more complex than fantasy magic, and the dangers of uncontrollable power form an important theme here. His settings and magical creatures provide surprise and drama as well as plenty of color. This substantial fantasy, in which moral and physical threats are serious and the actions of the characters have real consequences, will appeal to those tired of watered-down myth.' *Publishers Weekly*

Also by David Drake in Millennium

LORD OF THE ISLES

QUEEN of DEMONS

David Drake

This edition published in Great Britain in 1999 by
Millennium
An imprint of Victor Gollancz
Orion House, 5 Upper St Martin's Lane,
London WC2H 9EA

To receive information on the Millennium list, e-mail us at:
smy@orionbooks.co.uk

A CIP catalogue record for this book
is available from the British Library

ISBN 1 85798 823 X

Printed in Great Britain by
Clays Ltd, St Ives plc

To Jennie Faries,
a neat person and a cherished member of my
extended family

Acknowledgments

Among the people who helped on this one were Dan Breen, who would have graced the very finest of scriptoria; Mark L. Van Name and Allyn Vogel (yes, I worked another computer to death); Sandra Miesel and John Squires, who separately provided material that made it possible for *Queen of Demons* to develop the way it did; and my wife, Jo, who was unfailingly supportive while under the pressure of the project I diverged further and further from what passes for my norm. I should also mention that my editor, Dave Hartwell, practiced a policy of benign neglect under circumstances where less trusting people would have worried more publicly about when they would see the book.

Thank you all.

Author's Note

The readers who identify Celondre with Horace are correct; the translation is my own. My Aldebrand is not Macrobius but rather a less-able analogue of him. Macrobius' *Saturnalia* has given me many hours of pleasure and puzzlement. I was trained in history but my temperament is that of an antiquarian, a very different thing. Fiction is a better world for me than the snake pits of Academe could ever be.

As before, the general religion of the Isles is based on that of Sumer.

The words of power, *voces mysticae,* used by wizards in this volume are from binding spells of classical times. They are not part of my religion, but they *were* an aspect of the religious belief of millions of people who were just as intelligent as you and I are. Personally, I didn't care to pronounce the *voces mysticae* when I was working on the book.

Prologue

Valence III, crowned King of the Isles, shivered in the unseasonably warm night as the wizard Silyon scribed the words of his incantation on the transom of an age-crumbled gateway. The moon was two days past new and would be scarcely a ghost of itself when it finally rose. The only light came from the lantern whose wick gleamed through panels cut from sheets of mica so thin they were almost perfectly clear.

Nearby the sacrifice sighed in her drugged sleep. A silken bag hid the girl's outlines from a distance, but Attaper and the other Blood Eagles of the escort must have known what the king and his wizard brought with them whenever they visited the ancient ruins.

The Blood Eagles would be as silent as they were loyal: to the death. Even so, Valence had seen disgust in Attaper's eyes as the Blood Eagles' commander watched him and Silyon carrying their burden the last of the way alone.

Valence snorted with anger as he remembered that look. How *dare* Attaper judge him? A soldier's duties were simple: to kill or to die, but never to question. A king had to wrestle with more difficult situations, where right was never very different from wrong.

But for all that, Valence shivered again.

Silyon finished the incantation, a circle of words in the Old Script. His body was tattooed, and he wore slivers of bone through his earlobes. He set the small tripod within the circle, then pulled on gloves embroidered with silver thread. He smiled at Valence.

Valence suspected that the symbols picked out on the

back of the gloves had no meaning beyond decoration, despite the wizard's hints that they held dark truths. "Get on with it!" he snarled. He resented the fact that this ugly little man from Dalopo could treat him as an equal on the strength of the acts they performed together.

"As you wish, sire," Silyon said, still smirking. He removed the mirror, a fist-sized teardrop of greenish obsidian, from its wash-leather sack and fitted it carefully onto the silver hook hanging on a swivel from the tripod. Valence couldn't imagine how a hole had been drilled through the delicate tail of the volcanic glass without shattering it to dust, but that was the least of the object's wonders.

Silyon began to chant, touching an athame of black wood from his native Dalopo to each of the ancient words as he pronounced it: *"Hayad pikir tasimir . . ."*

A whippoorwill had been calling at a distance. It fell silent, but another took up the rhythm closer by.

"Wakuiem gabiyeh worsiyeh," the wizard said, twisting his lips around syllables with no human meaning. They were intended to be heard not by men but by the powers on which the cosmos turned. These forces were neither gods nor demons. They caused the stars to make their ceaseless circles, the seasons to change on Earth, and all things seen and unseen to move.

The Sun, the symbol of light and life, and Malkar, the symbol of dark and death, controlled all things. But how could a mere human being know which was which?

"Archedama phochense pseusa rerta . . ."

The ruined palace in which Valence and the wizard knelt was that of the Tyrants of Valles, a father, son, and grandson all named Eldradus. Through wizardry the trio had ruled the island of Ornifal for seventy years after the collapse of the Old Kingdom, then had fallen in turn to a revolt of the island's nobles. After the Tyrants, Ornifal had begun the rise from barbarism that now made the Dukes of Ornifal at least in name the Kings of the Isles.

The first Eldradus had built his palace a few miles outside the existing port of Valles. Those who overthrew the line had returned the seat of power to the city itself, so for nine hundred years the tyrant's construction had decayed without repair. Roots forced apart the stones of walls; roofs fell in when the beams supporting them rotted.

Nine hundred years. . . . But the underground vault at the center of the palace complex was older by ages beyond counting.

"*Threkisithphe amracharara ephoiskere . . .*" Silyon chanted. Shadows moved on the polished surface of volcanic glass, but it didn't reflect the legs of the tripod from which it hung.

The Tyrants of Valles had built their palace on the site of ruins buried deep in the loam of an ancient forest. Until Eldradus had the trees cut and the soil planed flat, no one—no one but the wizard himself—knew that below were foundations of black basalt laid on a Cyclopean scale.

At the center of the new palace the tyrants had raised a four-sided monumental arch over an ancient circular curb. The opening was the oculus, the eye, in the ceiling of a vast domed room buried underground.

That chamber could have been a tomb or a storage room or even part of a sewer system from the dim past. It was none of those things; or perhaps, now that Valence forced himself to think about it, all of them together.

"*Thoumison kat plauton!*" Silyon concluded, shouting out the final syllables. The cosmos itself tried to choke a wizard's voice when he spoke an incantation of this magnitude, thickening his tongue and rasping her throat to the texture of dry sand.

The obsidian mirror trembled with the sound of the Beast's laughter. "Greetings, humans," said the deep voice in Valence's skull. "Have you brought my meal?"

The Beast laughed again. Silyon's smile froze into a rictus; the king's visage had no more expression than a roughly sawn board. Valence hated himself for what he was doing, but the queen had left him no choice.

The green glass depths of the mirror were alive with bright mist, but thus far tonight Valence didn't see a specific image in them. Not long after the Dalopan came to the king with his mirror and his wizardry, Valence had dropped a blazing torch through the eye of the dome. The flaring light showed only stone blocks mottled by patches of lichen, exactly what one would expect in a chamber sealed for the better part of a millennium.

But halfway to the floor fifty feet below the surface, the torch had disappeared as suddenly as if it had never been. Valence assumed that the sacrifices he and Silyon lowered through the oculus vanished the same way, but he'd never had the desire—or the courage—to watch.

"The four whom the queen pursued have eluded her," the Beast said with no transition. "The two humans and two Halflings who come from Haft. I will draw them to me here."

Valence was kneeling, because his legs trembled uncontrollably if he tried to stand while conversing with the creature whom Silyon had summoned. "What are their names?" he asked.

"What do I care for the names of humans?" the Beast said. The king's ears heard nothing; the terrible voice thundered in his mind. "They all taste the same, whatever they call themselves!"

The mists within the obsidian parted. A wedge-shaped head like that of a serpent lashed out. Valence flinched even though his conscious mind knew the shape was only an image reflected in stone. Sometimes he saw this reptile head within the mirror; sometimes a creature equally monstrous but mammalian, a dog or a bear or perhaps a dog-headed ape.

And sometimes what Valence saw was a bulk whose vastness was only an impression. There was nothing in the mirror's vision to provide scale.

The Beast gave its grating laugh; the snake's head

blurred back into the mist. Valence's fear had amused the thing.

"They are Garric or-Reise and Sharina os-Reise," the Beast said. Humor still tinged the soundless voice. "The male is descended from King Lorcan, who hid the Throne of Malkar, which the queen thinks will bring her power over the cosmos. The Halflings are Cashel or-Kenset and Ilna os-Kenset. Their father was human and their mother a sprite. I will bring the ones I need here, and they will release me."

"I'll direct that they be arrested as soon as they—" Valence said. He paused. "As soon as possible."

He would have continued, "—come within my domains," but what did Valence III rule nowadays?

Certainly not the Isles as a whole; no one had truly been King of the Isles since the fall of the Old Kingdom a thousand years before. Twenty years in the past, when Valence took the throne on the death of his uncle, he could at least claim to rule Ornifal. Now, with the minions of the queen using wizardry to replace his officials in one post after another, Valence's will was obeyed without question only within the walls of his palace. He might not long be safe even there.

The queen left him no choice. For his own sake and that of the kingdom, he *had* to ally himself with the Beast.

"As you please," said the voice, echoing as if the Beast stood in the domed chamber below. "The male has a better right to the throne than you do. But all you *must* do is to feed me; I will do the rest."

Across the hanging mirror from Valence, the wizard's face spasmed in an involuntary grimace. Did he too regret the cost of this alliance . . . ?

A rope was fixed to a harness around the sacrifice. The two men lowered the girl hand over hand, feeling the unseen body swing gently below them. The coil of rope was only half used when the weight came off it; the sacrifice had reached the floor of the chamber.

The men looked at each other. Valence nodded and

stepped back. Silyon dropped the rest of the coil through the oculus and quickly packed his apparatus.

They walked as quickly as possible to where the guards waited with the horses. The lantern swinging in the king's hand threw distorted shadows across the ruins; the forest had long since recovered the site the Tyrants had cleared.

The Blood Eagles straightened to attention. The men's faces were as cold and still as the metal of their spotless black armor.

"Your Majesty," Attaper said, swinging the head of the king's horse around so that the beast was ready to mount.

A terrible scream reverberated from the ruins behind them. None of the men moved or spoke for the long seconds that it echoed in the night.

When the girl's cry had echoed to a halt, the commander of the Blood Eagles turned his head deliberately to the side and spat. Then he faced his king again.

There was no expression at all on Attaper's face.

Day 2 of the Fourth Month (Heron)

Garric or-Reise leaned on the rail of a balcony that existed only in his fancy, watching his physical body practice swordsmanship in the garden below. He wasn't asleep, but his conscious mind had become detached from the body's motions. In this reverie he met and spoke with the ghost of his ancestor who had died a thousand years before.

Garric gestured toward where his physical self hacked at a post with his lead-weighted sword. "It's as boring as plowing a field," he said. "And there at least you have a furrow to show for it."

"You've got the build to be a swordsman, lad," said King Carus from the railing beside Garric. He grinned engagingly. "At least they always told me I did, and my worst enemies never denied my skill with a sword. But to be really good, you have to go through the exercises till every movement is a reflex."

He pretended to study the clouds, picture perfect in a blue sky. "Of course," he went on, "you can always save yourself the effort and let me take over running your body when there's need for that sort of work."

Roses climbed a supporting pillar and flooded their red blooms across the balcony's solid-seeming stone. When Garric was in this state he had the feeling that nothing existed beyond the corners of his vision: if he turned his head very quickly, he might see formless mist instead of the walls of the building from which the balcony jutted.

Garric grinned at the king, pretending that he hadn't heard beneath the banter a wistful note in the voice of the man who hadn't had a physical form for a thousand years. "My father didn't raise me to shirk duties in order to save myself effort," Garric said. "And I don't care to be beholden to another man for work that I ought to be able to do myself."

Carus laughed with the full-throated enthusiasm of a man to whom the strong emotions came easily, joy and love and a fiercely hot anger that slashed through any obstruction. "You could have had a worse father than Reise," he said. "And I'm not sure that you could have had a better one."

He turned his attention to the figure below, Garric's body swinging the blunt practice sword. The men who guarded the compound of Master Latias, the rich merchant who was sheltering Garric and his friends here in Erdin, watched the exercises with approval and professional interest.

"You lead with your right leg," Carus said, gesturing. "One day a smart opponent will notice that your foot moves an eyeblink before your sword arm does. Then you'll find his point waiting for your chest just that much before your own blade gets home."

"I'm tired," Garric said. "My body's tired, I mean."

Carus smiled with a glint of steel in his gray eyes. "You think you're tired, lad," he said softly. "When you've been through the real thing, you'll know what tired is."

"Sorry," Garric muttered. Even as the words came out of his mouth he'd been embarrassed. He'd reacted defensively instead of listening to what he was being told. He grinned. "A scythe uses a lot of the same muscles, but I never had the wheat swing back at me. I'll practice till I've got it right."

The king's expression softened into bright laughter again. "Aye, you will," he said. "Already the strength you put into your strokes makes you good enough for most work."

The two men on the dream balcony were so similar that were they visible no one could have doubted their relationship. Carus had been a man of forty when wizardry swallowed down his ship. He was broad-shouldered, long-limbed, and moved with a grace that gulls might envy as they slid across the winds.

Garric would be eighteen in a month's time. He had his height and strength, but compared to the full adult growth of the king beside him he looked lanky. Both were tanned and as fit as an active life could make a man. Garric was barefoot with the wool tunic and trousers of a Haft peasant. Carus wore a blue velvet doublet and suede breeches, with high boots of leather dyed a bright red.

On the king's head was a circlet of gold, the diadem of the Kings of the Isles. It had sunk with him a thousand years before.

"There's more to being King of the Isles than just being able to use a sword," Carus said. His elbows were on the railing; he rested his chin for a moment on his tented fingers, an oddly contemplative pose for a man who was usually in motion.

He turned and looked at Garric. "Part of the reason I failed and let the kingdom go smash," he said, "was that my sword was always the first answer I picked to solve a problem. But you'll need a sword too, lad, when you're king."

"I'm not a king!" Garric said, grimacing in embarrassment. "I'm just a . . ."

What was he really? A youth from Haft, a backwater since the Old Kingdom fell. A peasant who'd been taught to read and appreciate the ancient poets by his father, Reise, an educated man who had once served in the royal palace in Valles and later had been secretary to the Countess of Haft in Carcosa.

A peasant who'd faced and killed a wizard who'd come close to assembling all the power of evil. A youth who had in his head the ghost of his ancestor, the last and greatest king the Isles had ever known.

"Well, I'm not a king," Garric finished lamely.

"But you will be," Carus said, his tone genial but as certain as the strokes of his mighty sword arm. "Not because you're of my blood; that just lets me speak with you, lad. You'll be King of the Isles because you can do the job. If you don't, the crash that brought down civilization when *I* failed will look like a party. All that'll be left this time will be blood and plague and slaughter till there's no one left to kill."

Carus smiled. "But we won't let that happen," he said. "On our *souls* we won't, King Garric! Will we?"

Two of Garric's companions had joined the spectators in the garden below. Cashel or-Kenset was nearly Garric's height and built like the trunk of an old oak. He and his sister Ilna came from the same village as Garric, Barca's Hamlet on the east coast of Haft. They and Garric's blond sister Sharina had been friends for as long as any of the four of them could remember.

Tenoctris, the old woman with Cashel now, was as complete a contrast with Cashel as Garric could imagine. A force that she refused to call fate had plucked her from her own time and carried her a thousand years forward to deposit her on the coast of Barca's Hamlet. Tenoctris was a wizard. She was a wizard with very little power, *she* said; but she understood where others merely acted—and by their actions brought destruction on themselves and those about them.

"No," Garric said. "We won't let that happen."

He'd have given anything to return to the life for which he'd been raised, the son of the innkeeper in a tiny village where nothing was expected to change except the seasons of the year. He couldn't go back, though.

The forces that ruled the cosmos were reaching another thousand-year peak. In the days of King Carus, a wizard with unbridled power had broken the kingdom into individual islands warring with one another and within themselves. Civilization had partly risen from that ruin; but if the cycle were repeated, Barca's Hamlet would be ground into the mud as surely as great cities like Carcosa on Haft, capital of the Old Kingdom of the Isles, had been shattered when Carus died.

"Join your friends," Carus said with a cheerful gesture. "Besides, you shouldn't overdo or you'll take more from the muscles than you get back from the exercise. Though you're young and you won't believe that any more than I did when I was your age."

The king, the balcony, and the sky above dissolved. Garric's mind slipped from reverie back into his sweaty, gasping body on the exercise ground. The shield on his left arm was a fiery weight, and all the muscles of his right side quivered with the strain of swinging the practice sword.

Garric reeled back, wheezing. Every time he'd struck the unyielding target, his hand had absorbed the shock. Garric's palm now felt as though a wagon had rolled over it. He stuck the sword down in ground he'd stamped hard.

"Ho!" Garric said, clearing his lungs. He fumbled with the strap that transferred some of the shield's weight to his shoulders. Cashel's big hands were there before him, lifting the buckler of cross-laminated wood away as easily as if it had been a lace doily.

The captain of the guards stepped forward. Serians like Master Latias were pacifists, unwilling to use force on another human being. That didn't prevent them from hiring men who had different philosophies, though. The men guarding this compound in Erdin were hard-bitten by any standards, and their chief looked to be the equal of any two of his subordinates.

"You said you hadn't any experience with a sword, sir," he said to Garric. "But that's not what I'd have thought to see you using one just now."

Garric had gotten back enough of his breath to speak. "An ancestor of mine was a great swordsman," he said, half-smiling. "Perhaps some of his skill passed to me."

He touched his chest. A coronation medal of King Carus hung from a silk ribbon beneath his tunic. Garric's father had given him the medal the day Tenoctris washed up in Barca's Hamlet. From that day everything started to change. . . .

"Tenoctris and I thought we'd go for a walk around the harbor," Cashel said. His voice was slow, steady, and powerful, a mirror of the youth himself. He shrugged. "My sister's got Sharina and Liane weaving with her. It's some special idea, she says."

Cashel and his sister Ilna had been orphaned when they were seven, making their way since then by skill and dogged determination. Garric was stronger than most of the men he'd met, but he knew his friend Cashel was stronger than anyone he was likely *ever* to meet.

"It's been a great many years since anyone called me a girl, and nobody ever mistook me for a weaver," Tenoctris said. She spoke with a bright, birdlike enthusiasm that made her seem only a fraction of the age Garric's eyes judged her to be. "We thought you might like to come with us, though if you want to practice more . . . ?"

She nodded to the post. Despite the blunt edge of the

practice sword, Garric had hammered fresh chips away all around the wood.

"No, I'm done for the day," Garric said. "Let me sponge off and I'll come with you."

He chuckled. "If you overdo with exercise," he added, "your muscles lose more than they gain."

Neither his friends nor the guards understood Garric's amusement, but the king lurking somewhere in the back of Garric's mind laughed his approval.

Cashel or-Kenset was satisfied with life as he sauntered along Erdin's busy waterfront with his friends. He was usually satisfied. Cashel didn't require much to be happy, and he'd found hard work would bring all but one of the things he needed.

The only thing missing had been Garric's sister, Sharina, the girl Cashel had secretly loved for as long as he could remember. Now he had Sharina too.

Cashel and Garric strolled at a pace Tenoctris found comfortable. Though she was a frail old woman, she nonetheless moved faster than the sheep who were Cashel's most frequent companions.

He'd watched flocks on the pastures south of Barca's Hamlet since he was seven years old. As he got his growth he'd been hired more and more often for tasks that required strength: ditching, tree-felling, moving boulders in locations too cramped and awkward to admit a yoke of oxen to do the work. Folk in the borough had quickly learned that you could depend on Cashel to do a careful job of any task you set him.

"Is that a shrine to the Lady?" Garric asked. He nodded toward an altar at the head of a brick quay stretching out into the channel of the River Erd. It would be discourteous to gesture too openly toward a deity, and in a strange place—as Erdin certainly was to a pair of Haft peasants—there was the chance someone would get angry with the boorish strangers.

Not that men the size of Cashel or Garric were likely to be attacked. Even so, they'd been well brought up and didn't want to give offense.

The altar was a carved female figure holding a shallow bowl. Three sailors were burning incense in it. The statue wore loose pantaloons and a sleeveless jacket that left her limestone breasts bare. Cashel had never seen garments like those, and certainly not on an image of the Lady, the Queen of Heaven. The incense surprised him into a sneeze.

"That's the Lady as she's worshipped on Shengy," Tenoctris said. She grinned ruefully. "I should say, in my day that was the costume the Lady wore on Shengy. But you have to remember that in my day, Erdin was an uninhabited marsh and the Earls of Sandrakkan were a coarse lot who lived like a gang of bandits in a castle on the eastern tip of the island."

"But the sailors aren't from Shengy, are they?" Garric said. "I thought folk from there are short and dark."

"Sailors tend to take spiritual help from whoever offers it," Tenoctris said. "They're more aware than most people of how much their safety depends on things they can't control."

In a softer voice, one meant as much for herself as for the ears of her companions, the old wizard added, "I sometimes wish that I could believe in the Great Gods myself. All I see are powers, and it's only because of my human weakness that I even call them Good and Evil. I'm sure that the cosmos doesn't put any such labels on the forces that move it."

"The cosmos may not care if people serving Malkar sink the Isles into the sea," Garric said as he fingered the medallion he wore under his tunic. "But we care, and we're not going to let it happen."

"I believe in the Lady and the Shepherd," Cashel said without anger. "I believe that Duzi watches over the flocks of Barca's Hamlet . . . not that the sheep didn't need me as well, silly beasts that they are."

Tenoctris was a good woman, and a smart one who was even better educated than Garric. She could believe whatever she pleased. But the truth for Cashel was usually a simple thing, and what other folk believed didn't change that truth.

Cashel was big. He moved with deliberation because he'd learned early that a man of his size and strength broke things by being hasty. He counted on his fingers, and the only reason he could write his name was that Garric had spent days teaching him to laboriously draw the letters.

A lot of people thought Cashel was stupid. Well, maybe he was. But a lot of people thought an ox was stupid too because it was strong and slow and did its job without the shrill temperament of a horse.

The people who thought an ox was stupid were wrong.

The three of them skirted a stack of hardwood being unloaded from an odd-looking twin-hulled freighter. The logs had a pronounced ring pattern that would stripe boards like lengths of Ilna's fancy weaving.

"Tigerwood from Kanbesa," Garric said in wonder. "Brought here, all the way across the Inner Sea to panel some merchant's house. Erdin's certainly grown since the Old Kingdom fell."

Cashel eyed the wood with critical appraisal. Pretty enough, he supposed, but he'd take oak—or hickory, like the quarterstaff he carried here in Erdin just as he had in the pastures back on Haft.

Cashel didn't carry the quarterstaff just for a weapon. He'd shaped the tough wood with his own hands. It was a part of Haft and a part of Cashel before he left Barca's Hamlet to wander the Isles. The smooth, familiar hickory made him feel more at home among these close-set buildings and a crowd as thick as fishflies in spring. Why shouldn't he carry it?

"Doesn't Sandrakkan have forests?" he asked. He found Garric's comments about the Old Kingdom odd. Cashel understood when Tenoctris said something about the world of a thousand years ago: she'd lived in it, after all. Sometimes Garric sounded as though he had too.

"There're a lot of forests, especially in the north," Garric said, "but they don't grow fancy species like tigerwood. It's just for show, so that a rich man can brag that he brought wood a thousand miles to cover his dining hall."

Cashel frowned as he planned what he wanted to say. A merchant passing in the other direction gave him a startled look. The man's bodyguard gripped the hilt of a sword that certainly wasn't for show. Cashel took no notice.

"There're goods from just about everyplace here," he said. He grinned slowly, the even-tempered youth from Barca's Hamlet again. "Bags of wool from Haft, I shouldn't wonder. People seem happy enough. It's peaceful and they get on with their lives."

Tenoctris nodded, waiting for Cashel's point. Garric was listening intently also.

"But if it turns to fights and demons and dead things walking, they all lose," Cashel said forcefully. "Why do they let that happen? Why do people *make* that happen?"

The old wizard shook her head. "Partly it's the way people are, Cashel," she said. "Not you and certainly not me. I never wanted any kind of power, just quiet in which to study."

She smiled broadly, shedding a decade with the expression. "I avoided power, all right, but it looks as though I'm not going to have the quiet study because we're trying to keep the world from going the way you describe."

She sobered instantly. "But that's the other thing: forces reached a peak a thousand years ago, and before they subsided they'd brought down the kingdom—what your age calls the Old Kingdom. The powers from outside don't cause disaster in themselves, but they amplify tiny imbalances, petty anger and ambition and jealousy."

Tenoctris looked out over the river. Cashel guessed she

was really viewing things more distant than the barges crawling down the brown Erd and the larger vessels that brought cargoes from all across the Inner Sea.

"Wizards with some power find that they have many times that power now," the old woman continued softly. "They can sink islands or raise demons who have the strength to wreck cities. But the wizards don't have any better understanding than they did before."

She looked at Garric, then Cashel, with eyes as fierce as an eagle's. "And they understood nothing before, though they thought they did. Because they were fools!"

"But you understand," Garric said, placing his big tanned hand on Tenoctris' shoulder. "And we won't let Malkar win this time. Evil isn't going to win."

Cashel scratched the back of his left ear, thinking. Sharina had left Barca's Hamlet; forever, it seemed. She hadn't known how Cashel felt about her because Cashel hadn't had—and wouldn't ever have had—the courage to tell her.

So Cashel had left home also, going no particular direction—just away from the place where so many memories tortured him. In the end he'd found Sharina again, and he'd saved her when nobody else could have. Nobody but Cashel or-Kenset.

"I think things will work out all right," Cashel said aloud. "Things pretty much do if you work at them."

The others looked at him in surprise. Cashel smiled slowly. Garric and Tenoctris were smart people who read all sorts of things in books. Cashel had nothing but the life he lived himself to base his judgments on. Other folks could believe whatever they wanted to, but that didn't change the things Cashel knew in his own heart.

They walked on, passing men who unloaded spices from a square-bowed Serian ship. Slim, brown-skinned sailors brought the sturdy chests up from the vessel's multiple holds, but local men loaded the goods on handcarts to be wheeled to a warehouse. A Sandrakkan factor oversaw the business. The cargo's owner, a silk-robed upper-class Serian who was taller and much fleshier than the sailors, stood impassively while at his side a secretary jotted the count onto a tablet of bamboo sheets.

"If the Isles were really united again," Garric said, "there'd be even more trade. Maybe that's just a dream."

It was Cashel's turn to look with curiosity at his friend. Not the sort of dream that came to Haft peasants, he'd have thought.

"The forces turned toward Malkar aren't in league with one another," Tenoctris said. Her train of thought didn't flow directly from what had been said before, but it fit well enough with Cashel's musings. "Evil people hate one another as bitterly as they hate what I suppose we may as well call the good. That's the real advantage good has over evil."

She smiled wryly. "Unfortunately," she went on, "there's very little that's purely anything. Including good."

They were passing a ship of moderate size whose deck cargo, dried fruit in pitch-sealed baskets, had already been unloaded. The crew was using the mast and yard as a crane to bring casks up from the hold one at a time, then swing them onto mule-drawn wagons.

A tin plate nailed onto the vessel's stem showed a gull and a name in cut-out letters. The captain was a red-bearded man as stocky as Cashel but not as big. He directed his sullen crewmen from the deck, while the merchant receiving the goods waited with the first in the line of wagons.

Cashel paused. His skin felt prickly as though sunburnt, something that almost never happened to him since he spent most of his time outdoors in all seasons. He stared intently at the ship.

"She's the *Bird of the Waves*," Garric said, thinking his friend was trying to cipher out the nameplate.

"There's something about it . . ." Cashel said. He slid his left hand slowly up his quarterstaff.

Garric started to speak but closed his mouth again instead. Tenoctris knelt on the brick quay and picked up a piece of straw that had been used to cushion cargo.

"Hey!" a carter shouted angrily. "Get out of the way or I'll drive over you!"

Cashel stepped between Tenoctris and the lead oxen. He set one of his staff's iron ferrules on the ground in front of him and stared at the carter.

"Ah, go back to your farm!" the carter said; but he swung his team to the side. Popping his whip he went around the trio with his load of grain packed in terra-cotta storage jars.

Tenoctris had drawn words in the grime of the street. Now she murmured a spell, touching each syllable in turn with the piece of straw. At the climax she released the straw, which spun away as though in an unfelt breeze. It landed on the cask being lowered to the lead wagon.

"I think . . ." she said in a shaky voice. She started to rise but would have fallen if Garric hadn't steadied her; the powers a wizard set in motion came with a price. "I think we should learn what's in that barrel."

"Right," said Cashel. He took a fresh grip on his quarterstaff. With Garric beside him, he walked toward the merchant.

They were going to learn what was in the cask. Like most other things, that should be pretty simple to manage.

Sharina paused to watch Ilna twist the shed stick, feed through a warp thread, and beat it flat in less time than it would have taken Sharina—or Liane on the third loom—just to make the shed. "You make it look so simple," she said ruefully.

Ilna looked up with a hard smile. Her fingers continued to feed warp threads from both sides of the loom frame with a speed and precision that would have been unnatural in any other weaver.

"It is simple," she said. "I've just got more practice than you do."

Which was true in a way. Any village girl on Haft learned to weave the same as she learned to cook, but in Barca's Hamlet for the past eight years or so Ilna os-Kenset did all the serious weaving. Most of the other women merely spun thread for her.

Ilna's fabric was tighter, her designs cleaner, and her rate of production ten times higher than that of her nearest rival in the borough, old Chantre os-Chulec. Even Chantre admitted that on the nights when she'd had more than her share of the beer in the taproom of Reise's inn.

But practice wasn't the whole answer, and the skill Ilna had when she left Barca's Hamlet was nothing compared to the genius she showed now. Something had changed, and from the look in Ilna's dark eyes more had changed than the way her fingers moved over a loom.

During the months Ilna and Sharina had gone their separate ways, Sharina had faced death and a demon. From the story Ilna's eyes told, she had seen far worse—and been worse as well.

"Ilna," said Liane, the girl Sharina had met at Garric's side here in Erdin three days before. "My father traveled the world. He brought Mother and me gifts when he returned. I've seen cloth from all over the Isles and beyond, but I've never seen workmanship to equal yours."

She called herself Liane os-Benlo, but Garric had told Sharina in a private moment that Liane was born to the noble house of bos-Benliman. Her father, a wizard, had died in a fashion that Garric didn't choose to discuss.

Liane's hair was as black as Ilna's, but she had the pale complexion of the Sandrakkan nobility whereas Ilna—like Garric—was tanned to the color of walnut heartwood. Either girl would pass as beautiful, but Liane was doll-like and delicate to look at, while Ilna . . . No one would ever call Ilna plain, but "severe" would be the first word a stranger used to describe her.

"Yes, well," Ilna said. "Perhaps it's compensation for my not being able to read books the way you and Garric do, do you think?"

Liane blushed.

"I'll teach you to read, Ilna," Sharina said sharply. "You know how many times I've offered before. You always said you didn't have enough time."

She didn't know Liane, but she knew Garric liked the girl and had gone through a lot with her. Sharina knew Ilna very well. She wasn't about to let her friend begin working on an undeserving Liane with a tongue as sharp as the bone-handled knife Ilna used for household tasks.

Thought of knives drew Sharina's mind to the weapon that was now hers, hanging behind her from a wall hook meant for cloaks in colder weather. The scales of the hilt were black horn riveted to a full tang, and the heavy single-edged blade was as long as her forearm.

It was a sealhunter's knife from Pewle Island in the Outer Sea, well north of the main circuit of the Isles. The man who'd carried it, Nonnus, had come to live as a hermit in the woods outside Barca's Hamlet before Sharina was born.

Nonnus ate the game he killed with wooden javelins and the crops he planted with a pointed stick. He set the bones of folk who injured themselves and could bring down a fever or soothe a cough with simples made from the herbs he grew. Beyond such help he'd had little to do with the community.

"Oh, I don't think I'd have the talent for reading," Ilna said, more with resignation than sadness. Her fingers worked as she talked, never hurrying but never putting a thread out of place. "And it's not a skill that a peasant needs, after all. Or a weaver either, so far as I've noticed."

Sharina got up for her frame loom. She'd go back to her design in a moment, but she wanted to stretch her muscles. She'd been raised as an innkeeper's daughter. Her duties had involved more moving and carrying than sitting in one place with her fingers doing most of the work.

They were staying in one of the buildings of Master

Latias' walled compound. It was a single room divided by folding paper screens with brush drawings of fanciful landscapes. The occupants had greater privacy than any peasant in a hut in Barca's Hamlet did.

Master Latias had provided the looms and thread also. Cashel had done the Serian merchant a service, and in return Latias treated Cashel and his companions as his own close kin. He'd offered silk, but Ilna said for her purpose wool would do as well.

Whatever that purpose was. Sharina had agreed when Ilna asked her and Liane to spend the afternoon weaving. She didn't understand the request, but Ilna asked very little—and never without an implicit promise to repay any favor many times over.

''Reading's a way to meet people of distant times and places,'' Liane said. She wasn't arguing, exactly, but she had her own opinions and she wasn't about to listen without response as things she cared about were disparaged. ''And when a work has survived the collapse of the Old Kingdom, it must have something special to it. Celondre said, 'My verses are a monument that will last longer than bronze,' and he was right.''

''There're plenty of people in this time and place that I haven't met yet,'' Ilna said. She gave a half-chuckle, half-sniff. ''And no few that I have met and sooner wouldn't have. My uncle Katchin, for example.''

Ilna sobered, though there'd been little enough humor in her tone before. She added, ''Well, there's some who'd say the same about having met me. They'd have good cause to feel that way too, I'm afraid.''

Sharina touched the hilt of the Pewle knife in its sheath of black leather waterproofed with seal fat. She hadn't intended to walk *here*. She'd just gotten up to stretch. . . .

But it wasn't in her muscles alone that Sharina felt an ache.

Pewlemen were a hardy lot, well used to weapons and brutal conditions. Generals hired them as irregular troops to accompany the main body of cavalry and armored infantry.

Nonnus had served as a mercenary soldier. While serving he'd done things that sent him to a forest on Haft, praying for the rest of his life to the Lady for forgiveness.

Nonnus had been closer to Sharina than to any of the other folk in Barca's Hamlet. He'd left the island with her when she needed a companion she could trust completely, and in the end he'd died for her in a mound of her enemies.

He'd done that because she was blond and beautiful; and because he couldn't do anything for the blond, beautiful child whose throat he'd laughingly cut one terrible afternoon when a king fought for his crown and nothing mattered but victory.

Sharina would have given all she possessed to bring Nonnus back, but she knew in her heart that death was the thing the hermit had wanted most after forgiveness. She could only pray, as Nonnus himself had prayed, that the Lady would show mercy to humans with human failings.

Sharina turned. The other women were staring at her, though Ilna's fingers continued to work across the loom frame.

"What is it that you're weaving, Sharina?" Liane said in a bright, false voice. She looked quickly down to her own project.

"A collar edging in red yarn," Sharina said, her lips smiling faintly. Her fingertips still rested on the hilt of the big knife. "A small thing, but one I could do well enough to pass. I could weave a whole lifetime and never be competition for Ilna."

Sharina looked at her friend. "Ilna," she said, "I don't know what you've done or think you've done, and I don't want to know. But you've got to remember that it doesn't matter, it doesn't make you bad."

She paused, swallowed, and blurted, "Nonnus did worse things than you ever could have, and there was never a better person in the world than him. Never!''

Sharina hadn't expected to start crying. Liane was a sensitive girl, brought up in a household where there was enough wealth to allow the luxury of sentiment. It wasn't surprising that she got up from her stool and squeezed Sharina's hand.

But it was a great surprise that Ilna held Sharina's other hand, the one that gripped the hilt of the Pewle knife.

The merchant turned from the cask swinging down to his wagon when he noticed Garric and Cashel walking toward him. His surprise quickly became concern as he realized just how big the two strangers were. ''Hey, who do you think you are?'' he cried.

The ship's captain took a mallet from a rack at the base of the mast. To Garric's surprise the six common sailors went on with their work as stolidly as so many plow oxen. He'd have expected more reaction from them if only because the strangers were more interesting than lifting barrels from the hold.

''We're friends,'' Garric said easily to the merchant. He nodded toward the vessel. ''Your friends at least, sir; I don't know if the shipper there is going to like what I have to say.''

''What do you mean by that?'' the captain roared. He hopped down to the quay. That was a mistake, because it made obvious how much smaller he was than the two youths. The oak mallet he brandished was no threat compared with the quarterstaff Cashel balanced easily in one hand.

''I'm an innkeeper's son, sir,'' Garric continued, ignoring the captain. ''Garric or-Reise from Haft. Are you paying for full casks here?''

''Of course I'm paying for full casks,'' the merchant said. ''What sort of question is that?''

He was wary but no longer frightened, and the angry edge had left his voice. The carters driving his half-dozen wagons had gotten down from their seats, holding their whips, but they kept a respectful distance from the discussion.

"See the bead on this barrel stave?" Garric asked. "It's not bilgewater, you know."

The cask had settled onto the bed of the wagon, resting on end. Garric wiped a finger across the wet patch he'd seen while the cask was still in the air. The sailors were loosing the sling as though nothing untoward was taking place on the dock.

Garric sniffed, noted the sharp tang of alcohol as he'd expected, and offered his finger to the merchant to make his own examination. It was cider royal—cider which had been left out in the winter. By skimming the ice that formed, a skilled man could create a drink much stronger than ordinary applejack. It was a drunkard's beverage, and one that Reise rarely stocked for his inn.

"Somebody's drilled this cask for a length of reed, I shouldn't wonder," Garric said, smiling nonchalantly at the furious captain. "The hole's plugged with wax, but if I were you I'd see how much was really left before I paid for the cargo."

"May the Sister drag you down to Hell for a liar!" the captain shouted. His beard bristled out like a bright flame. "These casks are just the way I loaded them at Valles!"

Men who've done heavy labor together learn to anticipate one another; otherwise a load slips and crushes the hand or leg of the fellow on the low side. Cashel and Garric had spent a decade shifting tree trunks and boulders. Neither needed to tell the other what to do now.

Cashel tapped the cask with the ferrule of his staff. It boomed, obviously empty or nearly so.

"Right!" said the merchant. "My name's Opsos, lads. Let's get this open right now!"

"By the Lady!" the captain said. "If you're going to start a cask, you're going to pay me for it first. You'll spill half of it over the docks, you will!"

Despite the captain's vehemence, he was by now only

going through the motions of protest. The black scowl he threw in the direction of his crewmen showed who he thought was responsible. They were lowering the sling into the hold for another cask.

Cashel stepped onto the wagon bed, using his staff as a pole to thrust himself the last of the way. The axle groaned a complaint as though a second barrel had been set on it.

"Sister take me!" the captain said, throwing the mallet to the ground in disgust. He looked furtively at the hull of his ship, perhaps considering how many more of the barrels his men might have tapped during the voyage.

Cashel raised his staff like a flagpole, then brought the ferrule straight down on the cask. One of the top's three boards flew into the air with the crossbraces still pegged to it, but there was no splash as there would have been if the barrel were full.

Opsos clambered onto the wagon with the driver's aid. Garric stayed on the ground where he could shelter Tenoctris against the press of spectators strolling over to see the show.

Cashel shouted. He tossed his staff down; Garric caught it without thinking. Hands freed, Cashel tilted the cask with one hand so that he could get his other under the lower rim. He lifted it overhead, an impossible task even for him if it had been filled with a hundred gallons of cider royal, and dumped the remaining contents onto the quay. Garric jumped back.

Only enough cider to darken the bricks remained. Doubled over, packed for preservation in the liquor the sailors had sucked out unknowing, was a corpse.

The corpse wasn't that of a human, or at any rate not wholly that of a human. It had two arms and two legs, but the skin was gray and had a pebbled texture between the scales.

The creature was hairless. Its head was the size of a man's but flattened and wedge-shaped, like that of a gigantic serpent.

"A Scaled Man," Tenoctris said as the bellowing crowd stampeded away from the scene. "Indeed, there's a great risk to the world if the Scaled Men have entered it again."

"I'm all right now," Sharina said. She snuffled deeply. Ilna nodded and stepped away. Liane offered the handkerchief she'd had ready since she jumped from her stool.

Sharina didn't notice the square of lace-fringed silk. She pulled a sturdier handkerchief from her sleeve and wiped her eyes before blowing her nose.

Ilna sniffed with amusement at Liane's quickly hidden discomfiture. The rich girl had yet to learn that other people usually didn't need help, or want it. Some other people, anyway.

"I'll tie off my collar band now," Sharina said, her voice under control again. She glanced over at Ilna. "Or would you like me to make it wider?"

"It's your design," Ilna said. She examined her friend's work.

The strip of red fabric would add color to the tunic a farmwife wore when she made her Tenth Night sacrifice: the splash of beer and pinch of ground meal sprinkled before the household altar with miniatures of the Lady and Her Consort the Shepherd. For major occasions—a wedding or the annual Tithe Procession, when priests came to the borough from Carcosa with mule carts bearing life-sized images of the Deities—the same woman would wear ribbons and garments of patterned fabric bought from a peddler. If she could afford purchased finery, that was; but Barca's Hamlet was a prosperous community in which anyone who was willing to work made out reasonably well.

"It's a nice piece," Ilna said. Sharina nodded, gratified by the praise.

As everybody in the borough knew, Ilna didn't lie about craftsmanship. The closest she came was silence.

Even then—and that slight kindness was the exception rather than the rule—anyone who pressed Ilna got the truth as Ilna saw it, with no more embellishment or delicacy than millstones show for the grain between them.

Ilna ran her fingers slowly across the collar band. Cloth spoke to her, telling her things which the folk who wove or wore the fabric often didn't know about themselves. She'd always had the ability, just as she'd always been aware of patterns where others saw only a loom frame and a mass of yarn waiting to be strung on it.

She'd never discussed her talent with anyone; not her brother Cashel, not Garric, whom she'd loved all her conscious life without giving the least overt sign of her feelings. Especially not Garric. If others thought at all about Ilna os-Kenset, it was merely that she wove well and that her assessments of other people were rarely charitable but were almost always accurate.

Sharina's fabric gave Ilna the feel of Barca's Hamlet, the simple houses and the warm tranquillity of a place where events had the virtue of being predictable even when they weren't desirable in themselves. Neither that nor the underlying strength and decency permeating the work were surprising to Ilna, who'd known Sharina since infancy.

The deep sadness was new, but Ilna had seen her friend cry as she remembered the protector who had died for her. Sharina's feelings toward Cashel were new also; Ilna jerked her fingers back from the fabric as though from boiling water. The truth can be an awkward thing.

"There," Liane said as she wrapped the selvage of the work she'd finished. Liane stood and swung the stool out of the way so that Ilna could get as close as she wanted to the frame.

After Ilna left the borough, her arrogant determination had brought her to a place she'd thought was gray Limbo but which she later realized was Hell. Ilna had come back from that place as a minion of Hell with skills no human was fit to wield.

The skills remained. She'd been rescued from the Thing that had possessed her, but nothing could ever rescue Ilna from the evil she'd done while the Thing used her the way her own fingers used a loom.

Liane stood as straight as a shed stick, waiting for Ilna to examine her work and pronounce on it. She met Ilna's eyes without flinching. She knew Ilna too well to expect mercy, but pride kept her even from wanting that.

Ilna smiled with a vague humor directed primarily at herself. She understood pride at least as well as the rich girl did.

She bent to examine the work without touching it. Instead of weaving a narrow band the height of the frame the way Sharina had, Liane had strung warp threads only in the center. She'd filled a square no bigger than her palm with an intricate zigzag design in rust-red and butternut yellow. The workmanship was painstaking and excellent.

The cloth buyers who'd carried Ilna's fabrics away for sale to wealthy folk all over the Isles made sure that she knew the fashions of Erdin and Valles, but this was like nothing she'd ever seen before. She looked at Liane and asked, "Is this a Sandrakkan pattern? Or did you see it when you were in Valles?"

"Neither," Liane said. "A panel like this hung over my crib when I was a baby. It's something my father brought back, I don't know from where. As I told you, he traveled widely."

Ilna's lips curved in what was for her a broad smile. "And the work itself? Did they teach you to weave when you were at your school for girls?"

"No," Liane said crisply. "Of course Mistress Gudea taught weaving in her academy along with all the other accomplishments proper to a young lady, but my mother had already taught me to weave. She was wonderfully talented, but she wasn't as skilled as you are."

Ilna sniffed. "Neither are you, Liane," she said. "But you're better than anyone else you're likely to meet. You missed a wonderful career."

And, as the other girls digested what they'd just heard her say, Ilna touched the square of fabric for the first time.

The hard thread and tight weave made the woven plaque feel slick. Ilna let her mind slip deeper into the fabric, merging with it.

Goats nipped the leaves from bushes as they wandered on rolling, rocky hills. In the distance lay the ruin of a castle built with Cyclopean blocks. Ilna was seeing the source of the pattern, though she had no more idea than the goats themselves did of where that source might have been.

The other girls murmured softly to each other. Ilna continued to stroke the cloth. She was aware of the world around her, but for the moment she wasn't part of it. There was a bustle at the door. Tenoctris and the men were returning, all three talking at once in the greatest excitement.

Liane's personality illuminated the fabric as the sun did the surface of the sea. She was calm, steadfast, and kind, with a spirit that could never be broken so long as life was there to sustain it. Everything Liane bos-Benliman seemed, so she was in fact.

Ilna stepped away from the loom and shuddered.

"We found a creature in a cask on the docks!" Garric said with keyed-up enthusiasm. "It was shipped here from Valles, but—"

He paused, his eyes on Ilna.

"Do you need to sit, Ilna?" Tenoctris said. Cashel, silent but more direct, had already hooked a stool closer with one hand as the other guided his sister onto it.

"I'm all right," Ilna said, though she allowed Cashel to seat her. It was pointless to resist when her brother decided that you needed to move.

She smiled at Garric, then Liane. "I'm quite all right," she repeated. "What did you find at the docks?"

Not that she cared. Not that she would have cared if the Isles and every soul upon them sank straight into the sea.

Garric would go far. He had strength, a fine mind, and—thanks to his father—an education equal to that of any noble from Valles. Besides all that, Tenoctris had said that Garric, not Sharina, was the real descendant of the ancient Kings of the Isles.

Fabric didn't lie to Ilna, and Ilna didn't lie to herself. She could no longer imagine that the rich, well-educated Liane bos-Benliman wasn't a fit companion for Garric.

As an illiterate peasant like Ilna os-Kenset could never be.

Garric looked at his companions, aware that there was one more person present than eyes could see: King Carus watched intently from somewhere between reality and dream. Carus grinned, as he generally did; but one hand generally rested on the hilt of his great sword also.

"The Scaled Men inhabit a separate plane of the cosmos," Tenoctris said quietly. "One so distant from ours that there was only once contact between them and humans. And even that contact is myth rather than history."

She smiled. "Was myth. I'm learning a great deal about things I used to think were myth. Including Good and Evil, I suppose."

"They're demons?" Cashel said, leaning minusculely forward. It was like seeing a boulder tilt. "Scaly men are demons?"

Cashel asked the question with anticipation. His huge hands flexed the way a wrestler loosens up for a bout. He'd fought a demon with his bare hands, Sharina said. Cashel hadn't talked to Garric about that or anything else which could be considered bragging.

The room's furnishings were of Serian style—spider-legged stools only inches off the floor, placed around a low table. Liane and Tenoctris used the stools, Liane more comfortably than the old woman, but the quartet from Barca's Hamlet squatted on their haunches.

They were used to that. Reise's inn and the ancient

millhouse where Ilna and Cashel lived had chairs, but many peasant huts had only a stone bench along one wall as furniture.

"No, they're not demons," Tenoctris said. "They're men, nearly enough, with no more powers than men have. But the story, the *myth*—"

She smiled again, her way of poking fun at herself for her former certainties.

"—was that a wizard in the time of the Yellow King brought the beast-god of the Scaled Men here. He thought the god, the Beast, could help him seize the Throne of Malkar. The Yellow King destroyed the wizard and bound the Beast in a prison of living fire."

Liane's lips pursed. "According to Ethoman, the Yellow King reigned for ten thousand years," she said. Her tone was dry and factual, letting the absurdity of the legend display itself without any help from her. "When he died, the waters rose and formed the Isles where before there had been a single continent."

"Yes, I said it was a myth," Tenoctris agreed, nodding.

"The Throne of Malkar isn't a myth," Garric said. Nor was it a myth that King Lorcan, the founder of the royal line of Haft, had concealed the Throne in a place that only his descendants could find. Wizards who sought power through Malkar, through evil, had hunted Garric and Sharina for that reason.

"The scaly man isn't a myth either," Cashel said. "I guess it's still lying where I tipped it onto the bricks. Though maybe somebody's dumped it in the river by now."

Tenoctris had said the Scaled Man wasn't important for itself, only in what it represented. Some traveling mountebank would probably claim the creature for an exhibit. Though . . .

The Scaled Man was so very nearly human that it disturbed Garric even now to think about it. Perhaps Cashel was right, and the River Erd was already tumbling the body toward the Inner Sea.

"The thing that concerns me is that if Scaled Men exist again in our world . . ." Tenoctris said. She straightened a pleat in her tunic while her mind considered distant matters. "Then the Beast they worshipped may exist too. If he's escaped from his prison, then this world has a serious problem. Because I'm quite sure . . ."

She smiled like the sun, though her words were grim enough.

". . . that the Yellow King isn't here to put him back."

"We're here," Garric said. "You can do something, can't you, Tenoctris? And we can help you."

"I don't know that I *can* do anything," the old wizard said, "but I may have to try. And I would certainly appreciate help."

"We'll need to go to Valles?" Liane said. "I have money left from my father's funds."

Garric noted with a feeling of quick pride that Liane simply assumed that she'd be part of the endeavor. Courage was to be expected in a noble, but Liane knew from past experience that she was letting herself in for dirt and nastiness as well as danger. In a girl brought up with all the advantages of wealth and position, that willingness was rare indeed.

"I think I should mention something else," Tenoctris said. "It may be that the corpse of the Scaled Man was sent here to bring us to Valles. That it's a trap set by someone of great power. Or some*thing* of great power."

"It doesn't really matter, does it?" Cashel said. "I mean, we want to get close to him. If he wants to get close to us too, well, we'll see who was right about being stronger, won't we?"

It didn't seem to Garric that all planning should be boiled down to the philosophy of a wrestling match: you bring the parties together and one slams the other to the ground. But despite doubting the theory of what Cashel had said, it really seemed that he was right this time. If the source of the threat wasn't in Valles, at least it had sent this missive through Valles. Therefore, that was the place they needed to start their search.

"*And Valles is the throne of the Isles, now, lad,*" a voice chuckled at the back of Garric's mind.

"When I left home," Sharina said, "I thought I was going to Valles. Father raised us to finish what we started, didn't he, Garric?"

She gave her brother a wistful smile. Deliberately, she put her hand on Cashel's shoulder. Cashel gave no sign of the contact except to become very still, even more like a rock than he usually seemed.

"I became wealthy from what I was doing here in Erdin," Ilna said, her hands folded on the table before her. "Evil's quite profitable. I haven't seen my business manager in the few days since I stopped ruining people's lives, but I'm sure I can provide you with funds in any amount you need."

She looked at Liane, then to Garric. Her gaze and voice were perfectly steady, as always. The passionate self-loathing in the cold words was evident to anyone who knew Ilna; but only to those few.

Garric reached across the table. Ilna jerked her hands back. She gave him a curt shake of the head.

"As I said," she continued, "I'll help in any way you request. I won't be leaving Erdin myself, though. I'm not such a fool as to believe that I can undo all the harm I've done—there were suicides as well as lives ruined from the work I sold here. But I need to try."

Garric stood. You didn't argue with Ilna when she'd made up her mind. He didn't understand her. He'd known Ilna all his life and he still couldn't guess what she'd do—except to know that Ilna os-Kenset would do exactly what she said, or die in the attempt.

"I'll look into buying our passage to Valles," Garric said. "Passage for five."

"Ilna, I wish you'd come with us," Liane said. She touched Ilna's hands with her own, as Garric would have done if she'd let him.

Ilna looked at the other girl. "Yes," she said, "I know you would. Well, I suppose without people like me for the background color, good people wouldn't stand out so clearly. Thank you anyway, but three would be a crowd. For the third one at least."

Cashel got up with the deliberate grace of a bear stretching to mark a tree with his claws. "I'll come with you, Garric," he said. "I never liked walls around me, even when there's as much room inside them as Master Latias has here."

They were all rising. Sharina offered her hand to Tenoctris.

"And I," said Ilna, closing the discussion, "will finish the fabric I started this afternoon. I want to have it done—"

She nodded toward Liane.

"—before you leave."

The 3rd of Heron

Even tied bow and stern to the quay, the *Lady of Mercy* quivered slightly as Garric stepped out of the cabin where he'd stowed the women's luggage. Reise's inn trembled in similar fashion during the worst of winter's easterly storms. Though harmless, the motion was vaguely disquieting.

The *Lady* was eighty feet long and probably carried about a hundred tons of cargo in her two holds. The roof of the three-cabin deckhouse was the platform on which the helmsman worked the steering oars. Liane and Sharina had one cabin; Tenoctris and the luggage were in another; and the captain himself would probably sleep in the third.

Garric and his friends were the only passengers. He'd

thought he and Cashel would share the third cabin, but when Cashel said he'd bunk on deck with the sailors Garric decided he would too. He'd liked the thought of the snug cabin; it reminded him of his garret room in the inn, but he was embarrassed at the thought of having the space to himself when the girls had to share.

"Tenoctris?" he said. "Does everybody do things because it'd look bad if they didn't, even though it's silly?"

The wizard ran her index finger along the pine decking. She looked up at Garric. "Well, in my day people wore clothes in public no matter what the weather was like," she said. "They did in my family's social circle, at least."

Garric laughed. "It is pretty common, isn't it? Anyway, I suppose we'll mostly lay up on little islands at night anyway, instead of running in the dark."

Tenoctris touched the beam again. "I didn't expect the ship to be so old," she said. "I'd say it was older than I am, but of course it's only older than I was a thousand years ago."

"Do you mean it isn't safe?" Garric said in surprise. He'd hired passage on the *Lady of Mercy* simply because she was leaving for Valles on the evening tide. She'd seemed solid enough . . .

"Goodness, I don't know anything about ships," Tenoctris said in surprise. "I don't know anything about much of anything outside of what's in books. I just meant . . ."

She gestured around them. "These timbers are over a hundred years old except where they've been patched. The sea prints itself on the things men put in it. I could feel that in your father's inn, because the main beams there were timbers taken from ships wrecked on your coast."

So quietly that Garric understood the words only because he was looking at the wizard as she spoke, Tenoctris added, "I'd much rather think about the ports this ship has seen in its lifetime than about what we're going to find in Valles. And what may find *us* there."

* * *

The *Lady of Mercy*'s mainmast was squarely in the center of the vessel. Sharina sat on the yard with her bare feet resting on the furled sail of coarse linen dyed the color of rust. From here, fifty feet above the deck, she could see all the way across the city.

Because Erdin was built in the river's floodplain, the buildings weren't more than two stories high, or three at the most. For a building of real height to be stable on this site, it would need impossibly deep pilings.

Barca's Hamlet had no harbor, so only fishing dinghies which could be pulled up on the gravel strand normally landed there. The sea was a presence just beyond the inn's east windows, though. When she was this high, Sharina could smell the familiar salt air rather than the river harbor's own mudflats, stinking with the very richness of the nutrients they contained.

Sharina had left Barca's Hamlet because emissaries of King Valence told her that she was the daughter of Countess Tera, murdered during the riots in Carcosa seventeen years before. Tera had been of the old royal line of Haft, the lineage of Carus, the last king of the united Isles. It was Sharina's destiny, the emissaries said, to take her place in the palace in Valles.

She didn't suppose she'd had a day of complete happiness since then, but it wasn't possible to go back to a world in which the emissaries had never arrived. Besides, Tenoctris said that forces were rising to a crescendo that could tear the Isles apart.

It wasn't merely that evil wizards turned toward Malkar to gain his Throne and temporal dominion. The forces of good were waxing as well, and they could be equally destructive of the present world. The world of men had never been of unmixed evil *or* good.

Barca's Hamlet couldn't escape the forces which shaped the entire cosmos. Sharina knew it was better for her to take a hand in the struggle instead of letting it sweep her away helplessly.

And if no day since she left home had been of unmixed happiness, then there were nonetheless moments of triumph . . . and the wholly unexpected awareness that her friend Cashel was a force in the greater pattern and a rock to whose strength Sharina could trust herself.

Cashel stood on the dock now, leaning on his staff as he chewed a blade of grass that he'd plucked from the margin of one of the canals that carried much of the city's heavy traffic. He seemed completely relaxed; unafraid and unconcerned. He'd faced enemies of this world and other worlds as well and had always defeated them.

Cashel turned and tilted his broad-brimmed shepherd's hat so that he could look up at her. He smiled as he waved.

Sharina waved back, feeling a tide of comfort. She couldn't return to the stable life of Barca's Hamlet, but she'd brought stability with her into the chaotic world in which she found herself.

She touched the horn hilt of the unladylike weapon she wore. The Pewle knife and Cashel might not be enough to defeat every danger she faced in the future; but between them, they'd been enough for everything she'd met thus far.

Water Street wandered along the River Erd. Its broad pavement served both for traffic and as open storage for the vast quantities of cargo passing through the port, unloaded from recently docked ships or hauled here from warehouses to fill the holds and decks of outward-bound vessels. Cashel watched the traffic around him, finding in it the same fascination that he felt in the sky as summer clouds built and changed over Barca's Hamlet.

Cashel couldn't guess where all the goods came from or where they were going. For seventeen years the borough had bounded his life. In the fall the Sheep Fair brought drovers and wool merchants to Barca's Hamlet to buy; the Tithe Procession in the spring brought bored priests from Carcosa to collect the due of the Great Gods, the Lady and the Shepherd. That was all.

Cashel's mouth spread slowly into a grin. He didn't know much about this wider world in which he found himself, but that had been true for him even in the borough. Garric and Sharina read and ciphered, their parents had served in great palaces, and Ilna with her weaving was only one of many residents who knew something that was completely beyond Cashel's experience.

But Cashel or-Kenset knew to do the task facing him, whatever that task was. That had been enough in Barca's Hamlet, and he guessed it would be enough for all the rest of his life.

The mate was on his way back to the *Lady of Mercy,* accompanied by one of the missing crewmen and half-supporting, half-dragging the second, who was still too drunk to walk by himself. The falling tide dragged the vessel hard against her mooring. They'd be under way shortly, Cashel knew.

He didn't look up to the masthead again, but his grin grew broader as he chewed the stalk of marshgrass. Now his task was to keep Sharina safe; and he would do that until the day he died.

''Ilna?'' said Liane to the girl beside her on the dock. ''Are you sure you won't . . . ?''

Ilna grimaced in irritation. She'd never had much use for people who nattered, even when their intentions were of the best. Perhaps the rich girl was used to folk who changed their minds frequently. There were enough of those in the world, the Lady knew.

''I have my own business to attend,'' Ilna said, trying to keep the bitterness out of her voice. ''You and . . . and the others, you have things to do. Before you leave, though, I want to . . .''

What Ilna really wanted to do was apologize. She couldn't say that, not because she was afraid of the words but because Liane wouldn't understand them. Liane was too decent a person to understand how bad other folk really were. She'd argue, and the last thing Ilna needed was *that* sort of argument.

Liane's eyes flicked to the side. The *Lady of Mercy*'s deck had been above the quay when the five passengers and Ilna arrived. Now the river had fallen on the tide so that the vessel's railing was level with the brick surface. Ilna didn't need to see Garric watching them with ill-concealed concern to know that it was time for Liane to board also.

"This won't take long," Ilna said crisply. "It won't take any time at all. I want you to have this. Wear it if you like, but at any rate try to keep it with you."

She handed Liane the sash she'd finished just as they left Master Latias' compound. It was of naturally colored wool, woven in an open pattern of brown on cream, recalling the gently rolling hills in which Barca's Hamlet nestled. Ilna wore its mate, woven as the same length of fabric and separated only when it left the loom.

"It's lovely!" Liane said. "I'll . . . I appreciate the token, Ilna. I . . ."

She looked from the sash to meet Ilna's eyes. "I wish we could be friends," she said. "I hope some day we will be."

"Yes, I'm sure you do," Ilna said with a sniff of amusement. "This has a purpose beyond clenching your tunic, though. If you're ever in need, real need, tear it apart. Just tear the cloth. If you do that I'll know, and I'll offer you such help as I can."

"I . . ." Liane said. Her fancy school had taught her to conceal surprise, but not quite well enough. "I . . . What sort of help do you mean, Ilna?"

"That'll have to wait on the event, won't it?" Ilna snapped. She couldn't help it. She'd wanted to be gracious, *sweet,* the way the rich girl herself was. It wasn't in Ilna to do that, even for these last few minutes. . . .

"Anyway," she added, "you probably won't need it. Good-bye, Liane. I wish you well."

Ilna offered her hand to clasp. Liane stepped close and hugged her. Ilna felt her soul shiver as Liane broke away and hopped onto the *Lady of Mercy*'s deck.

Ilna couldn't pretend that she liked Liane or that she wasn't bitter about losing Garric to the well-educated rich girl. But Ilna could make amends for the unjust hatred she'd borne Liane in the past. That was why she'd woven the paired sashes and given the one to her successful rival. Not that Liane had ever felt they were in competition . . .

"Fare well!" Ilna called to all the people in the world who mattered to her. She turned quickly and walked away before any of them could see her tears.

The 9th of Heron

Beltar or-Holman had been a moderately successful mercer when Ilna first arrived in Erdin. Ilna wove ribbons which attracted men to the women wearing them: she'd used Beltar as her agent. His business had grown enormously. He'd expanded into the adjacent premises, which had been a smithy where harness chains were repaired and horses were fitted with shoes to replace those they'd thrown on the city's hard brick pavements.

Ilna walked into the shop, smiling faintly. She wondered how Beltar expected to get on now that he had only ordinary cloth to sell. Well, she was here to save him from that difficulty.

Though it was late in the day there were several female customers, each with a maid in attendance with a basket for parcels. Two ladies chattered over a table of cut rolls;

the shop assistant was showing a third brocade of Serian weave.

The assistant looked up when Ilna entered. She was a pert little thing who wore an elaborate coiffure of false hair, combs, and amber-headed pins.

"I've come to see Beltar," Ilna said. She walked toward the doorway into the back, curtained not by fabric but with strands of carved wooden beads.

The assistant glanced at Ilna's simple dress and the roll of cloth in her hands. "Trade uses the back entrance," she said sharply. "But from the look of you, you'd be wasting your time anyway. *Our* customers are discerning."

Ilna smiled at her. "Then they have the advantage of you, you silly trull," she said mildly. "You must dress in the dark to wear shellfish dye and madder reds in the same outfit. And that silk you're trying to sell there—show your customer the edge you've folded under, why don't you, so that she can see the water damage."

"What?" said the customer's maid. She snatched the corner of the fabric lying over the assistant's arm and pulled it out straight for her mistress.

The assistant jerked back in horror. "Master Beltar!" she cried. "Master *Bel*tar!"

The beads clattered as Beltar or-Holman came out quickly. He still held the quill with which he'd been transferring tallies from wax tablets to a more permanent account on paper or thin boards. He stared at Ilna.

"Oh, Shepherd guard me!" he said in a husky voice. "I thought you were dead. When your house was destroyed . . . I prayed you were dead!"

The mercer had gained weight since Ilna first met him, but his red-blond hair looked sparser and his complexion was sallow. "I don't blame you," Ilna said without rancor, "but prayer never did me much good either. We'll talk in your office."

By sheer force of personality she drove Beltar ahead of her through the curtain. The women in the shop stared after them dumbfounded. Directly ahead were stairs leading up to living quarters. The room to the left had a stool and a slanted desk, a wall of deep pigeonholes holding scrolls whose winding rods were tagged for identification, and a table under the sole window where Beltar could examine fabric by natural light. A lamp shone on the accounts Beltar had been transcribing. Its translucent panels were cut from fish bladders.

"I've moved myself and my looms to a loft in the Crescent," Ilna said. "Living in a slum is cheap, and I have more important things to do with my money now than keep up a mansion on Palace Square."

Beltar sat heavily on the stool. A carafe and tumbler of faience stood on the adjacent sideboard. He poured but splashed more wine on the wood than he got into the tumbler. Gripping the carafe in both shaking hands, he drank directly from it.

"You have nothing to fear from me," Ilna said contemptuously. "You never did, you know."

Beltar lowered the carafe. Roundels sawn out of multistranded glass rods quivered in the lamplight. For the most part the mercer appeared to have his nerves under control.

"Your house was looted and there were so many bodies around it," Beltar said softly. "I saw it and I thought the sun had come out for the first time since I met you. Even though I didn't see your body."

"I'm not a great deal happier than you are about the reality," Ilna said. "But that doesn't change anything."

She laid the cloth she'd brought with her onto the examination table. "I still need you as agent to handle my business affairs," she explained, "selling what I weave. It'll be a different business, though."

"No," said Beltar. He stared into the carafe instead of turning to look at Ilna. "I won't work for you anymore. If you try to twist my mind again—"

He turned to her with eyes full of the terrified anguish of a rabbit facing a snake.

"—I'll kill myself! I will! I'm not going back to being . . . to selling . . ."

Beltar dropped the carafe. Wine splashed across the legs of the desk and stool. He cupped his hands over his face and cried into them.

The vessel's decoration had chipped, but its rugged stoneware core hadn't broken. Good craftsmanship, Ilna thought. She laid the tips of her fingers over Beltar's hands with a gentleness none of those who'd grown up with her would have credited.

"Poor Beltar," she said. "You've grown a backbone at last, have you? Perhaps there's more good in what I've done than I'd realized."

She stepped out of the room to fill the tumbler with water from the jar under the stairs. A little boy with Beltar's red hair peered at her from the upper hallway; a woman's arm jerked him back with an angry hiss. The shop assistant might not recognize Ilna os-Kenset, but the mercer's family certainly did.

Ilna gave Beltar the water, then tossed him a swatch of badly embroidered linen that deserved no better use than for the mercer to blow his nose on it. She waited with her hands folded in front of her while he mopped his face.

Beltar raised his eyes to her. "I'd rather die," he said softly.

Ilna nodded. "I won't force you to act as my agent," she said, "but I'll remind you that I didn't force you before. You sold my ribbons because they would make you rich. You kept selling them even after you knew beyond question that they ruined lives, ruined people. And they made you *very* rich."

"I'd give you all that money if I could go back to the way things were," the mercer said. "I'll give you the money now if you'll just go away."

"We have work to do here," said Ilna. "Oh, we can't put things right, that I know, but money in the right places can help. And the fabrics I'm weaving now . . ."

She picked up the bolt she'd brought into the shop and

let a yard of it fall free. The cloth was wool woven into a thin baize. The pattern was a series of gently curving stripes in brown and russet thread, almost but not quite parallel. It was like looking at a kelp forest when the tide drags the strands outward.

Beltar straightened on the stool. His expression was guarded but no longer one of hate and loathing.

"As you see, they make people feel better," Ilna said. "I suppose we'll be deluding them, but it'll be for their own good. A length of this in place of the bead curtain should be a good way to start."

The mercer swallowed. "There are others who could act for you," he said.

"Yes," said Ilna, "but they don't have sins of their own to deal with. Not involving me, at any rate. You do."

Beltar nodded. He got up from the stool, frowning in surprise when he noticed he was standing in the tacky lees of the wine he'd spilled. "Yes, all right," he said. He shook his head in puzzlement. "I'd convinced myself you were dead," he added. "I should have known better, I suppose."

Ilna dropped the bolt back on the table. "Come with me now so that you know where I'm living," she said. "At the start you can visit me every other day, but we may need to modify the schedule as word gets around."

Beltar marched out of the shop in her wake. She'd bullied him into agreement, Ilna knew; but it was for his own good.

The water of the Inner Sea was all the colors from green through violet; where seamounts neared the surface there were fish and coral of red, orange, and yellow besides. Garric leaned on the stern rail as though he were eyeing the dinghy which bobbed after the *Lady of Mercy* at the end of a twenty-foot painter. His mind watched with King Carus from the dream balcony, viewing preparation for a battle below them.

"The Isles are too big to rule except by the consent of the people being ruled," Carus said, eyeing the troops critically. He grinned and added, "Most of the people, that is; there're always going to be a few heads to knock."

The royal army was a force of lightly armored men with long spears, formed with unhurried precision into blocks sixteen ranks deep. They'd disembarked from the hundred warships that were drawn up on the beach behind them, protected by a palisade.

"And most people *are* willing to be ruled, lad, at least if you're doing a halfway decent job," Carus said. "Oh, they don't *want* to pay the Royal Portion any more than they want to pay any other debt. They'd sooner your father poured them beer for free in his taproom, right?"

The king turned to look directly at Garric. There were laugh-lines at the corners of his eyes, but the gaze itself had no more give in it than the edge of a sword has.

"But people don't want pirates swarming out of the sea to kill them all, either," Carus continued. "And they don't want a dozen of the local toughs deciding they're going to rape all the women and steal all the sheep."

On the ground below, a band of armored horsemen spurred from the enemy camp to disrupt the phalanx before it could complete its formation. Skirmishers met them, hurling javelins at the horses and scampering aside.

Horsemen slashed and wheeled like so many boxers beset by gadflies. The charge lost impetus. At last the horsemen returned to the ragged camp from which they'd come; some on foot, others nursing mounts restive from the pain of a dangling missile.

"They'll accept being ruled," Carus said, "if you're fair or fair enough, and if they think you're doing a job that needs to be done. Taking care of Count Hitto of Blaise—"

He nodded with satisfaction at the scene taking place beneath the rose-twined balcony he shared with Garric.

"—needed to be done. There were plenty of people on Blaise who didn't like paying taxes to Carcosa, but they liked that better than having Hitto strip them bare to raise an army to make him King of the Isles. Cavalry, lad! He was going to use heavy cavalry to conquer islands!''

A hundred and seventy free oarsmen drove each of the king's beached triremes. On land they traded their oar-looms for long pikes or three-foot staff slings and a wallet of pointed lead bullets that could outrange any peasant archer.

The phalanx shifted into motion with the leisurely implacability of the tide coming in. Parties of slingers sauntered between the blocks of pikemen. The skirmishers fell in on the flanks as the main force advanced.

At the rear, as a reserve and the hammer to strike the killing blow when the phalanx had pinned the enemy, was a party of five hundred armored swordsmen on foot. Their helmets and cuirasses glittered with gilt and gorgeous inlays.

On the shoulders of four burly swordsmen swayed a light platform like the frame of a sedan chair. King Carus stood on it, watching over the heads of his troops as the battle developed. Under his arm he held a helmet to don when the time came to lead rather than command; his mailed right hand rested on his sword hilt.

''Remember, lad,'' said the figure watching with Garric from the dream balcony. ''You can force any one man to do what you want.''

He chuckled. ''I could, at least, and you've got the size for it too. But when you try that with two, it's hard not to turn your back on one or the other sometime. If you've got a whole kingdom to rule, you'd best arrange that most everybody thinks it's good thing that you're ruling.''

Below, the count's armored horsemen were beating forward a mass of Blaise peasants armed with crude spears and the bows they used to hunt rabbits. Despite the threat of swords behind them, the peasant infantry scattered when the first volley of sling bullets slashed into them like hail on standing grain.

The phalanx strode forward briskly. The first three

ranks lowered their pikes; the points of the others wavered in the sunlight as a canopy of polished steel.

"But why me!" Garric said. "What right have I to be king? What right have I to be anything but a peasant on Haft?"

"It's not a right, lad," King Carus said. "It's a duty you have because your ancestor failed a thousand years ago. I failed. Not for lack of trying, but that wasn't enough. You've got to do it right, King Garric—"

He smiled. The Carus on the battlefield leaped off the platform to lead his shock troops into the enemy. His sword flicked like a serpent's tongue.

"—because if you don't, there won't be another chance. Not this time."

"Land ho!" a voice called. The words cascaded into Garric's consciousness, though it was a moment before he realized that he leaned against the wooden rail of the *Lady of Mercy* rather than a balcony of weathered stone.

"I make Pandah three points off the port bow!" cried the lookout at the masthead.

Liane sat a few feet away with her back to the railing. She was reading a codex of Celondre's *Odes*. When she heard Garric stir, she looked up with a smile.

A green light quivered momentarily at the corner of Garric's eye, near the northern horizon. He decided it must be a last echo of his reverie.

Cashel stood on the bow rail, bracing his left hand on the foremast which slanted forward at forty-five degrees. From what Cashel had seen during the voyage, the small sail hanging in front of the bowsprit was used mostly for steering. He couldn't see Pandah yet, but he knew the clouds piling in the center of the clear sky must have formed on the updrafts from land still beneath the horizon.

"Won't it be nice to be on solid ground tonight instead of some sandy hill in the middle of the sea?" Sharina said. "And fresh water!"

"What's in the ship's jars tastes of tar, that's so," Cashel agreed. He didn't mind being on shipboard. The motion didn't bother him, and he never felt confined so long as he had an open sky above him.

The lookout slid down the backstay of the mainmast, landing on the deck near Garric and Liane. Liane waved when she saw Cashel looking over his shoulder in her direction. Garric stared toward the northern horizon, shading his eyes with his left hand.

Sharina noticed her brother's interest. She ducked under the foremast and stood at the port bulwark; only the stern quarter had a railing. Cashel couldn't see in that direction because of the way the foresail was rigged.

"Cashel," Sharina said. "Come look at this."

Cashel stepped over the slanting mast instead of crawling through the cordage beneath. A sailor running to adjust the foresail bounced off his shoulder and shouted in anger. Cashel ignored him, watching the sea with a shepherd's eyes that were trained to spot hidden dangers.

The breeze moved the *Lady of Mercy* at a pace not much greater than that of sheep ambling to pasture. There wasn't enough wind to lift foam from the gentle waves.

A fish turned on the surface and flashed its silver flank before vanishing again into the sea. The scene was placid and practically identical to any other during the voyage.

The back of Cashel's neck prickled. He held his staff crossways at arm's length as though to form a barrier in front of him and Sharina. Nearby, sailors adjusted the sails under the captain's cheerful orders. They were eager to make port and unaware of any reason for concern.

"There was something in the sea," Sharina said, speaking with the deliberate calm of someone keeping strict control of her emotions. "It seemed to be a mile away. It was gray or green and I can't remember its shape. But it isn't there anymore, and there's no sign that it ever was."

Tenoctris came out of the cabin where she'd been resting. She glanced at Cashel, then looked off the port side.

"Maybe it was a whale or—" Sharina said.

A lens of gray distortion spread across sea and sky a hundred feet away. Cashel saw the waves and horizon through it, but they were shadowed and twisted out of their normal shapes. Lightning the color of rotten bronze leaped through the gray. A roar like bees swarming in unimaginable numbers smothered even the sudden screams of the sailors.

The lens swept down on the *Lady of Mercy* like a tidal wave.

Sharina gripped the gunwale with both hands as though she faced a storm. She didn't think of going inside. The lightly framed cabin would be no real protection, and even the ship's holds were unlikely to bring safety from this, whatever this was.

Cashel braced his legs apart, holding the staff as if he faced human opponents. He began to rotate it sunwise, crossing one hand over the other at increasing speed. Sparks skipped from the iron ferrules and hung in the air, forming a blue haze.

Ribbons hung from a crossjack on the stern to give warning of any change in the breeze. They slackened an instant before the sails also went limp in an unnatural calm.

The *Lady of Mercy* rocked violently. She entered the lens. Sunlight vanished.

Cashel continued to spin his staff. His face was calm, but he didn't look like the youth Sharina had grown up with. His visage now was one that might have looked down from the sanctum of a great temple, the Shepherd in His aspect of Protector rather than His more common depiction as the lithe, handsome Consort of the Lady.

Lightning spat from the grayness, then rebounded in a crash as it met the globe of blue light enclosing Sharina and Cashel. The gunwale shattered and the foremast flew out of the bitts. Cordage and the linen sail burned with wan red light until shadows swallowed them.

The *Lady of Mercy* was breaking up. The deck buckled and one of the great cross-timbers binding the sides of the hull together lifted vertically. The screams from sailors' open mouths were lost in the avalanche roar that followed the thunderclap.

Cashel and Sharina were in a cocoon of still air. Beyond them a gale ripped the mainsail. Sharina saw the captain fly from the top of the deckhouse, lifted by his billowing tunic.

Garric gripped the steering oar with one hand while he hacked at its rope pinions with his sword. Liane knelt beside him, tying herself and Tenoctris together with a brail from the shredded mainsail. The oar would float if Garric could get it free, but Tenoctris might be too frail to hold on to it alone until help could arrive from Pandah.

As for Sharina and Cashel—

The roar ceased abruptly. Sharina felt as though she were floating; perhaps she really was. She could see nothing but Cashel and the sparkling blue globe that the quarterstaff wove around them.

Sunlight blinded her. Sharina splashed into the warm, salty water of the Inner Sea. Cashel struck beside her. He still gripped the staff, but he wore the slack expression of a man who has worked beyond human limits.

Cashel's face dipped underwater. Sharina lifted his head with one arm. The dinghy floated nearby with only a tag remaining of the heavy rope by which the ship had towed it. Sharina swam to the boat, stroking with her free arm and kicking. When she lifted her head to breathe she could see that a galley had put out from Pandah. It was approaching on the rippling motion of many oars.

There was no debris on the sea's calm surface; no sign at all of the *Lady of Mercy*.

The 9th of Heron (Later)

The storm roared about them. Garric had cut the upper lashing, but he still couldn't get the steering oar loose. There must be a carrying rope deeper within the hull which he couldn't reach with the blade.

The wind pushed against him like the wall of a collapsing building. He braced his right leg against the rail, knowing the *Lady of Mercy* would break up soon. He sheathed the sword so he'd have both hands to wrench at the oar.

Carus must have been helping unnoticed: the swordpoint found the scabbard's narrow slot and shot home without hesitation. By himself Garric couldn't have managed that task one-handed, even without gusts tugging blade, sheath, and arm at different angles.

A split twisted halfway up the mainmast, following the grain of the wood. The mast parted just below the spar from which only scraps of cordage fluttered. Still linked by the lifts, the massive timbers spiraled off into lightning-shot darkness.

Garric leaned into the oarshaft. The gale roared from starboard, thrusting the *Lady of Mercy* into the gray maw. It was hard for Garric, facing in the opposite direction, to breathe. The carrying rope was bull sinew, elastic and enormously strong.

Liane had wound a rope under Garric's sword belt and through the brail that linked her and Tenoctris. She knotted the ends, drawing the heavy cordage as tight as possible. Tenoctris cuddled against the younger woman, gripping with all the strength of her frail arms.

Garric strained, using the whole strength of his body to

no avail. His eyes bulged, tendons stood out from his neck, and his triceps burned as though coated with blazing pitch.

Liane and Tenoctris should be all right so long as they hunched below the level of the deckhouse. Their tunics, longer and fuller than a man's, would snatch them away in a heartbeat if the wind—

There was a loud crash. Garric hurtled into the sea with the oar in his hands. He felt an instant's triumph when he thought he'd broken the carrying rope. The *Lady of Mercy* had disintegrated around him. Garric hit water whipped to froth by the storm, praying that the tug on his sword belt was the weight of Liane and Tenoctris.

The wind had been a burden, but the roiling water was the grasp of the Sister dragging dead souls to the Underworld. Garric wrapped both arms about the oar stock, shocked each time the heavy wood buffeted him as they rolled together in a maelstrom.

He didn't know when his face was above the water or if it ever was. He choked on saltwater every time he tried to breathe. His lungs burned, the tiller battered the side of his face numb, and he wasn't sure whether his leaden arms still held the oar.

Garric stopped moving. He supposed he was dead, but he didn't care anymore. There was soft green light all around him; and then there was nothing but black oblivion.

Garric's dream self stood on the marble balcony. Weathering had given the stone's exposed surfaces a gritty texture, though the undersides of carved moldings were mirror smooth.

He stared at his physical body sprawled unconscious on the muddy strand below. The steering oar lay beneath him, so he hadn't lost it after all. The women were beginning to stir. "I've got to get down there!" he said.

"Not yet," King Carus said, his expression more tautly

eager than Garric usually saw in these reveries. ''Your body needs as much time as they'll give you to recover, lad. You did more than any two men should have to do.''

The sky was sullen green. Half a dozen men were a hundred yards away, walking toward the castaways. They were armed with a mixture of clubs, axes, and spears. If any of them had come cadging around Barca's Hamlet during the Sheep Fair, he'd have been run out of the borough as a vagabond.

''There'll be time enough for them,'' Carus said judiciously. He stroked the railing in a gesture Garric recognized as the king's way to keep his right hand from grasping the hilt of his sword. Carus knew the truth of what he was saying, but his emotions were just as impatient as Garric's own.

''Hey, there's a body!'' one of the men called. ''Hey, he's alive! *She's* alive or the Sister take me!''

Liane struggled with the knot in the rope by which she'd tied herself to Garric's belt. As the men broke into a shambling run toward her, she drew a dagger from beneath her tunic. Its point was sharp enough to cut sunlight.

''Watch the sticker!'' a man said. The gang spread out as they advanced. Their feet splashed on the mucky ground.

''The other one's got a sword!'' bellowed a man carrying a club shaped roughly from a broken spar. ''The sword's mine! By the Lady, I'm due a sword! If Rodoard won't give me one I'll take it!''

The rope was thumb-thick sisal and salt-soaked besides. Liane parted it in three quick strokes of the keen steel. She helped herself up with one hand and faced the gang.

''Who-ee!'' said a spearman. ''You can have the sword, Othelm. There's what I want!''

''Maybe when Rodoard gets through with her,'' another man sniggered. ''If his bitch wizard doesn't decide to dispose of a rival first thing.''

''There's an old woman too,'' said the man who carried

a short-hafted axe, part of a ship's tool chest. "We may as well knock her on the head here."

"Now lad," King Carus said in a voice as soft as the rustle of a sword being drawn. "Now it's time."

The green sky wasn't as bright as it had seemed in Garric's reverie. He'd known as he looked down on his unconscious body how much every joint and muscle must hurt after the strain he'd put on them to survive, but *feeling* that pain was like hurling himself into a just-opened lime kiln.

Garric rose without stumbling. White fire flashed, blinding him at every heartbeat. He drew the sword, swinging it in a shimmering figure eight, and croaked, "Which of you wants to die first? Or shall I test the edge on the lot of you with one stroke?"

It was a good weapon. He'd bought it in Erdin, with King Carus nodding approvingly at the back of his mind. It wouldn't hack through six men at a stroke—or one either, the way Garric felt now. Though perhaps one . . .

"Sister take me!" a man shouted in terror. The whole gang leaped back as though burned. "I thought he was dead!"

Garric gripped the tip of his sword in his left hand and flexed the blade slightly. He wasn't sure he had the strength to hold the steel out with one hand; this gave him an excuse to use both.

Tenoctris whispered an incantation. Garric felt the spastic trembling of his muscle fibers calm. The old woman was giving him assistance from her own slight store of strength.

"You'll take us to Rodoard!" Liane said in a strong, clear voice; a noble, issuing commands as an instinctive right. She deliberately tucked the dagger away in its concealed sheath. "And you'll walk in front of us. Do you understand?"

The men looked at one another. None of them wanted

to take responsibility for the decision. After a moment the spearman turned without speaking and shambled off in the direction from which they'd come. The others joined him in a tight clot.

Garric and the women followed. Twice Garric would have fallen without Liane there to support him; but Liane was there.

Sharina sat in the bobbing dinghy, holding Cashel's head in her lap. His color was normal again, no longer the hectic flush it'd shown as he spun his quarterstaff against the lowering danger.

Sharina was exhausted. She'd not only towed Cashel to the dinghy, she'd had to lift him aboard. That meant standing in the boat while Cashel floated alongside, then pulling up his outside arm to roll him over the gunwale.

Sharina was a strong girl, but Cashel's sheer weight had almost been more than she could manage. Fortunately the dinghy was flat-bottomed and broad for its length, so she didn't capsize it during the process.

Sharina didn't know how Cashel had saved them. She suspected that Cashel himself didn't know either. But she was quite sure that without Cashel's action, the two of them would have been swallowed down with the *Lady of Mercy* and everything else aboard her.

The galley from Pandah had drawn close. It was a nobleman's barge, a lightly built craft with fifty oarsmen seated on open benches. A mast and a yard with the sail furled about it lay on deck parallel to the ship's axis. They could be pivoted up when the wind was favorable, but the oars were quicker for this short run from harbor.

In the bow a man of twenty-odd leaned eagerly on a rail of gilded bronze. His cloak of parrot feathers marked him as a noble. An older fellow, obviously a servant or aide, hovered close in order to catch the youth if he went over the side.

Beside the noble stood an even younger man who wore

a red velvet robe embroidered with silver astrological symbols. Neither velvet nor the feathers would have been Sharina's choice of garment for a sea voyage, but nobles and wizards seemed generally to feel a need to keep up appearances.

A large monkey clambered about the bow platform with the men; once it even hung nonchalantly from the railing and tried to dip a hand into the wave curling from the galley's bow. The rowers feathered their oars at an order from a helmeted officer in the stern. The monkey twisted up to stand between the men again. The beast spoke to the wizard; and, though the amazed Sharina couldn't make out the words of the exchange, the wizard replied.

"Back water!" the officer cried. The rowers rose from their benches, leaning forward to push their oarlooms instead of pulling them in the usual fashion. The galley halted twenty feet short of the dinghy. Around the hull swirled water spun by the perfectly judged oarstrokes.

Instead of the motley garb Sharina had seen on sailors from Sandrakkan and Ornifal, these rowers wore identical kilts with a saffron border around the hem. Their livery showed even more clearly than the feather cape did that the youth was the ruler of Pandah or the ruler's son.

"Throw them a rope, Tercis!" the youth snapped to the servant, whose utter amazement suggested he might as well be asked to fly.

"I'll do it, Your Majesty," the wizard said. He seized a mooring line and spun the coil out with an underhand toss that brought it directly to Sharina. She wrapped the line about the forebitt and let the wizard pull the boats together. The dinghy's oars had been in the *Lady of Mercy* when she went down.

Cashel was still comatose. "My friend will have to be carried aboard," Sharina warned as the dinghy thumped against the galley's port bow. It was disconcerting to be stared at by the ruler, his wizard, and the great brown eyes of the monkey, who was now hanging upside down from the rail.

"Captain Lashin!" the ruler said. "Get the man aboard. We'll take him to the palace."

He leaned even farther out to extend his hand to Sharina. "As we will you, mistress. I'm Folquin, King of Pandah. Someone as lovely as yourself must be of noble blood."

Without further orders, four rowers boarded the bobbing dinghy while one of their fellows held the stern firmly against the galley's flank. Sharina climbed onto the bow platform to get out of the way as the sailors lifted Cashel, a respectable weight even for all of them, over the side. Other sailors placed him on the furled sail.

"I'm not—" Sharina said to Folquin. The bow platform was far too constricted for comfort among strangers.

"A pretty female as humans go," the monkey said in a grating voice. "Is the big one her mate?"

"Zahag!" the wizard said. He was tall and gangling with the look of a colt who has yet to fill out. "You're not to disturb the lady."

Clearing his throat he went on, "I'm Halphemos, King Folquin's wizard. Can you tell us about what made your ship vanish, mistress?"

"I don't know," Sharina said. The galley was under way again. The rowers on one side backed while those on the other stroked forward, reversing direction in little more than the vessel's own length. "It just happened—like a storm, but it wasn't a real storm."

She looked at the excited, concerned faces of these strangers; staring at her, wondering about things she couldn't answer. "I'm Sharina os-Reise," she said. "I'm just . . ."

She didn't know how to go on. She wasn't a princess, but she wasn't just an innkeeper's daughter anymore either. She wasn't even Reise's daughter if what the royal emissaries had told her was true. "I'm . . ." she repeated.

And then, overwhelmed with worry, physical exhaustion, and relief she blurted what was at least the truth: "I'm very glad you came to rescue me and my friend Cashel!"

Garric gained strength as he and the women followed the gang through a forest of trees like none he'd ever seen before. He knew that in a day or two he'd feel the racking stress of his struggle with the steering oar, but for the moment the gentle exercise of walking was just what he needed to keep his muscles from cramping.

He sheathed his sword with a vibrant *zing/clank*! as the simple iron crosshilt met the lip of the scabbard. Othelm looked over his shoulder. Garric let his lip curl in something between a sneer and a snarl. Othelm's head jerked around again.

The sky remained a uniformly pale green. There wasn't a bright patch to suggest that the sun was above a layer of sickly clouds. The vegetation, both shrubs and the trees that reached sixty feet into the air, had knotted stems; branches kinked and twisted more like honeysuckle than any woody plants Garric had seen before.

He glanced at Tenoctris. She gave a quick shake of her head which Garric took to mean that their surroundings were new to her also. By common instinct the three were remaining silent until they knew more about what was going on.

Because the gang leading them cursed as they stumbled along with the massive steering oar, Garric doubted that the men could have heard the castaways' words. It still wasn't a chance he wanted to take.

He looked quickly every time he heard something scrabble in the undergrowth. This land didn't have true ground cover, grass or even ivy. The only animals he glimpsed were rats. They, like the humans, were probably survivors of ships engulfed the way the *Lady of Mercy* had been.

Garric smiled faintly. The same was true of the roaches

and flies buzzing and scurrying wherever he looked. He was glad he and his friends had survived, but that put them into a company which he couldn't regard with pride.

The path broadened. The watchman standing there looked as disreputable as the gang who'd found the castaways. He thumped a drum made from a hollow tree trunk several feet in diameter.

Garric's bowels trembled in sympathy with low notes which would penetrate for miles through the humid air. He straightened his back and noticed that his companions had reacted the same way.

More men—and a few women—came out of the forest to view the castaways. Most of their clothing was made from bark and fibers stripped from the long, sinuous leaves of the local trees, but many of the huskier and better-armed men wore an item or two which had been sucked here from outside.

''Why's he got a sword?'' a man asked Othelm in a challenging voice.

''Because I'd have killed all of them if they'd tried to take it!'' Garric said. He'd called sheep out of the woods of home. In this hushed, twilit place, his voice rang like a tocsin. ''Will you try me?''

The man who'd spoken was a squat troll with one eye and a ring through the septum of his nose. He spat on the ground but backed away when Garric came abreast of him.

They entered a broad muddy beach around a lagoon. Garric couldn't tell how far the water stretched. There were rafts on the reedy surface and dimly visible figures on the other side.

Hut-sized palisades lay along the treeline like lichen speckling stone, but the structures didn't seem to have roofs. There was no sun here and presumably no rain, so privacy rather than shelter was the only reason for construction.

Liane put a hand on Garric's shoulder and lifted herself close to his ear. ''The people in some of those boats aren't human,'' she murmured. ''There's fur on their faces.''

Guessing from the number of shelters, about a thousand humans lived in this twilight world. Perhaps a hundred had come out to meet the castaways. A similar number waited beside the pair of driftwood thrones standing in front of the largest enclosure, where a bronze gong hung from a gibbet-like crossbar.

''We've made a good haul, Rodoard!'' Othelm cried. ''This oar's seasoned oak, and there's a lot of iron in the straps, too!''

On the thrones sat a huge man and a statuesque woman who must be in her forties. She was still handsome, but there was a hardness around her eyes that revolted Garric at an instinctual level.

''So, a good haul for our beachcombers this time,'' the man, Rodoard, said. ''Come closer, boy.''

Garric stepped forward. ''Stay close,'' he murmured to his friends.

Rodoard wore several layers of silk and velvet clothing. The fabrics were sea-stained and muddy, and the assembled colors would have been hideous even in the sun's pure white light. Real cloth meant wealth in this place; that's all that mattered to Rodoard.

Metal meant wealth also. Rodoard wore a very serviceable short sword, and before him on the brocade-covered arms of his throne was a short-hafted polearm whose heavy blade was sharpened on the inner curve. There was a spiked hook on the back of the weapon.

''Demi-guisarme,'' Garric whispered, mouthing the name Carus whispered in his skull. *A clumsy double-handful that only a fool would carry in a real fight. . . .*

Garric stopped ten feet from the thrones. ''I'm Garric or-Reise,'' he said loudly. ''These are my friends Tenoctris and Liane os-Benlo. We've been shipwrecked.''

The enthroned woman stood and walked toward Garric. With a start of horror, he realized that her long dress was made of human finger bones: dried, drilled through the marrow, and strung on thin cords. They rattled faintly as the woman moved. She gave him a lazy smile.

"Leave him be, Lunifra," Rodoard said with what Garric heard as a tinge of irritation. "Later, perhaps. If he's a good boy."

A score of powerfully built guards stood close to the thrones. They carried both swords and spears, and several of them wore bits of armor as well. Even they watched the woman with disquiet.

Lunifra gave a throaty chuckle. She put her hands on her pelvis and pumped her hips in a gesture Garric found as disgusting as if she'd spit in his face. Standing so close, she stank of death.

"You're a sturdy-looking fellow, Garric," Rodoard said in a jocular tone which wouldn't have convinced even an infant of the ruler's good intentions. "We'll have use for you when we go after the Ersa for good and all. For now, though, you have to give over your sword and your woman. I decide who gets treats here in the Gulf."

"I'm from Haft," Garric said. He didn't raise his voice. "We don't own people there."

"Forget about Haft!" Rodoard said, leaning forward as his right hand tightened on the polearm's shaft. He was probably in his late twenties; almost as big as Cashel and, though puffy in the face and middle, beyond question a physically powerful man. "Forget about all the world you knew, because there's no way back to it. You're in the Gulf, now, and King Rodoard's word is the only law here!"

"As for my sword, though," Garric said as if he were still responding to the previous demand, "you're welcome to it—if you can take it from me. Do you care to try, Rodoard?"

Rodoard glanced to either side, reassuring himself that his bodyguards were in place. Garric rested his right hand lightly on his sword hilt. In Garric's mind danced a memory from the life of another man, his sword flashing through a mob of goat-footed creatures with bronze weapons. Limbs severed, horned skulls split, and over everything blood that was too red to be human. . . .

Rodoard jerked back in his seat at Garric's expression. He raised the demi-guisarme, then looked at it as though surprised to see it in his hands. He clashed the weapon down across the arms of his throne again.

Garric closed his mouth. His throat was dry and his hands trembled with bloodlust that shocked him even more than Lunifra's bone dress had done.

"Leave us be and we'll serve you!" Liane said. "But serve you as free citizens of the Isles. Do you understand?"

Lunifra was whispering. Her right hand dabbed a translucent wand over the ground. A handful of dirt squirmed upward into crudely human form and began to caper like a bear on a chain.

Lunifra looked at Garric. She was smiling again, but sweat beaded her forehead from the effort of her spell.

Beside Garric, Tenoctris murmured, *"Oreobazagra rexichthon hippochthon . . ."*

The figure of mud split in two, in four, in eight—each fragment dancing away from the others, halving and shrinking. In moments a patch of dirt a yard across shivered in ever-diminishing motion.

Lunifra tossed her head in fury. She crossed her arms in front of her to ward off a nonexistent attack. Her wand was the penis bone of a large carnivore, a bear or a giant cat.

"Sit down, Lunifra," Rodoard said. He deliberately lifted his hands from the demi-guisarme. "I told you to leave them alone."

The king looked at Garric without expression. "All right for now, boy," he said. "You can go. Josfred, find them some food and a place to sleep if they want it."

Rodoard's voice was indifferent—and far more menacing than any blustered threat could have been. There was a reason he'd become king of this assemblage of the worst sort of men.

A fellow so short and slender that Garric first mistook

him for a child came forward. He and others no bigger than him stood at the back and fringes of the crowd.

"And Josfred?" Rodoard added. "Make sure Garric meets the Ersa. I want him to know what he'll be using that sword of his on shortly."

The 10th of Heron

Cashel decided he was awake. He lay in a tight-stretched hammock. Intricately carven gratings covered the room's windows, and the vines which were trained across the openings diffused daylight into a cool, green glow.

He sat up. Over him hung a fan of brilliantly colored parrot feathers. The servant who was supposed to be making the fan swing with a treadle noticed Cashel move and began pumping his legs enthusiastically.

"Where am I?" Cashel asked.

Sharina entered through one of the two doorways, smiling like sunrise when she saw that Cashel was awake. "Don't strain yourself," she said as she stepped to the side of the bed. "Here, hold on to me—or I can get servants, men?"

"I'm all right," Cashel said. He smiled shyly; that was the sort of thing you said, after all. "I mean, I really do feel all right this time."

Cashel gave Sharina his hand, though he didn't put any weight on it, and stood up. He was light-headed but only for a moment; his body felt tinglingly refreshed. He had a confused recollection of having held the sky up for what seemed a lifetime; but it wasn't the sky, and it hadn't been his muscles that were doing the work.

He grinned at Sharina's hand in his. She was a tall girl

and not frail, but it still looked like he was holding a toy. She must have thought the same thing, because they laughed simultaneously as they stepped apart.

Sharina wore a beige linen tunic with a border of geometric blue embroidery. People in Barca's Hamlet usually wore the simplest sort of wool clothing, but Cashel had learned a good deal about fabrics and styles from living with his sister Ilna. Thinking about it, he supposed Ilna knew a lot about sheep, too.

He looked down at himself. He was in a similar tunic, but his showed signs of having been hastily pieced together from two garments. He smiled. Apparently people of his size weren't common here.

Wherever here was. "Are we on Pandah?" Cashel asked.

A monkey walked into the room on all fours. It stood upright and said to Sharina in a guttural voice, "Come on back. It's your move now."

"The monkey talks!" Cashel said.

The monkey drew its lips back in a sneer or a snarl. It was about as big as an average man, though its stumpy legs had deceived Cashel at first glance. The deep chest and arms layered with flat bands of muscle would make it a respectable opponent.

"Are all you humans too stupid to tell an ape from a monkey?" the beast said. "Maybe you should get Halphemos to raise this one's intelligence, Sharina. Though I think you'd do better to start with a dog. Or maybe an ox."

Cashel burst out laughing. "This is wonderful!" he said. "It really talks and thinks, then?"

"Idiot! Idiot! Idiot!" the monkey—the *ape*—shrieked. It leaped to a window and shook the grate in apparent fury.

Sharina was laughing too. "This is Zahag," she explained. "King Folquin of Pandah has kindly sheltered us after the—"

Sharina's frown was only a flicker, but her tone was

marginally more subdued as she went on, "After the storm wrecked the ship. His court wizard, Master Halphemos, has given Zahag the mind of a human. We've been playing chess."

Zahag hopped down from the window. "Come!" he ordered, reaching for Sharina's hand. His fingers were grotesquely long and covered with coarse reddish fur. "It's your move!"

The ape's anger a moment before hadn't been playacting. The window grating was made of some hard wood. Zahag's teeth had torn deep gouges on the center rosette.

The wizard's art might have given the ape a man's intelligence, but the creature still had a beast's *mind.* A Sandrakkan wool merchant had once come to Barca's Hamlet with a pet monkey, but that was a little thing no bigger than a cat. A pet with fangs the size of Zahag's didn't seem a very good idea, and a *smart,* strong pet that flew into rages was an even worse idea.

"In a moment, Zahag," Sharina said, twitching her hand away. "Cashel, are you ready to be introduced to King Folquin? There's no rush if you're not."

The servant—was he a slave?—watched as he continued to work the treadle. To someone watching, the man seemed to have no more personality than the fan itself.

"Now!" Zahag cried. He crouched as though to leap on Sharina.

Cashel, moving as he always did when there was need—faster than almost anyone else—swept Sharina behind him. He faced the ape with the silent resolution of a cliff face, just as he'd faced demons in the past.

Zahag gave a chirp of terror. He hopped onto the servant, flinging the startled fellow backward, and jumped to the fan itself. The suspension cords thrummed at the extra weight; feathers torn from the frame fluttered about like the petals of a giant flower.

Cashel backed away, keeping between Sharina and the ape. She wasn't wearing the hermit's knife today, he noticed. He supposed the weapon'd be out of place in a palace.

Zahag dropped to the floor of polished, dovetailed planks. He scratched himself nonchalantly, though he still watched Cashel with sidelong care. He muttered, "Well, the game can wait, I suppose."

Cashel cleared his throat. "Sure, I'd like to thank the king," he said.

They walked out of the bedroom with Sharina leading by a half step and the ape capering behind. The servant was holding the treadle-rope firmly to stop the fan's flailing.

Zahag's emotional swings were more of a worry to Cashel; but so long as he was around, Sharina didn't have to worry at all.

"How do you tell time here?" Liane asked as Josfred led them along a trail away from the settlement.

Garric guessed he'd slept a full twelve hours for his muscles to have recovered so well from their straining during the storm. Nothing in the sky or forest had changed since he collapsed from exhaustion in the shelter of woven saplings to which Josfred had led the three of them.

The guide shrugged. "You outsiders always ask that," he said. "Time doesn't mean anything in the Gulf. We can't understand you, the ones of us who were born here."

The track had once been a broad avenue skirting the lagoon, but shrubs like wormwood (though soft-bodied) had begun to cover it. Garric didn't know how fast vegetation grew here in the Gulf, but the diminution in traffic must have come within the past year or two.

"There!" Josfred said. "There's a bunch of Ersa harvesting plums. I don't suppose we ought to go much closer, but they probably won't give us any trouble. You've got a steel sword, Master Garric."

Bitterness dripped from the guide's voice. Garric

wasn't sure whether the rabbity little man envied him more possession of the sword or of Liane. Josfred didn't seem to have any conception of women as people. Garric had to assume that the guide's attitude was more or less representative of everybody here in the Gulf.

Though . . . Lunifra wasn't anybody's chattel, not even Rodoard's.

A dozen lightly furred humanoids picked dark blue fruit from waist-high bushes planted in regular rows. The ones Garric had eaten before he and his friends went off with Josfred were fist-sized and neither looked nor tasted anything like real plums; even the color would pale in real sunlight. Human castaways had given familiar names to the vegetation of the Gulf, but nothing else about "the plums" was familiar.

The Ersa stopped working and unslung the baskets in which they'd been putting fruit. They moved together, their eyes on the humans, while the males took up spears and clubs. The wooden weapons had points and edges made of shells from the lagoon.

The largest of the Ersa—Garric's height but more lithely built—had a spear whose slender iron tip had been forged from a nail. He waved it at Garric and said, "Go away, men." His accent was easier to understand than Josfred's.

"We'd better leave," the guide said nervously.

"I need to talk with them," Tenoctris said. She entered the field, stepping carefully between the waist-high bushes.

Garric opened his mouth to protest, then started after the wizard. Liane caught his arm. "Take off your sword," she whispered.

"I should've thought of that myself," Garric muttered. If he strode forward armed, he'd look like a threat even though nothing could be further from his mind.

He undid the sword belt. That wasn't a simple task: the buckle had two hooks and the tongue, left deliberately long, was looped about the belt proper. It was the way King Carus had worn his sword. . . .

"What are you doing?" Josfred said, his voice rising with concern.

Garric ignored him. He thrust the weapon into Liane's arms and hurried to join Tenoctris before she reached the scowling Ersa.

"This is our field," the leader of the Ersa said. "If you try to take our food, we will fight you."

From a distance Garric had thought the Ersa's features were catlike. Close up they didn't look like any animal he'd ever seen—nor did they look very much like furry humans. In fact, their gray-brown fur was one of the least *un*familiar things about the Ersa.

Their faces were round. Their ear openings were simple holes, but they signaled now among themselves with membranous external ears the size of a man's hand. Their mouths opened and closed sideways; and besides horny lids, nictitating membranes wiped their eyes in a quick, constant shimmer of motion.

"We aren't your enemies," Garric said. The Ersa looked alien, but they were clean and dignified—virtues in short supply in the human portion of the Gulf. "We mean you no harm."

"We've just come here," Tenoctris said. "Our ship was destroyed by a force that was new to me. Did you or your ancestors arrive in the Gulf the same way?"

The Ersa's eyes were closer to the sides of their skulls than a human's were. Like sheep, they could see in a broad arc behind them. Their ears fluttered in wordless speech like bunting in a windstorm.

"Our fathers made this place to escape enemies," the leader said at last. "We lived here alone for many generations. When the first men arrived, we let them stay. All was well for many generations more. Now new men have come with new weapons and take our fields. Humans, we are rulers here!"

He shook his spear in front of Garric. He had four fingers on each hand, two opposing two instead of fingers and a separate thumb.

"Go back now or we will kill you!" he shouted.

The stance of the whole group shifted slightly. King Carus was a presence in Garric's mind, analyzing the situation. An individual man would generally be a match for an Ersa, but a group of Ersa would fight in a united fashion that not even the most disciplined human army could manage.

"Thank you for speaking with us," Tenoctris said. She bowed low. "We will come and speak with you again."

Garric bowed also. Careful of the crops, he followed the old wizard back through the field.

"An Ersa wizard must have created this Gulf," Tenoctris said quietly to her companion. "There's no record of the Ersa, not even in the almagests of great wizards who searched all time for no better reason than to increase knowledge. Cadilorn and Mansel of Eyre; Uzuncu the Skull, too, if she wasn't just a myth like the Yellow King she served."

She smiled wanly at Garric. "I would have been one of that company if I'd had the power," she said. "Which of course I didn't. But because I'm with you, Garric, I'm learning things that not even Uzuncu knew."

Tenoctris laughed, a pure, cheerful sound that made the changeless day brighter for Garric. "Perhaps the folk who claimed it's better to be lucky than wise were correct," she added.

"I don't see that it's very lucky to have come here," Garric said. He was uneasy at the thought that their presence in the Gulf was because of him. "Especially if no one can leave once he's here."

"It's possible to leave," Tenoctris said with assurance that had nothing of bluster in it. "I don't know that it'll be possible for *me* to get us out, but I think I know how a sufficiently powerful wizard would be able to succeed."

They'd reached the others. Liane squeezed Garric's hand as she returned the sword.

Josfred had been shifting his weight from one leg to the other and back again. "You shouldn't have done that!" he blurted. "They might have killed you, and then what would Rodoard have said?"

"Nothing that would have been of any concern to Garric," Liane said, taking out some of her own previous nervousness on the guide. "And there's no point in talking about things that didn't happen."

Garric glanced over his shoulder. The Ersa had resumed gathering their crop. Since the Ersa were even more community-minded than humans, they had every reason to feel threatened by each member of a race which included the likes of Rodoard and Lunifra. Despite the threat with which the Ersa leader had ended the discussion, they seemed to accept that Garric and Tenoctris weren't personally hostile toward them.

"Josfred," Tenoctris said as they started back down the trail to the settlement, "you said you were born in the Gulf. How long have your ancestors lived here?"

The little man waved his arms in frustration. "I told you, the question doesn't mean anything!" he said. "We've always been here."

He paused as he suddenly realized that duration, even in the Gulf, could be punctuated in important ways. "Only we were slaves of the Ersa until the other men like you washed up on the outer shore with weapons. The outer shore was just mud before."

"Not in a thousand years, I'd venture," Tenoctris said with satisfaction. "Not since the previous time forces built to a peak. The Gulf is a closed world. I'm not sure that it was even part of our cosmos originally, because the Ersa exist only here in the Gulf."

"The cosmos is everything that was or will be," Liane said sharply. "Isn't it? There can't be anything more than that!"

"It generally seems that way from our human viewpoint," Tenoctris said. She smiled at Liane, taking the sting out of the implied rebuke.

Liane stopped on the trail and hugged the old woman. "I'm sorry," she said. "I shouldn't . . . I'm so afraid. Everything that I thought I knew is changing."

"Rodoard made us strong," Josfred said. "We aren't the Ersa's slaves anymore!"

Garric didn't need King Carus to tell him that Rodoard would be a very bad master indeed if he didn't have an external enemy like the Ersa to keep him in check. And even Rodoard's probable brutality would be better than the whimsical sadism that could be expected from Lunifra.

"Rodoard and six other men arrived together," Josfred said, reminiscing happily as they followed the trail back to the settlement. "They had steel weapons. One of the men thought he could give Rodoard orders, but Rodoard showed *him*."

Josfred chuckled like water dribbling from a cracked jug. "Rodoard cut his belly open, right there. And he squealed and squealed and then he died!"

"Was Rodoard this man's bodyguard in the outer world, Josfred?" Liane asked in an even voice. Garric looked at her, surprised both at the question and the calm fashion the girl asked it.

Josfred gasped. "Are you a wizard like Lunifra, woman?" he asked in horror. "How else would you know that?"

"Rodoard has the tattoos of a Blaise armsman," Liane said. In a tone of mild reminiscence she went on, "They often hire out to guard merchants. My father occasionally hired them."

In a terse, colorless voice she added, "And no, I'm nothing like Lunifra. Nothing at all."

"Lunifra is a skilled wizard," Tenoctris said. "*Skilled,* not just powerful, though she's respectably powerful as well."

She laughed. "More powerful than me, at any rate."

"Should you have let Lunifra know you're a wizard too?" Garric said quietly. Tenoctris usually kept her skills secret, so he'd been surprised when she openly displayed them by interfering with Lunifra's manikin.

"She already knew," Tenoctris said. "I saw it in her smile as she looked at me. She sees things instead of just forcing powers to her will. And she's quite intelligent."

Garric cleared his throat. If he understood what Tenoctris was implying . . .

"Tenoctris?" he said abruptly. The best way to get an answer to a question is to ask it. "Do you mean you want Lunifra to join us? To be our ally?"

Tenoctris halted in the middle of the trail. She put her hand on Garric's to cause him to face her. Josfred continued several steps farther, unaware of what was happening behind him, but Liane stopped and watched her friends with an expression of controlled concern.

"Garric," Tenoctris said, "when you look at Lunifra, what do you feel?"

"She turns my stomach," he said with his usual simple honesty.

"That's good," Tenoctris said. "Because I've never before in a long lifetime met someone who seemed so completely an assemblage of mindless evil. Lunifra isn't striving for power or doing any of the other human things that lead one to evil, toward Malkar. She's like lightning or a tidal wave: she smashes things just because she and they happen to come together."

"She's helping Rodoard now?" Liane said.

"He thinks she is," Tenoctris said. "When she's brought everything else down, she'll destroy him too."

Josfred had returned and was listening to the castaways in concern. "Lunifra came from the outer shore too," he said. "Not many women come from there. There've been over a hundred men since Rodoard, though, with steel and harder wood than what grows here in the Gulf."

The little man looked sidelong at Garric's sword. "The men who won't serve Rodoard all die," he whispered. "Everyone has to serve Rodoard so that we can be free of the Ersa!"

"Yes," Garric said. "I understand exactly what you mean."

Most of those swept into the Gulf would be sailors, men hardened by a brutally dangerous life. Humans born in the Gulf were stunted according to outside standards; the size and steel weapons of the recent castaways gave them unchallenged authority over the society they found here. The newcomers weren't necessarily bad men, but for most of them the Gulf would seem like Paradise; and some of them *were* bad men.

For those who wouldn't serve a thug like Rodoard, there was quick murder before the poison of decency took hold in the Gulf. Garric had been saved—thus far—because he'd reacted without hostility, but in a fashion that made him seem extremely dangerous if Rodoard insisted on trying conclusions.

From memory came an image of Carus dancing through a wall of enemies. His sword strokes had the speed and shattering power of so many thunderbolts.

A sailor wouldn't have had the presence to face down Rodoard, and a merchant wouldn't have the strength and skill to make the implied threat credible. Garric or-Reise, the peasant from Barca's Hamlet, couldn't have managed the act alone either, but—he touched the medallion on his breast—he hadn't been alone.

King Carus chuckled, unseen but always a presence now, even when Garric was awake and alert.

"We're going to finish off the Ersa," Josfred said, rubbing his hands in gleeful anticipation. "Many of your people have come to us, with hard wood and metal for weapons. We'll have the Ersa for slaves as they had us—or maybe we'll kill them all!"

If you do, Garric thought grimly, *Rodoard will show you what* real *slavery's like.* Though even that would be better than what Lunifra would bring to the Gulf.

"I have a better idea," Tenoctris said mildly. "I think we can all leave this place—leave it to the Ersa, at least—

and close it up behind us so that it doesn't trap other folk in the future.''

''Leaving this place,'' Liane said with forceful sincerity, ''is the best idea there could be. And it can't be too soon for me!''

Sharina touched Cashel's hand as she led him. The vines wreathing the colonnade were flowering, rich with perfume and alive with the deep hum of insects. It was an exotic setting to anyone raised in Barca's Hamlet, but it was peaceful in a reassuring fashion also.

''Hurry!'' Zahag demanded. His arms were twice the length of his stubby legs. He skipped ahead as though he were playing leapfrog.

''We'll get there,'' said Cashel, stilling Sharina's reflexive desire to speed up because somebody had told her to. She giggled and dropped back the half step by which she'd been leading. It was reassuring to be around Cashel. He moved quickly when it was necessary but he never hurried.

''Fagh!'' Zahag snarled in disgust. He jumped to the carved transom, then flipped onto the colonnade's roof. The thumps of the ape's leaping progress across the tiles faded.

King Folquin's palace was laid out as a square-bottomed U with on the outside a colonnade onto which each room opened. Corridors through both arms of the U led from the colonnade to the central court where the real business of the palace was conducted. Only the king's own apartments had an entrance directly onto the courtyard.

''It's nice of the king to help us like this,'' Cashel said. Another person might have let his doubt show in the initial statement. Cashel simply continued, ''Why is he doing that?''

''Because . . . ,'' Sharina said, just a sound to give her time to collect her thoughts on a difficult question.

"Whatever happened to our ship made a great spectacle from here. Flashes and thunder. Master Halphemos says that for a moment he saw a great disk like the night sky with stars. So they were very excited to find survivors, though I couldn't tell them much about what had happened."

The palace servants lived on the upper floor. Mothers called down to the children playing on the grounds beyond the vine-screened colonnade. Clothes dried in the sun on pole racks, while outside ovens spread the odors of cooking. People lived at closer quarters here in Pandah than they did in the borough, but they were people just the same.

The arched passage to the courtyard was lined by reed-shaped pilasters. The palace was built of stone, but on the way from the harbor Sharina had seen that the houses of common people were often made of tarred rushes.

"And also . . ." Sharina continued. The least she owed Cashel was complete honesty, even when it embarrassed her. "King Folquin is a romantic. Halphemos has told him that he'll marry a princess who comes to him as a result of wizardry. Folquin thinks that's me."

"Oh," said Cashel. He shrugged, an instinctive way to loosen his tunic about him. When Cashel flexed his huge muscles, he regularly split his garments. "Who's Halphemos, then?"

"The court wizard," Sharina said. She'd deliberately slowed her pace, but they were coming to the end of the short corridor anyway. "He's a boy, really—a nice one. I think he'd have fit in back in Barca's Hamlet. But he *is* a wizard."

"Let's go meet him, then," Cashel said mildly. "And King Folquin."

Sharina had never seen Cashel angry, not even when he was fighting for his life and her own. A giant oak doesn't get angry either, but when it begins to fall the only choices are to get clear or be crushed.

They stepped into the courtyard. Folquin sat on a stool

whose four legs ended in curved fishtails. He wore a linen tunic with only a plumed aigrette on his head to remind Sharina of the feathered state in which he'd rescued her. With him were several court officials—including Halphemos, who'd also discarded his formal robe. About a hundred citizens of Pandah and a scattering of foreigners stood at the open end of the court, either waiting to petition the king or simply watching the activities.

Three tumblers performed with a vaulting horse. They were skilled, but it seemed to Sharina that there was a desultory competence rather than real enthusiasm in their flips and handstands. They were present because court etiquette required entertainment. Waiting to follow the tumblers, a pair of trim young women with a xylophone chatted with a paunchy merchant and his secretary.

Folquin sat supporting his chin with a hand. A pair of women wearing baize shawls over their tunics argued a point of contention before him, each glaring as the other spoke. A court official stood beside each witness to keep her in check.

Zahag squatted near the chess table set up behind the king's stool, checking his fur for lice. Halphemos had been staring morosely into the distance. He brighfened and hurried over when he saw Sharina and Cashel.

"Master Cashel!" he said enthusiastically. "Mistress Sharina tells me that you're responsible for preserving her from the event that engulfed your ship. I'm honored to meet a wizard of your power!"

He reached out to clasp forearms with Cashel, hand to elbow like a pair of dealers meeting at the Sheep Fair. Together they looked like a stalk of bamboo growing beside an oak tree.

"I'm not a wizard," Cashel said. He shrugged with honest embarrassment. "I just . . . I don't remember really what happened. There was a big weight and I was trying to throw it off."

Cashel cleared his throat, turned to spit, and realized he was in a royal court. He swallowed instead.

Most of those gathered here were either watching the tumblers or talking to one another while they waited for the king to get around to their petition. An old woman with a cup in front of her told a story to a group at the back of the courtyard; a shabby-looking man in a corner was demonstrating a game involving three nutshells and a pea to a rustic.

The exception was a woman in a long white garment and tattoos on both cheeks. She squatted apart from the others, drawing with a pointed bone in the dust between her feet. Her eyes followed Cashel with the fixed intensity of a snake watching a vole. When she saw that Sharina had noticed her, she grinned inanely and looked down at the squiggles her bone stylus had made.

"Master Cashel," Halphemos said earnestly, "I'm not very learned in the art myself, but my friend Cerix understands everything there is about wizardry. Could I ask you to join us at our lodgings, perhaps tonight? He's been injured, so it's hard for him to get around."

The ape noticed them and came bounding over. He bumped Folquin's stool, drawing a black look from the king.

"Sharina!" Zahag said. "It's your move! Come!"

Cashel said, "Well, I don't mind meeting your Cerix, but what we really need is to find the friends who were on the ship with—"

The ape reached imperiously for Sharina's hand. Cashel stepped sideways to block him. Zahag hopped backward; a man would have collided with Cashel's massive form and recoiled.

Sharina glanced at the king. Folquin caught her eye and grimaced. He seemed determined to hear out this pair of complainants rather than start the whole business over again from the beginning.

"I'll finish the game," Sharina said with an apologetic moue to Cashel. "It shouldn't take long."

Sharina smiled as she trailed after the chortling Zahag. The ape was acting like an ill-tempered child, but he couldn't help it any more than the child could. A man—a man like Cashel, at any rate—was apt to react to bullying from someone of Zahag's size as if the ape were an adult who could control what he was doing. That wouldn't be appropriate.

Well, Sharina didn't think it would be appropriate. On the other hand, Cashel might be right in believing that if he once threw the ape over the roof of the palace, Zahag *would* find the ability to control his future behavior.

"That's part of the reason I'd like you to meet Cerix," Halphemos continued. "With his knowledge and your, well, our, strength, perhaps we can find your friends."

Sharina squatted before the low table. Pandah's court etiquette was fairly informal, but it forbade anyone to sit on a chair or stool while the king heard petitions. Squatting was no hardship to a girl from Barca's Hamlet.

She studied the board. Chess was a noble game which no one in the borough but Sharina and her parents, Lora and Reise, played. Lora had seen to it that Sharina learned chess as well as every other aspect of court procedure which could be taught in a rural inn.

Lora and Reise had been palace servants the night rioters killed the Count and Countess of Haft. Sharina grew into a willowy blonde who looked nothing like the solid, dark-haired natives of Haft, but was the very image of an Ornifal noble like Count Niard, ruler of Haft through his marriage. His wife, Countess Tera, sprung from the old line of Kings of the Isles. Lora had always been sure of what Sharina was told by the royal emissaries: Sharina was Tera's daughter, born the same night as Garric and fostered by Lora and Reise with their own son.

Lora was a bitter, sharp-tongued woman. All that sustained her was the hope that someday the child she raised would sit on a throne while Lora beamed from a seat one step below her. But when King Valence's emissaries took Sharina with them to what they claimed was her destiny, they left Lora behind—of no value to the king's plans, of no value to Sharina either. Sharina felt sorry for Lora, but she couldn't find any love in her heart for the woman she still thought of as mother.

Still, chess playing did seem to be a useful social skill here in King Folquin's court.

Sharina assessed the board's layout, then moved her gryphon out of the home row. Her pieces were carved from a deep red wood; Zahag's had been made from wood so pale that only by holding pieces at an angle could Sharina see the grain.

Pandah was the only major island in the heart of the shallow Inner Sea. There were many islets where a ship could be beached for the night, but few offered anything beyond a landing place. Food, good water, and all the entertainments of civilization were available on Pandah.

From being a general port of call, Pandah had grown into a major trading center where goods from all over the Isles were bought or bartered for transshipment. This chess set could have come from anywhere, though the grotesque carving made Sharina suspect the source was Dalopo.

Sharina eyed the crowd. The woman she'd noticed before was staring at Cashel again. Natives of Dalopo were supposed to tattoo themselves. . . .

Zahag cawed with glee. He slid his remaining wizard diagonally to take Sharina's tortoise. "There!" he cried. "You didn't see that!"

Sharina had indeed seen the move. She'd played several games with Zahag, and she'd correctly judged from past experience that the ape would be too hasty to see anything else.

Beside her, Folquin had adjudged a goat to one of the parties and a money fine for damage the goat did to the other. Both women wailed in shrill disbelief. Cashel and Halphemos continued to talk. The young wizard was showing Cashel his athame, a blade of yellow walrus ivory.

Sharina hopped her gryphon forward again. "Check," she said. "And mate."

"Ah, Mistress Sharina!" King Folquin said. "Would you introduce me to your protector, please?"

Sharina turned, starting to rise. Zahag exploded in an enraged shriek as loud as metal tearing. He flung the table to the side in a hail of chessmen and grabbed Sharina with hands strong enough to crack walnuts.

Folquin shouted angrily. The guards relaxing against the palace wall leaped to their feet. Most ran toward Sharina, but one in flustered excitement started to string his bow.

Cashel moved without a word or wasted motion. His great hands caught Zahag's forearms, squeezing hard so that the ape couldn't tighten his own grip. Zahag released Sharina and tried to bite Cashel's hand. Cashel snapped his arms apart, still holding the ape. Zahag raked Cashel's belly with the stubby claws on his feet.

The ape was frothing with rage; most of the spectators added their voices to the cacophony. Halphemos stood aside, chanting a spell with his eyes on the struggle. His athame beat the air. The wizard's mouth twisted to form ancient syllables; his face was pale.

Guards pushed through the crowd with their short, hook-bladed swords drawn. The leader's helmet had an erne-feather crest. Sharina stepped into their path, her hands raised. "Don't!" she cried. "Let Cashel handle it!"

She knew Cashel could hold Zahag until the ape's fury burned itself out. If nervous swordsmen got involved, there was no telling what would happen.

"Get out of the way!" the leader of the guards shouted, trying to thrust Sharina aside. She grappled with him, twisting his sword arm back. His brass helmet fell to the ground. The folk of Pandah were slightly built, and Sharina had fear as well as her native strength to aid her.

One guard dropped his sword and tried to pull Sharina away from his leader. The others hesitated, unwilling to act in a situation so confused.

Cashel raised Zahag overhead. He flexed to hurl the ape into the wall of the palace. Zahag was much stronger than a man of his size. He'd gotten a grip on Cashel's right wrist and wouldn't be shaken off. Cashel grunted and stepped toward the building, preparing to flail Zahag to jelly when he couldn't simply throw the ape.

"*Meueri puripeganux!*" Halphemos cried in the sudden stillness. His athame pointed.

The air surrounding Cashel and Zahag shimmered with a soap-bubble iridescence, then flashed red. Ape, man, and a section of the packed clay beneath Cashel's feet vanished.

Sharina and the gaping guards stepped apart. She looked at Halphemos in disbelief.

Halphemos stared horrified at the empty air. "I didn't do that!" he said. "By the Lady, I was just binding them!"

Behind Halphemos the tattooed woman stood up. The ball of her bare foot wiped out the signs she'd drawn on the ground. She walked away while everyone about her babbled in wonder.

The tenement where Ilna had a suite was so flimsily built that its foundations supported three stories rather the two to which walls of normal solidity would have limited the structure. Her rooms—one for her looms, the other for the normal business of life—were on the top floor. The roof above them didn't leak, and Ilna didn't consider that avoiding a walk up stairs was worth paying money for.

The walls and floor of Ilna's rooms were spotlessly clean for the first time in their existence: literally clean enough to eat from. The process had taken her a day and a half of scrubbing, and the odor of the lye she'd used still clung to the plaster.

Ilna thought about the past as her shuttle clattered back and forth across the double loom. She was weaving a thin fabric two ells across. It could be hung in the hall of a mansion—or over the light well of a tenement like this one. She hadn't decided which it would be: an object for sale to a noble who'd pay well for the benison the fabric brought his household, or a gift to some hundreds of people she didn't know and whose willingness to accept squalor disgusted her.

A debt was a debt, whether or not you liked or respected the creditor. The harm Ilna had done with her love charms had touched, directly or indirectly, every person in Erdin. The only present question was whether money or a gift in kind was a better means of repayment.

Ilna didn't think about the future. The past and the sores on her heart were bad enough.

Her instinct pressed the treadle to lift this or that grouping of warp threads into a shed for each pass of the shuttle. Because her mind was on the ship carrying Garric away from her, it was some moments before the subtle details of the pattern she wove reached her consciousness.

Ilna stopped, then ran her fingers over the closely woven cloth. The past, present, and future of the cosmos were a single fabric; and since Ilna os-Kenset came back from Hell, there was no pattern whose knots were hidden from her.

She snorted. During the days she'd been living in the Crescent, she'd managed to convince herself that people were better than she knew full well they were in reality. She'd still taken precautions, of course.

Ilna got up from the loom and put on a cape of dull blue wool. She'd woven the fabric herself; it had the consistency of warm milk. She took the noose made of the fine silk from its peg and concealed it under the cape. In a sense using silk for the purpose was a luxury, but Ilna had never been one to skimp on tools.

The windows were simply openings in the wall. Ilna didn't close and bar the shutters before she went out. The only reason she bothered to lock the door with its two-pin key was that it would seem suspicious if she didn't.

The tenement covered a square block with a light well in the center. There was a staircase in each corner, though the landings were usually choked with refuse.

A boy of ten or twelve loitered in the grubby hallway as Ilna locked her door. The rag wrapped over the boil on his left elbow had been filthy to begin with; now it was a mass of yellowish crystallized pus.

Ilna pretended to ignore the lookout as she strode to the nearer of the two stairwells. She was barely out of sight before she heard him give a piercing whistle.

The staircase was dank and stinking. Children played on it, shrieking excitedly as they jumped up and down over the gap where a tread was missing. They seemed happy enough, though Ilna couldn't imagine why.

Instead of going down to street level, Ilna got out on the second floor and walked to the stairs at the opposite end of the corridor. The passage had no windows of its own and most of the doors to either side were closed. It was like walking through a tunnel, lighted only by the glimmers around warped panels.

A couple were fondling on the landing. The man cursed as Ilna pushed by, climbing back to her own floor. She ignored them the way she ignored the excrement dried on the walls.

Ilna *could* change the world; she was doing so to the best of her considerable ability. But she couldn't change it all, and she couldn't change it all at once.

She stepped out into the corridor. Her door had been smashed open. The boy with the running sore stood beside the doorway, staring intently toward the stairwell by which Ilna had left. All the other doors on the hallway were shut: her neighbors were making sure that they saw nothing.

Ilna walked softly down the hall. The boy must still have heard the whisper of her bare foot on the boards, because he started to turn as her noose settled around his neck.

Ilna jerked the boy to her, choking the shout in his throat. With the free end of the rope she lashed his wrists and ankles together as though she were trussing a rabbit for market. The boy's eyes were terrified. His face was turning red, but he could still breathe if he pulled his head back to get a little slack in the noose.

Ilna touched an index finger to her lips in warning. Then she stepped to the door of her room.

One of the two husky men inside had his arms full of Ilna's yarn, two wicker hampers with loose-fitting tops. The other stood at the head of the double loom and said, "No, we'll get a lot more for this but we gotta get it apart—"

He saw Ilna in the doorway. "Sister take that useless kid!" he snarled. He pulled a cudgel from beneath his broad leather belt and started for her.

Ilna tugged the cord on the doorjamb, releasing the net of fine silk she'd fastened to the ceiling. It drifted over the thieves like mist on a meadow. Ilna stepped back.

"Sister bite your heart out!" cried the man as he swung his cudgel. The weapon tangled in the meshes, drawing other parts of the net closer about his head and shoulders. A sword would have done much the same: only the very keenest of blades could have cut the elastic fabric instead of being cocooned by it.

The men struggled like locusts caught in a spider's web. After a few moments, both of them fell over.

Ilna reached in carefully and drew out the cudgel which the owner had dropped when he tried to pull the net apart with both hands. He might as profitably have attempted to lift the building. Indeed, he was more likely to pick up this shoddy structure than he was to tear a net Ilna had woven. . . .

"You came for my property," Ilna said, looking down on her captives in cold amusement. "And you're going to leave with some of it: the net. I want you to crawl to the window together and jump out."

"You stupid bitch!" snarled one of the men. "You'd better let us go or—"

Ilna rapped him on the forehead with his own cudgel. The seasoned oak *toonk*ed like a maul driving a wedge.

The man's eyes rolled up in their sockets. His body went as limp as an empty sack.

The blow had opened a pressure cut in the man's forehead. Ilna glanced with distaste at the blood on the cudgel, then said to the remaining thief, "All right, you'll carry your friend to the window and jump out with him. If you're skillful, you may be able to cushion your own fall. Understood?"

"Shepherd guard me!" the man whispered with his eyes shut. "Shepherd guard me!"

He maneuvered carefully onto his knees and managed to lift his companion. Ilna judiciously plucked individual meshes away from where they were tangled, choosing each time the point that would have held the thief as he shuffled to the window.

He balanced his companion on the narrow ledge and looked back. "Up and over," Ilna said pleasantly.

It was the expression on her face rather than the waggling cudgel which broke the would-be thief. He lurched forward and disappeared with a despairing cry. Ilna tossed the cudgel after him.

She walked to the doorway, straightening items disarranged by the thieves or their capture. If she'd given them a few minutes more, they'd probably have managed to break the frame of the big loom. Well, it could have been repaired.

Several of the doors on the hallway were open. Heads ducked back when Ilna stepped out, but one frumpish woman continued working at the knots which held the lookout.

"Get away before you manage to strangle him," Ilna snapped. The boy's face was close to purple now.

The woman looked up. "You can't do this to Maidus!" she said. "He's my nephew!"

"Get back into your filthy sty or I'll do a great deal worse to *you,*" Ilna said with a smile as cold as a winter gale.

The woman flinched. She didn't move when Ilna lifted

the boy to her shoulder like a sack of grain and carried him, head hanging down behind her to lessen the noose's tension, to her own room.

Ilna loosed the knots as swiftly as she'd tied them, then slipped the noose and coiled the rope in readiness for any further use. The boy, Maidus, lay sobbing on her floor, massaging his throat with his right hand.

A slotted wooden box in the other room kept flies from Ilna's food. She took out the flask of cheap wine she used for sauces and the bone-hilted knife she used for household tasks. With them she returned to the boy.

Maidus squealed in terror as Ilna put a swatch of coarse fabric under his left elbow for a pad. "This is going to hurt," she said as she cut away the foul bandage. She flipped it out the window on the knife point. "Hold still or it'll hurt more."

"What're you—," the boy said. Ilna gripped his arm above and below the elbow, then squeezed the boil empty with the even pressure of both thumbs.

Maidus gaped at her. He didn't scream though, rather to her surprise. She mopped the skin around the boil with a clean corner of the pad. The mass of congealed pus had left a flat-bottomed pit as wide as a fingernail and deep in the boy's flesh.

"This will hurt too," Ilna said. She dribbled acid wine into the wound. Maidus began to whimper. He patted at his tears with his free hand.

Working methodically, Ilna packed the boil with a roll of thin fabric. She left a tag hanging out, then bandaged the work with a ribbon she'd woven in a pattern that would speed healing. She had to search for it; the thieves had jumbled her belongings in a fashion that would take her an hour to reorganize.

Ilna stepped away. "You can get up now, Maidus," she said. "Go home, I suppose. Come back in three days and I'll jerk the tape out."

She smiled at the look in the boy's eyes. "Yes, that'll hurt too," she said. "But it'll keep the boil from returning. This is one of those times when the hard way is really best.''

Maidus stood up cautiously. There were voices in the hallway, neighbors speaking to one another in frightened whispers. ''We didn't know you were a wizard, mistress,'' he said to Ilna.

''You don't know it now!'' she replied. ''But I hope your friends and all *their* friends realize Ilna os-Kenset isn't to be trifled with.''

She sniffed. ''And I suggest in the future you keep away from those two louts,'' she added. ''Their incompetence should bother you even if their dishonesty doesn't.''

Maidus nodded. He glanced toward the door. ''I can . . . ?'' he said.

''Yes, you can go,'' Ilna snapped. ''But I could use someone to run errands occasionally. If you'd care to do that, come see me in the morning.''

''Yes, mistress!'' the boy said as he sprinted into the hallway.

''It won't pay very much!'' Ilna called after him.

She picked up her door panel, considering the best way to hang it for the time being until she could get a carpenter to replace the hinges.

Not the whole world, and not all at once; but she *was* making changes.

The 11th of Heron

The moon should've been in its third quarter, not full as Cashel saw it above him when he opened his eyes. It shouldn't have been night anyway, though from the way Cashel felt he was willing to believe he'd been unconscious for a dozen hours.

He got carefully to his feet. Toads shrilled merrily. He grinned. They couldn't carry a tune any better than he could: toads, seagulls, and Cashel or-Kenset. Toads were a familiar sound, and in the near distance he heard the rattling grunt of a pig frog just like the ones in the marshes south of Barca's Hamlet.

Cashel looked at the night sky. The stars weren't quite right either. It was still spring—a thousand things told him that, from insect sounds to the feel of the wind—but the Tongs were already above the southern horizon.

If Cashel'd had his quarterstaff, he'd have rubbed the hickory just for the feel of it. He didn't, and he didn't guess it really mattered.

Something moved nearby among the low trees. Cashel turned to face the sound, hunching forward slightly. His arms were spread. "Whoever's there better greet me like a man, or I'll think I've got vermin to deal with," he rumbled.

"I was checking you were all right," Zahag's guttural voice claimed. "You've come around, then?"

"Come out where I can see you," Cashel ordered, relaxing somewhat as he straightened. He didn't have much reason to like the talking ape, but Zahag wasn't anything for Cashel to fear. He'd be a familiar face, though an ugly one.

"She nearly tore my arms and legs off, whirling us here," Zahag complained as he sidled into full view. He was on all fours and obviously ready to bolt for the trees if Cashel wanted to renew the fight.

"You don't have to worry," Cashel said with a degree of scorn. "It wasn't me started things in the first place. But my oath on the Shepherd, ape: you throw one of your hissies again and I *won't* half hurt you."

"You don't need to show your teeth," Zahag said gloomily. "I'd been around humans too long and I forgot how to behave with real people."

He scratched himself in the middle of the back. Cashel

blinked; it wasn't just the length of Zahag's arms but also the extra range of motion in the joints that made the maneuver possible.

"I wish I were back on Sirimat," the ape said. "I wish I were back the way I was before Halphemos made me talk."

Cashel worked his shoulders to loosen them. He felt as though all his limbs had been stretched. "Do you know where we are?" he asked quietly.

"Oh, this is still Pandah," Zahag said, squatting at Cashel's feet. "The shoreline's the same and the crayfish taste the same. The city's moved to the other side of the harbor, though, and the stars aren't right."

He put his long, unexpectedly soft hand on the inside of Cashel's knee. In a human, it would have been a gesture of pleading. Very likely it was the same in an ape. "I didn't want to let the people here see me till you'd come around," Zahag said. "See, I've brought you food already."

He swept up the handful of fruit and crayfish which had been left on a flat rock nearby. Cashel hadn't paid them any attention when he surveyed his surroundings. The crustaceans still twitched their tails, but they couldn't escape because the ape had plucked their legs off.

"Please," Zahag said. "Can I join your band?"

"It's a pretty small band," Cashel said. He wondered how he was going to find Sharina. He didn't doubt he would, he just wasn't sure how. "Sure, I'd be glad of your company. If you behave yourself."

The ape made a hollow *hoop! hoop!* deep in his throat. He pointed toward the opposite jaw of the land, outlined by the moonlit froth of waves. "That's where the city is now," he said.

"We'll wait till morning," Cashel said. "It's not polite to call on people at this time of night."

He thought back to one of the first things Zahag had said. "What did you mean about her 'whirling us here'?"

he asked. ''Do you know how this happened to us?''

''Oh, that was Silya,'' Zahag said. He twisted a sapling until the fibers tore between his hands with a loud crackle. Cashel could have done the same, but it was a reminder of how strong the ape was. ''She's the wizard from Dalopo who's been hanging around the palace the past ten days.''

He broke another sapling. He was weaving them into a sleeping nest, since Cashel had said they'd be spending the night here.

''I figured she was after Halphemos' job,'' the ape continued. ''He didn't even know she was a wizard.''

''Why didn't you tell him?'' Cashel said. His voice had a slight rumble that suggested thunder over the horizon. In Barca's Hamlet, people looked out for their neighbors.

Zahag stopped what he was doing and looked up at the human. He said, ''Halphemos made me what I am, chief. I'd have torn his throat out if I dared.''

''Oh,'' Cashel said. He thought about how it felt when you didn't fit in anywhere. He'd been that way when Sharina left the borough and took all his unspoken hopes with her. ''Well, that's between you and him, I guess.''

Zahag went back to weaving saplings, using his feet as well as his hands for the task. ''I guess Silya figured she'd get rid of you first because you're a wizard too,'' he said.

''I'm not . . .'' Cashel muttered, but he couldn't put any strength in the denial. He didn't know what the truth was anymore. Truth wasn't as simple as it had seemed when he tended sheep in Barca's Hamlet.

''And I guess King Folquin'll blame all the trouble on Halphemos,'' Zahag continued, ''so Silya may get rid of you both.''

He gave a soft, hooting laugh. ''Folquin's going to be angry enough to chew rocks, you know,'' the ape concluded.

* * *

"Folquin was wrong to arrest Halphemos," Cerix muttered angrily to Sharina. He paused to suck in more vapor from the pellet of black gum he was heating in a closed pot. "If the boy said he didn't do it, he didn't. Maybe there's more powerful wizards than Halphemos around, though by the Lady, *I* never met them. But Halphemos never put a foot wrong and got some effect that he wasn't expecting. Not once."

Cerix was a middle-aged man with a fringe of dark hair around a spreading bald spot. He had a paunch, but his powerful arms and shoulders would have been the envy of any hardworking farmer in Barca's Hamlet.

Cerix sat on a rolling chair with larger wheels in back than front so that he could grip them by the rims and propel himself when there was no one to push him. His legs had been cut off at mid-thigh; the drug he smoked might dull but could not eliminate the constant pain.

"I'm the one who made the mistake," Cerix said bitterly. He gestured toward where his knees should have been. "The boy never would have done this."

Cerix and Halphemos lived in a courtyard house with rooms on three sides and a wall across the other—much like the palace in miniature. Sharina would have expected the court wizard to live *in* the palace rather than nearby, but she'd realized immediately that Cerix was poisonously ashamed of being crippled.

He'd opened the door himself when she found the place, well after midnight. There weren't any servants, though a dwelling this size might have had several.

"Wizards who had very little power in past years are able to do great things now," Sharina said. "Could Halphemos have miscalculated?"

Cerix looked at her sharply. "You don't know anything about the art yourself, do you?" he said.

"No," said Sharina, meeting his glare with a steady gaze. She'd come to Cerix with the news—and to ask for help—as soon as she could after Folquin ended the uproar in his courtyard by having Halphemos imprisoned as the culprit. "But I have friends who do."

"You're right about the way things have changed recently," Cerix said. "You weren't listening to what I said about the boy, though. He had an instinct. Half a dozen times I taught him an incantation but he wouldn't use it, said it wasn't right. What did this hick kid know, I thought? So one day when I'd had most of a bottle of wine, I showed him."

The crippled man laughed, but the sound trailed off into a cackle of madness. He lifted the nosepiece of his inhaler and breathed deeply again.

The narcotic smoke scraped the back of Sharina's throat. She walked to the water jar and dipped herself a drink with one of the cups hanging from the rim. The attractively shaped jar was of low-fired clay. Water sweating through the porous container kept the remaining contents noticeably cooler than the air.

"How did you meet Halphemos?" she asked.

"I was the Great Cerix, whose key unlocks the wonders of the cosmos," Cerix said, lowering his inhaler. "I was giving a show on Sandrakkan. No place you've ever heard of, just a cluster of houses in the back of beyond."

Much the way Cerix would've described Barca's Hamlet, Sharina thought. She didn't speak aloud.

"A boy came up to me after the show," Cerix continued. "Alos or-Noman—Alos nobody's son. He said he wanted to join me, to learn wizardry from me."

He snorted. "I already had a boy to work the crowds for me—my sister's son, and a worthless little scut he was. But I didn't need a second brat. I told Alos that."

Cerix rolled his chair to the water jar. Sharina leaned forward to offer help but caught herself before she spoke. Even so, the cripple glared at her as he dipped his own water. He drank.

"One of the images I'd done during the show was the royal palace in Valles," Cerix said, shaking his head in marvel at the memory. "I'd got a bit of tile broken off the palace roof in a windstorm. From that I made the whole building appear. I was proud of that effect. Each time I did it was like pulling a plow through hard ground.''

Sharina nodded. In the borough, folk with plow oxen helped neighbors without; it's the way people were. But she understood the image very well, the wife on the plow handles as the husband pulled it; or worse, the little child guiding the sharpened stake that the widowed mother tried to drag forward.

''So this *boy* does the effect in front of me, parroting the words he heard me use during the show,'' Cerix said. ''There's the palace, hanging in the air, only when *he* does it you can see people walking in the courtyard and he's not raised a sweat. Alos the Bastard, twelve years old, taught himself to read but not the Old Script, of course. And he's a hundred times the wizard I ever thought of being. Funny, isn't it?''

Cerix started to cry. He mopped at his eyes with his free hand, then flung the mug against the well curb in the courtyard where it shattered.

''I wanted to hate him, but I couldn't,'' Cerix said. ''He'd dragged himself up from even less than I'd had, and all he wanted was me to teach him to use his talent. I just wish the Lady'd given me sense enough to listen to him instead of trying to prove I was just as great a wizard as he was—when I knew I wasn't, not even close!''

Sharina turned away. She cleared her throat and said, ''Halphemos thought that you could help me and Cashel find our friends who disappeared with the ship we all were on. Can you help me find Cashel first?''

Cerix had a napkin on his lap. He blew his nose fiercely on it, then rolled his chair out into the courtyard. He threw the wadded cloth accurately into a hamper by the open doorway of the adjacent room.

''Halphemos knew I couldn't work the spell myself,'' Cerix said in a tired voice as he returned with swift, powerful thrusts of his arms to where Sharina stood. He dipped water with another cup. "He said he'd find your friends when I taught him the incantation, didn't he? He still can't read the Old Script."

Sharina thought back to the young wizard's actual words in the moments before the royal court turned into a melee. "I guess that's what he must have meant," she said. "But you're a wizard too, aren't you?"

"Not anymore," Cerix said in a bleak voice. His inhaler was on the floor beside the charcoal brazier on which he heated it. He spun his wheeled chair back to it. "You won't understand, I suppose. The words of an incantation resist you. The greater the effect, the greater the resistance. That's why everybody isn't a wizard."

Cerix unscrewed the top of the inhaler and set it aside. The device was of fine porcelain decorated in green slip with a serpent coiling about the pot to swallow its own tail. Cerix turned up the container and scraped the crusted remnants of the pellet onto the floor with a wooden spatula.

"But you are a wizard," Sharina said evenly. She needed Cerix's help, and his drug-sodden weakness disgusted her. She touched the hilt of the Pewle knife. Nonnus had known nothing about wizardry except to avoid it, but Sharina would have given anything for the hermit's calm presence beside her now.

"I *was* a wizard," Cerix said sharply. He reached for the little box holding his pellets of black gum, then set it down and met Sharina's eyes again.

"I studied the art," he said fiercely. "I copied incantations from the works of ancient scholars, wizards of the Old Kingdom and before. I had everything I needed to be a great wizard—except the power to use my knowledge. Still, I was gaining power because the forces around me waxed."

He smiled in cold recollection. "Just as your friends told you. I knew Halphemos had the power I lacked, but I didn't understand that he had judgment I lacked as well. Good judgment mattered more than power."

Cerix shrugged his muscular shoulders. "I'd found an incantation that would open a window on another plane," he said. "Halphemos refused to speak it. This was two years ago, when we were giving performances in Erdin and I dreamed of becoming court wizard to the Earl of Sandrakkan. While Halphemos was gone from our lodgings, I worked the spell myself."

Tears began to drip from Cerix's eyes. Voice trembling, he continued, "It wasn't a window, it was a door. I started to slip through. Weakness was all that saved me—I couldn't finish the incantation, so the door closed before I was wholly inside."

Cerix picked up the box of narcotics. His hands were trembling so badly that he couldn't slide the top open. Sharina took it from him, opened it, and placed a gum pellet carefully in the center of the ceramic pot.

"My legs are still on the other plane," Cerix said more calmly. He screwed the top back on the inhaler and set the device on the brazier to heat. "Demons tear them. Every moment of every day, demons are ripping at my legs. And when I try to speak an incantation now, the words stick in my throat."

"I see," Sharina said. "I'm very sorry."

There'd been folk in the borough who'd lost fingers or whole limbs. Some of them complained of pain in the missing part for the rest of their lives. It had nothing to do with demons, but it was as real to the victims as any other pain.

Sharina frowned. She'd never *thought* that demons had anything to do with old Jael complaining about the foot she'd lost as a girl when a wagon rolled over her. Sharina had assumed Cerix had to be wrong when he told her something she hadn't known before. That was as foolish as accepting any "new fact" uncritically as the truth.

Cerix breathed vapor and set his inhaler down with a calm expression. "Halphemos brought me to Pandah," he said. "I taught him how to make a monkey talk like a man, and that caught the king's eye."

He shrugged. "King Folquin's been a good master until now. We have money saved, enough to buy passage to another island. For you as well."

The crippled wizard smiled at Sharina. "Get Halphemos out of prison," he went on. "It's just a cage for drunken sailors. Pandah is an easygoing place."

He lifted the inhaler again. "Free my boy," he said, "and between us we'll do whatever we can to find all of your friends."

"All right," Sharina said. "I'll be back when I've made plans."

She walked to the outside door, fingering the hilt of the Pewle knife. Behind her, Cerix sighed as he drew in another breath of anodyne.

"I never trusted wizards," King Carus said, watching with Garric as Tenoctris spoke an incantation in the glade beneath them. "I was afraid of them, though I'd never have admitted it."

Smoke from the punk of a soft-bodied tree mounted toward the sky's sunless illumination. Tenoctris had drawn a circle of words around the tiny fireset. The smoke staggered at each stroke of the twig the old wizard used as a wand.

"Most wizards didn't know what they were doing, and now they had more power than they'd ever dreamed of," Carus went on. "They were like so many blind men running around swinging meat cleavers."

Tenoctris, Liane, and Garric's physical body sat on a knoll some distance beyond where they'd met the Ersa the previous day. The trees ringing them were tall and branched in jointed sections instead of twisted curves like most of the native vegetation.

Carus shook his head in frustration at mistakes he'd made a millennium before Garric was born; the circlet of gold binding his thick, black hair winked. "I should've gotten a wizard to advise me on things I didn't understand,'' he said, ''not just ignored them. Ignoring wizardry let a wizard sink me and my fleet in the sea—and sink the kingdom, too. For a thousand years.''

The knoll was only ten or a dozen feet higher than the surrounding terrain, but even that eminence was unusual here in the Gulf. In the field below, a party of Ersa nicked the trunks of saplings with sharp-edged shells and harvested the inner bark with wooden spatulas.

''The wizards I've seen . . .'' Garric said. His dream self smiled at the life he'd led since leaving Barca's Hamlet. In the glade below, Garric's body sat with the sword across its knees; his eyes blinked, and his chest slowly rose and fell.

''The wizards I've seen,'' he said, ''would mostly have done you more harm than good. They strain to move things they don't really see, and they have a thousand times the *power* to move things than they did a few years ago. It was the same in your age, because the forces were peaking then too.''

The smoke from Tenoctris' fire crooked in the air as though a breeze had caught it. The Gulf was windless, and the smoke itself was a white unstained by the greenish sky.

''Tenoctris was around in my time,'' Carus said, nodding toward her. ''I didn't find her, lad; but you did.''

''She found me,'' Garric protested. ''She washed up on the shore of Barca's Hamlet. All I did was carry her up to the inn.''

''You found her, lad,'' the king said with a broad, satisfied smile. ''You found her, and you found me; and by the Lady! We're not going to let the kingdom fall again.''

Carus and the balcony on which he stood shimmered as though they were smoke, swelling and losing definition. They vanished into the ring of jointed trees.

Garric blinked, shocked at the sudden *heaviness* of his flesh. He clutched the medallion of King Carus with his left hand, then rose to his feet in a graceful motion. The

Ersa continued their labors, but their ears fluttered and their eyes tracked the humans.

Liane touched Garric's hand, glad that he'd mentally rejoined. She'd become familiar with his reveries. She didn't break into them and she'd never asked him what was going on.

Garric knew he ought to tell Liane what was happening, but he wasn't sure how to explain. He *knew* Carus was a real person rather than just a buried facet of his own mind—but he couldn't prove that, and it embarrassed him to claim that he spoke to somebody who'd drowned a thousand years ago.

Tenoctris smiled wearily. Garric and Liane together helped the old woman rise. She felt shockingly frail, her frame as delicate as a bird's.

"I've found the core around which this place formed," Tenoctris said. "I was a little afraid that the wizard who created the Gulf would have destroyed his source of power when he was finished."

Tenoctris continued to hold on to her companions, perhaps for the warmth as much as the support. Her hand in Garric's was cold. Wizardry must be as draining as digging a ditch—or fighting a battle.

"If he had," Tenoctris continued, smiling now with the self-deprecating humor that was so much a part of her character, "then there wouldn't have been any way out. I didn't mention that before. As it is, I can reopen the Gulf by speaking an incantation over the object."

"It's in the direction the smoke indicated?" Liane said. She nodded rather than pointing, a gesture the Ersa working in that direction might have misunderstood. A dozen more of the creatures, all males, had drifted out of the forest. They stood with weapons in their hands, silently watching the humans.

"That's right," Tenoctris said. "So we'll need Ersa permission to proceed."

Unless we wait for Rodoard to massacre all the Ersa, Garric thought. The thought made his lip curl in disgust.

"Then let's go ask now," Garric said. "Unless . . . ?"

"Now is fine with me," Tenoctris said. She straightened, her voice growing stronger with each syllable. Her wry grin flickered. "Though I'll need some rest before I carry out the incantation. The only reason someone of my slight power can even think of opening the passage is that the forces involved are in balance instead of being at rest."

"Like pulling a keystone from an arch instead of trying to lift the whole building," Garric said in understanding. "Well, let's go see if the Ersa will let us close to the arch, shall we?"

Garric began to whistle a love song as he led his companions toward the waiting Ersa. "Her hair was like the thundercloud, before the rains come down. . . ."

The sheep had liked the tune when he played it to them on his pipes in Barca's Hamlet. It reminded him of when he was a boy and life—looking back on it—was so simple.

The tall Ersa who'd spoken the previous day now led the group of armed males who'd joined the field workers. Garric walked toward him.

Tenoctris was on Garric's right. He put his sword arm around her shoulders, making explicit the fact that his weapon wasn't a threat to the Ersa. He wasn't going to leave the sword behind on the knoll where it might entice the Ersa or a human spy.

"I'm Garric or-Reise," he said to the tall Ersa. "Will you tell me your name, sir?"

The humanoids' ears fluttered like clothes hanging to dry in the wind. "You may call me Graz," the leader said. He lowered his spear so that the slender point aligned with Garric's chest. "Why do you come here? You must go!"

"We want to leave the Gulf," Tenoctris said. She touched Garric's hand on her shoulder. "We want to go home. To do that, I need to see and use an object that's within your territory."

She lifted her chin, a quick gesture in the direction the smoke had pointed. "I think you know where it is yourselves, but I can find it if you don't. I'll do no harm to it or you. It will open a door through which my friends and I can leave."

The Ersa twitched in great agitation. A pair of males, much shorter and perhaps younger than Graz, linked arms and began to keen wordlessly.

"Go back!" Graz shouted, jabbing his spear toward Tenoctris' eyes. "This is blasphemy! Go back now!"

Garric stepped in front of the old woman and linked his hands behind his back. "Give us access to the object," he said quietly, ignoring the needle of iron quivering a finger's breadth from his throat, "and we'll take all the humans out of the Gulf. You'll have this world to yourselves."

The words had fallen into a pattern in his mind even as he started to speak them. He didn't know whether the plan was his or that of King Carus.

"Yes," said Tenoctris, moving to Garric's side again. "I'll seal the opening so that it no longer swallows down folk from the outer world to start the problem again."

Garric knew—and perhaps the old woman did too—that if the Gulf were once emptied of humans, the next group of stragglers to arrive would be murdered at once instead of being bound into gentle slavery. Still, the Ersa had less of a bent to slaughter than men did, so a way that they could avoid the need would seem a benefit to them.

The Ersa's state changed from outraged horror to something equally tense but at the same time hopeful. The wailing pair calmed and faced the humans. The group signaled furiously with its ears; all but Graz. The Ersa leader remained as still as the trees of the windless forest.

"Can you open the way for us?" he said. "Can you send *us* home?"

"I can take you through the gate," Tenoctris said simply, "but you can never go home. The place you came from is nowhere I can reach. And I'm afraid you're better off in the Gulf than you'd be in a world of all humans."

It wouldn't have occurred to the old wizard to lie. Garric wouldn't have lied either, though he didn't know whether a politic answer, an answer that offered hope, might not have been—

No. The truth was always the better choice. Evil isn't done by evil people, most of the time. Evil is done by basically decent people who decide that a little lie, a little theft, a little slide down the black slope couldn't do any harm.

Graz thumped his spear butt on the soft soil. "Yes," he said. "You may use the Hand if you remove all humans from the Gulf."

Garric breathed out in a great sigh. "All right," he said. "We'll go now to explain the situation to the others."

He didn't need Liane's worried frown to remind him that convincing the Gulf's human community was likely to be a much more difficult task than negotiating with the Ersa.

The 12th of Heron

Ten donkeys with wicker panniers of cloves plodded just ahead of Cashel and Zahag; a similar train was not far behind. Traffic into the city was already brisk, though the sun was still a whisker's breadth beneath the cloudless eastern horizon. Local travelers looked at Cashel and the ape with friendly interest.

Cashel smiled. The pair of them probably looked like buskers planning to entertain in the city's squares. "The strong man and his trained monkey," he murmured to his companion. "Maybe we could earn the price of a meal while we get our bearings."

"Right," the ape said. The breadth of his lips emphasized his sneer. "You can lift a donkey over your head while I explain that you're a rare two-legged ox I captured on a distant island."

Cashel chuckled. "Sorry," he said. "My trained *ape*."

The limestone gates were twenty feet high. Carvings commemorated something or other, but they were low relief and the stone was too weathered for Cashel to make out more than the fact that they showed figures. The walls were plaster over mud brick. Where the plaster had cracked, crumbled brick dribbled out in rich brown fans.

Fields of cloves and other spices came up close to the city walls. Folk of both sexes tended the crops; leaves bruised during harvesting filled the air with a heady odor.

The scene was wholly alien to Cashel. It didn't make him uncomfortable, but he'd have liked to see . . .

"Do they have sheep here?" he asked Zahag. "Well, did they have sheep on the Pandah we came from?"

"What do you want with a sheep?" the ape said in amazement. "I've known frogs with more brains than the smartest sheep ever born!"

"I'm used to them, is all," Cashel said apologetically.

Zahag blatted his lips. "That figures," he said. "Well, I never saw a sheep since Halphemos took me from Sandrakkan, and I can't say I'm sorry about that."

All the traffic this early in the morning was toward the city: peddlers carrying garden trucks to markets within the walls, and larger-scale growers bringing spices to the docks for export. The gates constricted the flow, but the guards, wearing kilts and leather caps, appeared ceremonial rather than arrayed against a real threat.

The road bent to pass along the shore for the last fifty paces. Cashel glanced into the harbor as he waited for the congestion ahead to clear. There was an island, a low jut of rock, in the center of the harbor basin. On it was a windowless tower of pink stone that looked more like a confection than it did a real building. Red flames rose from the surrounding water.

"That's a funny thing," Cashel said. "What is it?"

"What's what?" the ape said. He followed Cashel's gesture and shrugged mightily.

"Well how would I know?" he said. "There isn't one like it in the other Pandah. No tower, no island. It's a stupid place for an island anyway. See how the boats have to work around it?"

Traffic shuffled forward. Cashel continued to look at the island. He supposed there was an entrance on the side he couldn't see, but that didn't explain the lack of windows. And where did the flames come from?

A figure appeared on top of the tower—a girl with auburn hair. She was a little thing, a doll of a girl, though pretty enough if you liked dolls. Sharina was slender, but she was nearly as tall as Cashel. . . .

The last of the donkeys clopped over the stone threshold. Cashel started to follow. He could see the houses within, narrow-fronted and three or four stories high. Wooden balconies jutted out from walls covered in pastel plaster.

Cashel eyed the houses uneasily. Streets built as narrow as this one made him feel like he was entering a cave, and he'd always preferred the open air.

"It's them!" said a guard in excitement. He put his lips to the mouthpiece of a set of bagpipes and wheezed a three-note call. Civilians looked surprised, and a donkey brayed a near equivalent to the bagpipes' sound.

Other guards came running, some of them were settling helmets on their heads or refastening sword belts they'd loosened for comfort while seated.

Cashel stopped and set his feet. He missed his quarterstaff. He'd like to hold it crossways in front of him to warn people that he didn't intend to be pushed.

Zahag bared his teeth, snarled, and tried to turn. Guards surrounded them. If Cashel had to fight, he'd grab one of the lightly built local men and use him as a club on his fellows. . . .

An officer with a fish-shaped tin medallion on his leather helmet appeared from a cookshop just up the street, sloshing the last of the wine from the drinking bowl he still held. "Sir!" he cried when he saw Cashel. He noticed the bowl and tossed it down in the street "Sir! Oh, the Mistress God has answered our prayers after all!"

Cashel looked over his shoulder to see if the fellow was talking to somebody on the road behind. Guards were blocking traffic so that the following train of donkeys didn't crowd him and Zahag. One of the men caught Cashel's eye and bowed in salute.

"What's all this about?" Cashel asked. Zahag had calmed; he sat on the packed dirt and searched his fur for fleas. Cashel himself was even more ill-at-ease than before when he'd thought they were being attacked. In a fight he *knew* how to behave.

The officer, a pudgy little man, was giving instructions to a subordinate. That man ran down the street shouting to be given right-of-way. The officer turned, knelt, and dipped his head to Cashel. "Sir," he said, "our court diviner Tayuta said that a great wizard accompanied by a monkey would appear to rescue Princess Aria."

"I'm not a—" Cashel began.

"I'm not a monkey!" Zahag shrieked. He leaped at the officer.

Cashel caught Zahag by the neck and jerked him back. "Behave!" he thundered. "I'll not have you embarrass me like this!"

Zahag hunched up, chastened. Cashel set the ape down and said, "I'm sorry," to the gaping officer. "He isn't really a man, you see."

"I see indeed," the officer said. He drew himself up—facing Cashel he looked like a sheep trying to be a plow ox—and went on, "Today is the last day before Ilmed comes to claim Aria as his bride. Please, if you'll come with us quickly to the palace? There's very little time."

"I—" Cashel said. He didn't have the faintest notion what the man was talking about. Certainly they couldn't have been waiting for him and Zahag because they'd—

The illogic of what Cashel was thinking froze his tongue. The fellow said some girl was in danger, and it sounded like time was short.

"Let's go," he said.

The officer trotted off with only a hand signal to his men. When the guards ahead and behind pushed the pace, Cashel scooped up Zahag—the ape wasn't built for running—and jogged with him along the narrow streets. Residents of the city crowded to either side of the narrow way, watching them go by with expressions of hope. A little girl and her mother even threw chrysanthemums plucked from a window box.

The streets of Pandah were a mixture of dirt and animal droppings. Cashel was glad of that, because walking—let alone running—on cobblestones or bricks jarred his joints all the way to the base of his skull.

The buildings here probably didn't last very long. The few that were stone-built and genuinely old—temples, all of them; one was circular with pillars on the outside—sat several feet down from the surface of the street and the surrounding structures. The whole city was raising itself on a mound of the last generation's ruins.

Zahag rode on Cashel's back, gripping his waist with feet as flexible as human hands and shifting his weight from side to side as he viewed the city. "Nothing like where we came from," the ape said. He didn't sound concerned, just interested. "The people look pretty much the same, but not the houses or anything else."

Cashel heard bagpipes and trumpets blare ahead of them. The street doglegged to the right—it'd never been much wider than a sheep track—and entered a paved square. There were stone buildings on either hand and a colonnade across the front to join them. At the far end of the pavement was another colonnade, this one on the harborside.

Guards and functionaries wearing bright silk and cotton were spilling from the buildings. They began to cheer when they saw Cashel.

A stately woman came out of the building on the right, wearing a fanlike headdress made of rainbow silk to match her gown. Two handmaids, dressed well but less expensively, attended her. A step behind was a fourth woman in a severe black woolen robe.

The officer of the gate guards, puffing and blowing from the run, saluted her and managed to cry, ''Lady Sosia! Your daughter is safe!''

The handmaids babbled in theatrical joy. The woman in the headdress—Sosia, beyond reasonable question—turned and hugged her black-clad companion.

''Pray!'' that woman said. Cashel judged her to be older than Sosia by a half a dozen years, though both were middle-aged. ''Give thanks to the Mistress God that She sent us both a true sign and a champion!''

Together they sank to their knees. The handmaids threw themselves down on the flagstones as well. It looked awfully uncomfortable to Cashel, who'd stopped at the edge of the pavement.

''Come forward!'' the officer said, trembling between deference and haste. ''Please, sir! The evil Ilmed may take the princess away at any moment!''

Cashel set the ape down and snarled, ''Behave!'' Zahag had become his responsibility when he said the ape could join him. Sheep were stupid, right enough, but you didn't have to worry about your ewe biting the queen. . . .

''Sir,'' said the officer, still struggling to get his breath, ''may I have your name? Then I can present you to Sosia, Successor and descendant of She to whom the Mistress God entrusted Pandah when She returned to the heavens.''

''There's no need of formalities, Gason,'' Sosia said. She'd risen with her companion but now bowed to Cashel's increasing embarrassment. ''I'm a mother today, not the Successor.''

She took Cashel's hands and continued, ''Will you

come within the palace, sir? We'll get you anything you require for your activities."

"I'm Cashel or-Kenset," Cashel said. "Please don't call me 'sir.' Please, I'm Cashel."

He wanted to jerk his callused hands away from Sosia's amazing delicacy. Nobody in Barca's Hamlet had skin as soft as the Successor's.

The woman in black touched the arms of both Sosia and Cashel. "Come inside please," she said. "I'm Tayuta, Master Cashel. Not a wizard like yourself, but the diviner who foretold your arrival."

They entered the building from which the women had come. Zahag ambled along behind. Cashel supposed that it was best that Zahag be inside where he could keep an eye on him. Now he had to worry about the ape climbing expensive draperies, though—or worse.

The thick double doors were pieced together from small sticks, none of them bigger than Cashel's arm. Pandah must not have big trees, or maybe the folk here just liked the look of cabinetry. Over the wood was bronze filigree, a single pattern repeated over and over again. If Sharina were here, she'd know if it was writing.

Thought of Sharina made Cashel's chest tighten. He'd find her, though.

All the servants must have left the palace at the announcement of Cashel's arrival. Now the pair of handmaids and at least a dozen servants of the ordinary sort rushed in after their mistress and bustled with furniture.

The main part of the building was a single room whose walls and ceiling were painted with geometric patterns in red and blue over a background of brilliantly white lime plaster. There were no tapestries or fabrics, but Cashel thought Ilna would like the interwoven symmetries of the walls.

Sosia sat on a high-backed chair of gilt wood. Tayuta stood behind and whispered in her ear. Cashel looked in confusion at the chair a servant offered him—styled like the Successor's but less ornate and without the gold leaf.

Zahag didn't have Cashel's instincts for politeness. The ape hooted in laughter and said, "Are all you humans stupid? Or do you just need kindling for a fire? That's all you'll have if my chief sits on *that* flimsy toy!"

"I'll stand," Cashel said. "I, ah . . . Look, what do you want me to do? So I can do it and go find my friend. Friends."

Sosia and Tayuta exchanged glances. "My daughter Aria was born eighteen years ago," Sosia said without further delay. "Eighteen years ago this evening. Three days later a man who called himself Ilmed appeared in my chamber. And I mean *appeared*; the usher swore he didn't enter by the doorway."

"I wasn't on Pandah at the time," Tayuta said. She stroked Sosia's hair below the splendid fan of silk. "Poor dear Sosia didn't have anyone skilled in the art to help her."

Cashel grunted. He didn't much like the airs Tayuta was giving herself. Also he couldn't help wondering who Aria's father was—and where he'd been when wizards were walking into the palace.

"So, you're a wizard?" he said to Tayuta with no more expression than a stone wall has.

Tayuta's lips tightened. She clasped her hands at her waist. "No," she said in a steady voice, "I'm not. I've studied the art, but my only ability is to divine the future. I foretold your arrival, Master Cashel, but I can be of no direct help to the Successor."

Cashel scowled at his own behavior. He hadn't any business getting his back up just because Tayuta had a good opinion of herself. "Look, I'm just Cashel," he said. "I herd sheep."

A pair of servants entered the room with trays of fruit and drinks. Zahag bounced toward them by leaping through his long arms. He reached up and began cramming his mouth with refreshments from both trays simultaneously.

The servants goggled. One of the handmaids cried "Stop that!" and stepped toward the ape.

"That's quite all right, Ivris!" Sosia said. "I'll tell you when I need someone to decide how food should be served in my presence."

The handmaid looked stricken. She ran out of the room, blubbering into her hands.

Cashel stood a little straighter. The girl had been wasting time when there wasn't much to waste, but Cashel didn't like to see one person treat another like a fool even though it was deserved. He knew folks would do that to him if it wasn't that he was so big.

"Ilmed said he'd decided my daughter was to be his bride," Sosia continued as though nothing had happened. "They'd be betrothed at once, but the marriage wouldn't be performed until Aria became eighteen. He was a powerful wizard, so we should feel honored—*he* said."

She smiled coldly at the memory. "I was in a bad temper from the pain," she said—and Cashel could imagine she had been, three days after giving birth. "I told the servants to flog Ilmed within an inch of his life and throw him into the harbor. Instead he disappeared. Into thin air."

Zahag shambled between Cashel and the women, slurping white fluid from a glazed cup. The contents were too thin for milk, even if it had been skimmed. Some sort of sap or juice, Cashel guessed.

"That night at full moon," Sosia continued, "Ilmed returned. I watched him but I couldn't move. None of us could move. He had several monsters with him."

"Scaled Men," Tayuta said. "They're the size of normal men, but—"

"I know the scaly men," Cashel said. "They took the baby, then?"

The diviner fell silent. For the first time her expression was tinged with surprise as well as respect for the power she hoped Cashel could wield.

"Yes," said Sosia. "They took Aria. When we could move again, there was an island in the middle of the harbor and a tower on it. The flames surrounding the island come out of the water, but they burn anything they touch—wood, metal; stone even. And flesh. We've tried everything over the years, but we can't pass through the flames to rescue Aria."

"As the child grew older," Tayuta said, "we saw her sometimes on top of the tower. At first with one of the Scaled Men, but more recently alone."

"Nowadays she comes out very rarely," Sosia said. "I saw her today, but only for a moment. I'm afraid that after today I'll never see my daughter again."

A tremble broke through Sosia's wall of control, though she didn't let emotion wholly defeat her. *Ilna would understand this woman. . . .*

And with that realization, Cashel understood Sosia as well.

"I'd help you if I could," he said. "But mistress, I don't know what I can do. I'd—"

He turned up his big hands. "Mistress, if it was a demon to fight, I'd, well, I've done that. But I can't wrestle a fire."

"You spun your wand," Tayuta said, her eyes focused on a memory. "I saw you in the water of my bowl. Your wand carved a path through the wall of fire. It closed behind you and I could see no more."

"A wand?" Cashel said in surprise. "Do you mean my quarterstaff? But I don't have it with me here, it's back with Sharina."

He frowned. Had it been lost when the *Lady of Mercy* disappeared?

He was shocked to realize that he was more concerned about a piece of wood than he was for Sharina and his other friends, but he was *sure* they would be all right. The staff was a thing he'd shaped himself when he was only a boy; and in a real sense, creating that solid tool was also the creation of a *man* named Cashel or-Kenset.

Zahag fluttered his lips in mockery. "Do you think they don't have trees on Pandah big enough for you to wave?"

the ape said to Cashel. "Use the mast of a ship, then! That ought to be your size, shouldn't it?"

The women looked at one another. The handmaid who'd run out of the room had returned, her eyes dry though a little reddened.

"Oh," said Cashel. "I didn't think of that. There'd be a flagstaff that balances right, I guess. Sure."

He laced his fingers together and hunched his shoulders, loosening his muscles for use. "Well, mistress," Cashel said, "I'll try what I can do."

He wondered whether this Ilmed would be in the tower or just the princess alone. A fellow who'd steal a little baby, well, he deserved whatever happened to him, didn't he?

Zahag scrambled back in sudden fear as he saw the expression on Cashel's face.

The guard rattled back the sliding door for Sharina, causing the two prisoners within to blink in the light of the setting sun. The prison's pair of tiny windows were in the east wall, behind the men.

"There he is, mistress," the guard said. "The other one's old Demito. Watch out that he don't upchuck last night's wine on you. He's usually lost it by this time of the morning."

"Mistress Sharina?" Halphemos said in surprise. "Oh, you shouldn't have come here, mistress. This is a foul place."

And so it was, though Sharina had seen worse. A girl brought up in a country hamlet doesn't get squeamish about filth, at least not after she's helped butcher a hog for the first time. She ducked her head and stepped inside.

The prison was a brick shed whose interior had been dug down several feet to rock. A stone bench ran the length of the long side opposite the door. There were leg irons in the floor and manacles set into the wall above the bench.

"Mostly we just get sailors from the foreign ships," the guard said apologetically. "Local people, they work off their crime to the victim. Or they're chopped, of course, if it was a man-killing and they can't pay the fine."

The prisoners—a drunk sagging against one end wall and Halphemos on the other—sat on the bench. Their left wrists were clamped to the wall and both ankles hobbled to the floor. They could feed themselves with their free hands, but their only possible movement was to slide a few inches to one side or the other along the bench.

"Master Halphemos," Sharina said in a cool voice, "your friend Cerix has sent you a scroll of hymns to the Lady. I suggest you use it while I share a skin of wine with your warder. He's kindly allowed you to read until sunset for your soul's sake."

Halphemos looked dumbfounded, as well he might. In Barca's Hamlet people were conventionally religious. Folk might not put much faith in the mealtime sprinkle of cheese and beer at the household shrine, but almost everybody did it—and though people muttered about the tithe to the Great Gods, they paid that also when the priests from Carcosa came through the borough once a year.

Cerix had a fierce *dis*belief in the gods. It was as much a matter of faith for the crippled wizard as a hermit's simple piety had been for Nonnus—and for Sharina now, in memory of the man who had died to protect her. Cerix was the least likely of anyone on Pandah to offer Halphemos a roll of hymns.

The guard had been friendly enough—as he should be, since Sharina had handed over the skin of wine she'd brought. He nonetheless watched to make sure that Sharina didn't pass the prisoner a file or a lockpick in addition to the parchment scroll. He'd opened the scroll, not to read—though the first ten columns were hymns to the Lady, just as Sharina said—but to make sure there was nothing concealed inside the parchment.

Nodding curtly to the prisoner, Sharina squelched up the three steps to ground level. The guard slammed the door shut behind her and set the pin in the heavy bar.

She'd wash her feet in the sea when their vessel got under way with the evening tide. "Have you sampled the wine?" she asked the guard brightly.

"Not yet, mistress," the man said. "Let's sit down and be comfortable in my hut."

The guard didn't have the keys to the prisoners' irons. If most of those held were sailors, there was an obvious risk that crewmates would attack the guard and use any keys he held to release their fellow. The leg irons in particular were so sturdy than any attempt to smash the locks open would be likely to crush the ankle as well.

Cerix had erased the text from the inner spindle of the scroll, creating a palimpsest on which he'd written an incantation in both Old Script and the square modern forms of the letters. Halphemos couldn't read Old Script, but he could copy the symbols onto the bench's slimy surface and speak the syllables as given in their phonetic equivalent.

Cerix wrote with a clean, legible hand even when he was in haste and in pain. Sharina wondered if he'd been a copyist before he became a wizard and a drug-sodden cripple.

The guard's kiosk beside the prison shed had a stool, a table, and a small brazier for heating food or mulling wine, but no bed and very little space. Sharina supposed another man took over, possibly at nightfall, but she hadn't wanted to risk a direct question that might seem suspicious.

The guard offered Sharina the stool and unstoppered the wine. It was a strong vintage from Shengy, laced with resin for travel. Sharina had crumbled a pellet of Cerix's drug into it. "You first," Sharina said to the unspoken question.

The guard took a long drink, his throat wobbling, then lowered the skin. "Ah!" he said with approval, handing the wine to Sharina. He frowned and with different emphasis said, "Ah? I don't have mugs, mistress. We could maybe . . . ?"

He looked doubtfully down the street. The lockup was among the warehouses on the harbor south of the residential parts of the city. There were a number of laden donkeys and human bearers even this late in the evening, but Sharina hadn't seen a tavern or cookshop when she made her way here.

"No, this is fine," she said, lifting the wooden mouthpiece to her lips. She plugged the opening with the tip of her tongue and pretended to drink as deeply as the guard had.

"What do you care about this fellow in there?" the guard asked as he gratefully retrieved the wineskin. He leaned forward and added conspiratorially, "I hear he tried to murder the king by wizardry!"

"I think it was an accident," Sharina said calmly. A bat fluttered low around the eaves of a nearby warehouse, then vanished into the night. The sky was still bright, but she doubted that Halphemos could see to read inside the prison anymore. "Anyway, it was my companion who vanished. And I doubt he was really harmed. Just sent away until I can find him again."

She gave the guard a false smile. In her mind she prayed, *Lady, Mistress of Heaven, be with Cashel. Shepherd, Protector of All Life, protect Cashel as he protected his flocks.*

The wineskin gurgled like a hungry man's belly as the guard drank again. He belched in satisfaction before he returned the skin to Sharina.

In the stillness Sharina heard, "*. . . esmigaddon maarchama kore . . .*" The shed's walls were thick, but Halphemos was shouting to force the words out against the inertia of the cosmos.

"Your job seems so exciting to me!" Sharina twittered in a bright voice. She hoped she wasn't overdoing it, but she had to say something quickly to conceal the young wizard's chanting. "Do you often have traitors to watch in your jail here?"

"Traitors?" the guard repeated in puzzlement. "Oh, you mean like this one, trying to murder the king. No, we don't—I mean, not *very* often. But we get lots of dangerous sorts here, you're right."

A rosy glow emanated *through* the bricks of the prison shed. Inside, the wards of the hand and leg irons clinked into alignment.

"You're very brave," Sharina said. She tried to pass back the wineskin though she hadn't mimed another drink. "I—"

The pin locking the prison door clanged to the ground. The drunk sharing the bench with Halphemos bellowed in terror. The guard leaped to his feet, also shouting. He snatched up his weapon, a club with a spiked iron collar around the end.

The crossbar crawled sideways. Nothing touched it except a tremble of magenta light. It slipped out of its staples and fell.

The door panel began to open. The guard raised his club and faced the door, though his face was twisted in a rictus of fear. Sharina picked up the stool by one leg and stepped behind the man, ready to club him senseless before he could strike Halphemos.

A figure of red light shambled up from the cell. It had the shape of the ape Zahag, but it was as large as an ox. Through the glowing semblance Sharina could see the jail and Halphemos himself. The wizard chanted, gesturing with the closed scroll in place of a proper wand.

The guard gave a great bawl of fear. He tried to run but his feet tangled and he toppled backward, losing his club.

The figure of light expanded like a smoke ring thrown out when a knot cracks in a fire. Sharina stood for an instant in a rosy ambience which then vanished.

Halphemos climbed the steps, wobbling with exertion. He tried to slide the scroll within the neckline of his tunic but he missed his intent; Sharina snatched the falling parchment with one hand and supported Halphemos with the other. It was reflex: a book was too valuable a thing to lose, even though as a tool it had already fulfilled its purpose.

"Quickly!" she said; half-guiding, half-pulling the exhausted wizard in the direction of Dock Street. Cerix had booked passage on a ship leaving for Erdin. There was nothing important about the destination, only that the vessel was leaving on the evening tide.

Sharina glanced over her shoulder as they turned the corner. The guard still lay on the ground, supporting his torso with his arms. He stared at the open prison door and bleated wordlessly.

The mist over the lagoon reminded Garric of those he'd seen rise on a thousand still mornings from swales in the meadows of the borough; but this was changeless. The sun would never brighten to burn off the haze, nor would a breeze come in from the sea to tear it to rags and wisps.

Wraithlike figures stood on floats made of bundled reeds to fish in the lagoon. Even Garric's keen eyes found it hard to tell whether individuals were human or Ersa if they were more than a hundred yards away. The Gulf had fixed limits, but at least for now there was room for both races to live without conflict.

"Maybe it's this place," Liane said quietly. Either she'd understood the thought behind Garric's glance and grim expression, or the same thing had occurred to her. "This green light makes me feel cold all the way to my bones. When we get people back to the real world, then they'll be . . ."

Garric looked at her, wondering what word Liane would settle on. *Better? Happier? Decent?*

Instead she grinned sadly. "Well, we can hope they will," she said, unable to complete the thought any better than Garric could have.

"The Gulf was created for a group of Ersa by one of their own kind," Tenoctris said. She looked at the roofless shanties of the human community with the same dispassionate interest that she showed for the forest's unique vegetation. "It should suit them better than it does humans, but I'm not sure it suits them perfectly either. The older I get—and at this point that's over a thousand years—"

She grinned. Liane hugged her.

"The older I get," Tenoctris resumed, "the more convinced I become that no wizard who had understanding equal to his power would do anything through wizardry. That was probably true of the Ersa who created this place, too."

Folk sitting in front of their shelters turned their faces away as Garric walked by with his companions, but they watched covertly from behind. Garric waved to a pair of women crushing roots in a mortar cut from a large tree trunk. They bent their heads and pounded faster, losing their previous rhythm and fouling each other's pestle strokes.

"How about yourself?" Garric asked. "You haven't made things worse. Not that I've seen."

Tenoctris laughed. "While I don't claim complete understanding," she said, "my powers as a wizard are so trivial by comparison to what I know that I suppose I'm a special case. I hope I am, at any rate."

They were nearing Rodoard's compound. The gate was closed, but a messenger had run ahead when Garric and his companions came in sight of the community.

The dwellings to either side of Rodoard's own belonged to his henchmen, toughs who'd arrived recently and had been allowed to live. They were alert, standing in their doorways with their weapons in hand. They met Garric's eyes but glared back in stony silence to his smiles.

Infants who'd earlier been playing in the mud peered now through the interstices of their woven shelters. Their mothers watched also, occasionally shadowing the palings as they moved.

When Garric's hand closed on his sword hilt, he felt King Carus swell in his mind until there were two of them, Garric and his ancestor, filling the same skin. He drew the blade with the liquid *sring!* of good steel flexing minutely. Othelm, the former sailor who'd have tried to take the sword on the beach if he dared, raised his huge club but jumped back.

Garric struck the gong with his pommel. The bronze bonged a deep bass note about which the swordblade whispered a descant.

"I have good news, Rodoard!" Garric called to the king's closed gate. "We can escape from here after all!"

He turned and waved to the community at large. The signal was bringing folk from their shelters and the nearby forest. Those born in the Gulf wouldn't look directly at the three newcomers, but they moved closer in a process as gradual as that of syrup soaking into coarse cloth.

Garric struck the gong a second time. "Come on out!" he said, knowing that his voice could be no more than a modulation of the metallic clangor.

One leaf of the gate jerked inward. Rodoard stood in the opening wearing helmet, breastplate, and his sword. He held the demi-guisarme at the butt and balance of its short shaft.

Rodoard's face was bleak with fury.

Garric stepped back. Rodoard swung his weapon in a high arc, past Garric rather than at him. The heavy blade sheared the crossbar as well as the cords holding the gong to it. The disk spun away and splashed to the ground. Mud quickly choked the quivering bronze to silence.

"I let you live, boy," the king said in an expressionless voice, "because I thought you might be useful. Maybe I was wrong, do you think?"

Colored smoke began to rise from the compound. Lunifra hadn't appeared, but Garric heard her voice from behind the palings as a chanting rhythm. At each syllable the smoke swelled, then compressed, as though it were the membrane of a beaten drum.

"This is good news, Your Majesty," Garric said. "My friend Tenoctris has found the key that opens the door out of the Gulf. The Ersa will let us use it to return to the waking world. All of us!"

Garric had known there was risk in taking a strong line with Rodoard, but the depth of the king's anger was unexpected. Still, if he'd gone to Rodoard pleadingly, Rodoard would have bullied him instead of listening to his proposal. By arriving with a sword in his hand, Garric forced Rodoard to treat him as an equal.

"So," said Rodoard, so close to Garric that either of them could reach out and pull the other's nose. "You've been dealing with the Ersa, have you? What did you offer the animals, Garric or-Reise?"

People were easing closer. The Gulf-born folk kept to the back so that they could scamper away if fighting started. Rodoard's henchmen were uncomfortably near. A part of Garric's mind remembered whirling, slashing melees in which the King of the Isles had cut his way out of similar presses, but the King of the Isles had never had to guard a girl and an old woman. . . .

Garric threw his head back and laughed. He couldn't save Liane and Tenoctris from so large a crowd of enemies. Therefore he wouldn't try: he'd strike off Rodoard's head and then hew his way into the mob of brutes and thugs until they brought him down.

You did what you could. Leaving fewer of such folk in the world was a benefit to everyone else.

Garric lowered his sword crosswise and pinched the tip of the blade between his left thumb and forefinger in order to look a little less threatening—without sheathing the weapon. His laughter had surprised Rodoard.

"All I offered the Ersa was the chance to be shut of us," Garric said, pitching his voice to be heard to the back of the crowd. "What I offer you—"

He turned to sweep the folk behind him with his eyes.

"All of you!" he cried. "All of us! Is the chance to see the sun again, the chance to feel a breeze and to be free! As nobody in this green underworld can ever be free."

Tenoctris had knelt and was drawing in the mud with her left index finger. She held a pulpy twig for a wand.

Liane stood between Tenoctris and the crowd. Her arms were crossed before her, the hands within the opposite sleeves. Three of Rodoard's henchmen were almost—but not quite—so close they touched her.

"So," said Rodoard. His voice was high-pitched for so big a man. He sounded peevish. Unlike Garric, he hadn't called sheep across the rolling dales and learned the trick of projecting his words. "Othelm, are you in a hurry to go back to Erdin? And Bassis? Do you suppose they've forgotten about you in Valles? Not to mention what you've done here!"

Fishermen whom the gong had called from the lagoon poled their floats up on the muddy shore. In some of the wicker creels flopped bottom-dwelling fish with armored heads. The men used wooden gigs with springy jaws that clamped to either side of their target rather than spitting it. With little metal and no stone to work with, these were better tools than true spears would be.

"How about the rest of you?" Rodoard cried. He'd regained his good humor, but there was a layer of enormous menace beneath his shouted banter. "Josfred, do you want to go to a place where the sun will burn the hide off you and you'll freeze in the winter—if you live that long?"

Tenoctris whispered as her wand flickered over the circle of power she'd drawn. To anyone else, even those who, like Garric and Liane, could read the Old Script, the symbols were no more than wormtracks in the mud.

"I've made you kings of the Ersa who enslaved you!" Rodoard said. "I've put your feet on their beast necks! Do you want—"

A child screamed inside the compound, a knife of sound that cut through his harangue. Rodoard didn't look around, though his face set in a scowl of anger at the interruption.

"Do you want—" he repeated.

The gate behind Rodoard was still open. A child of three or four years ran out, streaming blood from wounds in throat and abdomen. The child collided with Rodoard's legs and flopped onto the ground, thrashing as its heart pumped its body completely dry. Lunifra stood in the doorway, bathed in dark blood that had spurted from the child's carotid arteries.

Lunifra was naked. She held a knife of volcanic glass, and her smile was the gate to the Underworld. Because of the way the child had been mutilated, Garric couldn't tell which sex it had been.

Garric cut at Rodoard's ankles. The king leapt back as he tried to clear his demi-guisarme, but his feet tangled with the child's corpse. His mouth opened in a shout of disbelief as Garric's blade crunched through with the sureness of a hand used to jointing roasts for the inn's kitchen.

The cold fury that strengthened Garric's stroke would have taken the edge through Rodoard's thighbone as certainly as it cut the ankles' cartilage. *This* pair would kill no more children for their blood magic!

Othelm squealed, clasping both hands over the wound beneath his ribs. Liane flicked her bloody dagger toward the face of the other thug trying to grapple with her. He dodged the jab. Garric's blade lifted the thug's scalp and a disk of his skull beside.

The palisade sank into a mass of writhing fibers. The wood formed into a serpent three feet in diameter and as long as the stockade had been. Lunifra laughed hysterically. The wooden tail to Garric's left squirmed. The other end rose from the ground, gaping like a lamprey's circular mouth.

The crowd, Rodoard's henchmen as well as the Gulf-born folk, scrambled back in horror. Garric raised his sword, using the extra length of his hilt to add the strength of both arms to a cut that he knew would be useless.

The jaws of splintered wood engulfed Lunifra, then flexed closed. Because the jagged teeth were rotating, they flung her right and left feet in opposite directions. She screamed briefly.

Tenoctris collapsed from the effort of her incantation. Garric scooped her up in his left hand, in his haste holding Tenoctris more like a swatch of wet drapery than a cherished friend. All the community's residents were running. The thing of wood and wizardry writhed like an earthworm on hot stone.

"This way!" Liane said, pointing toward the lagoon. A coil of the wooden serpent swept toward her mindlessly. She leaped it with no more hesitation than a child playing a game.

Garric followed Liane, holding his sword high so that he didn't accidentally stab himself. He thought of his father shouting the day he'd seen Garric run with a sickle in his hands. This was far more dangerous, but there wasn't time to wipe and sheathe the bloody weapon.

The snake of animate wood clamped its jaws on its tail and began to swallow itself. Brown and yellow shreds spun from the mouth's rim. A network of strengthening fibers wove through the pulp of vegetation here in the Gulf, very different from the division of heart and sapwood Garric was used to.

Liane climbed aboard the largest of the fishing floats, three long bundles of reeds bent up at the ends and lashed together. She lifted the pole that propelled the vessel.

Garric dropped Tenoctris in the hollow of the float, checked to make sure no one was immediately behind him, and thrust his sword through the side of the outer bundle to keep it from slashing anybody. As soon as he had a moment he'd clean and dry the blade, then use the whetstone in the scabbard to bring the tip back to a working edge. Rodoard's ankles wouldn't have dulled the good steel, but the bone of the other thug's skull was another matter. . . .

Garric leaned his weight against the stern of the float.

His feet slipped in the mud; he dug his toes in and lifted, then pushed again. The float slid into the lagoon, bobbing much lower in the water than it ought to do. It was made for a single slight-bodied resident of the Gulf. Liane and Tenoctris together were more than its safe capacity.

Garric waded out, pushing the float, until his feet came off the slimy bottom. He began to kick, pushing the tiny vessel as Liane thrust with her pole over the stern past him.

"Make for the other side!" he said. He paused to spew out the muddy water he'd splashed into his own mouth, then added, "We've got to reach the Ersa before these humans get organized!"

One of the king's henchmen waded a few steps into the lagoon and threw his spear. It splashed within arm's reach of Garric. He continued to kick, ignoring everything but the need to cross the lagoon to temporary safety.

Tenoctris spoke to Liane. Garric heard her voice but his thrashing feet overwhelmed the words. The wizard was coming around again, thank the Shepherd. Garric knew that Tenoctris could never have raised a monster like the one devouring itself on the shore, but even the effort of redirecting Lunifra's powerful incantation must have brought the old woman to the boundaries of her strength.

When Garric raised his head he could see that Ersa on triangular floats were putting out from the other shore. The figures aboard them carried spears that he didn't think were fishing implements.

The Ersa were taking precautions, but nothing they could do would be sufficient if the human settlement got organized enough to attack. Garric could only hope that it would be days or at least hours for that to—

"Go wipe out the beasts now!" Rodoard screamed, his voice piping even higher with the pain of his amputated feet. A cut with a sharp edge, especially at a joint, was likely to clamp shut instead of bleeding the victim's life quickly on the ground. Garric realized he should have—

A murderously rational mind at the back of Garric's own slammed silence on that train of thought. *"There wasn't time to do anything but what was necessary—and you did that, no one better."*

"Kill them all!" Rodoard keened. "Kill them all before they work their wizardry against us!"

Garric kicked, concentrating on only what was necessary. And as soon as he reached shore he'd do the next necessary thing: he'd clean and sharpen his sword.

The 12th of Heron (Later)

The flame-bordered island was twenty feet from Cashel in the skiff. The captain of the Successor's barge stood in the bow. He halted the paddlers with a hand signal, then bowed to Sosia and said, "It's not safe for you to go any nearer, Your Highness. The wizard and his companion should go the rest of the way themselves."

The barge had a tasseled canopy made from cream satin. Sosia leaned out from beneath it to embrace Cashel in the skiff alongside. "Save my daughter," she said. "Whatever else happens, don't let Ilmed have her."

To Cashel's enormous embarrassment, she kissed him on the forehead. He kept his face rigid, but he felt the blush warming his skin anyway.

The red-orange flames rising from the waters ahead were as silent as swordblades, but their radiance already made Cashel's skin prickle. "Time we go, then," he muttered, refusing to meet Sosia's eyes. He turned his head over his right shoulder and said, "Are you ready, Zahag?"

The ape in the back of the skiff stared at his fingers. His lips moved as he muttered scraps of verse. Between

Zahag and Cashel was a coil of rope plaited from the attachment threads of giant barnacles. It was finer than bowcord, but Cashel had put his full strength against a loop of it as a test—and the rope had held.

"Zahag, answer me!" Cashel said. "Or I'll leave you. If you want to stay, stay."

Zahag flailed the water angrily with both hands. Sosia jerked back as harbor filth soaked the pastel silk of her dress. An attendant raised his baton, but Sosia prevented the blow with a curt gesture.

"I'll stay with you!" the ape said. "You're a fool and you'll get us both killed, but I'm afraid to be alone."

Cashel turned to his left and caught the eye of the barge's anxious officer. "Push us off," he said. He thrust one end of his staff against the side of the barge to bring the skiff's bow in line with the wall of fire.

Sosia and her diviner sat side by side on gilt seats in the center of the barge. The crew, a dozen men of matched physique, ordinarily stood facing forward in the bow and stern to work long paddles. Now a pair of them shoved the skiff toward the soundless flames.

Cashel rose to his feet. The skiff wobbled only minusculely; Cashel had a countryman's poise, practiced by a life in which every day meant walking the top of a wall or a path in which rocks were as apt to turn as not.

"Keep us going, Zahag," he ordered, sliding the pole between his hands to find the balance that would have been instinctive with the hickory staff it replaced. "We've said we'll do this, so we can't back out."

"Humans!" the ape said. "Sheep-stupid humans! Of course we could back out!"

Zahag dabbed the water, then splashed hard. His arms were so long that he could stroke with both paddle-broad hands at the same time.

The skiff slid toward the waiting flames. Zahag grumbled, but he continued to drive them over the still water.

A crowd stood on the shore of the harbor, to watch the event. Many waved scarves or their broad straw hats when they saw Cashel turn to glance in their direction.

"They must like her," Cashel said. People in Barca's Hamlet didn't give any thought to Count Lascarg in Carcosa, let alone to the King of the Isles across the sea in Valles.

"Fagh!" the ape said. "They're watching to see us burn. How many did Tayuta say the flames have killed before us? Wasn't it twenty-three?"

"Do you apes live forever, then, if you don't burn?" Cashel said. He adjusted his grip on the staff by an amount too slight for anyone else to notice.

The flames were hammering him, now; he could feel the fuzz on his upper cheeks curl tightly and his eyes were dry. He began to rotate the staff which palace artisans had hastily made to his directions.

The wood was fir, not hickory or another of the hardwoods. Some folk set store by the dense strength of cornelwood, but Cashel had always found that the springiness of his hickory staff made his blows easier on his palms without robbing them of their effect on his target. Nobody took a stroke from Cashel or-Kenset and stayed standing for another.

He grinned. He'd never fought a fire with a staff before. Maybe firwood was the best choice for the job.

The staff was eight feet long and as thick as Cashel's wrists. It spun easily, making a blurred circle in front of the skiff's prow. The workmen had rubbed and waxed the wood, but craftsmanship alone could never give it a polish like that which came from years of friction from Cashel's palms.

The new staff would serve, he guessed. Cashel had never been one to refuse a task because he lacked this tool or that.

The flames shot straight up from the water. There was no steam or bubbles, but Sosia had said that attempts to swim under the barrier were as certainly fatal as trying to penetrate it in a ship armored with vinegar-soaked bullhides.

A fish flopped to the surface and twisted under again. One side was silvery; the other was bright red, parboiled by contact with the wizard fire.

"Twenty-*four* stupid humans," Zahag muttered, "and an ape who's stupider yet because he knows better!"

The staff spun. Cashel no longer felt the heat. He'd found the rhythm, now, the same way he'd have judged the leverage in a weight he was bracing to lift. He wasn't sure how, but how didn't matter.

Faster, increasingly faster. Blue fire shot from the staff's ferrules, blending into first a ring and then a tunnel of light through which the skiff slowly moved.

The artisans who'd made the staff for Cashel had capped the ends as he'd asked—but instead of the simple iron cups he'd expected, they'd created bands of brass cutwork. One cap had a scene of whales battling, the other of eagles mating among the clouds. There wasn't a home in Barca's Hamlet with art as fine as what a trio of Sosia's workmen had created for an object as practical as a wagon wheel.

Hand over hand; wrists crossing and recrossing, letting the staff's inertia carry it around. A man, even a man as big as Cashel, could leap off the ground in a fight and the spinning quarterstaff would carry him around to face in the opposite direction.

Sparkling blue fire met orange flame. The flames roared now, but Cashel's staff bored through them like an auger into a plank. Hand over hand, neither faster nor slower, despite the drag of the snarling flames.

The work had its own rhythm. Just as seasons came and went, just as clouds spread across the sky and currents changed the color of the sea, so Cashel spun his staff in the pattern that was right for these conditions, for this need.

Zahag gibbered in the skiff's stern. Sometimes the ape shouted blasphemies in the name of the Sister and other human Gods, but mostly he squealed in bestial terror. Cashel ignored his companion and the bright spears of fire that stabbed against his spinning staff and splashed away.

They were wrong to call Cashel a wizard. He was a part of the cosmos, neither more nor less. Any task is a matter of leverage as well as strength; Cashel saw the point of balance and where to exert the necessary force.

The wall of lapping red fire surged behind him. The skiff had passed the barrier and scraped on rock at the base of the prison tower. Cashel staggered as he stepped to dry ground. Zahag, capering and crowing in triumph, supported him with one long arm while the ape's other hand waved the coil of rope.

Cashel raised his staff overhead and shouted, "Through! By the Shepherd's aid, through!"

The Gods *had* aided; but the strength that was the borough's wonder, that had been part of the victory also.

And if Cashel was proud to prove that he could do something that no one else could do, well then, he had a right to be proud!

Garric's chest touched mud an instant before the float grounded on the lagoon's far side. He rose to his knees, then retrieved his sword as he stood. Ersa on floats landed to his right and left. Graz waited onshore with an armed party. The Ersa were silent, but their mobile ears flared and waggled.

Tenoctris got out unaided before Liane could help her. She bowed to Graz with perfunctory politeness and said, "The humans have decided to stay in the Gulf rather than go to our world. Most of them were born here, of course. They'll kill you all if they can. Garric can better judge if that's possible, but Rodoard believes it is."

Garric realized that all the Ersa present were suddenly staring at him. It was a disconcerting awareness, because the humanoids' broader field of vision meant their heads didn't have to move.

"How many of you are there?" Garric asked. "Warriors, I mean."

Male Ersa were physically equal at least to the Gulf-born humans. If Ersa numbers were sufficient, then they might be able to withstand a hasty attack despite the greater strength and better weapons of the recent human arrivals.

"Two hundred and thirty-two," Graz said flatly. "And yourself, if you will fight."

"Oh, I'll fight," Garric said. He felt the cold death of hope. At the back of his mind, King Carus had analyzed the situation with the necessary dispassion of a herdsman deciding which animals to slaughter in the fall so that the remainder would have fodder through the Hungry Time in Heron before new growth came in. "But it won't do any good. They'll kill us all, I'm afraid."

Garric looked at his sword. He wanted to wipe the blade, but he didn't have any dry cloth for the purpose. Liane saw the glance and offered a handkerchief from her sleeve. An Ersa child darted past the warriors and gave Garric a wad of fruit rind. It was dried and as coarsely absorbent as the loofa gourds folk in Barca's Hamlet used for washing.

Graz nodded; a human gesture, just as he used human speech to Garric and his companions. His ears fluttered at the same time, however, and four Ersa warriors ran off along separate paths in the adjacent forest. Couriers, Garric supposed, warning the race of its certain doom. The Ersa females and children nearby left together by the broadest of the routes.

"If you let me use what you called the Hand," Tenoctris said, "then I can open a gate for your folk as well as ourselves. It isn't what I wanted to do, but it's all the hope I see now."

"Yes," Graz said. "I told my people to gather at the First Place anyway. Our ancestors entered the Gulf through that grove. It's fitting that our existence should end there as well."

He and the warriors beside him turned in unison and started off down a broad trail covered with planks. The local vegetation was too pulpy to make good structures, but by replacing slats when they cracked or wore through the Ersa provided dry footing in the Gulf's sodden expanse. There was nothing like this on the human side of the lagoon.

Garric dropped the wiping rag and sheathed his sword. Liane had given Tenoctris her arm, though the older woman seemed to have regained her normal sprightly animation. It was anybody's guess what another major incantation would do to Tenoctris after the strain of deflecting Lunifra's horror; but they were all doing more than reason said they could.

Liane gestured Garric ahead. There was no need for a rear guard. The humans hadn't pursued directly across the lagoon, so the attack would come from one side or both. Garric nodded to his companions and took long strides to join the warriors. The Ersa in the rear parted to permit Garric to walk alongside their leader.

"If my ancestors had killed the first humans and all other humans who reached the Gulf," Graz said without turning his head, "then we would be safe now."

"In Sandrakkan we have a saying," Liane called from behind them. Her ears were as sharp as those of an owl striking its prey through leaves in a nighted forest. "A man has as many enemies as he has slaves."

Graz stopped in the middle of the trail, so suddenly that even his warriors were taken by surprise. He turned, holding his spear at the balance.

Garric's face lost all expression. He spread his hands at his side, ready to act if the Ersa raised his weapon to thrust or throw.

"Four of you carry the old female," Graz said, speaking so the humans would understand at the same time his ears semaphored the command to his fellows. "If the Ersa are to survive beyond this day, it will be through her efforts."

He resumed walking. His stride was loose and his steps were shorter than those a human of his height would have taken. There was no reason for the party to weary itself running; the distance around the lagoon meant a delay of at least half an hour before the humans could attack.

"Do you think that if my people had treated yours as equals from the start," Graz said quietly, "that this would not be happening?"

Garric shrugged. "I'd like to say that, but I don't know," he admitted. "We humans don't have a perfect record, even with our own kind."

Graz squealed like a rabbit in pain. Garric gripped his sword, then realized the sound was laughter.

"We are not perfect either," Graz said. "Only death is perfect. Well, we Ersa shall hope to continue living and being imperfect in your world, human."

The board track passed through the forest and into a field of food plants and other vegetation which the Ersa exploited. Some of the fruits had shapes and colors that Garric hadn't seen on the human side of the lagoon.

"The First Place," Graz said, pointing ahead of him. Though the track was arrow-straight, the ground's surface even in the Gulf rose and fell enough that Garric's first sight of the twelve bulbous-trunked trees was completely unexpected though the nearest was only a hundred yards away. That didn't surprise him. Often enough he'd seen how a sheep could be concealed on a meadow so flat he'd have guessed even a vole would stand out like a flagpole.

Ersa of all ages were converging on the grove. Some of them spoke, particularly children and their mothers, but in the main the process was much quieter than a gathering of humans in a similar crisis.

Females and the older children carried a wide variety of baskets, chests, and bags made from bark fabric. There was no pottery, though Garric had seen some crude jars in the human community.

The adult males carried only weapons: clubs and spears. Few of the latter were metal-pointed. The mind at the back of Garric's mind noted the lack of projectile weapons. Apparently none of the available wood was springy enough to provide bowstaves, and slings were of little utility without stone, metal, or hard-fired clay for bullets.

"There's so many of the women and children," Liane said. She'd joined Garric unnoticed when the warriors lifted Tenoctris onto a platform of their spearshafts. "There must be two thousand Ersa, but so few soldiers."

"Right," said Garric. "Well, another time I'd wonder how their society works."

In fact, he didn't wonder. The proportion of adult males to females and offspring was pretty similar to the sheep he'd herded in the borough. With domestic animals the numbers were decided by culling. The owner slaughtered the young rams for meat but saved most of the ewes, which provided milk as well as the next spring's increase.

Garric didn't see any other likely way that the Ersa population remained the way it was. It made him think again about just how light a burden slavery to Ersa masters had really been for the humans across the lagoon.

Perhaps that doubt showed on his face. Liane touched his arm. "We've made our choice," she said. "Not that the Ersa are holy saints, but that they're the better of the two choices we had."

"Right," Garric repeated, smiling grimly. "I guess we should thank Rodoard for making the choice so easy."

Graz watched them with his left eye, but the Ersa leader didn't speak.

They entered the grove, brushing through silky foliage which hung to the ground in curtains of long strands. The leaves would have been colorless in normal light; here they had the same bilious hue as the sky. The trunks looked like water-filled bladders.

There was a broad track between the shrouding trees and a circular earthen mound higher even than Graz's head. The mound was the only structure Garric had seen on this side of the lagoon. Directly before them was a narrow opening, barely wide enough for Garric to pass without turning sideways. The Ersa females and young drifted through the trees to stand near the wall, but the warriors remained outside.

The warriors carrying Tenoctris set her on her own feet and went back to join their fellows in awaiting the human onslaught. Graz bent and touched the opening's threshold with the palms of both hands.

"Go in, humans," Graz said. He gave his hideous squealing laugh. "You needn't do reverence to the Hand, since it's the greatest blasphemy for you even to have entered the grove."

Tenoctris stepped briskly into the enclosure with only a nod to acknowledge Graz's religious scruples. The old woman saw the interplay of forces that others, even other wizards, did not see; but Tenoctris had never seen the Great Gods. Garric respected Tenoctris and understood her position, but he believed in many things which he hadn't yet seen.

Liane looked from Garric to Graz. "I'd better go . . . ?" she murmured.

"Right," said Garric. He didn't know *what* was right. Perhaps all they were doing was desecrating the Ersa holy place in the minutes before the whole race was exterminated.

"But we have to try," he said. He smiled. He wasn't sure whether he or King Carus had directed his tongue into the words, but either way it was the truth.

Graz looked at him straight on. Garric wondered what thoughts were behind the Ersa leader's expression.

Humans shouted in the near distance. Metal clattered on wood, a sound more like that of carpentry than the battle Garric knew it was. "Right," he said, and drew the sword he'd bought in Erdin.

The blade was good steel. It shimmered even in the changeless light of this sky.

He'd *killed* a man with it, less than an hour ago.

He remembered turning to see Liane struggling with

one of Rodoard's henchmen. The eye and arm of Garric or-Reise—not another man, not even a dead king using Garric's body—had brought the sword around in an arc calculated to miss the girl but to open the thug's skull and let his life out.

He'd done that thing, and not until this moment had the awareness struck him. His knees began to tremble so fiercely that he was afraid he was going to fall.

"Stay with your females," Graz said with an unreadable expression. "If you're needed, the fight will have to come to you."

Garric licked his dry lips. He was steadier already, due to his own natural resilience and the help of King Carus, whose life had been war.

"I'm not afraid to die," Garric said. The Ersa leader had already gone through the trees toward the sound of fighting. "I'm not even afraid to kill. I'm afraid of becoming a man who kills men."

"As well you should be, lad," whispered a silent voice. *"But it's worse to be a man who can't do what has to be done, no matter what it costs him."*

There was still confused shouting beyond the grove, but the battle itself had paused for now. The human vanguard had met the waiting Ersa warriors, had skirmished, and had fallen back to wait for reinforcements to arrive.

Most of the Ersa females faced the curtain of foliage, but the children turned their heads in all directions. One of them came up to Garric and fingered the hem of his woolen tunic. When the mother noticed what was going on, she snatched the child back with clucks of anger.

Tenoctris' voice rose in the rhythms of chanting, though Garric couldn't hear the syllables from where he stood. He looked again in the direction where the fighting had begun, then sheathed his sword. The First Place was a temple, so a drawn sword would be out of place.

Garric slipped through the entrance.

The interior of the roofless enclosure was forty feet in diameter, smaller than Garric had supposed. The mounded walls were a good ten feet thick. The ground had been dug out into a pit as deep as the mound was high, with only a central hub left at the original surface level. That pillar was bound with plaited withies to keep the soil from crumbling away.

On it was a human hand made of or covered with mother-of-pearl. Its luster was brighter than the dim green light of the sky could account for. It was an object of great beauty and great power, and of evil.

"*Archedama phochense pseusa . . .*" Tenoctris said. She had drawn Old Script characters in the dirt around the pillar. She walked its circuit as she spoke the syllables, marking each accent by twitching a wand made from a length of slender branch. "*Rerta thoumison kat huesemmigadon!*"

A cylinder of light the color of the glowing Hand was forming above the written symbols. Garric looked upward. He couldn't see the light meet the changeless sky, but neither did it appear to end at any point short of that presumed contact.

Liane watched the wizard, ready to act or speak if called to but otherwise silent. Her visage had the controlled stillness of a frightened person who's too iron-willed to give in to fear.

She met Garric's eyes and smiled. He winked, wondering what his own face looked like, and left the enclosure again. Behind him he heard, "*Maarchamma zabarbathouch . . .*"

The battle had been fully joined beyond the grove. Screams and curses from the human attackers and the clacking anger of the defending Ersa formed the background. Against those voices the clatter of weapons rose to a crescendo, fell away, and redoubled, accompanied by a shout from many throats.

Garric reached for his sword hilt.

"Garric!" Liane called. "Garric, it's time! Send them through while, while she can . . ."

"Come!" Garric said. Heads turned at his cry, but the

Ersa stayed where they were. Did these females even speak the human tongue?

Garric seized the nearest female by the shoulder. The bones beneath the light fur were thicker than he'd expected. "Come!" he repeated, waving his right arm high to summon the others. He dragged his—captive? victim?—dragged his example through the entranceway.

Liane had started to mount the flight of wooden steps from the enclosure's floor. Garric pushed the Ersa toward her, not harshly but with an awareness that if he had to carry each one in himself he'd be an old man before he finished.

Liane drew the Ersa toward her by the mere touch of her hands. The cylinder was now a translucent wall. Garric couldn't see the opposite side of the enclosure through it, but the Hand itself glowed like the sun in an empty sky.

"Zadachtoumar didume chicoeis," Tenoctris said, her face notched by lines of deep fatigue. She continued to walk around the circle of power. The old wizard would keep going until she dropped; but she would drop, perhaps sooner rather than later.

"Go through it now!" Liane said, gesturing the Ersa toward the column of cold radiance. "Quickly!"

The Ersa walked into the translucent surface without hesitation. She vanished through it as if she had fallen into night itself.

Garric turned. More Ersa, females and their children, waited in the narrow entrance which his body blocked. He jumped aside, stifling a curse at his own foolishness. He should have guessed that when the first of this sheep-like race moved, the rest would follow.

One by one the Ersa passed through the wall of the cylinder. The shuffling line blocked the entrance. The walls of the enclosure were low enough to climb, at least if Garric got a running start. He judged the angle, then saw something from the corner of his eye and stopped.

Tenoctris wasn't alone. A nude woman formed of shimmering, nacreous translucence like the cylinder itself walked beside her. Tenoctris appeared unaware of her ghostly companion.

Liane caught Garric's startled expression. She followed the line of his eyes, then looked back at him perturbed. "What's the matter, Garric?" she asked.

The ghost woman smiled lazily and stretched out an arm toward Garric. Her body was perfect and beautiful. Where her eyes should have been, Garric saw pits stretching all the way to Hell. He staggered back, stunned as if by a sudden hammer blow.

"Kill them all!" Rodoard's voice shrilled over the sounds of battle. "Slaughter them like the beasts they are!"

Garric took two strides along the inside of the enclosure, then leaped to the top of the mound. He drew his sword. He knew he was as much running from something he didn't understand as entering the fight on the side of those he'd joined, but he was needed in the fight as well.

The line of Ersa warriors had been forced back to the inner curtain of foliage. Carus' practiced eye judged that the Ersa had lost nearly half their original number. The survivors screened the females and children in a perimeter that shrank as the last of the noncombatants passed through the narrow entrance.

The human attack was disorganized but ferocious. A man nearly Cashel's size carried a heavy club in either hand; he had red tattoos on his right arm and blue on his left. Bellowing, he charged, swinging both clubs simultaneously.

The Ersa warriors moved to either side as smoothly as water parting before a dropped stone. Graz stabbed the tattooed man as he rushed past. The man continued forward, his clubs battering the Ersa females.

Garric jumped down in front of the man, who raised one club for a vertical blow. He held the other in front of his body on guard. Garric thrust, stabbing the hand holding the lower club. He'd used the trick a score of times in quarterstaff bouts during festivals in the borough: rather than stretching to reach your opponent's body, strike the hand holding his weapon and *then* strike the undefended body.

The tattooed man cried out in surprise and pain, dropping the club from his wounded hand. He stepped back and his eyes rolled up. Blood sprayed from his nostrils as he fell facedown like a toppling tree. Graz's thrust to his lung and heart had finally taken effect.

Garric was alone between the lines. The human attackers had fallen back for a moment; the Ersa females were all within the enclosure, and the warriors had taken a position on top of the mound. Garric backed quickly to stand in the entrance.

More humans came through the curtain of foliage. A party of eight Gulf-born men carried a litter on which Rodoard sat. Bandages of red silk tied off the king's lower legs.

"Kill them all!" Rodoard cried, pointing his demiguisarme. "Charge!"

His bearers broke into a shambling run toward Garric. Josfred was the lead bearer on the right side. His ratlike face glistened with sweat and fear.

"Garric!" Liane called desperately.

Garric glanced around. The Ersa warriors had jumped down within the enclosure, moving in silent unison. Garric, unable to see to the side or to read ear movements as speech, was alone again.

Three burly sailors came toward him with spears made by lashing knives onto poles. They had shields of cross-pegged boards, not very durable but sufficient against the light weapons of the Ersa. Other humans were starting to climb the enclosure to either side.

Garric backed through the entrance, hoping that the sailors would try to follow him carrying their shields. That would slow them long enough for him and his companions to escape through the circle.

"Kill them all!" Rodoard squealed.

Graz flung himself into the cylinder of light, vanishing as though he never was. He had been the last of the Ersa. Liane held Tenoctris around the waist and by one arm; the younger woman was helping the older continue her circle. Tenoctris' lips moved, but Garric couldn't hear the words of power anymore.

The Hand blazed with a fierce internal light. The object was the very sun to look at, but it neither cast shadows nor brightened the walls of the enclosure.

Garric jumped down to the floor of the pit. The woman of pearly translucence stood beside him. She caressed his cheek with fingers as soft as a butterfly's wing.

Garric jerked back in shock. The ghost woman laughed like chimes of crystal, pure and as cold as village charity.

"Garric!" Liane said. "What are you waiting for?"

Garric stepped toward her. Men had reached the top of the mound and were calling to their fellows to join them before they committed themselves by jumping down.

The woman of pearl took Liane's throat in both hands. Liane's weary frustration changed suddenly to horror. She let go of Tenoctris and tried to grasp the thing choking her. Her fingers met nothing.

Garric swept the pommel of his sword through the creature's head. Her form parted like smoke at the blow—and, like smoke, swirled together uninjured. She laughed as her grip tightened on Liane's throat. Liane's face was turning blue. Tenoctris staggered on, speaking the incantation by rote; perhaps she was unaware of what was happening around her.

The first of the sailors came through the entrance above Garric. Other men slid down the inner slope of the mound, their faces set and their weapons ready.

Garric stepped forward, his sword rising. The barrier of light made his skin tremble as he crossed it. *Someone walking on my grave,* he thought. He brought his blade down in a vertical cut that sheared through the Hand.

Something screamed. Perhaps it was the whirlwind that snatched Garric and whirled him into flaming darkness.

Light blazed. He saw Tenoctris and Liane; and then only the darkness, as deep as the ghost woman's blank hellpit eyes.

Sharina still held Halphemos' hand, but the young wizard was beginning to find the pace by himself. For the first several blocks after they left the prison, Halphemos had tripped himself every few steps. It was only Sharina's support that had kept him from falling. She couldn't imagine what it really was that a wizard did, but she'd seen the cost often enough to know that wizardry was work as brutal as scything in the hot sun.

"Where are we going?" Halphemos gasped, the first connected words he'd managed since he'd shouted out the final syllables of his incan-tation.

"There's a ship about to leave for Erdin," Sharina said, trying not to speak so loudly that passersby heard her. "Cerix is waiting aboard for us."

Cerix had written only a spell to loosen locks and bars on the palimpsest. The phantasm Halphemos sent out before him was of his own creation. Sharina supposed it was an illusion he'd practiced before, but it proved that the younger wizard had a stock of his own wizardry safe in memory.

Pandah's waterfront was just as busy and varied as what Sharina had seen in Erdin, the capital and port of entry for one of the most powerful islands of the kingdom. Serian ships with square bows and slatted sails were berthed end to end with catamarans from Dalopo, bulbous grain haulers from Ornifal, and small craft carrying wine or citrus fruit or metalwork from a dozen islands, some too small to have names to any but their own citizens.

A few months before Sharina had thought she'd never leave Barca's Hamlet. The variety she saw here seemed exciting and wonderful. While she imagined the wonders these ships implied, she could put aside for a time the darker mysteries of what had happened to her friends.

In contrast to the flimsy houses of mud brick and wicker which comprised most of the city, Pandah's quays were built of stone. A parrot squabbled with a seagull on the yard of a lateen-rigged coaster, and the chickens whose coop was being carried aboard a nearby vessel clucked a nervous counterpoint to the terns above.

A twenty-oared galley lay at wharfside of the nearest pier. Sharina knew enough of economics to be surprised to see such a vessel here.

Galleys were either military vessels or yachts for wealthy travelers who were willing to pay for the assurance of not spending weeks waiting for a favorable wind. They had very little carrying capacity and the crew was several times that of a sailing vessel. This one had neither military accoutrements nor the trappings of luxury to be expected in a yacht.

The *Porpoise,* the Sandrakkan freighter on which Cerix had taken passage, was berthed at the next pier. Sharina could hear the crew calling a chantey as they walked the capstan, raising the yard and sail which had rested on deck while the ship was in harbor.

A man stepped from behind a stack of timber, offloaded from an Ornifal vessel but not yet carried to its next destination. The sun was behind him, throwing his squat form into silhouette. He was blocking Sharina's path.

Halphemos continued a step beyond Sharina; he hadn't noticed the figure until she stopped. She drew the Pewle knife.

''Are you going to use that on me, child?'' the figure asked in a familiar voice.

''Nonnus,'' Sharina said. She began to tremble. She couldn't find the slot to resheath the heavy blade. ''Nonnus?''

''Who are you?'' Halphemos demanded on a rising note. Sharina suddenly realized how young he was. Halphemos was smart and able and a few years older than Sharina in simple chronology, but there was a good deal of boy still in his personality.

Nonnus had been mature. Nonnus had made decisions instantly but without haste. Nonnus had always been in perfect control of himself until the moment he died.

"Nonnus, you're dead," Sharina said as though she were whispering a prayer.

"Sharina?" Halphemos said, looking from her to the man who was a stranger to him. "What . . . ?"

"I was sent because I was the only messenger you would trust, child," Nonnus said. "We need to go immediately. More than the world depends on it."

Sharina moved closer so that she could be sure of the features even in the red light of sunset. The face and voice were beyond question those of the man who had died to protect her in a room full of hellspawn and slaughter.

"Cashel has disappeared," she said. "We were going to find him, and then f-find the others."

The crew of the *Porpoise* had belayed the falls to hold the sail in position. The captain shouted for the mooring lines to be taken in.

"Cashel will be all right," Nonnus said. "Your friend—"

He glanced calmly toward the quivering Halphemos.

"—can find Cashel without your help. And even if he couldn't, this is more important. I've got a ship here. We have to leave at once."

"I—," Sharina said.

Nonnus put a hand on her elbow. "You do trust me, don't you, child?" he said. He nodded to the galley. The oarsmen were at their benches and only the stern line was still around the mooring bitt on the quay. "We have to go."

Sharina turned to Halphemos. "I have to go," she said. "When you get to Erdin, find Ilna os-Kenset. She's Cashel's sister. She can help you."

"But—," Halphemos said.

Over her shoulder as she strode to the galley with Nonnus, Sharina cried, "You don't understand. Just go!"

The 12th of Heron (Later)

Cashel marveled to watch Zahag climb the tower with the coil of rope over his shoulder. From a distance Cashel had thought the structure was made from blocks of pink stone, but when he stood at the base he'd seen it was all one piece like a glazed pot. The ape went up it like a tree frog on the side of a barn.

"It's a *fool* thing to do," Zahag muttered, adding emphasis whenever his hand or foot gained a new hold. "When we *get* inside this Ilmed will *blast* us . . ."

His limbs were spread to their fullest extent. The ape's arms in particular spanned a considerable portion of the tower's circumference, though not enough that the hands were squeezing directly against one another.

"Or *else* we'll just *burn* . . ." Zahag said. Only one limb moved at a time, feeling its way upward for a new grip on what seemed to Cashel to be a smooth surface. The finish was weathered, the way even hard rock loses its polish if exposed to the elements, but that slight roughness was a long way short of anything a human could've hung on to. "In the *fire* going *back*!"

As Zahag spoke the last word, his hand reached over the top of the tower and snatched him out of sight. The swift, unexpected motion was like the flash of a frog's tongue, bringing back a victim to swallow before a man watching sees the mouth open.

"Ho!" Cashel cried in delight. The rope spun down the tower's side to him, uncoiling as it fell. He knotted the end around his staff, two half hitches on one side of the balance, leaving a long end which he tied off in another pair of half hitches to stabilize the pole.

"Well come *on*!" the ape demanded, peering over the tower's coaming with an expression Cashel couldn't read. In a human the snarl would have meant fury, but it seemed more likely that Zahag was grinning with delight. "Do I have to pull you up myself? Or shall we just get out of here now before the wizard comes back?"

"I'm coming," Cashel said. He gave the rope a firm, even pull while he didn't have fifty feet to plunge onto rocks. He thought of asking Zahag if he was sure the end was tied to something that would take the weight, but the ape was worse than a child. He might throw a tantrum if Cashel questioned his ability.

Palace servants had tried to give Cashel gloves along with the rope he requested. He couldn't understand why until he looked at their white, delicate palms and imagined what those hands would look like after hauling Cashel's weight to the top of the tower. A shepherd in Barca's Hamlet had calluses tougher than the calfskin gloves the servants offered.

When the line didn't cascade down at his first tug, Cashel braced one foot high up on the wall and used the full strength of his torso. The rope itself had a little stretch, but the loop at the other end was around something sturdy enough to stay planted. Cashel supported his weight with his grip on the rope as his feet walked up the sheer side of the tower.

The surrounding flames were a transparent curtain, but they seemed to block all sound from beyond them. People onshore cheered silently, waving hands and garments. Cashel wasn't used to that. In the borough folks didn't stare at other people any more than they stared at the clouds—though everybody knew what everybody else was doing and what the weather tomorrow would be. Erdin was a big city where nobody seemed very interested in anybody else, especially not bumpkins from a backward island like Haft.

But here on Pandah, *this* Pandah anyway, Cashel was the wizard who was going to save Princess Aria. He wondered if there was a soul in the city who wasn't watching him right now. He didn't much like the feeling.

When Cashel was six feet from the top of the tower, Zahag poked his head over the coaming. "Well, there you are!" the ape said peevishly. "I thought you'd gone back and left me!"

Cashel wasn't sure whether the ape was being sarcastic or if he'd really been worried. Cashel was used to people complaining that he was slow. It was all right if an ape took up the same song.

Nothing anybody said was going to make Cashel hurry, of course. He got jobs done in the time it took him. It was that simple, and he guessed Zahag would figure that out sooner or later. Folks in the borough had.

Cashel put a hand on the coping while the other kept its grip on the rope. He lifted his torso, then hooked his right foot over the edge and pulled himself completely onto the tower. He didn't suppose it looked graceful, but Cashel didn't care about that either.

The coping was ankle high—enough to trip somebody and trap rainwater, but not to do any good. The drain holes would let the water out—unless it froze, which it probably didn't very often on Pandah. It was still a stupid design. The little curlicues scalloping the edge of the pink material increased Cashel's scorn for the fellow who'd built the place.

Well, that wasn't a change from how he'd felt about Ilmed before.

In the middle of the roof was a tall post with glittering lenses all around the top. Zahag had looped the rope around it. Near the post was a trapdoor with two leaves, smooth and pink like the walls, lying open.

"What's inside?" Cashel asked as he drew the quarterstaff up to him. He wasn't sure how effective a weapon the fir pole would be, but he'd rather have it than nothing in his hand if trouble started.

"How would I know?" Zahag fumed. "You're the one

who wanted to come up here! I wasn't going to go into a trap like that alone."

Cashel walked to the open door and looked down. Helical stairs curled several flights below the floor immediately beneath, which seemed to be a dainty bedroom. The staircase was of pink filigree so delicate that Cashel thought for a moment of asking the ape to try it with his lesser weight first.

That would've been a waste of breath. Cashel put his weight on the top step, holding his staff crosswise. If the staircase went to pieces like ice shattering in the spring sunlight, the staff would support Cashel until he got his feet back on the roof and figured out what to do next.

The stairs didn't so much as tremble. The treads of Reise's inn, oak an inch thick, had more give in them than this tracery. Cashel rotated his staff upright and continued down.

The whole floor was a single circular room with a bed on one side and a series of fitted chests around the walls. What wasn't pink was white. The only other times Cashel had seen this much pink in one place were in occasional sunsets, and there the shade was mixed with more robust colors.

A mirror set between poles so it could tilt stood between a pair of chests. Cashel stared at himself. He'd never really seen himself before, not this way: the surface was more perfect than any pool or round of polished metal in the borough. If it weren't for the staff in his hand and the sight of Zahag climbing cautiously down the staircase behind him, Cashel would have taken the reflection as a real person: a big youth in a tunic more delicate than any part of the form it clothed.

The folding screen on the wall opposite the mirror was embroidered with roses and long-tailed birds of a sort Cashel had never seen in life. He walked over to it while Zahag watched from midway down the staircase.

Cashel jerked the screen aside, half-expecting a threat or a horror behind it. Instead he saw what looked for an instant like another mirror—but this one showed the landscape around the tower, from horizon to horizon.

The ape hopped down to get a better look. "See, there's the palace!" he said. "And the ship there in the harbor, it's moving!"

"Is it magic?" Cashel said, squinting to pick out the details in the image. He could see the folk on the harborside. Their lips moved as they spoke, if he brought his eyes very close to the image.

"No, no," Zahag said dismissively. "It's just light reflecting through a series of mirrors. The head is in the pole on the roof. Didn't you see it?"

"I didn't know what it meant," Cashel said simply. He walked to the staircase. They were here to rescue the Princess Aria, after all, not to watch people having a holiday on the harborside.

Cashel still didn't see how light could reflect through a solid roof—or, for that matter, how light reflecting through a solid roof was any different from wizardry. He was used to people getting angry because he didn't understand things, though, so when their voices took on that frustrated tone he didn't press them unless it was something he really needed to know.

Zahag usually sounded frustrated and angry when he tried to explain things to Cashel. That didn't make the ape any different from a lot of people.

Cashel went down the stairs to the next level. Zahag followed, munching an apple from the crystal bowl on the bedside table. The ape was a messy eater; seeds and fragments of crisp pulp spattered the back of Cashel's neck.

This room was a library. The walls were fitted with pigeonholes for scrolls lying end-out and cases in which codices stood. A pink rolling staircase would let a petite girl reach the highest shelves.

No one was on this level either.

Neither this room nor the one above it had windows. In the ceiling were bright panels across which Cashel could see clouds drifting. It looked like the panels were open to the sky—no glass could possibly be so clear—but Cashel knew that there was a thick rug over the floor directly above them. More wizardry, he supposed.

Tags dangled from the scrolls' winding sticks; the spines of the codices bore titles in gold leaf. A little wistfully, Cashel asked, "Can you read, Zahag?"

"Sure," the ape said. He tossed the remainder of the apple onto the white angora rug and pulled a codex off its shelf. "It's a waste of time, though."

Zahag flopped the book open, holding it from the top with his long, remarkably jointed arm. " 'Pasia os-Melte of Erdin was brought up as an orphan after her mother died in childbirth,' " he read. " 'Although Pasia was poor, she learned modesty and self-control. She regularly had a dream which prophesied good fortune for her, hinting at her future destiny.' "

Zahag tossed the book across the room. "What use is that sort of thing?" he asked. "Does it feed you?"

"Some people like it," Cashel said.

The ape scratched his armpit. "I tried to eat a book once," he said musingly. "It tasted like dried leaves. This one might be better in a pinch—it's animal hide, parchment. But not much."

He looked around the room. "Any more fruit down here?" he asked.

"I don't think so," Cashel said.

Only a few people in the borough could read and write. It wasn't a skill you needed to tend crops or herd sheep. Reise or-Laver, Garric's father, was an educated man, though. He'd taught his son and daughter to read the poets and historians who wrote a thousand years before, during the Old Kingdom.

Many times Garric had sat under the holly oak on a hillside south of the hamlet and read to Cashel. There'd been tales of battles and fantastic adventures as well as love songs written to girls who were dust and the dust of dust forty generations ago. Girls who might never have existed except in the poet's mind, Garric said.

Cashel was out in the greater world, now. He'd seen wonders as marvelous as anything in the books Garric read to him. And there'd been battles, too. . . . Cashel's grip tightened unconsciously on the quarterstaff.

But there was another world that only readers could enter. Garric and Sharina had shown Cashel a glimpse of that world, but he knew in his heart that he'd never be part of it himself.

Well, you couldn't do everything. "Have you ever herded sheep, Zahag?" Cashel asked as he walked toward the staircase again.

"What?" the ape said. "Why would I want to do that?"

"I don't suppose you would," Cashel said.

Because he was taking a last look at the shelves of books, Cashel didn't see the auburn-headed girl coming up the staircase until she said, "Who are—"

Cashel glanced at her in surprise. The girl screamed and ran back down the stairs.

"Help!" she cried. She wore a garment made from many thicknesses of white gauze; it drifted about her like a cloud. Each layer was so thin it seemed transparent, but together they were as opaque as a velvet robe. "Save me from the monsters! Help!"

"Princess Aria!" Cashel said. He clumped after her, putting a foot on each tread instead of jumping down because he was in a hurry. The twisting staircase wasn't built for someone Cashel's size; and anyway, he'd learned long since that his weight and strength meant he *had* to be careful when he did anything. There were plenty of people who thought Cashel was stupid, but nobody said he was a fool.

The stairs ended on the next level. Again it was a single room, this time a kitchen with a table and chair as delicate as all the tower's other furnishings.

The girl—she had to be Aria; there was nobody else here—had been eating when the voices of Cashel and Zahag brought her up to the library. On the table was a watercress/mushroom salad and tiny *somethings* fricasseed in a brown sauce. *Chickadee bosoms,* Cashel thought, though of course they could have been the breasts of any small bird.

Aria cowered beside a bronze door set into the curvature of the wall. Cashel was sure there'd been no opening to the outer wall of the tower.

The door opened toward him.

"Save me from the monsters!" Aria repeated.

A scaly man like the one Cashel had found in the barrel stood in the doorway carrying a curved sword. He rushed Cashel, raising the weapon for an overhand cut. Two more scaly men followed the first.

She called me *a monster!* Cashel thought. *Even Zahag's a lot more human than a scaly—*

He thrust his staff one-handed like a spear, crushing the creature's chest and flinging him back into his fellows. The sword, a wicked weapon meant for nothing but murder, bounced from the ceiling and back wall, then fell to the floor, where it quivered. The metal had the ring of bronze, not steel, but it had cut a nick from the hard substance of the wall.

The corpse bowled over another of the scaly men. The third dodged his fellows—*her* fellows; the scaly men wore studded leather crossbelts and armlets, but no real clothing—and came on with a murderous leer.

Cashel recovered his staff to the balance. He brought the other end around in a horizontal blow that spun the sword away an instant before dashing the creature's brains out.

His motions in a fight were as smooth and instinctive as those he'd have made while lifting a heavy weight. There wasn't time to think about what you were going to do; and for Cashel, there wasn't need either. It was just as natural as breathing.

The surviving scaly man disentangled himself from the first corpse. Blood and bits of other matter spattered the big circular room. The chair was untouched, but the table had smashed to tiny glittering splinters against the wall. Princess Aria stood with her eyes wide open, making gulping sounds.

"Look, we can—," Cashel said to the scaly man. It gave a guttural scream, the first sound he'd heard from any of the trio, and launched itself at him with its sword straight out at arm's length.

Cashel swept the creature's feet out from under it with another horizontal blow, this time widdershins. The scaly man hit on his back; Cashel finished it with a quick vertical chop to the head, just as he'd have used on a viper in a beanfield.

The new staff worked fine. It wasn't as heavy as what he was used to and maybe it wasn't quite as strong, but it had been strong enough for *this* job.

Cashel didn't take any particular pleasure in killing, but there were vermin and that was how you dealt with them. From their behavior, these scaly men were as mindlessly malevolent as so many horseflies, and they were a far sight bigger besides.

"Prin—" Cashel said. His mouth and throat were dry; he worked his cheeks against his tongue, wishing he'd brought an apple down from the bedroom, and resumed, "Princess Aria, your mother sent me to take you—"

Aria gave a despairing wail and tried to throw herself through the bronze doorway. Cashel grabbed her before she made it. All he could see beyond was swirling mist.

"Zahag!" he called. The ape seemed to have fled up the stairs when the scaly men appeared. That didn't surprise Cashel, but right now—with the princess shrieking and trying to bite his wrist—he could use some help.

Turning so that his body was between Aria and the door which he didn't have a hand free to close, he said, "We're *saving* you, Princess. There's a wizard—"

Zahag bounced down the stairs with screeches that weren't even close to being human words. He stopped beside the door, pointing back the way he'd come with one hand and covering his eyes with the other.

Cashel tossed the girl aside. If she wanted to run away, well, that might be a better idea than facing what had chased Zahag down the stairs.

A man with flowing white hair and a silver robe drifted down the stair shaft. His arms were folded across his breast, and his slippers of gilt leather floated above the treads.

"Ilmed!" Aria cried in delight. "You've come to rescue me!"

Ilmed's features were as perfect and hard as a marble statue of the Shepherd. He extended his right arm toward Cashel. His fist was clenched so that the great balas sapphire of his ring glinted at the youth.

Cashel held the staff before him in both hands. He began to rotate it before him sunwise. Instinct told him not to strike at the floating wizard.

"*Prokunete nuktodroma biasandra!*" Ilmed said.

Cashel spun his shaft faster. From the ferrules trailed light of the same trembling blue as a robin's egg. The streamers built into a hazy disk before him.

Cashel began to smile with the satisfaction of a workman who knew he was in command of his task. *When you've got your grip right and you feel the load start to come off the ground, then it's—*

"*Kalisandra katanikandra!*" Ilmed said. He cheeks were mottled with his effort; drops of spittle came off his tongue.

—just a matter of—

"*Laki!*" Ilmed shrieked. A bolt of blue fire shot from the wizard's carven jewel.

—time!

Ilmed's bolt struck Cashel's shield of purer blue light and rebounded. The blast shattered the stairs.

Cashel staggered back from the shock. His hands and wrists were numb, but he didn't drop his staff.

Ilmed screamed and fell to the floor. His robe was in tatters, and his hair and beard were burning.

Aria stood horrified, bending forward with both fists

pressed against her mouth. Zahag peeped out from between his knobbly fingers, then rolled to his feet with a broad smile. "Hoo!" he cried as he began to caper. "Great chief! The chief triumphs!"

A pattern of crazing dulled the walls' smooth pink surface. A crack shivered across the ceiling, spreading and branching like the top of an oak. A fist-sized chunk fell and shattered into sand on the floor.

Ilmed clucked, then stiffened. The wizard's breath no longer fluttered the stinking red flames that devoured his beard. His eyes were open, though the lashes had been singed off. Aria was bawling with her hand over her eyes.

Zahag hooted with sudden surmise. He sprang upward, catching the hole in the ceiling from which the staircase had hung. The material went to powder in the ape's grip, spilling him back to the floor with a despairing wail. Except for the bronze doorway, the whole tower was collapsing.

"Come on!" Cashel said. He grabbed Aria with his free hand and ducked through the doorway. "This way, Zahag!"

On the other side was a barren plain. The recently risen sun was the same sickly orange as the flames of burning hair. A trail wandered eastward through a landscape of rocks, boulders, and occasional spiky vegetation.

"Fagh!" said the ape, who'd followed Cashel out. "Where's this place, then?"

"Nowhere I've ever seen," Cashel said. The air was chilly, though from the look of the landscape the sun would heat it up very shortly. There wasn't any obvious shade.

He looked over his shoulder. From this side the doorway was a rectangle of twisted light: the ghost of a door rather than a real opening.

Cashel had released Aria's shoulder—he wasn't trying to hold the girl, just to get her out of a collapsing building faster than she'd have been able to manage on her own.

She gave a choked cry and leaped through the shimmering portal.

"Hoo!" cried Zahag, excited without being in the least dismayed by what the girl was doing.

Cashel threw himself after her, grabbing with his free hand. It wasn't so much a conscious decision on his part as the instinct of an animal to snap at movement. He caught Aria's ankle as his own head and shoulders passed through the frame of light.

He jerked back instantly. The girl came with him, though right now he didn't care about her.

Cashel was shivering. "Shepherd, guide my feet from danger," he whispered. "Lady, wrap me in Your cloak."

Aria whimpered. Her eyes were open, but they didn't seem to focus on anything.

"So what did you see there?" Zahag said, interested but as before unconcerned about the humans. "Isn't the wizard dead after all?"

"There's nothing there," Cashel said. "It's purple and it moves, but it isn't really there. There isn't even air to breathe."

The girl started to cry. Her dress, previously torn and spattered with the scaly men's dark blood, was now smeared with the gritty soil from this side of the doorway.

Cashel stood, smoothing the shaft of his quarterstaff clean with gauze he'd snatched from Aria's dress when he grabbed her. As his hands worked, his eyes surveyed the terrain.

The trail wasn't deliberately made. It was just a place where traffic had worn away the light soil and polished the rocks beneath. Still, it was the best choice they were offered.

"I guess we better get going," Cashel said. "The sun's going to make it too hot to travel soon."

He half-lifted, half-helped the girl to her feet. She continued sobbing but at least she didn't fight him.

And she didn't ask Cashel where they were traveling

to; which was good, because Cashel himself didn't have the faintest notion.

Garric stepped out of darkness, stumbled, and fell flat on a grassy hill slope. He'd never lost consciousness and he held his sword, though his right arm prickled all the way to the elbow.

Tenoctris sprawled beside him. Liane was nearby, already sitting up. She massaged her throat with one hand, but she could still give Garric a smile of pleasure and relief.

Garric smiled also, but he was pretty sure it looked shaky. He felt shaky, by the Lady he did!

They were in a meadow. Trees formed groves on the tops of the rolling hills. The landscape was a little more rugged than that of the borough; the trees were larger and more luxuriant also. Wood was a valuable resource in Barca's Hamlet. The right to take dead limbs in the common forest west of the community was valuable, prized as greatly as the freehold of a house and plowland.

The trees included oaks and beeches. There were dogwoods on the margins of the glades, though they were larger than Garric had ever seen on Haft and the leaves were notched rather than smooth-edged. Still, the tree was familiar even if the particular variety wasn't. The vegetation of the Gulf had been as alien to Garric as the changeless green sky.

As alien as the Ersa themselves.

The Ersa were walking in small parties. Scouting the new land, Garric supposed. Graz and a handful of the better-armed warriors stood at the edge of a glade fifty feet away. The Ersa leader bowed formally when he saw Garric glance toward him.

Within the stand of trees was a marble building; fluted columns supported a domed roof. Garric caught only a glimpse of it between the trunks. Having noticed one structure, though, his eyes picked out others: a sculpted niche from which a spring bubbled down a hillside; a grotto with an entrance of wedge-shaped blocks; on a distant hill, columns that he'd mistaken for dead pines. The entablature had fallen around the base like a tumble of boulders.

Garric bent and plucked a stalk of little bluestem. The seed head had tufted; it must be early fall here. He wondered what kept the meadow from growing into brush and being taken over by trees in a few decades. There was no sign of sheep droppings or those of natural grazers which might keep a meadow from becoming forest. People who thought the natural world was static had never lived in the natural world.

Which meant this place, wherever it was, was unnatural.

Sure at last that there was no immediate danger, Garric transferred his sword to his left hand. He flexed the right to return it to full feeling.

"What happened in the First Place?" Tenoctris asked. She was alert again despite the numbing effort of her incantation. She was sitting up, at least, cross-legged according to her custom. The pose still looked strange to Garric, raised in Barca's Hamlet, where people squatted instead.

Liane was coming back from the clear rivulet at the base of the hill, carrying water in a cupped sweetgum leaf. Garric could see bruises from the ghost's fingers beginning to appear on her throat.

"There was a woman in the pit with us," he said, speaking loud enough for both his companions to hear. "I guess . . ."

He didn't know quite how to phrase it. *He* wasn't a wizard.

"Nobody else seemed to see her," Garric resumed. "She, ah, waved at me. Then she started to choke Liane. And I thought because I couldn't touch her, that if I broke the Hand . . ."

Liane held the cupped leaf for Tenoctris to drink. It

wasn't much water, but it would moisten lips and a throat rubbed raw by syllables which were tools—and which, like tools, acted on the user as well as the work.

"I thought it was the air," Liane said. "I thought I'd breathed poison and it was going to kill me."

Garric shrugged uncomfortably. "I don't know why I cut the Hand," he said. "I guess because I'd never seen anything like the, well, ghost or the Hand either one. I smashed the one because I couldn't stop the other."

It had been his own decision, not that of King Carus. A peasant learns as surely as a king that the worst thing to do in a crisis is to do nothing at all; but the action Garric took could have meant—

"I could've trapped us all in the Gulf, couldn't I?" Garric said miserably. "Or between there and here, in the darkness."

"Garric," Liane said. She rose and put her arms around him, leaving the emptied leaf with Tenoctris. "It was killing me. I would have died if you hadn't smashed that evil thing."

"Yes," said Tenoctris, struggling for a moment before both young people helped her to her feet. "Though I suspect that would have been less unpleasant than what the creature had in store for Garric himself."

"You know who she was?" Garric asked.

Tenoctris shook her head. "No," she said, "but I think I know *what* she was."

The old woman grinned with a wry enthusiasm that meant she really had recovered. "It's all a myth, of course," she said, "and if I'm going to believe in demigods like the Temptress sent to lure the Shepherd from his duties, then I'd have to believe in the Great Gods themselves, wouldn't I? Where does my rational belief system go then, if you please?"

Garric examined his sword. Just below the tip, where the taper of the point merged into the straight blade's full width, something had eaten a piece out of the edge. The steel wasn't chipped or notched. Rather, a raised lip showed that metal had flowed under enormous heat. It looked as though Garric had tried to cut a lightning bolt instead of pearl and ancient bone.

"The Ersa who created the Gulf was more powerful than any human wizard," Tenoctris said musingly. "He or she was perhaps more foolish than any human would have been also. Though I've certainly seen my share of humans with more power than sense, we all have."

Her face hardened into an expression as implacable as that of Justice. "But to have used something as *evil* as that thing in order to create a sanctuary—that's utter madness!"

Garric thought about Rodoard and his henchmen; about the men, and particularly about Lunifra. They couldn't any of them have been saints before the Gulf swallowed them; but for that many people to have sunk to beasts so quickly—perhaps the cause was in part external.

"Maybe I did Rodoard an injustice," he said softly. "And Lunifra."

"No," said Liane, "you didn't. He was a monster and she was a worse one. However they got that way."

Graz started toward the humans. He walked with a stiff-legged gait that would mark him as alien at distances far greater than the Ersa features were visible.

"Tenoctris?" Garric said. "Do you know where we are?"

"Yes," the old wizard said. "The sort of place it is, at any rate; a bridge, I suppose you could call it. And I think we can return to our world from here. I'll have to study matters and choose the correct location from which to take the next step."

"What will happen to the people in the Gulf?" Liane asked quietly. She was tense, but Garric couldn't tell from Liane's tone whether she was afraid for the humans living in that green twilight or simply concerned that they would follow the escapees here.

"Nothing will happen to them," Tenoctris said. "Nothing that they don't do to themselves, I mean. That may be bad enough."

"They chose," Garric said. He thought of Josfred, dreaming of the day humans would slaughter the Ersa. "All of them chose, not just Rodoard."

"Yes," said Tenoctris. She shrugged. "When you destroyed the Hand, you sealed the Gulf forever, from both sides. The Gulf will no longer suck in people from our world, and those living in it can never leave. Not even if a wizard far greater than I am is born to them."

"I thank the Lady for Her mercy," Liane said as Graz joined the three humans.

The 16th of Heron

Sharina awakened in darkness, choking the scream in her throat. She didn't remember what she'd been dreaming, but she held the Pewle knife in a grip that threatened to numb her fingers.

She waited, taking slow, deep breaths until her heart stopped pounding, then crawled out of her tent. She still held the big knife, though no longer in a death grip.

"Mistress?" said the sailor outside the flap of her shelter.

"It's all right!" Sharina said, angry again that Nonnus kept a guard near her at all times, even the most private.

She glanced at the sky. The Oxen were above the eastern horizon, but only the great blue star of the Plowman's head had risen. At this time of year it meant that dawn was still an hour away, though the sky would brighten enough to tell dark from light well before then.

They'd landed on this nameless islet after sunset. The little vessel lay tipped sideways on the shore, resting on its port gunwale and a fence of oars thrust blade-down into the sand on the starboard side. Most of the crew slept under the sheltering hull, but Sharina had a cover of canvas hung on a brushwood frame.

The sailor guarding Sharina put two fingers in his mouth and gave a shrill whistle. She turned on him. "Why did you do that?" she snapped.

"Sorry, mistress," the man said. It wasn't an answer, but she knew by now it was as much answer as she'd get from him. She strode briskly along the shore in the direction Nonnus had gone after they ate together.

The Inner Sea was dotted with tiny islands. Few of them had freshwater, but they provided places for ships to lie overnight and their crews to sleep on dry ground. Many were covered in vegetation to the tide line. This one had a luxuriant growth of fig bushes, though the fruit would probably be small and bitter even in late summer when it had ripened.

Sharina noticed the flicker of red light only when it ceased. She stopped. She couldn't let herself understand what it meant, not yet. For a moment she wriggled her bare toes deeper into the sand for the familiar gritty feeling; then she walked on.

When Sharina had crawled from her tent there'd been a rosy haze toward the islet's northern edge. It was too faint to have crossed the threshold of her consciousness, but her country-trained senses were aware of it.

When the guard whistled, the light had vanished. That *change* in the previous ambience struck her though the mere fact of the light had not. The light was the sort of tremble-at-the-back-of-the-eyeball Sharina had seen in the past when a wizard worked.

She clasped both her hands about the hilt of the Pewle knife: not as a weapon, but as though she were in prayer.

A figure came out of the darkness ahead of her. "Sharina?" Nonnus said. "You're up early, child."

"We both are," Sharina said. The brush rustled. Some islets had populations of goats or pigs, landed in former times to provide meat for future travelers. This place had only rats. "I was having a dream, so I got up."

Nonnus nodded. "I was checking the weather," he said. His voice and manner were those of the man Sharina had grown up with, the hermit who prayed every day to the Lady to be forgiven for his past. "We'll have another fine day. We should make good time."

"As before?" Sharina said. "With half the rowers resting and changing shifts on the hour?"

"Yes, that's the best way to cover a long distance quickly," Nonnus said. "It's hard on the crew, but these men are trained for it."

"Where are we going, Nonnus?" Sharina said. "Please, can't I know now?"

They'd rowed east ever since they left Pandah, but Sharina couldn't guess how far they'd traveled. This driving progress by men rowing watch-and-watch would confuse even an experienced sailor, she thought.

"Not yet, child," Nonnus said. The sky had become enough lighter that she could see the square, familiar lines of his bearded face. "You'll have to trust me."

He gestured Sharina to turn. The arc of his arm cautiously avoided the Pewle knife she held before her. "Come, we'll see if there's porridge on the fire, yet."

"Nonnus?" she said in sudden surmise. "Don't you want to take your knife back? I only carry it in . . . because it helps me remember you."

"I don't touch iron since I returned to help you," Nonnus said smoothly. "You keep it if you like, though my men and I will make sure nothing happens to you."

As the sky brightened Sharina saw a shape under the rope belt of Nonnus' tunic. "You have another knife," she said.

"This?" Nonnus said, lifting the weapon slightly between his thumb and forefinger. His tone barely hinted at irritation. "Yes, but it's stone. Fossil bone, rather. Now let's go back to the ship."

"Yes, of course," Sharina said as she turned obediently. The guard stood close behind her. She sheathed the Pewle knife but continued to rest two fingers of her right hand on its black horn hilt.

The stone knife was no weapon: its hilt and blade were carved with symbols of power shaped in the curving style of the Old Kingdom. Sharina felt sick with fury. Did this creature who pretended to be Nonnus think that she wouldn't recognize a wizard's athame?

He hadn't intended her to see it, of course. She'd interrupted him while he was working an incantation, perhaps trying to foresee the weather. As if Nonnus—or any peasant in Barca's Hamlet!—couldn't have told without wizardry that the morrow would be fair!

Sharina had given herself into the hands of an enemy claiming to be the person above all others that she would trust. This islet was too small to hide on, even if she managed to escape for the moment from the men on either side of her.

But Sharina would escape. For her own sake. For the sake of Cashel, whom she'd abandoned because a lying wizard called to her.

And most of all, for the sake of the dead man whose memory she had stained by trusting an enemy who wore his semblance.

Ilna left her door open while she worked, so she heard Maidus running all the way down the hall from the stairwell. She tamped a last weft thread, closed the shed, and stepped out from behind the loom to face the boy when he burst into the room.

"Mistress Ilna!" Maidus said. "There's a man coming up for you. He's City Patrol for sure but he's not from this district. I think he's from the chancellor's office!"

Ilna glanced at the pattern she'd been weaving and saw nothing that concerned her. She frowned. If the chancellor sent an envoy to obtain Ilna's fabric directly instead of going through Beltar's shop, he wouldn't pick someone who frightened Maidus as much as—

"Ah," she said, smiling with appreciation. "A stocky man of forty or so? A solid fellow, and probably carrying a baton that's seen use?"

Maidus bobbed his head in furious agreement. "That's him, mistress," he said. "A terrible man!"

"A hard one, at least," Ilna said. "His name's Voder or-Tettigan. Well, I knew I'd see him as soon as he decided what he was going to do about me. You run along now, Maidus. I won't need you further today."

She smiled like plaster cracking. "At least for today."

"What's he going to do, mistress?" the boy asked.

"Go away, Maidus," Ilna said with wintry calm. "I won't tell you again."

The boy backed from the room, transfixed by Ilna's cold glare. She wasn't angry, but anger would have been easier to face than this detached analysis. It was like the look on the face of a cook determining where to start jointing a dead hen.

Voder came out of the stairwell even as Maidus vanished in the other direction. The patrol official clomped heavily on the sagging floor, deliberately warning of his presence. Doors along the corridor banged, leaving Ilna's the only one open.

Voder closed it behind him as he entered.

"Good morning, mistress," he said, glancing around the room in a deceptively casual fashion. He could probably have reported the number of warp threads strung on the double loom in the corner. "The last time I came to see you, I didn't have to walk up stairs."

He gave her a lazy smile. She didn't see any new scars, but Voder wasn't carrying quite as much extra weight around his belly as he had the day he visited her in the mansion on Palace Square she'd then rented. He'd probably lost the fat when Ilna had him imprisoned to prevent him from interfering with her schemes.

"The last time you saw me," she said, "I didn't have so many debts to repay."

She reached behind the loom and brought out the stool at which she worked. "I can't offer you a proper chair, I'm afraid," she said, "but you're welcome to this. I don't cater to visitors here."

Voder laughed. "I guess I get enough sitting done in the office, ever since they promoted me off the street," he said. He rubbed his waistline. "I didn't used to have a belly like this. Of course, I'm not as young as I used to be either."

Ilna straightened and crossed her hands behind her back. "Master Voder," she said, "I wronged you. I apologize for that. You'll have to decide on any further recompense yourself."

Voder shook his head, still smiling. "I threatened you," he said, "and then I turned my back. I've been off the street too long or I'd have known better than to do that with somebody of our sort."

He walked past Ilna to the window. He moved very softly now, despite boots with heavy soles and exposed nailheads. A man kicked with those boots would know it the next morning; or wouldn't, likely enough.

"We draped that hanging you sent us across the wall opposite the stove," Voder said without turning around. "We spend most of our time in the kitchen, you know. When I'm home, I mean. The wife keeps a room for company, but the Lady help me and the kids if we stick a toe in and muss it up."

"I gather there's a market for hangings of that size," Ilna said. "At any rate, Beltar keeps raising his prices on the ones I let him have."

"I could get a good price for one of my kids, too," Voder said, turning with the easy grace of a man in control of his body. "Especially the middle daughter. Quite a little charmer, she is. Nobody in my family or my wife's either was that blond before, but I don't suppose that's a question I ought to be looking into too carefully, hey?"

More people than Voder's wife and children had gone through hard times or worse because of Ilna's actions. That didn't make it any less wrenching for her to look at the man and think about the others she'd hurt without being more than casually aware of their existence.

Voder smiled. He was a cheerful man, one who'd smile even when he slid his cudgel out from beneath his broad leather belt.

"The wife's got kin here in Erdin and so do I," he said, answering the question Ilna hadn't asked. "They made out all right while I was away."

He grinned even more broadly. "She always told me I'd wind up on the wrong side of the walls unless I learned to kiss ass better than I did," he added. "I guess the only surprise for her was when they let me out again and promoted me."

Voder faced the window again. He cleared his throat before he continued, "Which I wouldn't have come here to thank you for, but since I *am* here—"

"You've no cause to thank me," Ilna said harshly. "For anything."

"Thank you anyway," Voder said without looking around. "What I came for was to say that there's a couple men asking around for you. Street conjurers, likely enough . . . but just maybe they're the real thing."

He turned. This time his smile was forced. Voder wouldn't say the word "wizard," because he was afraid of calling to himself the thing he named.

Ilna frowned in puzzlement. "I don't know any male wizards," she said. Her expression changed to a smile of a sort that Voder, at least, could understand. "None that're still alive, I mean. What do they look like?"

The police official shrugged. "The older one, Cerix, doesn't have any legs," he said. "The other one's a boy. He calls himself Halphemos but he was just Alos when he came here with Cerix a few years ago. Cerix had his legs then, too. They've been gone from Erdin for almost a year, but now they're back looking for you."

Ilna shrugged in turn. "I haven't the least notion as to what they want," she said. "You can direct them to me if you like."

"If you think there's going to be a problem," Voder said, turning sidelong so that he wasn't *quite* speaking directly, "they can leave town before they bother you, you know. What you've been doing these past weeks has helped a lot of people."

"I'm not afraid of them, Voder," Ilna said. She laughed harshly. "The only thing I'm afraid of are the things I'm capable of doing myself."

Nodding toward the room which she kept as living quarters, she continued, "Can I offer you something? I have bread, cheese, and some extremely bad wine. Also cistern water that a boy with a donkey brings by in the evenings. My major luxury. I haven't been able to bring myself to drink canal water yet—"

Her face hardened. "Though most of the people in this building have to."

Voder nodded. "I've drunk my share of canal water," he said. "I could say I miss the salt taste since I got some money, but that would be a lie."

He turned his gray eyes directly on her brown pair. "I still sort of wonder what you were doing, mistress," he said. "Before, I mean. I knew even then that you weren't in it for the money."

Ilna sniffed. "Let's just say I was making a fool of myself over a man," she said. "Not a new story, I'm afraid. Or a particularly interesting one."

Voder nodded. "Well, if you change your mind about Cerix and the other, let me know," he said, switching the conversation back so smoothly that it seemed never to have left its original channel. "You can get me through the central office. Or at home, if you like. We've got a second floor on Rush Street. My wife'd be pleased to meet you, I think."

He looked at a corner of the ceiling again and cleared his throat. "Speaking of work," he said, "there a watch captain here in the Crescent named Bonbo or-Wexes. He's told the chancellor that you're the mastermind of a gang of thugs who've half-killed a number of wealthy citizens while they were passing through the district in their sedan chairs. He didn't get much of a rise from the chancellor, but chances are Bonbo is going to keep trying until something happens."

Ilna flicked her head in disgust. "Your Bonbo was paying upkeep on his mistress out of the profits of a child brothel in the next building. The establishment is out of business now. Some of the local people took care of that themselves."

"Your doing?" Voder asked.

"I suppose," Ilna said. "I'd like to think so, at any rate. I've provided fabrics for the light shafts of most of the tenements nearby. The residents seem to feel better about themselves, and they're willing to improve their surroundings further by their own efforts."

She glanced out the window herself. "Some of the brothel's clients were roughed up when it went out of business," she went on. "Not as badly as they should have been, in my opinion."

She looked at Voder like a hawk facing a wildcat. "If Bonbo is going to be a problem," she said, "I'd best take care of him."

"No," said Voder. "No, you will *not* do that thing!"

He slapped the window frame for emphasis; his fingers were harder than the wood of the casement. "Look, woman," he said. "If a brothel keeper in the Crescent gets mobbed, nobody who matters is going to care. Chances are the particular nobles who got caught in that business don't have a lot of friends either. But if you raise a mob against a watch captain, that's revolution. The earl will send in the army if the City Patrols can't finish you off ourself."

"Well, somebody had better deal with Bonbo!" Ilna said. "Are you volunteering, then?"

Voder's anger vanished in a gust of loud laughter.

''Yeah, I suppose I am,'' he said. ''Bonbo is Central Office business, that's a fact.''

He slid out his hickory baton, looked at it, and twirled it experimentally between the thumb and two fingers of his right hand. ''Well, I didn't drop it,'' he said musingly. ''It's been a while, the Sister *knows* it has; but I guess not so long that I can't still teach Bonbo where he should've drawn the line.''

Ilna gave him a curt nod that was a salute. ''Just a moment,'' she said, walking to a wicker hamper near the door. She set aside the lid, considered the contents for a moment, and reached in with both hands to bring out a packet of considerable size, wrapped in black baize.

''Here,'' she said, handing the cloth to Voder. ''Master Beltar hasn't been by to pick up the Ten Days' weaving. If you give this to the chancellor, you may have less difficulty convincing him of why it was necessary to deal with Bonbo the way you did.''

Voder took the gift with the grin of one predator to another. ''It might at that,'' he agreed.

He put the baton back under his belt for the time being. ''I'll go about my business, then,'' he said. ''You know, I'm pretty much looking forward to it.''

Voder opened the door, then paused and looked over his shoulder. ''Mistress?'' he said. ''Does the fellow you mentioned know what he's walked away from?''

Ilna smiled. ''He's a special man,'' she said. ''He'll be very important, one day. I think he's done better for himself.''

"I haven't seen much of the world,'' Voder said. "I never left Erdin in my life. But I've met a lot of people and I'll tell you this, mistress: you're wrong. He couldn't have done better.''

Voder walked out of Ilna's room, leaving the door open as he'd found it. His feet didn't make a sound on the floor of the hallway, but he whistled a catchy tune about a milkmaid and her cat.

* * *

"This water tastes *awful,*" said the princess Aria. Her face screwed up as if she was about to cry.

"Well, what did you expect?" Zahag said. "Do you think we're back in the Successor's palace, is that it? I think I did pretty well to find anything to drink here!"

"I know I'm not in the palace," Aria said. "Because of you! Oh, Mistress God, how could you be so cruel to me!"

And she did start to cry. Again. Cashel didn't know where she found the fluid to refill her tear ducts, but somehow she managed.

"Don't pick at her, Zahag," Cashel muttered. "She's not used to this sort of thing."

"Oh, and I suppose I am?" the ape snarled. "Well, you can find your own water the next time!"

Zahag flounced to the other side of the outcrop beneath which he'd located the pool dripping between two layers of limestone. He wouldn't go far, Cashel knew; and it was hard to blame the ape for finding Aria a difficult companion. He sighed.

If you looked toward the horizon, the landscape seemed to have a lot of greenery. That's because it was pretty much flat. Tiny leaves of the low shrubs merged with distance into a solid carpet that looked remarkably sparse at any place you came close to.

There was grass: dead, dry stems but in such profusion that Cashel supposed there must be rain now and again. He tried to imagine the terrain after a storm when suddenly everything was lush and green. He'd woven the straw into sunshades for the three of them to carry on poles of brushwood from which he'd knocked the thorns.

He chuckled.

"What is there to laugh about!" Aria said, looking up in real anger. She thought he was laughing at her.

"If I wanted green grass and plenty of water," Cashel said quietly, "I should've stayed home in Barca's Hamlet.

And sometimes that's what I think: I *should've* stayed home in Barca's Hamlet.''

Aria looked at him like he was crazy. That was a change from her crying, at least. She stuck her head under the limestone and began to slurp more of the water they had no utensils to dip up.

''We could leave her here,'' Zahag said. He'd made a circuit of the outcrop to squat at Cashel's side. ''There's other females and anyway, this one isn't strong enough to be much use. She can't even pick berries!''

''I told her mother I'd bring her back,'' Cashel said. He'd stopped trying to argue with the ape about helping people whether you liked them or not. Aria wasn't part of Zahag's band—or Cashel's, she'd made that clear as springwater—and Zahag didn't figure he owed her anything.

The bushes that grew every double pace or two across the landscape were of a dozen or more varieties when Cashel examined them closely. They were all low to the ground; all thorny and small-leafed; but for a wonder, many of them carried dark berries the size of a woman's little fingernail on the undersides of their branches. The berries didn't have much flesh, but the kernels inside were crunchy and edible as well.

Berries had kept the trio going during the three days they'd walked across this wasteland. You'd have thought that Aria, whose hands and wrists were far more delicate than those of her male companions, would have had the easiest time picking berries from among the thorns.

That was true, in a way, because the first time Aria tried she'd pricked herself. She'd flatly refused to try again. Cashel and Zahag had to forage for her as well as themselves.

Aria drew her head back from the brackish pool and straightened. She glared at Cashel and the ape.

''You didn't tell her mother you'd bring her back,''

Zahag said deliberately. "You said you'd get her away from Ilmed. And you did that, right?"

"If you'd just left me alone . . . ," Aria said. Her tone started out angry, but it sank swiftly into bleak despair. "I would have married the most powerful wizard ever. Ilmed would have made me queen of all the world! And instead . . ."

She turned to survey the surrounding wasteland. Her eyes filled with tears and she sank to the ground again, sobbing.

"If you challenge the chief ape," Zahag said with gloating harshness, "then you'd better be stronger than him or able to run faster. Otherwise you get your neck cracked. I guess Ilmed learned that a little before he died."

Cashel cleared his throat. "Time we got moving," he said. He'd have liked to travel by night, but the track was so faint that he figured they'd get lost in the darkness. There wasn't even a moon in this place.

He leaned over and touched the girl's elbow to make sure she knew he meant it. Her dress was a mass of fluff and tatters like the seeds starting to spill from a milkweed pod. Her feet weren't hardened for this trek either, though he'd plaited her sandals of a sort from the gray-green bark of the shrubbery. Cashel would never have his sister's touch with fabrics, but he could make out.

Aria continued to cry. She clamped her arm close to avoid Cashel's touch.

"And as for Ilmed . . . ," Cashel said with a grating anger that he only half-regretted. Couldn't the girl even *try*? "He thought that because he had power, he could do anything he pleased. That's no way for a man to live, nor a woman either."

He cleared his throat again. "Now get up, mistress," he said. "I won't leave you here, but I might decide to drag you if you won't walk!"

The 17th of Heron

"'Silver hidden in the greedy soil,' " Garric read from the volume of Celondre, " 'has no luster, my wise friend Kristas. Only in wise use does the metal gleam.' "

He sat with his back to one of the four pillars across the front of the little temple. Inside, Tenoctris examined the carvings just below the roofline. If there had ever been a cult statue, it had vanished in the ages since the temple was built.

Liane sat cross-legged against the base of the next pillar over, facing Garric. She listened with a relaxed smile.

Garric believed Tenoctris that this land wasn't part of the world from which the Gulf had sucked them, but it obeyed the same rules. The sun rose and set, creeks ran downhill and breezes blew, and the tension he'd felt beneath the brooding green sky was absent. He was glad to have a few days of quiet; and glad also that he had someone with whom to share Celondre's *Odes*.

He was glad to know Liane. For most of Garric's life he'd never have dreamed of meeting a noblewoman. Now he was reading poetry to one, and she smiled at him.

" 'The man who masters his own appetites,' " Garric read, " 'has a kingdom greater than if he joined Haft to Bight and ruled far Dalopo besides.' "

In Garric's mind, King Carus laughed boisterously. Garric lowered the codex and grinned at his companion. "Of course," he said, "it's easy to say that if you're a poet with a country house in Ornifal and nobody would ask you to command a single trireme after the way you botched things the first time you tried."

"And if half the stories about Celondre's private life are true," Liane agreed, "he wasn't notable for mastering his own appetites either. Naked women posing in every room of his house in case the whim struck him!"

She giggled. "Of course we weren't supposed to read the *Lives of the Poets*," she added. "Mistress Gudea said each lyric should be appreciated for what was in its words alone. 'To import other considerations undermines a poem's innate ethos.' "

"How can it be wrong to get as much information as you can in order to understand something?" Garric said in amazement. He grinned, wondering how much the next thought that drifted through his mind had to do with the ancestor in his mind. "Of course, it gets harder to decide when you know a lot. The easy choices are the ones you make when you don't know enough to see how complicated things are."

Liane nodded, but the direction of her eyes led Garric to peer around the shaft of the column behind him. Graz had arrived, accompanied by the two females Tenoctris had sent as messengers to find him.

"Tenoctris?" Liane called as she rose gracefully. "Master Graz is here."

There were human structures scattered throughout this landscape. None was particularly large—this fane, a rich man's private chapel rather than a community temple, was typical. All showed the lichens and weathering of great age. Tenoctris' art had led her to this particular site, but it was Liane who'd identified it.

Tenoctris came from the building with a smile of satisfaction just as the Ersa leader reached the slab on which the structure rested. The chapel had been modeled on a full-sized temple with a three-step base, each layer so high that it would be cut by several human-sized steps to the central doorway.

This was a toylike copy and, to Garric's untrained eye, it looked ill-proportioned. Part of his mind wondered if real aesthetics had anything to do with academic pronouncements like the one Liane had just repeated.

He put the volume of Celondre away in his belt wallet and rose also. He smiled as King Carus would have done.

The humans bowed to Graz. Bowing didn't seem to be an Ersa custom, but the way Graz's ears flattened against his round skull was perhaps an equivalent.

"There was a connection between your First Place and the hillside where we entered the present world," Tenoctris said with her usual lack of small talk before getting down to business. "The temple here has a connection to a known part of the world which my companions and I left. Known to Mistress Liane, that is."

She nodded to the younger woman. Garric gave Tenoctris his hand and helped her to the ground as an excuse to step down himself.

There was an inherent challenge when an armed male stood above another, and the Ersa were inhumanly attuned to body language. Garric wasn't sure he'd have been quite so aware of that without Carus' guidance—but he *was* aware.

"The ruins of the palace of the Tyrants of Valles are outside the city of Valles," Liane said to the Ersa leader. "My teacher, Mistress Gudea, took us on a day trip there. She said that the study of history was just as important as that of literature."

She grinned. "Not as important as etiquette, of course, but very important. There was a temple exactly like this one in the grounds of the old palace, though the honeysuckle had grown over it."

Tenoctris touched the sandstone pillar. "This is a node that leads back to my world, our world," she said.

She gestured to Garric and Liane, but her eyes remained on Graz. "There are other nodes here also. I don't know where they lead. Some of them probably terminate in places which none of us would choose to see."

With a smile as hard as sunlight winking from the edge of a stone knife Tenoctris added, "We wouldn't want to live there either, but in many cases survival wouldn't be an option anyway. This is the only portal which I think it's safe to open."

"Valles is the capital of our world," Garric said. His words blurred over the chaotic political situation—there'd been no true King of the Isles since Carus drowned in a wizard's cataclysm a thousand years ago—but this was close enough for present purposes. "I won't say you'll be welcome there, but I don't know of any reason why you shouldn't be."

As if people had ever needed reasons to hate or kill!

"Anyhow," he concluded, knowing he sounded lame, "I don't know of a better spot you could come to. And the three of us will do all that we can to help you."

"I will look inside this place," Graz said. "There are more of them in your world?"

"Many," Liane said. "We live in buildings like this and much bigger."

Liane too was only hinting at a situation that was more complicated than words could explain. The Ersa had no concepts for what lay behind human descriptions of politics or artificial structures. Was the weather of the Ersa home world as changeless as that in the Gulf, or had they lost the knowledge of building when they exiled themselves into a place where the need was absent?

Graz and Tenoctris entered the little temple. The Ersa females walked silently to a nearby pine tree and began opening cones for the tiny nuts within.

"Mistress Gudea wanted us to remember that Valles had been a great city during the Old Kingdom," Liane said to Garric in a low voice. There wasn't enough room in the nave to hold four with comfort, nor did the younger people have any reason to join the senior pair inside. "She was particularly determined to drive that home in me, since I was from the upstart island of Sandrakkan."

She looked at Garric and added with a twinkle in her voice, "And unlike Carcosa on Haft, Valles had rebuilt after the Old Kingdom fell. Not that Mistress Gudea had any students from so backward as place as Haft."

"The great men of Ornifal . . . ," Garric said. The voice was his but the memories behind the words were not. "The landowners, the rich merchants—they didn't try to break the kingdom the way nobles did on some other islands. But they didn't help to hold the kingdom together, either."

Liane looked at him, her face suddenly without expression. She didn't back away, but he knew the cold anger in his voice had surprised her.

Garric couldn't help it. He tried, but his control meant only that he trembled with emotions that he couldn't release in the physical action they demanded.

"The *great* men just wanted things to stay quiet," he said. "They paid any shoeless usurper who demanded their support because they claimed it was cheaper than getting involved. Cheaper to stand aside and watch the Isles break up in chaos!"

Graz stepped out of the temple. His ears were extended so fully toward Garric that the Ersa looked as though he had three heads on his narrow shoulders. Tenoctris followed him.

Garric lifted his empty hands and managed a laugh. All the fury had washed out of him, but it left him weak with its passing.

"I was talking about ancient history," he explained. "Nothing that's worth getting angry about at this late date."

Graz fluttered his ears; they shrank to normal size. "My people will stay here," he said. "We have shared a world with humans in the past. I think it is better that we not do so again."

Tenoctris nibbled her lower lip. "Master Graz," she said. "I can understand your decision, but I think you're making a mistake."

She spread one hand in the direction of the meadow rolling away from the little temple. "This seems to be a lovely place and of course it is . . . but it's more than that too. A location where so much power comes together isn't a proper home for living beings."

"Nevertheless," Graz said, "we will stay here. I wish you well on your journey, humans. But do not return."

The Ersa leader walked away with his stiff-legged, mincing stride. His people wouldn't have an easy time on Ornifal or anywhere in a human world, Garric knew; but Garric knew also that when Tenoctris gave advice, the path of wisdom was to accept it. Still, the Ersa had the same right that humans did: to make their own choices, and to live or die by them.

"If you two are willing . . . ," Tenoctris said. She plucked a twig from the pine tree and stripped the needles off between her fingers. "I think it'd be a good idea for us to leave immediately. Graz has drawn a lesson from what happened in the Gulf, but it led him to a belief that I regret."

Garric and Liane exchanged glances. "Of course," Liane said. "We're ready now."

"You know . . ." Garric said, returning to the train of thought that he'd been following when Graz and Tenoctris returned. "The ordinary people on Ornifal wanted the Isles to stay united. They wanted to sleep safe in their beds and not have to take a spear with them when they went plowing for fear pirates would sweep the district. The people would've been willing to help hold the kingdom together, I think, if their leaders had let them."

The two women watched him in concern. His left hand squeezed a fold of his tunic and the medallion hanging beneath it.

Garric laughed. "Well, maybe this time their leaders will have better sense," he concluded in a voice shaky with emotion.

"Indeed they will, lad!" echoed a voice in his mind. *"Even if we have to knock that sense into their heads!"*

* * *

The false Nonnus crouched in the stern, talking with the steersman as they both eyed the shore forty paces off the dispatch vessel's port side. The oarsmen rested, adjusting their kit and swigging water from the basin the coxswain carried back between the pairs of benches.

One man stood and urinated on his left hand. A rower had told Sharina that urine toughened cracked skin so it healed as calluses.

She supposed the crewmen would know. They were a dour lot who didn't volunteer information and gave only short answers to direct questions, but they were skilled oarsmen.

This island was a shallow cone made of black basalt instead of the usual limestone or coral sand. It was bigger than most of the islets Sharina had noted as the dispatch vessel crossed the Inner Sea on the ceaseless labor of its oarsmen. The low sun illuminated occasional clumps of spiky grass, but most of the vegetation seemed to be groundsels shaped like huge cabbages, and giant lobelias whose shaggy flower columns stood taller than a man.

She stood in the bow as if to stretch. The vessel was designed for swift transit with no concession whatever to the comfort of its crew or passengers. The false Nonnus had landed the mast and sail, depending instead on the oars even when the wind might be fair. Sharina tried to visualize how crowded the ship would have been if the lowered mast and yard filled the narrow aisle between the benches.

"All right, we'll go on," the false Nonnus said in a carrying voice. "I don't like the shore here."

Oarsmen muttered and looked to the coxswain. He squared his shoulders and said, "*I* don't like being out at sea at night in a cockleshell like this."

The false Nonnus didn't stand—he didn't have the Pewleman's sense of balance, Sharina realized. Scowling, he said, "There's a sandy beach on the horizon. We can reach it with the light we have left."

The sun was fully down. The western horizon was still

pale, but stars were already visible in the direction the vessel was heading.

"And don't ever argue with my orders again!" the false Nonnus added in the real man's voice but not his manner.

Sharina went over the railing in a clean dive and stroked for the volcanic island. Nothing she'd seen there looked edible. There might not even be freshwater, but she had to get away.

Her tunic dragged at her. She would've alerted the false Nonnus if she'd removed the garment before she dived, and she didn't dare struggle in the water at the vessel's side while she stripped it off. She didn't think the crew would shoot arrows or javelins after her, but one of them might well have knocked her silly with an oar.

The thin wool fabric wasn't a serious impediment. Her powerful crawl stroke had brought her most of the way to shore before the men could organize their response.

The real Nonnus swam like one of the seals he'd hunted as a youth on the islands north of the main archipelago. The man who wore Nonnus' semblance only shouted orders while the coxswain bellowed a conflicting set. Both men were trying to turn the vessel after the escaping girl, but they were going about the process in different fashions.

Few sailors could swim. If one of the oarsmen had been the exception, and if he'd had the initiative to dive over the side after Sharina, well—

She had memories of how Nonnus coped with danger. And she had his keen-edged Pewle knife as well.

Because Sharina lifted her face between strokes only enough to gasp a mouthful of air, her fingers touched the shore before she saw it. She scrambled out of the water on all fours, dodging lobelias as she ran uphill. Her tanned limbs and the wet brown wool of her tunic were invisible against the background in this light, though her blond hair would be a beacon once the moon rose.

Sharina stayed below the crest as she worked to the left

around the island. The shrubbery didn't have thorns. Basalt fractured with sharper edges than, say, limestone, but Sharina's feet hadn't been in the water long enough for her soles to soften.

She'd have run across knife blades if that was what it took to escape from the monster wearing her friend's face.

The dispatch boat was a dark mass between two lines of oar-foam. It had turned in its own length and was putting in to shore. The false Nonnus was ordering the crew to fan out across the island as soon as they grounded.

When Sharina saw open water to the north she realized that the island was a narrow spine rather than the quarter-mile circle she'd hoped for. The twenty oarsmen could form a sufficiently tight cordon to find her by sweeping from one narrow end to the other.

They'd have to get organized first, of course, but the false Nonnus had shown he was capable of intelligent planning. And he was a wizard as well. . . .

The dispatch vessel grated onto the island. They must have touched parallel to the steep shore instead of driving straight in. For the sake of speed, the vessel's hull and frames were as thin as possible. Sharina had hoped they might break the ship's back when they landed, but she knew better than to expect that from a trained crew.

"Brace her to starboard!" the coxswain cried. "Use your oars!"

What Sharina expected was that she'd be recaptured. They'd carry her bound in the bottom of the vessel the rest of the way to wherever they were going.

The only chance she saw now was to get away from the island. Swimming outward would probably be suicide, but if she had a float of some sort for support there was at least a chance that she could reach another miniature landfall unseen in the gathering darkness. By now only the stars distinguished the sky from the sea below.

As the shouting sailors formed a line on the other side of the island, Sharina began to comb the northern shore for driftwood. The groundsels grew within a few feet of the water, though the lobelias seemed to be less resistant to salt. Fleshy leaves brushed her like dead men's fingers. She jogged through them, bent over to scan the ground more closely.

A figure stood in front of her. Her first thought was that a basalt outcrop had gotten to its feet, but it was a man—a huge man, holding vertically a spear whose blade was a hand's breadth wide. A weapon like that would let a victim's life out as swiftly as the heart pumped.

Sharina had the Pewle knife in her hand. She slashed upward. The big man's right foot moved in a smooth arc to meet her wrist, spinning Sharina away. Her forearm was numb, but she didn't drop the knife.

Sharina hit on her right side, half-cushioned by a giant groundsel. She twisted to get her feet under her as she tried to take the knife in her left hand.

The man planted the steel-capped butt of his spear in Sharina's solar plexus, paralyzing her diaphragm. She doubled up, unable to breathe.

She tried to hold the knife, but the man knelt beside her and plucked it from her fingers. He wore garments of leather with an unfamiliar, reptilian smell.

"Where'd you come by a Pewle knife, missie?" the man asked as he examined the weapon. His tone was conversational, but he pitched his voice too low to be heard more than a few feet away.

Sharina still struggled to breathe. "From a man who'd have you for supper if he were still alive!" she gasped.

The big man chuckled. "Then he was a right good man," he said without rancor. He handed the knife back to her, hilt first.

"My name's Hanno," he went on. "Now, it doesn't seem to me that the folks on the other side here are any friends to you. Is that so?"

"I'll die before I let them take me again," Sharina whispered. She put the Pewle knife back in its sheath, though she had to use both hands to do so. She trembled from exertion and the shocking blow to her abdomen.

"Now, missie," the stranger said. "I'm on my way back to Bight from Valles where I sold my horn. If you don't choose to stay here, you can come with me—but I warn you, you'll be living in a hunting cabin and I won't make another trip to Valles for six months or better."

"Let's go," Sharina said as she tried to stand. "One of the men's a wizard."

Hanno picked Sharina up in the crook of his left arm and strode down the shore. A twenty-foot dory, slimmer but otherwise similar to the two-man fishing boats that put out from Barca's Hamlet, was drawn into a notch in the basalt. Hanno set Sharina aboard, laid his long spear beside the crossed oars amidships, and shoved the vessel out to sea with a lurch and a grunt.

Hanno was carrying six months of supplies with him. The dory's hull fore and aft was packed with parcels wrapped in oilcloth and fastened securely with a web of horsehair ropes. Sharina could only guess at the weight the big man had just shifted into the water, but it must be on the order of three or four tons.

Hanno splashed after the boat for several paces, then climbed in over the upswept stern when they were out far enough that his weight didn't ground the keel. Sharina had her breath back. She squeezed aside as Hanno walked over the cargo and dropped onto one of the two thwarts amidships. The dory continued to bob away from the shore.

Hanno was an agile man—not just "agile for his size." Sharina didn't remember ever having met a man bigger than this hunter. He was taller than Garric and almost as massively built as Cashel.

He set the oars in the rowlocks. Sharina pinned them before Hanno could do so himself. He nodded in approval and perhaps surprise, then stroked outward.

"They have a twenty-oared ship," Sharina said in a low voice. She could hear sailors calling to one another and the false Nonnus trying to shout orders to all of them.

"They do for now," Hanno said. He sounded amused

rather than concerned. He turned the dory parallel to the shore. His oarstrokes were powerful, but they made no more sound than the ordinary slap of water against itself.

They were far enough out that Sharina saw the island as a black mass rather than a place. Lights began to bloom on the other side of the spine. The false Nonnus was passing out rushlights, pithy reed stems soaked in wax and ignited. They gave a pale, flaring illumination.

Sharina hunched instinctively. Hanno chuckled and said, "That's just made us safer. Them lights won't show anything beyond arm's length and it'll waste the fools' night vision besides. If they knew what they were doing, they'd spread out and hunker down to listen for you moving."

He chuckled again. "Of course, that wouldn't help them now neither," he added.

Hanno turned the dory. They'd rounded the tip of the little island and were headed back up the south side, staying about a bowshot from the shore. Sharina could tell land from sea only by the faint margin of foam where the two met.

Hanno rowed effortlessly, maneuvering by backing water with the one oar while the other took a full sweep. The dory didn't have a mast or even a mast partner on the false keel. He must row all the way from Bight to Ornifal and back. . . . Perhaps he set a triangular boat sail in the bow to run when the wind was dead astern.

A line of rushlights winked across the spine and over it. The lights began to move together toward the east end of the island, leaving the west for a second pass if necessary.

The crew had lit a small bonfire on the beach, just inshore of the dispatch vessel. Sharina saw one man or perhaps two tending the fire before the vessel's long hull blocked her vision.

Hanno grunted and pulled the dory's bow toward the island again. Sharina watched the hull of the silhouetted dispatch vessel loom past the oarsman. She could hear the voices of the men ashore, but only rarely was a word intelligible.

Sharina rubbed her aching abdominal muscles, then rested her fingers on the hilt of the Pewle knife. Starlight gleamed faintly on Hanno's teeth as he grinned at her.

Only at the last moment did Hanno glance over his shoulder. He backed water with one oar, then both, and brought the dory alongside the stern of the grounded dispatch vessel. He shipped his oars and touched a finger to his lips for silence. Sharina nodded curtly.

The false Nonnus' ship was tilted with the keel in the water and the port side lying along the shore. Because the ground sloped upward, any kind of a breeze could have flopped the vessel to starboard and possibly capsized it, but the air of the Inner Sea was normally dead still at sunset and sunrise.

The anchor hung from a rope stopper in the dispatch vessel's stern. The stock was iron, but the shank and arms were cypress wood bound with lead hoops for weight.

Hanno stood. The dory quivered, but the big man kept his weight centered. He gripped the anchor with one hand and severed the salt-encrusted stopper with a thrust of his spear.

The anchor's weight—as much as Sharina or perhaps even a man of middling size—dropped into Hanno's hand. The dory bobbed furiously, banging its starboard gunwale against the larger vessel's hull. Sharina held steady, knowing that if she tried to damp the oscillations she'd interfere with Hanno's own adjustments. The big man knew what he was doing.

A sailor on the other side shouted. "I'll take the spear!" Sharina cried.

Hanno slammed the anchor's lead-wrapped crown through the dispatch vessel just above the keel. The planks were pine and thin for a seagoing ship but were still two fingers' breadth thick. They splintered like glass hitting stone.

Hanno tossed the spear sidearm to Sharina. She was

braced for the weight, but it still felt like she'd caught a falling tree. The seven-foot shaft was oak, and a long steel butt-cap balanced the weight of the broad head.

A sailor carrying a rushlight came around the stern of the dispatch vessel and gaped at them. "What are you doing?" he shouted. He wasn't armed.

Sharina waggled the spear, holding it with both hands. "Get back!" she said. She had no quarrel with the sailors; they were obviously hirelings, not enemies for their own sakes. If the false Nonnus had stepped toward her . . .

Hanno dragged the anchor out of the hull, then swung it again into the siding like a mace. Frames as well as planking broke at the impact. The dory splashed like a whale broaching, but her beam and the weight of cargo kept her from going over.

The steersman stepped around the dispatch vessel. He carried a short, stiff bow with an arrow already nocked. "Hold the light up!" he ordered the other sailor.

Hanno threw the anchor at him. There was a wet crunch. Man and missile tumbled out of sight. The cable reeved through the anchor ring followed like the body of a striking snake.

Hanno took the oars, facing now toward what had been the stern. Sharina anticipated him, clambering out of the way without losing the big spear. The dory was double-ended and had neither rudder nor sail to impose a direction of movement.

They got under way gradually, the way a rock begins to fall. The weight of cargo made the vessel too massive for even Hanno's strength to accelerate quickly, though fewer than a dozen paired strokes were enough to get them out of sight of the shore.

Rushlights clustered around the dark line of the ship. Sailors shouted. Once Sharina thought she heard the voice of the false Nonnus. She smiled grimly. If he repaired the dispatch vessel's damage in less than a day, he was a wizard indeed.

"I don't much like to travel at night," Hanno said as

he rowed, now without the devouring effort that had taken them offshore, "but this time it's the choice. At least I'd had my supper before that lot landed on the other side."

"Thank you," Sharina said. She wasn't ready to explain what had happened—she wasn't really *sure* what had happened, what was happening—but Hanno didn't seem the sort of man who required explanations.

The moon had just come out of the sea over the big man's shoulder. Sharina felt the smile that she couldn't really see because of the darkness. He said, "You'll do, missie. You'll surely do."

"A forest!" Zahag cried enthusiastically. It was the first emotion besides peevish anger that Cashel had heard in the ape's voice since they'd escaped from the dissolving tower. "A forest at last!"

Zahag charged toward the dank, moss-draped trunks at a bobbling gallop. He looked remarkably clumsy because his forelimbs were so much longer than the back ones. He still covered ground pretty well.

Come to think, peevish anger had been the ape's usual attitude everywhere else Cashel had known him too.

"Have we come home?" Aria said as she twisted against Cashel's chest. Even she sounded hopeful for once. He'd been carrying her in the crook of one arm or the other since midday. It was that or drag her, and it was obvious the girl had been doing her pitiful best to keep up.

"Ooh!" Aria said in disgust as she took in the landscape ahead of them. "Oh, how could you bring me here?"

She started to cry.

"Well, it makes a change from the desert," Cashel said uneasily. The trouble was, he couldn't convince himself it was a change for the better.

"Oh, what a change from the rocks that were wearing my knuckles bloody!" Zahag called as he followed the trail out of sight. "And say, that's a lizard! That'll make a change from berries and more berries!"

"Can you walk now?" Cashel said, setting Aria back on her feet. "The going ought to be a little easier, and we'll be out of the sun."

The sun had been an unpleasant factor every day since they arrived in this place, but Cashel wasn't sure he wouldn't miss the glare before long. The light seemed hostile, but it didn't hide anything. This forest had a greasy, behind-your-back look to it, much like Cashel's uncle Katchin in Barca's Hamlet.

He grinned. The forest didn't have Katchin's windy pride, though. Maybe things were getting better after all.

"I wish I could die," Aria muttered, but she followed under her own power when Cashel started down the trail.

The trees weren't giants. They ran to ten or a dozen paces—double paces from left heel to left heel—in height, about as tall as you could expect for anything growing in boggy ground.

Cashel couldn't understand why the soil was so wet. They'd gone from grit and spiky bushes to trees draped in moss that dripped on the sopping ground. His footsteps squelched and the line of prints gleamed behind him like so many little ponds.

He tossed his straw umbrella away. It clung to a branch, wrapped in tendrils of moss. The dry grass began to soak through.

Cashel felt obscurely bothered. He tugged the umbrella out of the soggy veil and carried it back to the edge of the forest, where he threw it onto dry sand. If a breeze returned it to the bog, that was none of his doing.

"What on *earth* did you just do?" Aria said.

"Well, the umbrella did a pretty good job for me the past few days," Cashel said. "I didn't figure it deserved me to leave it here."

He resumed walking down the trail at his easy, shepherd's pace. He carried his staff at a slant across his chest, one hand above and the other below the balance.

He could feel the girl staring at him in amazement. Well, let her. Nothing Cashel had seen in his life had caused him to lose his belief in justice. Deep in his heart was the thought that a fellow who treated *things* badly was likely to be treated as a thing himself one day; and treated badly.

"Zahag, are you up there?" he called.

"What are you waiting for?" the ape replied. His voice sounded faint. The chirrups of unseen frogs and insects smothered ordinary speech over even modest distances.

The desert had been deathly still, except once and a while during the night when something howled in the distance. That sound had been pretty deathly too.

Branches twisted and forked. It was hard to tell which leaves belonged to a tree and which were on a vine or some lesser plant growing in a crotch.

The moss covered everything. Cashel used the staff to push through it, but even so dank strands brushed his shoulders.

"I don't like this place," Aria said in a small voice. It was an honest statement for a change, not an accusation. She must be really scared.

"Just stay close and you'll be fine," Cashel said.

Saying that made him feel so much better that he started to grin. "You'll be all right, Princess," he said. "This is what I do, you see. I'm a shepherd."

There was a *plop!* back the way they'd come. It sounded too loud to have been a drip hitting the ground, but who knew? Maybe a broad leaf had turned inside out and spilled a firkin of water all at once.

Zahag shrieked. Something crashed and splashed through the forest toward Cashel and the girl. Cashel slid his hands a span outward and lowered the staff slightly to a guard position.

Zahag threw himself at Cashel's feet and cried, "I didn't see anything! I didn't see anything!" Aria screamed too as she hugged Cashel from behind. Duzi! Didn't either of them have any sense?

The forest had grown silent. The normal volume of squeaks and chirping resumed. Nothing had pursued the ape.

"I think we better go on," Cashel said. Aria had already taken her hands away; Zahag twisted his head to look back the way he'd come. "I'd sooner be someplace else before we lose the last of the light."

They started on. It had been dark enough when they entered the forest. Cashel figured when the sun went down they'd might as well be deep in a cave. Aria walked right behind him, and Zahag stayed awkwardly close to his left side.

Cashel didn't suppose it was worth asking the ape what had frightened him. Out of sight, out of mind was pretty much Zahag's whole life. Whatever he'd seen or thought he saw in the dripping moss was nothing he'd be willing to call back to memory.

"I see things glowing," Aria said. "Out—there."

"Right," said Cashel, trying to sound hearty. Duzi knew he'd spent enough nights out in thunderstorms talking to sheep. Otherwise they might panic and smother themselves by piling up in a corner of the fold. "Foxfire, just like at home. I think we can keep on going a ways by it lighting the trail."

They were going to walk until Cashel dropped under the weight of both his companions if it came to that. There was no way he was going to suggest they bed down anywhere he'd seen since they entered the forest.

The path had a gray sheen. Tree trunks stood as greenish or yellowish ghosts across which other almost-colors wound themselves. It was hard to judge distances with nothing but fuzzy glows to go by. The moss was the only thing in this place that didn't seem to have its own light. Cashel couldn't keep it from dragging across him now.

Aria was crying softly. Cashel couldn't blame her. At least he didn't have to look back as he'd been doing during daylight to make sure she was still with him.

Trees rustled. At first Cashel thought that something—

or perhaps many lesser somethings—was above him, but when he looked up he could watch bare branches writhe against the unfamiliar stars. During daylight he hadn't been able to see the sky through the canopy of leaves.

Aria cried louder.

"Look!" said Zahag, tugging the hem of Cashel's tunic. He spoke with a desperate need to believe, a tone far removed from that of real belief. "Up ahead there—it's a *real* light. We're safe now, we just have to get to the light!"

"Well, we'll see when we get there," Cashel said quietly, scanning both sides of the trail as they ambled onward. He thought he'd seen the winking flames of a fire through the trees also, but there was too much strange in this forest for him to take anything for granted.

Cashel grinned. He was walking along with a talking monkey and a princess, but he wasn't sure the light he saw ahead of him was a real fire. People back in Barca's Hamlet would think he was crazy.

He didn't let the smile build to a chuckle. Aria and Zahag would think he'd gone crazy too if he started laughing now.

The branches whispered above them. A wave of undulating phosphorescence had paralleled their track almost since the sun went down. Cashel couldn't be sure how far out in the night it was, but it seemed to be drifting closer.

He was probably seeing a layer of marsh gas finding its level in the air. Nothing to worry about.

"It *is* a fire!" Aria said. "Oh, I can see it now!"

In a choked voice she added, "Oh, please, Mistress God, may it be a fire!"

They'd reached a clearing. Before them stood a tower of honest, lichen-stained blocks of stone—not pink confectionery that dissolved if somebody stumbled down the stairs.

And there was a fire as well, a beacon of wood burning in an iron basket lifted on a spike above the tower. Its flaring light silhouetted figures manning the battlements.

"Hello the house!" Cashel said as he stepped beyond the last clinging branches. Should he have said "tower" instead of "house"? He was so glad to see human habitation that he'd called as if he'd stumbled onto a farmhouse after being benighted.

"Go away, monsters!" a voice shrilled. "Or we'll kill you!"

The beacon dribbled a line of sparks; it sank to a throb of orange and rose. The fire had nearly consumed itself. The wood you found in this forest would be either too wet to burn or rotted into punk that didn't give a good bed of coals.

Cashel stepped forward. "We're not monsters!" he called. He held his staff upright at his side so that it didn't look threatening—not that anybody could make out details from the top of the tower. "We need a place to sleep for the night, that's all."

And maybe an explanation of where this place was. That would be nice.

"Go away!" the voice repeated.

Cashel heard a clicking sound from the battlements. *A gear,* he thought. *A ratchet and pawl—*

Somebody using a windlass to crank a powerful crossbow!

"Hey!" he bellowed, striding forward. He didn't pause to think about what he was doing. "You stop these silly games or I'll pull this place down around your ears. By the *Shepherd* I will!"

He slammed the butt of his quarterstaff on the ground before him. The staff flared blue fire, bathing Cashel in a moment of cold brilliance. Hairs prickled all over his body.

"He's a man!" somebody in the tower cried hurriedly. "What's a man doing out there?"

"Let me and my friends in right now," Cashel said, vaguely embarrassed at both his anger and the flash he'd created. The light had surprised him, but at least the folks in the tower had seen that he wasn't any monster. "We just want a place to sleep."

The beacon gave a last gulp and died. The bones of light that remained were scarcely enough to display the bars of the cage, let alone anyone beyond it.

"We're putting down the ladder," the first voice called. "Don't waste any time, though. They'll attack any moment now."

Something rustled and clacked down the wall of the tower. Cashel judged its location by starlight, then reached out. It was a ladder with rope stringers and wooden battens for steps.

"Come on!" he called over his shoulder in what he hoped was a carrying whisper. He hadn't wanted his companions close to him if somebody started shooting arrows, but he didn't want them left behind either.

He could well believe there were monsters in this forest, that was a fact.

Zahag scrambled past and grabbed the ladder; Cashel caught his hairy arm and held him back. The ape screeched with frustration but didn't quite try to bite.

"Can you make it by yourself, Princess?" Cashel asked. Instead of answering, Aria snatched the ladder and began climbing strongly. She quickly faded to a blur of pale fabric against the stone.

Cashel released the ape. "And don't try to climb over her!" he warned.

Though at the rate Aria was going up, that wasn't the danger Cashel had feared it would be. Her tower's steep steps had given her a lot of exercise. They hadn't done anything for her politeness, but that was probably true of a lot of princesses.

"It's a woman," a different voice on the battlements said. "Oh, is it really a woman?"

Cashel started to climb. He held the staff before him in the crooks of both elbows, making it a slow, clumsy job. If he'd kept the rope he'd used to climb Aria's tower, he wouldn't have to wobble up like an old man with pains in his joints. He didn't have the rope, and he *surely* wasn't going to leave his staff on the ground.

"Hey, a monster!" a man screamed. Steel clanged red sparks from the battlements.

Zahag was jabbering twenty to the dozen somewhere in the darkness, so he must be all right. It sounded like he'd jumped from the ladder to the side of the wall. The stones were so weathered that Cashel figured that in a pinch even a human could find enough hand- and toeholds between the courses to climb this tower.

"Hey!" he bellowed. He held the quarterstaff in one hand as he snatched his way up the last of the climb in a fashion that wouldn't have been safe if he weren't in such a hurry. "Stop that! He's not a monster, he's my friend!"

Cashel went over the battlements. The top of the tower flared out a little from the shaft so for the last two upward strides his toes weren't touching the wall anymore. It was good to have stone and not a wavering ladder under his feet; especially since the battens hadn't been meant for somebody Cashel's size in a hurry.

"Now you quit that!" Cashel said. "Who's the master here?"

He slammed his quarterstaff on the floor. The brass ferrule didn't spark on the stone the way the iron caps of his usual staff would've done, but the *whock!* was loud enough to get the attention of the dozen or so men present.

A squat, mustached fellow with a helmet and halberd cleared his throat. "I'm Captain Koras," he said. "You say that fellow with you's a true man? He looked pretty hairy to me."

"Hairy?" Zahag shouted in fury from close below the battlements. "I'll pull your scraggly whiskers off if you hate hair so much you'd take an axe to me!"

"Zahag, be quiet!" Cashel said. He cleared his throat and went on, "He's an ape, not a man, but he isn't any monster. And like I told you, he's my friend."

It was funny to think of Zahag as a friend. He guessed it was pretty much true, though.

Aria came out of the crowd and squeezed against Cashel's side, apparently uncomfortable with the soldiers around her. She'd be in the way if he had to use his quarterstaff, but he didn't think it'd come to that.

"We ought to get the ladder up," a man muttered. "They're going to attack any time, I'd guess."

Koras held his fist to his mouth and gave a rumbling cough. "Not to doubt you, sir," he said, "but it sounded like the creature was talking. Your friend, I mean."

"Right," said Cashel. There was no light but that of the stars, so the men facing him were merely dim presences. "He talks, but he's an ape. He used to belong to a wizard."

A man stepped close to Cashel, reached past him, and began pulling up the ladder. The battens tinkled on the blocks of the wall like a xylophone. A mummer, one of a trio who'd visited Barca's Hamlet during the Sheep Fair a few years ago, had played the xylophone. Cashel had been amazed that wooden tubes could make sounds so richly musical.

"Well, since you vouch for him," Koras said. "It's the first time I'd met an ape who talks, is all."

"Come on up, Zahag," Cashel said. "They're going to let us sleep here."

He stuck his staff down over the wall so that the ape wouldn't have to struggle with the top's flare. Zahag instead gripped an arrow notch with the fingers of one hand and flipped himself over by that contact alone. The ape was really strong for his size.

"Sleep?" said one soldier. "We only sleep during the day here, stranger."

"They'll be attacking soon," Captain Koras agreed. "You coming the way you did probably confused them, but—"

"Here they come!" cried a soldier.

Hideous screams came from the forest all around. A soldier resumed cranking his crossbow; another man drew an arrow from the quiver at his side and nocked it in his hand bow.

Cashel peered over the battlements. He could see motion on the ground but with no more details than if he'd been watching the tide on a moonless night.

A rosy flash danced through the soil to light the night like a thunderbolt. Against it Cashel saw the creatures attacking the tower. The angle foreshortened them, but it wasn't that which made them monsters.

Some had beasts' bodies; some had beasts' heads. They wore scraps of armor and human clothing, and their weapons ranged from long swords to stones gripped in one or more hands. They went on two legs or four; and one monstrosity undulated on more legs than a centipede and had a torso whose four arms waved axes.

Some carried scaling ladders.

The flash was there and gone, leaving only the impression of movement behind.

"Aria, get down inside if you can!" Cashel said. He slid his hands along his quarterstaff, getting the feel of it while he waited for the first of the screaming horde to climb to a level he could reach.

The plaza where three roads met near Ilna's tenement had a fountain that didn't work. She intended to get the water line repaired as one of her next projects, though she hadn't as yet determined whether to use bribery or extortion to bring city officials to her way of thinking.

Even without water the plaza was generally busy; it was as close to a park as the Crescent could boast. The magic act being performed there today would have drawn a crowd in any district of Erdin.

Ilna was at the front of the spectators. Folk in the Crescent knew Mistress Ilna and made way for her. If they didn't, one of their neighbors taught them proper courtesy with an elbow—or a brick. Ilna didn't encourage that sort of thing, but she couldn't have stopped it if she tried. And anyway, there wasn't enough courtesy in the world.

The young man wearing red silk muttered a word that Ilna heard but didn't understand; he struck down with his athame. A flower of ruby light grew, opened, and expanded into a sphere that Ilna couldn't have spanned with both arms outstretched. In its heart was a city of light—low houses and a harbor with ships moving on the water. Ilna could even see people walking along the streets.

"Oooh!" sighed the spectators.

"That's Pandah!" cried a man in the wide pantaloons and bright silk sash of a sailor ashore. "By the Lady's nose, that's Pandah or I'm a farmer!"

The image sucked in on itself and vanished. The young man stepped back and wiped his brow. He was sweating like a stevedore and looked tired.

As well he might. Most of the crowd probably thought they were watching an expert illusionist. Ilna had seen enough wizardry to recognize it when she saw it again.

Voder had said the young man's legless helper was named Cerix. He propelled his little cart into the crowd with thrusts of one hand on the right wheel while his left held up a wooden bowl. "While the great Master Halphemos rests before his stunning climax," the cripple said, "it's time for you good people to show that you appreciate his art. Give to the master who gives to you!"

To call the Crescent a poor district was to praise it; half the residents were probably planning to flee at the end of any given week to avoid the rent collector. Despite that, several folk dropped coins into the bowl. Copper, of course, and in one case the clank of a wedge-shaped iron farthing from Shengy—but more money than any street entertainer had seen in this plaza since the mud was bricked over.

It wasn't a fraction of what the show was worth. Halphemos—and his helper, who'd drawn the circles of power before each incantation—could have performed before the earl himself for a fee paid in gold.

The cripple shoved his cart up to Ilna. "Will the

wealthy lady show her appreciation of Master Halphemos?'' he said as he rattled the bowl.

Ilna nodded curtly. Her clothes were clean and hadn't been patched; in the Crescent, that made her a member of the elite.

She dropped a silver coin in the bowl. Several of those nearby gasped when they heard the unmistakable chime. The cripple snatched it out and put it in his mouth for safekeeping, giving Ilna a look of amazement as he did so.

''I'll see you after the show,'' Ilna said. ''I believe you're looking for me.''

The cripple skidded his cart back to Halphemos even though he'd only worked half the crowd. The two whispered. Ilna smiled grimly at them. She didn't know why a wizard should be looking for her; but one was, and she saw no reason to delay learning.

It was probably bad news. There was never a reason to delay getting bad news. That was cowardice.

The cripple quickly scratched a new pattern on the bricks, using a bit of charcoal as before. During the performance the ''stage'' on which Halphemos performed had moved steadily to the right so that his helper had unmarked bricks on which to write the next time. Ilna didn't think the symbols were actually legible even to someone who could read, but they were apparently necessary for the incantation to have effect.

Halphemos stood and made a slight bow of acknowledgment to Ilna. He still looked tired, but there was a nervous enthusiasm in his voice as he began to murmur sounds that were not words to human beings.

Light swelled from a ruby-colored bead in the air. For a moment, Ilna thought there was nothing but swirling mist. A serpent of bloody light struck outward—

''No!'' shouted the crippled helper. He reached for the circle of power to smudge the words out of existence, but Halphemos had already thrown down his athame.

The image vanished like blood soaking into dry sand.

Ilna's fingers had twitched her lasso out by reflex. She tucked the silken coil back beneath her sash.

The crowd reacted with screams, gasps, and—when the image vanished—cheers and foot-stampings of applause. They'd been frightened, but they thought the shock was all part of the entertainment. When it passed, they were delighted.

Halphemos sat. Ilna winced to see his silk robe on the filthy pavement. His athame, a length of spiral horn or possibly tooth, lay before him. He reached for it absently, then jerked his fingers away before he touched the tool.

Cerix was gray-faced. He waved to move the spectators away and cried, "The show is over! Master Halphemos must rest now!"

A prostitute with a room in Ilna's tenement leaned forward to drop a coin in Cerix's bowl. The cripple glared so fiercely that she backed away in surprise.

"What in the name of all gods did you do?" Cerix said to Halphemos, his voice harsh with fear. He felt Ilna's presence and jerked his head around to snarl before he recognized her.

"Let's get him into Anno's," Ilna said. "That's the tavern behind you. We can use the room in back."

"It should have been King Valence in his palace," Halphemos said, as much to himself as to Cerix or Ilna. "I'd used the Earl of Sandrakkan when we opened, so I just switched the names to have something different for the close."

"Come," Ilna said, putting her hand on the young man's arm. She gave it a tug when he didn't react quickly enough.

Halphemos was wobbly, but he rose obediently to his feet. With her free hand she picked up the athame.

They staggered the few steps to the tavern. Four pewter mugs were chained to the stone counter facing the street. The back was the family's living quarters, but Anno would set up a table and stools whenever somebody was willing to pay three coppers instead of two for his wine.

Anno's wife—or perhaps sister, Ilna didn't choose to inquire—flopped the wooden gate in the counter back to let them through. She must have been listening.

A man wearing broad gold rings on both his thumbs plucked Halphemos' sleeve as he started to follow Ilna within. "My good young sir!" he said. "With a man like me who knows local business conditions as your agent, you can become richer than you dream!"

Ilna looked at him. "Get out of here, Mangard," she said. "And while I think of it—don't ever let me hear about you threatening one of your girls with a knife again. If I do, I'll put a knot in a place you'll notice more than if it was your throat. Do you understand?"

"I, ah . . ." Mangard said. He thought the better of whatever he'd planned to say, which meant he probably did understand.

Ilna scowled as the pimp scuttled away. What she thought she'd seen in Halphemos' last vision must have disturbed her more than she'd realized. Normally she didn't make threats of the sort she'd spoken to Mangard. Not because she couldn't carry it out; rather, because now that she'd used the words she'd *have* to carry it out. The thought disgusted her.

Halphemos sat, though he seemed still to be in a daze. When Cerix wheeled his cart close, his chin rose just above the level of the table. It made for an awkward way to carry on a conversation but a practical one.

"Wine for the two men," Ilna said. She took a pair of coins from her purse. They were silver-washed bronze, minted in Carcosa a generation ago. Here they passed at three Sandrakkan coppers each.

"You don't have to pay, mistress," the tavern-keeper said.

Ilna smiled. "On the contrary," she said, "I do. And I wish I had nothing worse to pay for than two mugs of your wine."

"You're Ilna os-Kenset, aren't you?" Halphemos said, accepting the athame which Ilna handed him without comment. He'd gotten his color back; when the wine arrived, he drank normally instead of the greedy slurping Ilna'd expected.

He didn't choke at the taste, either. Halphemos might wear silk now, but it wasn't the first time he'd drunk watered lees in a dockside tavern.

"Yes," Ilna said. She probably wouldn't have been any good at small talk even if she'd seen a purpose in it. "Why were you looking for me?"

Cerix frowned slightly, considering how to respond to Ilna's bluntness. Halphemos simply nodded toward his mug—they weren't chained here in the back, though they didn't appear to be washed any more frequently either—and said, "Mistress Sharina, that's Sharina os—"

"I know her," Ilna said without inflection.

"Sharina said we should come to you," Halphemos said. "I made your brother vanish by mistake. She thought you could—"

"It wasn't your fault!" the cripple said furiously. "I keep telling you, you've never made a mistake like that. Look how you stopped yourself today!"

"I spoke an incantation, and your brother Cashel vanished," Halphemos said in a self-damning tone that Ilna had heard often enough in her own voice. "With your help Cerix thinks we can find him again. And be sure he's in a place of safety."

In the Crescent, taverns didn't waste money on the rushes or bracken which more pretentious inns spread on their floors. There were some strands of rye straw which had broken from the truckle beds on which Anno and his family slept, though. Ilna picked a few of them up and began plaiting them, only half conscious of what she was doing.

"There should have been three other people with my brother and Sharina," Ilna said. "Garric or-Reise, an old woman named Tenoctris, and . . . a girl my age. Quite an attractive girl."

"The ship Cashel and Mistress Sharina were on was

swallowed by a monster," Cerix said. "Anyone with them must be dead now."

Ilna looked at her sash, the twin of the one she'd given Liane. It remained precisely as she'd woven it. "I doubt that," she said, "but it needn't concern us now. What do you want of me?"

She looked at what her hands were doing. The straw was filthy. She slapped the pattern she'd woven down on the table, wondering if there'd be a rag here that wouldn't make her fingers dirtier than they were already.

"If you have an object of your brother's—" Halphemos said.

"Wait!" the cripple interrupted. He picked up the twists of straw so that he could see them squarely, then looked at Ilna in wonder and surmise. He said, "Why did you write 'Valles' this way, mistress?"

"I didn't write anything," Ilna said, controlling her anger with some difficulty. "I can't write. Or read either, if you think that's any of your business."

"You wrote the word 'Valles,' mistress," Cerix said. He held the straw pattern out to Ilna in the palm of his hand. "In the Old Script."

Halphemos quirked a smile toward her. "I can read," he said—admitted? "But I still have to sound out the words, and I don't know the Old Script."

"I don't know anything at all," Ilna said, glaring at it in irritation. But she *had* woven the straw into its present pattern.

"Are you a wizard yourself, mistress?" the legless man said softly.

"I never thought so," Ilna said. She grimaced. "I don't know."

"Nevertheless," Cerix said, "I think we should go to Valles. I wish the notation had been a little fuller so that we knew what we were looking for there, but perhaps it will become clear in time."

Halphemos nodded three times, as though he were batting his head against an invisible wall. He looked at Ilna.

"Will you come with us, Mistress Ilna?" he asked.

He had a pleasant smile. It seemed a natural expression for him.

"Yes, I suppose I have to," Ilna said as she stood. "I'll make arrangements to take care of my responsibilities here, but I should be ready to leave in a few days."

Cerix cleared his throat. "There's a question of finances," he said. "The boy and I saved enough to—"

"I can take care of our passage," Ilna said. "He's my brother, after all."

She nodded a cold farewell and walked out of the tavern. She'd spent most of her life caring for Cashel, so it was easy to keep her duty to him at the front of her mind.

And that was good, because otherwise Ilna knew she'd be thinking about Garric, in the belly of a sea monster.

The 17th of Heron (Later)

"*Arsenoneophris miarsau,*" Tenoctris said, her voice steady. This time she had written the words of power in an equilateral triangle on the temple floor.

"*Arsenoneophris miarsau,*" Liane said, reading the phrase in turn. She and Garric both knew the Old Script, though the words of the incantation meant no more to them than did the chatter of finches fluttering among the milkweed heads in the nearby meadow.

"*Arsenoneophris miarsau,*" Garric said. Even at this early stage of the process, it felt as though he were trying to talk with his mouth full of stream-washed pebbles. The words were as simple as an axe helve, but turning them to human purposes was just as difficult as swinging an axe with strength and skill.

This portal was of another sort than the one which had

reached from the Gulf to here, though Garric and Liane understood merely that it was different. Tenoctris explained that she could open it only for herself; for her companions to enter, they must speak the words as well. Once they were inside the passage, Tenoctris would keep it from collapsing by herself—if she had the strength.

Shepherd, shelter me with Thy staff, Garric prayed silently as he waited for the next phrase. *Lady, guide my steps.*

"*Barichaa kmephi,*" Tenoctris said. At every syllable she dabbed her wand, this time a willow whip. Garric had trimmed it neatly with the iron knife he carried like any other peasant in Barca's Hamlet.

"*Barichaa kmephi,*" Liane said.

"*Barichaa kmephi,*" Garric said. The pebbles had swelled to the size of clenched fists; his throat was dry and choking.

The triangle scribed on the floor of the temple was bright, but everything beyond it seemed dim. Garric no longer heard birds, nor could he see the walls. The stained marble should have been close enough for him to touch.

"*Abriaoth alarphotho seth!*" Tenoctris cried. Garric saw the old woman start to rise. She vanished like salt in water.

"*Abriaoth alarphotho seth!*" Liane said, her voice staggering between the fifth syllable and the sixth. Darkness swallowed her as it had Tenoctris before.

Garric was alone in emptiness. A voice he almost recognized laughed at him.

"*Abriaoth alarphotho seth,*" he said. He rose, straining at the words as though he were trying to push a boulder uphill. Only when his feet came down on a solid surface did Garric realize that he'd succeeded.

The path they stood on gleamed like silver through a barren waste. Tenoctris had stumbled to her knees; Liane was helping her up. Ahead the path was fading, but its cold majesty returned as Tenoctris took up the incantation again.

A wind blew across the waste, though Garric didn't feel the tug of the gusts that made the stunted bushes writhe in furious agony. The three of them would be separated from the landscape for so long as Tenoctris continued to speak.

Liane tried to guide Tenoctris forward. Garric stepped past and lifted the old woman in his arms. She seemed to weigh no more than a newborn lamb.

Garric started walking. His pace was that of a man who doesn't know the distance before him, but who's determined to cover it regardless. "*Iao el nephtho,*" Tenoctris whispered against his chest.

The path was as slick and unyielding as cobblestones. Sheep would bruise their hooves on a surface like this. A fellow could lame himself easily, even a callused peasant who wore shoes only after the ponds froze.

Garric heard the laughter again. It was cold as the unfelt wind that whipped this wasteland. He looked over his shoulder. Liane followed close behind, her lips working. She forced a smile when she felt Garric's eyes. He wondered if she was praying.

The woman of pearly light walked beside the path.

The phantasm blew Garric a kiss, then mimed reaching for Liane's throat. Her laughter rang again. Each peal was a frozen knife to Garric's heart.

Duzi who watched over me at home, help me in this place too. My need is great.

Tenoctris' lips continued to move, but Garric could no longer hear the words even faintly. The old woman's eyes were closed. She described herself as weak. Perhaps she was—as a wizard. Garric had never met a person with greater strength of will.

He walked on. The laughing wraith kept pace, but she never reached over the silvery path.

Liane seemed unaware of what accompanied them, not that Liane would have showed fear in any case. With companions like these two women, how could a man do other than be brave?

"A little farther, lad," murmured a voice in Garric's mind. *"Steady, just the way you're doing it. Never let them move you at their pace. And never,* ever, *run when you don't know what's over the next rise. You can be sure that the first time you do, you'll learn something the hard way."*

Garric no longer saw the tortured bushes. They were still there and he knew the ghastly female creature still strode alongside. She laughed like light dancing from the edge of a headsman's sword.

None of that mattered. Garric put one foot in front of the other, feeling an old woman's heart beat strongly against his own.

The last step was one Garric didn't remember taking. His toes touched stone rather than the harder silver gleam and he sprawled forward. Liane stumbled onto him. They all three lay together, gasping wordlessly.

Leaves and pine needles, some of them in clumps still attached to branch tips the wind had blown off, lay on the floor. They were in a miniature temple like the one where Tenoctris had drawn the triangle of power.

An owl called, and the moon visible through the doorway had waned to a sliver.

More time than Garric would have guessed must have passed *somewhere* since the Gulf swallowed the three of them. They were back now, though, back in the world into which they had been born.

And Duzi guard me that I never leave it again!

As Hanno prepared to pull the dory farther up the sandy beach, Sharina took the coil of mooring rope and walked ahead. A pine grew on the ridge marking the tide line; it was stunted, but to survive here it must have roots into something firmer than sand.

"Now, don't you get in the way and get trampled, missie!" Hanno said. He set himself, gripping the forebitt with one hand and the stem low enough that he could lift as well as pull with the other. "I can shift this old girl without you helping."

Sharina ignored the insult to her intelligence. From working at her father's inn she'd gotten used to men thinking that because she was pretty, she didn't have the sense of a kitten. Half the merchants and drovers at the Sheep Fair, and all the badgers who actually drove live sheep for the drovers who bought them, seemed to believe that.

For that matter, some of the men in Barca's Hamlet acted the same way when they surely ought to have known better.

She knelt and looped the end of the rope around the base of the pine. Hanno grunted; even for him, dragging the laden dory across sand took real effort. Sharina drew in an arm's length of slack and twisted the end around itself for the first of the pair of half hitches.

She grinned. Occasionally a man treated Ilna as if she didn't understand anything. That rarely happened twice with the same man.

Hanno gave a final *hunff!*—a mixture of labor and triumph. Sharina pulled the rope taut, slid the first loop closer to the tree, and locked it with a second half hitch inside as Hanno approached. She stood, striking her palms together to brush off fibers of salty rope.

Hanno grinned. His great spear was in his right hand. "I need to watch the way I talk to you, don't I?" he said.

"Or not," said Sharina. "I guess you've got as much right to make a fool of yourself as any other man."

The big man nodded. "And as much talent, I shouldn't wonder," he said. "Well, I try to learn."

Hanno looked over his shoulder at the moonlit sea across which he'd rowed. The island where they'd left the false Nonnus was well below the western horizon. Without checking the knot in the mooring rope—as he might reasonably, Sharina thought, have done—he walked back to the dory.

"Would you like a proper supper, missie?" he asked

as he tugged out a bundle of tanned hides that had ridden amidships instead of under the rope netting. "I've got fire in a gourd and I can get a pot boiling in no time."

"No, the dried fish you gave me on the way was enough," Sharina said. She felt herself beginning to tense. She deliberately kept her hand away from the Pewle knife. "All I really need now is sleep."

Hanno tossed one hide down, then the other at a slight distance. "You can have your choice of wrappers," he said. "Or both of them if you like. It's so mild this time of year that I mostly sleep in my clothes unless it rains."

He slammed the butt of his spear into the sand between the hides. It sank deep enough to stand like a tree when he took his hand away from the shaft.

"You won't be troubled in the night, missie," he said.

"I didn't think I would," Sharina lied, looking straight into Hanno's eyes. She felt herself relax all the way to her bones. Deliberately she laced her fingers together and stretched them backward.

She really was tired, physically and mentally both, but her mind was racing in too many directions for her to go to sleep at once. Besides, the hides—thick leather covered on one side with coarse white hair rather than fur—stank badly, though she didn't want to offend the big man by refusing his gift.

"Hanno?" she said. "What is it you do? How do you live, I mean."

"I hunt hides on Bight and sell them in Valles, missie," Hanno said. "I sell the scutes, really. The plant-eaters there have horn plates in the leather. They polish up like tortoiseshell—and prettier than that, some of them, like butterfly wings only hard. They use them for inlays, they tell me."

Hanno sat by crossing his ankles and lowering himself till his buttocks touched the hide blanket, then straightened his legs one at a time before him. He wore a round cap; a jerkin cinched by a broad belt from which hung tools, including a pair of butcher knives; fitted leggings;

and soft slippers on his feet. All his garments were made of leather.

"I didn't know Bight was inhabited," Sharina said, sitting also. "By real people, I mean. I know about the Hairy Men."

The truth was, she didn't know much about the present-day world despite—and partly because—of the excellent education in the Old Kingdom classics that she'd gotten from her father. She'd read the *Cosmogeography* of Katradinus—but Katradinus had died a century before the Old Kingdom ended with King Carus' death at sea.

"The Monkeys, we call them," Hanno said with a nod. "They ain't people, though I guess they ain't really monkeys neither."

He paused, looking either toward the sea or away from his companion. "There's a market in Valles for Monkey eyeteeth, too," he said, "for them as want to fill it. Myself, I let the Monkeys go their way so long as they give my cabin a wide berth. Though like I say—"

Hanno turned toward her again.

"—they ain't people."

Sharina unbuckled her belt and set the Pewle knife beside her. She switched it from one hip to the other on alternate mornings. The weapon was sufficiently heavy to bring twinges to her lower back if she kept it always on the same side.

"My friend Nonnus told me that it was hard enough to make decisions for your own life without trying to decide how somebody else should behave," she said. She smiled at her companion. "I'm glad you don't hunt men for their teeth, though. Even if they're Hairy Men."

Hanno stretched out on his back. "We folk that hunt on Bight," he said, "there's plenty who don't think we're people any more than the Monkeys are. Myself, I come from Ornifal. My father was a cobbler. He had thirteen kids, and I didn't fit in much in the village anyhow. I went looking for another place, and I wound up on Bight nigh twenty years ago. I already knew how to work leather, you see."

Sharina lay on her blanket. Either she was getting used to the smell or she was too tired to care anymore.

"Best get some sleep, missie," Hanno said. "We'll be up at dawn."

If he said anything more, Sharina didn't hear it because she was already asleep.

The soldier holding the crossbow leaned so far over the battlements that Cashel put a hand on the man's back to keep him from falling. He wondered why the square-headed arrow didn't fall out since the fellow was pointing almost straight down.

"Kil-l-l them-m-m!" shrieked a three-headed monster. Its body was like a bladder standing on one hairy leg.

The crossbowman squeezed his trigger lever. It released with a *whang!* shockingly loud. The bow hummed as the soldier straightened; the echo danced from the tower's stone wall and back from the forest.

The arrow struck just below the midmost of the monster's three necks. The body blatted like a collapsing bladder, but no blood spurted. "Kil-ll . . . ," the mouths said, the word dying to a whisper.

Scores of other monsters capered about the base of the tower. Another flash of pinkish lightning ran through the soil deep in the forest. Cashel saw trees and monstrous figures in silhouette; but he wasn't sure which were which, nor whether there was really any difference.

A ladder clashed against the battlements beside him. The stringers were wood, but for an arm's length they were plated with iron.

Cashel grabbed the top rung and pushed outward. The ladder already shook with the tread of creatures mounting it. He could move it despite its weight, but his arms weren't long enough to fling it over on those climbing. A brick grazed his head as he struggled.

He dropped the ladder and stepped back. His head rang. The crossbowman was cranking furiously on his bulky weapon; the defender to Cashel's other side hacked at the stringers with a blade the shape and weight of a butcher's cleaver. It sparked but didn't cut.

Cashel set one ferrule of his staff on the ladder's top rung. He leaned into the shaft, feeding it outward hand over hand.

A creature with four arms and the head of a viper scrambled to the top of the ladder. Its scythe slashed toward Cashel's face. He didn't flinch. The blade missed him by a hand's breadth.

The ladder toppled backward in a hellstorm of shrieking. One of the stringers snapped, flinging rungs into the air like a juggler's batons.

The strange lightning flared through the stones of the tower. Cashel thought he saw the bones of his own arm against it. He touched his head and felt the tackiness of blood. *Bleed like a pig, a scalp wound does. . . .*

Steel, stone, and wood clashed together on the other side of the tower. The attackers must have thrown up a ladder there too. Cashel thought of going to help, but monsters were climbing the tower itself. In the latest flash he'd seen a thing with the tentacles of an octopus below the torso of a four-breasted woman. She had axes in her hands and her fangs were as slender as a cat's.

A rock bounced high from the battlements, then fell onto the floor within. Zahag grabbed it and hopped screaming to an arrow notch. He hung down, gripping the sides of the notch with his feet, and hurled the missile with both hands.

Before Cashel could reach over to steady him, Zahag twisted himself back into the interior of the open space beside Aria. He continued to gibber.

Cashel couldn't tell anymore which shouts were the defenders and which came from the throats of the monsters climbing the walls. Some of them were perfectly human—in part.

A headless thing with arms like a spider came over the battlements. The crossbowman shot it through the middle of the dog-shaped torso. The creature probed the hole in its chest with delicate, pincerlike hands. Cashel struck the monster with the butt of his staff as though he were trying to batter in a door; it flew back from the wall. More pink lightning rippled through the forest floor.

A bow twanged at the base of the tower. The soldier beside Cashel swore and stepped back. An arrow dangled loosely from his wrist. The shaft was a length of blackberry cane with grooves rather than proper fletching to make it fly straight.

The soldier tugged it out. The point, a dog's tooth, fell onto the floor. He broke the shaft against the battlements, then tossed the pieces over the side.

The forest stilled except for occasional whoops. The trees were dark, but sometimes there was a quiver like heat lightning in the far distance. The eastern horizon seemed brighter, though the fight hadn't gone on near long enough for that to be dawn coming. Had it?

"Well done, men!" Captain Koras said. He sounded weary. Weapons scraped as they were sheathed.

Cashel heard the princess weeping. He knelt by her and said, "It's all right now, Princess. We're safe."

He hoped he was right. It was the right thing to say to Aria, anyhow.

Zahag squatted beside Cashel and said, "We showed them! They'll know better than to mess with *our* territory again, won't they, chief!"

Cashel blinked at the smell. The ape must have been flinging his own excrement at the monsters when he had no better missiles. Well, Zahag had done what he could. Nobody could fault that.

Aria opened her eyes doubtfully. When she saw for sure that nothing was coming over the battlements with a knife, she looked at Cashel. "Oh!" she cried. "You've been killed! You're all over blood!"

"What?" said Cashel. He remembered the brick that

had grazed him; he patted his head gingerly. It was still oozing some. He hated to get cuts on his scalp, though on the good side they healed pretty quick.

"Let me bandage that for you, young man," said Captain Koras as he stepped close with a wooden bucket of water. In his other hand was the pulp of a large mushroom, dried and turned inside out, in place of a sponge. "Would your lady care to rinse you off first?"

"Mistress *God*!" said Aria, covering her face in disgust.

Koras cleared his throat in embarrassment. He began daubing away the blood. The water had a slight sharpness to it, as though there was vinegar mixed in.

"If you died," Aria said without looking at Cashel, "*then* what would I do? Oh Mistress God, how *could* you be so cruel?"

"What is it that you're doing here, sir?" Cashel asked. He kept his hands in his lap and his eyes on the horizon as the captain worked. "In the tower, I mean."

"Griet, you've got the packet of thorns, don't you?" Koras said. "Bring them here to our wounded comrade."

In a milder tone he went on to Cashel, "We're defending against the monsters, good sir. I should have thought that was obvious."

The sky really was getting brighter. Rosy light gleamed on the crests of the defenders' helmets, those who wore helmets.

"But why are you defending here?" Aria demanded. She didn't usually seem aware of her surroundings—beyond the injustice of her being among them.

"Well, this is where we are," Koras said. He seemed puzzled by the question, but there was a tinge of embarrassment in his tone as well.

He pinched the sides of Cashel's pressure cut together between his thumbs and forefingers. A soldier with oddly round eyes poked thorns through the paired edges of the skin. Each jab was a hot spark that festered, then slowly cooled. Cashel had never seen a wound closed this way before, but it seemed to work.

Dawn was certainly breaking. As it did, leaves swelled from the twigs about which they'd curled themselves during the hours of darkness. Though—was it really hours?

"Ooh," said Aria. Cashel glanced to his left, following the line of her eyes. She was staring at a stocky fellow with a spear and a breastplate of iron hoops.

He had the face of a cat, complete to the whiskers.

When he saw the princess looking at him, he ducked away. The soldier with hairy arms who'd been using the crossbow had hairy legs as well. They ended in the hooves of a goat, and the two bumps on his helmet were placed just right to cover stubby horns.

"Dulle, get the ladder down and start gathering breakfast," Captain Koras ordered. "Meg, you go too."

He stepped sideways so that he blocked Cashel's view of the cat-faced soldier. In a falsely hearty tone he continued, "We eat a shelf fungus that grows here in the forest, good sir. It's quite delicious. Our service is arduous, but we eat better than kings!"

The cat-faced soldier and his goat-footed fellow scuttled down the rope ladder. The rest of the defenders milled in front of them until they were over the side. Now that Cashel was looking more closely, he could see things about most of the soldiers that would have surprised him back in Barca's Hamlet. Even the captain had a faint pattern of scales on the backs of his hands and his throat above the line of his cuirass.

"I was impressed by your manly courage, young man," Koras said. "Would you and your companions care to join our band? You'd be among brave fellows, and you'd know you were doing the most important work there is: standing as a firm bulwark against monsters and the night."

Aria stared at the captain in mesmerized horror. She looked like a rabbit toward whom a viper slithers with slow inevitability.

Cashel cleared his throat. He didn't want to embarrass Koras and his, well, men. But—

"Ah, sir," he said, rising to his feet. "I thank you for your offer, but I think we'll take ourselves off now that it's daylight. I, ah, promised to return the princess here to her mother."

The thorns in his scalp held, though they twisted a little. He didn't feel pain from the wound, just a dull ache and the sharper throb from the blow itself.

"Didn't, didn't, didn't promise that!" Zahag muttered. "But *I'm* ready to go, you see if I'm not!"

"Well," said the captain, "I understand that such a duty takes precedence. We'll see you off, then. And you can be sure that the good wishes of humanity's defenders go with you."

The rope ladder was fastened to a pair of thick iron eyebolts on the inner face of the wall. Cashel motioned Aria to it; she moved faster than he'd ever seen when he wasn't slinging her around himself. Zahag was already over the battlements, ignoring the ladder in his haste.

"I've been, well, honored to meet you, sir," Cashel said. "I, ah, hope your fight goes well."

He hoped it wasn't obvious that he was guarding the ladder so that the soldiers wouldn't cut the ropes while Aria was still on them. Not that they'd been anything but friendly, but . . .

A soldier reached from behind Koras with a wedge of saffron-colored mushroom. It smelled like fresh bread. Cashel's stomach quivered in delight.

"To eat on your way, good sir," Koras said, passing the offer to Cashel. The first soldier's hand had long, very hairy fingers. It would have been hard to tell them from Zahag's, as a matter of fact.

"Thank you," Cashel said. He tucked the mushroom into the front of his tunic. Aria would complain, but she'd complain anyhow. He bowed.

His companions were safe on the ground. Cashel tossed

his quarterstaff over the side to thump down at a safe distance from them.

"The Shepherd guard you, sirs," he said. He climbed over the side and lurched to the ground as swiftly as even a pretense of safety permitted.

Cashel waved over his shoulder as he and his companions started off in the direction they'd been going all along—eastward along the trail. Aria tugged his arm to speed him until they were out of sight of the tower.

"When Silya sent us out of King Folquin's court . . ." Zahag said. There was an emotion in his voice that Cashel hadn't heard before, though he couldn't have said exactly what the emotion was. "It was night, and it was nowhere I'd ever been. You remember that?"

"I remember waking up there," Cashel said.

"I was glad you woke up, chief," Zahag said. "And I guess those folks in the tower woke up somewhere strange too. It's good not to be alone at night in a strange place."

Cashel cleared his throat, but there wasn't a lot to say. They kept walking, the three of them.

Together.

The 19th of Heron

Garric sat on a fluted stone barrel, a piece of the little chapel's front colonnade. The pillars had fallen, carrying the pediment and the roof of the porch with them. Garric was breathing heavily and the big muscles of his thighs trembled.

He hadn't had a chance to relax since they'd entered the fane in the other place, a lifetime ago.

Liane walked over to him from the temple's interior.

She seemed a trifle wobbly but nonetheless in better condition than Garric was.

His nerves were on the edge of failing him. Every time he looked into the undergrowth, he saw a figure striding toward him with a smile straight out of Hell on her shimmering face.

"Tenoctris is all right," Liane said. "She wanted to check on something."

Garric gave her a quick look. Liane nodded. "An incantation," she said softly. "I didn't want to listen quite yet."

She sat beside Garric. He shifted, though the round of stone was still close quarters. "Garric?" she said. "There was something with us, wasn't there?. When we were coming here."

"She couldn't get to us as long as we stayed on the path," Garric said without meeting the girl's eyes. It wasn't a direct answer, and he couldn't even be sure it was true. He prayed it was true, though.

"And as long as Tenoctris could keep speaking," Liane said. She looked at the partial moon. It had the same luster as the nude woman who'd followed Garric with cold, silvery laughter. . . .

"These must have fallen recently," Garric said brightly. He patted the section of pillar next to the one on which they sat. "The honey-suckle's grown around them, but there're no pine seedlings taller than my knee."

Liane grinned wanly at his change of subject. She reached for his hand and squeezed it.

"That was in the earthquake two years ago, I suppose," she said. "I was still at Mistress Gudea's Academy. There wasn't much damage in Valles, but the site of the old palace was badly shaken."

"Two years?" Tenoctris said from the doorway. The younger people jumped up, surprised. Garric jerked his hand out of Liane's.

"I would have guessed a little longer than that," Tenoctris went on, "but the force may have been obtruding for months or longer before it began to have an effect in the physical world.''

''Effect?'' Garric said.

Tenoctris smiled. She looked as though she'd been dragged a mile behind a wagon, but she was standing on her own legs. She held the willow whip Garric had cut into a wand for her.

Tenoctris let Liane take her hand, but the old woman walked to an adjacent fragment of column and sat as though she didn't need the help. ''Something's come here,'' she said. She patted the stone with a hand which showed the delicate veins. ''I mean this very place, not just our world. But I don't know what it is.''

Garric and Liane faced the old wizard. Garric stretched his arms. Tenoctris didn't weigh very much, but he'd been carrying her for an unguessably long distance along the silver path.

''The thing that brought us here?'' Liane asked.

Garric straightened. ''Nothing could have brought us here!'' he said.

Even he was surprised by his vehemence. Coughing, he went on, ''I mean, it was all random that we came here. We were on the way to Valles, sure. But the Gulf, and then Liane happening to recognize the chapel in the other place where we were—that was just chance.''

Tenoctris smiled vaguely. ''As you know,'' she said, ''I don't believe in the Great Gods—''

''I do,'' Liane said forcefully. ''Tenoctris, this can't be just luck making these things happen. Luck doesn't work that way!''

Tenoctris shrugged. ''Nor do I believe in fate,'' she continued in her usual calm tone. ''But if I thought all these events were being manipulated by an enemy, the queen or some other person trying to work his ends through Malkar, the best advice I could give us is that we should surrender. An entity which can move us with such precision through such complex gyrations isn't going to be defeated by anything we or any other humans can do.''

Garric smiled. The women looked at him with determinedly blank expressions.

Garric's smile grew slowly until it was as broad as it'd been the afternoon he'd won a bout at the Sheep Fair against a merchant's guard. The fellow fancied himself with quarterstaves—and fancied his chances with Sharina, for all she'd made it clear she didn't want him to bother her further.

"Well, that makes it easy," Garric said. "I mean, we're not going to quit, are we?"

"No," Liane whispered. Tenoctris merely began smiling herself.

"So we may as well believe the Great Gods are on our side," he explained. "Or fate, or we've got some—"

Garric lifted his hands palms-up in a gesture of doubt. "—some friend, some *player,* who's smart enough to make all this happen. We're going to go on, so we may as well believe we're going to win eventually."

He'd always been conventionally religious, like everybody else in the borough. Atheism and free-thinking were for wealthy cities, not for hamlets where a hard winter or a bad storm could mean starvation for whole households.

Real belief was something different, though. The Lady and the Shepherd were far too fine for a little place like Barca's Hamlet.

As for Duzi, well, it did Garric good to believe there was someone with him when he watched sheep grazing the borough's meadows. Maybe the someone was named Duzi, and he—He—really appreciated the garlands and nibbles of cheese Garric and other shepherds offered to the stone carved with His rough image. A bit of cheese or a garland was no great expense, even for a shepherd.

Garric hadn't changed his beliefs, but he felt the same as he had about Duzi back home. If you're responsible for things that are too complicated to really control, no matter how hard you try, then it's good to feel that there's somebody watching alongside you who knows a little more.

"I'd offer a bite of cheese," he said, letting his smile return as a wry quirk of his lips. "A whole round of cheese, even. I just don't know where to leave it."

Liane stared at him with the expression of someone who's afraid her companion has gone mad. Tenoctris continued to smile; and somewhere in Garric's mind, the tall, tanned figure of King Carus was laughing.

"Will you need to carry out more, ah, researches here, Tenoctris?" Liane said stiffly. She thought she was being laughed *at,* which she certainly wasn't. Garric squeezed her hand again.

"I'm looking forward to researching a bed," the old woman said. "I've learned something by arriving in this place, but there's nothing more that I need do."

She half-smiled. Tenoctris wasn't a jolly person, but for the most part she seemed to Garric to be both contented and happy. That was a remarkable tribute, given the chaos and danger he'd seen threaten her many times.

She stood up carefully. "Everything seems to work," she said. "As well as it did before, that is. Though I wasn't an acrobat even when I was the age you two are now."

Garric frowned. "We're a mile from Valles proper?" he asked Liane.

She nodded, seeing at once what he was thinking. "At least," she agreed. "Half again as far from the harbor, where most of the inns are. I'll go hire a chair—a carriage, do you think?—while you watch Tenoctris."

She patted her waistline, hearing a softly reassuring *clink*. Liane carried the remnants of her father's wealth in gold, rolled within a sash beneath her tunic. There were enough Sandrakkan Riders in the silk to buy a ship, let alone rent a sedan chair and four bearers.

"I'll go," Garric said. "You'll be safe here till I get back. Unless Valles is a paradise compared to Carcosa and Erdin, it's not safe for a lone girl with a beltful of money to hire a chair at a drover's tavern."

The coins in Garric's purse were silver and bronze, but

they were more than sufficient for the purpose. Except for his father, Reise, and perhaps Katchin the Miller, no one in Barca's Hamlet had ever seen as much money in coin as Garric carried; and in Reise's case, not since he'd left burning Carcosa with a wife and two newborn infants the day after the riots.

Liane's expression was technically a smile, but there was no humor in it. "No, Valles isn't a paradise," she said. "Particularly not the north side of the city where we'll be coming in. I forgot that in the past I always had either my father's servants or ushers from Mistress Gudea's Academy with me when I went out at night."

She nodded to indicate the chapel by which they'd arrived. "The door is aligned with sunrise on the equinoxes, of course," she said. "There's a paved road coming into what were the palace grounds only a hundred paces or so south of here. Mistress Gudea had to send a party out with brush hooks to clear a path before each field trip because it's so overgrown, but—"

"I think I can find my way in the woods, Liane," Garric said. "Even in the dark."

He was a little nettled at the girl acting like he was a city-bred fool who'd get lost on his way home without a street to guide him. Though—

Just maybe what bothered him wasn't Liane telling him things he already knew, but rather that she'd assumed he knew something he didn't. That temple doors faced east wasn't "of course" to Garric, though he'd felt a current of agreement from Carus. There weren't any temples in Barca's Hamlet; nor, for that matter, within a day's journey of Barca's Hamlet.

"Oh, I'm sor—" Liane began.

Garric hugged her fiercely. "*I'm* sorry," he said. "I'm scared that there's something I'll need to know that I don't. And we'll fail because of what I don't know."

Liane kissed his cheek. "We're not going to fail," she said. "The Lady and the Shepherd are on our side, remember?"

"Right," said Garric as he stepped away. "Right!"

He strode off quickly, so quickly he almost walked into a full-sized beech tree. That'd be a fine answer to the way he'd boasted about being a countryman!

Garric laughed, happy down through to his heart, and then began to whistle a jig called "The Merry Plowman." He'd piped it a hundred times at weddings and harvest festivals. Danced it, too, hopping high and spinning in the air as Lupa os-Queddin rang the tune with a wooden spoon on three part-filled jugs. Had Mistress Gudea taught her charges to dance jigs?

The old road was closer than Garric expected. In truth, he hadn't been thinking much about what he was doing. Even the vines that caught in his long sword's crossguard and looped the scabbard couldn't put him out of his present good mood.

Roots had tossed the paving blocks into a pattern as irregular as the sea's surface. Garric tried walking on them, then decided to push through the undergrowth alongside instead. The old road helped with his direction, but the forest soil made easier going.

He heard dogs bark; hounds, he supposed, yipping to be let off their keeper's leash. This tract would make good hunting—though what Garric meant by hunting, wandering in the common woods with a bow and blunted arrows listening for squirrels, was very different from the vast royal drives that Carus recalled.

A stray thought from an earlier age made Garric wonder if the site of the old palace was still royal land. That would explain why it hadn't been built on again. Property so near Valles must be valuable for more than brush and ruins.

He continued to whistle. He thought about making himself a set of pipes when he got a moment. There must be reeds and wax on Ornifal. . . .

A hound bayed, sounding birdlike and excited. Garric looked over his shoulder. The dog was very close by.

Three hounds burst from the undergrowth barking in

shockingly high-pitched voices as they closed on Garric. Their mottled hides made them wraithlike in the dappled gloom.

"Hey!" Garric shouted. He wished he had a staff. "Get back from me, you!"

He wasn't frightened, just surprised and a little angry. They were good-sized animals, all together probably weighing more than even a large man like Garric. In Erdin savage, spike-collared guard dogs were chained in the door alcoves of wealthy houses or walked on leashes in front of sedan chairs to make sure that nobody jostled the woman of quality within. These were just hunting dogs, though.

Garric put his back to a tree. When two or more dogs were together, there was always a risk that they'd do things that none of them would do by itself. In that they were very like human beings.

These hounds had better go back shortly to their proper business—raccoon, deer, or whatever it was folk hunted on Ornifal. Otherwise Garric was going to trim a sapling with his sword and start rapping noses until they got the idea.

A huntsman in tight-fitting jerkin and breeches came out of the woods. He held a silver-chased hunting horn in one hand and, in the other, a spear with a bar just below the head to keep a boar or other dangerous game from slipping down the shaft onto him. The hounds redoubled the raucous yapping that was driving Garric wild.

"Are these yours?" Garric said. "Get them off me, will you?"

Instead of answering, the huntsman blew a two-note signal. His horn's twisted shape wasn't that of any cow Garric had seen, and if it came from a sheep or goat it was of a much larger breed than those raised on Haft.

"I said get your dogs away!" Garric said. "Is this the way you treat travelers on Ornifal? Sister take you all if it is!"

Carus' spirit coursed close to the surface of Garric's

mind, as it always did when the youth was angry or frightened. He put his hand almost unconsciously on the hilt of his sword. The huntsman backed a step, leveling the boar spear on Garric's chest.

He shouldn't have done that. Garric imagined with perfect clarity his sword coming out of the scabbard in a quick sweep to behead the fellow. A right and left to the hounds, two of them flying sideways, their yelps silenced in gouts of blood, and a quick thrust behind Garric's back to settle the third beast, who'd be going for a hamstring. . . .

A nobleman burst from the night. With him were six other men in helmets and mail shirts. The latter were soldiers, not huntsmen. Three held spears with slender points for piercing armor, while the others had drawn their swords.

Hand weapons were a better choice than bows with the undergrowth so thick, noted a coldly professional mind at the back of Garric's own.

"Watch him, Lord Royhas," the huntsman cried to the noble. "He's got a sword!"

"Whip your dogs away!" the noble said. "How can anybody hear themselves think?"

Garric was uneasily aware that his clothing, though of good quality to begin with, was very much the worse for wear. They'd been able to wash their garments in the place they'd gone when they escaped the Gulf, but the tunic had stains that wouldn't come out in plain water and they weren't able to mend tears properly.

The huntsman threw down his equipment. He caught two hounds and dragged them back by their collars. The third followed her master and companions, still whining with excitement.

"I thank you, sir," Garric said. He reached down to tap a clink from his heavy leather belt purse. "My name's Garric or-Reise from Haft. Though I'm afraid I look a little bedraggled, I'm not a vagabond."

He was glad to relax. The barking had gotten on his

nerves in a way that an open threat wouldn't have done. The dogs hadn't been *doing* anything, so Garric couldn't properly respond to them.

"Yes, I thought you might be," the noble said pleasantly. "I'm Royhas bor-Bolliman, the Master of the Royal Hunt."

The soldiers moved in from either side, acting without haste. They were already too close for Garric to draw his long sword. Two had sheathed their own weapons. The spearmen were a pace back where one or both could easily stab Garric if he tried to struggle with the other four men.

"Let us take this, sir," a soldier said, kneeling to unwrap the sword belt's long double tongue as the first step to unbuckling it. The swordsmen put their free hands on Garric's wrists. Their blades weren't precisely threatening him, but the points were still close to his face.

"What's the meaning of this?" Garric snapped. He wasn't frightened; part of him was actually surprised at the feeling of cold analysis that drove all emotion from his mind. A year ago—a few months ago—he would have been shocked and afraid. The man he'd become since leaving home merely looked for the way out.

At this moment there was no way out.

"King Valence was informed that a pretender claiming to be a scion of the old royal line would be arriving here," Royhas explained. He was in his thirties and moved with the ease of a man who spent more time outdoors than he did at the table. "The Master of the Hunt was the obvious person to apprehend him. These men are members of my own household, by the way—not royal troops."

Royhas gestured to the men holding Garric. The kneeling soldier had the belt off. The swordsmen bent Garric's arms back with firm pressure but not violence; he didn't resist. The fourth man bound his wrists with a soft, strong cord. It was silk, Garric supposed.

"I'm not a pretender to anything," Garric said. He tensed his wrists as the soldier drew the bonds tight. The men knew that trick: the pair holding Garric's arms rapped his elbows with their sword hilts. As the youth's muscles spasmed, their fellow pulled the slack out of the knot.

How had Valence known that Garric would arrive *here*? And what did the king intend—

"Master Silyon, the king's wizard, apparently feels differently," Royhas said without concern. "A nasty piece of work, that one. But he was right about you appearing, wasn't he?"

The cord binding Garric had arm's-length tags. Two soldiers looped the ends around their own belts, attaching Garric to them though he could still walk by himself.

"We'll get you into a closed carriage and then sweep the grounds for the friends you're supposed to have along," Royhas said. He smiled. "My royal master has ordered that you all be quietly put out of the way. As though you'd never existed."

Sharina squatted where the ground became flat enough to support a grove of giant tree ferns. Rhododendrons poked hard green leaves through the fronds. "Give me a moment," she called ahead to Hanno.

Sharina wasn't precisely winded, but her legs hadn't gotten much exercise during long days on the ship and Hanno's boat. The terrain from the cove on the shore of Bight where the dory sheltered was more a cliff than a slope. Previous travelers had notched handholds into the particularly steep portions. That made the climb possible, but Sharina wondered how the hunter was going to carry up his tons of supplies.

"It's not far, missie," Hanno said. "The rivers here flow north and east, but me and my partner Ansule figure it's better to climb a bit and save an extra two days of rowing to Valles. There's others that feel different, but they mostly use sails on their boats."

Butterflies with wings the size of Sharina's hands fluttered through the grove, dabbing into the flowers of air plants growing along the branches of the tree ferns. One of them landed on Sharina's shoulder. It felt heavy, and its spindly legs gripped with uncomfortable strength.

She sucked in her breath with surprise. The giant butterfly uncoiled its long mouth parts and prodded her skin.

"Looking for salt," Hanno said nonchalantly. He carried only his weapons, the huge spear and the knives in his belt. "I figure if there was a way to get the wings back to Valles, I'd be a rich man. They lose their pretty color if they get knocked around, though."

The insect on Sharina's shoulder was too close for both her eyes to focus on it. Its wings were striped black and white, and there were red dots on the bottom lobe.

Compared to many others in the grove, the butterfly was positively chaste in its patterning. The thought of it being pulled apart for a rich lady's headdress disturbed Sharina.

The butterfly stepped into the curve of Sharina's neck. "Ouch!" she said. Her index finger brushed it into the air with a determined shove. Scales like tiny feathers spun from the creature's wings, dancing in a beam of light.

Sharina grinned at herself. Aloud she said, "If I were a better person, I wouldn't let one pinch wipe away all my kindly thoughts."

Hanno smiled, more or less. "Don't get worked up about butterflies," he said. "They never helped a soul but themself, I figure. There's plenty of people who think it's good enough to sit around looking pretty, and I never had much use for them neither."

He rose to his feet. "Ready to go on?" he asked. Sharina stood in response.

"Me and Ansule'll rig the cable and pulley tomorrow to haul the goods up to the cabin," the hunter said. "No point in worrying about it so late in the day. Missing griddle cakes along with our meat for another day ain't going to kill us."

He led Sharina into a belt of pandanus trees. A skirt of stilt roots rising as high as Sharina's waist supported each scaly trunk. The ground was noticeably lower than at the cliff's edge, so the area probably flooded during storms.

"What about the boat?" Sharina asked. They'd left the dory tied bow and stern in a cove overlooked by giant palms. There wasn't even a hint of a shoreline. While the vessel could ride where it was during fine weather, the first storm from west or northwest would batter it to splinters against the rocky walls.

"Haul it straight up the trunk of one of them palms and lash it till we need it the next time," the hunter said. "With the mountain so close behind, the wind don't get enough of a run to pull down trees. That's how they got so big. There's the corniche to keep the waves off, all but the spray."

Sharina heard buzzing; she turned to look. A fungus the size of a man's head bulged from the stem of a woody vine. "What—" she began. When she spoke, a cloud of flies rose from the fungus cup with a terrible odor.

Hanno laughed. "You don't want to bump them stinkpots, missie," he said. "Though I tell you the truth, it gets mighty ripe around the cabin sometimes when we're curing a good crop of horn."

They crossed a slight ridge, noticeable more for the fact Sharina heard a brook purling than because the slope reversed significantly. The path Hanno followed didn't show on the ground. Thin soil and lack of light penetrating the forest canopy meant there was no ground cover to be marked by traffic.

The watercourse was a rivulet through blocks of basalt. Ferns, giant philodendrons, and knee-high curls of moss covered both shallow banks.

Sharina smelled wood smoke; she sneezed. "We must be getting—" she said.

The stench of rotting flesh hit her, shocking her mouth and nostrils closed. She thought, *Hanno warned me, I guess, but this is awful.*

Barca's Hamlet was no more fastidious a place than any other rural community, but meat was a valuable commodity. Very little offal remained after a hog or sheep had been butchered, and that was composted with vegetable waste to decompose before being spread as fertilizer on the house gardens. This was—

The hunter had disappeared. "Hanno?" Sharina called. She walked two paces upstream with her fingers resting on the butt of the Pewle knife. Her skin tingled.

She heard the flies.

The clearing lay under a beetling knob covered by bamboo and wisteria. The cabin had backed against the rock so that the brook washed one side of its foundation. The timbers of the wall on that side still smoldered, though the remainder of the building had burned out completely.

Flies rose in a dozen separate clouds. There were three complete bodies and the scattered remains of a fourth.

Sharina drew the big knife and felt behind her for a tree. She backed against the trunk. Her mouth was open, but she didn't speak.

Hanno came out of the foliage on the other side of the creek. His appearance hadn't changed in any way that Sharina could describe, but his face was as bleak as a tidal surge.

"They've been and gone," he grated softly. "Not so long ago that I can't catch up with them, I guess."

"Who, Hanno?" Sharina said. Her voice was steady; it was like listening to somebody else speak. The Pewle knife didn't tremble in her hand.

"Monkeys," the hunter said. He prodded with the metal-shod butt of his spear, levering one of the bodies up so that Sharina could see it clearly.

The body was more like a man than not, but it was covered with coarse russet hair. The chest was deep, the arms long, sinewy, and muscled like the forelimbs of a cat. By contrast, the bandy legs looked deformed, and the skull showed scarcely a shallow dome above the thick brow ridges.

The creature's lips were drawn back in a rictus of death. The yellowish teeth included long canines in both upper and lower jaws, though one of the latter had been broken to a stump.

"Hairy Men," Sharina said. "The Autochthones of Bight in Katradinus' *Cosmogeography.*"

Hanno let the corpse flop down. A powerful stroke had opened its belly. Coils of intestine, purple-veined and swollen in the damp heat, spilled onto the moss beside the body.

"Monkeys," he repeated as he walked to a lump of the corpse that had been dismembered. He lifted the severed head of a young man with a scar up the right cheek. The dead man's hair was a butternut color except where the scar tissue continued across his scalp; there it was white and exceptionally thin.

"You're looking poorly, Ansule," Hanno said. "I guess you should've gone to Valles after all. The sea voyage would've been good for you."

Sharina squatted, using the tree's presence for support. She's seen worse, but not when all the victims had been living humans. And this was bad enough in all truth.

Hanno set the head of his partner back on the ground. "We've got a stash up the trunk of that big monkey-puzzle tree," he said, nodding toward a huge araucaria across the creek from the burned-out cabin. "For all they look like monkeys, they don't like to climb. You can stay there till I get back."

He disappeared into the forest with the smooth silence of a shadow moving on the ground when a cloud slides across the sun. From the green luxuriance his voice returned, saying, "Or take the boat if you think you can handle it, missie. I won't be any longer than I need to be."

Then the only sound was the brook, and a spit of steam that came from the ruins of the cabin.

Sharina considered her surroundings. She wasn't frightened. Rationally she supposed she could trust Hanno to know whether there were any dangers in the vicinity, but her lack of fear went well beyond reason.

What Sharina *really* felt was irritation at the way the hunter had abandoned her, but she knew she didn't have any claim on his time. Besides, she could read Hanno's behavior as a compliment, proof that he thought she could get along without him.

And so she could.

Rainbow bark—orange and yellow tags flaking from the chartreuse underlayer—marked a nearby eucalyptus sapling that was about the diameter of her upper arm. She walked to it, put tension on the trunk with her left hand, and struck not far below the crotch with the Pewle knife.

The wood was soft with sap. Sharina reversed the angle and struck again. The sharp, heavy knifeblade hurled away a large chip. At home, Sharina's tasks included cutting kindling for the inn's fireplaces. She was used to making strong, precise cuts.

The fourth stroke severed the trunk, though its branches interlocked with those of neighboring trees and kept the sapling from toppling. Sharina pulled and shook the eucalyptus loose, then paused to listen for any change in the surrounding forest.

A tree behind her cried, "Fool you! Fool you! Fool you!" Sharina spun around, then realized she'd heard a bird or maybe a lizard. She grinned. Not that she felt like arguing with the creature's opinion.

She lopped off one of the trunk's branchings just above the crotch, then severed the remaining portion four feet higher. After a few judicious blows to shape the lower end into a paddle, Sharina had a serviceable digging stick.

She dug on the other side of the creek where stream-deposited sediment created a deeper layer of soil than elsewhere in this rain-leached land. The understratum was yellowish clay, dense and difficult to dig even when it was sodden. When it dried, as it did on the roots of toppled trees, it became a coarse, crumbly limestone.

Sharina's family had a real shovel whose hardwood blade was shod with iron, but less wealthy households in Barca's Hamlet did all their digging with sticks like this one. The branch she'd trimmed short made a shelf for her foot to bear down on. A pair of wooden-soled clogs would have made the task more comfortable, but Sharina's determination and calluses between them were sufficient.

She didn't try to make a proper grave, just a shallow pit to hold the fragments of Ansule's body. He'd been killed no more than two days before, but his flesh was already softly ripe in the steamy climate. Sharina gathered the parts without squeamishness, then wiped her hands on the hard, jagged leaves of a bamboo before she took up the digging stick again.

Ansule's bones had been gnawed, then cracked for marrow. Sharina's face was emotionless as she resumed digging, this time a trench between the sprawling buttress roots of a great tree.

It was good to have work to do. Hard work saved you from feeling sick or angry or desperately lonely and afraid.

The Hairy Men had been killed by a broad-bladed weapon wielded with strength. The wounds were terrible: a male disemboweled, another nearly decapitated, and the dead female split all the way from collarbone to diaphragm. The survivors—how many were there in the band Hanno was pursuing?—had left the corpses where they lay. The only sign of kinship with the dead was that those bodies hadn't been eaten.

Sharina levered the Hairy Men into the trench with her digging stick. It wasn't deep, just enough that the corpses lay below the surface level when she covered them with broad leaves and scraped loose dirt back over them.

She didn't owe anything to the Hairy Men, but if she was going to stay here she needed to do something about the smell.

When she'd closed both graves, Sharina carried head-sized stones from the stream and laid them in a simple cairn over Ansule's remains. She didn't know what kind of scavengers lived in this forest, but the cool, black blocks were heavy enough to keep out even pigs.

She didn't bother to protect the Hairy Men. Nothing would dig them up while she was staying nearby, and what happened afterward was no concern of hers.

Sharina leaned on the digging stick, breathing through her mouth. Her shoulders ached, her hands were raw, and the ball of her right foot throbbed even though she'd switched feet at intervals. She must not have used as much strength with her left foot. . . .

Nonnus had planted his garden every year with a digging stick.

The thought twisted Sharina's mind out of the safe channels she'd been keeping it in. She knelt on the ground, sobbing uncontrollably. After moments, minutes—time no longer mattered—she began to pray to the Lady; and as she did so, she felt the placid, sturdy presence of Nonnus close by her.

Sharina raised her eyes. The forest chirped and hooted to itself, but the only movement she saw was mites whirling in a stray beam of sunlight.

She wasn't alone. Her friend Nonnus had died, but he hadn't left her. It was easier to remember that here in the immense green peace of the forest.

Sharina got up, smiling again. She'd seen fruit growing out of the trunk of a smooth-barked tree as she followed Hanno here. Bright-colored birds had been squabbling over the red pulp, so it seemed likely enough a human would find it safe to eat. If she didn't like the taste, well, going to bed hungry was no terrible thing.

The sun had been past zenith when she and Hanno found the cabin. It must now be low, but she should have time to weave a simple booth of leaves and saplings against the rain she expected.

She'd smooth a slab of wood, too, and carve the Lady's image on it for Ansule's grave. The headboard wouldn't last long in this climate, but it was what she could do.

Sharina whistled a soft tune, a lullaby that her father had brought with him from Ornifal to sing to his children.

The words were nonsense, but they soothed her mind as no others could.

She needed to set a network of lines and pebbles to rattle if anyone tried to creep up on her in the dark. The inner bark of the eucalpytus would strip into suitable fibers.

Sharina wasn't really worried about being surprised in the darkness, though. Nonnus would be with her.

And nobody *ever* took Nonnus unaware.

Ilna had expected difficulty in finding a ship sailing direct from Erdin to Valles, since the Earl of Sandrakkan and King Valence were as hostile as they could be without open warfare. There was no difficulty at all: a lounging stevedore had immediately directed her and Maidus to the *Pole Star,* leaving on the ebb tide tomorrow afternoon.

The stevedore hadn't propositioned her—or the boy—after he took a good look into Ilna's eyes. She knew her duty to her brother and she'd do it—of course; but she was nevertheless irritated at being dragged from the path on which she'd set herself. Shadows from the low sun might have made her look angrier than she really was.

Ilna grinned. Or again, maybe they just underlined the truth.

Her nose wrinkled. Erdin was a river port. Though people in Barca's Hamlet weren't overcareful about what they dumped in the water, there weren't enough of them for their sewage to have the impact Erdin's did.

"I don't think I'll ever get used to this smell," Ilna said. "Well, if I don't return, I won't have to."

"Mistress," Maidus said miserably, "don't talk that way. You've got to come back!"

If Ilna had wanted to, she could have woven a tapestry that displayed her entire future and the lives of everyone she knew. She smiled, a grim expression even by her own standards. As if things wouldn't be bad enough when they happened, without worrying about them beforehand as well!

Ilna glanced down at the boy. "You'll be fine with Captain Voder," she said. "Better than you would with me, at any rate. Just remember to do what he says the first time. He's not one to threaten, that one."

Maidus sniffed. "*You* think he's scary, Mistress Ilna?" he said. "Ask anybody in the Crescent who they'd rather go up against, Voder or you!"

"Then they're fools," Ilna said mildly. "Though if more people behaved properly, Voder and I might find our lives quieter."

She wondered if that was true. Well, it wasn't a notion that was likely to be tested in her lifetime.

Ilna had bargained for nearly an hour to get passage for three at twelve Sandrakkan silver Earls—new-minted so that the earl's head and the wheat sheaves stood up sharply from the unworn surface. The *Pole Star*'s captain had first demanded a golden Rider, twenty-five Earls in value, for each passenger.

Ilna sniffed. She could have paid the extortionate price; paid it a dozen times over, if she'd chosen to. That wasn't the problem. For a moment her anger that a *worm* of a sailor thought he could cheat her had almost overwhelmed her. She'd reached for a tuft of rope yarn to bind the fool's mind to whatever purpose she chose—

And then caught herself. The bargain took longer by haggling in normal fashion, but it was fair on both sides when Ilna and the captain spat on their palms and shook hands.

Her powers would pave a road straight back to Hell if she ever let her anger rule her.

"If I'd known what those wizards were planning," Maidus said, "they'd never have—"

"They came to tell me my brother was in danger," Ilna said sharply. "Would you have concealed that information from me, Maidus?"

The true answer to that was "Yes, in a heartbeat;" but

the boy had the decency instead to mutter, ''No, mistress.''

Halphemos and Cerix had been smart enough to realize after a few preliminary inquiries that there were people in the Crescent who wouldn't want Ilna os-Kenset to leave. Instead of trying to find her by asking directly, Halphemos had worked a series of small locating spells, coming closer with each one.

''I wish I could come along,'' Maidus said.

''To get in my way?'' Ilna said. ''No thank you.''

That wasn't true, but it was a reason the boy would accept with only an occasional sniffle of despair. Maidus had proved himself a clever fellow and a determined one.

The truth would have been ''I don't want you with me because anything powerful enough to swallow Cashel is too dangerous for me to involve you with.'' If Ilna had said that, the boy would have managed to come along even if it meant tying himself to the blade of the *Pole Star*'s steering oar.

Erdin's port didn't shut down completely when the sun set, but most of the remaining activity was from crews stowing the last of their cargo for a departure at dawn. Lanterns and the light of flaring torches were a poor substitute for the sun, and the risk of sparks on sun-dried wood and fabric made late work dangerous as well as difficult.

The sky was still bright enough to reflect from the brick wharfs. Delay in hauling or loading meant that some goods remained on the docks, piled under nets to deter pilfering. Each mound was guarded by a watchman with a lantern. Well before dawn the tallow lamp candles would have burned down and the men would be dozing in crevices among the bales and barrels, but by then the thieves would likely have gone to sleep also.

Ilna chuckled. ''Mistress?'' Maidus said.

''Laziness prevents more crime than conscience ever did,'' she said. The boy looked at her with a puzzled expression.

They were nearing a moderate-sized ship, much the same as the one which Ilna had watched carry her friends away. This vessel had a tin plaque nailed to the curving stem; the pattern punched onto the white metal was a gull touching a wave top, though Ilna doubted she'd have known that except for her familiarity with equally stylized designs in fabric.

Most of the docked vessels had a crewman on watch to rap the deck with a cudgel if anyone passed nearby. This one was silent. Either the watch was asleep, or the vessel was in such bad condition that the captain didn't worry about anyone stealing his cordage.

"I'll be back as soon as I can, Maidus," Ilna said in a gentler tone than she'd used on the boy previously. "My first duty's to my brother. Though—" She threw back one wing of her cape and examined the sash cinching her tunic. Despite the poor lighting, she could see that the pattern remained smooth and unharmed.

Ilna laughed without humor. "My *first* duty," she corrected herself, "I should rather have said, is to Liane bos-Benliman. I treated her worse, and with less cause, than I did most people in the recent past. But Liane seems quite capable of taking care of herself."

"Mistress Ilna?" the boy said in a small voice. He was staring at his feet. "If I promise to—"

Four figures leaped from where darkness had hidden them in the bow of the adjacent ship. They weren't men, though they wore sailors' clothing and were man*like* except for their bestial features and the faint shimmer of scales where their skin was exposed. Ilna hadn't seen the creature her brother had found in a cider royal cask, but she could recognize Scaled Men from his description.

The noose was free in Ilna's hands before she was consciously aware of danger. The Scaled Men carried hardwood belaying pins from the ship's furniture. All of them had daggers as well, and a curve-bladed sword was tucked beneath one's leather belt.

Maidus gave a shriek of anger that stopped with the

toonk! of a head blow. Ilna turned, casting the noose as she did. There were two more Scaled Man behind her. She didn't know where they'd concealed themselves. Maidus was on the bricks, bleeding from a torn scalp, and the Scaled Man who'd struck him was raising a belaying pin for another blow.

The silken loop settled over the neck of the creature who'd knocked the boy down. Ilna jerked the Scaled Man into the path of its fellow, ducking as she did so. The club aimed by one of the quartet from the ship slashed past. The noosed creature flailed like a headless chicken, choking as it tangled its fellow.

Ilna snatched Maidus up by the sturdy tunic she'd given him. Her own cape pulled away, delaying her for an instant she couldn't afford. She dropped the noose and had her paring knife half out of its bone case when scaly hands caught both her wrists.

The creatures were silent. The Scaled Man on her right didn't make a sound even when Ilna drew her sunbeam-sharp blade across its arm.

Hands gripped her hair. She squirmed and bit flesh as dry as a snake's skin.

She didn't feel the club hit her, but she heard the hollow ring of the blow. The night went white. She was as blind as if she'd been staring into the noonday sun.

Ilna hadn't called for help. No one was likely to run to a frightened woman on the docks, except perhaps to demand a turn for himself. She would be *damned* before she wasted breath on a vain exercise.

Hands lifted her. She thought her wrists and ankles were being bound, but she wasn't sure even of that. She could hear voices, and they weren't human.

She was lowered again. She lay on a wooden grate, smelling bilge water below. She was sure her limbs were bound, but the light behind her eyeballs still blinded her.

Mooring lines thumped on the deck. Wood squealed, a sound Ilna identified after a moment as sweeps being fitted into oarlocks. She felt the ship rock.

The River Erd was unbuoyed as a defensive measure: no enemy could sail up its winding reaches by night to take Erdin unaware. To attempt it was to go aground on a mudbank or nose into a blind slough.

But the Scaled Men were unquestionably under way, taking Ilna os-Kenset with them.

The 20th of Heron

Garric hadn't been blindfolded, but the lanterns on the arched gateway were only orange sparks as Royhas' coach pulled into the enclosure. They must have been just extinguished.

The coach pulled around the back of a mansion and halted. The two guards who'd ridden as postillions threw open the vehicle's left door.

Lord Royhas was opposite Garric, facing the rear of the compartment; the remaining guards sat on the outside of both benches. The nobleman's hand, a pale blur, flicked toward the opening. "Quickly," he said to Garric. "And don't make any noise."

Garric's hands were still bound, but he didn't need King Carus' insight to know that Royhas didn't plan to have him killed. Not just yet, at any rate. He stepped down without comment and followed the guards into the house.

A servant opened the door but hid behind it as the passengers from the carriage entered. Garric saw only a vast stone bulk as his guides bustled him inside. Royhas and the others were close behind.

The corridor was unlighted, but a candle glimmered through an open doorway at the end. The floor creaked underfoot like the puncheon floors of his father's inn. The walls were paneled to waist height and frescoed above that, though in this illumination they were differences in shading rather than pictures.

Or again, maybe he was mistaking water stains for art. He grinned.

The chamber was intended as a winter dining room, but the broad windows along the south wall were now covered by heavy velvet. Not drapes, Garric realized: the fabric had been tacked to the casements so that no one could possibly look in, nor would any gleam of light escape.

Royhas was taking no chances anyway. Only a single wax taper was lighted in a wall sconce holding nine.

The table and twelve chairs were of a dark wood Garric didn't recognize, but from growing up in an inn he could appreciate the amount of rubbing required to bring out this luster. A man wearing an outfit of mauve silk—sober to look at, but it must have cost the price of a good horse—waited inside the door with his hands crossed over his plump belly. From his combination of obsequiousness and wealth he was of the better class of servants, probably the majordomo.

The guards led Garric inside, then turned to face their master. Garric looked over his shoulder.

Royhas said, "Loose him," to the guards. He spoke with a tinge of irritation as though it was their fault Garric was still bound. One of the men tugged at the cord. The knot slipped open immediately, though Garric's surreptitious twisting during the coach ride hadn't gained him so much as a hair of slack.

"Maurunus," the nobleman said to the servant, "some other gentlemen will be arriving shortly. Show them here when they arrive."

Garric kneaded his wrists. The soft cord hadn't chafed his skin, but his fingers tingled as blood returned to their tips. Though the guards watched him with expressions of bland innocence, they were tautly ready to hurl themselves on Garric if he suddenly attacked their master.

"Lord Waldron arrived a few moments ago, sir," the majordomo said. He nodded toward the chamber's other door. "I put him in the buttery since I didn't think you'd want him waiting in the main hall. Shall I—"

"Sister take the man!" Royhas snarled, the first honest emotion Garric had seen him offer. "Is he a wizard himself, then? The courier must have met him on the way here."

Maurunus waited with a look of polite attention, his hands still folded. He didn't speak.

Royhas shook his head in exasperation. "Wait for the turn of a glass, then send him through," he said. "I'll speak with my guest here in private."

The servant bowed and went out the other door. His steps were so small and quick that he seemed to be gliding.

"Leave us," Royhas said with a curt gesture to the pair of guards who'd preceded Garric into the chamber. A slight tension at the corners of their mouths was their only sign of protest.

"And shut the door, you fools!" the nobleman shouted at their backs. The second man had swung the panel to the jamb but hadn't fully closed it.

"Well, Master Garric," Royhas said with a smile Garric would have known was false even without watching Royhas deal with those who served him. "I suppose you're wondering why I've brought you here."

"*I* suppose," Garric said, "that you're hoping to use me as a willing puppet in a plot against King Valence."

He smiled without warmth at the startled nobleman.

Garric had met men like Royhas before, in the borough and more often among the drovers and their guards at the Sheep Fair. Fellows like that ran roughshod over everybody who didn't push them back—hard. Garric had learned early that he felt better after a fight than he did after backing down to somebody.

What had been true in Barca's Hamlet was true here in Valles. Royhas could have Garric killed out of hand—but if he'd been willing to do that, Garric would be buried in the grounds of the ancient palace. Garric had nothing to gain by cringing and a good deal to lose, including his self-respect.

"I'm not a traitor!" Royhas said. He'd thought he was dealing with an ignorant peasant—and because he was a nobleman, he didn't realize that a shepherd had more experience than civilized folk about how members of a group jockey for position. Rams or men, it was all the same at the most basic level.

The medallion of King Carus was a warm presence on Garric's chest. Cashel would have known what was happening just as Garric did. Because Garric drew on the memories of his ancient ancestor, though, he also understood how to deal with this particular *form* of dominance behavior.

He raised an eyebrow as though he were amused by a child denying the obvious.

"Listen, boy—" Royhas said.

"You'd best bring your flunkies back before you next call me 'boy,' Lord Royhas!" Garric said in a voice that made the candle flame quiver. In a quieter tone he went on, "Alternatively, you can treat me as the scion of kings and the man on whom your plot depends. In that case we'll get along better."

He didn't know how much of that was Garric or-Reise and how much came from Carus, but he did feel the king's personality bellowing with laughter deep in his mind. The guards had taken Garric's sword belt away, but he hooked his thumbs behind his hipbones and splayed his elbows out, grinning at the amazed nobleman.

Royhas was a solidly built man, but he was neither as big nor as young as Garric, and he wasn't as strong by a half. For a moment his face was contorted with anger; then he considered what Garric had said rather than just the fact that a peasant had talked back to him.

In a careful voice Royhas said, "We're all under a degree of strain, Master Garric. My associates and myself are as loyal as any men to King Valence. It's quite obvious that Valence is unable to respond to the threat posed by the queen, however, so we've been forced to consider other courses of action for the sake of the kingdom. And for Valence too, I shouldn't wonder."

"Go on," Garric said. Royhas must originally have planned to tell him to agree with whatever Royhas said during the meeting of conspirators and otherwise to keep his mouth shut. Still, if Maurunus had turned over a sand glass the size of those Garric had seen used on shipboard to judge speed against a drag line, there was still a little time to talk.

Royhas grimaced in frustration. He'd been knocked off his line, and he wasn't any happier than a young ram whose fellow had spilled him on the meadow.

Garric smiled. Of course, most years *all* the young rams were slaughtered come fall. That was something a shepherd understood too.

Royhas probably thought Garric was laughing at him, but he swallowed his anger and said, "The queen is sending her own minions to take over important positions in the city. Gate guards, the customs assessors in the port. The chancellor's office, even. There's always somebody willing to do a monster's dirty work if the money's good enough."

Garric cleared his throat. Carus' agreement with the last statement was such a fierce, angry surge that for a moment it took Garric's breath away.

"She can't be buying everybody's support," Garric said as soon as he could. A thought that wasn't entirely his own floated into his consciousness. "Or do the common people support her?"

"Nobody supports the queen!" Royhas said. "She's a demon in all truth, a wizard and worse. Mobs stone her officials, but that just makes it worse. Whatever the reason, riots mean shops are looted and people are mugged because they looked like they had the price of a drink in their purse."

Someone tapped softly at the door by which the majordomo had left. Royhas looked up and started to speak.

Garric raised a hand to forestall him and said, "My friends? They're to be brought to me immediately."

Royhas scowled. "I don't even know if they've been found," he said. "You were our real concern."

"When you find my friends Liane and Tenoctris," Garric said, "they're to be treated like the noblewomen they are. Because you're a gentleman, Lord Royhas, I'm not concerned that you'd think of using them as hostages to compel my acquiescence in your plans—but because some of your co-conspirators may *not* be gentlemen, please make it clear to all concerned that I would fly into a berserk rage if anything of the sort were to happen. I doubt that any number of guards could prevent me from killing the culprit."

Royhas flashed Garric a smile of some amusement. "I'm not in the habit of taking hostages from peasants, young man," he said. "Perhaps things are different on Haft."

Garric laughed aloud. He wasn't hysterical, but the release of tension was greater than the tension itself had seemed a moment before. "No, Lord Royhas," he said. "Things aren't different: Haft peasants are just as capable of overvaluing themselves as the highest nobles on Ornifal are."

He nodded to the door. "We should let them in," he said. "So long as you oppose the queen, we should be able to get along between ourselves."

Royhas took his position behind the chair at the head of the table and motioned Garric to stand on his immediate right. "Enter!" he said.

Maurunus opened the door, but he stayed outside when the four cowled figures who'd been waiting in the hallway pushed past. The last of them slammed the door behind him, then searched for a bolt. There wasn't one.

"I don't lock myself in to dinner, Sourous," Royhas said tartly. "If you like, we could meet in the old slave pen in the subcellar."

"There's no need for names!" Sourous said. He was a

surprisingly young man with delicate features, from what Garric could see. Unlike the others, Sourous hadn't thrown back his cowl when the door closed.

"There's every need for names," Garric said. "Mine is Garric or-Reise of Haft, and I'm a direct descendant of Carus—the last *real* King of the Isles."

The words weren't his own, though they rang with bell-like clarity from his lips. Carus was speaking through him, but he was speaking the words Garric would have used if he'd had the experience to choose them.

"So you say," said the first man to enter the room. He had chiseled features and the thick wrists of a swordsman. Though about sixty and the oldest of the five conspirators, he looked extraordinarily fit.

"So the wizard Silyon said, Waldron," Royhas snapped. "I don't trust that Dalopo savage any more than you do; but since he was right about Master Garric's appearance, I think we have to assume he knew something about the gentleman's provenance as well."

There was no love lost between these two men. Garric supposed that was an advantage, since he could stand as the keystone between their competing pressures, but he didn't imagine it would make his coming tasks more pleasant.

The plump man in green pulled out a chair and sat. "If we fight among ourselves," he said, "the queen won't have to waste effort hanging us, will she?"

He spoke with a wheeze. To Garric he seemed more peevish than frightened.

Royhas smiled tightly and nodded to the seated man, "Lord Tadai bor-Tithain," he said, "and—"

He gestured to the last man, a haggard fellow who looked as though a cancer were eating his bowels.

"—Lord Pitre bor-Piamonas. You've met Waldron and Sourous already, Master Garric."

"We'll all hang," Sourous muttered. "Or worse, who knows what that she-demon will do to us? What if one of her fire wraiths appears here right now?"

''What happens if the sun goes out right now?'' Waldron said without trying to hide his disgust. He shook his head. ''Your father and I had our differences, Sourous, but at least I never doubted that I had a man to deal with!''

Tadai wheezed with laughter. ''What did I say?'' he remarked to the air. ''We should hire ourselves out as buffoons for the Feast of the Lady's Veil.''

''I was explaining to our friend from Haft,'' Royhas said, rechanneling the discussion with a skill that Garric could appreciate, ''that the danger isn't simply from the queen's hirelings. When she wants to replace the proper officials with her own men, she sends a phantasm with them.''

''They can't do any real harm,'' Waldron said in irritation. ''They're uncanny, I grant, but nothing that should make a brave man leave his place.''

''Perhaps King Valence should hire only men with the courage of a bor-Walliman to collect his port dues,'' Sourous said, his face turned toward the wall. Waldron's hand twitched in the direction of his sword hilt, then checked. The motion was so slight that Garric wouldn't have noticed it without his ancestor reading the tiny cues.

''What do you mean by a phantasm?'' Garric said, doing his part to keep the conspiracy from flying apart in mutual insults. If King Valence wanted his life—and there was no reason to doubt Royhas' claim—these men were the best chance Garric and his friends had of surviving for more than the next few hours. ''Ghosts?''

Tadai glanced up with the first real interest he'd given anything except his perfect, almond-shaped fingernails. ''Demons, I would rather say,'' he said, ''but only in appearance. As Waldron notes, they don't do anything except look ugly. I might say the same about my wife . . . and unlike my Trinka, the queen's little friends don't bring a dowry of ten thousand acres.''

''People who've faced them say the phantasms remind them of things,'' Royhas said. He flashed the bitter ghost of a smile. "They don't say what memories are involved, but one can make some assumptions from the fact the witnesses refuse to discuss them. I have more sympathy for those who don't choose to resist the queen's hirelings than Waldron does."

"And there's the fire wraiths," Pitre muttered. He'd taken a spherical limewood puzzle from his purse and was rotating it between his hands. "*They're* not harmless!"

"Fagh!" Waldron said. "How many times have they been seen? Four times? Five? In almost a year!"

"Once has always been enough, hasn't it?" Tadai said, looking up from his nails again with an expression of polite inquiry. "For the victim, at least; which seems to me good reason why there've been so few victims. The five of *us* have certainly chosen to conceal our opposition to the queen."

Garric glanced at Royhas. Royhas nodded and said, "They—or that, there's never been more than one fire wraith seen at a time—appear near someone who's been opposing the queen in a particularly open fashion. The first was a gang boss named Erengo who was raising a mob to attack the queen's mansion. I dare say he expected to get particularly rich from the loot, once a few hundred cattle from the slums had broken down the defenses."

Pitre tittered. "He should have hired himself to the queen instead," he said. "His sort's where she gets most of her servants."

"Erengo may have come to that conclusion in his last moments," Royhas said grimly. "He hadn't made any secret about his plans, though he'd intended to be some distance from the actual event. A thing like a fiery lizard on its hind legs appeared out of the air. His bodyguards attacked it with no effect—"

"No useful effect," Tadai said sardonically. "I gather it made quite a colorful display."

Waldron looked down at the seated man with a cold expression and a tightness in his sword arm. Tadai folded his hands in his lap, pursing his lips slightly.

Garric guessed it would take a great deal of irritation before Waldron lost his temper enough to physically attack a coconspirator. It was a silly risk to take for no purpose, though, and this business already involved risk aplenty.

"The fire wraith put its arms around Erengo's neck," Royhas continued. "It burned him to a blob of greasy ash. Then the wraith vanished again."

"The common herd would follow King Valence if he'd just lead them!" Pitre said, hunched over his puzzle. His fingers were recombining the separated pieces into a sphere. "Everyone hates the queen, even the scum who work for her."

"And Silyon could protect King Valence!" Sourous said, sounding like a child in his eagerness to believe what he hoped was true. "After all, the queen would have disposed of *him* if he weren't protected, wouldn't she?"

Tenoctris might be able to answer that question. Garric couldn't, but he knew that there were fights that you avoided as long as possible even if you thought you could win them. That might be why the queen hadn't attacked Valence directly—and it was even more likely that Valence *feared* that was why the queen had held back.

"My colleagues and I are loyal subjects of King Valence," Royhas said with a tinge of irony. "We've been forced to consider alternative ways to preserve the kingdom—"

Through Garric's mind ran the thought *Their part of the kingdom.* He grinned wryly.

"—and when Valence told me to dispose of the would-be usurper I'd find in the grounds of the Tyrants' palace, the possibility of a way forward occurred to us."

"So you claim to be Countess Tera's heir, boy?" Tadai asked. He was no more supercilious to Garric than he was to his fellow nobles; but Garric *wasn't* one of Tadai's fellow nobles.

Garric placed his left hand flat on the table and leaned onto it, bringing his face closer to Tadai's. "I'm a free citizen of Haft, fat man,'' he said pleasantly. ''And my lineage goes back to Carus, though the place where you'd find the proof of that isn't one you'd return from—even if you could get there.''

In Garric's memory, a black throne rose from a black plain into a black sky: the Throne of Malkar, the source of all evil and of universal power. Lorcan, the first King of the Isles, had hidden the throne where only his descendants could find it . . . as Garric had found it, in a nightmare whose illusions were real enough to kill the soul.

Tadai said nothing. He drew a handkerchief of green and black silk from his left sleeve and wiped his forehead. His hair was so fair that in brighter light he would seem to be bald.

Pitre flung down the bits of his puzzle. ''Where did he come from?'' he said to Royhas. ''May the Lady shield me! This isn't the bumpkin from a sheepwalk you told us you were bringing!''

''He's the man Valence told me to watch for!'' Royhas said. ''The name was right, the age was right. We've never doubted Silyon was a powerful wizard, have we? He was right!''

''I think . . .'' said Tadai. He carefully folded the handkerchief away as everyone watched him.

''I think Valence was right to fear that this youth could usurp his throne—with the right backing,'' he continued. Tadai's tone was still light, but the mockery was gone. ''And I think we were right, gentlemen—''

He looked around the taut faces of his fellows.

''—to believe that he could rouse the populace against the queen in a directed fashion, as Valence will not.''

Garric's legs were wobbly, but it was probably because of Carus that he chose to pull out the chair in front of him and sit. They had to break the tension. This last exchange had sent the nobles' minds spinning in more directions than there were men in the room.

''Talk to me like a peasant from Haft who doesn't

know anything about the queen and why King Valence married her,'' Garric said calmly. He gestured the others to seats with an assurance that made him marvel—but they all obeyed, even Royhas, whose house it was. ''But I can start by saying that I have no designs on the throne of the Isles so long as Valence is on it.''

He grinned. ''I'm a loyal citizen too, albeit Valence seems to have been misinformed on the matter.''

Garric's grammar and diction were as good as those of any man in the Isles. Reise had seen to that, with a fierce determination that no paid schoolmaster could have matched. Still, his voice had a lilt that would always set him apart from the clipped accents of Ornifal or a Sandrakkan burr. That was as surely a mark of Haft today as it had been in the time of King Carus.

''The princess Azalais was the daughter of the King of Sirimat,'' Pitre said. Garric had expected Tadai or Royhas to take up the story. ''Valence had just fought the Earl of Sandrakkan for the throne—''

''For the title,'' Waldron spat. ''It could have been a real throne if he'd been a real man.''

Pitre's eyes surveyed the floor during the interruption, looking for the pieces of his puzzle. The bits of pale wood were hopelessly concealed among the black and white tesserae of the mosaic.

Waldron grimaced. ''Go on,'' he said to Pitre. To Garric he added, ''Pitre was there.''

''Valence and I were great friends at one time,'' Pitre said softly, toward the stones of the flooring. He continued, ''He needed to marry because unless there was a clear succession there was a certainty of more trouble from men who were positioning themselves for the future. Rather than a wife from one of the great houses of Ornifal—''

''Which would have made all the other nobles his enemies,'' Tadai said. Garric already understood that, from reading history and from Carus' own vivid recollections.

''—Valence accepted the offer from Sirimat, quite outside the struggles for power over the past millennium,'' Pitre continued. ''Azalais brought an enormous dowry, and she was strikingly beautiful besides.''

A pale smile flickered over Pitre's lips. ''Not that her beauty was a matter of great concern,'' he said. ''Nor that Valence saw much more of it than any other wedding guest did, as matters worked out. Certainly there are no offspring.''

''She was a wizard,'' Waldron said. ''She used wizardry to get Valence to marry her.''

Pitre shrugged. ''Perhaps,'' he said, ''but not all bad decisions come from wizard's work. At the time some of us thought it was quite a brilliant way out of the tangle of Ornifal nobles struggling for advantage.''

''My niece—'' Waldron said. He stopped when he saw the broad, hard grin Royhas was giving him. Sourous tittered nervously. Waldron slammed the edge of his fist into the wall, shaking the candle.

Garric nodded to show that he understood what he'd been told. ''The first task is to remove the queen's people from the government of Valles,'' he said. He smiled faintly and went on, ''I don't see how that can be done without me winding up the way Erengo did, but as tired as I am I'm doing well to see the table.''

He patted it. The smooth wood felt good beneath his fingers.

''One of my friends will have some ideas,'' he said. ''Both of them, I shouldn't wonder.''

Liane had lived in Valles as a wealthy outsider. Her experience might provide insights that the conspirators missed simply by being too close to the problem.

''We have a plan—'' Royhas said.

Garric stood, feeling his head spin at the sudden movement. He needed food, and he particularly needed sleep.

''Not now,'' he said. ''I want to be able to go over matters with a clear head and with my companions present to advise me. It may be that planning you've done in my absence will have to be modified now that you've met me in person."

Now that you know I'm not going to get burned alive by a fire wraith if there's another way to defeat evil, he thought but did not add.

"Kings die, just as other men," whispered a voice in Garric's weary mind. *"And sometimes a king dies that his people may live."*

Garric smiled, though the nobles facing him wouldn't have understood the reason. Wouldn't have agreed either, he guessed.

The conspirators looked at one another. Royhas nodded curtly and said, "Yes, all right. I'll have Maurunus put you in my private suite on the top floor. And your companions, if they've turned up."

Pitre bent and picked up a piece of his puzzle, then placed it on the black wood of the table with an unfathomable expression. "Call us when you're prepared to act," he said to Royhas.

"With a real leader instead of Valence," Waldron said harshly, "the Kingdom of the Isles could be very different. We could return to a Golden Age as it was during the Old Kingdom."

He strode to the door, the first to leave as he had been the first to arrive. Garric had noticed that Waldron said "a real leader" instead of "a real king."

Through the waves of fatigue filling Garric's mind, a voice murmured, *"The Golden Age they dream of looked a lot like this one when I was living in it; and it'll take some work to keep this age from going the same way mine did. But we'll manage."*

Ilna supposed she must have been unconscious. She came awake prickling as though someone had filled her skin with live coals. It took a moment for her to realize that the buzzing she heard wasn't the sound of blood in her ears but rather Scaled Men chanting. Their voices rasped like those of mating toads, harsh and insistent.

Ilna could see again, though her head throbbed and slow ripples drifted across the field of her vision. The pain brought on nausea. She fought down the surge of vomit, but it burned the back of her throat before it subsided.

The six Scaled Men squatted in a circle on the afterdeck. In their midst was a small pot buried in a tray of sand. It was the sort of simple brazier used on shipboard to keep live coals without risk to the vessel. They'd brought it out of the small aftercabin where the tray was normally pinned between frames.

The ship rocked in a sluggish current. The yard was raised with the sail furled about it. Ilna couldn't see over the gunwale, but an owl calling in the darkness indicated they were still within the river's winding course.

A Scaled Man wearing a headband of red and green silk pinched powder from an alabaster jar and threw it onto the fire. Purple smoke rose, as luminous as the throbbing afterimages caused by looking directly at the sun.

The creature added more powder as his fellows chanted. Though the powder came from the same container, the second plume was as orange as a fire's heart.

The Scaled Men chanted louder. Rising to their feet and joining hands, they began a grotesque step-dance circling the brazier.

Instead of dissipating, the plumes wove together like breeding serpents. The colored elements remained distinct in the merged column. It rotated sunwise, opposite to the dancers' motion.

The column began to swell, losing definition. The vessel shuddered. Ilna thought they must have gone aground, but she could tell by the motion of stars against the ship's mast that they were still moving. Her flesh tingled, much as it had in the moment when she'd regained consciousness.

Thin smoke enveloped the ship. Ilna sneezed at the dry, astringent odor, but it wasn't anything she would have described as unpleasant.

In the glowing mist the Scaled Men continued to circle, raising and lowering their arms as they stepped to the rhythm of their chanting. Ilna could still see a few bright stars above her.

The ship yawed. The motion had a greasy feel, like stepping on a flagstone coated with black ice. Ilna thought they were capsizing. She tried to sit up, but her wrists and ankles were tied behind her back. She managed to twist to where she could see through a scuttle, though nothing was visible except the haze.

A wave of distortion shimmered through the sky. Something cold as a knifeblade touched Ilna's marrow, then vanished before she could tense for the scream she would never have uttered.

The fog was gone. The hull rocked gently. The cloudless sky had an odd twilight appearance. None of the many stars were in constellations that Ilna recognized.

Muttering among themselves, the Scaled Men loosed the sail with a rattle of blocks. They worked expertly, sailors in all truth as well as in their manner of dress.

Ilna didn't feel a wind. Another pair shook out the small triangular sail on the foremast. It too expanded in the unfelt breeze.

The sea was faintly phosphorescent. The light had color, but it was so pale that not even Ilna's trained senses could be certain whether she saw green or yellow.

Spikes of rock stuck out of the calm sea. Some towered hundreds of feet in the air; others were little more than fangs, black exclamations against the luminous water. The tallest were flat-topped and looked like the metal nails which saw only occasional use in Barca's Hamlet, where wooden tenons served their place.

The ship got under way with a smooth motion that the gusty turbulence of a normal breeze could never impart. Froth curled around the cutwater, drawing eddies in the patch of surface Ilna could see through the scuttle.

The Scaled Man at the steering oar began to sing. His voice was the same shrill toad-croak as the chanting had been. The words weren't meant for any human throat.

The ship slid onward, carrying Ilna through the twilight. She was tied too tightly for her fingers to find purchase on the ropes, but by slacking and tensing individual muscles she was able to affect the knots minusculely.

Everything had a pattern. Eventually Ilna would find the pattern that would free her. What would happen then depended on circumstances, but the image in her mind involved six nooses slowly tightening.

The 21st of Heron

The causeway was corduroyed, but the logs had rotted so badly that at each step Cashel's feet crunched through after a momentary hesitation. It was as bad as walking on a snowdrift. The bark, like a snowcrust, gouged at Cashel's legs as he withdrew them for the next step. His shins were bleeding.

"Oh, Mistress God, thank You!" Aria cried, raising her hands sky-ward in joy. "Oh, please forgive me for taking so long to understand Your plan!"

The princess and Zahag were light enough to walk on the logs so long as Cashel's weight hadn't smashed them to pulp and splinters first. Cashel had made them go ahead of him ever since the path turned into this causeway across a slough. Aria kept drawing back. Cashel had already decided that he was going to prod her the next time she stopped, and he wasn't going to be overly delicate about *where* he prodded her.

This transport of joy was about as unlikely as Aria sprouting wings. Instead of extending the quarterstaff, Cashel said, "Understand what, mistress? And try to keep moving, please."

Aria turned and threw her arms around Cashel's neck. "I understand that you're testing me, silly! Like Patient Muzira!"

"There's not been enough sun for it to be sunstroke," Zahag called down. "My guess is that one of the bugs bit her and she's delirious."

The ape was searching for eggs in the nest in an upper fork of a tree growing out of the slough twenty paces ahead. Or beetles, Cashel supposed; Zahag wasn't a particularly delicate feeder.

Cashel carefully detached Aria. Zahag's guess about why the princess was behaving this way seemed likely enough, but there weren't any swellings or hectic spots on her skin that Cashel could see.

"Let's keep walking," he said in a neutral voice. He made a little shooing motion with his left hand.

"Of course, Master Cashel," Aria said. She attempted a delicate curtsy. Her right foot was on a log that had already crumbled under Cashel's weight. The rim of bark gave way as the princess bent forward; her leg plunged into wood pulp, swamp water, and the insects that thought a mush like that was a *great* place to live.

Aria's expression went from shock through fury—to a bright smile that wasn't entirely forced. Cashel was amazed to see how she took the mishap, though he kept his own face blank. He lifted the girl out so that she wouldn't scratch her leg as well as covering it with muck.

"Of course, Mistress God," Aria said to the dull blue sky. "I understand that the test must go on longer."

She patted Cashel on the cheek—for a horrified instant he'd thought she was going to kiss him—and danced on off down the causeway. Shaking his head, Cashel resumed crunching his way along behind her.

Something belched in the stagnant water. Cashel glanced toward the sound. In a normal swamp it would have been a bubble of foul-smelling gas bursting to leave ripples and a flag of mud in the water. Here he stared back at a creature with human arms and its head and body all together, like a face drawn on an egg. It picked its triangular teeth with a fingernail, grinning like a human after a satisfying meal.

Cashel sighed. There wasn't any law against being ugly, especially here. If the thing crawled up the causeway at them, Cashel would see if it smashed like the egg it resembled. None of the other monsters in the water had attacked, though, so he didn't expect his one would.

Zahag hopped from the tree and ambled to Cashel's side. His jaws worked on the last of whatever he'd found in the nest. The ape was their forager. He had a better eye for potential food than Cashel, and several times his broad, flat nose detected poison in fruits and mushrooms. Zahag made sure to gulp down particularly tasty bits before he brought the remainder to be divided.

That was fair. The ape's idea of "particularly tasty" wasn't Cashel's, and offering Aria her choice of—for example—a handful of grubs would give her dry heaves for the rest of the day.

"Have you got a good look at the bugs here?" Zahag asked. He eyed a miniature squadron buzzing low enough over the marsh to riffle the black water.

"Yes," said Cashel. He didn't want to talk about it. They weren't insects, though a number had lacy wings or jointed legs like the bugs in Barca's Hamlet. Some of them had riders who looked awfully human, except they were about the size of a fingernail.

"They're quick," Zahag said, "but they're not as quick as me!" He smacked his lips with gusto.

Cashel grimaced and stumped onward. The line of smashed logs in his wake stretched all the way to the western horizon. He wondered if anybody repaired the causeway. Somebody'd built it, after all.

"So who's this Patient Muzira that you're testing?" Zahag asked. The ape was walking with a rolling gait on his short hind legs alone. He stayed a half step ahead so that he wouldn't be on the next log when Cashel's foot plopped through it like a battering ram.

"Never heard of her," Cashel said. Garric would probably know, or Sharina. Not that his friends were much like the princess in any way *except* that they'd all read a lot of books.

Aria turned and continued walking—backward. That wasn't the best idea on a corduroy surface, but Cashel wasn't going to complain so long as the girl kept moving. She could turn somersaults if she liked.

"Patient Muzira was the most perfect lady ever," Aria said. Her face shone with animation. "She was so perfect that the greatest king in all the land decided to marry her, but first he carried her off and treated her like a slave. He made her sleep on the ground and gave her only—"

Aria missed a step and toppled backward. Cashel stuck his staff out for the girl to grab, but she didn't know to do that. She landed on her back with a thump. Water spurted from the soggy logs.

"Eek!" she cried.

Cashel leaned forward and set her on her feet again. The good thing about Aria's dress being so filthy was that at least he didn't have to listen to a rant about this latest stain.

"My, wasn't that clumsy of me?" Aria said. She tittered a laugh. It sounded as false as the stories Katchin the Miller, Cashel's uncle, used to tell about his private dinners with Count Lascarg when he went to Carcosa.

Zahag stared at her, then looked at Cashel. Cashel shrugged.

"Anyway," Aria resumed, "the king made Muzira scrub all the floors of the palace and didn't give her anything to eat except lentils with worms in them."

"Yeah, that's a nice thing about lentils," Zahag said reminiscently. "A lot of times you get your meat right along with your vegetable."

"And after seven whole years," Aria said, ignoring the comment or perhaps blessedly unaware of it, "the king called Muzira out in front of all the people and ordered her to kiss his feet before he beat her in public with a horsewhip. She did, and then he told her all the discomfort had been a test to see if she was worthy to be her bride. She'd passed, so he married her right then and made her queen!''

''That's disgusting!'' Cashel said. There were bad husbands in Barca's Hamlet—more than there were good ones, if you listened to Ilna; not that she had any use for the wives either—but the sort of behavior Aria chirpily described was unimaginable. Even the biggest drunken brute had to sleep sometime, though the odds were that a few of the huskier men in the borough would have taught the fellow a lesson before then. In a rural village, everybody's business *was* everybody's business.

Aria started walking again. ''I wonder, though, Master Cashel?'' she said, this time without turning to look at him. ''You aren't the king yourself, are you? You're his faithful servant.''

Cashel cleared his throat. ''I'm a shepherd,'' he said. ''I don't know any kings, Princess. Well, your mother's a queen, sort of, I guess.''

''I understand,'' Aria said. ''You can't say. Well, I won't tell anybody that I figured it out before it was time.''

''She's doolally, huh?'' Zahag muttered.

Cashel shrugged again. ''Seems that way, I guess,'' he said.

Boy, he'd take it, though. Aria crazy was a lot nicer to be around than she was in her right mind.

In the far distance, the sun glinted on the peaks of high mountains. Last night Cashel thought he'd seen blue light winking from that direction. He didn't know how far it was, but he guessed they'd make it eventually.

He plodded on with a crunch/*squelch* at every step.

Eventually. Which was good enough.

A bird in the canopy trilled variations around a central theme as Sharina sharpened the Pewle knife. It never repeated itself and never—it seemed to her—took a breath.

Sharina drew the blade across a block of fine-grained basalt from the creek, edge toward her, in long, smooth strokes. She paused as she reached for the dampened wad of moss she used to keep the stone's surface wet. It struck Sharina that in this forest she couldn't be sure that what she was hearing was really a bird.

Haft was a backwater, and Barca's Hamlet was isolated from even the minor alarms and excursions that took place in Carcosa. Life in the borough went on much as it had done for centuries. Individuals were born and died, but the round of activities stayed much the same.

Now Sharina was out in the wider world where things were different to begin with and were changing besides. She couldn't *assume* things the way she had in the past. She might get killed by doing that—and worse, she might fail the ones she loved and who depended on her.

She'd assumed that a man who looked and sounded like Nonnus had to be Nonnus. She'd stopped searching for Cashel in order to follow the impostor.

Sharina felt the tears start. *Oh Lady, I am so alone. I am so alone.*

Nothing that she could have described changed, but Sharina knew suddenly that she was being watched. That wasn't the sort of companionship she'd been hoping for, but it gave her something to do besides cry about the past.

Sharina got up from where she'd been working in the patch of sunlight that fell near Ansule's grave. Wiping the knife's blade on fluff she'd pulled from a large seed case, she walked nonchalantly past the headboard she'd carved with a figure of the Lady.

The path to Hanno's tree nest wasn't really marked, but the hunter had cut a few rhododendron stems off flush with the ground. The remainder of the thicket twined dark leaves and sweet magenta flowers above the tunnel, but a human could easily pass through what would otherwise have been a solid barrier.

Sharina ducked into the rhododendrons. She crawled

halfway down the passage, then hunched out of sight in the nook she'd made before going to sleep the night before. Those watching her would have to come through the thicket one by one, and the leader would be almost on the point of the Pewle knife before he realized—

Someone was behind her.

Sharina twisted. She'd thought the rhododendrons were impenetrable, but the bulk among the twisted stems proved that she'd been fatally—

"Morning, missie," Hanno said. He was belly to the ground. "I thought I'd surprise you since you hadn't listened when I told you to shimmy up the tree. Guess I been so used to the Monkeys that I forgot there's folks beside me who know what they're doing in these woods."

She couldn't imagine how a man so big had wormed through the thicket, but even Hanno had had to leave his great spear behind. To reach her with his butcher knife would require that he crawl closer yet; in the time that took, Sharina could have run out the open passage to freedom of a sort.

"I didn't know it was you," Sharina said in a shaky voice. "I'm glad you're back, Hanno."

She nodded to the passage, then backed down it to the clearing. The hunter joined her moments later. She hadn't heard the leaves rustle this time either.

Hanno glanced at the graves and the whetstone; he smiled with grim approval. He looked much as he had when he vanished into the forest two days ago, but he carried a set of steel weapons besides his own: a slender-bladed spear, and a short-hafted axe with a head whose smooth curve made it a thing of lethal beauty. Because the helve balanced the light head, the axe could be either thrown or swung.

"Ansule don't need his gear now," Hanno said with the deadpan humor Sharina already knew to expect, "but I didn't figure to leave it with the Monkeys."

He tossed down a crude bag. He hadn't been carrying

that when he left either. "Not that the Monkeys needed it neither, when I left them."

Sharina bit her lower lip. She knew what she was going to find, but she squatted to open the bag anyway. It was a swatch of knobbly rawhide which she supposed must have come from a reptile. The corners had been twisted over the contents, then bound with a length of sinew.

The sinew was probably human.

"I see you dug the pot out of the cabin," Hanno said conversationally. "That's good, though I guess we could boil these clean in the little pan that's still down in the boat."

Sharina had found a five-gallon bronze kettle in the ashes, twisted but not split when the cabin's roof collapsed. She'd hammered out the worst of the dents with lengths of wood as punch and mallet, then filled the container with water and put it on a low fire.

She opened the bag. It held eyeteeth, about thirty sets of them. The roots were still red with the flesh from which they'd been ripped a few hours earlier. Sharina's rush of nausea wasn't a reaction to the stench, but the stench was bad enough.

"They was heading straight away from here," the hunter said. "Never saw Monkeys act like that before. Mostly they wander all over the landscape."

Sharina stood up. "They're not Monkeys," she said in a clear voice. "They're men. Human beings!"

Hanno shrugged. "All right, missie," he said. His voice was calm, but beneath that surface he was as tense as Sharina herself. "They're men. Who burned my cabin and ate my partner before they moved on."

"Some of them were children!" Sharina said.

"Every one of them that was weaned to solid food is right there!" Hanno said, pointing to the bag of teeth. "The baby ones, well, they're with their mothers but I didn't take the teeth. There's no Monkey going to grow up to tell the rest how good a human being tastes!"

Sharina took a deep breath and turned away. She didn't

know what was right. She knew what was right for her, but she hadn't lived in this jungle.

If the body had been hers, not Ansule's . . . what would Nonnus have done to the band who killed and ate her?

She unbuckled her belt and knife and set them on the ground. She walked to the grave's headboard with tear-blind eyes and knelt. "Lady, guide me in Your ways," she whispered. "Lady, forgive me for the wrongs I do others, and forgive others for the wrongs they do for my sake."

"I don't take the teeth normal times," Hanno said behind her. His voice was thick with embarrassment. "There's a good market for them in Valles, they sell them on to the Serians to grind up for medicine, but not me. Only, for Ansule, I figured I ought to do something special. Guess I'll string the lot and hang them on his grave."

"No," Sharina said. She stood and turned to face the big hunter. She was no longer crying; she wiped her cheeks with her fingers unself-consciously. "Or do—I won't tell you how to remember your friend. But first take the Lady away. She has no part of that sort of thing."

Hanno frowned, in concentration rather than disagreement. He knelt beside the cairn and ran his finger over the headboard. Sharina had stained the fresh, white wood with the juice of nut hulls, then used the point of the Pewle knife to carve the Lady's outline.

"A pretty piece of work, missie," he said to the eucalyptus wood.

"Thank you," Sharina said tightly. The grave marker was simple and wouldn't last long in this climate, but she too thought it was surprisingly attractive.

Hanno stood and shrugged. "Guess we'll leave things stay the way they are," he said. He picked up the piece of hide, carried it to the trench where Hairy Men lay, and spilled the raw teeth onto the dirt.

"Thank you, Hanno," Sharina said. She paused, then stepped over to the hunter and hugged him. Both of them kept their faces resolutely turned away from the other. As they parted Sharina added, "I'm sorry about your friend."

"I never thought Ansule was careful enough," Hanno said. He coughed to clear his throat. "I figured it'd be one of the hunting lizards got him, though, not a Monkey. He'd go after them with this toy—"

He'd butted the spears in the soil when he knelt at the grave. He plucked Ansule's out, balancing it in his right palm. Only to a man like Hanno could the other hunter's seven-foot spear be considered a toy, though it weighed barely half what his own broad-bladed weapon did.

"—and I tell you, missie, some of them big lizards take a right lot of killing."

Hanno gazed reflectively at the spear, then back to Sharina. "Do you want Ansule's gear, missie?" he asked. "I don't figure to pack it back to his kin—and anyhow, they didn't bury him."

"The spear's too big for me," Sharina said. That she might have need for weapons for as long as she stayed on Bight was beyond question. "As for the axe, I think my knife will do me. My friend's knife."

The hunter nodded noncommittally. He set the spear-shaft across the eucalyptus stump, then struck it a foot from the butt with Ansule's axe. Sharina could see that Hanno's blow was delicate for him, but a chip sailed up from the seasoned hickory. He rotated the shaft and chopped cleanly through from the opposite side.

Displaying the shortened weapon to Sharina he said, "Like this? Or another hand's breadth off? I'll fit the butt spike once I've rubbed away the wood whiskers."

"It should do very well as it is now," Sharina said. The offhand strokes had been as precise as the movements of the stars. Hanno's strength was perhaps less amazing than the way he controlled that strength.

"Guess I'll keep the axe myself," he said judiciously. He slid the helve under his belt. "I'm like you, missie, I'd sooner use a knife for the close work, but I guess Ansule'd like to know it had a good home. Set great store by this axe, he did."

"I brought a peck of grain up from the boat," Sharina said awkwardly. "Would you like me to fix ash cakes? Or porridge?"

She wasn't such a fool as to doubt that Hanno cared about his friend's death despite the nonchalant way he discussed it, but she didn't know how to respond. She supposed it was best to ignore the matter and let Hanno deal with his grief in the way he chose.

"Ash cakes would be a treat!" the hunter said. "I'll see if I can find us some meat for one meal, at least. And we can decide what we do next."

He squatted, rubbing the shortened spearbutt against the side of Sharina's whetstone. He worked absently, keeping his hands busy while his mind was elsewhere.

"I don't know what's happening since I've been gone to Valles," Hanno said. "Ansule maybe wasn't so careful as me, but he'd been here five years. I'd never have thought Monkeys would get him the way they did."

He bobbed his bushy beard toward the surrounding forest. "They crawled up in the night and laid around the clearing, waiting for him to come out in the morning. If they'd charged the cabin straight, the door and walls would've held them till Ansule was good 'n' ready to come out. Chances are he'd have cut his way through."

Hanno looked at the grave and shook his head. "He was a quick little fellow, I swear he was."

"Is it unusual for them to attack hunters?" Sharina asked, showing that she was interested. The fact that there was a trade in the Hairy Men's eyeteeth suggested that hunters on Bight regarded them more as prey than as enemies.

Hanno shrugged. "It can happen," he said. "But you can have a limb drop on your head, too, and that's more of a reason to worry. Anyway, even if they wanted to, they couldn't think far enough ahead to lay up for Ansule like that. Only they did."

He rose and tossed Sharina the spear. "You going to be all right while I find us a lizard?" he asked.

"Yes," she said.

Hanno nodded. "Figured you would," he said. He looked around the green wall of jungle that surrounded the clearing. "I ought to talk to some of the other fellows who hunt this end of the island and see what they've got to say. I'll sleep here, and then maybe the next few days I'll spend visiting."

He grinned. "That's if there's anybody alive to visit, I mean," he said.

Sharina grinned back at him, though there was a knot in her stomach. "I'll get some more headboards ready," she said. "In case there aren't."

"Are you sure you're ready for this, Tenoctris?" asked Liane as she carried the silver serving dish onto the roof garden. Royhas hadn't objected to the old wizard scribing symbols of power around the platter's rim so that she could use it in her incantation.

Garric set a small intarsia-topped table between a miniature fig and a planter in which narcissi were already blooming. He shivered. Royhas' town house was taller by half a story—the extra height of the third-floor banquet room—than the buildings around it, but the servants had strung the sunscreen of saffron-hued canvas overhead as well. The cool spring afternoon wouldn't usually have required the cover.

Garric supposed the caution was reasonable. The chill in his bones didn't have much to do with the weather anyway, and sunlight wouldn't have warmed it.

"I believe I've recovered well enough for a simple scrying ceremony," Tenoctris said as she seated herself on the curving bench that faced the table. She looked at her companions with a faint smile. "And I certainly believe that we have less time than I would wish."

Liane swallowed. She placed the dish in the center of the low table. *Almost* the center of the table: Liane hadn't been raised by an innkeeper who expected perfection.

Garric grinned, his bleak mood broken. He sat across from Tenoctris, leaving room for Liane to sit between them.

The platter was polished to a smooth luster. Garric saw Tenoctris reflected in it. Beyond her was the garden wall, topped with a trough from which ivy spilled down the building's façade.

Tenoctris touched the cool metal. "Silver should prevent the queen from coming to us through my spell," she said, "unless her wizardry's of a more benign form than I expect."

She looked at her companions, her smile fading to an expression of quiet concern. "I won't need your help with the incantation," she said, "but I can't be sure that I'll remember what the silver shows. I hope you'll be able to help there."

"We're fine," Garric said heartily. "You do the hard part and we'll sit here and watch."

Tenoctris was talking to put off the task a few moments longer. Garric didn't think the old woman was afraid. Tenoctris had said she didn't care about her life or her body, and Garric had never seen any sign that the words were false; but she was very weary from the trek along the shining road to here. He knew that he found it easier to face danger than to return again and again to a grinding task that wouldn't be finished any time soon.

Tenoctris grinned. *"Sasskib,"* she said, turning the platter with her index finger. The smooth metal rotated easily on the smooth wood. *"Kabbib sady knebir."*

Garric was afraid. Since the incantation in the First Place of the Ersa, he knew firsthand of the things that waited at the fringes of the paths between the planes. Somewhere that Garric couldn't see, a female of pearly light waited for him. Tenoctris was a careful craftsman; she didn't leap into darkness hoping for a good result. Even so, this spell might open the waking world to the force whose Hand had formed the Gulf.

Liane feared the same thing. She sat with her fists

clenched beside her. When Garric touched her she linked fingers with him fiercely.

"Sawadry maryray anoquop," Tenoctris said. She lifted her finger from the platter's rim but the silver disk continued to revolve. *"Anes paseps kiboybey."*

Royhas had provided everything Garric asked for, including a valuable dish to be scratched into a magic mirror. Neither he nor any of the other conspirators wanted to be present at the scrying, though; and only very senior servants, Maurunus and two others, were aware that Garric and his companions were in the house.

The guards knew, though; and the huntsman. Word would get out one way or another. If Silyon could predict the trio's appearance in the palace ruins, he could surely find them again if he turned his art to it.

"Banwar!" Tenoctris said. The dish spun faster, too fast for anyone to read the letters scribed around its rim. *"Nakyar nakyar yah!"*

The silver dish was a blur. In it—*through* it—Garric saw the queen, a coldly beautiful woman, standing in a gown of rainbow silk before a slab of polished tourmaline. The crystal staff in her hand glittered. Around the tableau, words of power were set as a circular mosaic in the floor.

Tenoctris continued to mouth her incantation. The image held Garric the way a weasel holds a rat.

The queen was chanting also. No sound passed to Garric's side of the silver dish, but he felt the rhythms. It was their compulsion rather than his own desire which forced him to watch the scene.

The queen raised her staff of flashing crystal. As if severed by its stroke, a ghastly image drifted from her body. The thing had the features of a demon. Its body was gray, and its eyes were yellow hellfire.

The queen continued to chant, tapping the air with her wand. Beyond the circle was a columnar table. On it Garric sometimes thought he saw a chessboard, but the image wasn't clear. Another phantasm shivered away from the woman, penetrating the chamber's wall unhindered.

A third phantasm separated and passed from the field of polished silver. The queen stood, imperious and cold, but her flesh was losing definition as each avatar sprang from her substance. Tenoctris' voice had dropped to a murmur.

"In the mirror," Liane whispered. She was struggling vainly to stand. "Look in the stone mirror."

Garric forced himself to rise. He stepped over the bench, moving clumsily because he was unable to look away from the spinning platter. When he stood behind Tenoctris, he looked into the mirror just as the queen herself did.

Tenoctris gave a sigh. She rubbed her eyes, looking dazed. The platter wobbled from the table and clanged onto the stone flags of the roof garden. Though the silver continued to quiver with one pure tone and a dozen harmonics, the images vanished as soon as Tenoctris ceased intoning the words of power.

The old woman toppled forward, asleep or unconscious. Garric caught her by the shoulders to keep her from cutting her face on the inlaid table.

"Did you see it?" Liane demanded. Garric was swaying also. Only his need to hold Tenoctris kept him from falling over himself. "What did you see in the stone?"

"I didn't see the queen," Garric whispered. "All I saw was a demon. And it was looking at me."

Maidus hadn't cried since the night his mother's current boyfriend beat him almost senseless and he crawled from her door, never to return. He was crying now as he sat, head bowed, on the floor of the room Cerix and Halphemos rented by the day.

"Put my last pellet in wine and give it to him, Halphemos," Cerix said as he concentrated on sewing up the boy's scalp. The club had left a cut a hand's breadth long. It had resumed bleeding profusely as soon as the two wizards sponged away the blood clotted in the coarse, black hair. Without attention, the boy would faint or even die from blood loss.

"He's not crying from the pain," Halphemos said tightly. "I knew I should have gone down to the docks instead of Ilna!"

"Give him the pellet!" Cerix repeated. "It's not only the body's hurt it dulls, boy."

His left thumb and forefinger pinched closed the wound; his right guided the needle through the twin edges of skin. The suture was a thread unraveled from Halphemos' robe. Because the silk was red, the fresh blood soaking it wasn't noticeable.

"You wouldn't know that, Halphemos," the crippled man said as his companion obeyed him. "Be thankful that you don't."

"You're wizards, good masters," Maidus said. He didn't flinch as the needle pricked, then dragged the thread through his skin, but the tears continued to run down his cheeks. "I hated you for taking Mistress Ilna away, but now it's only you who can help. Please bring her back, masters. She's the best thing that ever happened to the Crescent. She's the best thing that ever happened to the world!"

Cerix snorted. Halphemos glanced at him warningly, but Maidus seemed to ignore everything but his own misery.

"And as for negotiating in Ilna's place . . . ," Cerix said as his fingers worked. He'd lived for twenty years as a traveling entertainer; first aid was one of the skills that had kept him alive during that time. "Even if it weren't her own money involved, she'd think you were mad to suggest you could get a better deal than she would. As for her safety, I dare say she's in less danger now than whatever it is that captured her."

Cerix pulled the needle off the end of the thread. "All right," he said. "You can take a drink before I knot it."

Maidus straightened and took the drugged wine. He swallowed it in three convulsive gulps. Breathing hard, he looked from one man to the other. "But can she come back?" he asked. "Can you bring her *back*?"

The cripple's hands were trembling; they hadn't been while he stitched the cut. The boy had come to them as soon as he regained consciousness, blurting his story of Mistress Ilna's abduction by scaly monsters. Cerix could close his wound, but for the rest—for the real need that had brought Maidus to them—he was helpless and knew it.

"We have her cloak," Halphemos said brightly. "We can use a location spell, don't you think?"

He picked up the garment that Maidus had been clutching to him. Dried blood crackled from the fabric. The wool was so tightly woven that drips from the boy's scalp hadn't penetrated.

Cerix looked at the box, empty now, where he kept his pellets of anodyne. "The spells we used to locate Ilna before would work again if she were close enough," he said. "With your strength as a wizard we could probably find her anywhere in the Isles, though getting to her is another matter. We don't have the price of the room left."

Or the price of Cerix's drug. He would willingly sleep under a stormy sky if he had half a dozen pellets to soften the spasms of his demon-tortured legs.

"We've earned money before!" Halphemos said. "I don't want to waste time, but we can earn our way to wherever she is. We owe it to her and to her brother."

Cerix didn't know what was owed to anyone. He doubted that Ilna had been taken because of anything he and the boy had done; he doubted even that Halphemos was responsible for casting Cashel out of the waking world.

But he knew that he would have died long since if the boy who owed Cerix *nothing* in Cerix's own terms hadn't cared for a man whose arrogance and stupidity had left him a legless cripple.

"We can earn money, yes," Cerix said. "Enough to take us anywhere in the Isles, I suppose. But if the creatures who took Ilna are what I think they are, she's no longer in the world we walk—"

His mouth quirked at the unintended humor.

"You walk, that is," he said. "And she's not in a place where my knowledge can find her, let alone bring her back."

Halphemos gave the older man a stricken look. "But . . . ," he said. "We have to get her back!"

Maidus had curled up on the floor of the room, sleeping from trauma and exhaustion as much as from the drug. They'd have to get him to the watch captain whom Ilna had appointed his guardian.

A single pellet was a sizable dose for a boy who wasn't used to it. Perhaps they should have given him half or even less. Then Cerix could have—

He laughed harshly at himself. "Yes," he said, "perhaps we do. But I don't know. . . ."

His voice trailed off because he'd noticed the pattern on the cloak in Halphemos' hands when the light of the room's single candle slanted across it. "Stop!" Cerix said. "Don't move."

Halphemos lowered the cloak fractionally. It was an unconscious twitch.

"*Don't* move the cloak!" Cerix said. He shifted the chair on which he sat, then cocked his head so that he could again see what he'd thought was there.

Halphemos stood like a statue. He was used to repeating incantations precisely, though the sounds meant nothing to him. He was calm, waiting for his friend to explain when there was leisure to do so.

Cerix leaned back in his chair. "Put the cloak down on the floor," he said in a soft voice. "Don't fold it, though I doubt it would make any difference. Mistress Ilna doesn't do work that won't stand up."

"The cloak?" Halphemos said as he spread it on the table.

"The fabric was stressed when the Scaled Men pulled

it off her," Cerix said. "Or perhaps she did it herself, I don't know."

He wondered what it would be like to have such power. He couldn't imagine it. All the power Cerix really wanted now was the power to get a large enough supply of pellets to make his pain go away. Perhaps forever. . . .

"Cerix?" Halphemos said.

The cripple smiled at him. "There are symbols in the Old Script in the weave, now," he said. "When the light is right, I can read them. I suppose they'll form an incantation that can lead us to Ilna."

Joy transfigured Halphemos' face. "The Lady has blessed us!" he said. He fell to his knees. "Oh, Cerix, I knew there'd be a way! There had to be!"

"I don't know about the Gods," Cerix said. "I particularly don't know about them having anything to do with Ilna. I think she has more in common with the winds and tides than she does with anything you'd worship."

Halphemos crawled around the spread cloak. He was trying to find the angle that would bring out the writing, not that he could read it. He wasn't listening . . . and that didn't matter, because Cerix knew he'd really been speaking to himself.

To have such *power* . . .

"I'll parse out the symbols," Cerix said wearily. "It'll probably take days, so we'll have to go back on the street tomorrow for the rent money."

Halphemos nodded without looking around. "No more visions of King Valence this time," he said.

"No," Cerix agreed. But he knew now what he'd seen in the globe of red light. An incantation that led him and Halphemos to Ilna would risk bringing them to that Beast in more than image.

Ilna os-Kenset might survive such a meeting. Ordinary humans couldn't possibly do so.

Such power . . .

The 22nd of Heron

Sharina awoke. The rain had stopped. She thought the time was probably closer to dawn than sunset, but the forest canopy concealed the moon and stars so she couldn't be sure.

Hanno slipped out the other side of the leaf-roofed shelter which Sharina had built wide enough for two. The hunter moved soundlessly, though his spear made a soft, sucking motion when he drew its butt from the ground.

Sharina joined him, tensely conscious that her feet squelched on the wet soil. A frog changing position on a leaf made more noise, but it wasn't frogs against which she judged her performance on this night.

A demon of gray light slid into the clearing. It passed through the buttress root of a forest giant. Though the phantasm's legs moved, its feet stepped sometimes over, sometimes under, the surface of the soil.

Its bright yellow eyes were almond-shaped and slanted. They were the only part of the creature that were real.

The phantasm paused. Neither Hanno nor Sharina moved. Sharina had left her own spear inside the shelter; she wasn't used to having it. She slid the Pewle knife from its case of black sealskin and waited.

The creature glowed enough to be visible, but Sharina could see the wrinkled outline of the tree's bark through the elongated torso. A dozen Hairy Men, all males, appeared at the edge of the clearing. They carried unworked stones or lengths of tree limb which had been pounded short to make usable clubs.

The phantasm extended its arms to the side, then swept

them forward in command. The Hairy Men lurched toward the two humans.

"Watch my back!" Hanno said.

The hunter let the leaders reach the creek, then rushed them. Instead of stabbing, he hooked his spear in a broad arc as if he were a reaper using a scythe. He jumped back, leaving a tangle of corpses in the rivulet. Three of the Hairy Men were dead; only one of the trio was long enough about his dying to scream before blood choked his throat.

Hooting with fear, the survivors recoiled from the carnage. Several of them had dropped to all fours in their panic. The heavy blade of Hanno's spear had cut sideways through the ribs of one of the victims, leaving the upper and lower portions of his chest joined only by the spine. The humid air stank of gore and feces.

Hanno drew deep breaths through his open mouth; Sharina panted quickly. Neither of them spoke.

The phantasm swelled and subsided. If smoke could have an expression, it was furious. It gestured the gibbering Hairy Men forward again.

Hanno bellowed. He leaped the creek and brought his spear around in another terrible cut, this time aiming at the shining wraith. The blade sliced the phantasm like water and drove all the way to the shaft in the tree behind.

The trunk shuddered. Hanno grunted with the shock of hitting something too massive for even his great strength to thrust aside. Two Hairy Men leaped toward him.

Sharina stepped forward, raising her knife to chop rather than stab. Hanno caught the club swinging toward him from his left. Simultaneously his right foot lashed out, flinging his other attacker sideways with a broken breastbone. The hunter pulled the club forward and put a hand on the wielder's rib cage. He flailed the Hairy Man against the tree and hopped back.

Hanno's victim slipped down the trunk, every bone in his torso smashed. The great spear still quivered in the living wood. Even a giant like Hanno would need to work the blade back and forth edgewise to free it.

The remaining Hairy Men crouched snarling, but the phantasm's gestures could no longer drive them forward. Sharina used the lull to snatch up her spear. ''Here,'' she said, holding the weapon out so that Hanno could grasp it at the balance.

''Keep it,'' the hunter growled. He slid Ansule's axe from beneath his belt with his right hand and drew one of his long butcher knives with his left.

The phantasm paled and vanished except for its yellow eyes. The Hairy Men mewled in abject fear. One of them pressed his face on the ground and covered his head with both hands.

A corkscrew of fire bloomed in the air where the phantasm had stood. It was the dirty red of burning tar. In a moment the flames had filled a portion of air in the shape of a man.

The fire wraith staggered forward, moving with the stiffness of a stilt-walker. Its extended hands rained blazing droplets.

''Sister drag you down!'' Hanno screamed. He leaped toward the creature, swinging the axe in a stroke so swift it was a glitter rather than a motion. The steel struck the wraith where a human's neck would have joined his shoulders.

The axe head exploded into white sparks. Hanno somersaulted backward. The hairs of his scalp and beard stuck out like the fluff of a ripe dandelion. Half the axe's wooden helve had been blasted into splinters. They burned a cleaner red than the wraith.

The creature moved forward. The wet soil popped and sizzled.

Hanno lay at Sharina's feet. His eyes and mouth were open, and his limbs twitched uncontrollably. The fire wraith hopped over the creek.

Sharina dropped her knife and spear. She lifted the kettle by both handles. Three gallons of water and the bronze container besides made a considerable weight.

The fire wraith reached for Hanno's throat. Sharina threw the kettle into the center of the creature's chest. There was a roar like water hitting boiling oil. Gobbets of flame blew in all directions.

The forest crashed as Hairy Men galloped away in blind terror, colliding with trees and tearing their way through lesser vegetation. Fires winked in a score of places, some of them high in the canopy. Damp foliage would shortly smother the flames.

The fire wraith had vanished. For a moment Sharina thought she saw the phantasm's almond eyes glaring from the empty air; then they were gone as well.

She didn't remember being knocked backward, but she sat on the ground several paces from where she'd been when she flung the kettle. The Pewle knife lay before her. She grabbed it and half-walked, half-crawled to Hanno.

The hunter was moving his arms with volition, but he wasn't strong enough to roll onto his belly. His beard smoldered. Sharina smeared it with a handful of muddy clay.

Hanno sighed and seemed to relax. He turned over with less effort than he'd expended in his failures moments before. He lifted his torso onto his hands and said, "Did you kill it, girl?"

"It's gone," Sharina said. "I don't know if it'll come back."

Sharina had bits and pieces of memory, like the fragments of a shattered glass bowl. She wasn't sure if she'd ever be able to join them into a connected memory of the attack.

She wasn't sure she wanted to.

The kettle's rim was of doubled thickness. It and the ring handles lay nearby, warped from the heat. The rest of the bronze had been blasted into streaks of green fire.

Hanno chuckled. "You'll do, missie," he said. He got to his feet with the care his size demanded but with no sign of pain or stiffness.

He spread his right hand, the one that had swung the

axe into the fire wraith. "Will you look at that?" he said, flexing it slightly.

Already Sharina could see the puffiness. Dawn would show the red of a bad burn, even though two feet of hickory had separated Hanno from the thing his axe struck.

Hanno grinned. "Well, it won't keep me from rowing," he said. "Missie, I figure you and me are heading back to Valles in a couple days when my hands're in shape to climb down the cliff to the boat. Have you got any problem with that?"

"No," Sharina said. The air of the forest was already brighter.

She used a wad of dry moss to wipe mud from the blade of her knife. "No," she repeated, "I'd be glad to do that."

Garric and his companions sat with the five conspirators at a semicircular table in the dining hall of the Glassblowers Guild. The room was rented anonymously for the meeting. They wore oversized theatrical masks of papier-mâché and robes of nondescript brown velvet which concealed their features and even sexes. The trumpet built into the lower half of each mask was intended to project an actor's voice; it had the effect of distorting normal speech as well.

The man standing at the hub of the table's arc was in his early twenties. He wore his chestnut hair and mustaches long, and he dressed in a flashy mixture of silk, velvet, and gilded bronze.

His name was Gothelm or-Kalisind. He was one of the sixty servants in the queen's mansion, and his gambling had left him in debt to men who were more than willing to make an example of him.

"First the money!" he said. "I won't tell you anything without the money!"

"He's broken already," said King Carus, watching the proceedings from the balcony at the side of Garric's dream self. "He's looking for an excuse to talk."

"Why?" asked Garric. Because he needed to understand what the traitor was saying more than he needed to question the man himself, Garric had allowed himself to drift into a reverie. His fatigue had helped the process, but experience made him increasingly comfortable about sharing a psyche with his ancient ancestor.

The figure on the right end of the table—Tadai, though the full robe made his plump form indistinguishable from Waldron's lean muscularity—dipped a hand into the opposite sleeve. He came out with a purse which he tossed contemptuously to Gothelm's feet. The gold clanked musically on the stone floor.

"He's angry with the queen—or her steward, I suppose," Carus explained, "for not bailing him out of the mess. It's their fault that he had to give information to these conspirators, you see. Not his. It's never the fault of Gothelm's sort."

Carus was smiling. It looked as though the king really thought the situation was funny.

Gothelm bent to pick up the purse, dropped it, and then snatched it with both hands. He tried momentarily to open the drawstrings, but his fingers were trembling too badly.

"All right!" the traitor said, speaking loudly to conceal his fear. "What do you want to know, then?"

Garric grinned at Carus. It *was* funny if you looked at it the right way. A rural village was a hard enough school that Garric could appreciate the sort of humor that Carus had picked up on battlefields. There were times that the only jokes were grim ones—and then especially, it was better to laugh.

''Describe the path to the gate by which you enter,'' the midmost conspirator asked. The mask made Tenoctris' voice resonate. Oddly, the gravity of the false sound better fit Garric's impression of the old woman than her real birdlike tones did.

''It's bare cobblestones for the ten feet nearest the walls,'' Gothelm said willingly. His hands continued fondling the purse, framing the outline of one coin after another through the thin suede. ''When you step in, it's a hundred times that wide and it's a garden. The plants, I guess you'd call them plants, have teeth on the leaves and faces in their petals.''

''This is the same view that you see from outside when somebody else walks toward the gate?'' Royhas asked. He kept even his hands hidden within his robe's loose sleeves.

''Yes, yes,'' Gothelm said in irritation. ''You can see it from inside too, when there's somebody in the garden. And you can see the stepping stones. You walk on them and you're all right. Only if you're not supposed to be there the stones let you get into the middle and poof! they're gone. I've seen that!''

Sourous nodded his head. The exaggerated height of his mask gave magisterial importance to the gesture. ''Yes, yes,'' he murmured. ''It's a terrible thing.''

''How do you identify yourself to the maze?'' Tenoctris asked.

''Maze?'' said Gothelm. ''It's just a path—there's no maze.''

''The path, then,'' Tenoctris snapped. ''Do you speak a word or make a gesture?''

''I told you, you just walk through to the gate,'' Gothelm said peevishly. ''You don't have to do anything. And the gate opens by itself too.''

''He's hungover,'' Garric said. ''Though I'll bet he usually snarls like that.''

''I'll bet he's usually drunk or hungover,'' Carus

said. "The trouble with making people obey because they're afraid is that the folks who're willing to work for you usually aren't worth dulling your blade on."

The king's fingers played with the pommel of his own great sword. He didn't grip the hilt, just gave it the sort of touch that one lover might give another in a moment of repose.

Tenoctris glanced to her right, then left. "I've heard all that I need," she said.

"What?" Waldron demanded. "We've paid this insect a hundred crowns for *that*?"

"Look, I have to get back to the mansion!" Gothelm said. Both hands clutched the purse against his red sash. "I've told you what you want!"

"He'll be of more use to us if we let him return," Tenoctris said. "Quite apart from the fact that we made that agreement with him."

"*I* say we haven't got a hundred crowns' worth of information from him!" Waldron said, rising to his feet. The stool on which he'd been sitting toppled behind him.

He didn't care about the money—Tadai had made the payment from his own resources, and all five of the conspirators were too wealthy for the sum to matter, though it was huge by the standards of Barca's Hamlet. Disgust at the traitor and anger that a venal commoner had dared raise his voice goaded Waldron to grope for the sword beneath his concealing robe.

For an instant Garric saw with two sets of eyes—his own, through the pupils of the mask, and the eyes of his mind viewing from the balcony. The dream vantage dissolved like smoke in the wind. He stood up from the table, his muscles trembling with the emotions coursing through his bloodstream. The king's knowing grin was still a presence in his mind.

"Our word is not a small thing!" Garric said. "If we lie to him, then with whom do we keep faith?"

"Boy—," Waldron said, clutching at the unfamiliar

robe. It opened down the back. Waldron's hand found his sword through the thick velvet but couldn't draw the weapon.

"Enough!" Royhas said. "She says we have what we wanted. What use is there to stay here?"

"We have use for Master Gothelm," Tenoctris repeated in a surprisingly firm tone. Though all the men were getting to their feet, she sat with her fingers tented before her. "But he can't help us here."

"Fagh!" said Waldron, turning away. He kicked his fallen stool aside and strode through the door into the member's robing room, where the diners donned their guild regalia.

"Go," Royhas said, gesturing the traitor toward the stairway door that led down to the street. "We'll contact you when we have further need."

Gothelm bolted from the room. "He'll never come to us again, not unless we snatch him like a prisoner," Pitre said in a tone of despair. "What did Waldron think he was going to accomplish?"

Tenoctris laid her robe on the table. "He has nothing further to tell us," she said. "Or tell anyone, I suspect. I want to watch as he returns to the queen's mansion."

She nodded to the door. "There won't be much time. Garric, Liane?"

Liane was already in her street clothes. Garric was still struggling with the ties behind his back, but he started for the robing room.

"No, this way," Tenoctris said as she walked around the table to the stairwell door. The hall was a warren. That, and its location near the queen's mansion, were why Royhas had chosen it for the meeting.

"You'll be seen!" Pitre said. The conspirators had entered through the Guild chambers, each by a separate entrance.

"That doesn't matter," Tenoctris said. "I have to watch what happens, and I much prefer to do it directly rather than through my craft!"

Garric tossed his robe onto the floor behind him as he followed the women.

He found the afternoon sunlight a relief. Royhas had ordered guild servants to curtain the clerestory windows which could have lighted the dining hall at this hour, knowing that Gothelm would as quickly sell the conspirators to the queen as unveil the queen's secrets to the conspirators. It would have been safer still to interview Gothelm during darkness, but the traitor's duties—he was an underporter—required that he be within the mansion all night.

The Glassblowers Hall stood in a wealthy residential district. Marble swags and lintels set off the soft yellow limestone of the walls. The effect was pleasing where the materials had aged together, and strikingly brilliant when the surfaces had been recently cleaned with lye and stiff brushes.

Many buildings of the neighborhood—the hall included—dated from the Old Kingdom. Images out of Carus' memory flickered through Garric's mind, frequently coinciding with the three- and four-story structures still standing.

Streets in Valles were cobblestoned and straight, though here in the center of the city they were also narrow. The houses on either side of the road were owned by rich merchants or guilds, but the right-of-way was less than two paces wide. The front entrances were on the first floor rather than street level, so stone staircases encroached still further on the pavement.

"Liane?" Garric asked. "How did the queen come to live in this district? The ducal palace was on the northern city wall."

Liane looked at him, puzzled as often before by the way Garric's questions showed a familiarity with the structures of former times. "The royal palace still is," she said. "The queen built a separate residence here not long before I came to Mistress Gudea's Academy five years ago."

"Was there space open?" Garric asked. Carcosa, the ancient capital of the Isles, was a vast ruin where the present population used the monuments of the Old Kingdom as quarries for new construction. Valles seemed to have suffered relatively little in the past millennium. It was hard to imagine space available for a building as big as he'd heard the queen's mansion was.

"There was a fire," Liane explained. "Limited to properties which the queen's agents had tried but failed to purchase. There were rumors, of course, because the blaze had flared up so suddenly that no one got out of the buildings alive. That was before the first fire wraith had appeared in public."

She looked at Garric with an expression as bland as her tone. "All the heirs were willing to sell. More than willing."

Tenoctris set the trio's pace. Gothelm was drawing slowly ahead, even though he'd slowed down as soon as he was out of the guild hall.

A six-horse carriage came toward them, filling the street. Gothelm disappeared around the corner while Garric and the others sheltered behind a staircase.

The carriage passed, its iron tires roaring and sparking on the cobbles. There was a coat of arms on the door panel, but the isinglass windows were too cloudy for the passengers to be more than shapes.

"In a properly governed city," Liane said in a cold voice, "coaches wouldn't be allowed till after sunset. Along with delivery wagons."

"We know where Gothelm's going," Garric said, "but we still ought to hurry if we're going to watch him arrive."

By "properly governed," Liane meant "governed like Erdin"—where she was born, and the sole present rival to Valles for the title of greatest city in the Isles. The fact that Liane had finished her education here—where local girls treated her as a Sandrakkan barbarian despite her wealth, culture, and noble birth—had reinforced her parochial feelings.

It wasn't something Garric needed to discuss with his friend. After all, Carcosa on Haft (though now decayed into a backwater) had been the capital of the real, unified Kingdom of the Isles. Nothing today could compare.

Tenoctris smiled as though she knew what Garric was thinking. He grinned back at her.

When they reached the intersection—three streets met at skewed angles and a fourth joined the widest a few paces down—Garric was surprised to see Gothelm just ahead of them. The traitor was hesitating before he stepped onto the clear pavement around the mansion.

The mansion was an even greater surprise.

The basalt building was five-sided. The street down which Gothelm had turned led to a gateway with rebated arches, the sole opening on this side of the ground floor. There was only a single upper story, but the stone railing about the mansion's roof was as high as the nearby multistory buildings.

A dozen glazed windows pierced the second-story façade; flames leaped behind them. Garric had a moment of vertigo when he looked at them, as though he were hanging over a pit that plunged all the way down into the Underworld. He could understand why Gothelm paused, and why also those passing through the nearby intersection averted their eyes.

Gothelm put his hands to his cheeks. He didn't dare cover his eyes, but he obviously wanted to. He lurched forward.

"He looks as though he's jumping off a cliff," Liane whispered.

"It would be a cleaner death," Tenoctris said. "But it wouldn't help us."

"Why do you—" Garric began. As Gothelm entered, the ten feet of pavement changed suddenly to a deep expanse of statues and dark-hued vegetation. Garric fell silent.

He'd been told what to expect, but the reality nonetheless amazed him. The mansion looked the same, though it seemed enormously larger because the foreground had increased. A line of pentagonal stones led to the entrance. Gothelm followed them, stepping deliberately.

"I thought he'd run," Liane said. She had crossed her hands over her stomach, an instinctive response to tension—just as Garric found his right hand resting on the pommel of his sword.

"He's afraid of missing his step," Tenoctris said. "Being careful won't help him. If the queen didn't bother to provide a password to keep her enemies out, it's because the maze itself can read the hearts of those within it."

Yew trees and basalt planters bordered the path. The statues on low plinths within the landscape were basalt as well. Details of the carving were hard to make out because of the stone's dull surface; but from what Garric could see, he was happier for his relative ignorance.

Though the path seemed straight, Garric's view of the man walking down it shifted with each step. It was as though Gothelm were wandering through—well, through a maze, as Tenoctris had described the defenses when she questioned him.

Gothelm sometimes seemed to face Garric and his companions, but he obviously didn't see them. Each step the man took ended with his foot on the next stone nearer the mansion, even though the apparent motion of his leg should have taken him off the path or back the way he'd come.

"We're sacrificing him, then?" Liane asked. She kept her eyes on Gothelm.

"I want to watch the defenses in action," Tenoctris said. Liane's question hadn't been an objection, quite; the old wizard's reply wasn't defensive. "To a degree I suppose I regret what's going to happen, but all men die."

She smiled faintly. "I have greater responsibilities than to protect Gothelm from the consequences of his own dishonesty."

"Better men have died," Liane said. Garric agreed with her, but the harshness of Liane's tone would have surprised him—if he hadn't realized she was thinking of her father, gutted in a tomb by the demon her father had summoned.

Actions had consequences. Gothelm was about to pay for his actions, as others had paid for theirs.

As though the stones were hoarfrost and the sun had come out, the path vanished. Gothelm froze. His right leg was outstretched. He drew it back and clutched his arms to his body, slowly turning his head. He still didn't appear to understand what had happened.

Gothelm wore boots of red calfskin, but the toes were no longer visible. "His feet are sinking into the ground," Liane whispered.

"The ivy's growing over him," Tenoctris said. "It's harmless. Most of the effects are probably harmless, but I need to know which ones to prepare for."

Gothelm screamed and began to run. His voice sounded as though it came from half a mile away. The traitor's course roughly paralleled the building's front wall. A willow waved tendrils toward him, though no breeze moved the other foliage.

"Why doesn't he come back this way?" Garric asked.

He didn't like watching cats toy with a vole. He understood the need sometimes to kill, but the quick snap/*crunch* of a dog's jaws were more to his taste. His hand gripped his sword hilt lightly, bringing the fierce strength of King Carus a little closer to him.

Tenoctris shrugged. "He can't see us," she said. "Or the mansion. If he did happen to run in the right direction, something would drive him back like—"

A statue with the torso of a man and legs like the writhing tails of serpents stepped off its base. It slithered into Gothelm's path. He screamed, as mindlessly as a baby shrieking in a tantrum.

"That's harmless also," Tenoctris said dispassionately.

"Oh, it could crush you if you fell asleep in front of it, but it can't move with any speed."

"Perverts!" someone called behind them.

Garric glanced around. A woman with a basket of fresh bread had paused in the intersection. "Perverts!" she repeated and hastened on.

"We have to know," Garric said, his lips barely moving.

An outcrop of stone, apparently natural, had been carved into a demon's face. From the open mouth gushed a rivulet meandering through the landscape. Gothelm ran toward the humpbacked bridge, though the stream was narrow enough to jump.

When the traitor was in the middle of the bridge, the stone fabric flexed and flung him off. The water beneath lifted from its bed and caught him in midair.

Gothelm's limbs thrashed. His voice rose into a despairing wail like that of a rabbit with its legs in a snare. The water coiled like the tongue of a toad, sucking Gothelm with it into the stone mouth.

The gargoyle's jaws closed. The scream stopped. Bones crunched.

Garric swallowed. He'd thought a quick killing would be the result he preferred.

The stone face turned and looked at them. The jaws opened and belched. The gargoyle and all the landscape around it faded from view. Garric and his friends were looking at the flame-eyed mansion across a stretch of cobblestones no wider than a man in good health could leap.

On the stones lay half a red leather boot, bitten off in the middle of the shaft. Gothelm's foot and part of his leg were still inside.

"We've learned all we can here," Tenoctris said quietly. "And I for one will be glad to put some distance between myself and what we've seen."

* * *

Ilna os-Kenset was aching, hungry, and angry. Still, when she cast her mind back she couldn't remember many times that she wouldn't have described herself as angry about something. She'd ached and gone hungry often enough too.

She barked a laugh. The sailor trimming the sail looked down at her. She thought of kicking his ankles but nodded instead, the sort of limited courtesy she'd have offered a neighbor in Barca's Hamlet.

The sailor wrapped the luff rope another turn around the bitt and walked forward. The Scaled Men had faces like frogs. It was impossible to tell what they were thinking or whether they thought at all.

Ilna had enough slack that she could have sat up, but that would have warned her captors of what she was doing to their knots. She was normally an active person; being forced to lie on her side made her stiff in every muscle.

The sun was slower making its way between the horizons than Ilna was used to. For the most part the sail shaded her, but even the direct light was reddish and only vaguely warm.

Her captors had twice let her drink by dipping a rag in a puncheon of water and putting it in her mouth so she could chew the moisture out. They'd have had to let her sit to use a cup, and they were taking no chances.

The water tasted foul. The rag had come from the breechclout of a man who'd been killed by a falling spar a decade earlier—the fabric told its story to Ilna whether she would or no. The drink would keep her alive; that was all that mattered.

She particularly wanted to survive for the next while. She had scores to settle.

Something drifted across the sky high above, shadowing them. She looked up. Among the clouds hung a creature with a pink body many times the size of the ship. Diaphanous wings undulated along both its sides like the fins of a turbot. Ilna couldn't see any eyes or other sensory organs, but jointed rods and cavities trembled within the pink envelope.

The sailors grunted in agitation. One of them opened a chest built into the front of the deckhouse and distributed arms. The sailor who took the crossbow cocked it by putting his foot through the loop on the forestock and pulling back the ears of the short wooden bow until the cord slipped over the nut of the trigger mechanism.

It didn't look like a particularly powerful weapon to Ilna. She guessed the ordinary bow that Garric and most Haft countrymen used for hunting would send an arrow farther as well as being quicker to use.

But only an archer could use a simple bow with skill. Any fool could point a crossbow and send a missile in more or less the right direction by pulling the trigger bar.

Ilna sniffed. Human beings were good at finding ways around their lack of skill.

The creature took no notice of the ship. It entered a drifting cloud not much larger than itself, then came out the other side. Vaporous tatters quivered behind in the currents stirred by its long fins. The rest of the cloud had been swallowed.

The Scaled Men became calmer. The crossbowman uncocked his weapon and returned it to the arms chest, though several of the others continued to wear cutlasses hanging from loops on their broad leather belts.

Ilna heard a rhythmic thumping from the hold beneath her. There was a voice as well, but she couldn't hear well enough through the cover even to be sure that it was human.

The sound wasn't a major concern to her. Whoever or whatever made the commotion obviously couldn't free itself, so she needn't expect help from that quarter.

She continued working on her knots. A sailor was generally watching her, making the job more difficult, but Ilna had never expected her tasks to be easy.

She did expect them to be successfully completed, though. This one would be no different from any of the others.

The 24th of Heron

Cashel didn't know what had awakened him. It was a warm night and quiet except for the ape beside him.

Zahag snored. Also his lips flapped each time he breathed out. Aria still complained about the noise, though it no longer kept her from falling asleep.

To Cashel it was a homey sound. Dantle—Dantle Longleg, not Dantle Squint at the other end of the borough—had a sow who snored just the same way while she slept under the wagon shelter beside the sheepfold. Many a time Cashel had heard that snore as he helped Dantle shear.

He got to his feet. Though he moved quietly, he was still surprised that Zahag didn't wake up. Cashel had seen the ape jump from midsnore to grab a scorpion crawling across the pebbles an arm's length from his head.

Zahag had swallowed the scorpion, then looked up to check whether his companions had seen him bolt the tidbit. Cashel wouldn't even have smashed the creature with his bare hand, let alone eaten it, so he'd pretended he hadn't been watching.

They were out of the swamp, and the landscape, though dry, wasn't the desert they'd found when they first escaped from Aria's prison. Cashel wouldn't have wanted to pasture sheep here, but goats shouldn't have a problem. He'd seen squared stones near the path today, the first sign they'd had of people since the causeway.

Of course, he couldn't be sure "people" was quite the word.

A fox whooped in the distance, sounding like something much bigger. Cashel slid the quarterstaff between his hands, reminding himself of how it felt. He still missed the hickory staff he'd left in Folquin's palace, but this one was serviceable.

He didn't like goats. They were smart, but brains weren't high on Cashel's list of virtues. Goats had nasty, peevish temperaments and were prone to doing things out of pure cussedness. A sheep would walk through an open gate to browse a garden. Goats would crawl through a fence that looked proof against mice and nibble the greens to the ground, even if there was plenty of proper fodder available.

Protecting Aria reminded Cashel powerfully of the times he'd had to tend goats.

The coals of the brushwood fire flared suddenly, then sank to their previous dull glow. Flames rose again, but this time they were a blue as pale an autumn sky. There was no sound at all.

"Zahag," Cashel said. He didn't exactly shout, but even Aria—who slept like a seal—should have jumped to her feet. "Princess."

His companions didn't awaken. Their chests were still. The only movement in the night was the fire's unnatural flickering.

Cashel heard the soft crunch of feet on dry soil. He looked into the darkness but saw nothing. Crossing his staff before him he called, "Who's there?"

Three women, not quite giants but as tall as Cashel could reach at full stretch, came into the firelight holding hands. Though they went barefoot like peasants, they wore tiaras and their robes were of silk so fine that it flowed like water.

"We've been waiting for you, Cashel," the woman in the middle said. Her hair must have been ash blond because its present color was the same ghostly blue as the firelight. "Come dance with us."

The woman on the left had black hair and white skin. "We should be four when we dance, Cashel," she said in a voice as melodious as a distant trumpet.

They were beautiful. They moved with as much natural grace as Sharina did. When Cashel looked at them, he found it difficult to remember Sharina's face.

"Where do you live?" he said. He stretched his leg out and prodded Zahag in the ribs. It was like toeing a rock. The ape's hairy side was as hard and cold as a statue's.

"We don't live here, Cashel," the third woman said. She beckoned him with her free hand. He felt a pull like the current of a brook at flood. "We came to visit you."

"Dance with us," the women said together. They began to circle slowly, stepping with the majesty of rams preparing to fight.

"No," Cashel said. He tried to speak, anyway. He wasn't sure the intention made it as far as his lips.

The women joined hands as they danced, then parted. Each in succession pirouetted, but all the time they continued the common sunwise circle. Each gestured to Cashel as she turned. *Dance with us. . . .*

Cashel couldn't see the moon, or the fire behind him when he tried to turn his head. The dance was quicker now. Over the calm, lovely women lay a pale light that cast no shadows.

Cashel held the quarterstaff before him as though it were a rail overhanging a pit. The dance was approaching its climax. Motion continued but the three women were still and imperious in his mind's eye. They gestured to him.

Join us, Cashel. We should be four for the dance. Join us. . . .

Cashel forced his head away. Aria was curled in the bowl of earth he'd scraped for her beside the fire, sleeping like the dead. He didn't like Aria, but she was in this place because Cashel or-Kenset had brought her here.

Sharina was a faint memory. His other friends and the struggle against Malkar's agents were empty names like fragments from an epic Garric read to him as they tended sheep in Barca's Hamlet.

Duty remained.

"I can't," Cashel whispered. "I'm needed here."

The dance accelerated. There were no figures any longer, only a pillar of indistinct light.

The light expanded slowly, enveloped Cashel, and lulled him into dreamless sleep.

"We've done as you asked," Royhas said. "Over a hundred of our agents are coming into the city with the rumor. By this time tomorrow, there won't be a soul in Valles who hasn't heard that King Carus is returning to put paid to the queen."

He laughed cynically. "They'll believe it too, the mob will. And they're the ones we need."

The bell on a barge riding at anchor rang nearby. They were walking along the River Beltis, down which goods from the interior reached Valles. Royhas didn't understand why Garric had insisted on meeting this way rather than in his mansion or at least a carriage. The noble's bodyguards were a dozen paces behind and not happy with the situation; though even unguarded, two sober men with swords would probably be safe enough from the low-class footpads who frequented the river path.

To Garric's right, an embankment supported the rear of a temple to the Lady of Abundance. The Beltis flooded in early spring; the great limestone blocks of the retaining wall were mud-stained for twenty feet above the roadway. This temple and the other public buildings to either side of it faced Merchants' Plaza—the center of Valles when it was a village.

"Some of them will believe," Garric said. "More will believe when I appear. And eventually—"

He looked at his companion. He didn't speak for a moment to draw Royhas' eyes.

"—everyone on Ornifal and across the Isles will believe and join us, I hope. I don't believe in golden ages, Royhas. But I do believe in a government that tries to give everyone justice, and a King of the Isles who rules."

Royhas was both intelligent and active; there wouldn't have been a conspiracy without him, though none of the others would have granted him primacy. His foot hesitated for a heartbeat; then he resumed walking.

Garric and the noble didn't have a linkman to light their way. The moon was sufficient here along the river, since the sky wasn't blocked by buildings rising shoulder to shoulder.

"You don't talk like a peasant from Haft," Royhas said. His eyes were on the road in front of him. The hood of his cape hid his face from Garric. "You haven't from the beginning, as a matter of fact. I wonder if I should simply have had you buried in the woods, as I swore to Valence that I did?"

Garric chuckled. At least the sound came from Garric's throat. The memories were those of Carus. *A sword that flickered until it clanged on bone; a cloak wrapped around the left forearm in place of a shield. Enemies too close to understand what was happening, gaping in surprise at wounds opening so suddenly that they died before they knew they'd been struck. . . .*

Bats chittered as they coursed the insects above the surface of the river. Occasionally a splash and heavy wingbeats indicated a larger predator. The rural boy in Garric had already noticed Ornifal's night-fishing owls.

"No," Garric said. "You shouldn't have given that order, Royhas."

The nobleman gave a humorless bark of laughter. He'd understood the distinction between the question he'd posed and the answer that Garric gave. There'd have been slaughter in the forest if Royhas had ordered Garric's death, but it might not have been Royhas who walked away from the result.

Voices rose in singsong argument on the temple platform above. A bowl or bottle smashed. One speaker shouted louder recriminations; the other subsided into drunken sobbing.

The vaults that supported public buildings in Valles

provided shelter for vagrants. On nights when the weather allowed, the denizens sat on the monumental steps to eat, drink, and fantasize in a society of their peers.

And how were they different from folk like Royhas bor-Bolliman and Garric, late of Barca's Hamlet on Haft, who dreamed of being King of the Isles?

Garric laughed. He couldn't even be sure that his dreams were greater than those that came out of wine bottles on the temple steps.

"What do you want?" Royhas said. "What *do* you want? I swear, you're as uncanny as the queen herself!"

"But I'm not evil," Garric said, hoping that was the truth. He smiled again. It must be true: he wouldn't have friends like Liane and Tenoctris if he were a creature of Malkar.

"Lord Royhas," he continued softly. "I intend to be King of the Isles. *All* of the Isles, ruling and serving all peoples of the Isles."

Garric knew this was the moment he'd been waiting for. He'd maneuvered Royhas into a place where the noble felt alien and alone, despite being in the center of the city where he was born.

"I'm not going to do that because my ancestor was King of the Isles—though he was, just as Silyon told you," Garric said. "I'm going to do it because if I don't, our whole world is going to sink into mud like the bottom of this river."

He and Royhas continued walking; if they stopped, the guards would be on them in an instant, silently questioning. The two men, the noble and the youth with the insights of an ancient king, stared at each other, disregarding the stones missing from the pavement and garbage that had floated up from the river.

"Why are you telling me this?" Royhas said. He sounded unsure, perhaps even frightened. Garric represented something that the noble didn't understand, in a situation where ignorance was dangerous and the known risks for the conspirators were overwhelming.

"Because I want you to believe," Garric said. "I want everybody to regain belief in the Kingdom of the Isles. The Old Kingdom fell because people stopped believing when Carus disappeared. If people can believe again in something more important than the size of their own money chest or the number of troops they can put in the field, then we can have real unity and peace."

"Waldron will never serve you," Royhas said. That was more proof he was the man King Carus had judged him to be: quick-minded, decisive, and brave in a way that had nothing to do with willingness to draw his sword. "My family are merchants for twenty generations. Waldron and the other northern landholders, though—their honor's the only thing that really matters to them. They'll never bow to a shepherd from Haft."

By implication, Royhas was saying that he—and the city nobles like him—would bow or might bow. Garric smiled faintly.

"Will they bow to the crown of the Isles?" he said. "They acknowledge Valence, don't they?"

"Oh, yes," Royhas agreed. "Valence is one of theirs, after all: his estates in the north and west are bigger than some islands, after all. And they fought for him at the Stone Wall, because whatever they might have thought of Valence as a man, he wasn't a pirate from Sandrakkan."

"I want the Isles to be united in peace," Garric said. He smiled. "Well, as much peace as humans are likely to have. As I said, I don't believe in golden ages. Bad as the queen is—and bad as the thing Valence serves, as you know—"

"I don't know!" Royhas said, his voice jumping unintentionally louder. "I don't know anything about Silyon or whatever they're doing!"

"As you know," Garric said, "for all your attempts not to know, because you wouldn't have preserved me unless you did know . . . All of that, I tell you, is minor compared to what we really need: a united Isles. Not everybody can be expected to help, especially at the beginning; but those who try to stop us out of local pride or personal honor or any of the other words people use when they mean they don't care about anything except their own will—they're just as much of a problem as the queen, Royhas."

There were lights ahead of them. They were approaching a ferry landing serving the suburbs on the other side of the river. A bridge and causeway crossed the Beltis south of here where marshes split the channel into three streams, but there was a good deal of water traffic even at this time of the morning.

"I'm not a soldier," Royhas said.

Though you're a good judge of them, if your guards are anything to go by, Garric thought. Aloud he said, "We'll have soldiers. What we'll need are people who can organize, who understand money and supplies, and who can make hard decisions fast when there's no time to refer to, say, the King of the Isles."

Royhas laughed in open amazement. In a voice that still held a tinge of self-mockery he said, "You're asking me to be your chancellor, King Garric? What about Papnotis bor-Padriman, who wears the seal now? Quite apart from the fact his family can raise a thousand men with half-armor or better, he's rather good at the job. Considering what he has to work with."

Royhas and Garric wore tunics with striped hems and light capes, nondescript clothing for a merchant out at night. The scabbard of Garric's long sword was unusual; Royhas wore a slim-bladed court sword that was as much statement of rank as weapon. Garric might have been an off-duty soldier, though.

They were close enough to the ferry landing to see the faces of the half-dozen people waiting for the next boat. At this time of the morning most traffic was inward—farm families bringing produce to the city's markets on donkey-back or their own.

Garric continued at his previous slow pace. He'd timed things well, or Carus had.

"Papnotis is chief administrator for Ornifal," he said. "That's as much as the present kingdom governs, after all—on a good day. Ornifal will need an administrator in the future too."

He hadn't known the chancellor's name until this moment; there hadn't been time. Carus' silent urgency drove Garric as surely as the king's measured advice guided him in moments of reverie. If Garric took the time to learn everything he needed to know before he acted, nothing would happen—except the complete and irrevocable end of civilization and perhaps of life in the Isles.

Royhas laughed quietly. "I think we've gone as far as we need to tonight," he said. "After all . . ."

He made a hand gesture before turning on his heel. The guards stopped, dividing three and three to either edge of the path. They waited for their employer to pass before falling in behind again.

"After all," Royhas resumed, "it's all moot if a fire wraith incinerates you tomorrow, isn't it? If you don't mind my saying, the survival of the man who led the uprising against the queen wasn't a major concern of ours when we were planning events."

"If you're suggesting your priorities have changed tonight," Garric said dryly, "then I'm particularly glad we've had this discussion. Tenoctris says the wraiths can't be formed quickly and can be quenched if you have enough water handy. You can even run away from one if you have room. And if you don't panic."

"My personal experience," Royhas said, looking straight ahead as he walked, "is that wizards generally aren't to be trusted."

"I trust this one," Garric said. "I trust her with my life. As I have before."

Royhas nodded, as though he'd been discussing the menu for tomorrow's dinner.

"As for the defenses of the queen's mansion more generally," Garric said, "Tenoctris says it's mostly a matter of not losing our way. The individual effects aren't very complex."

"Your Tenoctris is the queen's equal, then?" Royhas said mildly.

Garric laughed wryly. "Tenoctris says she's not sure anyone is the queen's equal. Any human, that is. Tenoctris isn't sure the queen *is* human."

Royhas looked at him. "You're serious, aren't you?" he said. "You're not just vilifying an enemy."

"Tenoctris doesn't do that," Garric said. "She believes that the . . . person claiming to be Princess Azalais is really a changeling—a demon in human semblance."

He shrugged. "Tenoctris wants to understand her enemy so that she can counter her," he said. "All I want to do is to lead the risen populace against the queen's mansion and remove the queen from Valles and from our world."

Garric grinned. "And also to survive," he said. "I'd like to do that."

He sobered. "So long as civilization can survive too."

The men walked on in silence. Above on the temple steps, men and at least one woman were singing about the vintage. Grapes weren't grown on Haft, but Garric had played the same tune at dances after the shearing.

"I'd appreciate the loan of a couple of your men to stay close to me tomorrow," Garric said. "If they're willing to volunteer, that is. I suppose you'll be well out of the city yourself."

"That was certainly my intention," Royhas said easily. "No point in the five of us making ourselves targets for the queen's vengeance should you fail, after all. It's not as though we, the principals so to speak, would make much difference in a mob of thousands."

Garric looked at him. "But . . . ?" he said.

"But I suppose the duties of a chancellor involve some risk," Royhas said. "Realistically, if you fail there won't be safety for anyone in the Isles before long. I've lived these past two years afraid of what the queen might do to me when it suits her whim, and afraid of what Valence's creature would do otherwise. My men and I will be with you tomorrow. *King* Garric."

Garric touched the medallion on his chest. The words "King Garric" echoed through his mind. With them came the boisterous laughter of the last and greatest King of the Isles.

"Not the last, King Garric," Carus' voice whispered. *"And as for greatest, well, we'll see, you and I!"*

Hanno paused among the palms growing from the base of the cliff, leaning on the shaft of his spear. He looked so much like Cashel, watching the flock from a vantage point in the meadows south of Barca's Hamlet, that Sharina's throat swelled with longing.

She missed Cashel and she missed her home. She missed *having* a home.

"Well, I'll be," Hanno said in a tone of mild surprise. He scratched his neck idly with a fingertip.

Sharina stepped to the side of the big man to see what he'd been looking at. Because the context was unfamiliar, it took her a moment to understand what she was seeing.

A shipwreck, she thought. Storms threw debris onto the steep gravel shore of Barca's Hamlet: driftwood but also ships' timbers and sometimes deck cargo washed or cast from a vessel as the waves broke over it.

Once at dawn Reise had found a body on the black shingle. They'd buried it in the community graveyard. Every year at the Solstice Ceremony they'd fed meal and beer to the sailor's spirit along with the borough's dead. Perhaps other communities cared in the same fashion for fishermen who'd never returned to Barca's Hamlet.

"Them little beggars," Hanno said wonderingly. "If I didn't know better, I'd say they'd got brains. There's never been a Monkey with brains!"

"Oh," Sharina said, feeling her stomach congeal into a lump of cold lard. She was looking at the wreckage of the dory. The Hairy Men had dragged it onto the corniche and methodically smashed to bits. At first she hadn't associated the fragments with the dory because there wasn't a piece remaining as long as her forearm.

For hammers they'd used head-sized lumps of rock, which now lay among the wood and scattered supplies. Hanno touched one of the rocks with his spearbutt; Sharina had already noticed that the hunter used his weapon the way a mouse tests the shape of the world with its whiskers.

"They're strong little beggars when they get worked up," he said musingly. "They sure did a job here, didn't they?"

Sharina squatted to examine the end of a shattered thwart. The dory had been built of oak. As the hunter implied, destroying the vessel so thoroughly with crude tools had required enormous strength.

"The phantasm leading them probably told them what to do," she said. By focusing her mind on little questions, she was able to avoid the huge doubt from which she shied away trembling.

Could they get off Bight, now? Would bands of Hairy Men and the accompanying creatures of wizardry hunt them to eventual death through these wilds?

"Well, I figure there's two ways for you, missie," Hanno said as he turned to face her. He was calm, nonchalant even. "First choice is I build you a raft and you float to Ornifal, because that's how the currents trend. Now—"

He raised a hand the size of a bear's paw to forestall the protest she'd had no intention of making. Hanno had peeled off the blistered skin; the layer beneath looked healthy though tender. His ointment smelled like tar rather than the lanolin Sharina was familiar with from the borough, but it seemed to work.

"—I know that don't sound like much, but I know for a fact it'll work if there's not a storm. We can salvage enough food so you can eat, and there's fish to catch besides."

He shrugged. "I can't tell you it won't storm, but a bad storm here in spring would be the first one since I been on Bight, and that's past eighteen years."

The hunter smiled. His remaining teeth—one of his upper canines was missing—were yellowish and as strong as a mule's. "Of course," he added, "the Monkeys getting together this way, that's a first too. So you have to decide for yourself."

"What are you going to be doing?" Sharina said. Hanno had offered only one option, but she thought she could guess what the other was.

"Well, I figure if the Monkeys are so fond of me they'd bust up my boat to keep me here," he said with a grin as hard as the blade of his great spear, "I'd give'em reason to know I'm here. Beside that, Bald Unarc had his territory a couple days north of here. Unarc's boat is cypress and he sinks it in a creek's mouth to keep it safe between times he needs to use it."

Hanno prodded a fragment of gunwale with his spear-butt, then flipped it high enough in the air for him to catch it with his free hand. The hunter moved with remarkable economy, just enough to accomplish the task he set himself.

"I always thought Unarc was a donkey who wouldn't trust the sun was going to rise in the east," he said, shaking his head in wonder at the plank. Not only were the ends splintered, the whole length of the piece was dented and cracked from additional blows. "Just goes to show, don't it?"

He grinned again. "Mind, I don't figure Unarc was so careful that he's going to be around for me to ask his permission formal-like."

Sharina wasn't afraid of the sea. This jungle's sounds and smells were as alien to her as the world beyond the sky, while in the past she'd spent weeks adrift in a dugout almost as crude as the raft Hanno said he'd build.

If Nonnus were here, he'd be searching for the answer to the puzzle of what was happening on Bight. Unless Sharina misread the man's character, the hunter was doing the same thing.

And for Sharina to drift away seemed—

"Cowardly" might not be quite the word, but it was close enough to stand until she could convince herself there was a better one.

"I'll go with you," Sharina said, her voice steady. "If you'll have me."

Hanno chuckled. "I'd move faster if it was me by myself, that's true," he said. "But I wouldn't be moving much at all if you hadn't fixed that fire-thing. I'll tell the world! So I'd admire to have you along."

"I'm glad you feel that way," Sharina said. She felt better for the decision even though it was against her own deep wishes.

And she knew that so long as she survived, a part of Nonnus was present in her.

Ilna had been dozing. When her eyes snapped open, she saw that the full moon had risen. The cratered face was much the same as hung over Barca's Hamlet, but it was three times as large and as red as the coals of a dying fire.

The vessel was sailing between towers of rock. The islands were little more than bowshot to either side, closer than Ilna had seen them by what passed for daylight in this place. Pits and crevices marked the shafts. She didn't see how rock so soft could support the mushroom tops that swelled hundreds of feet above. They should have crumbled under their own weight.

The Scaled Men grunted in fear-muted voices. They were armed again. The ship drove on, the sail still filled by a wind Ilna could not feel. One of the sailors crouched at the steering oar, but the others scanned the sky instead of paying attention to the vessel or its course.

Something flew past the moon.

The crossbowman capered in a clumsy circle, his weapon lifted as he tried to find his target against the stars. The others waved cutlasses and a spear, shouting in guttural panic.

The flyer had looked like a man to Ilna. A man with bat wings.

The sail blocked much of the view from the deck. The sailor with the striped headband started to climb the rigging; there was a bucket fixed to the masthead for a lookout to stand in. He paused midway in an agony of indecision, looking over first one shoulder, then the other.

The flyer swooped up from sea level to skim the starboard railing. Clawed fingers sprouted from the joint at each midwing. They clutched at the man on the rigging. He gave a hoarse cry and slashed with his cutlass.

The flyer lurched away and down. The broad wings were of membrane so thin that Ilna could see the moon's face through it.

The crossbowman leaned over the railing and squeezed his trigger. The bowcord cracked loudly as it released. Scaled Men hooted in delight, hugging one another and stamping their feet on the deck.

The sailor who'd started toward the masthead jumped down. He was holding his right shoulder with his left hand. Across his back were three long slashes that looked black in the unnatural moonlight. He called out to his fellows.

Two of the others put down their weapons and examined him, clicking and muttering. The shoulder wound was a deep one. When the sailor took his hand away, blood quickly spread down his arm. If the wound wasn't closed quickly, the victim would die as surely as sunrise.

In this place, perhaps more surely yet.

A Scaled Man gave a cry like that of an ox dying. He pointed his cutlass upward. The towering island to port now overhung the vessel. From rookeries in the pitted rock, winged men like the first were launching themselves into the air.

There were scores of them. Ilna thought of mayflies swarming in the moonlight.

The sailor at the steering oar shouted to his fellows. One leaped toward Ilna with his cutlass raised. He chopped, severing the rope that bound her to the stanchion.

For a moment Ilna thought the Scaled Men were about to free her. Two more sailors were unlacing the canvas cover that held the hatch grating in place. They lifted it; the sailor who'd cut Ilna loose dragged her toward the opening like a sack of millet.

She smiled faintly. It would have complicated her future actions if she felt her captors had begun to behave decently.

A flyer dived, showing a birdlike mastery of the air. It slid between the mast and the forestay, its right wing up and the tip of the left pointing almost straight down toward the deck.

The thing's mouth was open. Its face was human—handsome, even, in a high-boned hollow-cheeked fashion—but the teeth were pointed and unnaturally long. The moonlight stained them red.

The flyer bit at the Scaled Man pulling Ilna. The fellow screamed and threw himself across her. His right ear was missing and there two long gouges across his scalp.

As the flyer banked away, the sailor with the spear thrust upward. The rusty point missed the torso, as thin and muscular as that of a skinned squirrel, but it pierced the fabric of the creature's wing and tore a four-pointed star. The material was as tough as fine parchment. The flyer flapped free, climbing with labored strokes.

The sailor who'd lost his ear rose, holding his scalp with one hand and waving his cutlass with the other. The pair crouching for safety behind the grating took Ilna by her bound ankles and neck of her tunic, then dropped her unceremoniously through the opening.

She hit hard. For a moment all she was aware of was numbing pain and the sight of a man silhouetted as he tried to squirm up through the open hatch without using his arms. A Scaled Man kicked him in the face. He fell back into the hold with Ilna; the grating slammed above them.

Through the ventilation slots, Ilna saw the red moon. Across its face more and more winged humanoids flew.

Like mayflies swarming . . .

Ilna began working on her remaining bonds. The man with her in the hold shuffled over on his knees. His arms were tied behind his back and there wasn't height enough below the grating for him to stand.

"Sister take me!" he said. "It's a girl!"

"It's a woman," Ilna said. "And if I were you, whoever you are, I'd be careful what names I was speaking right now. It may be soon enough that you'll be answering to the Sister herself for them."

She had a hand loose. She'd kept her frustration buried as long as she was bound, but with freedom all the emotions welled up and a wave of fierce triumph shook her.

"Well, you're better than nothing," the man said. "Can you maybe chew my knots loose with your teeth? If my hands were free, I'll bet I could figure a way to get the cover off. They didn't lace it down proper after they threw you down here."

He turned awkwardly as he spoke. The hold was half-filled with what felt to Ilna like sacks of gravel. The moonlight coming through the grating wasn't bright enough for her to see details, even if she'd cared.

"Get back and I'll untie you after I've gotten myself free," she said. "Who are you?"

Ilna twisted onto her other side to get a better purchase on the remaining wrist. The Scaled Men had tied her limbs individually and then together. Their knots were hard and expert, as was to be expected from sailors. The knots weren't of types that she had come across before, though; and knots were to Ilna as weather was to a husbandman.

"Captain of this ship, that's who *I* am," the man said.

"Cozro or-Laylin of Valles on Ornifal. I'm to have an eighth share of her as my pay for this voyage—or I was."

He spat in disgust. "The scum above are my crew, at least before they got the plague or whatever happened."

The grating crashed with the weight of a winged man landing on it. The creature's big toes hooked back to grip against the other four on each foot. The claws tore splinters out of the hardwood grating as the flyer struggled with someone on the deck. Its flapping vans concealed all details of the battle.

Cozro bellowed in surprise and flung himself prone. "Sister drag me to her cave! What's going on up there?"

Ilna had her left wrist free, though a tag of rope still dangled from it. The ship's cordage was woven from spar grass, but to bind her the Scaled Men had used a well-carded flax. She supposed she should be thankful, but the coarser, stiffer rope would have been easier to untie.

She sat up. "Your ship is being attacked by bats with the bodies of men," she said succinctly. "We aren't in the world we were born in, though I have no idea where we are."

She smiled coldly as her fingers worked on the knots binding her ankles. "Your suggestion that we're in the Underworld is as likely as any other. Certainly I've seen nothing to disprove that."

The flyer lifted, then slammed chest-down onto the grating. The spear and at least one cutlass blade hacked through its wings, slicing great gares out of them.

The creature's teeth gnashed wildly, tearing finger-sized bits from the wood. In a final dying convulsion it writhed off the hatch cover and mostly out of sight. One foot continued to clamp and release with the regularity of the surf coming in.

"Lady preserve Your servant Cozro," the captain muttered with breathy sincerity. "Also preserve the *Bird of the Waves*, and cause Mistress Arona to deed over the eighth share of the vessel as she agreed—the skinflint!"

Ilna loosed her ankles. She scissored her legs sideways

and back, luxuriating in the pain of stretching her cramped thigh muscles.

"The *Bird of the Waves*?" she said. "You're the ship that brought the Scaled Man to Erdin. I suppose that explains it. Your crew drank the liquor that the body had soaked in."

"I had nothing to do with that," said Cozro, suddenly defensive. "I didn't put a body in the cask, and I don't know that there was any cider in with it from the first."

"Turn around and hold your hands out as much as you can," Ilna ordered. The binding ropes would make a satisfactory weapon once she'd spliced the pieces into a single noose, the work of only minutes for her skilled fingers.

The crossbow released again on the deck above. There was a high-pitched cry like steam lifting a tight lid. She didn't know whether it came from one of the Scaled Men or their winged attackers. She'd never heard its like from the throat of a living creature.

"Sister take me, that might be how it happened, though," Cozro said. He gave a low growl at the memory. "I told Mistress Arona that carrying cider royal was more trouble than it was worth, but would she listen? What do you expect sailors to do? Do you think saints crew a vessel that pays no better wages than Arona does?"

"Hold still," Ilna snapped. "I wouldn't need your help even if you were capable of helping."

"We were on the way back to Valles with a cargo of oil nuts," Cozro mused. "I could tell there was something wrong with the crew. Oh, the first day out they were still hungover from port leave, I could understand that. But they kept getting quieter. Wouldn't say a word to me, and when they talked to each other I couldn't figure out what they were saying."

There seemed to be a lull in the fighting on deck. Ilna heard the sailors' grunted speech. One of them sobbed with pain or desperation. The Scaled Men's stiff, froglike features didn't fit with openly expressed emotion.

"Every night when we anchored," Cozro said, "they'd

go off together. Sometimes we tied up to a spit of land so small I could watch them. They'd all kneel facing toward Valles. I thought they was praying, but I don't know. I swear, it was like they was listening to something. Every night."

"There," said Ilna, coiling the rope into a neat hank like the others and placing it in her tunic sleeve. "Now turn your feet toward me and I'll free them."

Cozro clapped his hands with delight. Ignoring Ilna's direction, he hunched forward to work on his ankle ties himself.

"If you like, I'll have you loose in a few minutes," Ilna said, each syllable as edged as a shard of broken glass. "Otherwise you can continue what you're doing—and keep wasting your time like a fool until the ship sinks or you die of old age, whichever comes first."

Cozro jerked his head around. "What did you say?" he demanded.

"If you were capable of untying these knots by moonlight, you'd have done so days ago," Ilna said. "But it's your choice."

She took a length of cord from her sleeve. The Scaled Men had taken her knife when they captured her, but her fingers alone easily spread the rope-end for plaiting.

"All right, you do it," Cozro said in a sulky voice. He rotated and leaned backward so that Ilna could reach the knot.

The flyer's foot clenched on the grating for a final time. The claw on the big toe was by itself as long as a man's thumb.

Ilna bent to work. She didn't need even the light that penetrated to the hold; the pattern and its solution were in her fingertips.

"They did their work," Cozro said. "I can't say they were taking orders, but they were sailors all of them. They didn't need me to tell them how to trim the sail. Their skin got rough and the color, well . . . Sister, they were turning blue! I knew it though I pretended I didn't. I was afraid of catching it myself, you know.''

Scaled Men croaked in fear. The crossbow whacked. Something struck the ship.

''Hold *still,*'' Ilna said as the captain twisted to look at the other corner of the grating.

The ship rocked the way a pond stirs when the first heavy drops of a thunderstorm hit and call down thousands more. Dozens, scores of the flyers were landing, on the deck and in the rigging. Their thumping impacts drowned the sailors' cries.

''Three days out from Valles,'' Cozro said, his face tight with fear, ''they lined up in the bow to pray like before. I didn't say anything. I'd pretty well stopped talking to them anyhow. Then they turned around and came for me.''

There was a choked shriek above; a sailor fell spreadeagled across the grating on his back. Winged men covered him, their bodies writhing like grubs in a week-dead rabbit. The killers blocked the light as their jaws crunched on and through bone. Blood dripped into the hold, and there was a charnel stench.

''There wasn't a thing I could do,'' Cozro said. He was shouting as much to conceal the sounds from above as so that Ilna could hear him. ''I thought they were going to kill me. They argued and I think that's what it was about. Finally they tied me and threw enough oil nuts out of the hold so there was room for me.''

The deckhouse door slammed. The flyers shifted away from the sailor's body, permitting a little moonlight to enter the hold. Only disarticulated bones and tags of cartilage remained of the corpse; that, and the fluids still dripping through the grate.

''There,'' Ilna said. ''You're free.''

''Lady save me,'' Cozro muttered. ''*Please* Lady save me.''

Ilna took out a second hank of linen rope and frayed the end for splicing. She heard the rasp of teeth on wood;

the flyers' fangs weren't meant for gnawing through a ship's timbers, but she had no doubt they'd succeed before long.

"There's a butt of water forward in this hold," Cozro said. Sweat gleamed on his forehead. He refused to look up. "I stove the end in and let me tell you, *that* was a job with my hands and feet tied!"

A flyer thrust the remains of the corpse aside and pressed its face against the grating. Its nose wrinkled like that of a horse scenting water. With increasing fury it began to bite the wood, all the time making a mewling sound.

"I don't understand what's happening!" Cozro said. "I don't understand!"

From the deckhouse came the sound of hoarse chanting. A whiff of bitter smoke drifted through the grating. The Scaled Men were at their rites again.

More of the flyers dropped onto the grating. It was like watching foxes chew their way into a chicken coop—from the viewpoint of the chicken.

Ilna sniffed. Her fingers spliced a third length of cord onto the growing noose. It wasn't the perfect weapon for tight quarters like this, but it would serve for a time.

That's all you could say of anything or anyone, after all.

Cashel sat up, stretched mightily, and grinned at his companions. "Umm!" he said. "I haven't felt this good since I don't remember when. Guess I needed that sleep."

Aria and Zahag were staring at him like—

Like he was a ghost.

Cashel stood, absently brushing gritty soil from his quarterstaff. "Look, I slept a little late," he said defensively, "but I'm usually the first one up."

He glanced toward the horizon. The sun was still pretty low. "It's not like I slept half the morning—"

The sun was low on the *western* horizon. He'd slept for the whole day.

"Oh," Cashel said. He shifted his posture, working all his muscles enough to know that he didn't have any stiffness. "Well, I don't know how that happened."

"You're all right?" Aria said. She continued to kneel near where he'd lain, some distance from the hole he'd scraped for his hipbone. "You're sure?"

The princess held a wet rag—another scrap torn from her fluffy gown. She looked like a dandelion head after a thunderstorm, so bedraggled had the journey left her.

"I'm fine," Cashel said. He touched his forehead; it was damp. Aria had been mopping his brow to bring him out of what must been a deep stupor. He wouldn't have thought the girl had it in her. She must really have been afraid that he'd, well, left them.

"We thought you were dead," Zahag said, uncharacteristically subdued. "Your heart didn't beat but once in a great while. We couldn't rouse you any way we knew."

Cashel rubbed his right cheek, then his left. He'd been slapped hard—and pinched, he shouldn't wonder. Well, he might have done the same if it'd been Aria unconscious. The two of them sure weren't going to carry him like he carried Aria when she couldn't walk.

He smiled broadly at the thought of him dangling over the princess's shoulder as she trudged up the mountain they had ahead of them. "Well, I'm all right now for sure," Cashel said.

His mood sobered. His image of the princess had brought to mind the three women of the night before. Any of them *could* have carried him as easily as he did Aria.

"There's water close by here," Zahag said, getting up on all four limbs and pacing a slow circle. "I guess we're not in a hurry, so another day isn't—"

"The water tastes awful!" Aria said. She was still kneeling. "Oh, I thought something terrible had happened. I thought you were . . ."

She couldn't get the word out. "Yeah, we both did,"

Zahag said. "Dead as a stone. Your heart was going to stop the rest of the way and bing! you'd start to rot."

The ape shrugged, a gesture which the length of his arms amplified. "I didn't know what was going to happen next."

"Zahag?" Cashel said. "When you woke up, did you see tracks around the fire?"

He waved a hand toward the patch of ground where he remembered the women dancing. Was that in a dream? "Over there, maybe?"

"Huh?" said the ape. "What kind of tracks? I didn't see anything except you were sprawled on your back instead of your side like usual. And you wouldn't wake up."

Cashel walked into the brush in the direction from which the dancers had come. His legs pushed crackling stems aside. He didn't recognize the bushes, though they seemed pretty normal. He didn't suppose there was rain enough here to water the sorts of plants that grew near Barca's Hamlet.

"Where are you going?" Aria cried on a shrilly rising note. "Cashel!"

She started after him. This dry brush would catch on the gauzy remains of her dress and strip her stark naked if she wasn't careful.

"I'm not going far," he called. "I just want to see something."

It was closer than he'd imagined—a circle of pitted stone that might have been a well curb, only two or three double paces from the edge of the trail. If there was a shaft, windblown dirt had choked it long ago.

"What are you doing, Cashel?" Aria said from just behind him. It was the first time he remembered her showing interest in what somebody else was doing except as it involved her.

Come to think, she was probably worried he was going off and leaving her. He wouldn't do that. Of course, he'd never slept the sun around before either.

"I'm just looking at, at this," Cashel said. "I thought there might be something."

"Oh," said Aria, moving around to his side. "It's a sacred precinct."

Cashel looked at her in puzzlement.

"She means a temple!" Zahag snarled from across the little ruin. He muttered something else that might have been, "Strong back, weak mind!"

"They're not statues," Aria said. "They're caryatids. They held up the roof instead of columns."

The temple's roof had been tiled; at any rate, fragments of curved red tiles poked out of the soil nearby. The statues, the caryatids, had toppled, but the square bases were still in place on the curb.

Cashel walked closer. Two caryatids lay on their backs. The marble had weathered to the point that all he could tell for sure about them was that they'd been women in flowing robes.

The statue between those two lay facedown. Wind and rain had eaten the upper side as badly as it had those of the others, but the face was unmarked when Cashel rolled it over.

He recognized the blond dancer's features from his dream the night before.

Cashel laid the figure back the way he'd found it, then straightened. It was getting dark. When he looked up the slope ahead of them, he saw pale blue light wink.

"Cashel?" the princess said in a subdued voice. "What are we going to do now?"

Cashel thought he saw a light, anyway. There were a lot of illusions in this place.

"I know it's late," he said to his companions. "I think maybe I'd like to go on some tonight anyway. I, well . . . Maybe I see something."

"Nothing to keep us here," Zahag said, sounding unusually agreeable. He clambered over the stone curb on his way back to the trail.

Cashel and Aria followed him. Cashel glanced over his shoulder once.

There were four bases but only three statues on the ground. He sort of wondered what had happened to the fourth one.

The 25th of Heron

Maurunus led two pages carrying a helmet and cuirass into Royhas' crowded stableyard where Garric and his immediate entourage were readying to attack the queen. "We've brought Master Garric's armor, sir," the majordomo said to Royhas.

Garric looked at the equipment winking in the early dawn. The pieces were silver-plated and decorated with scenes from the mythical founding of Valles: on the breastplate the Shepherd guided Val and his band of survivors from sunken Xadako to the mouth of the River Beltis, whose personification bowed to the newcomers. The helmet was chased with battles between Val and the autochthonous giants of Ornifal; on the crest, the Lady waved Her blessing over the carnage, an image Garric found blasphemous.

Besides, the reliefs could catch a spearpoint. Not to mention that he'd feel like a poncing courtier wearing that gear.

"It's beautiful," said Liane, looking up from the slanted writing desk moved into the yard. She was checking off the messengers coming in from each district of the city. A pair of servants with short swords stood to either side of the small strongbox, but Liane paid each new arrival herself as soon as he'd given his information.

"I can't wear that!" Garric blurted.

"We've had it sized by eye," Royhas said. "The straps have enough play in them that it ought to fit."

The nobleman was keyed up, but he wasn't peevish or frantic as somebody else in his place might have been. With the rebellion—attack, anyway—being launched from his town house, he'd at best be a fugitive if they didn't defeat the queen. Given the stories about the queen, death was by no means the worst possible result of failure.

"Look," Garric said. "If I've got to wear something, get me a proper set of battle armor."

Everyone in the stableyard looked at him: the six guards with dawning respect, most of the others in surprise.

Royhas was simply irritated. "This isn't about a battle," he snapped. "As you said last night when you were thinking more clearly, we can get people to do the fighting. Your job is to lead, and for that you have to be seen."

"Ah," said Garric. Carus, very close to the surface of Garric's mind in these preliminaries to chaos, understood and agreed; though the disdain for the ornate gear had been as much his as Garric's own. "Yes, I see."

He unbuckled his broad sword belt without being asked. The cuirass rode on the flare of his hipbones as well as his shoulders. It wouldn't be a problem to wear the belt over the armor, because the long tongue had plenty of excess. The mind that had guided Garric as he chose his equipment was that of a consummate man of war.

A guard took Garric's sword so that the pages could put the cuirass on him. The shoulder straps were riveted to the backplate and fitted onto hooks with pin closures on the front.

As the pages started to lace the sides together, Garric said, "I'll do that myself. How can you decide how I want it to ride?"

Liane gave him a tiny smile. Royhas frowned slightly and said, "Of course. We didn't realize you knew how to adjust armor."

Garric did up the leather laces—tight at the bottom but increasingly looser up the sides, trading the risk of a spearpoint through the gap for the greater flexibility the rig gave him. His fingers moved in practiced reflex—not *his* practice, but his reflex now.

He smiled. Since Garric had begun wearing the medallion of King Carus, he'd had no privacy. No matter what he did, he'd had an awareness of another figure standing closer than his shoulder, watching through his own eyes.

But there wasn't any real privacy for a boy growing up in a rural village anyway, so Garric didn't feel he'd lost much. He'd gained a world of knowledge and abilities.

His fingers paused. His face must have changed, because Royhas said in concern, "Is there a problem with the armor?"

Garric tied off the lace with a double knot. "No," he said. "I was just thinking about the number of things I wouldn't need to know if I'd stayed the rest of my life in Barca's Hamlet."

"If you'd done that," said Tenoctris, sitting on the cushion of the sedan chair in which she would ride, "there wouldn't have been a Barca's Hamlet for very long. Not that the parties who brought you into the wider world would have let you stay."

She smiled. "I'm afraid I'd have prodded you myself, if I'd had to."

Garric's laugh was an echo of Carus' own. "Well, what's already happened doesn't matter now," he said. "There's enough in the future to worry about, of that I'm sure."

Royhas spoke to a groom with a mustache whose tips drooped below the level of his chin. The man bowed and disappeared into the stone-built stables behind them.

Garric took the helmet from the page, though for the moment he tucked it under his arm instead of putting it on. Helmets were miserably uncomfortable to wear. Carus had often gone into battle with only a diadem on his head, leaving the helmet in his tent.

"I took risks I didn't have to, lad," a voice murmured at the edge of Garric's consciousness.

"Sometimes there're risks you do have to take," Garric said aloud, looking around the company that was waiting for him to lead them. The others thought he was speaking to them; and so he was, in part. "Liane, how are things looking?"

"We've had at least one report from all the districts but Fourteen and Sixteen," she said. "The rumors have gotten around. People are out in the streets, and several of the queen's officials have been attacked."

Districts Fourteen, Fifteen, and Sixteen were across the Beltis, cut off from the general business of the city. The queen's presence was light there anyway.

The mustached groom came out of the stables, leading a tall gelding whose coat was colored a gray so pale that only a purist would refuse to call it white. It carried a parade saddle; the high pommel and crupper were covered in chased silver plates.

Garric started to open his mouth, then caught his words and laughed again. He didn't need to be told twice. "Royhas, is that my mount?" he said.

"Yes, ah . . . ," Royhas said. "Ah, have you ridden a horse before?"

"I'll ride the horse," Garric said. "I understand. But get that rig off him—indeed, I'll be safer bareback."

"This—," the nobleman said.

"That's designed to keep me from falling off a horse's back," Garric said, overriding the explanation. "It'll keep me from jumping off in a hurry if something panics the horse, too."

"Ah," Royhas said. "Yes, I can imagine a horse being less steadfast than you, Master Garric."

He gave the groom a curt nod. The man shouted something incomprehensible into the stable and uncinched the parade gear. A boy staggered out of the building carrying a saddle designed for light city use, perfectly satisfactory for the present tasks.

"That may mean horses have better sense than men do, Lord Royhas," Garric said. Somewhere close, King Carus was grinning broadly.

There were at least fifty people in the stableyard: guards, servants, bearers for Tenoctris' chair—the effort of wizardry would be bad enough without the old woman trying to run over cobblestones in the midst of a jostling crowd—and the principals themselves. Garric frowned when he noticed that not only stablehands but also the house servants, even pudgy Maurunus, carried wooden cudgels.

"They're to defend the house while we're gone?" Garric said in Royhas' ear. He lifted his chin slightly to indicate the majordomo.

Royhas snorted. "The house can burn," he said. "I won't need it if we fail. Every man in Valles who owes me service will be with me this morning to make it less likely that we *will* fail. This is neck or nothing, Master Garric."

Garric clapped the nobleman on the shoulder. Royhas wore a cuirass also, plates of blackened iron riveted to padded leather backing. The cap he held was brown plush, but it had an iron cup under the soft exterior. It was excellent equipment for an urban riot: good protection without making the man wearing it stand out from the crowd.

Standing out was Garric's job, after all.

"This isn't a fight about who calls himself king," Carus whispered. Garric could almost see his ancestor standing on the dream balcony, looking down on the courtyard with his face as calm as a boulder but his right hand playing with the hilt of his sword. *"This is about having a chance to live in peace and die in your own home; and it isn't only for people with 'bor' or 'bos' in front of their names."*

Female servants were coming out of the house also; not all of them but most. Some carried kitchen knives, and a woman's arm could fling a cobblestone.

Garric grinned at Tenoctris and Liane. The younger

woman had folded her account book and put it in her sleeve. She took the silver water bucket that she insisted on carrying herself and nodded to Garric.

As for Garric, well, his horse was resaddled.

The people of Valles were the key to success or failure. Liane had sensibly suggested they wait till midmorning so that the populace would be up and dressed; it was midmorning now, or close enough to make no difference.

Garric took the reins from the page who'd intended to hold the gelding's head, put his foot in the left stirrup, and swung himself into the saddle. His technique was flawless, but a twinge in his thigh muscles reminded him that riding a horse—like swordsmanship—was a matter for the body as well as for a mind that understood the process at a reflexive level.

"All right!" Garric said in a voice that rang from the walls surrounding the stableyard. "Let's go show the people in the Customs House that there's no room in Valles for anybody who serves the queen!"

A pair of guards walked the heavy gate-leaves open. Garric rode into the alley. It wasn't the most inspiring start, but it was the only practical one unless they'd wanted to prepare an insurrection in the porticoed formal entrance to Royhas' town house.

"Valence and the Isles!" Garric shouted as he led his entourage from the alley into one of Valles' major boulevards; this portion was called Harmony Street, but it became Monument Avenue half a mile west in the vicinity of the queen's mansion.

Garric drew his sword. Despite its size, the gelding was of a more phlegmatic disposition than some of the thoroughbreds Garric had cared for in his father's stables. He obeyed Garric's reins, and his hooves didn't slip as they clashed over the cobblestones.

Garric was the only one mounted. A horse for Liane or Royhas would have put them at risk without helping the endeavor. They were far better off on their own legs.

"Valence and the Isles!" Garric cried. He waved his

sword toward the row of expensive houses across the street. The faces of householders as well as servants were peering from windows.

"King Carus and Freedom!" bawled the nomenclator who normally announced visitors at the levees where Royhas accepted petitions from his clients.

"King Carus and Freedom!" the rest of the entourage shouted at the tops of their lungs. Liane and Royhas marched on either side of the horse. If not as loud as the frog-voiced nomenclator, they were still clear and easily audible.

Garric walked his mount forward. People came out of houses farther down the street to see what the commotion was about. The helmet flare cut off Garric's peripheral vision, and he didn't want to turn his head to look over his shoulder. That might send the wrong signal to those watching.

"They're coming!" said Liane. "They're joining us, Garric!"

"Carus and Freedom!" Garric shouted. The noise was making the horse restive; he swayed his head and stutter-stepped. Garric jerked the reins hard to straighten the beast's line.

Emotions rushed through Garric's blood. He wanted to thud his heels into the gelding's ribs and rattle down the street at a canter. He fought that instinct and the horse as well: they had to move slowly so that enough ordinary citizens could join the mob to give it unstoppable weight.

"They're coming!" Liane repeated exultantly.

Harmony Street bent to the left at an intersection and narrowed slightly; a block of three- and four-story apartments replaced the noble residences of Royhas' immediate neighborhood. Even so these were dwellings of prosperous or at least comfortable citizens, not tenements.

People spilled out of the arched entranceways, joining the march. Some newcomers were actually ahead of Garric, though most of them swelled the crowd that followed.

"King Carus!" shouted part of the growing mob. Other

throats screamed, "Death to the queen!" and "Burn her alive!" The slogans merged into a sound more like the snarl of a huge beast than anything from a human throat.

Rumor and sometimes the conspirators' paid agents had readied the ground, but universal hatred of Queen Azalais did more for the response than plotting had. Garric's presence was the spark in this district, but trumpet calls and occasionally smoke plumes from elsewhere in the city showed that riots had broken out at dozens of other points as well.

A squad of the City Guard with polished brass helmets and gorgets trotted from a side street into the triangular plaza twenty paces ahead. The leader carried a spontoon with a broad, filigreed blade as a rank insignia. He called an order. Four of his men spread to the sides, raising their long, knob-headed staves to receive the mob, while the cornicene raised his coiled horn to summon support.

"Down with the queen!" the nomenclator shouted. Garric swept his sword in an arc, pointing to the street branching toward the Customs House.

The squad leader grabbed the cornicene before the man could blow; the staff-bearers looked uncertainly at one another and their commander. Garric, seeing the hesitation, waved his sword in a broad flourish as though he had a signal flag in his hand.

"Down with the queen's lackeys!" he cried, and rode past the Guards. They didn't try to stop him.

"Down with the queen!" the squad leader said as he and his men joined the mob.

The Customs House was a monumental gateway standing where the main north-south road entered the esplanade around the harbor's margin. The structure was a square of red sandstone with a twenty-foot arch on each side. For the most part the inspectors worked on the surrounding pavement, but for paperwork and storage there was a second story served by inside staircases. Swags and pillars of colored marble decorated the walls, and on the crenellated roof stood a gilded bronze statue with a scepter in one hand and a stalk of rice in the other, symbolizing Valles.

The customs officials wore linen tabards over their tunics. Instead of red and black, the royal colors, these were in shades of orange—as close as dyes made from pollen and red earth could come to the hue of fire.

A grotesquely fat man on top of the gateway shouted an order as he saw Garric approach at the head of the mob. There were a dozen officials on the pavement. They drew the swords they carried but wavered back into the shelter of the building when they appreciated the numbers they were facing. A second mob spilled into the plaza from the slums to the south.

The air before Garric congealed into a gray shape with glowing eyes. The gelding shied with a scream of terror. Garric swung his leg over the saddle and pushed himself away from the animal. He hit the cobblestones hard and might have fallen if Royhas hadn't supported him. He was glad for once that he was wearing boots.

The phantasm drifted forward. Its face was a demon's, and its clawed hands reached toward Garric's eyes.

Garric had seen the phantasms in Tenoctris' scrying mirror, but this was his first direct experience of them. He walked forward with his sword raised.

"It's an illusion!" he said. His voice was a frightened squeal in his own ears—but he kept walking.

The phantasm's jaws opened; its very silence made it the more frightening. From the corner of his eye Garric could see that the other mob had halted before a similar creature.

"It's an illusion!" Liane said in a clear, melodious voice as she advanced at his side.

Even so, Garric couldn't force himself to walk straight through the phantasm. He reached out with his left hand instead.

His skin tingled. For an instant he stood on a barren plain. All around him were the bodies of his friends and kin, impaled on stakes of rough-hewn cedar. Their dead eyes cursed him.

"Illusion!" Garric shouted. He stumbled forward. He could see again. The phantasm had vanished. Garric ran across the cobblestones with a thousand screaming citizens at his back. The queen's officials threw down their weapons; some knelt begging for mercy, others fled northward up the plaza.

Royhas' guards cut a pair of the queen's men down with quick sword strokes. Stones dropped those running; citizens, some of them wearing expensive clothing, pounded the fallen to death with clubs and their feet.

"We don't have to kill them!" Garric shouted, but he knew no one would listen. The slaughter made him sick to watch, but he'd known when he agreed to the plan that a mob is a beast with an appetite for blood.

He ran under the gateway. "To the queen's house!" he called. The plan was for the mobs to converge on the queen's mansion, but only after they'd swept her minions out of every district of the city. King Carus had recommended that course, so that those involved would be flushed with victory before they reached the place where resistance would be more than will-o'-the-wisps and a handful of thugs.

Garric was hot and already panting. Sweat soaked his armor's padding, and he felt the impact of each stride over the cobblestones. He wondered what the horse was doing—and laughed at the thought, because the muscles of his inner thighs ached from even the short ride he'd had.

There was a scream from above, then an enormous wet impact like nothing Garric had ever heard. He turned. People who'd passed under the monumental gateway looked up, waving their fists and shouting curses.

Garric lifted his helmet with his left hand so that the silvered brim didn't get in his way when he looked up. Men—and a few women—leaned over the ornamental battlements, laughing at those below.

Because the crowd had scattered, Garric could see what

had happened when he lowered his eyes again. Citizens had climbed to the top of the gateway and flung the queen's customs chief to the pavement forty feet below. The impact had crushed the fat man so completely that his clothes were sopping red with blood.

Liane looked at the garbage which had recently been human. Her face had no expression. "To the queen's house!" she cried, trotting up what was now Monument Avenue. Royhas and his guards fell in alongside.

Garric and his fellows were no longer leading the mob. The citizens who'd chased the fleeing officials were well ahead, and another limb of the insurrection had joined three blocks up the broad expanse.

A large crowd had broken into an imposing residence with lions carved in low relief to either side of the front door. Garric glanced at what was going on. A bed burst through a third-floor window casement from the inside, fell, and shattered into splinters of ivory and exotic woods when it hit the stone planter below.

Garric supposed the house was owned by one of the queen's officials. Before long, though, there'd be looting and death without any political excuse, let alone reason. There was nothing to be done about it—except to finish the queen as quickly as possible so that order could be restored.

"Worse things happen in wartime, lad," the king's voice murmured; but there was no joy in the words, only grim acceptance of what couldn't be changed.

Statues of statesmen of former days stood on plinths to either side of the avenue. Some were so old that verdigris had eaten holes in the bronze.

Garric remembered scenes his own eyes had never beheld in the Voting Field in the center of Carcosa. Since the day when Comus had imposed a monarchy on the oligarches of ancient Haft, statues and other monuments had filled the plaza. Now it was weeds and rubble. Modern Carcosa hadn't rebuilt the area after pirates and dynasts sacked the city repeatedly when the Old Kingdom fell.

The queen's mansion was directly ahead. A mob already surrounded it, though the black walls and flame-wrapped windows were unharmed.

Garric looked behind him; he had to turn his whole body, because the cuirass prevented him from twisting to glance over his shoulder the way he normally would have done. Tenoctris looked composed as she sat in her sedan chair. The four bearers moved at a sliding trot that made the vehicle sway but didn't jounce the passenger significantly.

Garric and Liane reached the back of the crowd around the mansion. At a command from Royhas, the guards jogged ahead of Garric with their spears reversed.

"Make way for King Carus!" the nomenclator shouted. His lungs were so powerful that he could actually be heard over the mob's noise. Spearbutts or an armored shoulder moved folk out of the way if they didn't take the hint.

The guards halted just short of the queen's perimeter. Their commander, a stolid veteran named Enger whose short beard was the same iron gray as his eyes, nodded Garric and Liane forward. Tenoctris dismounted to join them a moment later, but Royhas remained with his guards in an armored semicircle behind the three.

The ground cover across the sharp demarcator was the pale yellow of light-starved grass, but the hairlike leaves weren't flattened into blades. The cherry tree nearby was in bloom; the petals were black. A twisted branch beckoned to Garric like a diseased whore.

Tenoctris seated herself on the cushion a bearer slid between her lanky buttocks and the pavement. Another bearer handed Tenoctris the length of pine board they'd carried lashed to the chair's back. She'd already scribed it with a circle inside a six-pointed star.

Thirty feet to their right, a muscular young man who'd shaved the back of his scalp bare stepped across the margin between cobblestones and wizardry. He waved a staff taken from a City Guard and shouted, "Come on, anybody who's a man!"

Several other fellows with their hair cut like his followed him. After a moment's pause twenty-odd men and a few women plunged after the leaders crying, "Death to the queen!" in loud, drunken voices.

Tenoctris took a bronze stylus from her sleeve. With the pointed end, she began to scratch words in the Old Script around the edge of the circle she'd prepared. The stylus marked the soft wood easily, but it was intended for wax tablets: the other end flared like a fishtail for smoothing over mistakes.

She seemed oblivious of the people running toward the mansion. Everyone else outside the perimeter, Garric and Liane included, watched them in fearful anticipation.

The half-shorn men were members of a street gang. Very possibly they'd worn the queen's colors in the past, but the lure of disorder had caused them to revert to their old ways this morning—and thereby saved their lives, because it was very unlikely that anyone caught wearing orange in public had fared better than had the customs officials.

Their lives were forfeit now, along with those of the ordinary citizens the gang members had drawn across the perimeter with them.

They intruders had lost their way already. From drunken bravado, their demeanor had changed to confusion and fear. They stopped running. Their voices grew thinner, as though they were at a great distance, and they obviously couldn't hear the directions shouted by friends outside the zone of wizardry.

"Can't we . . . ?" Liane said, looking down at Tenoctris. She caught herself before Garric could hush her.

No, they couldn't disturb Tenoctris in order save a score of people guided by wine rather than sense. Garric and Liane knew the only hope for the insurrection was that it succeed before the queen could marshal her enormous, scattered powers to deal with them, the three of *them.* He, Liane, and Tenoctris were the only present opponents with knowledge enough to be dangerous to the queen's power.

Those who'd entered the garden had drawn into a tight group. A statue that was half-man, half-woman stepped from its base. Its face was perfect but inhumanly cold. It walked toward the interlopers at the measured pace of an officiating priest.

A man flung down his stoneware bottle and threw himself on the ground beside it, kicking like a child having a tantrum. He covered his head with his hands. The remainder of the interlopers bolted away from the androgyne as a group—

With one exception. The husky fellow who'd led the others into the garden now swaggered toward the oncoming statue.

"*Kaias,*" Tenoctris murmured. "*Saseri tayam. . . .*"

The bravo's staff had a fist-sized knob on the end of a six-foot shaft, a murderous weapon if used with that intent. He swung it into the androgyne's head with a sharp *whock.*

The dense wood cracked and a few chips flew away. The staff rebounded, quivering like a lute string. The bravo screamed curses but kept his grip despite the numbing vibration.

The statue came on. Its expression, a faint smile, did not change.

"*Daya quayamta alista . . . ,*" said Tenoctris. A wisp of light spiraled slowly from the center of her circle. It looked like the shaving that rises when an auger bores soft wood.

The group trying to flee the garden was twenty yards from the man they'd left crying behind them. The ground gaped beneath them.

Victims screamed. Those closest to the collapsing edges tried to climb to safety, but the turf crumbled like wet sand when their hands clutched it.

An athletic youth took a running leap. His fringed tunic,

popular among the fashionable elite, fluttered behind him. He'd have cleared the trap except that a cedar tree's root squirmed from the soil to grip his ankle. It flipped him into the cavity with a motion much like that of a man tossing tidbits to his dog.

The earth closed. There was no sign that it ever had opened, nor of the score of humans it had swallowed down.

The bravo with the staff stood his ground, laughing in a cracked, high-pitched voice. He swung again. The knob shattered. He flailed at the androgyne with the shaft, splitting it the long way.

The statue caught the laughing man's wrists. He continued to struggle, but flesh was no match for stone. The arms encircled him.

The bravo's spine cracked in the embrace; his legs flailed to the sides, then hung limp as burlap sacks. Ribs splintered through his skin and tunic. The arms continued to close until the victim's torso fell in two pieces.

The smiling androgyne walked back toward its base.

"*Horan,*" said Tenoctris, "*elaoth!*"

The helix was faintly blue. It bent at right angles and began extending itself over the perimeter of the queen's domain.

Tenoctris set the board on the stones in front of her. When she started to rise, Garric and Liane quickly offered their arms for support. The tight coil of light continued to bore its way slowly toward the mansion.

"Now it's up to us," Tenoctris said quietly. She gave her companions a smile.

Black petals from the cherry tree covered the man who'd thrown himself to the ground in panic. There was no sound or movement from within the somber mound.

"Right," said Garric. He drew his sword and led the way in the direction the helix pointed.

* * *

"I need another pellet first," Cerix said. They'd slid the table with his paraphernalia against the wall to make more room for the circle of power on the floor. He gripped his wheels to roll the chair toward it.

"Cerix?" Halphemos said. He laid his hand over the cripple's. "I think we'd better do the spell now. We need the moon at zenith, and . . ."

The air of the small room was gray with cloying residue from the drug the cripple had smoked while he transcribed the words from the cloth to the floor they'd whitewashed for the purpose. The container had been full when the wizards began their preparations; only half a dozen pellets remained. The older man's fragile control had broken under the weight of the spell they were attempting.

Though rural labor had given the younger man considerable wiry strength, Cerix's arms did the work of other men's legs. From the waist up, he could wrestle down youths half again his size. He batted away Halphemos' hand with childish fury and gripped his wheels again to spin himself forward.

"Cerix?" Halphemos said.

The cripple didn't move. He closed his eyes; tears crawled down his cheeks. "You don't know what it's like!" he pleaded. "I can *feel* the demons gnawing on my legs. Every day, every breath, every moment. You don't know!"

"Cerix," Halphemos said softly. "We owe it to Ilna and her brother. We have to do this."

Cerix gave a shuddering sigh. "So you say," he said in a savage whisper. He shook himself, then wiped his face with his sleeve. He looked at his friend with a forced smile.

"Well, I suppose you're right," he said. "I'll be needing something to steady me afterwards, won't I? Sure, let's get this over with."

Halphemos clasped hands with Cerix. They took their places beside the circle of power, Halphemos squatting and the cripple beside him in the chair. The lamp hanging from the wall bracket behind them shone on the parchment which Cerix held in his left hand.

"Can you read it?" he asked. He tapped the sheet with the length of rye straw he was using as a pointer.

"Yes," Halphemos said. He cleaned the athame he used for private incantations by running his left thumb and forefinger over the blade of walrus ivory. As a showman he used a narwal's tusk for the broad motions of his public displays. "You've taught me well, Cerix. I won't fail you."

The cripple grunted. "I'm not worried about you," he said. He touched his pointer to the first of the syllables he'd written on the parchment in the blocky modern script which Halphemos could read.

The younger wizard tapped the corresponding symbol drawn on the floor in cursive Old Script. *"Phasousouel,"* he intoned, his voice strong but laboring against the power of the word he spoke. *"Eistochama, nouchaei. . . ."*

The circle and the words around its rim were written in soot congealed with olive oil. Each time the athame touched the floor, the symbols rotated to bring the next in front of Halphemos. Cerix, his face stiff and gray, drew his straw along the parchment at the rate the chant itself set.

"Apraphes einath adones . . ." Halphemos said. He flexed his torso unconsciously as though he were shouldering a heavy weight, but his voice remained firm. *"Dechochtha iathenouion."*

What had been a circle on the floor opened slowly into a pit with white sides whirling like a maelstrom. The syllables in Old Script stood stark and black against blurred chaos. Cerix continued to deacon out the chant, but even he could no longer be sure of the words on the parchment. Halphemos didn't miss a beat.

"Chrara!" he shouted. *"Cherubin! Zaaraben!"*

The room had vanished. A hot, violent wind roared from nowhere, and the pit was a corridor before them.

There was no floor or existence except for the shimmering tunnel beyond their world. Against its blazing white light, objects were forming.

"*Namadon!*" Halphemos shouted.

The wind was a hurricane, an unstoppable torrent. The parchment flashed from Cerix's hand, shredding into fragments as it disappeared down the tunnel.

The wind whirled the wizards after the parchment. Halphemos continued to shout the incantation.

Cashel eyed the bulge of rock above them as best he could by the light of a few stars. It didn't look very high. At least it wasn't as high as it was steep. "Zahag, you go up and I'll hand Aria to you," he said.

Something was chuckling in the darkness to their right. It went on the way a brook runs, mindless and gurgling.

The chuckling thing had been keeping parallel with Cashel and his companions all the way up the slope. It could've been any distance away, from miles to close enough to hit if Cashel spat into the encircling night.

"Well, I don't know," the ape said in a subdued voice. He was hunched at Cashel's feet—literally: he pressed his coarse-furred flank against Cashel's shin. "I don't think I want to lead."

"Get up there," Cashel said. He wasn't going to raise his voice, but his hands squeezed his quarterstaff *hard*. "Or go your own way, Zahag. And may the Shepherd forsake me if I have any more to do with you!"

Well, maybe he'd raised his voice a little after all. The chuckling stopped briefly while the echoes died away.

"Yes, chief," the ape said. He clambered up the rock face as easily as he'd have walked the same distance on the flat. His arms covered an amazing span. With his short legs gripping also, Zahag looked like an enormous crab spider.

"Send the female up!" he called from close above. An arm reached down; the ape's hand was half again as long as Cashel's own.

"I'll show you that I'm worthy, Cashel," the princess said in a tiny, frightened voice.

Instead of making a stirrup with both hands, Cashel put his left palm against the rock and said, "Hop onto the back of my wrist, Princess. Then grab Zahag's hand, all right?"

"Whatever you say, Cashel," Aria piped in a desperate and completely failed attempt to sound cheerful. She stepped on his arm in a gingerly fashion and waved her right arm overhead until Zahag caught it. She must have closed her eyes.

Cashel didn't blame her for being frightened. He hadn't been willing to lean his staff against the rock so he had both hands free to lift her.

Besides, she didn't weigh anything. Purple finches sometimes landed on Cashel's shoulder while he waited to turn the oxen at the end of a furrow. Aria didn't seem much heavier.

"I can see the light!" Aria cried. "It's right ahead of us. It's coming from a cave but there's a rock in the entrance!"

The moon came out from behind the high clouds in which it'd hidden for most of the night. Cashel didn't have any great affection for the moon. When it was full, the animals got restless.

Cashel had never thought of moonlight as being hostile before, though. Maybe it was the things it shone on in this place.

The slope had been a succession of crags, each a barrier but no single one so high that Cashel couldn't climb it. Even Aria could manage with help. The path they followed was barren, but on either side scrub pines found soil enough in crevices to grow.

Among the pines below Cashel stood hulking, two-legged figures. He couldn't tell their numbers in this light; some of what he saw were probably the shadows of misshapen trees.

There were likely a dozen of them, anyhow, and any

one of them bigger than Cashel was himself. Like Zahag their legs were much shorter than their arms, but they had long skulls and were as hairless as so many eggs.

"Do you want us?" Cashel shouted. His back was to the crag; he held the quarterstaff across his body and a little advanced, ready for use. "Come and get us, then!"

One of the figures stepped into the full moonlight, half a dozen paces below. It resumed its gurgling chuckle. None of the others advanced.

"Cashel!" the princess cried. "Please come up! Please!"

Goodness, she must be scared to say please like that. And surely she had a right. . . .

Cashel turned to the crag. He butted his staff firmly so that it wouldn't slip, put his left foot about knee-height up the rock face, and lifted himself on the quarterstaff.

Zahag had one arm stretched back to hang on to a knob of rock. With the other he caught the crook of Cashel's left elbow. The ape's flat grip was as strong as a hook of strap iron. Cashel flung himself to the top of the outcrop, drawing his staff up after him. The cap of bronze cutwork gave him a better grip than the polished iron ferrules of the staff he'd left in Folquin's palace.

The moon went back into the clouds. The chuckling seemed louder, but that might have been Cashel's imagination.

"Quickly!" Zahag said, tugging Cashel along by the hand still holding his arm. "Maybe you can snap their chief's neck, I don't say you can't, but what if the rest of them come for us?"

Cashel shook his elbow free. "Right," he said. "We're almost to what we were seeing."

It was a night for first times. Zahag had just included Aria in his band, or whatever it was that apes had.

The blue light Cashel had seen the night previous was up a last slope, no more than forty paces long and gentle enough that even the princess could walk it unaided. Crawl it, maybe, but Cashel didn't intend to take a hand away from his staff just to keep Aria from skinning her knees.

The glare was so fiercely bright that the air around it glowed. It seeped past the irregular surface of the great boulder crammed into the mouth of a cave. Cashel heard a faint whine like that of a distant mosquito. It made his skin tingle.

He looked over his shoulder. He couldn't see the huge not-men who were following, but he'd have known they were there even without the continuing chuckle. Why did only one of them make a sound?

Zahag and Aria were scrambling ahead. Cashel lengthened his stride, leaning well forward to keep his balance without having to dab a hand down. The slope's weathered surface gave his feet a firm grip.

His companions had reached the cave mouth. Aria was weeping from fear. She leaned against the boulder, trying to move it. "I'm worthy!" she said. "Oh please Mistress God, I'm worthy!"

Cashel didn't laugh. He didn't remember ever seeing anything so silly as this: the princess struggling to move a boulder that Cashel knew was beyond his own strength.

But she was trying. Cashel didn't think he'd ever come to like the princess, but it wasn't hard to respect her.

"Zahag, keep an eye behind," Cashel said, running his left hand over the seam where the boulder was wedged against the cave wall. "Let me know if I need to . . ."

He didn't finish the thought. It'd have bothered Aria still worse; and truth to tell, Cashel didn't much fancy seeing a dozen or more of those brutes hoisting themselves over the lip of rock himself.

He wondered what they were called. He'd have to ask Tenoctris when next he saw her. *When.*

The boulder's fit was closer than Cashel had seen between house beams in the past. He tried the weight, pressing one palm against the boulder just in case it was balanced to shift at a touch.

Well, he hadn't figured it would be.

Cashel itched all over, he supposed from the glare. He'd felt this way when he spun his staff as he and Zahag had gone through the wall of flame to rescue the princess.

Who didn't want to be rescued—then. She sure did now. Since Cashel had taken the job, he guessed he'd better get on with it.

He set the butt of his staff into the seam and leaned against it cautiously. As he'd expected, the lever flexed without any effect on the boulder. This fir staff might not have quite the strength of the hickory he was used to, but Cashel was pretty sure that even an iron bar as thick as his arm would bend without doing a blind bit of good.

Zahag began to jump back and forth, shrieking at the night in ape language. Cashel could pretty well guess what he was saying. Prayers might be a better choice, but who knew? Maybe swearing would keep the others off for a little longer.

Cashel set the quarterstaff beside the cave. He spread his arms to grip the boulder well around the curve on both sides. He knew he couldn't lift something so heavy, but he had to try.

Cashel braced himself and started to pull. His grip on the rough surface stayed firm, but the boulder didn't move. He kept leaning his weight back. His pulse was singing in his ears.

"I'm worthy!" Aria screamed over the ape's gibbering curses. "I'm worthy of a king!"

She must have picked up his staff. Cashel couldn't see it any longer in the corner of his eye, even before the red haze of blood filled his vision.

The boulder didn't move. The boulder would never move.

"Duzi, save my flock!" Cashel shouted. His world exploded into crackling blue fire.

By using the spear as a balance pole, Sharina was able to dance across the fallen tree to keep up with Hanno ahead of her. The bark beneath the layer of wet moss had rotted enough that sheets of it threatened to slide away beneath her; Hanno, twice her weight, seemed to have no difficulty.

The bottom of the gully was rock-strewn and forty feet down. Sharina didn't really expect to slip off . . . and as much at home as Hanno seemed in this rain-drenched world, he'd probably reach back and grab her before her feet had left the trunk.

"Unarc keeps a snare or two down there," Hanno said as he hopped to the solid ground. His spearbutt gestured into the gully. "The hornbacks travel the easy way, so once they've made a trail you can take them from the same snares till you're old and gray."

He laughed. "Not that Unarc's got hair enough to get gray," he added. "Don't expect he's been getting older this past while neither, not the way the Monkeys are cutting up."

Sharina stepped to the ground instead of jumping; she was afraid that the bark would slough and spill her if she put that extra strain on it. The hunter's balance must be perfect, because she knew that though her own was quite good she couldn't equal the big man's ease on dangerous footing.

A beetle with a jeweled carapace droned between her and Hanno. It moved slowly with its wings blurring to support a body the size of a man's fist.

The forest floor squished, but Sharina's toes could find a hard substrate not far beneath the leaf litter. They'd passed stands of giant horsetails in particularly wet sections but the trees here were araucarias, conifers whose trunks were visibly conical and whose branches started horizontal but bent up sharply on the tips.

"Are the animals you hunt dangerous?" Sharina asked, as much to show interest in her companion's life as because she cared about the answer. She'd been raised to keep an inn. If the customer thought of you as a friendly peer, he was more likely to pay his scot without objection than if he considered the inn staff to be surly menials.

Although some interest was justified. The Hairy Men might be a new danger, but Sharina was pretty sure they weren't the only threat to hunters—and castaways—on Bight.

"No, not unless you happen to be standing in the place a hornback's bound and determined to go," Hanno said. He carried what he'd described as a light pack: it nonetheless weighed at least fifty pounds, mostly of grain and dried fruit. "They don't have no more brains than a cockroach, but they weigh a ton or better, some of them. But that's like felling a tree on yourself: if you pay attention to what you're doing, it won't happen but maybe one time in a thousand."

"And predators?" Sharina asked. They were paralleling a body of water shallow enough that horsetails of ordinary size grew most of the way across its fifty-foot width. If there was a current, it was a sluggish one. That a pond—or marsh—should stand so close to a deep ravine proved that the underlying soil was an impermeable clay.

"There's lizards that run on their hind legs," Hanno said. "Half a ton each and they've got a righteous mouthful of teeth, but they rush straight on. You just butt your spear against your right boot and let them run right up it. Anyhow, they ain't common."

"I'll keep that in mind," Sharina said. She grinned, trying to imagine herself awaiting the charge of a half-ton monster with a mouthful of teeth. Well, since she'd left Barca's Hamlet, she'd done other things she'd never have expected she could.

"We cross the lagoon up here," Hanno said. "There's a ford. And then—"

A lizard—a baby crocodile, all scutes and bony plates, Sharina decided—splashed from the horsetails into the water as they approached. It swam with strong, sinuous curves of its flattened tail; its clawed feet were against its sides.

"Anyhow," the hunter continued, "Unarc's place is

just over the rise. He's got a hide in a hollow tree that I figure you can lay up in while I check on the boat alone.''

''Well,'' Sharina said. ''If you—''

Water roared. The little crocodile vanished in a whirlpool. A flat-headed monster with eyes bulging on the top of its skull swept to the surface, turned, and vanished again into the tannin-dark water. It was huge. Its skin was the slimy black color of a rotten banana.

Sharina stopped. ''What was that?'' she snapped.

''Oh, they're no danger neither,'' Hanno said. ''Not to something our size. They're salamanders, I reckon. They lie on the bottom of a pond. When something swims overhead, well, you saw what happens. I don't recall I ever saw one leave the water except when a pond dried up. Even when they have to they can't walk far.''

His spear pointed. ''Here's the ford,'' he said, and strode into the water without concern.

Sharina followed, keeping close. At least the salamander had just gotten a meal. *That* salamander had, at least.

''I'm wondering about heading for Sirimat after I get you back to Valles,'' Hanno said. He strode into a tangle of roots and tree boles on the other side of the lagoon. There wasn't anything Sharina would have recognized as a path without him, but the big hunter slid between obstacles instead of forcing his way against them. ''If the Monkeys are acting up—''

He shrugged, then moved his spear in a serpentine arc. It threaded through a knot of upturned roots that Sharina had thought was completely impervious to an object so long.

''—well, I can't work my trap lines and fight Monkeys every night. So I need to find another place I can hunt.''

Sharina blinked, then giggled. Hanno wasn't inventing little concerns because he was afraid to face the major question of survival. He took survival as a given and was puzzling over how he was going to make a living in the future.

That wasn't a little concern, come to think—*if* you assumed there was going to be a future. She wasn't sure Hanno had good judgment, but he was better company than a realist would have been.

"I don't know much about Sirimat," she said. A week ago she hadn't known much about Bight. "Rigal—the poet—says trees walk and the people there don't worship the Lady, but he wrote two thousand years ago."

Spiky roots like the teeth of a snake faced her from both sides of the trail. She shoved her way through, wondering how the hunter had managed not to disturb them.

"On Sirimat there's trees with jewels at the heart," Hanno said, "or so I hear. Well, I'll see what I can learn in Valles. There's always somebody along the Valles waterfront who's been any place you please, though the trick is staying sober enough to remember what they tell you."

They were on an upward slope distinct enough that Sharina's feet twice slipped on matted leaves. The soil beneath was bright red. High on the branches Sharina caught glimpses of flowering air plants and the occasional brilliant flutter of birds, but color, other than shades of green, was the exception in this portion of the forest.

Hanno halted and stepped aside for Sharina to join him. He was looking into the clearing before them. "Well, that's where Unarc's cabin was," he said. "I'd have bet we'd find him under that slate roof he always strutted when he talked about, but I'd have lost my money."

A few charred logs stuck out from the pile of rock slabs at the edge of a spring. Lowering trees, one of them a baobab that must have been twenty paces in circumference, bounded the clearing.

Hanno glanced at Sharina. He grinned and added, "We'd still smell him if he was under that. It takes a good month, even in this climate, before you can't smell a dead man."

"Oh," Sharina said quietly. She walked into the clearing.

Underfoot was a shale outcrop unusual in a landscape which was mostly forms of coarse limestone. Apparently the local vegetation found the surface uncongenial: the leaf canopy hundreds of feet in the air was at least as thick as that anywhere in the forest, but the saplings and lesser plants that elsewhere created a second and third layer beneath the main blanket were absent. Sharina felt as though she were in a room of enormous height.

"It's very peaceful," she said.

Hanno nodded. "Unarc felt that way about it," he said. "Me, I like hearing the water when I'm lying there at night."

He chuckled. "I guess Unarc's finding it pretty peaceful wherever it is he's at now."

Hanno glanced upward. There wasn't enough sky visible at any point through the leaves that a fingernail wouldn't have blocked it, but darkness was already leaching the hues from the trees.

"Unarc's hideout was in that baobab," he said, pointing the spearbutt. "There's a crack in the trunk you can slide through, and inside it's a regular cave. I'll leave you with the pack."

"You're not coming in with me?" Sharina said, careful not to put any particular weight in the question.

The hunter slipped off his pack and held it by the straps in one hand as he strode across the clearing. "I'm going to check on Unarc's boat," he said. "I know the way well enough to go there now, though I'll lay up there till the morning."

He stopped at the side of the baobab where the pale bark gaped in a seam. Sharina would have assumed the scar closed deeper in the trunk had she not been told otherwise.

"You going to be all right?" Hanno said.

"Yes," said Sharina, holding her spear point-forward so that she could enter the narrow gap. "Of course."

The 25th of Heron (Later)

Garric?'' Royhas called, his voice already attenuated.

Garric looked over his shoulder. The crowd seemed half a mile distant, though Garric knew he'd only taken two steps into the garden. The air was warm and still, with an odor like that of overripe fruit.

''I'll send the men with you,'' the nobleman said. His face was distorted with the effort of shouting. ''I'll lead them if you like!''

Tenoctris shook her head minusculely. ''I couldn't protect them,'' she said. ''My powers won't cover more than three people at once. That is, I very much hope . . .''

The three of them grinned at one another. They all knew what Tenoctris meant, though it was Liane who actually finished the thought aloud: ''We'll *all* hope that three people aren't more than you can protect. Anyway, we're with friends.''

''I'll keep that in mind when the stone tiger swallows me,'' Garric said. He cupped his left hand and his right fist around the sword hilt to his mouth for a crude trumpet. ''Wait as we agreed!'' he called. ''Nobody enters until we've made it safe!''

They walked on, side by side. Their glowing guide, a helix outside the perimeter, was a dot of blue light here. It bumbled through the air with the aimlessness of a crane fly in the twilight, passing between a pair of planters in the shape of dragon heads. Hostas grew out of the stone mouths, looking like green flames.

''That way?'' Garric said. He felt his helmet wiggle as he frowned. He'd have given the planters a wide berth if the decision were his.

"Yes," Tenoctris said crisply. "Ilna could pick a pathway through these illusions better than my wizardry can, but I think my abilities are sufficient."

Garric strode ahead, resisting his instinct to slash at the hostas as he passed them. He'd been raised not to trouble those who didn't trouble him. That was a good plan for life. Striking out because he was scared—which he surely was, scared even by the *plants* in this terrible place—was a bad one. He wasn't going to let fear drive him.

Garric couldn't see the queen's mansion. He turned to look for the spectators he knew were watching the scene, but they were gone too. Shrubs whose stems twisted in groups of six or seven from a common base waved tiny leaves at him. He didn't remember having seen them as he entered the garden with his companions.

"We'll bear to the left here," Tenoctris said in gentle reproof. She gestured. Garric noticed that she still held the stylus in her right hand.

"Sorry," Garric said contritely. "I won't let my attention wander again."

The dot of light had curved to avoid a bed of purple daffodils at the foot of a small magnolia and a boulder. The tree was in flower; its perfume had a heady attraction that made Garric think of women wearing brass spangles and little else.

He obediently followed the guide through sedums whose flowered heads humped like giant toadstools in his path. The outcrop lifted itself onto short forelegs. Knobs opened into eyes which watched with toadlike malevolence as the human intruders kept beyond its reach.

Liane still carried the pail of water. Her eyes darted about their surroundings, but her face showed only aristocratic unconcern.

"Pretending you're not afraid is a good way to keep going on, lad," murmured King Carus. Ever since Garric entered the garden, the king's tall, sturdy form had been with him. *"But if she's really that brave, she's more of a man than I ever was."*

Garric smiled. He wouldn't bet against Liane being truly fearless, but neither did it matter. Garric knew that Liane would go on no matter how frightened she was.

And so would he.

The guiding light drifted past the statue of a three-headed ogre. The creature moved on its plinth, making a grating sound. "Wait," Tenoctris said. She knelt and plucked a fern crosier which sprang from the crack between two skull-shaped rocks.

The ogre's three single eyes glared at the humans. It began to step down, lifting the saw-bladed sword in one hand and the axe in the other.

"Thesta," Tenoctris said. *"Eibradibas!"*

She struck the crosier's stem sharply with her bronze stylus. The fern broke.

The ankle still supporting the ogre on its base snapped loudly. The statue toppled forward and hit the ground, shattering into a dozen major pieces and a pile of gravel. Garric wouldn't have expected so much damage from stone hitting soft turf.

The old woman wiped fern juice from her stylus with a satisfied smile. Liane helped her rise.

"Quite a simple effect," Tenoctris said. "All the queen's effects are, really. But what *amazing* power she has to project so many presences at once, and over such distances!"

Garric's boots crunched on bits of the broken statue. One of the heads was upturned. He saw the stone eye swivel to follow him. His mouth twitched in an involuntary grimace.

The bead of light turned at right angles from what looked like a smooth, stone-bordered path and crossed instead a stream gurgling noisomely through reeds. Garric didn't ask this time, but his stomach tightened as he followed. He remembered very clearly what had happened to Gothelm at a watercourse that might well be this one.

Garric splashed through the creek. Water soaked through the uppers of his boots almost instantly. It felt clammy and his feet squished for the next few steps, but none of the horrors he'd imagined—none of the horrors he'd *watched*—occurred.

The light skirted a pair of weeping cherry trees, neither of them twenty feet high. Their flowing blossoms weren't the usual white or magenta but rather a red as bright as arterial blood.

Trailing branches shivered as the humans passed just beyond their reach. Garric felt a wave of dry, bloodless hatred directed at him.

"Ah . . . ," Liane whispered.

Garric had been watching the light. He raised his eyes slightly, following Liane's line of sight. On the slight rise ahead of them, he could see the queen's mansion. Its windows fluttered baleful flames.

"We're there," Garric said. He restrained his instinct to run forward. The king in his mind feared covered pitfalls, sharp stakes hidden in the ground, iron caltrops forged so that one of the four spikes was up no matter how the object fell—all the material traps that a wily general strews in front of a hostile army.

But the queen wasn't a general and didn't fight on a material battlefield. Besides, the guide would warn them of—

The light vanished. It was gone with none of the lingering glow that a candle wick offers as it smokes itself cold. Tenoctris whispered what Garric thought was an incantation; he couldn't be sure.

"The door is opening," Liane said. Her voice had the emotionless timbre of rigid control.

The high door leaves creaked inward; the iron hinges sounded like the souls of the damned. Garric expected a gush of flame-colored light as the windows above showed, but for the moment there was only darkness.

"We've penetrated the queen's illusions, so she'll send her living gatekeeper," Tenoctris said. She seated herself on the pale-leafed grass. "This won't be an illusion."

"I didn't think it would be," Garric said quietly. He was two persons now, a peasant and an ancient king. Carus no longer displaced Garric from his own body at times of violent crisis, but the king's knowledge and reflexes were intertwined with the youth's own. As with a rope, the whole was far stronger than the separate strands.

With his left hand Garric unclasped his red velvet cape and snapped it twice around his forearm. The cloth would be some protection; slight, perhaps, but sometimes the difference between life and death is no wider than the thickness of the stabbing blade. He moved forward on the balls of his feet, waiting for the thing that would come through the doorway.

Tenoctris' lips were moving; Liane stood beside her, holding a bucket of water in one hand and a dagger with a blade as sharp as a snake's fang in the other.

The queen's gatekeeper hunched to pass beneath the twenty-foot archway. When it straightened it was manlike save for its size and its single eye.

The cyclops wore a corselet and greaves of black iron. The armor was molded with images of demons rending human victims. The shield on the cyclops' left arm had a dragon-head boss; its eyes gleamed. A crested helmet added to the height of a monster already thirty feet high.

Garric laughed with a glee that was just this side of hysteria. He'd seen a cyclops before, that one a prehuman corpse which a wizard had reanimated for his protection on a beach beyond the waking world.

That wizard was dead, and the queen would die also.

The cyclops came toward him, striding with the heavy inevitability of a river flooding. Its legs were relatively thicker than a man's, vast pillars that made the giant appear pyramidal despite the breadth of its chest and shoulders. It held a spear all of iron over its right shoulder, poised to stab down; the scabbard of a sword half again as long as a man clanged at its side.

"Haft and the Isles!" Garric cried as he broke into a run. That war cry from a former time was drowned in the monster's hooting bellow, louder than that of the long trumpets coastwatchers in Carcosa blew to guide mariners in time of fog.

"Haft and the Isles!"

Garric unrolled his cloak again for a better use. A man couldn't carry armor that would be proof against the thrust of the cyclops' spear, but the brain within the thick bones of the creature's skull should be no bigger than a lemon. It was a beast, not a warrior.

Garric fluttered the cloak through the air to his left. His body shifted right. The iron spear, flashing like a thunderbolt, spiked the velvet to the ground; Garric, slashing right and left, drove between the massive legs.

His sword hit bone with the forestroke, cartilage with the back. A huge foot kicked out, catching Garric in the ribs as he tried to slide clear. He flew twenty feet from where he'd intended to land. He'd lost his helmet. Half the studs holding the right seam of his cuirass together were broken as well.

A creature so large hadn't a right to be quick besides. . . .

Garric rolled to his feet. There was blood on his swordblade and more blood gushing from the cyclops' right ankle. The blow had severed a small artery; what Garric wanted, needed, was to cut the Achilles tendon.

In time the monster would bleed out. Garric, already gasping with effort, didn't believe he had the time.

The cyclops stabbed the cloak repeatedly with the single-minded determination of a mother smashing the viper she'd spilled out of the cradle. Garric took two deep breaths, glad the cuirass had loosened and wishing he could fling the useless burden away. He took a step toward the monster. It turned to face him, pivoting on its left heel.

Garric paused. The cyclops turned, bent, and stabbed down at him. Garric stepped sideways. The point of his long sword clashed against the monster's right gauntlet as the spear plunged deep in the soil.

The monster's index finger spun away in a dance of

sparks. The gauntlets had to be thinner metal so that the sections could slide over one another at the joints. The good steel of Garric's blade had sheared like a cold chisel to the spearshaft beneath.

The cyclops hooted on a sustained note that made Garric's bowels quiver. It came toward him with its shield advanced and the spear rising again to thrust.

Garric backed quickly. The monster was deceptively fast because the strides, though taken with deliberation, were each as long as several paces by a human being.

"Garric!" Liane cried. "Your helmet!"

Garric hopped back, past rather than onto the headpiece of silvered bronze. He hooked the tip of his long sword between the neck flare and earpiece, then flipped it in a glittering curve over the cyclops' head.

The creature shied like a man attacked by a hornet. The spear licked out but missed the tumbling helmet. Garric rushed in, using his left hand on the pommel this time to add force as he chopped the outside of the advanced right leg. The blade crunched, sinking its own width in the cyclops' ankle.

The cyclops roared. It swung its shield downward as a weapon. Garric dived under the blow instead of trying to back away from it. He'd cleared his sword with a jerk; bits of cartilage and vascular bone clung to the edge, as sometimes happened when he jointed a roast with a cleaver in his father's inn.

He was between the monster's legs. It raised its right foot to stamp him into the ground. He stabbed deep into the left ankle as he twisted his body back.

The hobnailed boot slammed down. It missed Garric, but he had to leave his sword behind as he scrambled free.

The cyclops paced toward Garric, step by titanic step. Garric was gasping, his lungs a furnace. His hands were free because he'd lost his sword. He clutched at the half-opened seam of his cuirass, trying to wrench the armor completely loose.

The laces resisted him. The right side of his chest was still numb from the kick.

Garric backed away. He couldn't turn and run, because then he wouldn't be able to see if the cyclops threw its spear. Even facing the monster, Garric wasn't sure he'd be able to dodge the huge missile.

He was going up the gentle slope. When he reached the mansion, the cyclops would crush him like a bug against the pilastered stone wall.

Because Garric was concentrating on the monster's eye, a truer predictor of its intentions than the point of its weapon, he didn't see Liane until the girl grasped the sword projecting from the cyclops' ankle. Holding the hilt in both hands, she pulled back with all the considerable strength of her small body. The blade rotated through the joint like a knife slicing into a head of cabbage.

The cyclops shrieked. It turned, poising its spear. Liane tumbled backward, still holding the sword hilt. Blood gushed from the wound.

"Here!" Garric shouted, running toward the monster and waving his arms to distract it. The cyclops couldn't have heard him over the sound of its own cry. Shreds of red velvet fluttered from the spearpoint. "Look at me!"

The monster lunged forward. Its left foot twisted out from under it, still attached to the leg by glistening tendons that stretched under the creature's weight.

The cyclops fell, missing Liane by so little that Garric's heart stopped till he saw the girl still scrambling away. She held the sword. She stabbed inexpertly with it at the gauntleted hand as the creature flailed in her direction. The iron spear was rammed two yards deep in the soil.

The cyclops was howling. Blood fountained over the foot that stuck sideways from its leg. On the other side of the creature from Garric, Tenoctris mouthed an incantation.

Liane stumbled uphill, holding the sword in both hands. Her face was white except where blood spattered it; her arms were drenched in the creature's gore.

Garric turned. The mansion doors were open. A sparkle of purest blue dusted the gap between the leaves, though the air within was orange flame.

"The gate!" Liane gasped as she pushed the sword hilt into Garric's hand. "Tenoctris says take iron through the gateway!"

Garric strode toward the curtain of fire. The basalt threshold was hot to step on, even with his thick boots. He thrust his sword as if stabbing for the eyes of an enemy he could not see.

He felt a tingle, no more. In place of the flame was a brooding entry hall lighted by windows on the upper level. It was empty save for suits of armor that hadn't been designed for humans.

Garric looked over his shoulder. The cyclops' huge skeleton lay in a pool of its liquescent flesh, and the mob, thousands of Valles' citizens, ran across the cobblestones shrieking for the queen's blood.

Garric tried to stand aside. He wanted to make sure Tenoctris was safe, but first he had to get his breath. He saw everything as a blur of color and motion.

A man clasped Garric's free hand and slapped the backplate of his cuirass enthusiastically. "King Carus!" he cried. "Hail Carus!"

A woman old enough to be Garric's mother threw her arms around his neck and kissed him on the mouth. She wore a perfume of heliotrope and her layered garments were silken.

"Please!" Garric said. Most of the crowd was pouring into the mansion, but an increasing number of people pressed about him. He tried to move away. Liane had squeezed to his side. She stood with her fists raised to either side of her jaw.

Two of Royhas' guards forced their way through the crowd. The nobleman himself and Tenoctris joined a moment later, protected by the other four guards. The armored spearmen forced citizens away from Garric and Liane the way a froe splits shakes from a cedar log.

"The other members of our group will be with us shortly," Royhas said. His mouth quirked in a wry smile. "Here at the mansion, I told them. They weren't very pleased, but they didn't have a great deal of choice, did they?"

Shouts echoed inside the mansion. From the brief glimpse Garric had gotten of the interior, the mansion was constructed around a courtyard. The style was familiar to King Carus, but it hadn't been used in Valles either in the present day or during the Old Kingdom.

Liane held Tenoctris' hands and talked, her face close to that of the older woman. Tenoctris looked tired, but she smiled warmly when she felt Garric's gaze on her.

Royhas noted the exchange of glances. His smile tightened and he went on, "I should have offered my congratulations first, Master Garric. No one who watched you—and that's much of the populace of Valles—could doubt that you're a returned hero of former times."

"The heroes of former times failed," Garric heard his lips say. "We—you and I and all the rest—need to do better, Royhas. And so we shall."

Smoke belched from a mansion window. It was the natural gray-white billowing of wood and cloth because some *idiot* had set furnishings alight.

"Can you stop that?" Garric said to Royhas. "Do you have enough men that we can restore order?"

The nobleman shrugged. "We can try," he said.

"Where's the queen?" Liane demanded. "Is she—"

Screams of terror came from within the mansion, though it wasn't until the many thousands of citizens outside joined that the sound reached Garric's awareness.

The sun darkened. He looked up.

The thing lifting from the mansion roof had translucent gray vans that spread to the size of small clouds. The body, relatively small, was soot-colored and shaggy. It reminded him of cobwebs hanging in the common room of an ill-kept inn.

On the creature's back was a woman of coldly perfect

beauty. She looked at Garric without expression as she swept no more than fifty paces overhead.

"If I had my bow . . ." he muttered.

All around the mansion, people fell to their knees. One of Royhas' guards chanted a hymn to the Lady in a childish singsong, a vestige of the last time he'd prayed.

"It would take much more than an arrow," Tenoctris said quietly. "But now that we've driven her from her lair, we may have time to find a permanent solution."

The winged creature rose gradually as it flew out over the sea. Its wings rippled like those of a stingray, not a bird. It was visible for miles as it continued on toward the southeast.

Sharina felt the strangers' presence before she heard them. She held still, wondering if her heartbeat echoed as loudly as it seemed to her to do.

The acoustics within the great tree were remarkable. The narrow, twisting passage through the trunk led sound in the way a human ear does; she feared it might also, like a human throat, amplify any noises she made.

"She's in there," a voice whispered. It was the false Nonnus.

The baobab's interior was faintly lighted when Sharina first entered. The cavity opened to the sky somewhere high in the canopy, though the amount of illumination even at midday was less than that of the stars on an open meadow. It had been enough for Sharina to get a sense of her surroundings.

The cavity was twenty feet in diameter and unfurnished except for the sleeping bench Unarc had hacked into the spongy wood of one side. Since there was ventilation, Sharina had been surprised not to see a flat rock for a cooking fire.

A moment's reflection reminded her that this was a refuge, not a home. The hunter wouldn't have risked giving away his location by even a hidden fire.

Besides, the wooden interior with its narrow crack for ingress and egress made Sharina's stomach tighten as she thought of being trapped by a blaze; though she didn't imagine the real danger was as great as that of a wattle-and-daub hut in Barca's Hamlet. There'd been disastrous fires during several winters within Sharina's memory. Families had died before they could escape.

"Sharina?" said the false Nonnus. He'd raised his voice and was probably standing near the entrance. "I've come to rescue you, child. You can come out now."

"She's not coming," another man muttered. Sharina thought she recognized the voice as one of the dispatch vessel's crew, but she couldn't put a name or face to the speaker. "If she's even there."

In all likelihood, the false Nonnus and his fellows didn't realize how well the girl within could hear them, but that was no help to her. There was only one way out of the baobab: into the arms of her pursuers. The upper opening was probably too small for even a supple human to squirm through, and it was completely inaccessible besides. Sharina guessed she could climb ten or a dozen feet using main strength and splits in the wood, but the cavity's inward slope would prevent even a monkey from reaching the peak hundreds of feet above.

"Come out, child," the false Nonnus said in a cozening voice that made Sharina's skin crawl. "The wild man who captured you won't return till tomorrow night, if then."

Sharina squeezed her hands against the hilt of the Pewle knife. "Lady, cast your cloak about me," she whispered. "Lady—"

She realized that she was calling on the Lady of Peace while she gripped a weapon. She snatched her hands away, then froze.

With a tiny smile, Sharina drew the big knife and held it ready. She'd pray later, if she was able to.

"She's not coming out!" the second voice repeated. "I say we go in and get her if she's there."

"*I* say, Crattus," said the false Nonnus in a tone of

menace the hermit had never *ever* used, "that'll you'll obey me or regret that you did not."

The voice became bantering as the impostor continued, "But if you want to enter, go ahead. It'll be pitch dark unless you hold a torch in one hand, and the girl had a knife the last time I saw her."

"What do you want to do, then?" a third man asked. He sounded tired and vaguely angry. Sharina wondered how many men altogether were in the band.

"We'll camp here and wait for daylight," the false Nonnus said easily. "At dawn, I'll be able to illuminate the interior through my art. You shouldn't have much difficulty subduing our runaway safely."

"That's easy to say for somebody who won't be in there facing the knife," a man rumbled.

"Yes, Osan," the impostor hissed, false again to the mind of the man whose face he wore. "And easy for you to accomplish, or you shouldn't have taken the queen's gold. Do you want to explain to her that you were less afraid of her wrath than you were of a peasant girl?"

"I'll do my job," Osan said. "I always have, haven't I?"

"We'll camp here," the false Nonnus said briskly. "Crattus, make sure two men guard the opening at all times. In the morning we'll take care of the matter and get off this foul island."

A hand rasped the outer lip of the opening. "We can block this hole with a couple spears rammed into the sides," Crattus said. "Even if she's got the strength to pull them out, they'll squeal loud enough to wake the dead."

"Yes, a good idea," the false Nonnus agreed. "Do that as well."

A spear thunked into the wood. Echoes shivered about Sharina. Moments later a second spear struck and a human grunted loudly.

"That'll hold her!" said a voice Sharina hadn't heard before.

"What about the big guy she was with?" the third man asked.

"I told you, we'll be long gone before he returns," the impostor said. "I'm a wizard, remember?"

"I'm not bloody likely to forget that," Osan muttered. Sharina suspected he was facing the opening into the tree and that she heard more than his companions did. "I'm not bloody likely to work for another wizard, neither!"

"Osan, you and Denalt watch until moonrise," Crattus ordered. "Bies and Seno, you take over till the moon's a quarter up, and then Bayen and I take the last watch."

"Say, what if I can't see the moon?" Osan demanded. "It's as dark as a yard up a pig's backside here!"

"Then watch till dawn!" Crattus said. "The rest of you, get as much sleep as you can."

The men bedded down with only a scatter of further mutterings. They were obviously professionals, though this jungle seemed as foreign to them as it was to Sharina. The false Nonnus said nothing; perhaps he'd gone off to work his wizardry alone.

Sharina didn't know what to do. The tree soughed with the breath of the forest, moist and faintly tinged with decay. She walked across the cavity in darkness and lay down in the alcove.

She considered the possibility that Hanno would return during the night, then rejected it. If the false Nonnus was wizard enough to track Sharina down in this jungle, he was also wizard enough to determine the hunter's whereabouts.

She was physically and emotionally exhausted, as much from the preceding weeks as from the events of the day just ending. Morning would come. Her only choices then would be capture or suicide.

The Lady turned her face from those who took their own lives. And yet . . .

Sharina began to doze. The blade of the Pewle knife was beneath her cheek like a steel pillow. In a dream she saw herself stand and walk through the door that opened for her into a woodland like that of home.

A hut stood by a stream whose bed had been scooped deeper to create a basin for filling pots and washing. The man who'd been planting in the garden knocked dirt from the tip of his dibble and walked toward her.

"Nonnus?" Sharina said.

"Such of me as there is since I died, child," the stocky, smiling man said. "Sit down, please. It's all the hospitality I can offer you here. That and my company."

Sharina squatted on her haunches as she'd done hundreds of times beside the hermit's hut. Nonnus sat across from her.

"I watch you always, child," he said. "I hope you know that even when you can't see me."

On the ground beside them, colored pebbles from the creek picked out the Lady's image. In the woods near Barca's Hamlet Nonnus had carved the Lady on the trunk of a great tree. Though he wore his familiar black goat-hair tunic, the Pewle knife Nonnus had taken off only while praying was nowhere to be seen.

Sharina looked at the knife she held, then met the hermit's eyes again. He smiled again. "I don't have any need for it here," he said. "Besides, it's in good hands."

Sharina slid the blade back into its sealskin sheath. "There's a man outside who . . . ," she said. She swallowed. "Who claims to be you. He's a wizard."

Nonnus nodded. "He's Nimet or-Konya," he said. "And for perhaps the first time in my life I'm thankful for a wizard's work, child. I doubt we'd have been able to visit if it weren't for the magic Nimet and his mistress used to borrow my semblance. They made the barrier thinner than I suspect they knew."

He chuckled with grim humor. "Wizards aren't the only ones to neglect the side effects of their actions, of course," he added. "If I'd understood that when I was younger, I might have less to beg forgiveness for now."

Sharina leaned forward and caught the hermit's powerful, sinewy hands. She was crying. "Nonnus," she said, "can I stay here with you? Please!"

He held her with the delicacy of a mother with her infant. "This isn't your place, Sharina," he said softly. "When the time comes, and I pray to the Lady that it will be a long time, you'll have another home."

"Nonnus, what shall I do?" she cried. She squeezed his hands, knowing she could no more hurt this man than she could a hickory tree. "I'll fight them, but I don't think I can . . ."

"Kill six soldiers and Nimet himself as well?" Nonnus said. He detached one hand and put it on top of the other, sandwiching Sharina between. "No, I don't suppose you could. Which I think may be why you're here."

Sharina mopped her face on her tunic sleeve. She met the hermit's eyes and smiled. Trying to control her tremble of relief, she said, "Will you come back and help me, Nonnus? *Can* you?"

"I don't have flesh, child," Nonnus said. "But you do. If you permit me, I can use your flesh in ways you yourself could not."

He gave her a smile as hard as the crags that broke the seas off Pewle Island. He said, "I've repented of many of the things I did when I was young. But I haven't forgotten how to do them."

They stood, still holding hands and laughing at the pleasure of each other's company. "I knew you'd help me, Nonnus," Sharina said. She didn't know why she'd ever felt alone.

The hermit sobered and withdrew his hands. "This isn't a small thing for you to do, child," he said. "This is a violation like no other you'll ever feel. You might be better off to go with Nimet to his mistress, the queen."

"Nonnus," she said. "I need your help. Do whatever your conscience permits you to do. I'll do the same. And may the Lady shelter us."

Nonnus smiled; this time the expression was as gentle as a snowflake's touch. "For the last eighteen years of my life, Sharina,'' he said, ''the only thing besides mercy that I wanted was to be able to help you. I think the Lady has just granted me both.''

He touched the girl's cheek with the fingers of his right hand. ''Go and sleep, child,'' he said. ''And we'll see what happens when the dawn comes.''

The Scaled Men's chanting rose to a grunted crescendo; Ilna felt a ripple shiver through not the ship alone but also the world it rode in. Cozro shouted and the flyer which gnawed the grating inches from Ilna's face turned with an angry snarl to look over its shoulder.

The *Bird of the Waves* fell out of the twilit world and splashed jarringly as it landed. The hatch cover broke loose from the quick-and-dirty lashings the crew had applied after they flung Ilna into the hold. Sunlight lanced through the grate and around the frame lying askew on the coaming.

The winged creatures twisted upward like seared leaves. Their flesh turned black and sloughed away. The cartilage that articulated their bones shrank, knotting the skeletons into tight masses like the indigestible casts vomited beneath an owl's perch.

Ilna put her hands and right shoulder to the grating to shove sideways. Cozro simply flung it up, though without Ilna's direction the heavy cover might have toppled back again: the captain hadn't allowed for the weakness of muscles bound for days.

Ilna stepped out of the hold with the noose loosely coiled in her hands. The brazier, still dribbling the last of its varicolored smoke, sat in front of the deckhouse. The Scaled Men had set their fire and left it before they retreated to the poorly ventilated deckhouse. The flyers, beasts for all the humanity of their features, hadn't known or cared to quench the brazier as they swarmed over the craft.

The creatures in desiccated profusion hung from the

rigging and littered the deck. *Like mayflies,* Ilna thought again, smiling grimly. The corpse of the sailor she'd seen devoured lay beside the hatch where it slid when Cozro raised the grating. It had been chewed to red bones. The skull was very broad and flat, and the remainder of the skeleton differed more from that of a normal man than the Scaled Man had when alive.

The door to the deckhouse rattled as the crossbar was withdrawn inside. Cozro freed a cutlass that a desperate blow had driven into the mast.

The sky was a pale, cloudless blue. The sun was near the western horizon, but it still hammered the sea and the ship rocking on it.

The sail hung limp, its deep belly empty of the wizard-wind that had filled the linen across the sea of that other world. An island, small but heavily overgrown, broke the surface half a mile to starboard. A flock of seabirds startled by the vessel's splashing entrance rose into the air above.

The Scaled Men had to force the door open against the flyers piled before it. The shrunken corpses stuck to the decking as though melted into the wood. Cozro snatched up the brazier in his left hand.

Ilna had been ready to noose the first of the sailors while the captain dealt with the next. "Take the one on the right!" she said. She was furious that she'd so nearly committed herself by assuming that other people thought the same way she did in a crisis.

The first two Scaled Men out of the deckhouse had cutlasses. They were bleeding from deep bites but both looked well able to fight. Behind them came a third sailor with the spear; last was a heavily bandaged fellow struggling to cock his crossbow.

"None of this scum could swim when they were men!" Cozro shouted. "We'll hope they haven't learned since they changed. The dinghy's still astern. Swim to it and we'll paddle to that island with our hands."

The four Scaled Men arrayed themselves in front of the

deckhouse. They were apparently waiting for the crossbowman to cock his weapon so that they could either shoot their escaped prisoners or threaten them into surrender.

"I can't swim either!" Ilna said. If the two of them rushed *now,* they might overcome the sailors; but it had to be both of them together. The Scaled Men were wounded to a greater or lesser degree, but she and Cozro were weak from days of hunger and tight bondage.

"Then I'm sorry for you!" the captain said. He turned and scattered the brazier's burning contents into the sail. The parched linen flared like tinder.

Cozro dived over the side. The Scaled Men shouted in guttural fear. Ilna was between the sailors and the roaring heat of the sail. The mast, cracked by long exposure to salt and sun, was beginning to burn also.

The sailor with the spear stepped forward. Ilna's noose settled about his neck and pulled tight. She'd acted on reflex rather than according to a plan. The only options that *swine* Cozro had left her were drowning or burning alive; she supposed she preferred to drown, but she wasn't quite ready to make that decision.

She kicked the spear free of the Scaled Man choking on the deck at her feet. Another sailor came for her with his cutlass raised; she whipped the free end of her rope across his bulging eyes. He jumped back with a blat of despair.

The air beyond the ship's port rail congealed into a disk of blue radiance, intensely cold.

Ilna looked at the disk over her shoulder. She kicked again, this time at the Scaled Man's crotch. She could see figures moving within the disk of light.

Without hesitation, Ilna stepped onto the railing and hurled herself into the blue glare. The disk might mean death, but staying with the *Bird of the Waves* was certain death.

Ilna regretted leaving her noose behind; but she'd had

many regrets in her lifetime and she'd learned to live with them.

Cashel could see his bones through the crackling blue radiance that suf-fused the night. He continued to concentrate on the boulder. It was moving, and any other considerations could wait till Cashel had finished the job at hand.

Zahag and the princess were shouting but their voices only buzzed like distant wasps over the roar of Cashel's pulse. He had the boulder over his head. He shouldn't have been able to lift it.

He rotated his body carefully. A load that was safe while it was poised could tear your back and knees apart if you shifted the wrong way. It was all a matter of balancing forces. . . .

When Cashel had turned just enough that the boulder wouldn't fall back on him and his companions, he rolled it off his spread fingers. It bounced away as he staggered forward.

Cashel's legs were too weak to support him; when he put a hand to the ground to steady himself, his elbow started to buckle. Aria grabbed his arm, but he didn't know if she was trying to hold him up or merely clinging out of fear.

The mountainside below them shook as though wracked by an earthquake. Blue fire crackled, splitting the rocky soil as far down the slope as Cashel could see. A skeleton bathed in sizzling light humped up from the long trench like a horse rising to its feet. It had the body of a lizard, but it stood on two legs the size of the largest oaks in the borough.

The creature turned with a dancer's grace, each joint sparkling with azure lightning. The tail of stiffly articulated bones swung, balancing the weight of the monster skull. It roared, shaking the heavens; then the jaws snapped shut on the nearest of the trolls who had pursued Cashel and his companions.

"Is is yours, chief?" Zahag cried. The ape was hopping up and down as the ground shook. "Did you call it up?"

"I didn't . . . ," Cashel said. "I don't know. . . ."

"Please!" Aria said. "Please, can't we go now?"

The creature stepped across the trench from which it had risen. Its tail was a whip of savage light. Clawed forelimbs snatched a troll, splintering his club and casting the mangled whole into a mouth easily able to hold him.

"My staff," Cashel mumbled. He tried to stand. He wondered if he was dreaming that he was helpless while fantastic things went on around him.

The creature of stone and light followed the fleeing trolls, snapping with the precision of a serpent hunting mice. The saw-toothed plates along its spine waved from side to side.

"I have the staff!" Aria said. She did, too, though she'd just now picked it up. "Please! Please!"

His companions couldn't lift him, but they weren't willing to leave him behind. That was all right. He could walk. He could!

Cashel turned on all fours and began to crawl toward the cave mouth. The creature that had risen from the rocks shook the earth every time its foot came down. Like Cashel himself, it controlled its weight with a graceful delicacy that belied the strength involved.

Trolls bawled in helpless terror as the creature hunted them down the slope. Its strides were thunder against which the trolls' deep voices sounded like the cheeping of tree frogs.

The monster didn't seem to be hostile to Cashel and his companions. There wasn't much he could have done about it if it were.

Cashel chuckled at the thought of waving his quarterstaff at a creature hundreds of feet long. The laughter washed some of the fatigue from his muscles. He tried again and this time he *did* stand up. Zahag ran ahead but paused at the blazing entrance to the cave.

"Oh thank you Mistress God!" the princess babbled, stumbling along at Cashel's side. "Oh thank you!"

Cashel lurched into the cave. His companions were behind him; he could feel their presence though he didn't turn his head to make sure. His skin sizzled and crawled with immense power. He went on, feeling as though the skin and not the flesh it covered moved his limbs and drove him unstoppably forward.

He could see forms ahead through a cascade of blue fire. King Folquin sat in his court, flanked by courtiers as he listened to a petition.

Cashel stepped toward them, but the cave branched suddenly. To the right Ilna stood on the deck of a ship, fighting with monsters like the corpse Cashel had poured out of a barrel on Erdin's waterfront.

"Ilna!" he cried. He couldn't hear his own voice over the cave's own pulsing thunder. "Ilna, I'm coming!"

Ilna turned away from him. She jumped toward a pair of men Cashel saw vaguely in the air beyond her, a cripple he didn't recognize and the gangling youth who'd been Folquin's court wizard. "Il—"

Ilna vanished. The ship disintegrated in a flash of azure lightning that rent fiber from fiber and plucked apart the scaly men like flies in a boy's hands.

The cave walls opened. Cashel and his two yammering companions fell into a sunlit sea whose foaming surface tossed with body parts and splintered wood.

The 26th of Heron

Let me say right now that I won't have anything to do with harming King Valence!'' Pitre said. ''If you're going to talk about that, I'll leave the room until you're finished.''

Garric sat at one end of the dining table they'd moved from the servants' refectory into the vast circular room that had been the queen's private suite. He looked at Pitre in expressionless amazement, wondering what went on in the mind of a person who could mouth those words.

''There were more cowards than brave men in my day, lad,'' said the voice in his mind. *''I wouldn't expect that to change in the next thousand years either.''*

''We needn't hurt Valence,'' Waldron said curtly. The conspirators were undisguised and the members of their entourages present wore their colors openly. ''Not if he'll listen to reason, anyway. I won't even demand that he abdicate immediately, though of course we'll appoint a regent. Valence's line still has a lot of respect among the lower orders, and I don't see any call to borrow trouble before we've consolidated the real power in our own hands.''

Before Garric and his companions had reached the queen's sanctum, members of the mob had pushed the tourmaline mirror over on the stone floor, cracking it across. Tenoctris had nodded approval at the result, saying that destroying the mirror had been her first priority.

The large room was under a dome in the center of the one of the five wings. There were no tapestries on the granite walls, and no furniture save for the great mirror and an empty circular table standing waist high. The queen had existed without chairs, wardrobes, or even a bed.

It was a little past midnight in Valles. Outside, the sea breeze had blown clouds over the sky and only a few stars managed to sparkle down. Inside, the windowless room would have been equally dark with the sun at zenith.

Garric remembered that the scene he viewed in Tenoctris' scrying mirror was suffused by soft light. The conspirators' servants had brought in lanterns, but their smoky flickering accented the gloom they were intended to dispel.

"Appointing a regent might lead to the mistaken impression that one of us was somehow superior to the others, Waldron," Lord Tadai said, holding his hands before him as though he were examining his perfect manicure. "I think we'll call ourselves the Council of Noble Advisors and avoid the sort of awkward discussions that would otherwise result, don't you?"

Waldron flushed. Besides their aides and advisors—nobles like themselves—each conspirator was accompanied by his personal bodyguards. Waldron himself might be the only real man of war among the five, but all the liveried soldiers looked tough and competent. Whoever started a fight under these circumstances guaranteed his own slaughter by the combined forces of his former allies.

Garric smiled faintly. He drew his long sword down the whetstone he'd set on the table before him.

"Does he have to make that noise?" Sourous said loudly. The young noble rubbed his hands over themselves as though he were washing. He indicated Garric only by a sideways tic of his goatee.

"Yes he does, Sourous," Royhas said, speaking for the first time since the conspirators convened in the queen's suite at his insistence. "While I stood in the crowd here and the rest of you hid in your town houses, Master Garric single-handedly slew the giant whose skeleton you passed to enter this mansion. He's readying his sword for the next time he needs to use it."

In truth, the blade was in better shape than Garric—or Carus within him—had expected after the vicious fight. The cyclops' bones hadn't dulled the edge significantly. More important, the blade had snapped back straight after the brutal twisting it got while levering the monster's ankle apart.

All eyes were on Garric. He smiled, reversed the sword, and drew it down again with a sliding motion which in its course passed the whole length of the edge across the stone.

There'd been a tiny nick in the tip where the blade had lopped off the cyclops' armored finger. A few strokes on the stone had restored the steel's smooth line.

"I have servants to do that!" Waldron snarled, speaking to Royhas rather than Garric. Garric was still beneath Waldron's consideration, but the northern landowner knew Royhas to be his most serious rival among the conspirators.

"The presence of our young associate does raise an interesting possibility," Tadai said, turning slightly to include Garric in his comment. "King Garric, the true heir of Carus and the Old Kingdom, might look better on the throne than Valence. Under a Council of Noble Advisors—"

Tadai smiled thinly.

"—of course."

"Valence is insane," Sourous muttered. "Completely mad!"

Garric found his bitter tone surprising. He hadn't realized the young man was capable of anything but fear for his own person—though something, come to think, had brought Sourous into the conspiracy. Garric realized again that he could never know all he'd like to know about those with whom his fate was now twined—even about Liane and Tenoctris.

Garric wiped his blade with a coarse woolen rag, then glanced over his shoulder. Behind his chair Liane and

Tenoctris filled the place of the dozen retainers assisting each of the noble conspirators.

Garric grinned. He'd trade the two women and Carus, closer yet, for a hundred times their number of the sort of advisors the others had in their service.

''No, no,'' Pitre said. He twisted and untwisted a silk handkerchief as he spoke, a replacement for the wooden puzzle he'd spilled across Royhas' floor. ''Valence will stay king, but we'll get rid of that wretched wizard Silyon. Now the queen's gone, and when Silyon's gone too everything will go back to normal.''

''I say—,'' Waldron said.

Garric stood. He shot the sword into its long sheath with a *zing/tunk* as the crossguard slid home against the mouth of the scabbard. Everyone in the room stared at him again. Though in fact Garric had put up his weapon instead of drawing it, the action had clearly been aggressive.

''We aren't rid of the queen, gentlemen,'' he said. His mouth spoke his own thoughts, but King Carus' experienced direction gave Garric's tone and stance their present assurance. ''We've bought time by driving her from Valles, but the first thing the revived Kingdom of the Isles needs to do is to meet the queen's counterstroke and crush her utterly.''

Tadai raised an eyebrow—half-mocking, but only half. Pitre looked at Garric in amazement, Sourous looked at his hands, and Royhas smiled faintly as he sat in a posture of apparent relaxation. His ankle was crossed on his knee and his right arm sprawled languidly on the table.

''Yes, of course,'' Waldron said with a dismissive flick of his hand. To his fellow nobles he continued, ''I'll take charge of mustering the royal forces, of course. We can decide later whether my title will be—''

''Gentlemen,'' Garric said. He deliberately didn't raise his voice, though he noticed Tadai's gaze flick appraisingly from Waldron to him.

''—warlord or regent,'' Waldron continued. The chief

of his guard contingent, a craggy man whose hair, beard, and eyes were all the hue of cast iron, ignored his master and watched Garric intently. "Now—"

"Gentlemen!" Garric said in the voice that had called sheep from distant hills.

Waldron's hand gripped his sword hilt. His guard commander laid fingers on Waldron's wrist, preventing him from drawing the weapon. The other nobles, even Royhas, started in their seats. A secretary dropped his handful of ledgers on Tadai's feet.

"Gentlemen," Garric continued, pitching his voice to carry but no longer at threatening volume. "You can't trust any one of yourselves with supreme power or what looks like it might become supreme power. You can trust me."

He grinned, a wolfish but not unfriendly expression. "Trust me not to be in the pocket of another of you, at any rate."

"This is absurd!" Waldron said; his tone showed that he realized that the suggestion was by no means absurd. He made a quick, angry gesture, brushing his guard away, but didn't put his hand back on his sword.

"I don't think it is," Tadai said judiciously. "Though—"

"What of Valence?" Pitre said. He met Garric's eyes, making the youth wonder if possibly Pitre had a backbone after all.

"He's not an evil man," Garric said. Tenoctris couldn't speak at this gathering, but she and Liane had coached Garric on how to handle a question that was certain to arise. "There's no need to supplant him—once we've removed his wizard, who *is* an evil man or at least one who does evil willingly."

He paused, sweeping his eyes across the nobles at the other end of the long table. It was a measure of the authority Carus' spirit gave Garric that none of them interrupted him.

"Valence has no issue," Garric continued. "He can

adopt me as his heir, uniting the old royal line of Haft with the present line of Ornifal."

"Ho!" said Tadai, clapping his hands as if at a keenly struck blow at a cockfight.

Pitre snapped his handkerchief out. "Yes," he said, nodding with sudden enthusiasm. "Yes, Valence is a good man. The trouble's none of his doing, not really."

Waldron went livid but he didn't speak. His right hand clasped and opened, clasped and opened.

"It seems to me," Royhas said, still affecting a languid appearance, "that in the short run this solves all our problems. Master Garric's fame has already spread over the city as the man who slew the giant. Indeed, much of the populace probably sees him as King Carus reborn rather than merely the descendant of the old line."

"That's right!" said Sourous with unexpected animation. "We'll give the mob a hero, while we run the kingdom as it should be run!"

Even Waldron looked at Sourous in amazement. Liane drew in a hissing breath at the young noble's effrontery. Garric simply laughed. How could he get angry at a fool who was so dismissively insulting to a man standing well within the reach of his just-sharpened sword?

"Lord Sourous," Garric said. He nodded with a slight, friendly smile toward Waldron and the blank-faced guard commander at Sourous' shoulder. "Friends all, I hope. You gentlemen know more of Ornifal than I could ever hope to. Your lineage, your wealth, and the patriotism that led you to act when your king would not—these all mark you as the sort of advisors any ruler would wish to have."

Tadai's plump face wore a watchful expression in place of its usual mocking humor. Pitre looked expectant, and Sourous showed a degree of startled-bunny fear; *his* guards had moved close to the table on either side of the young man, and the reason for their concern had apparently dawned in Sourous' limited brain.

"You must realize, though," Garric continued, speaking the words an ancient king whispered in his mind, "that though I'll listen willingly to your advice and that of other wise and noble folk throughout the kingdom, I will not be taking your orders. You'll be taking mine."

Waldron until that moment had held himself tense as a bent spring. He leaped up, kicking over his chair.

"In this room," Waldron said, "you see some of the oldest blood on Ornifal."

He looked at the cowering Sourous. In a snarl he added, "Sadly decayed though some members may be! But not even Sourous is fool enough to take the orders of a shepherd from Haft!"

Garric stepped around the corner of the table and walked deliberately toward Waldron. Pitre, seated between the two standing men, jumped to his feet and backed away. His guards formed a hedge in front of him.

"Waldron bor-Warriman . . ." Garric said. His hands were spread open at his sides. "I see three choices for you. You can accept me as your leader by birth, because I'm directly descended from King Carus."

"You say!" Waldron said. His guard commander's posture was very like Garric's own, open-handed but tense as a drawn bowcord.

"Second," Garric continued, his voice rising in volume but remaining a thunderous tenor with no touch of shrillness, "you can decide to turn your hereditary lands over to the folk tilling them, because you have no title on the basis of heredity if you refuse to accept *my* rule."

"If I bowed to every madman who called himself king, I'd never be able to straighten up!" Waldron said.

"As for your third choice, Lord Waldron . . ." Garric said. He was trembling. The body he wore was no longer his alone. The muscles quivered with the fierce, channeled bloodlust of King Carus.

"If you think I'm a lying Haft shepherd rather than the King of the Isles," Garric/Carus said, "try to prove those lies on my body. We'll duel in front of the mansion, by torchlight or we'll wait till dawn. And no one who watches will doubt that every word I've said since I came to Ornifal is the truth!''

''We'll do it now,'' Waldron said in a grating voice. He seized his sword hilt and had half-drawn the weapon when his guard commander stepped in front of him and grasped the noble by both elbows.

''Let go of me, you fool!'' Waldron said. ''Do you think I'm afraid of a shepherd?''

''Sir, look at the way he moves!'' the guard cried. ''If he's a shepherd, then I'm a gravedigger. And I'd be your gravedigger if I let you fight him, I swear by my soul in the Lady's arms!''

Waldron tried to shove the man away. The guard, blocky where his master was tall, and very, very strong, kept his grip. He pushed Waldron toward the wall. The other men wearing the Warriman cat's-head crest on their tabards stepped between Waldron and Garric, though they were unwilling to put hands on their master as the guard commander had.

For a moment, the only sounds were wheezing breaths and the scrape of boot soles on the granite floor. Waldron let go of his sword and lowered his arms; his retainer released him.

''Lord Waldron,'' Garric said quietly, ''I need you and I'll hold you in the highest honor; but I *am* your king.''

Waldron continued to gasp for breath; his face looked gray. The nobleman was more than three times Garric's age. Waldron knew—as Carus did—that courage and skill counted for more than youth on a battlefield; but the old man had seen enough battles in his years to be able to size up Garric as surely as his guard commander had done. A fight between the two of them would no more be a duel than a hog duels the butcher who holds its nose in a hooked clamp as his knife slices the beast's throat.

Garric knelt and righted Waldron's fallen chair. ''Please, Lord Waldron,'' he said.

Without waiting to see what the nobleman decided, Garric walked to his own seat at the end of the table.

Liane gave him a tiny nod. When Garric turned and sat down, Waldron was seating himself also. His guard commander held the chair for him.

"We'll need to discuss the situation with Valence as soon as possible," Royhas said, continuing the previous conversation. "Pitre, you're probably the person to make the arrangements, don't you think?"

"I wonder what it's going to be like living under a real king," Tadai said. His laugh held a strain of hysteria.

The powdery soil broke Ilna's fall instead of her bones, but it rose in a plume that threatened to choke her. She clawed her way up, swimming as much as climbing. When she finally burst clear of the pit her impact had dug, she found it was still desperately hard to breathe.

She was on a barren plain which stretched to the horizon in every direction. The sun shone with bitter intensity, but the sky was black and the atmosphere so thin that she could see the stars. None of them looked familiar.

Halphemos, coughing and wheezing, dragged the cart with Cerix on it from another soft-rimmed crater nearby. Ilna strode over to them, trailing her toes at each step as she would have done were she walking in mud. The dust neither clung to her feet nor hung in choking clouds—the latter a small benefit from the thin air.

"Where are we, Halphemos?" Ilna said. Her voice was a bat squeak. She smiled faintly. "I'm not complaining. It isn't on fire, so it's a better place than I was standing a moment ago."

"I don't know," Halphemos mumbled. He looked numb and exhausted. He'd been working his wizard arts; he *must* have been, to have saved Ilna this way. "I don't . . . Cerix, do you know?"

Ilna helped pull the wheeled chair up from the hole it had splashed when it landed. The wheels were too narrow for this dust: they sank to the hubs, like those of farm carts after the spring thaw. A sledge would be better, but there was no wood in this wasteland from which to fashion one.

Cerix spat out a gobbet of phlegm and the dust he'd swallowed when impact flung him out of the cart. This landscape's harsh light drew the lines of the cripple's face deeper, but Ilna judged he'd have looked terrible under any illumination.

"The boy didn't bring us here," Cerix said. He shook his head, either to clear it or from anger; Ilna couldn't be sure which. "We were opening a passage to you through a circle of power, but before we arrived you entered the circle. And brought us here."

"I saw you in the air," Ilna said. She kept her tone even. She'd heard rebuke in the cripple's tone, but she'd lived in her own head long enough to know that she sometimes heard rebuke where none was intended. "I went to you because the choices were to burn or to drown."

"She entered the circle after we formed it?" Halphemos said to his mentor. "That isn't possible, is it?"

He wiped his face with the sleeve of his robe. The cloth was dark with rich gray silt because the boy had caught himself on his arms when he landed. Halphemos looked like a mummer in blackface playing a minion of the Sister.

"It wouldn't be possible for me or even you, boy," Cerix said, "but it's what she did, clearly enough."

He looked up at Ilna. "Who are you, mistress? And *don't* tell me you're a weaver from some village in the back of beyond. We have to know where we are if we're ever to get out!"

Ilna's nose wrinkled. Breathing this thin air was like being half-smothered by a pillow. No matter how Ilna's lungs strained, she couldn't draw in a satisfying breath. It made her irritable and she supposed she should make allowances for her companions being irritable for the same reason.

She'd never been good at excusing bad behavior in herself *or* other people.

"If you think I'd bother to lie to you," she snapped, "then you've lost more than your legs. If you didn't rescue me from the ship as I'd thought you did, then neither of us owe the other anything. I'll see if I can find more congenial company."

Ilna turned to walk away. One direction was as good as another—and all of them bad. The rolling terrain was completely barren. The landscape could stand as a symbol for life; at least life for such folk as Ilna os-Kenset. She smiled like a razor at the thought.

There was something in the middle distance. The odd sharpness of the light here made it hard to identify shapes with those they had normally, but she thought she was seeing the bones of some vast creature.

"Mistress, please!" Halphemos said. "Cerix didn't mean to accuse you of anything. We were trying to go to you. If instead we came here, it must have been a mistake of mine. Like the one where I made your brother vanish."

Ilna looked over her shoulder. She was letting anger rule her. That was worse than anything Cerix thought—or believed.

"Mistress," the cripple said. "I'm afraid. I don't know where we are, but I don't think we can live here. I think, I *pray*, you have the power to get us out of this place but I don't know how. I misspoke because I was a fool."

He touched his stumps with a bitter smile. "As these legs already prove," he added.

"Yes, well," said Ilna. "I've acted the fool myself often enough that I should have greater charity for others, I suppose."

She didn't think anything of the sort, but Cerix had apologized and it behooved her to do the same. She grimaced. "I know nothing about how we got here or how we can get out. If no one has a better idea, I suggest we walk in that direction—"

She indicated north with a tic of her chin.

"—because that puts the sun at our back. My skin is

prickling already. The light scarcely seems bright enough for sunburn, but that's what it feels like.''

''We may as well,'' Halphemos said doubtfully, squinting toward the northern horizon. It was just possible that there were hills in that direction, but they were probably an illusion.

''If she says we go north,'' Cerix said, ''that's where we go.''

He scowled and admitted, ''I can't move myself. I can turn the wheels, but they won't bite in this dust. If you want to leave me . . .''

''Don't talk nonsense,'' Ilna said. ''Halphemos, we'll use your sash as towline. It's silk and long enough, I'd judge.''

As the youth unwrapped the garment, Ilna continued to the cripple, ''As for who I am—my father drank himself to death after he brought my brother and me home to Barca's Hamlet as infants. I never knew my mother. I ask only the respect due a decent woman who pays her debts. That's all the discussion I intend to have about my private business. Do you understand?''

Cerix burst into hacking laughter. Halphemos rose from tying the end of his sash to the chair's front axle. He watched his mentor in concern.

The fit ended when Cerix brought up another mass of filth from his lungs. He wiped his mouth and looked at Ilna with a smile of self-mockery. ''I don't understand anything at all about you, mistress,'' he said. ''But as for my respect—on *that* score you need have no doubts.''

Ilna nodded curtly. To Halphemos she said, ''The sooner we get moving, the better our chance of finding water while there's still daylight. Not that I see the chance as very good.''

The youth gave her a hopeful smile and leaned into the makeshift towline. Ilna gripped the silk from the other side and fell into step.

The cart cut a wide furrow. Halphemos had rigged the sash to lift the front edge when they pulled, so at least they weren't digging deeper with every step.

It was still hard work. Carrying water from the well to the laundry cauldron, two buckets at a time on a yoke, was punishing for a lightly built woman; but the task ended when the cauldron was sufficiently full. This trek wouldn't end until the three of them died.

She smiled to think of the well back home. Her thoughts and those of her companions were the only place there was going to be water in this desolation. Occasionally they trudged across bands of discoloration around a central hub. Perhaps lichen had grown there once, but the stain and a slight firmness to the soil were all that remained.

They walked. Ilna didn't know how long. The sun moved more slowly here than it did in the waking world. Sometimes they rested, but there was little rest to be had in this wasteland.

"We're on the bottom of the Outer Sea," Cerix said. "It's like this all the way from the Ice Capes to the southern lands where men have their faces on their bellies."

Ilna risked a look over her shoulder; "risked," because she knew that when she was so tired any change of routine meant that she might stumble. Getting to her feet again would be as difficult as climbing a mountain in her normal state of health.

Cerix was grinning as his chair rocked over the rolling landscape. He made swimming motions with his arms and his eyes watched stars move in the black sky.

Ilna faced forward again. Delirium wasn't a bad response to their situation. It was a form of weakness, of course; the drug in which the cripple saturated himself and whose stench clung to his clothing like the dye itself had obviously sapped his will.

Strength wasn't going to save Ilna, but weakness wasn't an option for her either. She walked, setting the pace now. The soil dragged like the surf, retarding each step without gripping.

For all the cripple's madness, this plain did look much

as Ilna supposed a sea bottom would. Twice in her lifetime a neap tide had drawn the water back half a mile from the gravel strand at the eastern margin of Barca's Hamlet.

There was no wind. The chill air was so thin that the sweat of effort didn't evaporate quickly. A drop trickled like the touch of a cold knife down Ilna's backbone. She breathed only through her nostrils though each inhalation seared like the fumes of a bonfire; gasping with her mouth open would dry her body even faster than was happening already.

"What's that?" Halphemos croaked. He nodded toward the scatter of objects a few hundred paces to the right of their aimless course.

Metal ribs similar to those of a wooden ship stuck out of the silt. A few scraps of hull sheathing clung to the uprights, but not enough to give more than a hint of the vessel's original size. The panels were still bright despite their advanced decay; the sun and stars glinted from them.

"Nothing that helps us," Ilna said. Her voice rasped worse than the youth's did. It would be a relief to die.

"We're sailing through the air," Cerix caroled in cracked cheerfulness. "See how we dance in the clouds, Halphemos? Oh, I've never been so free!"

The youth winced. He looked at the ground before him and paced onward as if oblivious of his friend's raving.

Ilna kept going because that was what she'd always done. Her lungs burned, her shoulders felt as though the strain of pulling would dislocate them, and the throbbing pain of her headache put a halo around anything she tried to focus her eyes on.

There was no purpose in going on, but there was no purpose in life either, not that Ilna had found. She went on anyway.

"Oh, look at the fountains playing!" Cerix said. "Have you ever seen anything as beautiful as the way the water sparkles in the light? We've found paradise, Halphemos! The Lady took flesh and rescued us!"

Ilna thought of gagging the cripple with a strip of his tunic. She wondered if she still had enough strength to tear cloth. Strangling Cerix would be even more satisfying than simply stopping his mouth.

"So graceful!" Cerix said. "All golden and so beautiful!"

Halphemos was beginning to weave from side to side. His tug on the sash threw Ilna off her line. "Wake up!" she said. "Watch what you're doing."

She wasn't sure the words came out of her mouth. Her lips were as dry as the dust that caked them.

A circular trapdoor opened in the surface ahead of them, spilling radiance the color of a winter dawn. Humans climbed out and walked toward the trio. They were golden, beautiful; glowing with their own internal light.

Halphemos stumbled and fell as though heart-stabbed. He didn't throw out his hands to catch himself. Ilna dragged the cart a pace onward without noticing. When it jammed against the youth's feet, it jerked her to her knees.

She fumbled, trying to lift Halphemos' face. The dust would suffocate him as surely as the ocean Cerix kept maundering about. She finally laced the fingers of both hands in his hair and tugged his mouth and nose clear.

The golden folk of Ilna's hallucination gently lifted the youth. Other hands helped her rise. Her body felt as light as dandelion fluff.

"Relax, just let us carry you," said a melodious voice. Ilna drifted across the landscape toward the trapdoor and its spire of light. She couldn't see her companions. She supposed she was dead.

A sponge soaked in sweet wine bathed her lips. The alcohol bit where the dry skin had cracked.

The pain seemed real. Her eyes focused again. A male figure, tall and slender, passed her through the trapdoor to a statuesque female. Similar figures carried Halphemos and Cerix down a curving ramp ahead of her.

Beyond, all was light and vegetation and architecture

as delicate as sugar sculptures. Water danced in scores of streams and fountains among the greenery. The illumination soaked through Ilna's being. She could hear singing voices more pure and rapturous than those of cardinals in springtime.

Her consciousness sank into the pool of golden radiance and vanished beneath its warm surface.

The wizard Nimet, who called himself Nonnus the Hermit when he wore his present guise, had scribed his circle of power on a roof slate from the ruins of Unarc's hut. He tapped his athame of fossil bone as he intoned, "*Barbliois eipsatha athariath. . . .*"

Nimet's six soldiers waited at the entrance to the baobab's interior. Osan pretended to be studying the rim of his round buckler, unaware of the wizardry going on a few paces away. None of the others looked uncomfortable, though their expressions ranged from boredom to the concern of Crattus, their commander. The girl was active and resourceful, and a Pewle knife wasn't a joke no matter who wielded it.

"*Pelchaphiaon barbathieaoth io,*" Nimet said. The sun had risen a few minutes before, though no light had as yet penetrated to the forest floor. A spherical effigy of the dawn sky formed above the circle of power, complete with clouds and a line of fruit bats straggling home. The great bats were tiny as dust motes in the illusion.

The soldiers held small shields in their left hands. They had simple bronze helmets and cuirasses of stiffened linen, already soaked with their sweat. Denalt and Bies held their spears reversed to use as clubs since they'd be the first into the cavity. Osan and Seno had their swords drawn; they would follow.

"*Marmarauoth ieaoth,*" the wizard said. As he spoke the illusion of sunlit sky rose to the height of a man's head. It began to drift toward the opening into the baobab.

Its cold illumination, faint in absolute terms, was as bright as a torch in the gloom beneath the canopy.

Crattus and Bayen were veterans of thirty years' experience. They'd pin the girl's shoulders to the wall with their spears if they had to, trusting the Goddess Fortune to keep them from fatally nicking an artery. Nimet wanted the girl captured alive, but he'd made it clear that he was even more concerned to stay alive himself.

Crattus didn't quarrel with an employer's priorities. Besides, his own were similar.

"*Achrammachamarei!*" Nimet cried. He staggered up from his seated position. The sympathetic illusion, in all ways an image of the sky above the jungle, trembled through the slot into the baobab. It illuminated the wood as it passed.

"Time to earn our pay," Crattus said, nodding to Denalt. The leading soldier eased into the tree, holding his buckler sideways until the opening widened sufficiently for him to straighten it before him.

"You mean we haven't been already?" Bies said with a morose grimace. He followed Denalt. Osan, then Seno, slipped through behind them. Each waited just long enough that he didn't tread on the heels of the man preceding.

The illusion hung in the center of the cavity, casting its soft radiance on the living wood. A lump covered by a blue cloak lay in the sleeping notch on the far side. A sturdy javelin leaned against the wall beside it.

"Is she dead?" Denalt said. He took a careful step toward the cloak, his buckler well advanced.

"*Watch—*," Bies screamed.

Nonnus leaped down from where he clung to the wall above the entrance. He landed between Osan, just squirming through the opening, and the soldiers already inside. The Pewle knife severed Osan's throat.

Nonnus turned on the balls of his feet. Bies was trying to face around and reverse his spear for use. The Pewle knife, sharp and as heavy as an axeblade, entered beneath the lower edge of Bies' short cuirass and continued through the way a scythe cuts wheat. The same stroke severed the tendons and arteries at the back of Denalt's knees before the man had fully realized the debris rolled in Sharina's cloak wasn't his real enemy.

Osan bolted into the cavity, spewing blood like a headless chicken. He tripped on a coil of Bies' intestines; both men fell, tangled with the screaming Denalt.

"What?" cried Seno, pushing ahead to see why Osan had jumped forward that way. His head was slightly lowered. Nonnus chopped through his spine from behind and slipped into the opening like a gory shadow.

"Get back!" Crattus said. The shouts within the cavity were meaningless, but he could smell fresh blood.

Bayen stepped sideways to let Seno through the narrow slot. He'd opened his mouth to say something to Crattus. Nonnus gripped Bayen's spear just behind the head and jerked the soldier to the side. Bayen dropped the spear, but he was still off-balance for the instant it took the Pewle knife to stab up through his throat. His severed tongue flew out in a red spray.

Crattus thrust over the body of his toppling comrade. Nonnus had gone under Bayen instead.

Crattus shouted a curse and jumped backward. The slashing Pewle knife opened the side of his left thigh, nicking the bone. Severed muscles shrank back to their attachments, leaving the ends of the femoral artery writhing unsupported. The lower portion oozed; the upper end spurted, draining the soldier's blood in powerful gouts.

Crattus fell on his back. He was a good man; he managed to throw his spear in Nonnus' direction, though he can't have imagined he had any chance of success.

Instead of ducking, Nonnus ticked the point aside with the back of his knife. He'd have liked to finish Crattus quickly for mercy's sake, but the old veteran drew his sword while his left hand tried to clamp his wound closed.

It wouldn't do him any good, but Nonnus respected his

willingness to try. Crattus wasn't a man to take chances with.

Nimet had run away blindly when he saw a bloody demon spring from the opening into the tree. Nonnus bent and wiped the Pewle knife on the hem of Bayen's tunic before he sheathed the weapon again. He followed the wizard at an easy pace. The jungle wasn't a familiar environment to him, but the laws of every place were the same: stay aware of your surroundings, and don't do anything hastily.

He found Nimet fifty paces away. The wizard had run into a stand of bamboo. Nonnus grinned faintly. He'd have had as much luck pushing his way through a granite boulder as he did with a grove of thumb-thick bamboo.

Nimet had penetrated several feet into the wiry mass; now he was clawing his way back and finding the springy stems just as determined a barrier in this direction as the other. He saw Nonnus waiting under the broad leaves of an elephant-ear plant.

Nimet screamed and tried to draw his sword. His arm was tangled with the bamboo stems. The leaves, tiny but saw-edged, had covered his bare skin with a tracery of cuts.

"Do you recognize me, Nimet?" Nonnus asked. His left hand reached into the bamboo, caught the wizard by the neck, and jerked him out. They stood nose to nose; Nimet's fingers clutched at the hand choking him but without loosening its grip.

The men's features were identical, but blood from the hermit's victims had bathed his skin and clothes. His free hand touched the knife hilt but did not draw it. Nimet's mouth blew bubbles as he tried to speak.

"You'd foul my steel!" Nonnus said. He twisted, flinging the wizard facedown on the leaf litter. Before Nimet could rise, Nonnus had stepped on the back of his neck.

"I'll—" Nimet screamed.

Nonnus caught a handful of the wizard's hair and jerked upward. The neck broke with a sharp crack.

The hermit stepped back, breathing hard. His job was done.

He looked upward, toward a star-shaped patch of clear sky. He smiled faintly. The change came with the suddenness of a tropic sunset. Flesh and bone flowed back to their original semblance.

Where a man in his forties had stood, a tall, willowy young woman sank to the ground unconscious. Her arms and clothing were red with the blood of her enemies.

Cashel couldn't breathe. Spiders were crawling on his face. He moved a leaden arm to brush them away.

He was facedown in saltwater, drowning. Aria screamed in his ear as she tried to tug his nostrils to the surface. He turned, blowing like a whale, and went under again. He didn't have any strength and he couldn't remember how he came to be in the sea.

"Zahag! Help me!" the princess cried. She was pulling on the neck of Cashel's tunic now.

Cashel tried to breathe, sucked water, and thrashed his arms in frustrated anger. This time his head and shoulders came up. He saw a dinghy bobbing a dozen paces away. The man in it—

The man in it was Cozro, the master of the ship that brought the corpse of the scaly man to Erdin. What was he doing here?

Cozro sat in the dinghy's stern, paddling clumsily with both hands. He rigidly ignored Cashel and the girl. She was screaming like she hoped to be heard back on Pandah.

Zahag swarmed over the dinghy's gunwale. Cozro stopped splashing and raised a rusty cutlass. The ape hopped backward into the bow, swinging his body between his long arms. His shrieks rose into an insectile chirping.

Cashel swam toward the dinghy in a walloping breaststroke. He was so tired that he heard but did not feel the sea he splashed through.

Cozro saw him coming and settled back in the stern of the rocking dinghy. "Who are you?" he shouted.

Cashel caught the gunwale. He wasn't sure he could lift himself into the boat. He'd only been able to swim this far because he was worried about Zahag. "Put that sword down!" he shouted to Cozro.

Aria grabbed the side also. "Zahag!" she shouted. "Help Cashel get in!"

The princess floated like thistledown, buoyed up by her gauzy garments. If they became saturated they'd take her to the bottom like an anchor, but so long as air was trapped between the layers they were a benefit.

"How did I know you were human?" Cozro said. He lowered the cutlass though he didn't put it away. "I thought you were more, were more . . ."

Zahag grasped Cashel by the arm with one inhumanly strong hand and started to drag him upward. Though the ape also held the opposite gunwale, the dinghy still threatened to turn turtle. Cozro shouted in fear and threw his considerable weight to the other side. Cashel, finding the strength after all, rolled into the belly of the boat.

No one spoke for a moment. The dinghy rocked as Aria crawled in with assistance from Zahag.

"Who are you?" Cozro repeated. He'd put the cutlass down and seemed afraid to pick it up again. That showed he had an idea of how Cashel felt about the captain's apparent intention of leaving them to sink or swim as he paddled to the island alone.

Cashel was breathing hard. He wasn't quite ready to sit on a thwart instead of sprawling across it, but the abnormal exhaustion was draining away.

He raised his head from the hollow of the dinghy and looked at Cozro. In a voice that grated with controlled anger, Cashel said, "You were headed for the island. You go ahead and paddle there now. My friends and I will watch."

Cozro nodded, swallowed, and began lashing the water

with his hands. He probably thought that if Cashel got angry enough, he'd find the strength for anything he chose to do.

Cashel thought he was right.

The 27th of Heron

Garric rested his head on his hands, feeling as tired as he'd ever been. Rural labor was sometimes back-breaking and often brutally long—harvesting went on from dawn to the dusk of long summer days, because the next morning might bring rain.

What he felt now was a sort of mental exhaustion, though, that was completely different but no less punishing. For the past ten hours, he hadn't been out of his chair.

He smiled faintly. That wasn't quite true. He'd used the close chest in an alcove off this room, the queen's former reception hall and now his office. Liane had suggested it was more politic for Garric to make his headquarters in the queen's mansion rather than Royhas' town house.

"The next petitioner is Nimir bor-Nummerman, a land-holder from the Routan Peninsula, that's on the west of the island," Liane said, holding the wax tablet on which she'd jotted notes at a slant to the three-wick oil lamp. "He told me he was here simply to offer loyalty on behalf of his district, but Tadai says that he's in an inheritance struggle with his two half-brothers."

"We may still want to support him," Garric muttered into his hands. "His brothers could have gotten the inheritance through the queen. May the Lady guide my steps!"

Garric hadn't thought so often about the Great Gods since he was a little boy watching the Tithe Procession.

Priests from Carcosa drew carts with giant statues of the Lady and the Shepherd around the borough annually, collecting the temples' due. Garric knew now that the images were only painted wood, but their colored silk robes and gilt accoutrements looked dazzlingly divine to eyes that hadn't seen much of the world.

Now he thought about the Gods because he needed to believe there were powers who understood the things that he did not.

"Shall I send him in?" Liane said. Royhas—any of the conspirators—would have provided Garric with an experienced secretary who already knew the ins and outs of Ornifal politics. Liane was a better choice. Garric could trust her to have her first loyalty to the same things he was loyal to, fuzzy though the concepts were.

Garric rubbed his temples. "Liane," he said, "I don't think I can talk to anybody else today."

He took a swig of water laced with citrus juice from a jug decorated with a pair of heroes fighting winged demons. It was Sandrakkan ware, red figures on a black background rather than black on cream as was the convention here on Ornifal.

He looked up and smiled at Liane. She'd bought all the office furnishings the day before. "Has the shipper you found to take the letter arrived yet?"

"His name's Ansulf," she said, rising. "I don't think so but I'll check the waiting room. Shall I tell the others you won't see anyone else today?"

"Would you?" Garric said. Of course, the petitioners would be back tomorrow, along with hundreds of other people who thought they had something to gain from Garric or-Reise. "I haven't written the letter yet. I . . ."

"I'll leave you alone," Liane said, responding to the request he hadn't voiced. He needed some time to himself; to himself and Carus. "When Ansulf arrives, I'll knock on the door. All right?"

Garric nodded. Prince Garric, he supposed he was. It made his stomach knot to think of that. *Lady, please guide my steps,* he whispered as the door closed softly behind Liane.

He walked to the window. The street beyond had been dark for hours. The other conspirators were busy in the work of government—Royhas, Tadai, and Waldron were, at any rate. Pitre should be contacting the king to arrange a meeting, and Sourous was supposedly arranging an assembly of the city's trade guilds. His family controlled the Ornifal cloth trade. Royhas said that whatever one thought of Sourous himself, his staff was excellent.

No matter how good an underling was, and even if the underling was a noble who traced his lineage back two thousand years, there were going to be people who insisted on dealing with the man in charge. Garric groaned. Things were going to be awful when he really *was* in charge.

He leaned on the window ledge and grinned tiredly. He let his mind go blank, then slipped into the reverie that brought him to the side of King Carus.

Below them was a crowded plaza bordered by monumental buildings. Garric thought he recognized the temple in front of him, though only three of the six high columns still stood in the Carcosa of the present day.

"The temple of the Shepherd Who Guards the Kingdom?" he said.

Carus nodded.

"That's my adoption ceremony," Carus said. "King Carilan adopted me as his son and heir presumptive. I was only a second cousin. He had closer kin, but he and his advisors thought I'd provide the strong hand necessary to hold the kingdom together in a time of rising stresses."

Smoke rose from the altar built on a low platform midway up the temple steps. Priests and courtiers in gold and varicolored robes of state stood to either side. Carilan and the teenaged Carus, kneeling before him, wore the bleached white wool of ancient formality.

"How do *you* like being king, lad?" Carus asked with a grin.

"I hate it," Garric said flatly. "The people I'm dealing with now are the ones who're so desperate that they're coming to me because they couldn't get redress from Valence."

He laughed without humor and added, "Or much of anything else from Valence, apparently. Royhas says the king hadn't been seen in public for six months, though occasionally he'll call in somebody to assign a special task. The way he told Royhas to murder me, for example."

Carus nodded, his face no longer smiling. "You say you hate it, lad," he said bitterly. "I hated all the business of governing so much that I looked for excuses not to do it. Any excuse would do, but going on campaign was the best one. That's what I'd been made king for, wasn't it? To be a strong hand!"

Carilan was a slender man who looked seventy years old, though Garric knew from Adiler's *History* that the king was barely fifty though in bad health. In the vision below, Carilan took a massive gold ring from the middle finger of his left hand and placed it on Carus' finger while the youth continued to kneel.

"The ring weighed half a pound," Carus said, shaking his head in bemused memory. "It was only worn at these ceremonies. It disappeared when Dalopan pirates sacked Carcosa after my fleet and I sank. I suppose some slave hammered the ring into foil to cover the throne of a king with bones through his nose."

"But you *were* crowned to be a strong hand, weren't you?" Garric asked, troubled by the anger he'd heard in the voice of a king who laughed even in situations where others ran screaming. "You had to be."

"I had to be," Carus said, "but I had to be more than that. And I wasn't. If the only tool you have is an axe, then you turn all your problems into trees to be chopped."

He shook his head, wistful but no longer angry. "I told the lords of Ornifal that I'd harry their island from one end to the other if they didn't stop bribing my enemies to spare Ornifal's trade. What was I thinking of? Why couldn't I see what would happen, the way I understand it now?"

"They stopped sending taxes to Carcosa?" Garric guessed. "Because they thought they'd just be braiding a rope for you to hang them with?"

"*And* they doubled the subsidies they were paying under the table to the Earls of Cordin and Blaise," Carus agreed ruefully. "Figuring if they were ready to revolt, I wouldn't dare take my fleet across the Inner Sea to Valles."

"But you did," Garric said. On the temple steps, Carilan raised Carus by the hand. They stood, their arms lifted together. Underpriests came carefully up the steps leading a garlanded bullock with gilt horns. "You crossed the sea to crush the Duke of Yole."

"I wasn't the only one who could miscalculate," Carus said, grim again. "I figured it could smash Yole with a surprise attack, hang a dozen nobles in Valles on my way back, and then deal with Blaise and Cordin. It might have worked. Moving faster than the other man expects wins campaigns as surely as it does duels, lad."

"Only the Duke of Yole had a wizard," Garric said. He thought of the Hooded One, standing in black majesty as the world crumbled about him. "Or the other way around, perhaps."

"Either way, they put paid to me and my fleet," Carus said. "*And* the kingdom, *and* all society higher than three huts together and an ox to plow with. If it hadn't been Yole, it would have been another place I overreached, using my sword when I should have used my tongue."

A priest brought a spike-headed hammer down on the bullock's forehead. The animal kicked out in a death spasm, then collapsed on the platform. An underpriest drew a gilded knife across the beast's throat while another priest caught the blood in a flat bowl.

Blood sacrifice had disappeared in the poverty following the collapse of the Old Kingdom. Garric was just as glad it hadn't returned as wealth increased during the ensuing millennium. Pans of hot, fresh blood had nothing to do with the Lady he envisioned, and wanton slaughter was even more alien to a Shepherd's duties.

"I made enemies of the Ornifal nobles," Carus said softly, "when all they'd been before were fools. Though not so great a fool as I, to think my sword could solve all my problems. You'll do better, lad. You're doing better already."

The scene below them was dissolving. From far away Garric heard the sharp tap of Liane's bronze stylus on the door. "Master Ansulf is here," her voice whispered.

"But for the problems that do need a sword," said Carus, smiling again, "they'll find there's a strong hand on the throne to swing one. By the Shepherd and the honor of Haft, they will!"

Garric was alone in a high-ceilinged room of the queen's mansion. The stone under his palms was polished alabaster, as cool and smooth as the visage of the queen as she fled Valles two days before. A night breeze blew through the open casement. On the streets below, linkmen guided a happy group who were caroling about sunshine and freedom.

"Bring him in please, Liane," Garric said, turning from the window. He still hadn't written the letter.

He sat at the desk but smiled over his shoulder in greeting to Liane and the man with her. Ansulf was blond and sallow. His tunics, the inner one hanging a hand's breadth beneath the outer, were of Ornifal style and bore Ornifal embroidery, but the man himself was from Cordin or just possibly Tisamur.

"Master Ansulf," Garric said as he dipped and wiped his pen nib, "forgive my delay. I'll have this for you in a moment."

Ansulf had spent most of his adult life in the service of Serian merchants. The Serians, separate by both culture and religion from the rest of the Isles' population, were always viewed askance and often the subject of persecution. Their industry, craftsmanship, and business acumen made them more, not less, hated.

Serians were nonviolent as a matter of religion and used pygmy cannibals from their isle's highlands to guard their ships and buildings in the outer world. In much the same way they hired men like Ansulf to act as business agents where native Serians would be robbed or killed. Liane's family had used Serian bankers, and it was through that contact that she had found the messenger Garric required.

Garric wrote in the swift, neat hand his father had taught him:

If you are well, it is good. I also am well.

In this place I have some friends and many who call themselves my friends. If the Gods permit, I will tomorrow be a prince and will act in all ways as though I held the office of King of the Isles. I have an abundance of people who say they can teach me to run a kingdom; but I have a palace to staff and run as well, and there is no one here whom I trust to do that for me.

I need you. The bearer of this letter will provide whatever funds and facilities you request for the journey. I cannot overstate the dangers you will face, but there is no one else whom I can ask. I hope you will come at once.

Garric or-Reise

Given at Valles on Ornifal, the Queen's house.

Garric folded the letter into three crosswise. He wrote the address on the flat side, then turned the document and reached for one of the candles to seal the folded edge with wax. He paused, then opened the letter again and blotted *or-Reise* from his signature. Above his given name he wrote in tiny script, *Your loving son*. Only then did he seal the letter and give it to Ansulf.

The shipper looked at the document with professional appraisal, then tucked it into a pouch whose leather was stiffened by iron wire. "I've discussed the anchorage with merchants who know the district, Your Lordship," he said.

"At Barca's Hamlet?" Garric said in surprise. "There isn't an anchorage. I mean, not for anything bigger than a fishing boat."

Ansulf shrugged. "I think we can manage," he said. "Landing on the east coast will save at least a week over going overland from Carcosa. It's in the hands of the Lady, of course, but—"

He smiled with the sort of quiet confidence Garric had seen on the face of every man he'd be willing to dignify with the name professional.

"—you've been recommended highly to me. I dare say the same people have told you I can be trusted."

Garric laughed. He stood up and clasped arms with Ansulf, gripping one another hand to elbow. "May the Shepherd watch over you," he said. "And—when you're in Barca's Hamlet, would you crumble a bit of cheese on my behalf to Duzi? My father can show you the hill where he stands."

The shipper grinned. "I've never been too proud to ask the Gods for help," he said as he opened the door to leave. "And it's never done me harm that I can see."

The latch clicked behind him. Liane leaned against the door and said, "We've had messages from all the others except Waldron. Basically, the reorganization of the bureaucracy is going even better than we'd hoped. Sourous has arranged for you to meet Papnotis tomorrow in the king's palace. If matters go well, you'll see the king immediately."

Garric nodded absently. He was dizzy from trying to remember everything he'd done and said today.

"I don't know what Waldron's silence means," Liane said, watching Garric closely.

He shrugged. "That Waldron is as proud as any three other men," he said. "Which we already knew. If there were a real problem with levying troops in our name,

Royhas would have told me. He's got spies close to Waldron, I'm sure.''

''Then—,'' Liane began.

''I wonder if he'll come?'' Garric said. He hadn't noticed Liane starting to speak. ''I'm not really his son, after all.''

''The man who raised you,'' Liane said quietly, ''isn't going to refuse his duty. And as for not being Reise's son—why do you say that?''

Garric frowned, feeling awkward. He was sure that he'd told Liane that . . . ''I'm Countess Tera's child,'' he said carefully. ''Reise was just her secretary. He pretended I was his son to save me as he fled Carcosa during the riots when the count and countess were killed.''

Liane nodded. It suddenly struck Garric that Liane, raised as a noble while he was tending sheep in Barca's Hamlet, was enormously more sophisticated than he was.

''I know Countess Tera was your mother,'' she said. ''That doesn't tell me who your father was, Garric.''

She stepped close, hugged him, and backed quickly away. ''Anyway, Reise will come as quickly as he can. Now—''

The door opened, fast and without warning. Garric, driven by reflexes honed in another man's lifetime, had his sword clear of the scabbard before Royhas halted with a startled expression. Waldron, half a step behind him, eyed the tableau with a hint of the first amusement Garric had seen on the old warrior's face.

''Sorry,'' Garric said as he slipped the long blade back into its scabbard.

Royhas was in court robes, plain beige silk with the broad red stripe of the chancellery sewn down the right side. The stripe was a recent addition to a garment which, though not shabby, was well broken-in. ''Lord Waldron's brought news,'' he said, nodding to let the other man speak for himself.

''The commanders of the four regular regiments—not the Blood Eagles—had agreed to join us,'' Waldron said.

His face worked in disgust. "Though the cowards weren't going to *do* anything until Valence capitulated on his own. I was waiting for the first installment of the bribe to arrive from Tadai's bankers."

Garric nodded in understanding. The Ornifal standing army—calling it "the royal army" gave Valence too much credit—was ill paid, ill led, and badly understrength. The four regiments based near Valles totaled only about fifteen hundred troops when they should have had a thousand apiece.

They could make the next days difficult if they opposed the conspiracy, though. If the local regiments backed the king, he might resist at least until levies from the northern landholders reached Valles to give Waldron the muscle to overawe them. Without their open support, Valence would have to come to terms with Garric.

Garric didn't expect fighting. Besides, he wasn't—nor was Carus—concerned about the outcome if it *did* come to sword strokes; but he believed Tenoctris when she warned that there was very little time.

"The cart with the money chest was in *sight,*" Waldron said bitterly. "Then a messenger came from the Naval Arsenal saying that the fleet on Eshkol had just proclaimed Admiral Nitker King of the Isles and that he'd be arriving shortly to take charge. The regiments marched to the Arsenal. 'To await developments,' that brainless twit Pior who commands Harken's Regiment told me."

"There's ten thousand men in the fleet base on Eshkol," Royhas said with a frown.

"Eight," Liane said, reaching for one of the score of notebooks in her valise but sure of the figure without it. "They're understrength as well, though not as badly as the army."

"We'll crush them like bugs when the levies from the north get here," Waldron said impatiently. "The nobles are coming with real soldiers, not rowers with swords in their hands."

Garric had both history and Carus' vivid memories to

warn him that Waldron was making the sort of assumptions that could lead to disaster. A body of disciplined men experienced in working together might be more than a match for a ragbag of noble retainers, even though the latter had better armor and perhaps more experience in fighting on land.

Aloud he said, "Well, in the short term it doesn't matter to us. We'll—" The hallway behind the two nobles was packed with their armed guards and the petitioners who hadn't gone home despite Liane's attempt to dismiss them. Smoke from the extra lamps brought in by the newcomers merged with that of the wall sconces. The haze hovered a foot beneath the coffered ceiling.

"What?" Waldron said, more in anger than surprise. "Nitker isn't as great a fool as most of the naval sort and he's obviously ambitious. If—"

"In the short term, I said," Garric resumed. Fatigue had ground away the layers of civilized politeness that might have softened his response. Waldron being Waldron, politeness would have gotten in the way of the necessary message. "Our concern was that the regiments in Valles not support Valence against us. Who they do support is immaterial for the moment, so long as it's not him. We'll come to terms with the king tomorrow, as planned, and deal with Nitker—"

He grinned, then broke into a booming laugh that was as much that of his ancestor as it was Garric's own. " 'Deal with him at leisure,' I was going to say," Garric continued, "but I don't expect any of us will have leisure for longer than I care to guess. What I will have—"

Garric grinned again, a rakish but not unfriendly expression that raised Royhas' eyebrow and cooled Waldron's anger into wariness. They were wondering if stress had driven Garric mad.

"—is sleep, which I need if I'm going to be of any use when I see Valence. I hope you'll forgive me, but for the moment there's nothing I can do that will more greatly benefit our cause."

He bowed. Liane stepped between Garric and the nobles; and they, nodding, closed the door behind them.

Sharina waited until she was sure that one of the two men was Hanno. She half-hopped, half-swung down from the hiding place she'd found for herself, the stub of an araucaria whose trunk had sheared a dozen feet in the air. "It's all right," she called. "There are no enemies here."

Hanno stepped out from behind the buttress roots of a silk cotton tree where he'd sheltered when he heard the flies. "Unarc," he said, "this is the girl I told you about. Guess I wasn't lying when I told you she was a perky one. Missie, here's Unarc, and I guess he's not quite as dead as I figured him."

The man with Hanno was short and built like a stump. He was completely bald. His beard and mustache were so full that his head would look more normal if it were mounted upside down on his neck.

Unarc held a knife the length of his forearm; its heavy blade curved inward like that of a pruning hook. His right arm was bound to his chest by leather wrappings which were both sling and bandage.

"He'd got his boat raised when the Monkeys who'd burned his hut caught up with him," Hanno explained. "There was more fuss—"

His spear dipped toward Unarc's injury.

"—and when it was over, the boat was farther out than a fellow with one arm could swim to it."

"Pleased to meet you, miss," Unarc said. It was perhaps the most obvious lie Sharina had ever heard from the mouth of an adult. The bald hunter dug his big toe into the soil and stared at it all the time he was speaking. "Guess I'll look. . . ."

He didn't so much drift away as jump toward the baobab tree. The presence of a woman embarrassed him beyond words.

Hanno's spearbutt touched the body of a soldier with a sword in his hand. The skin of the corpse looked sallow;

the pool of blood beneath the deep slash in his thigh was still tacky.

"I see you kept yourself busy while I was gone," the hunter said. Apologetically he added, "If I'd thought there'd be trouble, I'd not have left you."

"By the Shepherd's holy staff!" Unarc said from the echoing interior of the baobab. "There's four more of them here!"

Hanno raised an eyebrow, though he didn't speak.

"It wasn't me, exactly," Sharina said. "My friend Nonnus . . . Nonnus helped me."

She was tired and uncomfortable at talking about the slaughter. She slid the Pewle knife into its sheath and stood, wishing that she'd had time to bury the bodies. She couldn't have hidden what had happened, of course.

Unarc came out of the tree's shelter, his mouth open to shout some further revelation. He saw that the others were talking and remained silent.

"You mean he taught you to use a knife that way?" Hanno said.

A creature in the treetops began to call: who-*oop,* who-*oop,* over and over. The hunter glanced upward with a hard glint in his eyes. Just as suddenly his spear arm relaxed from the insane cast it was about to attempt. He gave Sharina a faint smile. He was uncomfortable too.

"No," Sharina muttered, looking away. She'd washed her tunic in the stream. Cold water had sluiced out most of the blood, but the hunters' practiced eyes weren't going to be deceived. "He came back and did . . . what he did for me. Alone. But he's gone again now."

Hanno nodded as though he understood. Unarc quietly rejoined them. "Nonnus," Hanno said reflectively. "He'd be the friend you said could have me for supper, would he?"

"I'm sorry," Sharina said. "I shouldn't have said that. I was upset and I thought you were another enemy."

The big hunter smiled in a sort of humor. He toed the soldier's hand to see if he could loosen the sword, but the hilt was in a death grip. "Oh," he said, "I don't know that you misspoke, though it'd be a fight folks'd pay money to see. What do you figure, Unarc?"

"Horsefeathers, Hanno," the bald man said uncomfortably. "You could take him. Unless he got inside, and then, well, it'd be a fight."

"Anyhow, missie," Hanno said, businesslike again, "your Nonnus is a right good man. I'm proud to know a friend of his."

He gestured with his spear. "Now," he said, "Unarc and me figure that since we can't get off the island for a bit, we ought to learn something about what's going on. Are you up to joining us?"

"It don't seem she'll be slowing us down as much as I'd figured," Unarc admitted, speaking to the ground. "Sorry to doubt you, Hanno."

"Yes," Sharina said. "I think we need to learn what's going on. And maybe to stop it."

When they'd landed the previous afternoon, Cashel had been so glad to have firm land under his feet and an ordinary sky overhead that he hadn't given much thought to where they were. This is, he hadn't wondered whether they were back in the world he and Zahag had been booted out of in the courtyard of King Folquin's palace.

The sea rolled in much the same way as the surf did on the coast of Haft. The constellations were right, more or less; the common ones were much higher in the sky and there were stars on the southern horizon that even Cozro had never seen before, though he said he'd sailed as far south as Shengy when he was younger. All that meant was that they were a distance beyond where the captain had been, not that they were in another world.

But Cashel's skin still prickled in a fashion that he'd come to associate with things being . . . wrong. With wizardry. There, he'd gone and thought it.

"Wow!" called Zahag, who'd ambled up the beach out of sight. "Come see these eggs!"

Cashel looked up from his work. They hadn't found sign of anything more dangerous than stunted pigs on this island, but it wasn't as though they'd had time to really explore. Zahag wasn't in danger and Cozro—even without the cutlass, which Cashel was using as their only woodworking tool—was probably safe as well, more's the pity; but Cashel didn't like leaving Aria alone.

"Would you like to take a walk, Princess?" Cashel asked.

Aria sat in the shade, gripping her knees and staring at the sand between her feet. She looked up without enthusiasm. Saltwater had gummed her hair and made her eyes bloodshot. Abrasion wherever cloth rubbed skin had raised rashes and even welts.

"What does it matter?" she asked. She got up, though.

"Here, you carry the cutlass," Cashel said, handing her the weapon. "I'll take the staff, hey?"

Cashel was planing a length of palm trunk into an oar. The result was pretty good. Better than he'd counted on being able to manage, anyway. He hadn't decided whether he was going to build a larger boat or if they'd just leave the island on the dinghy when he'd made oars and had stepped a mast.

"You'd drag me if I didn't, wouldn't you?" the girl said bitterly. At some time in the recent chaos she seemed to have lost the belief that she was being tested like Patient Muzira. That was a shame, but Aria was a lot sturdier now than the fluffball Cashel and Zahag had rescued from the wizard's tower. She'd done things and she could do more, though she thought it was terribly unjust that she had to.

They set out along the sandy beach in the direction Zahag had called from. There must be a vein of sweet water somewhere under the island, because the vegetation was lush instead of the bitter, small-leafed tamarisks Cashel had seen on similar islets in the Inner Sea. For now the castaways had quenched their thirst with fruit, but maybe he could dig a well for drinking water when they sailed away from the island.

Cashel wasn't sure they could carry enough food and water for four in the dinghy; but neither was he sure that he could build a serviceable boat all by himself, and it looked very much like that's how it would have to be made. Aria was worthless; Zahag wouldn't pay attention to anything for as long as two minutes straight; and Cozro . . . well, Cozro had found a fruit the size of a peach with a hard rind. Opened, it fermented in a couple of hours, and that was all he'd shown interest in from that moment on.

"I wondered if you were coming!" Zahag said angrily when Cashel and Aria appeared. The ape stood on a six-foot mound of seaweed just above the tideline. He'd tossed away the top layer and was grubbing down into the interior with both hands. "If you think I'm going to do all the work, you'd better think again!"

"I didn't think that," Cashel said dryly. He'd gotten used to the ape. Zahag and Aria both did about the best they could. A lot of times that wasn't very good, but the contrast with Cozro made Cashel appreciate his longtime companions better. "You've found eggs, you say?"

For answer, Zahag raised in both hands a pale cream egg the size of a watermelon. "What kind of bird laid this, do you suppose?" he asked. With the question, he looked skyward in sudden concern.

Cozro strode out of the foliage toward the interior of the island. "Say!" he said. "But that's not a bird egg, it's a turtle. A bird that big couldn't fly."

The captain was drinking his punch from a scooped-out coconut shell. He had a line of similar containers fermenting in the sun near where Cashel had dragged the dinghy up the beach. Preparing the coconut shells and filling them with fruit pulp was the only work Cozro had done since they landed.

Zahag set the egg on the mass of vegetation which had

been keeping it warm. It didn't look like any bird's nest Cashel had seen either, but—

"It's got a hard shell," he said. "Turtle eggs are leathery. Besides, it'd be a *real* big turtle."

Cozro snorted. "There's plenty of things in the sea bigger'n what laid that," he said, slurping a draft of his punch. "You won't see a bird bigger'n an albatross, though, and for all their wingspread they don't weigh much more'n a chicken. Turtle eggs are fine eating, though."

He finished his cup of punch, belched, and walked away without taking further notice of his companions. Off to get the next shell in the line, and perhaps to refill the empty.

Cashel had tried the punch. He knew his tastes were pretty narrow compared to those of people who'd lived in bigger places and traveled more, so he tried to make allowances.

The beer Reise brewed for his inn was bound with germander from the woodlands of the borough, not hops imported from Sandrakkan. Germander made beer dark and bitter, but it was the taste Cashel had grown to expect.

Wine was rare and expensive in Barca's Hamlet. He'd had sips and didn't much care for it, though cider mulled with spices could be a pleasure on winter nights.

Making allowances didn't help. Cozro's punch tasted like rotten fruit, it was that simple. Cashel would've drunk seawater before he'd suck down more of that oily, sticky liquid.

"Are there many of them?" Aria asked, stepping closer to Zahag but unwilling to climb onto the mass of decaying vegetation. "Can we really eat them?"

The princess could be peevish with Cashel and the ape, but she didn't seem to recognize that the captain even existed. So far as helping was concerned, he didn't; but Cashel figured Cozro would be quick enough to claim a share of the egg after Cashel had lit a fire with the firebow he'd made as his first project after landing.

"They're four to a layer," Zahag said. "I'd say three layers."

He hopped down from the mound with the egg in his arms. "As for eating it," he went on, "I don't see—"

"Don't smash it!" Cashel shouted. He was too late. Zahag dropped the egg; it crunched but didn't smash. The ape quickly rolled the dished-in portion uppermost.

"What's the matter?" the ape said in puzzlement. He thrust his hand through the broken shell and drew it up dripping with both white and yolk. "I didn't lose any in the sand; and anyway, there's plenty more."

"Ugh," Aria said as Zahag started to lick the egg's contents off his hairy hand with a tongue like a blanket. She turned her back.

"Yeah, but I wanted to save the shell," Cashel said. "To hold water when we get away from here."

"Well, there's plenty more," the ape repeated with his usual unconcern. He climbed the mound, sucking at his fingers.

"No, they can stay in the nest for now," Cashel said, organizing their escape in his mind. Maybe he could build a raft to hold the supplies. He'd been wondering what to do for water butts, so the giant eggs looked like a gift from the Gods.

Cashel couldn't understand the ape. Though he could read and talk as well as Garric, Zahag just didn't see why you planned for the future.

"I'm getting hungry," Aria said, looking over her shoulder toward the egg. "But all runny like that . . . ?"

Cashel scooped the egg up in both hands; he could carry it in one, but he was afraid the crack Zahag started in opening the shell would spread and spill the contents on the ground.

"I'll put it on a slow fire," he said to Aria. They didn't have a pot to boil it in. Even back in Barca's Hamlet, the only containers big enough would be the laundry cauldrons that several of the wealthier households had. "And maybe we can fry some if we can find a rock flat enough."

They trudged back toward the fireset and the upturned dinghy. Cashel could hear Cozro swearing as he pricked himself while gathering more fruit for his punch.

Three would be easier to plan for than four were, but Cashel knew in his heart he wouldn't make that decision. Once in a while, though, he wished he was the sort of man who could leave the captain behind—and sleep nights afterward.

Ilna was drowning. She reached up a hand with glacial slowness. It broke surface. She thrashed violently, awakening as her head thrust upward. Sputtering and suddenly conscious that she was nude, she looked around her.

Several willowy, perfect humans stepped back with grave smiles as liquid splashed from the trough Ilna was lying in. It wasn't water but something thicker. It was as viscous as olive oil to the touch, but it vanished into miniature rainbows when it dripped from Ilna's body. She hadn't been drowning, either, though all but her nose and lips must have been under the surface until she awakened.

"Where am I?" Ilna demanded. "Who are you?"

The bearded man holding a cup and ewer opened his mouth to reply. Before he could get a word out, Ilna added, "And where are my clothes? I want my clothes!"

She was even more determined about that because none of the strangers around her were clothed. The air was balmy and breathed perfumes like those of flowers at evening. Her skin tingled with a healthy feeling when she stepped from the trough.

"Of course, we'll bring your clothes as soon as they're ready," the bearded man said. "They're being cleaned now. But you're welcome to fresh garments if you'd like, though we ourselves don't see the need."

"This is the Garden, mistress," a girl of about Ilna's age said. "I'm Cory. This is Wim—"

The bearded man nodded.

"And I'm Bram," said a youth who might have been Cory's twin brother. "Ah . . . we call ourselves the People of Beauty, but that sounds pretty boastful, I guess. You don't have to call us anything."

"Except friends," Cory said with a bright smile. She stepped close and hugged Ilna. She looked so perfect that Ilna expected her flesh to be as cool as beeswax, but in fact Cory felt completely normal.

Another slender woman walked toward them, carrying Ilna's tunics draped over one arm. She wasn't running but her clean strides covered ground swiftly. A herd of deer with long, backward-sloping fangs in their upper jaws ran across the meadow behind her.

"The Garden" seemed as good a name for this place as Ilna could have come up with, not that it told her anything she wanted to know. Fruit trees grew, separately and in small groves. Goats and miniature deer browsed beneath them but didn't seem to strip the bark as Ilna would have expected from her own experience.

Water ran in profusion. From the large pond in the near distance sprang a fairylike pink fountain that was all spines and curlicues. Birds rested on it and occasionally dived into the water. When they rose again, they carried fish or frogs in their bills. The Garden wasn't entirely a place of peace.

Though it seemed very close to that. A giraffe, a creature Ilna recognized as a motif on fabrics from Cordin but which she'd never before seen living, walked to the pond in stately fashion and splayed its forelegs out to drink. A pair of scimitar-horned antelopes moved aside but continued drinking.

Ilna looked up. The sky burgeoned into rich color in the west, while the eastern horizon sparkled with what looked like stars.

"Where are we?" she demanded. The woman had come up with her tunics; Ilna took them, but it was somehow more embarrassing to dress in front of these strangers than to stand here nude as a plucked chicken. "I thought I was being taken underground."

"That's right," said Wim. "That's the cavern roof above us. It's covered with flow rock that glows according to the time of day it would have been in the upper world, back in the days before we had to come here to the Garden to survive."

He poured fluid from the ewer into the goblet of chased metal and offered it to Ilna. "This is wine," he explained. "It will help your throat and lips. They're terribly dry."

"That's why we put you in the bath when we brought you down," Bram said. "Your poor skin had been scoured, just *scoured,* by being on the surface unprotected for so very long."

Ilna grimaced. She lifted the inner tunic over her head and wriggled into it quickly.

With the cloth covering her eyes, she could think. This whole place was wrong. Not hostile, not dangerous, but wrong—it shouldn't be here. It didn't fit the pattern of the world across which she and the wizards had been walking.

Ilna's head reappeared from the neck of the tunic. The fabric had been cleaned perfectly—better than Ilna herself could have done. The tunic was cleaner than when the wool first came from the bleaching vat, she would have said.

"Where are my friends?" she asked, suspicious again. "Halphemos and Cerix?"

Bram offered Ilna his hand. "We'll take you to them," he said. The four People of Beauty—the woman who'd brought the garments was tagging along—set out toward another pond a quarter mile distant.

A group of young men and women passed in the opposite direction riding bareback on a variety of animals, none of which were horses. A deer with Y-shaped horns branching from its nose, and a griffin with a beak and bird's legs in front and the hindquarters of a dog, were among the stranger mounts. The large billy goat wasn't unusual in itself, but the fact that a laughing girl controlled it by ribbons was more amazing than the griffin.

The second pond was fed by a pair of streams running from pink tracery fountains which poured water out of dozens of holes. Ilna could follow the pattern which the pink strands wove among themselves, but she doubted that anyone else in Barca's Hamlet—and perhaps anyone else in the world—could have done so.

She smiled grimly. Wherever "the world" *she* meant by the term was, it wasn't here. And she very much doubted that the Garden was really a part of any world, even the one into which the wizards had flung her and themselves.

At the pond's edge grew a wrist-thick vine which sprouted translucent growths like pea pods the size of human beings. Several of the People of Beauty stood nude near one of the pods; with them but clothed in a red silk robe was another man.

"Halphemos!" Ilna called, louder than she'd meant to. Ever since she awakened she'd been suppressing the fear that she was alone in this place.

The youth stood and turned with a beatific smile. "Ilna!" he called. "Come and look what they're doing for Cerix!"

Ilna lengthened her stride. Her companions kept up with her effortlessly. It was worse than when Ilna walked with long-limbed, free-striding Sharina on the beach at Barca's Hamlet. These really *were* the People of Beauty—and of grace, and of kindness, and apparently of all manner of other desirable attributes that Ilna was too honest to claim for herself.

Halphemos gestured toward the pod. The People of Beauty with him moved aside to afford Ilna a clear view. Though the sky was growing darker, the structures from which the water poured were suffused with a soft pink glow that lighted the meadow around them.

Ilna bent to look into the pod. A man floated inside with his eyes closed. For a moment Ilna didn't recognize him, though Cerix's face should have been familiar enough.

Cerix didn't have legs, though. This man did: hairless and the same color as the light itself, but unquestionably legs.

Without speaking, Ilna looked up at Halphemos.

"Isn't it wonderful?" Halphemos cried while the People of Beauty looked on with indulgent smiles. "They're giving him back his legs! He'll be normal again!"

Ilna nodded to show that she was listening. She was trying to organize her thoughts, trying to find the pattern; and the pattern wasn't there.

In the pond, a gloriously blond mermaid cavorted with another creature that was half-fish. The upper parts of the second form were insectile, a chitinous carapace and a head with great multifaceted eyes.

"Yes," Ilna said at last. "Our hosts appear to be very skillful. They cleaned my garments better than I could have done myself."

Her comment probably sounded inane to anyone who didn't know her well. Anyone who *did* know Ilna's fierce pride in her own skills would see how deep was her praise.

She gestured Halphemos to follow, wondering if the People of Beauty would fall into step. They, as tactful as they were lovely, turned their backs and murmured among themselves in soft, cultured voices. The youth, puzzled but too cheerful to object, walked along the margin of the pond with her.

"I came around sooner than you did, mistress," Halphemos said apologetically. "I'm afraid you must have been doing most of the work during the last hour or more, even though you're . . . I mean, I'm bigger than you."

Ilna waved her hand in disinterest. Lights glimmered in the depths of the pond. Tiny human forms rode fish that looked like swollen bladders. They glowed in a variety of pastel colors.

"I don't think this garden is real," she said bluntly. "Or the people who live here."

"But . . . ?" Halphemos said. He pinched the flesh of his arm, then offered his hand to Ilna. "Touch me," he said. "I'm real and you are too."

Ilna squeezed the youth's hand perfunctorily and released it. "I dare say we are," she said. "But what we see around us . . ."

Above them a creature like a vast winged fish floated across the starlit sky. Trills of laughter drifted down from the riders on its back.

"Halphemos," she said, "I think we're in a hallucination. Your friend's hallucination. His delirium is so strong that he's woven a dream of paradise around all three of us. It's almost the only thing that could fit the pattern."

"But . . . ," Halphemos said. They were nearing one of the streams which fed the pond. They slowed slightly. "What do you think should we do, mistress?"

Ilna shrugged. "We set out to find my brother," she said. "I can't tell you what to do, but I intend to keep looking until I find him; or I die. And I won't find Cashel here."

"Yes, I see that," Halphemos said. A lizard with three heads swam down the stream into the pond, singing multipart harmony as its tail oared from side to side.

Halphemos straightened with a firmer expression. He turned on his heel, forcing Ilna to turn with him. "You said that us living in Cerix's hallucinations was almost the only explanation," he said. "What are the other possibilities?"

"There's one," Ilna said. She smiled faintly. "That we're dead. That my brain is drying out on the bottom of a sea older than time, and this place is the last thought that goes through it."

Black and white swallows in equal numbers traced a

curving line across the sky. They chittered merrily. Halphemos looked up at them as he walked.

"I see," he said at last. The pod had opened and Cerix, waving enthusiastically, was getting out.

The 28th of Heron

The banners of the two heralds riding at the head of the procession bore the black eagle of Ornifal, but against a blue ground instead of the red of the present royal line. The soldiers, a mixture of armed retainers provided by all five conspirators, wore tabards with the same device.

"King Carus!" the crowds cheered as they saw Garric. "Long live Carus!"

At the back of Garric's mind, a normally cheerful presence glowered at the flags. Garric turned to Liane, being carried in a sedan chair which put her head almost level with him on horseback, and said, "We ought to use the Gold Ring of the Old Kingdom. It symbolized both the diadem of kingship and the whole circuit of the Isles, not just one island."

Liane looked at him. "Did it?" she said. "I didn't know that. Where did you learn it?"

Garric coughed. "I think it's in Aldebrand's *Dinner Party,*" he muttered.

It probably was somewhere in Aldebrand's massive collection of bits and pieces of information from the literature of the Old Kingdom—which had fallen four hundred years before Aldebrand compiled it in the form of conversation at a dinner party of savants of the former age. Because Aldebrand had the run of the vast temple library at Wist on Cordin, long-since burned and dispersed, he provided information which had survived nowhere else. Unfortunately Aldebrand was also a superstitious fool and a careless copyist, so his information was as likely as not to be wrong.

In truth, Garric had learned about the Gold Ring while watching a priestess of the Lady instruct Carus in the spiritual underpinnings of kingship a decade before Carus donned the diadem. Had anybody tried to teach Valence about kingship? If all being King of the Isles meant was privileges and politics, alliances and bribes . . . who could expect anything better than the upheaval and injustice of the present day?

"But you know better," a voice whispered through the ages.

The crowd had been cheering all the way from the queen's mansion in the center of the city. Many of the people who'd seen the procession passing had fallen in behind it; as many more were already gathered here at Garric's destination. Their shouts and the morning sunlight were dazzling.

One of the heralds rode to the gate of the royal compound and rapped the butt of his flagstaff on the ironbound oak. "Open for Prince Garric!" he called in a voice like a silver trumpet.

The complex was on what had been the northern edge of Valles five centuries before. The city had overgrown the district, but the buff stone walls enclosed several acres of gardens and widely spaced buildings.

Royhas ordered his eight-bearer palanquin up on Garric's right side. Tenoctris, in a sedan chair behind Liane's, caught Garric's eye when he glanced around but continued whispering an incantation. On her lap was a limewood board chalked with symbols in a triangle. The line of spear-carrying footmen on either side were to keep enthusiastic spectators from seriously impeding the progress of Garric and his companions.

Garric looked down onto his chancellor, reclining on

the palanquin's cushions. "I wish Pitre had come," he said. "Since he was so close to Valence."

Normally the gates of the royal compound would have been open with a squad of Blood Eagles on display in the archway. Today and for the past week, the compound was guarded like a fortress.

"Don't wish that," Royhas said. "The best he'd do is dither. It's just as likely he'd break down and cry here in front of the mob."

Royhas couldn't ride a horse in the normal way because of his long robes of state. The choices had been a palanquin or a sidesaddle; sedan chairs were for women or images of the Gods at religious festivals, and arriving at the palace in a carriage would break both the law and—more important—tradition.

Garric looked at Liane and they exchanged smiles. He'd like to have squeezed her hand, but he didn't suppose that was fitting. He didn't suppose it was what he ought to be thinking about, either.

The viewport on the right gate-leaf opened. The man inside said something to the herald in a voice Garric couldn't hear over the crowd noise. The herald replied.

Garric wondered what the purpose of Tenoctris' incantation was. She was using a swan quill rather than the bronze stylus to strike the symbols as she mumbled them out. An object gathered power with each use and thereby became harder to control with the precision that safety demanded. Tenoctris couldn't do as much as many wizards, but she never did anything beyond what she intended. No power was truly uncontrolled; what the user didn't control was left to the cosmos to decide, and the cosmos was no friend to humankind.

The herald turned his bay mare and rode back between Garric and Tenoctris. "Your Majesty?" the man said. He came from Waldron's household. "They say you can enter, but it has to be alone."

"I'll talk to them," Garric said curtly. He dismounted—he needed Carus' reflexes for better things than keeping his seat on a horse—and strode to the gate, brushing past the herald before the man could back his horse out of the way.

Royhas started to protest, then ordered his bearers to put down the palanquin so that he could join Garric. Out of the corner of his eye, Garric saw Liane's chair also lower; Tenoctris continued to concentrate on the words of her incantation.

They four were the only principals present. Waldron was organizing the first units of household troops arriving from the north of the island, and Tadai said he neither needed nor wanted to meet Valence under these conditions. Tadai's refusal gave Sourous an excuse and Pitre the opportunity to stay away as well.

Because Royhas knew the king's advisors, he could provide Garric with a viewpoint from within the ruling elite. At base, though, success or failure would be up to Garric himself.

He grinned. It was always nice to know where the blame lay if things went wrong.

The eye of a man wearing a nose-guard helmet watched from the other side of the thick panel. Garric was dressed in red breeches, high boots, and a short blue tunic cinched by his sword belt. That was flamboyant garb which had more to do with Carus' taste than it did with that of Garric's upbringing, but it didn't threaten violence.

"I'm Master Garric from Haft," Garric said, trying to be more diplomatic in addressing the king's men than the herald had been. "My advisors and I have a meeting with the king and his chancellor."

"Chancellor Papnotis has gone back to his estates," said the guard. "You can come in, but only alone."

"I'll come with Lord Royhas, whom you know," Garric said. His voice took on a grating edge, like ashlars slipping over one another. "Also two women. And I'll enter now, as agreed. I keep my oaths, and I assure you I have a short way with oathbreakers!"

Threats of violence wouldn't work against the Blood

Eagles. Men who'd remained with Valence this long weren't going to blanch because a boy threatened them with death or torture. But calling them oathbreakers, that was another matter, even though the arrangement had been with the chancellor who'd already fled.

Garric couldn't see what Royhas was doing. "Open!" the soldiers accompanying Garric shouted. "Open! Open!" The crowd bellowed with wordless anger.

Garric turned and raised his hands for calm. Tenoctris, still chanting, stood above all those around her.

Only those in the front of the crowd could see Garric; they continued to shout anyway. That was fine. The whole gesture was playacting to convince the guards that Garric was a force for moderation.

Facing the viewport again, Garric said, shouting to be heard, "Your duty is to keep King Valence safe from attack. Your few swords can't accomplish that. Letting me and my advisors in to speak with His Majesty is the only way to save him."

The man at the viewport turned to talk to someone who'd arrived behind him. The wicket in the other panel opened abruptly. It was only large enough for one person to enter at a time, which also was fine. The last thing Garric wanted was for the main gates to swing back. They'd draw an uncontrollable mob into the palace grounds like a bass sucking in prey by opening its jaws.

Garric stepped through, ducking to clear the iron-strapped transom. He was ready to hold the wicket by main force if the guards tried to close it before Tenoctris, Liane, and Royhas could follow.

"Let them by!" ordered an officer in gilded armor.

The officer looked Garric over. "I'm Attaper bor-Atilan," he said. For all the richness of his accouterments, the ivory hilt of Attaper's sword showed the wear of real use. "Legate of the Blood Eagles."

He nodded to Royhas, entering last behind Tenoctris, then gave Garric a grin of disgust. "My men and I appear to be the entire palace staff, as well. Everybody else ran when Papnotis scuttled away last night. The wizard Silyon comes and goes, so it's probably wishful thinking to believe he's gone for good now.''

A troop of forty Blood Eagles was drawn up at the gate. There were three hundred in the regiment at full strength, not enough to guard the compound's long perimeter if it came under real attack. Garric could see squads stationed at intervals among the plantings and walkways. They wore half-armor that was no less functional for being buffed to a high polish.

''I mean our king no harm, Lord Attaper,'' Garric said, speaking words that were only partly his. ''And as for you and your men—no kingdom has so many honorable citizens that I would permit those under my control to harm such.''

He grinned, a wolfish expression, veteran to veteran, that took the legate aback to see on Garric's youthful face. ''Not that I believed you were afraid. The Blood Eagles stood at the Stone Wall.''

Attaper's left index finger absently traced a scar that ran from the jaw hinge down the side of his neck. ''That was a long time ago,'' he said. ''A lot of things have happened since then.''

Harshly, though the anger didn't seem directed at Garric, the legate continued, ''Come along, then. I'll take you to His Majesty.''

''Shall I . . . ?'' Garric said, putting his hands to the buckles of his sword belt. Royhas in court robes wasn't wearing a sword. For anyone but his guards to enter the king's presence armed was an insult even when it wasn't a threat. Either was punishable by death.

Attaper looked at Garric. In a voice that quavered with a disdain shared between equals he replied, ''I choose to believe that you're a man of honor, Master Garric. In the event that you're not, you'd scarcely need a weapon to dispatch His Majesty in his present condition.''

Garric looked over his shoulder and asked, ''Are you all right, Tenoctris?'' He knew what wizardry could take out of the old woman, and he had no idea how difficult was the incantation she'd performed on the way to the meeting.

She smiled and said, "Quite all right, thank you." Her voice was pert enough. She turned to twist off a forsythia twig to replace the quill she must have abandoned when she got down from the sedan chair. Liane took the older woman's arm in a comradely gesture.

Attaper led Garric and his three companions down a walk paved with slabs of soft, yellow limestone, worn by centuries of use. The remainder of the guard detachment stayed at the main gate. Grape vines that had leafed out but hadn't yet set fruit covered the trellis overhead.

Liane missed a step, then skipped over the slab before her. Garric looked back. Frozen in the limestone was the coiled shell of an ammonite. It was small, no larger than a clenched fist, and its dozens of waving arms had rotted away long ages since. This ammonite hadn't been one of the house-huge monsters Garric had seen often in nightmares and once in a storm-tossed sea.

But he noticed that Tenoctris, walking alongside Liane, avoided the fossilized creature also.

Attaper turned into a one-story bungalow with a fanciful roofline and outer walls decorated with blue-figured Serian tilework. It looked new compared with most of the buildings nestled among the gardens. Although the taste that designed the structure was more delicate than Garric's own, he found attraction in the fact that it *was* designed to an individual's taste rather than as some sort of monument to posterity.

Two Blood Eagles stood at the front door; another peered around the back corner when he heard people approaching, then withdrew when he saw his legate leading the newcomers. The guards stiffened to parade rest, but they'd been attentive even before their commander appeared.

"Any change, Melus?" Attaper asked.

"Nothing to report, sir," one of the guards said. He

and his partner exchanged quick glances. ''Ah . . . ,'' Melus added. ''The situation at the gate is . . . ?''

''Is under control,'' Attaper said. He grinned crookedly at Garric. ''For the moment.''

The guards stepped aside so Attaper could open the door of tiger-striped wood. ''Your Majesty,'' he said, ''I've brought some citizens to see you.''

''What?'' said a querulous voice from the interior. ''What are you talking about? And where's Papnotis?''

Attaper gestured Garric and his companions inside, then closed the door behind them. His face was perfectly expressionless.

Valence III, King of the Isles, was younger than Garric's father. He looked ancient: thin and gray-faced, with wine stains on his goatee and the cerulean silk tunic he wore.

''Who are you?'' he demanded. His eyes glanced over Royhas with a flicker of recognition, but they focused on Garric's sword. ''Who sent you?''

He looked at the nobleman and continued on a rising note, ''Royhas, who sent you?''

''The people of the Isles sent us, Your Majesty,'' Garric said. ''We're here to save the kingdom, for you and for all citizens.''

Valence turned away with a cracked laugh. This large room was fitted as a council chamber with tables, couches, and a bare wall against which aides could stand while ministers discussed matters of state. Two doors led off it: one of burl walnut standing ajar, through which Garric glimpsed a bed; and a discreetly curtained portal which probably led to servants' quarters and a kitchen, unless that was in a separate building.

The king appeared to have been sleeping on one of the couches here. Fruit stood untouched on a sideboard, but empty wine flasks lay on the floor. One of them, ticked by the opening door, was still rolling.

The king opened the lower cabinet of the sideboard and peered inside. ''Oh, Lady help me,'' he moaned. Straightening, he shouted to the world at large, "Bring me wine! How dare you leave me without wine?"

Tenoctris walked to the king's side and brushed his forehead with the twig she'd plucked. "Sit with me, Your Majesty," she said in a gentle voice. "You'll feel better."

Valence let Tenoctris lead him to a couch covered in the hide of an antelope with soft taupe fur, but he began to cry. Tenoctris held the twig against his forehead and whispered words Garric couldn't hear. A faint rose glow formed over the king's head like fuzz on a peach.

"I'm going to die," Valence said. "I was supposed to feed the Beast three days ago, but the servants ran away because of the riots. The queen will come for me or the Beast will come for me—it doesn't matter which. I'm going to die!"

"We've driven the queen from Ornifal," Garric said. "Tell us about the Beast."

"It has all power, Silyon told me," Valence said. His eyes were open but he spoke like a sleepwalker. "It would save me from the queen, he said, and nothing else could. But if it was so powerful, why do I have to feed it? Why couldn't it find girls for itself? It isn't fair!"

Garric saw Liane's face go very still. He hoped he kept his own expressionless, because the disgust he felt wasn't the proper emotion to display to the man whose assent was necessary to Garric and the kingdom.

"Where is he?" Garric said aloud. "The man you call the Beast?"

"Man?" Valence repeated, then cackled another burst of mad laughter. "*It,* not he. And I don't know where it is, but we speak to it through a well in the ruins of the Tyrants' Palace. There's nothing there if you look down, but Silyon shows me the Beast in his mirror. And the girls, it finds the girls we lower down to it."

Valence tried to rise to his feet. Tenoctris' touch, gentle as a kitten's, thrust him back onto the couch. "Oh, dear Lady help me," he said. "Please give me wine. Please."

"Tenoctris?" Garric said. "Is there anything else we need to know about the Beast?"

The old wizard continued to whisper her incantation. She shook her head minusculely in negation.

"Your Majesty," Garric said, "for your own sake and for the kingdom, you must go out to the gate with us and tell the citizens that I am your son and successor. Then we can keep you safe from the queen and from other enemies. Even the Beast."

"Nothing can save me!" Valence shouted. "Are you a fool? You don't understand: the Beast has all power! I thought it would save me, but now I know it never meant to do that. But if only I could feed it, perhaps it would eat me last. Do you see? It would eat me last!"

"I see, Your Majesty," Garric said. He held his hands open in front of him, but in all truth he had no wish to grip his sword. He felt toward Valence as he would feel toward a roach scuttling across the floor of his mother's pantry.

"Come, Your Majesty," Royhas said, offering Valence his hand. "Prince Garric will save you. You'll tell the people that you've adopted him as your son and heir, and then we'll take care of all the rest."

"What?" the king said in a return of his original peevish tone. "Who is he, anyway? And why is he wearing a sword! I'm King of the Isles!"

"Indeed you are, Your Majesty," Garric said, taking Valence's other hand. Gentle pressure from the two men brought the king to his feet like a child learning to walk between its parents. "My sword is here to defend you against all enemies. Tell the people to obey me in your place, and we'll do the rest."

"There's riots," Valence said as they walked him slowly forward. "They'll kill me! They know I couldn't protect them from the queen!"

Liane silently opened the door. Tenoctris followed behind the three men, still chanting softly but no longer stroking the king's forehead. The glow had faded to what might have been a flush on Valence's skin.

"We've dealt with the queen in your name, Your Majesty," Garric said. "We'll keep you safe."

He found he couldn't hate so abject a coward. Males are formed to react to challenges—and a broken reed like Valence was no challenge to anyone, however much evil the king might have done in his weakness.

Attaper led them. At his signal the four guards followed, their eyes scanning for threats in the plantings to either side.

"Loyalty can't be bought or even earned, lad," a voice whispered in Garric's mind. *"It has to be given. And it really doesn't matter that Valence is unworthy of it. As the Gods know he is!"*

They reached the gate and the larger detachment of Blood Eagles. The crowd rumbled through the masonry and thick wood, like a nearing storm.

"Let me out the wicket," Garric said to Attaper. "I'll order them to stand back. Then open both leaves wide and bring His Majesty through to make the announcement."

"Make it so," Attaper said to the soldier with his hand on the wicket's separate crossbar. Garric noticed that the legate hadn't so much as glanced at Valence for confirmation.

Garric stepped into the street. The noise was deafening. The guards from the conspirators' households stood two deep. Their spears were crossed before them to bar the press of people.

Garric hopped onto Tenoctris' sedan chair and said to the bearers, "Lift me up so that I can be seen!"

When Garric rose into general sight, barely wobbling, he raised both arms. The crowd roar redoubled, then fell away slightly. He'd never seen so many people in one place before—except in the memories he had from King Carus, similar gatherings and similar occasions.

"Citizens of the Isles!" Garric shouted. Some of the people could hear him. They would tell others, and anyway the most important thing was to be *seen*. "Your king has an announcement to make!"

The main gates opened. Garric motioned the other sedan chair to the side of his, then risked a look backward.

The Blood Eagles were drawn up five ranks deep and eight files wide, filling the archway with their armored bodies. Between the fourth and fifth file tottered Valence, wearing the circlet of gold Royhas had brought for him: they hadn't been sure they'd have time to find the ornate crown of the present dynasty. Tenoctris followed the king, leaning on Liane. She continued to chant the words that kept Valence from collapsing in blubbery incapacity.

Attaper helped Valence onto the chair, then gripped the king's thigh with a powerful hand to steady him as the bearers lifted him into full sight of the crowd.

"Citizens of the Isles!" Garric shouted. "His Majesty King Valence the Third has adopted me as his son. He has proclaimed me regent of the Kingdom of the Isles!"

Valence was gaping like a hooked perch. He trembled dangerously despite the legate's support. Liane stepped to the king's other side and added her help, but Valence was likely to buckle at the knees at any moment.

Garric lifted the diadem and put it on his own head. He'd tried the circlet on when Royhas brought it to the queen's mansion, to make sure it would fit without looking ridiculous. Then it had been no more than a band of metal, heavy despite being so thin, and vaguely uncomfortable. Now—

Golden light suffused Garric's mind. In it sparkled images—not from his memory or even that of Carus alone, but from scores of generations of kingship. All the rulers of the Old Kingdom were with Garric momentarily, united like the facets of a diamond.

His vision cleared. The crowd shouted like a god trumpeting. Through the joyous sound Garric heard Tenoctris' voice.

He turned. Liane looked around also. Neither of them could understand Tenoctris' words, but Garric from his higher vantage point could see over the heads of the Blood Eagles.

A scrawny man wearing a robe embroidered with symbols in the Old Script had come up the path from the bungalow where Valence had hidden himself away. He had bones in his earlobes. Through the open gateway he saw Garric crowned and Valence beside him.

Garric pointed. "Stop that man!" he cried. "Stop Silyon!"

But the wizard, doffing his heavy garments, had vanished into the shrubbery in his loincloth before the Blood Eagles could turn to see him.

Halphemos wore a garment of gold. It weighed less than gossamer, but because each strand scattered light like an invisibly thin mirror, the youth was as modestly clothed as if he'd been wearing his own robe of silk brocade.

Cerix wore nothing at all. The older wizard was too delighted with his regenerated body to cover any part of it. The hair on his legs from mid-thigh was fine and blond in contrast to the black curls on his arms and torso, but the bones and musculature were complete. In the middle of a comment, Cerix was likely to lose his train of thought as he watched his toes stretch.

Ilna wore the tunic she'd woven in Erdin, cinched with the twin of the sash she'd given to Liane. Watching the men prance in what they'd gotten from the Beautiful People—Cerix no less than Halphemos—offended her, though of course she didn't interfere in the way her companions chose to act. Besides, she knew in her heart that she was a fool to feel the way she did.

So be it. Ilna os-Kenset didn't want to change.

Ilna swallowed the slice she'd cut from a strawberry the size of her head, juicy and meltingly delicious. She looked at the two wizards and the three People of Beauty who'd greeted her when she awakened here, then said, "I intend to return to the world from which I was kidnapped.

by the Scaled Men. If there was a way into this garden, there's a way out of it. Which I will find."

"But mistress," Wim said in puzzlement. "Why do you want to leave? Is there anything you need that we haven't offered you?"

Halphemos looked distressed; he fidgeted with the cuff of his vaporous tunic rather than meet Ilna's eyes. Cerix glared at her angrily, knowing where the discussion was going to go and furious about what it would mean to him.

Ilna's nose wrinkled. Cerix could see the right of it as clearly as she did, but he was letting personal considerations prevent him from acting.

"My brother's gotten into trouble," she said to Wim. Glancing aside toward Halphemos she added, "Or been put into trouble by others. I'm going to try to help him, and for that I need to be back in my own world."

"The boy wasn't responsible for what happened to your brother!" Cerix said.

"It doesn't matter," said Ilna; and it really didn't. She didn't believe Halphemos had harmed Cashel or anyone else deliberately. "Can you help me, Master Wim, or must I find the path myself?"

A slim girl passed, playing a twin-necked theorbo to half a dozen youths who walked with her entranced. Ilna marveled at the girl's intricate fingerings—but though the lute strings vibrated, they made no sound.

"We can show you the path you seek," Bram said. "But mistress, there's no place on that plane as full of joy and contentment as the Garden."

Ilna almost laughed at the humor of it. "I daresay you're right," she said, "but I can't imagine what bearing you think that has on me."

She stood. She'd eaten her fill of the huge strawberry, but most of it still remained. The waste disturbed Ilna, as much as anything because it underscored the Garden's vast abundance, but there was nothing she could do. Perhaps the deer-footed unicorn walking slowly through the nearby orange grove would finish the fruit.

"Will you lead me, then?" Ilna said to Bram. The harshness of her voice and manner was out of place. The world didn't provide something for nothing. This place, this *Garden,* did. Therefore so far as Ilna was concerned, the Garden didn't and couldn't exist.

As a matter of faith, Ilna os-Kenset couldn't believe in a place so obviously good.

"I'll take her, Bram," Cory said to the troubled-looking youth.

"We'll all go," the bearded Wim decided, rising with the grace of a cat stretching. The People of Beauty reclined on the grass rather than sitting. The sward felt as soft and springy as a sack of wool beneath Ilna's bare feet. "We don't spend much time in that grove, Mistress Ilna."

"It's cruel to remind ourselves how wretched the existence of others is compared to our own," Bram said. He lowered his eyes from the horizon to look straight at Ilna again. "I really wish you'd reconsider."

He reached out to take Ilna's hands. He was as tall as Garric. Though slimmer, he had a supple strength as all the People of Beauty did. Bram's features were as perfect as those of the image that the Shepherd's priests brought to Barca's Hamlet for the Tithe Procession.

Ilna stepped back quickly. "Good day to you, then," she said to Halphemos and Cerix.

Halphemos stood. "I'm coming with you," he said. He looked at the ground as he spoke.

"Sister take you, boy!" Cerix said as he too jumped to his feet. "You're not responsible! You didn't harm her brother!"

"Please," said Cory. "We're all *friends* here and the trouble—"

Halphemos raised a hand to silence her. He faced the older wizard, his mentor, with a steadiness that wasn't a boy's expression. "Cerix," he said, "I spoke an incantation to hold Zahag and her brother. They vanished instead. Neither of us believe that was coincidence."

"But . . ." said Cerix. There was a tear in the corner of his left eye, and another running down his right cheek. "Alos—"

"And even if I didn't think I was responsible," Halphemos said, "I'd go with her. As she would go to help us, even though I don't think she likes us—"

He gave Ilna a wry grin.

"—very much."

Cerix shook his head in frustration and sadness. "Yes, of course we'll go," he said.

He glared at Wim. The People of Beauty had drawn back from the strangers, the way sensible folk do from a dogfight. "You said you were going to lead us," Cerix snapped. "Let's get it over with, then!"

Ilna looked at her companions, suddenly disgusted with herself. She'd maneuvered Halphemos and Cerix into a decision she and they knew they were fools to make. Because they were men of honor, despite the flaws they had because they were human, it had been easy.

"For what it's worth," she said, "I like both of you better than I like myself. Though that isn't much of a recommendation."

"Of course we don't want to prevent you from making your own decisions," Wim said uncomfortably. "I . . . But of course, we'll take you to the grove."

He gave a hand each to Bram and Cory. Without looking back to see if the strangers were following, the three People of Beauty set off toward a nearby hill. Its perfectly rounded aspect looked as artificial as the bridge which crossed the stream at its foot.

Though not particularly tall, the trees on the hill's crown were thick-trunked. That made them unique in this place, where everything else Ilna had seen, plants and animals including humans, was willowy and graceful.

"There aren't any birds in the trees," Halphemos said. "They don't fly overhead either."

"It's the first place I've seen here that looks natural," Ilna said. Cory glanced over her shoulder, just enough to see Ilna out of the corner of her eye. She didn't speak.

"What do you think, Cerix?" Ilna said deliberately.

"I don't think," Cerix said. The slope was gentle; they'd almost reached the grove. The trees were oaks of many varieties. Some of them already carried budding acorns. "If I thought, I wouldn't be doing this."

The People of Beauty stopped beside a pin oak and murmured among themselves. The younger pair stepped back. Wim turned to Ilna and said, "I'll take you the rest of the way, mistress and masters. There's no danger, and I don't suppose you'll even find it particularly unpleasant."

Ilna gave him a curt nod. Bram looked at her imploringly as she passed, but she didn't turn her head. She could hear the feet of her companions rustling the dry leaves as they followed her.

Vertical cavities as high as a man split the trunks of each tree. Though light dappled the bark and the forest floor, the openings were swirls of dark mist.

"There's something inside here!" Halphemos said in excitement. Ilna glanced back. The young wizard tugged Cerix's arm to show him the landscape of gleaming metal shapes that formed if you focused on the mist in the cavity of a burr oak. Wim paused, his expression resigned.

Cerix refused to turn his head. He and Ilna exchanged glances. She resumed walking, stepping over a surface root writhing through the litter. Wim nodded gravely and went on.

Ilna had seen that image and all the rest, one at the heart of each tree they passed. For the most part the worlds inside didn't affect her: they were as inhuman as the interior of a flint nodule just cracked by a mason's hammer.

Some of the images were unspeakably foul. Ilna didn't let her expression change, but now she understood their hosts' reluctance to enter the grove.

"How much farther?" she asked.

"Not far," said Wim. He looked over his shoulder. "You're sure . . . ?" he said.

"Yes," Ilna replied, but her tone was softer than it had been when she was first driving the People of Beauty to guide her. Perhaps they couldn't see any real difference between the world where Ilna had been born, and a world in which a monster with two legs and a spiked tail looked up from the human infant it was devouring in the ruins of a mansion.

Ilna smiled without humor. She knew there were places in her world where that scene, or scenes very like it, was just as real as the mud streets of Barca's Hamlet. Perhaps the People of Beauty were correct.

It didn't matter, of course. Ilna's duty wasn't in the Garden; and she would do her duty.

"This one," Wim said, gesturing to the bole of a white oak not very different from one that grew on the western outskirts of Barca's Hamlet, a tree that lightning had struck long before Ilna was born. The thunderbolt had torn off a branch and ripped a serpentine path down the bark to the ground. Here, instead of weathered sapwood, haze curled in the tear.

"If you don't mind," the bearded man said, "I'll take my leave of you now. But I'd rather that you come back with me."

Ilna nodded curtly, intent on the pattern in the mist, glimpses of a street in an unfamiliar city. She could see steeply pitched shingle roofs and downspout decorations in the shape of fanciful animals.

"Thank you," Halphemos said earnestly. He gripped Wim's hand and wrung it. "For your hospitality, and especially for what you did for my friend Cerix."

Wim hurried off, striding as though to escape an unpleasantness. The wizards watched him go and faced Ilna only when he was out of sight.

"You don't have to come," Ilna said. "I suppose you shouldn't come."

Without a word, Halphemos stepped past her and vanished into the mist. "Sister take—" Cerix said in surprise and anger.

Ilna stepped into the heart of the tree. There was no sensation except the touch of a cool breeze blowing down the street between wooden buildings. She stumbled.

The street was dirt, though there was a stone-lined open sewer in the middle. A dust devil curled around the corner, then dissipated.

A woman stood halfway through the doorway of the house to the left, holding buckets of slops which she was carrying to the sewer for the next rainstorm to flush away. She'd stopped, staring in horror at Ilna and Halphemos.

"There's nothing wrong!" Ilna said. She glared at the woman, holding her by sheer force of will. She noticed that Halphemos was wearing his own robe, not the one the People of Beauty had given him.

"What is this town, mistress?" Halphemos asked in a pleasant, worried voice. "Here, let me help you with your pails."

"Why, this is Divers on Third Atara," the woman said. She held the cypress buckets for a moment, then let the youth lift them away and walk to the sewer. Halphemos was simply being his natural self. That was more calming than anything Ilna could say.

The street wasn't busy, but a handcart rolled across the intersection two doors down. "Where did you come from?" the woman asked. "You weren't there, and then—"

Cerix appeared out of nowhere and tumbled into the street in front of her. His ragged tunic was black with the silt of an ancient sea bottom. He clasped the stumps of his legs and began to scream.

At that, the Ataran woman screamed also.

Cashel stared at the straight-trunked tree, considering how it would fit into the raft he was building. Zahag sat nearby, crunching red seeds he'd excavated from a fruit he'd found. The pulp was tasteless, but apparently the seeds were delicious—at least if you had molars like Zahag's.

A soft-leafed cactus curled up the tree bole. Several of the multipetaled white-and-crimson flowers dangled flaccidly, like cuttlefish hung to dry. The blooms only lasted for a few hours, but last night their spicy perfume had drifted across the inlet to where the castaways slept beside the dinghy.

Cashel looked over to the camp. Cozro lay in the shade on a mattress of withies while Aria tried to plait narrow leaves into a hat for herself. She was absolutely useless at the task, but at least she was trying.

The princess had even let Cashel show her the basics of rowing this morning before the sun got too high. She had something of a talent for that, though of course she'd have rubbed her soft palms raw on the oarlooms if they'd kept at it for more than a few minutes.

No doubt about it: the Princess Aria had changed a lot since Cashel first met her. Maybe someday she'd even forgive him for rescuing her.

Cashel pushed through undergrowth to the next tree inland, a eucalyptus of some sort. The trunk divided about four feet up. He guessed he'd be better off to use it as two poles than to take the tree down at ground level as he'd intended.

Kneeling, Cashel swiped the cutlass through brush that would otherwise get in the way of his cutting strokes. It was bad enough having to use a cutlass instead of a proper axe, but he'd make do.

Zahag hopped onto the latticework stems of a strangler fig. The tree which the fig had used for support during its first decade of life had rotted completely away, leaving no sign of its presence save the woody vine that had murdered it.

"What was wrong with the first tree?" the ape asked. His words slurred around the seeds he continued to munch.

"The cactus that grows on it," Cashel said, feeling vaguely embarrassed. "There's—"

He paused. Numbers were a problem for him.

"Well," Cashel said, "there's more buds on it than there ever was sheep in a flock I was tending. I figure most of them are going to bloom tonight."

He wiped the cutlass blade with a palm frond, cleaning the steel of juices that might be corrosive. It wasn't a particularly well made weapon even if you liked swords—which Cashel didn't, not even a little bit—but it had a full tang and wasn't going to snap during the tough work of cutting trees.

Zahag turned to look at the cactus, wrinkling his long, expressive face in concentration. "So what?" he said.

"Well," Cashel muttered, "I liked the smell last night. And in the moonlight the flowers were pretty as can be."

He didn't want to talk to the ape about why he liked flowers. He didn't know why, he just did. Most of the people in Barca's Hamlet would have been as amazed to hear him say that as Zahag was.

He drew the cutlass back, using one hand over the other on the stubby hilt so that he could get the strength of both arms into the blow. Aria screamed.

Cashel stuck the cutlass point-first in the hard soil and left it as he lurched back to the edge of the beach. He didn't think of it as a weapon. It would just get in the way of using his quarterstaff, now leaning against the cactus-covered tree.

He didn't know what he'd see when he looked across the embayment toward Aria: maybe seawolves, great carnivorous lizards, squirming out of the water; maybe some sort of land predator, though they hadn't found any traces of one during the days they'd been on the island; maybe even a demon sent by Ilmed or some other wizard to snatch the princess away.

What Cashel saw was Aria holding an oar like a club and Cozro picking himself up from the sand. It wasn't hard to figure back to what had gone on during the time Cashel couldn't see his two companions.

Cashel's *one* companion. Cozro had just become a problem Cashel was going to solve very shortly. "Cozro!" he bellowed across the water. "Touch her again and I won't leave enough of you for the fish to finish!"

Cozro turned to look at Cashel. They were less than two hundred paces apart, but the water separating them was deeper than a man was tall. Cashel could swim, more or less, but if he tried to swim this distance he had a much better chance of winding up on the bottom of the inlet than he did of reaching Aria in time to be of service.

It was several times as far to the princess around the curving shoreline as it was across the water. Cashel started running.

Cozro shook his head to clear it. Blood dripped from the pressure cut over his left temple. If he'd heard Cashel, he'd ignored the threat. He started after Aria again, his arms spread wide.

Because Cashel intended to go out clamming in the inlet later, he hadn't dragged the dinghy up the beach after he and Aria returned from rowing practice. Instead of running as Cashel expected her to do, or fighting as a man might have done, Aria leaped into the little boat and flipped away the mooring line.

Cashel saw at once that she was right. Cozro wasn't fast, but he was a lot stronger than the princess. If she ran inland, the island's vegetation would tangle her before she'd gotten twenty steps. Cozro was between her and Cashel, and running the other way down the beach would take Aria to the giant nest at the tip of the cape with nowhere to go but into the water.

Cozro roared angrily and stumped into the sea after the dinghy. Aria teetered in the stern as she pushed the boat deeper into the inlet, using the oar like a barge pole. Cozro could swim: his third splashing breaststroke brought him almost close enough to grab the gunwale.

Aria whacked his head again with the oar. Cashel, using

the staff for balance as he ran—he ran better than he swam, but it still wasn't a talent he was known for—shouted in triumph.

If the princess had known to use the oar's edge like a wooden sword, she might have put Cozro down for good. As it was, a swat with the flat didn't do the captain serious damage but it did convince him there was no future in trying to climb aboard the dinghy. Cozro scrambled out of the water again.

"I'm coming, Princess!" Cashel cried with what breath he had left over from running through soft sand. He really hoped Cozro would try to fight him. Otherwise Cashel was going to have a moral problem about what to do with a man who'd proved he was too dangerous to live with on the same small island.

Cashel's first guess was that the captain was going back to shore to get a pole to fend off Aria's swipes. Aria must have thought the same thing, because she settled both oars in the rowlocks and clumsily stroked farther out. If she got beyond the jaws of the inlet, she might not be strong enough to get back. . . .

Cozro continued to run up the beach. Cashel wondered if there wasn't something in the captain's punch that ate his brain away. Cozro might be able to finish his business with Aria before Cashel caught him, but he couldn't expect to escape except possibly by rowing an empty dinghy out into an empty sea. That was an end as final as facing Cashel, and a good deal more unpleasantly slow.

Cashel had his stride, now. He wasn't fast, but he could keep going as long as he had to. Aria had found her rhythm too and was pulling with both arms together. Cashel tried to imagine what the princess would be like if she'd been born a fisherman's daughter in Barca's Hamlet. He couldn't get his mind around the thought. It was too much like imagining the sun rising in the west.

Zahag chattered enthusiastically, watching events from high in the strangler fig. Cashel knew the ape couldn't either swim or run well enough to reach Cozro before

Cashel did, but it gnawed him that it wouldn't even have occurred to Zahag to try. Zahag would probably say that the tribe's females were the chief ape's business, not his.

Cozro ran off the tip of land into the sea. Well, if the captain wanted to drown himself that was just fine with—

The dinghy grounded. The shock tipped Aria backward into the bow. Her legs waved in the air for a moment before she could clamber onto the thwart again. Cozro shouted in triumph. He was well out from the shore, but the water was only ankle-deep.

Cashel stopped. Pounding over the sand didn't help him think, and he knew he had to grasp what was going on before he could do anything about it.

Though it was simple enough, really. Aria got out of the boat and tugged at it without success. She was standing on a firm surface just beneath the water. Cozro was certainly drunk and possibly mad, but he was a sailor. He'd noticed, as Cashel had not, that there was a bar between the jaws of the inlet. Even the shallow dinghy would ground on it when the tide was low.

The princess turned and splashed toward the shore where Cashel had been working. Cozro was gaining on her. Cashel had gotten almost to the base of the inlet, about as far away as he could be. If he'd just stayed where he was . . .

Cashel didn't even sigh as he started back. He'd made a mistake and not for the first time. He'd do what he could, even though he could see that he wouldn't get to Aria in time for anything but revenge.

Which he would take.

Zahag started to shriek pulsingly like a wagon wheel spinning on its hub while a smith tries to balance it. The ape clung to the fig's woody stems with both hands and thumped his feet up and down on lower strands, setting the whole tall lattice to vibrate. He was staring out to sea.

"Help Aria!" Cashel bawled. If Zahag put himself between Cozro and the girl, he could hold the captain off until Cashel arrived to finish matters.

If, but Zahag wasn't human and he surely didn't think like Cashel. He continued to call, letting go with one long arm so that he could point out to sea.

The princess was fifty feet from shore; Cozro was twenty feet behind her and gaining. She looked over her shoulder and froze where she was. Cozro shouted, "*Now* you'll learn, you little tease!"

Cashel thought Aria had panicked when she saw how close her pursuer was. He shouted, "What are you—"

His attention was so wholly focused on Cozro and the princess that he didn't see the long toothed heads coming in from the sea until the captain did. Cozro turned screaming. He splashed three steps back toward the dinghy before the monsters reached him.

Only when they slid onto the bar did Cashel realize that the creatures were birds—or their forefathers had been birds, at any rate. Their belly feathers were creamy, while those of their upper surfaces were slate gray speckled with white. The only traces of wings were tiny stubs that stuck out as the birds reared upward.

Tip to tail, the creatures were twenty feet long, and each toothy orange beak measured a yard by itself.

Cozro bawled in terror and raised his arms to cover his face. The Sister only knew what he thought that would accomplish. The birds struck simultaneously. They grabbed Cozro at the knees and shoulders, then jerked apart, shaking their heads like a pair of hens struggling over a worm. Blood splattered the foam.

After a time, Cozro stopped screaming.

Cashel continued to run along the shore. He understood now why Aria had stopped where she was. She stayed still and the captain was moving: the birds landed on Cozro like black on coal.

A smart girl, smart and quick-witted besides. Nobody was going to call Cashel either of those things, but he knew his job didn't mean hiding in the bushes while the princess was stuck out there in the water, as plain as a boil on your bum.

Cashel reached the strangler fig, twenty paces or so from where Aria would come to dry land when she next could move. Zahag had dropped to the ground and was hunching like a fur-covered rock. His bulging eyes stared at what was happening in the inlet. Cashel paused also, breathing through his open mouth and leaning forward slightly so that his diaphragm could expand his chest more easily.

The birds had just about finished with Cozro. They rose, chest to chest, hissing like water on hot rocks as they both tried to gobble down the last tidbit. Their feet were huge and orange. Scales projected from both sides of their toes in place of the skin webs that helped the geese of Barca's Hamlet swim.

One of the great birds overbalanced the other with a sly twist of the neck, a maneuver that Cashel, a wrestler, could well appreciate. Both birds slipped sideways with a great splash, but the one who'd thrown the other swallowed Cozro's leg as they fell. Fragments of the shattered dinghy flew out from under the squirming bodies.

Simultaneously and in apparent good humor, the birds flopped into the deeper water of the inlet and swam to the opposite shore where their nest stood. They slid along with their heads and long necks raised, making contented hissing sounds.

Aria began to crawl toward land. Behind her, the wreckage of the boat floated in water whose bloodstains were being quickly diluted. A small fish leaped with a bit of something in its mouth.

Cashel started toward the point where she'd arrive, moving stealthily so he wouldn't draw the birds' attention to this side of the inlet. Zahag mewled as he crept along at Cashel's side, more afraid to be alone than he was afraid to move.

The birds slid up on the beach beside their looted nest. Their cries of rage were like nothing Cashel had ever heard: high-pitched, penetrating, and louder than should come from anything alive. They dipped their heads into the pillaged mass of leaves and seaweed, lifting out each remaining egg for examination. The beaks that had ripped Cozro to bloody fragments were mother-gentle with the softly gleaming ovoids.

Aria reached the shore. Her mouth was open and her eyes stared. She was terrified, but not too terrified to think and even act. Cashel felt a surge of warmth toward a girl he hadn't imagined he'd ever like, let alone respect.

Cashel held out his free hand to her. Tags of skin dangled from her oar-scraped palms, though the saltwater had sluiced away the blood.

A bird hooted. Aria turned her head and screamed. Both the huge creatures dived into the water with sinuous grace.

Cashel swung the princess behind him; there wasn't time to be dainty about it. ''Stay close but don't get in my way!'' he said. ''Zahag, you too!''

His wrists set the quarterstaff spinning. The brass end-wraps blurred into a gleaming, golden circle as the staff speeded up with each twist.

If there'd been one bird, and if Aria and Zahag stayed squarely behind him, Cashel thought there might have been a chance. He'd seen what the beaks could do. The teeth were like a seawolf's and the very length of the gape meant it clopped shut like the door of a fortress slamming.

One bird alone, though, would have run into a barrier of spinning firwood every time it tried to peck through to the delectable flesh beyond. The birds each weighed as much as a dozen plow oxen. One *could* squirm on through despite Cashel's defense—but there'd have been pain for it on the way, and maybe a broken beak besides. They would have had a chance, Cashel and those he defended.

Two birds working together as this pair had proved they could, well, it would be over in moments. Aria and the ape would be gone in two snaps, and the birds would quarrel over Cashel's fragments at only slightly greater length.

Blue light crackled in the circle of spinning brass. Cashel felt the world around him starting to fade. He thought Aria was saying something, but he couldn't be sure.

The birds had crossed the inlet beneath the surface. Now they lurched up from the water. Their beaks were open and their pink tongues vibrated, but Cashel didn't hear their hissing cries. His quarterstaff was a disk of sizzling blue fire, roaring and popping and filling the world. He could see figures on the other side of it, but the giant birds thinned into shadows.

The disk was an open pit before Cashel. He fell through it; Zahag and the princess were tumbling after him.

Cashel lay in the dust of King Folquin's palace on Pandah. "Guards! Guards!" someone screamed. Cashel felt his vision blurring.

Zahag was gibbering, Aria wailing for the Mistress God, and King Folquin kept shouting for his guards. A woman with Dalopan tattoos bent and stared into Cashel's face. He recognized her from the crowd of petitioners the morning he and Zahag had been flung out of this world into the first of the places they'd trudged through before this return. Now the Dalopan was wearing a robe of silk brocade embroidered in silver thread with astrological symbols.

The woman straightened. "Stand back!" she said. "I have need of this one for my art!"

The blackness of utter exhaustion spread over Cashel like the surface of the sea.

Something in the forest canopy went *ka-ka-ka-ka* as Sharina and Unarc passed below. She didn't bother to look up. She knew by now that she wouldn't be able to see anything; and anyway, she didn't have the energy to spare for sightseeing.

Sharina had been following the wounded hunter for . . . she couldn't be sure. It probably hadn't been many miles, but it had been longer, harder work than she was used to.

Unarc moved like a ghost. Only occasionally did the

hunter remember to look back to see that the girl was keeping up with him. It was a matter of fierce pride to Sharina that she always *was* there when Unarc checked.

She hadn't seen Hanno since the three of them set off this morning. She hadn't expected to. Unarc could guide the girl, while the big hunter scouted unseen for anything that lay in wait or followed them. Nonnus would have done the same.

Sharina smiled. Indeed, perhaps Nonnus was *doing* the same.

Unarc paused in a grove of elephant-ear plants and raised his knife in warning. The wicked hook caught enough light to wink like a snake's eye.

Sharina stopped in place. She opened her mouth to breathe silently, then turned her head to watch their back-trail.

Nothing. She felt no hint of danger. Thanks to Nonnus, she was sure she could trust her instincts—not that she wouldn't continue to use her conscious senses the best ways she could.

Sharina looked at Unarc, then crept to his side when he nodded her forward. The knife gestured into the tangle of mangrove roots growing out into a great river. They'd been paralleling the water for most of the day, but this was the first time Sharina had seen rather than merely heard it.

A strikingly ugly animal waddled into sight through the mangroves. It was probably the weight of an ox but it was built more along the lines of a giant hedgehog, broad and low to the ground. Horny spikes stuck out along both sides of the creature, with particularly long ones projecting from the shoulders. It was munching the last of a cycad frond as it ambled along, drawing in more of the tough vegetation with each front-to-back motion of its broad jaws.

"That's where we get the horn," Unarc whispered. Once the bald hunter came to believe that the slaughter at the baobab tree was Sharina's doing, he'd treated her with respect—but no longer as a source of the crippling embarrassment with which he viewed women. "And you might know, we'd run across one as fine as I've seen in seven years on Bight right now when I'm outa the horn business."

The browser vanished into foliage on the other side of the root maze. It amazed Sharina that something so large and apparently clumsy could move unhindered through the dense mass.

She whispered, "Its armor looks—"

Ugly as tree bark was the phrase her tongue started to form.

"—dull."

Unarc nodded. "Likewise tortoiseshell," he said. "You take the outer rind off and polish her up and in the sunlight you never seen anything so pretty. Which we don't do, since it'd get scratched to hell in the shipping, like enough, but you take it from me that was a first-quality critter."

Sharina jerked around, grasping the Pewle knife's hilt. Hanno, emerging from between a pair of ginger bushes without disturbing any of the dew-dripping pink flowers, grinned in wry approval. "Good thing you got her along, Unarc," he said. "If I'd been a Monkey, I guess you'd be dinner now unless they decided to cook you first."

"Sister take you, Hanno!" the bald man said. "I knowed it was you all the time!"

Sharina took her hand away from the knife. She didn't know if Unarc's statement was true. Anyway, she was glad to see the big hunter again.

"There's no Monkeys up or down the river," Hanno said, setting aside his humor. "I figure we can get to the top while there's still daylight. Sister take me if I don't think every Monkey on the island's walked this way in the past month! And no tracks going back."

Unarc shook his bald head. "Well, something had to be happening or—"

His knife waggled in the direction of his strapped arm.

''—I wouldn't be sporting this. Let's go see what it is.''

''The top of what?'' Sharina said. She didn't need her hand held, but the two hunters were so used to acting alone and with similar uncommunicative men that they didn't tell her things that she might need to know for all their sakes. The men were apt to speak in a monosyllabic code that an outsider lacked the background to break.

Hanno nodded to indicate he understood and approved of the question. Under other circumstances Sharina would have liked to throttle the hunter—but she was here by his sufferance and free because of the risks Hanno had taken in the same unthinking way that he sometimes treated her as a dim-witted girl-child.

''This whole north end of the island is volcanoes,'' he said aloud. ''The bay where it seems the Monkeys're headed, that's one too, only the north wall's been eat away by the sea. We're going up a cone on the side of that one, and we're going up in style where the critters won't see us coming.''

Unarc nodded solemnly and said, ''The lava came up the top and made a tube when it ran down the side. The outside froze to rock and the inside run on till it hit the river and the water carried it away. I seen it happen—not here, I mean, this is old, but the other side of the island the first summer I come to Bight.''

It struck Sharina forcibly that though she thought of the hunters as unsophisticated—even by her own rural standards—they'd seen things with their own eyes that the scholars of this and former times had never dreamed of. They were savage—she'd seen proof enough of that in Hanno's collection of teeth—but they weren't savages, and they were neither of them stupid. Even before this change in the Hairy Men's conduct, the forests of Bight would have shown little mercy for fools.

''We go into the river,'' Hanno said, ''duck underwater to get into the tube, and then we just climb. Hope you don't mind getting a little wet.''

He grinned at the joke. A bath in the river wouldn't make Sharina any wetter than the daily rainstorms did.

Sharina grinned back. "Looks like there's enough mud in the current," she said, "that I won't get nearly as wet as when it rains. My friend Cashel would want to plow it."

Cashel's name gave her a pang. She'd let a wizard's false semblance lead her away from searching for her friend. What had happened to Nimet later didn't change the fact of Sharina's own faithlessness.

"You hold on to my spear while I find the entrance underwater," Hanno said. "It's black as a yard up a pig's—"

He caught himself and cleared his throat. "Well, you can't see a thing in the water. Though come to think, why don't you hold on to my belt instead. And Unarc'll follow us."

The bald man nodded agreement. "You can't see nothing when you're inside neither," he said. "Not till you get most of the way up where there's holes. But it's not like you can lose your way once you get started."

Sharina wondered what sort of creatures might lair in the utter darkness of the lava tube. She smiled faintly. Nothing nearly as terrible as Hanno and his great spear, of that she was certain.

"I'm ready," she said aloud. She wrapped the fingers of her left hand around the hunter's lizardskin belt.

They stepped into the river. The unexpectedly fierce current pushed Sharina's stiffened left arm against Hanno until she could catch herself and lean backward against the flow. The hunter didn't seem to notice.

They walked twenty yards downstream at a deliberate pace. The water rose to Sharina's mid-chest and once—briefly—to her neck, but she was never in danger of going under. They passed the intruding mangroves. If Sharina had been alone she'd have picked her way hand over hand, clinging to the roots in the same fashion she'd have used a similar web on a vertical climb if it were available.

Beyond was a mass of palms whose trunks sprang three and four together from a common center, but between the mangroves and the palms was a hump of black rock to which only ferns and lesser growth clung. It climbed the slope to vanish in the taller vegetation.

"Here we go, missie," Hanno warned. He walked deeper into the stream, then—as Sharina's head started to go under—deliberately ducked. She followed, trying to keep her feet on a slick clay bottom scoured by the current's rush.

The water seeping between Sharina's tight lips had a brackish tang. She closed her eyes, gripped the hunter's belt, and kept her other hand on the pommel of the Pewle knife for the comfort the contact gave her.

She couldn't be sure, but she thought Hanno had changed direction. The current lessened. The bottom became rock and rougher, a good surface for the feet of a girl from Barca's Hamlet.

Sharina's head broke surface again. "Lady, I thank you for Your blessings!" she said. Her shout echoed as a trembling chorus up the lava pipe in darkness.

She let go of Hanno's belt and walked up the slanting path. The slap of the tiny waves her motion stirred grew into the mutterings of a crowd. Even Sharina's breath and that of her companions swelled like the winter wind.

"Nothing keeping us here," Hanno said. His soft leather boots squelched as he began walking. Sharina followed, and behind she heard Unarc.

The roof of the lava tube was too high for Sharina to reach with her fingers outstretched; the floor was a boulevard on which the three of them could have walked abreast if they'd chosen to do so. Sharina kept track of her companions by cues she couldn't have put precise names to. Sound was one of them, of course, though the echoes and counterechoes of her own feet would have made that alone a treacherous guide. Sometimes she thought she could feel the warmth of the hunters' bodies; and sometimes she just *knew.*

She smiled. Nonnus would have understood. She could feel his nearness in this physical darkness as she had in the spiritual darkness when she waited for death in the baobab's heart.

The way upward was no steeper than the meadows where the sheep of the borough grazed. The companions didn't speak to one another, but Sharina became aware of both the soughing of wind that blew across the open mouth of the tube and the subtle changes in pressure on her eardrums as the river swelled and sank below them.

It didn't matter that they couldn't see. "Up" was a direction as good as any their eyes could have given them. Occasionally there was a pothole where a deep-rooted tree had survived long enough that, burned to carbon and powdered by the following ages, it left its mark in the rock. Sharina learned to avoid those also, though she couldn't have told how.

She became aware of light. At first she thought it was a trick like the flashes that traced sometimes across her closed eyes. This was a gray paleness, though. Hanno's body was a powerful silhouette against it. They were nearing openings into an outer world that she'd almost forgotten.

Early in its course down the mountainside the lava had splashed over the roots of a pine. When the organic remains decayed, they left holes through the tube. Sharina might have been able to stick her arm through a hole and waggle her fingers in the outer air, but neither of the men could do even that.

Hanno got down on his belly to look through a hole just above ground level. Unarc squatted and peered through another. "As I hope for the Lady's grace!" he said. "Hanno, what're them crazy Monkeys doing down there?"

"I know what it looks like," the other hunter muttered. Without speaking further, he got to his knees and edged sideways, gesturing Sharina to the viewport.

She rotated her belt so that the sheathed knife wasn't

between her and the rough lava surface. She was looking down on a bay some five hundred feet below. Felled timber of all sizes and descriptions covered the water's surface. Vast numbers of Hairy Men clambered over the floating debris, guided or directed by phantasms like the one leading the Hairy Men who'd attacked her and Hanno.

She couldn't guess how many of the brute men she saw. Their squirming reminded her of the day early each Heron when the termites came out of the ground in swarming profusion, preparing to fly to new homes while the crows and jays gorged themselves on the sudden bounty.

"Has there been a storm?" Sharina asked, lifting her face from the opening to meet Hanno's eyes. "To wash all those trees into the bay?"

"That's not storm-swash, missie," Unarc said as he also straightened. "They've been felled. All of them. You see the branches but there's no root balls like a storm would've done. Besides, there's been no storm."

Hanno nodded. "The Monkeys did it," he said. "They—"

"Monkeys *couldn't* do that!" Unarc said. "They don't have the brains!"

"They had the brains to cut you good and mash both our boats!" Hanno said. "Things ain't the same, Unarc. The fuzzy ghosts down there talk to them. Put fear of the Gods in them, from what it seemed when they came after me!'

He grinned reminiscently. "Though not so bad as me and missie there put the fear to them later on. Such as were left."

"There are thousands of Hairy Men down there," Sharina said. "Tens of thousands."

She looked again down into the natural harbor. A mass of timber was sliding toward the mouth of the bay. The trees must have been tied together as well as bound by their entangled branches.

"They must've cleaned both banks of the East River

for leagues to get all that wood," Unarc said. "I noticed some trees down when we followed the West River too—"

Sharina hadn't noticed any cut trees. The river itself was merely a thrum in her consciousness for most of the day's journey.

"—but I didn't think much about it."

Over the raft swarmed many hundreds of Hairy Men. They were—

"They've built rafts," Sharina said as she rose again to a squat. "They're pulling themselves out to sea by ropes or something. More Hairy Men at the jaws of the bay are holding the other ends of the ropes. I think there's more rafts in the open sea already."

Hanno dropped so suddenly that Sharina almost fell as she squirmed clear. "Well I *will* be fricasseed in a pot!" the big hunter said. "That's what they're doing, missie. That sure is."

Unarc's brow wrinkled. "They're drownding themselfs?" he said.

"Hanno?" said Sharina. "You said the current carried west all the way to Ornifal. Could they . . . ?"

"There goes another lot," Unarc said from his viewport. "May the Shepherd shear my bum if they don't!"

"Yeah, it might be that," Hanno said as he got to his feet. "I don't know what they'd figure to do on Ornifal."

"There's a powerful lot of them," the bald man said reflectively. He rose to a kneeling position, but he checked the edge of his hooked knife in the light before he stood completely.

Hanno nodded. Both hunters resumed climbing the steep slope. Sharina, caught by surprise, took long strides to fall in between them again before the light faded.

Breathing was easier now. A breeze past the tube's unseen mouth higher up the mountain drew air in through the root holes. Sharina recognized the mustiness of the tube's stagnant lower level only now that she was past it. Any air after being submerged in the mud-black water had left her lungs too grateful to complain about the quality of what was available.

At first Sharina thought the sound she heard, *felt*, was the crosswind reverberating in the depths of the tube. Garric played a shepherd's pipe of reeds stoppered at the bottom with wax so that each different length vibrated at a graduated note.

Sharina climbed higher. She began to hear unintelligible words in the pulses of sound. Light seeped from above. The rush of molten rock had drawn striations down the lava tube while the walls were still plastic. Hanno held his spear crossways. His right hand was at the balance and his left just below the broad head, prepared to thrust or throw.

Sharina could see the opening above them. The lava had poured from a notch in the lip of the volcano, cooling as it plunged downward. The eruption that formed the tube must have been a later one since it had engulfed full-sized trees that grew from the existing cone. The walls were thinner at the top of the tube than they became by the time they reached the river. They'd crumbled away for a distance of twenty feet below the lip, but the notch had weathered deeper also.

Sharina drew the Pewle knife. Without looking around, Hanno gestured her and Unarc to wait.

The big hunter crept to the tunnel mouth. His limbs didn't seem to move at all; it was like watching a snake climb a tree. He glanced around, then slithered fully into the open to peer over the edge of the notch.

He signaled the others forward. The air throbbed with the sound of the huge voice chanting, but Sharina still couldn't understand the words.

She stepped out of the sheltering lava, bending low but not attempting to crawl because the porous surface would scrape her to the bone. Hanno must have some technique that even Unarc lacked, because the bald hunter hunched out just as Sharina did. Though they were at the top of the volcano, part of the cone now blocked their view of the harbor.

Sharina looked over the lip of rock, expecting to see a hollow filled with bubbling magma. Instead, the volcano had been dormant so long that grass covered the bottom of the crater. The walls were weathered to the color of rust.

"Oh . . . ," Sharina whispered. She squeezed her knife hilt for the comfort it gave her.

A fifty-foot outcrop had remained in the center of the basin when the surface around it slumped back into the earth. Someone had shaped it into the form of a Hairy Man with a ball in his right hand.

"It wasn't like that six months past," Unarc whispered. "Hanno, *what* are the Monkeys up to?"

Sharina swallowed. The idol's eyes and mouth were carved deep. Wisps of colored smoke drifted from the openings to form a cloud like faded rags above the brutish head.

The sound of chanting came from the huge effigy. Though the words were still meaningless, Sharina now recognized the rhythms of wizardry.

"There's no Monkeys down there now," Hanno said. "Except for whoever's inside the statue making that noise. I guess they're all gone to the harbor."

"The cloud," Sharina whispered. "It's shaped like a demon."

She should have recognized the smoke image immediately: the cadaverous body; the limbs like wires knotted at the joints; the long skull and undershot jaw. The phantasms directing the Hairy Men were in the same mold and of similarly insubstantial fabric, but the scale of this semblance had deceived her.

"I don't see any point in—" Unarc said as he started to back toward the concealing tube.

The smoke-demon moved. *Drifting in the breeze*, Sharina thought, but there suddenly was no breeze.

The smoke stared at them with yellow eyes.

"Run!" Hanno shouted as he jumped to his feet. When Sharina paused to let him lead as before, the big hunter grabbed her and half-shoved, half-flung her toward the mouth of the tube.

Sharina ran through the darkness in exaltation. The crisis had so taken her out of herself that she wasn't aware of her footing, let alone concerned. In Sharina's present state she was as much a part of her world as a fish swimming; and as with the fish, she instinctively *knew* the environment through which she moved.

She'd sheathed the knife. The sturdy blade would be useless against the present dangers and she didn't need the feel of the grip to remind her of Nonnus.

She reached the light diffusing from root holes across the passage and leaped it in the same gazelle-like bounds that she'd been making in the pitch blackness above. The two hunters padded along at their own best speed, but for once they seemed noisy and slow compared to the girl they'd sent ahead of them.

Sharina wasn't thinking about what she would do when she reached the river. Did religious folk ever reach the sort of closeness to Godhead that she felt now? All existence was one, and she was one with all existence!

The lava walls began to glow with red light as though she were running through a cloud lit by sunset. She heard Hanno and Unarc shout in surprise from far away. They must see the light also.

Sharina took another leap. Ahead of her the walls of light bulged inward. A huge clawed hand, smoky but still more substantial than the rock it penetrated, reached through and began to close.

Hanno shouted again. Sharina would have liked to stop, but the momentum of her spirit no less than her body carried her forward.

She was trying to draw the Pewle knife when the demon hand clamped shut, squeezing Sharina into darkness again as it drew her back the way it had come.

2nd Day of the Fifth Month (Partridge)

"Ah, there's the baron's brontothere coming!" said Ascelei, letting out anger as well as informing Ilna and Cerix, "You could buy every house on this street for what that animal cost, and out of our taxes!"

Cerix squirmed to get a better look at the great beast pacing slowly around the angle of the street. Ascelei's house stood on the Parade, the broadest thoroughfare in Divers, but even the Parade bent and wriggled on its course from Baron Robilard's palace to the harbor.

Ascelei the Mercer, Ilna's host and employer for the past four days, was one of the most prosperous men in Divers. He'd added an ornate railing to what had probably been an open balcony when the house was built a century or more in the past. The flat, pear-shaped banisters were attractive and made the balcony safer for people who needed mechanical help to avoid falling into the street. Cerix in his cart could see more through the slats than if he'd been at street level behind the legs of the other spectators, but only a little more.

"Do you want me to lift you?" Ilna said. She kept her eyes on the procession so that the cripple could avoid embarrassment by pretending she hadn't spoken if he wanted to.

The brontothere resembled a horse more than it did any other animal Ilna had seen, but it weighed several tons and its head looked like a gigantic saddle. A broad, side-forked horn stuck up from the nose like a pommel, and the forehead was dished in to curve upward to the thick neck. Despite the beast's great size, the skull didn't have much room for a brain.

"No, I can see," Cerix muttered, drawing himself up to look over the railing. He had to use the strength of his upper body to keep his weight off his stumps, but he clearly preferred that to accepting help from somebody else.

Ilna smiled wryly. She didn't have a lot in common with the cripple and she despised the weakness that caused him to drug himself for the pain; but she could at least applaud his desire to do without the help of others.

The crowd cheered to see the brontothere, though there was less enthusiasm than Ilna would have expected for a spectacular parade. There'd already been a troop of cavalry in polished armor—only twenty of them, but Third Atara was a small island which had to import the grain that horses needed to stay healthy. Then came a band with horns, cymbals, and even a copper kettledrum carried in a frame between two men and beaten by two more who walked to either side. Next were nearly two hundred sailors keeping step as they marched in tight companies.

The sailors surprised Ilna till Ascelei mentioned that they were from the baron's war galleys. The fixed rhythms of rowing made them better able to keep pace than most folk.

And now the brontothere, a striking sight even had it been alone. The only folk in the street who seemed to be cheering unreservedly, though, were ragged fellows who probably had nothing to be taxed on. Very possibly it wasn't just wealthy merchants like Ascelei who felt the burden of Robilard's shows.

"He claims to be descended from the Elder Romi," Ascelei said bitterly. "Him! His grandfather was a bodyguard for my grandfather when he was trading to Sandrakkan. If Robilard's a real noble, then I'm the Lady! And everybody knows Romi was celibate anyway."

Cerix cocked his head to look up at Ilna. "Romi was the wizard who ruled Third Atara after King Carus drowned," he explained. "During the hundred years

Romi lived, he kept Third Atara peaceful while the rest of the Isles fell apart.''

''You know about the Elder Romi, Master Cerix?'' Ascelei said with for the first time a degree of respect for the cripple. He'd allowed Cerix to view the procession from the second story—the sleeping loft—of his shop only because Ilna had insisted and Ascelei was afraid to lose her services.

The mercer was a sour man, though astute and scrupulously honest in his dealings. Ilna had gained a place in his household minutes after she and the two wizards had arrived in Divers four days earlier. The mercer was having a gastric attack. Ilna had cured it with a quickly knotted pattern that settled Ascelei's stomach as no healer's nostrum had managed in the decades previous.

''I've visited Third Atara in past years,'' Cerix said. ''But Romi I know from my studies. He was one of the greatest wizards of all time.''

The brontothere paced stolidly down the center of the roadway, crushing the coarse limestone gravel into dust with its three-toed feet. Two men walked beside the creature holding beribboned cords attached to its collar, but no one could imagine that they'd restrain it should it decide to bolt. The horsemen riding to either side with lances leveled at the brontothere's rib cage were the real control on its behavior.

''Robilard, Baron Robiman,'' Ascelei said. ''He claims he's going to regain the glory of his ancestor the Elder Romi. If it would bring back Romi and the golden age, I wouldn't grudge the way taxes have risen, but all we get for our money is pomp like this, gilded armor and brontotheres from Shengy!''

He gestured down toward the handsome young man with a goatee, a spike mustache, and—as the mercer had said—gilded armor, brilliant in the sunlight. Ilna had thought the chariot in which Robilard stood was harnessed to the brontothere, but she saw now that the double line of footmen following the vehicle pushed it along by means of a pole. The baron was apparently doubtful enough about the brontothere's tractability that he didn't choose to tether himself to the beast.

"What a ridiculous display!" Ilna said. She'd seen too much human folly to claim that this example surprised her, but familiarity didn't keep her from feeling disgust at each latest manifestation.

"Romi isolated Third Atara from the rest of the Isles," Cerix said. He'd exhausted the strength of his arms, so he lowered himself awkwardly onto his chair again. Breathing heavily he continued, "While he lived, he could do that: no ship reached the island without Romi's permission. If they tried, though they sailed forever the island would move away as quickly as they moved forward. But when Romi finally died, Third Atara was no different from any other place, and the pirates came here too."

Ilna saw movement behind the line of spectators. She leaned over the railing for a better view. Because the lofts of this and other houses facing the Parade overhung the ground floors, it was difficult to see pedestrians who walked close to the building fronts.

She'd been correct in her identification, though. "Here's Halphemos coming at last," she said. "He wasn't required to, of course. An invitation isn't a command."

She heard the bitterness in her own voice and grimaced. "A truth that I should listen to myself, I see," she added.

Halphemos and Cerix had lodged at an inn, the Dog and Cat, with the last of their money. Ilna had become the guest of her employer as part of her wages. The wizards had held street shows while Ilna returned to weaving as a way to earn a living until she got a sense of the situation.

Ascelei had quickly judged the value of the feelings of well-being which Ilna's woven panels brought. He'd have advanced her money to lodge at the Dog and Cat if she'd wished to. She didn't see any reason to do that; but she *had* expected both the wizards to accept her invitation to watch the spectacle from the vantage of the mercer's house.

Cerix had wheeled himself to the house under his own power, explaining with some embarrassment that Halphemos had another engagement but would be along shortly. Cerix hadn't been willing—or perhaps able—to say what the other engagement was. Ilna assumed it involved a woman. Though she didn't have the least romantic inclinations toward Halphemos (the boy!) she was irritated to note a flash of jealousy in her reaction.

"Your other guest, mistress?" Ascelei asked.

The chariot had passed Ascelei's house and was nearing another bend in the Parade that would take it out of sight. Baron Robilard had remained perfectly still during his progress.

Ilna's lip wrinkled. The baron might better have dressed a statue in his glittering armor and used the time to do something useful himself—like clean the palace chamber pots.

Behind Robilard's chariot came a dozen or so litters and sedan chairs carrying courtiers of both sexes. Some of the nobles had the decency to look embarrassed—though from what Ilna knew of the nobility, those were probably folk who feared their display wasn't as splendid as that of their rivals in other conveyances.

Ilna hadn't had any contact with the nobility when she lived in Barca's Hamlet; if she thought about them at all, it was to wonder why people believed that what their ancestors had done somehow made them better than anybody else. Nothing she'd seen since she'd entered the wider world had given her a better opinion of the class.

Third Atara, the last of the smaller islands trailing Atara proper, exported its wines and the colored marbles of its quarries all over the Isles. Ilna noted that perhaps as a result of its far-flung trade, court dress here ran to marine colors. There were blues, greens, and even a pale violet that must have come from eggplant rind. The aubergine's smooth consistency impressed her with the dyemaster's skill.

Silks purchased by the nobility's agents on Seres and Kanbesa predominated among the fabrics. Ascelei's clientele came mostly from the class to which he belonged, wealthy merchants who favored woolens and fur trim. The small panels Ilna had been weaving from fine wool were already bringing queries from the palace, though—a matter of considerable satisfaction to the mercer.

The majordomo stepped onto the balcony and whispered in Ascelei's ear. The mercer gave an irritated wave of his hand and said, "Yes, of course he should be admitted. It doesn't matter that he came separately!"

He looked at Ilna in apology. She nodded curt understanding. Ascelei had a dozen servants in addition to the clerks in his shop below. He needed them because of his position in society, he'd explained to Ilna. Her opinion was that if Ascelei had at least ten fewer of the officious busybodies in his house, his position would have been a great deal more comfortable.

The very tag-end of the procession was passing, a pair of drummers and a body of palace servants on foot. The latter were probably only those who could afford impressive clothing, but there were still scores of them.

Ilna grinned. She imagined a horde of ragged scullery maids, stableboys, and undergardeners following to demonstrate just what it took to maintain one young fop in gilded armor in what he deemed his proper state. From what Ascelei had said, at least the taxpayers of Third Atara were already well aware of the cost.

"Master Halphemos, who does not give his patronymic," the majordomo announced, making clear his disdain for a man he classed a common mountebank for all the young wizard's silk robes. To be fair, the red brocade was considerably the worse for wear since Halphemos had been jailed in it.

Ilna wasn't in a mood to be fair. Halphemos had left what he thought was paradise for her. In a cold rage she turned and grasped the collar of the majordomo's robe. She ran her fingers across the fabric, lace over a tight serge. With closed eyes she let its patterns flow into her conscious understanding.

Ilna opened her eyes again, taking her hand away from the garment and reentering the waking world. The majordomo was gabbling; Ascelei watched with questions but no concern in his expression, and Halphemos slid past the tableau with his right hand in his left sleeve.

"Do you know who *your* father was?" Ilna asked harshly, her eyes holding the servant's. "I do."

"I'm Othem or-Almagar!" the majordomo said. "My father was Baron Orde's personal valet!"

He patted his collar to make sure that Ilna hadn't torn it. As if she'd take her anger out on innocent fabric!

"Your father was named Garsaura and he was a groom in the palace stables," Ilna said, raising her voice so that the several servants standing beyond the balcony door could hear clearly. "Would you care to learn more about your real ancestry, Master Othem?"

"That's not—" the majordomo said. He didn't finish the thought. His mouth remained open as he turned. He left the balcony faster than his dignity of a few moments before would have allowed him to do.

Halphemos grinned appreciatively, though he seemed a little embarrassed to have needed a woman to stand up for him. "Thank you, mistress," he said. He nodded in the direction the majordomo had vanished and added, "He won't sleep till he's proved there wasn't a groom named Garsaura in the palace forty years ago, will he?"

Ascelei's eyes moved in quick increments from Halphemos to Ilna. It was Cerix, looking over his shoulder because there wasn't room on the balcony for him to turn his chair, who said, "But there *was* a Garsaura in the palace then. Wasn't there, mistress?"

"Yes," said Ilna with a smile that could cut glass. "As a matter of fact there was, Master Cerix."

"She doesn't bluff, boy," the cripple said to his gaping

ward. "She doesn't lie. And by whatever gods you believe in, *don't* get her angry."

"I apologize, Master Ascelei," Ilna said, feeling the knot of self-loathing begin to form in her stomach. It always did after she realized she'd used her abilities for an end she couldn't justify as having made the world a better place. "I'm a guest in your household. It isn't my place to discipline your servants, and I shouldn't have done it in that fashion anyway."

"Othem has been known to insult guests—friends and good clients of mine—when he doesn't feel their lineage is sufficiently exalted," the mercer said. He spoke with perhaps more care than he would have shown if he didn't understand what Ilna had just done. "I didn't know how to break him of the practice without dismissing him, and in general he's a very useful servant. I'm still further in your debt, mistress."

He dipped his head to Ilna in gesture that was almost a bow.

Ilna grimaced. It bothered her obscurely that she appeared to have done exactly the right thing when she knew perfectly well that her intentions had been bad. She didn't expect to find justice, but it seemed deeply wrong to be unjustly good.

Halphemos, his right hand still clutching whatever it was he hid in his other sleeve, sidled close to Ilna. "I have something to show you in private," he announced in a barnyard whisper.

Ilna could have slapped him. Instead she said in a voice that came all the way from the Ice Capes, "My host Master Ascelei invited you here as a favor to me. If you have secrets you don't wish to share with him, boy, please take them and yourself out of his house. I'll join you when I'm able to stomach your discourtesy—which won't be in the near future, I assure you."

Halphemos opened his mouth to protest, then looked stricken. He'd let his excitement run away with him, but he did know better.

"I'll leave the three of you here," Ascelei said equably. "I'll see that you're not disturbed."

He smiled. The mercer's sense of humor—indeed, his personality—were not dissimilar to Ilna's own. "I don't think Master Othem was going to be intruding anyway."

Ilna started to protest, then shrugged. This balcony was as good a place to talk secrets as any in Divers. The spectators were dispersing, but the normal traffic along the Parade formed a blanket of noise to smother words quietly spoken in the open air. Of course a servant might lean against—

"But do explain to your household . . . ," Cerix said loudly. He'd backed his cart around into a corner so that he could look directly at the others on the narrow balcony. ". . . that Mistress Ilna would never use her powers to strike a spy deaf and blind."

"What?" said Ascelei, looking at the cripple in surprise. He smiled again. "Yes, I see. I'll inform them."

The mercer closed the balcony door behind him. When Ilna had quenched the instant's anger at what had been implied in her name, she smiled also. It was a clever trick, and harmless.

Halphemos knelt and withdrew a bag of soft red leather from his sleeve. "Look at this!" he said as he opened the drawstrings. "When I sell it, we'll have passage for three to Valles and a fortune leftover besides!"

He poured a pearl the size and shape of a pigeon's egg onto his palm. It was mounted as a pendant with a gold cap, though the chain or cord was missing.

"Have you ever seen anything so beautiful?" Halphemos said.

"Occasionally," Ilna said, though the pattern of light through the jewel's iridescent layers spoke to her as to few others, she suspected. "And I've seen things that were even more dangerous for castaways in a foreign land to hold, Halphemos. Occasionally."

"Where did you get it, Alos?" Cerix said quietly. The

cripple's hands kneaded his thighs just above the stumps. He looked as worried as Ilna was furious.

"I can't tell you that," Halphemos said, defensive against his companions' unexpected lack of enthusiasm. "It's not stolen, that's all that matters."

"No," Ilna said coldly, "it's not all that matters. The best thing you can do with that is throw it in the sea."

Halphemos stuffed the pearl back in its bag with trembling hands. He stood, white with anger. "You're just jealous!" he said. "Well, *Mistress* Ilna, it's time you realize that there's other people who can do things even when you can't! I'll buy us all passage to Valles. You can decide if you want to come search for your brother or stay here and sulk because *I* earned the money. By my art!"

He jerked the door open. Seemingly, Halphemos had forgotten the small sack he now held openly in his hand. "Cerix," he said, "come along with me. The mistress doubtless has things to discuss with her wealthy friends."

Cerix wheeled himself into the loft proper, bumping over the sill. He threw Ilna a worried look; Ilna nodded a reply. Halphemos flounced out angrily without meeting her eyes again.

Ilna hoped the boy would allow Ascelei's servants to help Cerix negotiate the stairs instead of doing it himself. In his present state, Halphemos was apt to tip his friend all the way down. That would be *all* the situation needed!

Though flinging Cerix down the staircase was less dangerous to the cripple and all of them than what Halphemos proposed to do with the pearl. Jewels like that one screamed an owner's name louder than a summonsing bailiff did.

Maybe Cerix could talk the boy out of his foolishness. Ilna didn't see a better hope.

Though it wasn't a very good one, as determined as Halphemos had sounded.

* * *

"Awaken, Cashel or-Kenset," the cracked voice said. "Your body is renewed, your spirit is refreshed. Awaken now and aid me as I have aided you!"

Cashel was drifting in a fog of purple smoke. He wasn't worried; the smoke buoyed him up like salt water, but he could breathe its tendrils as well.

"Awaken, Cashel," the voice said. "I, Silya, command you by the virtues I have arrayed to tend your hurts!"

"Who are you?" Cashel demanded groggily. He felt his lips move, proving that he was speaking aloud. He opened his eyes, though the effort to do so amazed him.

He lay on his back on a board. He patted the surface with his fingertips, noted the chill, and realized it was polished stone instead of wood. So. He lay on a stone slab, stark naked, in a vault lighted by braziers which puffed rich-colored smokes as well as a lurid glow into the air.

He was lying like a corpse laid out for burial.

"Hey!" Cashel said. He kicked his legs over the edge of the slab and stood, looking around wildly. No one was in the room with him except for Silya, the woman wearing the bones through her ears in Dalopan fashion. She was naked as well, but tattoos covered her body like a garment of knobbly lace.

"Cashel or-Kenset," she said, waving a bone rattle at him. The box was made from a dog's skull, but the thigh bone laced to it for a handle was human or Cashel was blind. "I've brought you back from the portal of death. Now you will help me and—"

She thrust the rattle directly at Cashel's face; he suppressed an urge to crush the ugly thing in his fist.

"—between us we will be the Beast's overlords in this world!"

"Where are my clothes?" Cashel said. The smoke was making him gag, though he supposed it was meant to be soothing. "And where are my friends, Zahag and Aria?"

He looked around without seeing his tunic or anything else he could throw over himself for the moment. The braziers' flickering illumination hid as much as it revealed. On the floor about the slab was chalked a many-sided figure with words on the margin.

The wizard looked puzzled. Cashel supposed Silya had expected some other response than simple disgust and a desire to leave her presence. He wasn't afraid of her, and he certainly wasn't grateful. "You're the one who sent me and Zahag to the other Pandah, aren't you?" he said. "Keep away from me with that toy you're holding or I'll feed it to you, by the Shepherd I will!"

"That was a mistake," she said. "Here, I have clothing for you in the next chamber."

Silya walked to a door which, with its frame, seemed to have been knocked together recently: the wood was still oozing sap. Similar wooden barriers closed the five other archways, though they didn't have doors set into them. The vault had been blocked out of the foundations of a large building, probably Folquin's palace.

Cashel slammed the door behind him, thankfully closing off the still-smoldering braziers. He coughed loudly to clear the cloying fumes from his throat.

This room was also a vault walled off by partitions, but here the bricks were covered with mats of colored grasses woven in attractive geometric designs. *Ilna would be interested in those,* he thought.

A hammock hung from hooks set across one corner. Patterned baskets with covers stood along the walls, and a pole stand held a variety of tools. Those could be intended either for cooking, torture, or wizardry.

A bronze oil lamp lighted the space. The lobes for the three wicks were each shaped like a man's private parts. Cashel's nose wrinkled.

"I thought your woman Sharina was the important one," Silya said as she lifted the lid from a storage basket. It was cunningly made, requiring a twist rather than a straight pull to release it. "That's because my brother believed the girl was the scion of the old line who could lead him to the Throne of Malkar."

She paused, then plucked a tunic from the basket and shook it open for Cashel. It was of simple pattern—indeed, it had probably been sewn from an awning—but that was fine with him.

He took the garment. Cashel knew he didn't owe anything to this woman, but he always felt good toward somebody who was helping him. Of course, it was Silya's interference that had caused all the trouble to begin with. . . .

Cashel draped the tunic over him. As he shrugged the heavy cotton down past his shoulders, he digested what the Dalopan wizard had just said.

When his head emerged from the tunic, Cashel looked at her. In a very quiet voice he said, "What have you done to Sharina?"

He took a step forward. The world he saw was gray except for the startled wizard and the expanse of brick wall behind her.

Silya's eyes flicked toward the stand of tools, then wisely met Cashel's again. She even tossed aside the bone rattle in her hand. "The girl's unharmed!" she said. "She was nothing to me after all, so I let her go with the boy wizard I replaced here on Pandah."

Cashel took a deep breath. "But you said . . ." He tried to remember exactly what Silya *had* said. Everything had blurred for a moment. He looked at his hands and clenched them to work the tension out.

"My brother thought she was important," Silya said, taking quick, relieved breaths herself. "He was drawing her to him. I traced his work and thought I'd forestall him here on Pandah. But he was wrong, so I let her go."

She wasn't lying. Cashel was used to people trying to lie to him. It wasn't as easy as strangers thought, but sometimes they succeeded.

They never succeeded when Cashel was angry, the way he was now. He could see right to their heart.

Silya started to pick up the garment she'd draped over the hammock, then dropped it to return her attention to the young man before her. "My brother Silyon stole the Stone of Connection from me," she said. "He communicates with the Beast through it. You and I will take the Stone back from him and *we* will be the Beast's viceroys!"

Cashel wasn't sure hold old the wizard was. At first he'd thought she was quite old, fifty at least, but Silya's voice was that of a much younger woman. The tattoos aged her. Besides, travelers' tales claimed that the folk of Dalopo looked ancient by the time they were thirty—which was old enough in all truth.

"Where did Sharina go?" Cashel asked. "And where are Aria and Zahag?"

"Don't you hear me?" Silya shouted. "I offer you half of all power and you ask about girls and beasts. You can have every woman in the world if you join me!"

Cashel stepped toward her again before he was even conscious that he was moving. She shouldn't have talked about Sharina that way.

"The girl Aria is fine!" Silya said hastily. "She's with the king and quite the favorite. The ape's probably all right too, though why you should care is beyond me. The meat's stringy at best, and the males are gamy besides."

Cashel forced himself to relax. "And Sharina?" he asked.

"She went off to Valles with the other wizards," Silya said. "The boy and the cripple. My brother was drawing her, as I told you, but he was wrong about her power. She's just a girl."

"Yes," said Cashel in a guttural voice as he started for the door out of this chamber. "She is."

"Cashel or-Kenset, wait!" the wizard said. She raised both her hands, palms outward, though she stepped out of Cashel's way. "You broke through the planes by your own main strength. With me to guide you, no one can stand against us! We'll take the Stone, and perhaps we'll be able to rule the Beast instead of ruling this world beneath him!"

"I'm going to find my friends," Cashel said. His tongue was so thick with anger and disgust that he could barely understand his own words. "Don't get in my way."

He turned the latch and pushed the door. It stuck. He pushed harder, smashing the whole wall down. The door had been meant to open inward, he saw, as he glanced down at the ruin of heavy balks.

"Don't ever get in my way!" Cashel repeated as he strode toward the light glimmering from outside the vaulted basement.

A group of children giggling with fright ran out of the basement ahead of him. Cashel's crashing exit had scared them away. They'd been playing, not spying, among the brick pillars.

Cashel grinned. It'd scared Silya too, if she had as much sense as the Lady gave a goose. The grin faded. It'd be good to hold his own hickory staff again, though the fir replacement from the other Pandah was a fine piece of work too.

The steps up to ground level were littered with dirt, leaves, and human debris. There were holes in the stone sill where doors had once pivoted, but the panels were long gone.

Cashel paused at the top of the steps, slitting his eyes against the bright sun as well as shading them with his left hand. It was near noon, though he realized he didn't know what day it was. He was at the back of the palace; the children and adults socializing in the large open space were all looking at him.

Though Cashel smiled to show he was friendly, children gathered close and their parents circled them with their arms. He wondered what sort of stories were going around about him. It bothered him to realize that people probably thought he was a friend of the Dalopan wizard. He'd as soon be friends with a seawolf.

The walkway around the palace was railed off from the grounds, a mental barrier though not much of a physical one. Cashel put a hand on a vine-wrapped pillar to hop over.

Zahag dropped from the roof in three spider-limbed jumps. They were very nearly the last moves the ape made in this life. Cashel, still tense and a lot more angry than he'd realized, shouted "Hey!" and threw his great hands up to meet what reflex was treating as an attack.

"Hey!" Zahag echoed in fear. Instead of landing at Cashel's side, the ape bounced upward from the railing to grab a pillar five paces distant.

Children and adults too were stampeding away from the bellow. Cashel rubbed his forehead in embarrassment. It was as bad as the day a horsefly stung Piri's off-ox under the base of the tail.

"I didn't mean . . . ," Cashel mumbled. He'd known before he was seven years old not to get angry. Now look at him! All because he was worried about Sharina, but Sharina didn't need an ox running around kicking and goring, that was sure.

"I had to hide all the time you were sleeping," Zahag said in the hurt tone which had quickly replaced his fear. He dropped off the pillar and sidled toward Cashel, ready to flee again if he found he'd misjudged the situation. "Now you come after me too. It's not fair, you know!"

Cashel didn't speak for a moment. Then, as the ape started to wilt, he said, "I'd rather you didn't surprise me that way, Zahag. I'd feel bad if I'd swung you into the ground so hard you splashed, the way I started to do."

"Oh, no, chief, no, that'll never happen again!" Zahag said. He turned his back and peered at Cashel upside down from between his own legs. From a human the posture would've been insulting, but there wasn't anything but belly-crawling submission in the ape's tone. "No, no, no!"

Cashel nodded. "Where's Aria?" he said. "Is she all right?"

"Oh, you're going to fix him now!" Zahag said, capering in joy. "Come on, chief, he's up in the courtyard. Oh, he's going to be sorry now!"

He grabbed Cashel's right hand and tugged with friendly enthusiasm. The ape's mood changed about as quick as a summer breeze, but that didn't bother Cashel. Sheep were the same way, so he was used to it. Farmers wouldn't need to pay shepherds if all animals were as solid and mannerly as oxen. Most times.

Cashel climbed over the railing. Zahag hopped from the ground to a pillar to the walkway—and back, all nervous motion like flies over a fresh side of meat. The children and palace servants in the plaza whispered among themselves, now that there didn't seem to be a prospect of immediate bloodshed. They ducked away when Cashel swept them with his eyes, even though he smiled as warmly as he knew how.

Cashel paused. "I asked if Aria was all right," he said to Zahag. "Who's this that's going to be sorry?"

The ape was already halfway into the passage to the courtyard. He turned and momentarily wrinkled his lips in a snarl of frustration. "Folquin, of course!" he said.

Even as Zahag growled his words, he remembered who he was talking to. He gave a grunt of apology and went on clingingly, "King Folquin, who told his guards to kill me for the trouble *I* caused, when it was all that Dalopan savage's doing. And *she's* his new wizard, wouldn't you know? Folquin who's trying to take your female, chief!"

"Take my—" Cashel blurted. He blinked. "Oh," he said, "you mean the princess. Well, let's go see her."

He hummed a jig as he sauntered down the passage behind Zahag. He was remembering the dances at the very start of Heron when the plowing was over.

Cashel didn't play pipes or the lyre, and his steps were simple ones in contrast to the hops and handstands some of the more agile youths demonstrated to the crowd's applause; but Cashel could dance the feet off the other lads in the borough, and any of the girls save Sharina herself. Many's the time he and she turned and turned about in

Finnan's Reel while the others cheered in exhausted amazement.

The ape hunched along on all fours, frequently glancing over his shoulder at Cashel. A servant with a tray of empty cups came the other way, saw them, and bolted back into the courtyard. He could have squeezed by; there was plenty of room.

Aria Cashel's female indeed! How long would the princess have kept her feet as the hamlet danced?

Zahag stepped aside and let Cashel enter the courtyard ahead of him. It was already in commotion. Folquin had jumped up from his backless stool. The servant stood beside him; a line of cups sprinkled on the ground from there back to the passage showed what haste the fellow'd made to warn his king that Cashel was coming.

The six guards stepped between Cashel and Folquin. One of them put his knee against the belly of his bow to string it, but his officer snarled, "*Put* that down and stand straight!"

Aria had been seated beside Folquin. She rose with regal grace. She wore a tunic of violet silk gathered beneath the bosom and again at the waist. The excess material wobbled like breeze-blown moss dangling from a tree branch.

To Cashel's utter astonishment, the princess held his fir quarterstaff in front of her like a flagpole. Its sizable weight wavered even though she'd butted one end on the ground. She turned to Folquin and said in a carrying voice, "Your Majesty, I see that Master Cashel, my champion, has regained consciousness. May I have the honor of formally presenting him to you?"

"It's all right, Aria," Cashel said. "The king and me met before. Before, you know, I met you."

The idlers and petitioners were all watching him, just like they had when he'd grabbed Zahag that morning a lifetime ago. Silya wasn't in the crowd, though. Cashel looked over his shoulder to make sure the wizard hadn't followed. She hadn't, but Zahag was backing his chief with bared teeth and a growl that made bubbles of spit form on his lips.

"Yes," Folquin said. He cocked his head to the side, apparently trying to peek around Cashel's solid form to find the wizard also. "Ah, Master Cashel kept that horrid monkey from attacking me at considerable risk to himself. I trust you're well, Master Cashel?"

"I, well, I'm glad to be back," Cashel said. "Zahag's all right, though."

He turned his head and snapped, "Zahag, stop that! Mind your manners!"

The guards parted for Cashel at their officer's whispered command. That man stood sideways, his eyes darting from Cashel to his king, tense as a drawn bowstring in hopes that he'd made the right decision.

Aria gave Cashel the quarterstaff. "I trust you're well, Cashel?" she said. She really did seem glad to see him, but there was more than just formal reserve in Aria's careful words. She was wearing sandals of silvered leather that laced high up her calves.

"I'm fine," Cashel said; because it was true, and anyway he had to say something. He smiled at the staff. He'd have liked to spin it to make sure he hadn't gotten out of shape during his long sleep—too long for nature, it must have been more of the wizard's doing—but he was sure to start a panic and maybe clip somebody.

Cashel frowned and looked at the king again. A secretary standing beside Folquin gave a squeak of terror and closed his eyes.

"Ah," Cashel said, "not to be picky, but I wonder if the hickory staff I left when I was here before is still around? I made that myself when I was a boy and I'd hate to lose it."

Aria looked at the servant holding the tray from which the cups had spilled. "You heard Master Cashel!" she said. "Find that staff and bring it to him at once. Go on! Why are you standing there looking at me?"

Folquin opened his mouth, apparently to repeat the

princess's order. The servant didn't wait for it. He even flung away the tray as he scampered toward the passage into the building calling, "Wyckli! Abdorn! Her Majesty—"

He plunged into the passage. His voice reverberated back, "—wants the pole from the big barbarian's room!"

Cashel smiled. He'd been called worse, though the folks who did so generally had reason to regret it before the bout was over.

Aria was sure in her element, here. That was the awkward part about what had to happen next.

"Ah, King Folquin," Cashel said, "you've been kind enough to guest me and the princess. I think you ought to know that it was that Dalopan woman Silya who caused the trouble before she was in your service, not Zahag; but I didn't hold it against you anyhow."

"Silya?" said Folquin, frowning. "No—"

To shut the king off, Cashel thumped the staff against the packed soil. He was frustrated with himself. He wasn't a speaker and he'd let himself wander off the track.

"Anyhow," Cashel went on, "I appreciate all you've done. But now I've got to go on, because I need to find my friend Sharina."

He took a deep breath. "And I need to take Princess Aria with me," he continued, "because I told her mother—"

Folquin, Aria, and about six other people started to speak at the same time. What Cashel actually heard, though, was Zahag's growled, "No, you didn't, chief. You told her mother you'd get her away from Ilmed. That wizard hasn't been the least trouble to Aria since he met you."

"Ah," said Cashel. "Well, but what I meant . . ."

He wasn't sure what he *had* meant way back then when he stood before Queen Sosia. It was hard to get his thoughts straight because the others kept chattering at him, most of them.

Princess Aria had listened to Zahag also. "Be quiet, all

of you!'' she said. ''Remember you stand before your king!''

Cashel grinned wryly. True enough, but King Folquin fell silent with the rest of those who'd been yammering away.

In the silence Aria put her hand on Folquin's wrist for attention, then nodded him toward Cashel. There wasn't much doubt about which of that pair would be guiding the plow and which would be pulling it; assuming they were a pair, which at the moment Cashel didn't see them being.

''Master Cashel,'' the king said. From the many times Cashel had carried Aria he knew she was just a wisp of a girl, but right now her presence shrank everybody else around. ''I regard Princess Aria's arrival on Pandah to be a manifestation of the will of the Gods. She is clearly the woman they intend for my wife and to become Queen of Pandah. Therefore—''

''You were sure as sure that Sharina was meant to be your queen too,'' Cashel said with a touch of anger that he hadn't been expecting. ''You were wrong that time, and I'm not about to call you right this time either. I'm no clerk to play with words, what I said to Queen Sosia—''

He looked over his shoulder. The ape was combing himself for fleas and cracked those he caught between the backs of two claws. He didn't seem to notice his chief's threatening frown.

''—or anybody else. I'm going to protect—''

Aria began sobbing. Cashel stopped as short as if somebody'd felled a tree on him. Aria flung herself into his arms and wailed, ''Oh, Cashel, do you have to test me more? Even Muzira didn't have to go through the things I've done!''

''But Aria . . .'' Cashel muttered helplessly.

''If you tell me I have to go, I'll go,'' the princess said. Her tears were already spreading into a wet spot on his new tunic. ''But *please,* Cashel!''

King Folquin exchanged a glance with the captain of his guard. The soldier frowned and patted his left cheek, the gesture that meant, ''No,'' here on Pandah.

Half of Cashel regretted the soldier's warning, because a fight would be a lot simpler to figure out than the mess he'd somehow managed to get himself into. Why *wasn't* life simpler?

''I'd say there were plenty of females with more meat on their bones,'' Zahag remarked as he continued to crack fleas. ''But this one's better than I used to think. She kept the guards off me when we came back, not that I trusted them when I was out of her sight.''

Cashel looked at the ape. Zahag resolutely paid him no attention. Two servants bustled out of the passageway, carrying the hickory quarterstaff between them with as much pomp as if they were hunters with a deer instead of a bare pole.

Aria stepped back and raised her face to Cashel. It hadn't been a trick, her saying she'd go on if he told her she had to. And it hadn't been a joke, either, saying that she'd gone through more than Patient Muzira had. No, *sir,* it hadn't.

''Aria,'' Cashel said. ''Princess? Are you really sure staying here is what you want to do? Because I don't care how many there are, I won't let—''

Aria laid her finger vertically across Cashel's lips to silence him. ''I know you wouldn't, Cashel,'' she said. ''This is where I belong. I think Folquin will make a very nice husband. Just the sort of person the Mistress God would choose for me.''

''Ah, Master Cashel?'' the king said. Folquin was Cashel's senior by a little. Right now he seemed just a mite of a boy, barely old enough to wear a rag over him when he ran around in the summer. ''I want you to know that you're welcome to any position you wish in my palace. Captain of the Guard, perhaps, or—''

''No, no!'' Cashel said. He had to laugh at Folquin's earnestness. Why, the boy would probably buy the first flock of sheep ever to graze on Pandah if Cashel said he wanted to be the royal shepherd! "Your, ah, Majesty, I really need to leave as quick as I can. For Valles, I guess, if that's where Sharina went."

"You won't be staying for the wedding?" Folquin said with a suspicious enthusiasm. "Of course, the preparations for an event like that will take some time."

Cashel caught Aria's sharp glance at her husband-to-be, so he needed to speak fast before the princess decided to speed the preparations. The only thing Cashel wanted speeded was himself getting off Pandah and then back to his friends. "If there's a ship in harbor that'll take my labor for the passage, I'll board right now," he said.

The servants with Cashel's hickory staff were standing close, but they didn't want to interrupt the proceedings by speaking. Cashel reached out with his right hand and took it. The smooth, denser wood felt like coming home.

"Master Cashel," Folquin said, "if you can wait till the morning, I'll put one of the royal biremes at your disposal."

Apologetically he added, "It really will take that long to prepare the crew. But it will be a great deal faster than any sailing vessel could be."

"Ah, well," Cashel said. "That'd be good, I guess. I'd be beholden to you if you'd do that, ah, Your Majesty."

Folquin turned to one of his aides. In a crisp voice, very much the king again, he said, "See to it, Mousel. At once."

"Well, I . . . ," Cashel said. He felt pretty silly holding both quarterstaves, but he wasn't sure what to do with the extra one. "If there's a place I can get something to eat, I'm famished with hunger."

If he'd been sleeping for four days, it was that long since he'd had anything to eat. His last breakfast had been a mess of egg and fruit, tasty enough but not the sort of thing to stick to your ribs for the time it'd had to.

The king didn't even bother to speak an order this time. He gestured to a servant, who trotted off like dogs were chewing at his heels. ''Well, I'll—,'' Cashel began.

''Cashel?'' Aria said. ''You aren't going to keep the staff you had when you rescued me, are you?''

''What?'' he said. He held the fir staff out at arm's length and examined it closely. The brass end bands winked in the sunlight; they'd been polished a treat while Cashel was asleep in Silya's chamber. ''Well, it's a nice piece and it's lighter than my hickory, but . . .''

He paused without completing the thought. ''Thing is,'' he said, ''I'd hate for it just to prop up somebody's fishnet. I know, it's just a piece of wood, but—''

''It won't prop up a fishnet,'' said the princess. ''If you would give it to me, Cashel, I would be honored.''

''And of course I'll pay you—'' Folquin blurted.

Aria turned to look at her husband-to-be. ''Be silent,'' she said without raising her voice.

Cashel couldn't help but grin. Ilna couldn't have done it better, no sir. ''Sure, of course you can have it, Princess,'' he said aloud. ''I wish I had something better to give you for your wedding and all, but . . .''

He shrugged. He didn't even own the tunic he was standing in.

Servants were coming from the passage with trays of food. Cashel hadn't meant to eat here in the courtyard since it was more or less Folquin's throne room. As hungry as he was, though, it didn't seem to call for objection.

''Cashel?'' Aria said. ''Is your Sharina beautiful?''

Cashel paused with a ball of fried dough halfway to his mouth. ''Is she ever!'' he said. ''And graceful? You never saw anybody so graceful!''

''She's very lucky,'' the princess said as she turned away and began talking to Folquin about nothing in particular.

Cashel—with Zahag's help—was nearly done with the first tray of food in dainty bits, sitting in a corner of the courtyard, when Aria's words went through his mind again. He frowned.

"Zahag?" he said. "She must have meant *I'm* lucky, didn't she?"

"Chief," the ape said through a mouthful of flat bread smeared with nut paste, "I told you before I've met sheep that were smarter than you are. But it doesn't seem to matter."

Sharina stood in a red-lit chamber cut from the living rock, as motionless as an image of the Lady in its niche by the hearth. She could see and hear. The thrum of chanting voices was deeper than ears alone could sense, so perhaps ears were no part of the impression.

There were vertical slits in the walls around her. Beyond each opening was a different scene, viewed as though through a panel of flawless ruby. Of the half dozen Sharina could see from her frozen vantage point, four were or might have been of the world she knew; two were certainly not.

On Sharina's far left, a plain stretched to the horizon under a black sky. A jumble of long crystals covered the surface like straw on the threshing floor.

There was no movement anywhere in the scene. The stars remained static in their unfamiliar patterns, and their reflections along crystals lay in lines as rigid as those of door lintels. The sky was airless so that not even the light trembled.

The next opening looked down on a town of some size. Not very long ago Sharina would have thought it a metropolis as huge as Carcosa or Ragos on ancient Cordin—places Sharina had read about in the epics, but which she'd imagined in the form of Barca's Hamlet writ large because her home was the only community she then knew.

A single figure hunched his way along the moonlit streets: Cerix, rolling his wheeled cart over the gravel with thrusts of the short poles he used when outside. A dog roused by the clatter of tires lunged to the length of its chain from a doorway, barking silently and pawing the air.

The same chill that kept Sharina motionless seemed to lie on her heart as well. She could see, but she didn't care about the events taking place beyond the ruby curtain.

The third slit showed figures carrying dirt from a pit and up the slope of a mound. It had taken Sharina hours with nothing to do but look at the scenes in front of her before she realized that this vision was not of an anthill roiled by disaster. Rather, humans were laboring under the control of demons with claws like hands full of knives.

Then, because she had visited Erdin on Sandrakkan, she recognized the ruined buildings on the far horizon. When Sharina last saw them they had been the residences of wealthy nobles fronting Palace Square. The image was an hallucination, not reality; an hallucination, or perhaps a prophecy.

Through the fourth window Sharina saw Cashel lying on boards from which he'd thrown all the bedclothes. At home in Barca's Hamlet Cashel slept on the ground or the stone floor of the rooms he shared with his sister in the ancient millhouse. The softness of feathers and fine-spun fabric was foreign to him, and the night must be warm besides.

At the foot of the bed, curled in a nest of the cast-off blankets, was an ape—perhaps the one Sharina had played chess with in Pandah. Sharina remembered him, just as she remembered the emotions she had felt toward Cashel after he fought a demon to save her; but she felt nothing at all in her present state.

A web of bright lines quivered about Cashel, though he was unaware of them. A tattooed woman with bones through her ears chanted and danced where the lines conjoined, at a point outside Cashel's chamber by the laws of normal space and relationships.

The naked wizard spun, shaking her bone rattle, and the net of red light tightened over the sleeping youth.

Cashel tossed fitfully but neither he nor the ape at his feet awakened.

The fifth opening showed a building of black stone which Sharina recognized, though she had never seen it in waking life. She viewed not only the exterior but also saw through the thick basalt walls. A pair of humans prowled in the vaults many levels below the ground.

The thing that watched in the darkness was not in the same plane of the cosmos as the human intruders. It interpenetrated the stones of. waking reality. Its heads bobbed and its tongues tasted the edge of the insubstantial wall separating it from Tenoctris and Garric.

The old woman sat cross-legged, scribed a circle on the stone, and whispered an incantation. The watcher tensed. Its mouths opened and its claws slipped in and out of their sheaths. Barriers thinned, but never quite did they fail completely; and Garric, squatting beside the wizard in the vaults of the queen's mansion in Valles, rested his hand on his sword pommel by habit rather than concern.

Tenoctris rose. Garric replaced the stub of his candle with a fresh one and followed, holding the lantern for her. The watcher slavered; and Sharina shifted her attention to the remaining window, as unmoved as a statue of ice.

The view through the final opening had remained the same from the time Sharina had found herself frozen in this rock chamber. It was a room containing only a waist-high stand on which rested a game board. She couldn't tell for sure how many stone pieces stood on the vast expanse. They were of unfamiliar shapes, no two of them the same; but each time Sharina's attention returned to the motionless tableau, the arrangement seemed different. The question didn't concern her, because now nothing caused her concern.

Sharina looked again at Cashel, whom the tattooed wizard was binding even closer in meshes of light. Motion touched her peripheral vision. Sharina's mind—for not even the pupils of her eyes could move—focused on the sixth opening in the rock.

A woman with features as cold and perfect as the glint of a hawk's eye had entered the chamber. She wore a long-sleeved white gown, gauzy but as opaque as the granite walls of the room in which she stood. A girdle of golden silk cinched her waist, and the hem and throat of her garment were of gold lace.

She looked at Sharina and smiled. "Do you know who I am, Sharina os-Reise?" she asked. Her voice was a liquid contralto that made the very cosmos quiver to its sound.

"You are the queen," Sharina said, but she knew her lips did not, could not, move.

"Yes, Sharina," the queen said. "And soon you will take me to the Throne of Malkar."

She touched one of the tourmaline game pieces. Sharina felt ice tremble through every cell of her being.

The queen laughed and lifted her finger. "But not quite yet, Sharina," she said. "I have other business first."

The perfect female form shriveled away like frost in the bright winter sunlight. For a moment an armature of something else, a thing only vaguely human, stood in her place; then that too was gone.

But the game board remained; and the queen's laughter hung in Sharina's mind, echoing down the chill corridors of memory, eternal and inescapable.

There were no rats here; no insects even. That surprised Garric.

"Tenoctris?" he asked, raising the lantern so that her shadow and his didn't cover any of the expanse the old wizard was viewing. Pillars supported square-sided vaults. So far as Garric could tell, each one was identical to every other vault on this level and on the two basement levels above it. "Are we looking for anything in particular, or . . . ?"

He didn't mind being in the cellars of the queen's mansion; in fact, it was the closest thing he'd had to relaxation since he and his friends had arrived in Valles. He could have sent an escort of soldiers with Tenoctris when she said she needed to search the building's lower levels. A prince, a king in all but name, had more important things to do than prowl through dust and darkness while creatures skittered out of sight.

But Garric had gotten used to being the physical arm on which Tenoctris' unbreakable spirit depended. It made him feel needed in a way that talk could never do. He understood the need for planning, and he accepted that "Prince Garric" was a symbol of the new government to members of the priesthoods, of the Valles guilds, and of the nobility who might be inclined to go their own way at a time of crisis if they thought they'd been relegated to an underling.

But standing with a sword on his hip, supporting and protecting a frail old woman on whose wisdom rested the fate of the Isles—that was real.

King Carus chuckled at the back of Garric's mind. *"You're not the first to feel that way, lad,"* he said, whispering down the corridors of time. *"And so long as you keep it under better control than I did, there's no harm done. Neither I nor the Isles would have much use for you if you thought talk was the thing that mattered most."*

Garric smiled. Besides, there were threats that might paralyze even a battle-tested veteran. Garric had faced wizardry in the past, and faced it down or cut it down.

Tenoctris settled herself on the floor of basalt hexagons. The pavers had been cut from naturally six-sided columns rather than shaped by the hand of man. "I'm looking for passages, Garric," she said. "And I'm determining where they lead."

She looked up with the grin that never failed to brighten the world about her. "I don't mean secret passages in the walls. I mean my kind of passages, routes through planes other than the one on which we're standing. The queen fixed her mansion in a node with several such connections and I think built more. She's very powerful."

Tenoctris scratched a circle on the floor with one of the bundles of bamboo slivers Garric carried for the purpose. "I suppose I could use the same one for each incantation," she muttered apologetically. "It's such a slight thing I'm doing, after all. But even a twig gathers some degree of power with each incantation, and in this place particularly I'm afraid of doing more than I intend."

"I don't mind the load," Garric said mildly. Each sliver was the length of a man's hand. All together the bamboo weighed about as much as the buckle of Garric's sword belt, a massive construction of iron ornamented with tin and niello. "And I *surely* don't mind the fact that you don't take chances you can avoid."

Tenoctris marked a few words of power around the margin of the circle. He heard her murmur, "*Asstraelos chraelos phormo . . . ,*" but the rest of her chant was as lost to him as it was empty of meaning.

Faint blue glimmers formed and fled in the air around the two of them. They never lasted as long as the sparks struck off by a blacksmith's hammer, and some were so brief that Garric wasn't sure whether it was his eye or his mind that witnessed them.

Garric looked about him as he waited, though he didn't expect there to be anything visible to his eyes. According to Royhas, human laborers had built the queen's mansion; and perhaps that was true for the portions above the ground. These cellars were far too extensive to have been built by men in a few months. The volume of earth and rock excavated would have been sufficient to fill the harbor if it had been dumped there. Instead, it had simply vanished, and the very existence of the lower levels had remained unguessed until Garric led the assault that drove the queen away.

Tenoctris sighed and laid down the sliver she'd been using. She put her hands flat on the floor to help push herself to her feet. Garric quickly reached out to support her, keeping the lantern at arm's length so that the hot metal frame didn't burn either one of them.

"No luck?" he asked. He lifted slightly, but for the most part he simply provided a firm post on which the old woman could pull herself erect.

"Oh, no, my problem's the other way around," Tenoctris said. "From what I've found thus far, the queen had at least a dozen routes to other locations in this plane and elsewhere in the cosmos. Simply tracing which entrance went where is . . ."

She grinned again. She always looked a generation younger when she smiled. "I was about to say that it was impossible, but I'm going to have to do it if we're to be safe. If the Isles are to be safe."

Tenoctris nodded Garric toward the next archway. He walked alongside her, still providing support if she needed it. He wondered how many more examinations she intended to make in this cellar, and whether there was yet another level beneath them.

Their shadows trembled in a score of fanciful patterns on the stone. The pillars' contours distorted the human silhouettes. Garric was almost sure that was all he was seeing.

"Tenoctris?" he said as they passed beneath the round-topped arch into a nearly identical vault. Seepage glistened along the junction of two hexagons in the center of the floor. "The queen meant to travel through the passages you're finding, didn't she?"

"Yes," Tenoctris said crisply. She looked around her, analyzing aspects of a reality Garric couldn't see. She nodded him forward again instead of seating herself here. "That was certainly why she constructed her mansion at this location."

"But that isn't what happened," Garric said. "She flew away when we broke in. She didn't, well, go through a passage. Didn't she have time to chant the right words? Or . . . ?"

Tenoctris paused directly beneath the next arch and settled onto the cold basalt. "I should have brought a pad," she murmured, "or at least a thicker robe."

She turned her face toward Garric again. "I don't think the queen's concern was time," she said. "Opening a passage is quite a simple matter, even for a person with no more power than I have."

She smiled; Garric tried to smile back. He failed because of the tension.

"I think the problem," Tenoctris continued, "is that one of the passages leads by a short route to another . . . being. A being that even the queen was unwilling to face, and which she feared was strong enough to break through to her if she opened the passage from her side."

"You mean the Beast," Garric said.

Tenoctris began drawing another circle of power. The bamboo left a silvery tracing on the coarse black stone. Only the person who drew the symbols could recognize them with any certainty; that person, and the forces which the symbols commanded.

"Yes, the Beast," Tenoctris said as she drew. "I would guess that the queen was waiting to gain some additional article of power before she attempted to return the Beast to a place that would hold it. She's a great wizard, but she wasn't sure she was powerful enough to defeat that creature alone."

"But we have to defeat her *and* the Beast," Garric said. His index finger touched the pommel of his long sword.

Tenoctris smiled at him again. "Well," she said, "we have to try."

The 3rd of Partridge

Ilna made her bed on the shop level of Ascelei's dwelling in a cupboard with a slatted door. It had previously been used for extra storage, but the tags of cut rolls removed to make room for her should have been used long since for garment edgings or to stuff pillows.

She recognized the clatter of iron tires on the stone doorstoop. Rising immediately, she donned a daytime tunic over her sleeping garment of fine linen. She'd have gotten up soon anyway; and the anger Ilna felt now was primarily because she knew she'd driven Halphemos to do something stupid.

Ascelei's doorkeeper was supposed to sleep between the inner and outer doors, but he and the cook—a widow—had paired off. He spent most nights in her hut attached to the oven behind the main house. That left Ilna as the real doorkeeper, and Ascelei would never have a better one.

Cerix hammered on the front door. "Open up!" he shouted. "I have to speak to Mistress Ilna!"

The inner panel was of larchwood planed smooth and decorated with rosettes of copper nails. Ilna jerked it open and stepped into the narrow alcove that separated it from the outer door of iron-bound oak. Servants were already chattering in alarm. She heard one of them wonder in a loud voice, "Should someone rouse Master Ascelei?"

Their racket would raise the dead. "Be silent!" Ilna said toward the upper hallway. "I'm taking care of this."

It was her fault, after all. She'd treated Halphemos like a child, and quite naturally he'd acted childishly as a result. You can weave humans into a pattern as surely as you can wool; but you can't use the same technique, for humans balk at direction in a fashion that threads do not.

Cerix fell silent when he heard Ilna's voice within. When she threw out the latch cord he rolled his little cart aside so that the outer panel didn't hit him when she pushed it open.

Cerix looked at Ilna. His fear was so intense that it overcast the scowl of physical pain that usually dominated his features. "The baron's men came for him, mistress," he said. "He'd made an amulet for Lady Tamana to use on Robilard."

Cerix rubbed his mouth with the back of his hand, then went on, "Tamana used to be the baron's favorite, but he's got another friend now."

Someone tried to open the door Ilna had closed behind her. She slammed it back with her heel. "I'm handling this, if you please!" she said.

Cerix had thrown a rough wool blanket as a wrap over the tunic he'd slept in. In the confusion of Halphemos' arrest, the cripple had managed to make off with part of the inn's bedding. Well, his host probably considered that a cheap price for getting rid of an associate of the criminal.

"Halphemos made an amulet to harm the baron?" Ilna asked without inflection. If that was the case, then Robilard could pull the boy's guts out and drag him through the streets before Ilna would stir a finger to help her former companion.

"He wouldn't do that, mistress," Cerix said chidingly. "Alos may be a fool, but you know he wouldn't harm anyone."

He rubbed his mouth again and mumbled, "He might have made a love charm, though. He watched me do that in former days."

Cerix's chin bobbed in a quick gesture to his stumps.

"And the Lady Tamana would have offered a great deal for a path back into the baron's affections."

If it weren't for love, there would be far fewer fools in the world, Ilna thought. *As I well know.*

Aloud she said, "I see. Halphemos sold the pearl pendant to a jeweler. He recognized it, as who on Third Atara would not? The jeweler told the baron a vagabond had a pearl belonging to the baron's former mistress; and the baron asked the lady about the matter in a fashion that brought the truth from her."

"I saw Tamana when she first came to Halphemos," Cerix admitted sadly. "I wasn't worried. I thought she just wanted her fortune told or, well, he's a good-looking boy. It's not my place to object to him having a good time.''

Ilna sniffed. ''No doubt,'' she said. Her tone would have suited a response to someone who'd admitted that he liked to rob blind beggars. ''Will the Lady Tamana have told the truth, or will she say that the idea came from Halphemos?''

''That one might have said anything,'' Cerix said with a grimace. ''I don't imagine Robilard even had to slap her before she started blubbering whatever first came into her head.''

''Yes, there are women like that,'' Ilna said without emphasis. ''Well, I'll see what I can do.''

She pulled the latch cord, but someone pushed the door open from the inside before she started to tug on the ornate iron handle. Ilna's tongue was ready to snap a comment until she saw Ascelei silhouetted against the rushlights the servants behind him held.

''Master Ascelei,'' she said with a contrite nod. She'd been about to snarl at her host. ''I apologize for this disruption. I have to go out and I don't know when I'll be able to return.''

''I heard,'' the mercer said gravely. ''Ilna, I have a cousin with an inn on the west of the island, a quarrying village. If you'd care to stay there for a few days until you know more about the situation, that would be all right. No one would have to know your real name.''

''Hide, you mean?'' Ilna said. ''It hasn't come to that, thank you, nor will it while I'm still alive.''

Ascelei stiffened. Ilna heard her angry words play back in her memory. She knelt on the threshold, took the mercer's right hand in hers, and said, ''Master Ascelei, your offer was meant as a kindness and I behaved as my uncle Katchin might have done. I apologize.''

She rose to her feet again and added, ''If you knew my uncle, you'd understand how sincere that apology was.''

The mercer gave a nod of satisfaction. ''I never doubted your sincerity, Ilna,'' he said. ''And while I don't apologize for making the offer, I should have known better than to imagine you might accept it.''

Ilna glanced down at the cripple. ''Ascelei,'' she said, ''could you shelter Master Cerix while I'm gone? This is none of his doing, but I doubt he'll be welcome at his lodgings.''

''I should go with you,'' Cerix said in surprise. ''I can help—''

''No,'' she said sharply, ''you can't. I'll have enough to worry about without you to push around also.''

Ascelei winced. ''Yes, of course,'' he said. ''Cerix, if you'd care to come in . . . ?''

The cripple looked stricken. Ilna wasn't going to apologize for her comment, though. Cerix *would* have been in the way, and if the older wizard hadn't shown the boy how to make love charms then none of this would have happened. Love charms were abominations.

Ilna smiled. Ascelei had stepped out as Cerix poled himself into the dwelling without further comment. ''Mistress?'' the mercer said, surprised at Ilna's expression.

''I'm tempted to say that love itself is an abomination,'' Ilna replied; an honest answer if not a particularly informative one. ''But this isn't the time to talk philosophy—if there ever was one.''

She took a deep breath. ''I'll be off to the palace, sir,'' she said. ''I appreciate your actions on my behalf and wish I were able to better repay them.''

''There's money owing you,'' the mercer said as she turned. ''And would you care to use my litter? It won't take a moment to rouse the bearers.''

''An honest woman like me would look a complete fool riding in a litter,'' Ilna said, more tartly than she'd intended. ''You can give any money I'm owed to Cerix. Or keep it yourself, Ascelei.''

She reached into her sleeve to check that the hank of yarn was there. ''I have everything I need,'' she called over her shoulder as she strode along the Parade.

Servants were up in most of the houses, sweeping and

emptying slops. The majority of buildings had a residence above and shop below; from these, night soil was carried out to the central gutter. Folk who didn't expect customers to be entering their front doors were less fussy about what their servants dumped where.

Ilna's nose wrinkled in disgust—at the practice, not the smell. In a decent community like Barca's Hamlet where folk kept house gardens, manure wasn't wasted.

She walked briskly. There were other pedestrians out already. The sky had grown pale enough to tell black from white, so folk who didn't care to pay for lantern light were on the road.

Baron Robilard's palace was half a mile south on the Parade; no distance at all to walk, though Ilna found the gravel unpleasant. Folk in Divers wore slippers with soft leather soles, adequate for this coarse crushed limestone.

It amused Ilna that she and Ascelei had been talking as though Ilna wasn't coming back from her meeting with the baron. Anything was possible, but Robilard didn't have a reputation for wanton cruelty. The baron had every right to be furious with Halphemos, but in her heart of hearts Ilna was sure that she'd find some way to buy the boy free. They'd have to leave the island, of course, but they'd been planning to do that anyway.

The palace of the Barons of Third Atara was a more modest structure than Ilna had expected. Oh, it was more building than the ego of any one man should have needed, but she herself had lived in a larger mansion in Erdin during the days when evil had no more skillful craftsman than Ilna os-Kenset.

A porch with huge columns of striped marble was under construction. If Robilard ever got around to rebuilding the rest in scale with his new porch, he'd have a residence larger than that of the Earl of Sandrakkan.

She turned down the semicircular drive to the porch. Here pavers of patterned limestone replaced the gravel. Grit clinging to Ilna's soles crunched against the slick, chill surface.

She grinned. Not as slick *or* as chill as the mud of early spring at home in Barca's Hamlet, though. Things weren't necessarily better simply because they were familiar.

There was light and bustle within the palace. The glass in the small-paned windows wasn't clear enough to show details, but figures moved by lamplight with more agitation than Ilna imagined was the usual thing at this hour of the morning.

Beneath a lantern fashioned in the form of a three-headed dragon, two soldiers guarded the door. The lamp's appearance made Ilna's guts tighten for no reason she could fathom; she scowled at herself.

The soldiers watched Ilna long enough to be sure that they didn't recognize her. One of them then knocked on the wicket set into one of the huge, bronze-plated door leaves. An officer came out, settling his plumed helmet on his head as he and the men murmured among themselves.

Ilna drew the hank from her sleeve, measured a sufficient length of yarn, and snapped it between her index fingers. That left the ends frayed, but this was no time to flash a knife even for the purpose of cutting thread.

The officer's breastplate was molded into the form of a demigod's muscled torso; the dawn light gleamed on it and on the tips of his waxed mustaches. He stepped forward and said, "Sorry, mistress. There's no peddlers being admitted today."

"I'm not a peddler," Ilna said as she walked to within arm's length of the man. "I'm here to talk to the baron about the wizard he's arrested. I think that after he talks to me he'll be willing to release the boy."

"*Especially* nobody sees the baron about the wizard, mistress," the officer said in a noticeably colder tone. "And if you've got anything to do with him, then I suggest you use what time you've got to leave the island. Swim if you don't find a better way."

"If she wants to come back after midday when we're

off duty,'' one of the soldiers said, ''I might find the price for what she's got.''

The other soldier and the officer laughed. Ilna's expression didn't change as she worked the yarn among her fingers.

She raised her eyes. ''Look at me,'' she said crisply.

''What?'' said the officer, turning toward Ilna again. She spread her hands, drawing the yarn into the pattern she'd chosen. The officer gave a smothered ''Urk!'' and went stiff.

''Take me to Baron Robilard,'' Ilna ordered. The officer bowed, turned, and marched toward the wicket. He'd left it open when he came out.

''Hey!'' said the soldier who'd joked about enjoying Ilna's favors. ''What's happened to the captain?''

The soldier snatched at the halberd he'd leaned against the marble doorframe. He fumbled the weapon, which fell with a ringing crash on the lintel. He knelt to pick it up.

''Nothing that will harm him,'' Ilna said. ''If you act the fool by getting in my way, I'll deal with you in a different way. Do you understand?''

The soldier stared up at Ilna as his fingers felt for the halberd shaft. The other guard gripped him by the shoulder and pulled him out of the way. Neither man spoke as Ilna followed their officer into the palace.

The anteroom was empty except for the chair where the officer had sat with his back to the door, watching events in the audience hall. The latter was a room of some pretensions, rising the full height of the building to a vaulted ceiling. The pillars along both sidewalls were decorated with bands of low reliefs portraying scenes from the island's history.

Ilna assumed it was history, in any event—there were no obvious deities among the figures. The carvings were very ably executed, a fact that made her feel better-disposed toward Robilard. She knew it was foolish to assume that decency was connected with appreciation of craftsmanship—but emotionally she *did* assume that.

Dawn streamed between the support pillars on the east side of the hall, but oil-fed sconces flared on the walls as well. Servants were still lighting the last of these. The scores of people present didn't fill the large room, but their shuffling and whispers echoed like cicadas on a summer night.

Baron Robilard sat on a throne of patterned marble. It looked uncomfortable but old, and Ilna could appreciate the value of tradition. This morning Robilard had dressed in a doublet and trousers of velvet, well-cut and worn with a flair. Even though the emotion that animated him was anger, the baron looked far more attractive than he had as a supercilious statue in the procession of the day before.

In his left palm Robilard bounced a small wash-leather sack; he glared at the dark-haired woman who knelt between two soldiers before the dais on which the throne stood. Tamana, past a doubt. She was blubbering, and her broken sentences were scarcely intelligible anyway.

To the left of the baron's throne sat his wife, Cotolina. During the procession she'd ridden directly behind Rodilard's chariot in a chair with an azure awning. Her hair was pale blond, and her perfect features remained composed as she pretended to watch the twins under the care of a nurse beside her.

Lady Regowara, a buxom brunette in the same mold as Tamana but younger by five years, stood with her left hand on the throne's armrest in a gesture of ownership. She watched Tamana with an expression of greedy delight. That showed Ilna that the baron's current mistress was as great a fool as the former one had proved herself. A woman with any sense would have seen her own future in Tamana's present. Few women had any sense—and fewer men, so far as Ilna could judge, at least as far as their taste in women went.

The folk in the hall were soldiers, servants, and courtiers, in equal proportions. They watched with nervous anticipation. The soldiers flanking Tamana had the grace to look embarrassed. The poor woman seemed barely capable of standing, much less posing a threat that required her to be guarded.

The soldiers who held Halphemos were much more serious about their job. The boy's arms were tied behind his back, and he'd been knocked about enough to blacken one eye and cut the cheek below the other.

The guard captain pushed a path through the spectators, though the crowd wasn't so dense that Ilna couldn't have made her own way to the front. The slight commotion caused Halphemos to glance around. "Ilna!" he cried. "You shouldn't have come here!"

One of the guards hit the boy in the pit of the stomach. Halphemos doubled up, gasping, and would have fallen except for the soldiers gripping his arms.

Ilna looked at the man who'd struck Halphemos. The soldier opened his mouth to snarl at her, then got a good look into her eyes. He turned his head abruptly.

"Snuggles," Tamana whimpered toward the floor on which her tears were dripping, "it wasn't to harm you, it was just a little something so you'd love me the way you used to. And I wouldn't have taken it, only he bewitched me to get my pearl pendant. You know I'd never have parted with any of the jewels *you* gave me except for a wizard's spell!"

"Lift the wizard's face up," Robilard ordered in a voice of cold anger. A guard seized a handful of Halphemos' hair, but the boy had already managed to straighten despite the blow to his stomach. He met the baron's angry glare with a quiet pride that did something to redeem him in Ilna's opinion.

Robilard dropped the amulet onto the dais and stood to grind it under his heel. Objects within the wash leather crunched. "You polluted my court with your wizardry," the baron said. "I'll put you where the fish will end your pollution forever."

He gestured to one of the front rank of courtiers, an older man and the only noble wearing a breastplate as well as a sword. "Lock him in an iron cage, Hosten, and dump him into the sea. Well beyond the harbor mouth."

The courtier bowed in agreement. The cicada-rustling of whispers rose to nearly a roar.

Ilna stepped forward and said, raising her voice to be heard, "Baron Robilard, I understand and share your anger, but we both know that Master Halphemos is guilty of nothing more than being a fool. If you'll release him to me, I will see to it that he works no more wizardry here—and I'll provide you with something of value in return. Certainly greater value than fish food."

"Who is this?" Baron Robilard cried into the sudden tumult. "What's she doing here?"

"She is Ilna os-Kenset," said the guard captain in a toneless voice. "She has come to see you."

Ilna smiled faintly. The captain staggered as he completed her injunction, then looked around him in growing incomprehension. He had a horrified expression, as though he'd found himself in court wearing nothing but a ribbon on his private parts.

"In a week," Ilna said across the shocked babble, "I can weave you a panel that will force everyone who comes before you to speak the truth."

And so she could, though the reason she didn't think such a pattern was a work of evil was her certainty that Robilard would destroy it after a few days. The only folk who thought they wanted to know the truth were those who had no experience of it—and those few, like Ilna os-Kenset, who were willing to live with the consequences.

"Or another pattern that will benefit you and those around you," Ilna added. "I realize that Halphemos misused his power, but you might take that as a warning not to make the same mistake yourself."

Offering a pattern that compelled truth was a compromise between what Ilna thought Robilard would want and what he *should* want. She would much rather provide the baron with a panel like those she'd been spreading about Erdin before Cashel's disappearance called her away. The value of cheer and feelings of well-being wasn't as immediately obvious to most people as sex, wealth, and revenge. Those last were things Ilna wouldn't provide.

Wouldn't provide any longer.

"You're a wizard," Robilard said. His voice rose with each syllable.

"I'm a weaver," Ilna said. "I'm a decent woman of Barca's Hamlet on Haft, and I will do what I say."

The buzz in the hall had silenced, though folk shuffling to get a glimpse of the newcomer raised rasping echoes of leather on stone. The guard captain had skulked around the edge of the hall to vanish outside again. Other soldiers looked confused; those who held polearms shifted them from one side to the other as they waited for orders.

"Another wizard," Robilard said, his voice returning to normal. Cotolina looked at Ilna with cool appraisal; Lady Regowara had moved behind the throne and was fingering an amulet of her own. "You must be mad to have come here. Well, the same cure will do for both, I suppose. Hosten—"

"No!" Halphemos shouted. "She has no part in this!"

Halphemos tried to pull away from his handlers. They had a struggle to hold him but they didn't, Ilna noted, begin hitting the bound prisoner again.

"Halphemos, be quiet," Ilna said. "I'm taking care of things now. You've caused enough trouble already."

"She's completely innocent!" Halphemos shouted at the baron. "If you harm her, I'll—"

The Gods only knew what the boy thought he *could* do. Make empty threats, she supposed, and make the situation still worse.

She stepped in front of Halphemos and jerked the pattern of yarn taut. "Stand silent till I release you!" she commanded.

Ilna was furious, with herself and with the injustice of the universe. The boy had good instincts—and all the trouble he caused stemmed from those good instincts. It wasn't fair that someone like Halphemos should do so much harm!

The soldiers had flinched back when Ilna spoke. When she faced Robilard again, he spread a hand before his eyes. Ilna sneered and flung the length of yarn onto the dais.

"Baron," she said, "I come to you for justice, not mercy. Release Halphemos to my custody and I will pay any reasonable price."

It crossed Ilna's mind that she and Robilard might mean different things by "reasonable." Well, he'd learn her definition quickly enough if they varied excessively.

Robilard lowered his hands. He was trembling with fury—because he'd been afraid, and because this girl wizard had seen his fear.

"All right, weaver!" he said. "This is what you can trade me for the freedom of your friend, here. Tonight I'll celebrate the anniversary of my rule as Baron of Third Atara. Go to my ancestor, the Elder Romi, and ask him to grace my dinner. If he comes, I'll release—"

Robilard gestured toward Halphemos, struck mute and motionless between his guards.

"—that one, who thought to aim his wizardry at me. Otherwise, you'll join your friend if you haven't managed to get out of my kingdom by that time."

"All right," Ilna said. She was furious: at Robilard, at Halphemos, and not least at herself for what she'd committed to do. She didn't fear death, but she knew that doing what the baron demanded would bring her very close to the boundaries of evil and darkness which she'd sworn to avoid. "I'll need a guide."

Hosten, the soldier, looked up at his baron with a worried expression. "Milord," he said, "were you serious about . . . ?"

Robilard glared at the noble imperiously. "Make it so, Lord Hosten!" he said. "Unless you're afraid?"

Ilna smiled faintly to hear the youthful bravado. It settled her own fear. She might be doing the wrong thing, but she'd said she would do it. Therefore the discussion was over.

Hosten's lips tightened. He turned to the nearest guards and said, "You four, come with me," in a colorless voice. He walked over to Ilna, bowed, and said, "Mistress Ilna os-Kenset? We'll escort you to the Tomb of the Elder Romi."

"Yes," Ilna said. Ignoring the rest of the gaping, whispering crowd, she touched Halphemos' forehead and said, "You can awaken now, Alos. Don't cause any more trouble. I'll be back."

She took two steps toward the door before she paused and turned. "On my honor," Ilna said to Halphemos and the rest of the gathering, "I *will* be back."

Cashel stepped onto the walkway behind the palace. Back in the room Zahag grunted and complained about the hour. In a world where servants provided food, the ape saw no reason to get up before noon.

Cashel wasn't forcing Zahag to rise. The ape wasn't quite sure of his safety on Pandah except when Cashel or Aria was there to protect him, though. He might be right, but Cashel wasn't about to change his own schedule because an ape was lazy.

Silya sat cross-legged on the railing, bowered among the grapevines. Because she was in public she had clothing on, a light cotton tunic instead of the richly decorated robe that she'd worn when Cashel fell back into King Folquin's court.

He stopped. "I said I didn't want to see you," he warned.

Silya spread her empty hands in a gesture of unconcern. "I understand, Master Cashel," she said. "Still, you're going to be dealing with my brother, whom I have no reason to love. I can give you some advice on that. It won't delay you since the ship won't be ready till the middle of the afternoon. But of course if you're afraid . . . ?''

She gestured again. Whatever the wizard's age, she was remarkably agile to be able to balance on the narrow railing while shifting her weight as she spoke.

Cashel grinned, imagining Silya as a wren. They were pushy, quarrelsome birds apt to use their strong beaks on the eggs of their neighbors. . . .

But Cashel wasn't an egg, and he wasn't afraid of Silya or anybody else on earth. ''What do you want to show me?'' he asked, holding his quarterstaff out to the side so that he wouldn't seem to be sheltering behind it.

''Come down into my quarters,'' Silya said. ''Don't worry. You proved you could leave easily enough, and I've only hung some matting for privacy instead of replacing the wall.''

''I wasn't worried,'' Cashel growled.

He lifted himself over the railing, feeling as awkward as a hedgehog in comparison to the wizard's birdlike motions. Still, hedgehogs got where they were going, and so would he.

The palace cooks were already at work on the tables behind the main building. Stewards were chaffering with peddlers, mostly women, carrying fruits, vegetables, and some fish in baskets.

Cashel hadn't seen meat being eaten on Pandah. Here at the palace, at least, it couldn't have been a matter of cost alone.

He followed Silya into the basement. She hadn't brought a lantern, but light came from the rooms she'd closed off in the far corner. That was illumination enough to show Cashel where the pillars were. Sometimes his foot splashed in an unseen puddle, but he wouldn't have gone out of his way to avoid so minor an inconvenience in broad daylight. Mud and worse were so much a part of rural life that Cashel didn't really notice them.

''Hey!'' he heard Zahag call from somewhere. ''Wait for me!''

Silya had rearranged objects in the chamber where she'd kept Cashel; where perhaps she'd helped him recover. He didn't much care for the wizard, but he knew that when he fell back into Folquin's court he was about as wrung out as he ever remembered being.

Now the slab on which Cashel had lain supported a large tray covered with colored sand. Triple lamps of simple, unobjectionable design hung from all four of the pillars framing the chamber. As Silya had said, she'd provided a grass mat to replace the timber wall Cashel had wrecked. When Cashel entered behind her, she drew the mat across the opening.

"Or I can leave it open if you're . . . ?" she said.

"No," Cashel replied curtly. He knew Silya kept hinting that he was afraid so that he wouldn't back out the way he *knew* he ought to do; but her trick worked anyway.

"Very well," Silya said. She shrugged out of her tunic, then took the bone rattle from the equipment rack. "I'll call out the incantation that I've written here."

She gestured with her empty left hand toward symbols drawn in white sand against the tawny background. Cashel couldn't read anything beyond his own name and that with difficulty. Garric talked of the differences between Old Script and modern squared characters, but they were both hen tracks so far as Cashel was concerned.

"Occasionally I'll stop and ask you a question about what you see. You'll answer the question in your own words, and then I'll go on."

"Why should you do that?" Cashel said. The many burning lamp wicks filled the air of this enclosure with a thick warmth he found disquieting. "And why should I?"

"This will protect you against my brother's wizardry," Silya said. "He'll try to bind you to do his will."

Cashel grimaced. Silya said, "You can leave any time you want to. You may not need my help. *I* can't be sure of the future, though. I don't see how you know what you'll need when you reach Valles either."

''Go ahead,'' Cashel muttered. ''I'll watch for a while.''

Silya bobbed the rattle down. Dried peas rustled in the brainbox. *''Barouch ino anoch,''* she said. At each syllable her rattle indicated another of the sand-written symbols. *''Uoea eanthoukoia . . .''*

The room grew warmer. The heat shouldn't have been enough to bother a youth who'd plowed in the summer when the furrows quivered, but Cashel found himself getting a little dizzy. It was probably because he'd been so tired from, well, the way he'd come back to Pandah from wherever it was that he'd been before.

''Arthaemmiem,'' Silya said. She walked slowly around the long table, never looking at Cashel. *''Thar barouch maritha.''*

The sand in the center of the tray humped as though a hidden breeze had caught it and swirled it upward. There was a face in the moving specks. As the wizard continued to chant, the features of the sand image sharpened and became as clear as those of a real person standing before Cashel. ''Garric!'' he said in amazement.

''Cashel or-Kenset,'' Silya said in a voice taut with strain. ''Is the figure before you your friend?''

''Yes,'' said Cashel. ''Where's he now?''

The whirling sand collapsed into a mound, then smoothed like water poured into a pan. The wizard resumed her walking and chanting. *''Uoea eanthoukoia, arthaemmiem. . . .''*

Cashel felt very warm now, though his body wasn't sweating. He rubbed his thumb against the dry wood of his staff, reminding himself of its reality and of his past life in Barca's Hamlet.

The sand rose again, this time in the image of Tenoctris. The glint of lamps on tiny whirling crystals was exactly like the twinkle in the old wizard's eyes when she looked at Cashel.

''Cashel or-Kenset,'' said Silya. ''Do you entrust yourself to the craft of the figure before you?''

"Yes," said Cashel. He was feeling dazed, but he knew what he was saying. "I trust her. I wish she was with me now."

The sand blurred. The table's surface was now in constant motion. The writing itself shifted without losing definition. The white symbols spun about the margin of the table. Silya continued to chant, her rattle striking down at signs that rotated past her instead of her walking to reach the signs.

"*Thar barouch maritha . . .*" the wizard said.

Lamp flames guttered as the mat behind Cashel moved. He didn't look around. He heard Silya's incantation, but the words no longer came from her lips. The dog-skull rattle twitched up and down in seeming silence.

An image was forming on the sand table. Blond hair, flowing the way honey rolls from a comb; laughing blue eyes, a high forehead, and the mouth from which came the sweetest voice in all the world.

Cashel started to whisper Sharina's name.

"Cashel or-Kenset," Silya said. "Do you pledge your life to the figure before—"

Zahag hopped chattering onto the table. The tray was wider than the stone bier it rested on and tipped, spraying sand across the floor.

Silya shrieked and swung her rattle at Zahag. The ape, gibbering back at her, leaped to a lamp hanger on the opposite wall.

A welcome chill washed over Cashel's frame. Everything was in focus again. The tray had fallen with one edge on the floor and the other leaning against the bier. The colored sands were still shifting to reach a natural contour. The edge of the spreading pile covered Cashel's toes.

On top of the bier where the table had hidden it was a painting on silk. The toppling sand tray had rippled the fabric but Cashel could easily make out the remarkably good likeness of the wizard Silya.

"Yield to the figure!" Silya screamed in empty desperation. "Yield to me, Cashel or-Kenset!"

"I warned you!" Cashel shouted. He thrust his quarterstaff like a spear, not at Silya but at the wizard's silken portrait.

The staff's iron ferrule clashed against the hard stone and skidded off, throwing sparks onto the thin cloth. The fabric ignited with an unnatural violence; red flames rose and twisted as they devoured the silk.

Cashel braced himself with his staff before him. This chamber wasn't big enough for the full spinning dance of an expert with the quarterstaff, but solid hickory thrust by solid muscle could crush its way through any foe Cashel expected to meet. His hands tingled from striking the unyielding granite, but he could still grip his weapon.

Zahag shrieked, "There was nothing there! You weren't seeing anything that was really there, chief!"

Silya screamed on a rising note. A black blotch had appeared around her, not in the air but in the cosmos itself. Cashel saw both the wizard and the wall beyond, but he was seeing as though with different pairs of eyes.

Tentacles of red light emerged from the darkness. They fastened about Silya like the arms of an octopus pulling open the shell of a clam. Where the tentacles touched her, Silya's flesh turned black and shriveled.

"Say you yie—" Silya's voice wailed from the infinite distance; then the sound too was gone. The chamber was lighted only by the quivering lamps. The one the ape had swung from still gyrated wildly, splashing oil onto the stone floor.

The fire had completely devoured the silk portrait; not even ash remained on the slab. The mat Zahag had pulled aside to enter dangled askew from the remaining hooks.

"Let's get out of here," Cashel muttered. He could see the gleam of daylight creeping through the forest of pillars. "Maybe the ship will be ready earlier than they said."

"What was it that happened to her, chief?" the ape asked as he hunched through the cellar, keeping very close to Cashel's side. He sounded chastened. "Was it something you did?"

"I don't think so," Cashel said. "I don't know what happened."

He stopped just short of the outer door and took the ape's long hand in his. "Zahag?" he said. "Thanks."

Cashel didn't remember daylight ever feeling better than it did as the two of them left the cellar.

A warmth that was more than physical flooded through Sharina, melting the frozen lethargy in which she'd been held since the smoky hand snatched her from the waking world. She turned. The slit window to her right was sweeping toward her, swelling to become her whole environment.

She stood in a windowless room of white marble. Before her was the board set with pieces of varicolored tourmaline. Even now that Sharina was alert, she couldn't view the full array of counters.

The queen stood across the board from Sharina. Her smile was as perfect and cold as every other aspect of her appearance.

"Good evening, Sharina," the queen said. The voice was as Sharina remembered it from what now seemed the dreamworld in which she'd been held: a rich contralto that covered all feelings the way a velvet drape can cover the door to an execution chamber. "It's time for you to help me now. I'll have no difficulty in recovering my position against physical opponents. . . ."

The walls of the room were marked only by minor imperfections. Faint gray flecks lurked within the whiteness, though the surfaces were polished to such a sheen that the play of light across them varied more than the stone.

The queen gestured minusculely with an index finger. The walls, floor, and ceiling faded to shadows, then became as transparent as a flawless diamond. Sharina gasped. Her feet rested on an unseen hardness fifty feet above the slow swells of an ultramarine sea.

She and her captor looked down on a raft as tangled and formless as the mats of seaweed that drifted slowly around the seas south of the Isles. More of the surface was open water than was timber, but the downed trees spread over an expanse too vast to encompass even from Sharina's high vantage point.

Twists of vine and interlocked branches bound the floating trees together. Some parts of the mass separated from others, only to merge with similar fragments into a larger mat again.

It was like watching water spread across the furrows of a flooded field. Individual rivulets might follow different tracks, but the whole was as surely one as an open-meshed net. All the portions moved on the same currents, at the same slow rate; and with the same certain destination.

The raft swarmed with Hairy Men in numbers that Sharina couldn't begin to count. They crawled over the branches, nursed their infants on the trunks, and shrieked at one another across the open sea in spats as fierce as those of two-year-olds.

The queen remained silent. Sharina refused to call the folk Monkeys even in her mind, though their antics on the raft made the hunters' term more innocent.

The Hairy Men were eating fruits, nuts, and tubers they'd brought with them. In some cases they plucked food still hanging from the branches of trees floating as part of the raft itself, though generally that source had been exhausted by this point in the sluggish voyage.

"What do they drink?" Sharina asked. In her wonder, she almost forgot whom she was talking to.

"They've brought along trees that store water in their trunks," the queen said. "I intended the migration to take place during fall when they could suck rainwater from their fur, but this is satisfactory."

The smile she gave Sharina could have frozen a bonfire. "They'll be thirsty enough to drink blood by the time they reach Valles," she added. "That suits me quite well."

Occasionally a Hairy Man and a gull wheeling above the raft screeched insults at one another. Sharina and the queen remained invisible from the raft even though they themselves could see for miles in every direction.

Sharina imagined the raft and its occupants landing on the shore of Ornifal. She'd seen the savagery with which the Hairy Men attacked and she knew what the results of those attacks would be on the stunned population of Valles. She'd buried the gnawed remains of Hanno's partner, after all.

With that image in her mind, Sharina lunged for the queen's throat. Before the thought had even reached Sharina's muscles, her body stiffened into stony rigidity. She was back in the marble room and the queen, with her usual faint smile, had her index finger on a game piece of carven tourmaline.

"As you see," the queen said in her smoothly pleasant voice, "I've made arrangements to deal with my physical enemies. There's another problem, though. The king's wizard looked for a servant and managed to summon a master. That master will not be easily put down."

She lifted her finger from the piece. Sharina could move again, but she rubbed her arms instead of attempting another vain attack. Her skin twitched and prickled as it had after lightning struck a nearby pine when she played in the woods as a child.

The queen's smile widened like a cat's claw slipping from its sheath. "You're going to help me, Sharina," she said. "You're going to lead me to the Throne of Malkar, which your ancestor concealed in a place only his blood can find."

"I'll die before I help you," Sharina said quietly. Her fingers kneaded her forearm muscles.

For an instant, something happened to the figure facing Sharina over the game board. The queen's perfect features became translucent. Beneath the flesh was another visage, this one snarlingly inhuman.

The image was gone as suddenly as sun flashing from

a gull's white wing. Everything was as it had been before, except for Sharina's doubtful memory of the moment.

"I could make you *beg* me for death, Sharina," the queen said in tones that flowed like honey. "I plan to take another course instead. But you will do as I require, of that you may be sure."

Sharina felt the chill pervade her body. The white room was receding; she stood frozen at the hub of the windowed chamber again, watching with detached interest as scenes evolved in the distance.

The game board remained beyond the sixth window, but the room was otherwise empty. The queen's clawed smile still hung across Sharina's mind, though.

"I've heard people say that the only difference between the regulars and the Blood Eagles," Attaper said disdainfully to Garric as they rode up to the Naval Arsenal and their meeting with Admiral Nitker's envoy, "is that we have better officers."

A hundred soldiers from Harker's Regiment of what had been the Ornifal standing army stood with their commander, Pior bor-Pirial. The adjacent quays, normally used by vessels bringing naval stores which for one reason or another couldn't be accommodated within the vast brick shed of the Arsenal, were empty now. All ships that could sail had done so when the riots started, and Nitker was blockading Valles from his base on the island of Eshkol close offshore.

Attaper spit past the polished toe of his left boot. "That's crap," he added flatly. "But I'll agree, having decent officers might help some."

A grinning figure at the back of Garric's mind murmured, "*Officers* and *training will take you further than just recruiting will, lad. But recruiting on Haft or the northern counties of Ornifal, that'll take you a ways.*"

Garric and the eight Blood Eagles escorting him were mounted, but the horses were just transportation. Like

Garric himself, the royal bodyguards were most comfortable on their own feet. Ornifal's military strength had always been in its heavy infantry. The nobility swanked it on horseback, but when it came to fighting the troops who covered the flanks of an Ornifal army were hirelings, either cavalry or light infantry who could break up a cavalry charge.

The River Beltis was at its greatest width here; the far shore was barely visible through the haze sucked from the water's surface by the late-afternoon sun. The warship hanging a bowshot off the end of the quay was a trireme with nearly two hundred oars in three banks. A few dozen men stroked to keep its bronze ram pointing into the slow current.

A skiff with seven men aboard put off from the trireme's stern. The rope ladder by which they'd descended dangled there; at the railing above, officers in red cloaks watched along with off-duty oarsmen.

"Here they come," Garric murmured. He gripped the saddle pommel and swung his right leg over the cantle, settling thankfully to the ground. Two Blood Eagles held the horses while Garric and the other six strode up the quay to meet the incoming skiff.

Garric noticed to his amusement that his stride, that of the Haft phalanx of the Old Kingdom, put him a finger's breadth farther ahead of his escort at each double pace. Attaper gave a muffled curse, then growled, "Route march, Sister take you!" to his men.

Garric had used Pior, still holding neutral in the Arsenal with his regular troops, to broker this meeting with the admiral's representatives. Pior would like to think of himself as holding the balance—perhaps even being a kingmaker.

He was nothing of the sort. As Attaper said, the troops of the regular regiments were, if not a joke, at least no threat to Garric and his new government. Waldron could crush them or ignore them, pretty much as Garric chose.

The six marines accompanying Nitker's representative

were much more impressive. They wore bronze helmets and cuirasses of stiffened linen that could turn a sword slash or even an arrow sent from a distance. Four of them rowed despite their armor; the other pair held the squad's spears crossways on the thwarts, long boarding pikes rather than javelins designed for throwing.

The Blood Eagles sized up their potential opponents as the skiff reached the end of the quay; and behind Garric's eyes, King Carus did the same. *"I could always use more of that sort, lad,"* the king's voice whispered. *"They'll be planning to snatch you if they think they can get away with it. . . ."*

"They can't," Garric said.

Attaper said, "What was that, sir?"

Garric didn't realize that he'd spoken aloud. "Stand back for a moment," he said instead of answering. He took two strides ahead of his escort and waited, arms akimbo, for Nitker's men to climb the stone steps from the landing stage to the top of the quay.

The envoy was a balding, middle-aged man who looked as though he was more familiar with court robes than the cuirass of iron scales which he wore for this occasion. The fact he was in armor underscored Carus' warning. Attaper realized the same thing and said, "Sir, be careful!"

Garric drew his long sword. The marines instantly formed a close rank, their pikes facing out in a lethal hedge. "What is this?" the envoy cried from behind his men. "This was to be a peaceful parlay!"

Garric tossed his sword spinning into the air. The burnished steel caught the afternoon sun to flash like a deadly jewel. Garric glanced up, judged his moment, and raised his hand. The sword hilt slapped into his palm. Light trembled for a moment as the blade moaned softly back to silence.

Garric shot the sword home into its sheath and grinned at the marines. "Don't even think about it," he said to their officer in a lilting voice. The shadow of an ancient king laughed with gusto in his heart.

The trick was Carus' own, though Garric and Cashel had practiced similar displays with quarterstaves as they chatted and watched their sheep in the borough. A sword was shorter and lighter than a staff, but it spun faster and the edges added an element of danger to the embarrassment of a missed catch.

Garric didn't intend to make a mistake, and the effect of such flashing skill did more than any number of threats to insure that the parlay *would* be peaceful.

Raising his hands to shoulder height, palms out to demonstrate that they were empty, Garric said, "I was told to expect Matoes bor-Malliman. You're Lord Matoes?"

The envoy snarled something in a low voice to his escort; the marines parted so that he could face Garric directly instead of peering over the armored shoulders of his men. "I'm Chancellor Matoes," he said, giving himself the title Garric had withheld. "Duke Nitker sent me to receive your proposals of alliance, ah, Prince Garric."

One of the Blood Eagles muttered in disgust at Nitker's airs. Garric's mouth twitched in a smile. The admiral probably thought he was being moderate not to claim the throne of the Isles.

"Admiral Nitker stepped into what he thought was a vacuum in Valles," Garric said, speaking calmly and crossing his arms before him. "That was the action of a patriot, and neither I nor the king who adopted me could blame the admiral for what he did. But for the sake of the Isles, Matoes, Admiral Nitker has to make it clear immediately that he's a loyal subject of the government of King Valence. Otherwise he can only be considered a traitor."

Royhas had suggested that he or perhaps Waldron should represent the new government, since Nitker was sending an envoy instead of coming in person. For Prince Garric to attend the meeting would confer too much status on the admiral's minions.

Garric wasn't interested in status. He alone of the new government really understood the danger that faced Ornifal and the whole Isles, so he was the one to treat with the envoy.

As for the risk that Matoes and Nitker would think Garric was weak because he'd come to the meeting himself—Garric and the king within him laughed at the thought. Whatever tale the envoy and his bodyguards took back to Eshkol, it would not be that they'd met a foolish young lout just off the farm.

Matoes bumped the man to either side as he stepped through the rank of marines. He wasn't allowing for the bulk of his unfamiliar armor. The marine officer frowned slightly, then spread his men with a hand gesture. He'd have liked to keep his charge behind the line of guards, but he didn't have the authority to order that.

Matoes stopped a pace from Garric and fumbled absently at the side lacings of his cuirass, now unnecessary. The armor had been to protect him if he ordered his men to kidnap Garric; the government would gain nothing by grabbing an underling like the self-styled chancellor.

Matoes was clearly not a stupid man. Instead of posturing with statements about Nitker's lineage and mandate from heaven to rule the Isles, he said, "Eshkol—the Duchy of Eshkol, shall we say?—could quite easily retain its independence, Prince Garric. There's no naval force in the Isles to match the Royal Fleet—"

Garric smiled. The envoy grimaced when he realized he'd used the old term for the ships which Admiral Nitker commanded.

"The fleet, that is," Matoes resumed. "You may not believe that Duke Nitker could capture Ornifal from you, but you certainly can't invade Eshkol successfully with the forces at your disposal. The obvious solution is an alliance of equals. King Valence has wisely adopted a son. He might well—"

Matoes held out a hand and appeared to examine his perfect manicure. Garric noticed that the envoy was watching from the corners of his eyes to see how his next statement was received.

"—adopt another prince and cosuccessor."

"And sheep might well learn to fly, Lord Matoes," Garric said pleasantly. "But not in Admiral Nitker's lifetime, or my own."

One of the marines stifled a snicker. The envoy spun in fury, but his escorts were all straight-faced by the time he met their eyes.

"The reason that Admiral Nitker should return to his allegiance," Garric said, "isn't that the kingdom will crush him if he doesn't—though assuredly the kingdom *will* crush him if one of our common enemies doesn't do it first."

Matoes opened his mouth to protest. Garric flicked his left hand up to cut off the objection. "The reason Nitker should rejoin the government is the same one that caused him to rebel, Lord Matoes: the Isles face enemies greater than at any time since the fall of the Old Kingdom. We decent men—men who oppose chaos—all have to join together or evil will destroy us severally."

Gulls wheeling over these waste-laden lower reaches of the Beltis called shrilly. On the quay, the only sound was creaking equipment as the men of both escorts moved slightly. Matoes stroked his left cheek with his index finger as he considered what next to say.

"Admiral Nitker was adamant that he would accept nothing less than a coregency," the envoy said at last. "You need him and the fleet to enforce your rule."

"Lord Waldron was just as adamant that he should be king in Valence's place," Garric said mildly. Noble courtiers like Waldron and Matoes had certainly known each other before the current troubles, so the envoy would understand what Garric was saying. "In the end he realized that the threat to the Isles was too great to ignore for the sake of personal ambition. Waldron became commander of the Royal Army, just as Admiral Nitker will remain as the honored commander of the Royal Fleet."

In the plaza two blocks away, the regiment which accompanied Garric and his immediate bodyguards at a distance was going through evolutions. One company at a time advanced, wheeled, and countermarched while the remaining troops stood ready in case the admiral's men attempted something.

The supporting regiment was made up of household troops from a dozen of the northern landholders commanded by one of Waldron's noble friends. Attaper had provided each of the new regiments with drillmasters from the Blood Eagles.

The nobles supplying—and paying—the troops had complained, some louder than others, but in the end they'd accepted Waldron's insistence that the mixture and joint training of troops from individual households was necessary. Garric had King Carus' memories of usurpers' undisciplined levies of breaking before the steady precision of his royal army.

Waldron had something more vivid than that: the old warrior had been with King Valence at the Stone Wall on Sandrakkan. There, when the Ornifal militias panicked, only the Blood Eagles' steadfast courage and the atrocious ruthlessness of Pewle mercenaries who butchered women and children within the Sandrakkan camp had saved the throne for Valence. Waldron had no intention of allowing indiscipline in the forces *he* commanded.

Matoes looked toward the drilling troops. At first Garric thought the envoy was simply staring into the distance while his mind worked, but Matoes' eyes were really focused.

"I'll carry your message," he said to Garric at last. "I don't know how the admiral will respond. He's quite rightly confident in the strength of his position . . . for the time being, that is."

"Lord Matoes," Garric said, fixing the envoy with his eyes, "I'm not nearly as concerned about the time being as I am about the entire future of the Kingdom of the Isles. The future, or the lack of future."

He turned and pointed to the troops going through their exercises. "Tell the admiral," he said, "that it isn't about rank, his or mine or anyone at all's. It's about the survival of civilization. And very shortly he'll realize that there aren't any neutrals."

Matoes nodded. "I'll tell him," he said. "But I'm very much afraid—"

He laughed without humor. "I believe you, Prince Garric," he said, "though I can't imagine why I do. And I really can't hold out much hope that I'll be able to convince the admiral, but I'll do what I can."

Matoes turned and nodded to the commander of his escort. The envoy and four marines started briskly down the quay. The other two stood where they were long enough for the envoy to reach the steps to the skiff.

"We all have to try," Garric whispered. The setting sun painted the clouds piling up on the eastern horizon into a wall of blood.

"And this time," said the king in Garric's mind, *"we're going to succeed, lad."*

The 3rd of Partridge (Later)

I'm sending an extra bank of oarsmen, seventy-eight instead of fifty-two, Master Cashel," King Folquin said. He sounded both pleased with himself and defensive at the same time. "That way you'll be able to change half the crew every time the glass is turned and keep up full cruising speed all the way to Valles."

Cashel considered the trim warship and the men wearing only kilts or breeches who boarded her. There was surprisingly little confusion despite the crowding. He tried to imagine the sailors as sheep so that he could better judge their numbers, but men moved too quickly for that trick to work either.

Fifty-two and seventy-eight were just words to Cashel. When he counted above five, he notched a tally stick or—for preference—dropped pebbles or dried peas into a pan. Garric and Sharina could count to any number, and Garric had even showed Cashel how he could measure the height of a tree by taking sights from the ground.

"There won't be room enough to scratch your bum," Zahag said, considering the bireme. As he spoke, he scratched his bum. "Well, I guess anything that gets us back on dry land quicker is a good choice."

He rotated his head to look at Cashel. "Of course, some of the dry land you've taken me to, chief, isn't much to brag about either. You're not going to do that again, are you?"

"No," Cashel said. "Well, I don't think so."

"It does look very squeezed," said the Princess Aria, her eyes narrowing as she regarded the vessel. The ship's name was the *Arbutus* and Cashel was willing to believe the king when he said that she was the finest vessel in the squadron which kept pirates out of the waters surrounding Pandah. "Perhaps—"

"Master Cashel is in great haste to rejoin his Sharina in Valles, my dear," Folquin said. A tinge of desperation had entered his voice. "I'm sure that he'd prefer minor discomfort in order to reach Valles in a single stage. He'll be with his beloved before morning dawns."

It made Cashel acutely uncomfortable to hear Sharina referred to as his beloved. She was, right enough—he certainly wasn't going to correct the king—but it wasn't something he talked about.

Cashel gripped his quarterstaff harder. He'd *sure* never used the word to Folquin. Did everybody in the world see what to Cashel was the most private feeling there was?

"Yes, I appreciate exactly how you're looking after my friend Cashel, Your Majesty," Aria said. Judging by her tone, she didn't think much of Folquin's word choice either.

Aria turned to Cashel and put her fingertips on the backs of his hands. "Cashel," she said, "I know you'll succeed in whatever you set out to do. You brought me here where I belong. No one else could have done that."

She looked to the side for a moment as if collecting her thoughts. Without meeting Cashel's eyes again she continued, "Still, I'll pray to the Mistress God for your well-being. And you know—"

Aria faced him squarely. She was a tiny little thing but by Duzi! he'd seen weasels that weren't half so fierce as the princess when she was in the mood.

"You *know* that you'll always be welcome on Pandah," Aria said. She looked at Folquin. "Doesn't he, dear?"

"Yes, absolutely," the king said, staring at the pattern the toe of his sandal was tracing on the brick quay. "Ah, I think the captain is ready to cast off now, Master Cashel."

"Right," said Cashel, thankfully turning away from his hosts. The gangplank creaked and the ship rubbed her bumpers of coir matting against the quay as Cashel's weight shifted it. "May the Lady keep you well, Princess. And you too, King."

Crewmen bow and stern had already singled up the lines. The piper seated cross-legged in the far stern blew a shrill note; all the oarsmen along the right side shoved the vessel away from the dock with the ends of their oars.

Cashel looked for a place to sit; there was barely space to stand on the narrow deck with the extra rowers all squeezed aboard. Zahag hopped onto the sternpost which curved up over the steersman and captain. The former yelled in surprise, but the captain shushed him with a snarl.

The piper began a two-note call, changing it by fingering the stops in his single reed pipe. The oarsmen fell into a rhythm, though their strokes were short ones until the ship began to slide forward.

Cashel waved once toward the figures on the quay, then eased his way back to stand beside the piper. There wasn't really room, but by gripping the sternpost with his free hand he could sit on the gunwale and lean out safely enough.

Zahag was still looking shoreward. "Except for being so scrawny, Aria isn't bad at all," the ape said. "I'll be interested to see what this Sharina's got that Aria didn't."

Cashel looked up. "Don't say anything like that again," he said, "unless you want to swim to wherever you're going. Understand?"

The ape hunched to the post as tight as a barnacle. The water was already hissing past the bireme's hull. "You bet I do, chief," he said. "No, no, never again."

Princess Aria was wearing a layered white dress as much like what she was used to as the seamstresses on Pandah could make. It was funny how far away Cashel could see that white speck in the sunlight, still waving.

Ilna paused to get a closer look at where her guides were taking her. The afternoon sun slanted across an entrance porch set into the face of a limestone hill. The delicate carvings on the roof were thrown into sharp relief despite the effect of long weathering.

One of the six pillars supporting the porch had fallen into the road leading up to it. Ilna's eyes narrowed when she noticed that the shaft had split at an angle instead of falling into separate stone barrels.

"This whole place was cut out of the front of the hill," she said. And very ably cut, too. No one could fault the craftsmanship of Third Atara's stonemasons.

"Yes, that's right," Hosten said. He and his troops had become more and more taciturn as they approached the tomb. "The Elder Romi had it built before he died."

"It was finished the very hour he died," one of the

soldiers said. "He'd foretold his death that close."

"That's a legend," Hosten said sharply. "It may have happened, it may not."

He looked at Ilna and added, "There are many stories about the Elder Romi both before and after he died, mistress. If I were you, I'd go back to Divers immediately and find a ship."

"That's *if* he died," muttered another of the soldiers. This time Hosten didn't rebuke him.

"It hasn't been such a pleasant jaunt that I'd care to have had it for nothing," Ilna said as she strode toward the entrance. "Besides, I said I'd do it."

They'd come most of the two miles from the palace by carriage. Hosten had offered her a horse, but Ilna had never ridden an animal before and didn't think that making a fool of herself by falling off during the journey was going to improve her mood.

They'd walked the last hundred paces. Earthshocks like the one that threw down the pillar had broken the roadway into tilted blocks. The jumble was hard enough for humans to traverse, let alone a horse or the wheels of a carriage.

"It's a natural cave," Hosten explained as he followed a short distance behind her. "Only the entrance was shaped. People say that it goes all the way down under the sea."

The Inner Sea wasn't visible from where Ilna stood, but she could hear the whisper of waves on the shore now that it was called to her attention. She wasn't concerned about the cave extending underwater. If the stone walls had lasted this long, it wasn't likely that the sea would rush in just in time to drown Ilna os-Kenset.

She smiled slightly. That event would end her responsibility to Halphemos and Cashel and all the people she'd wronged in the past year, of course. Well, if the Gods existed, she doubted that they were going to let her off so easily.

"The coffin was ice cold," a soldier said. "They—"

"That's enough!" Hosten snarled.

Ilna turned her head. "Let him speak," she said. "Legend or not, I want to hear it."

Hosten turned his back, his hand squeezing and releasing the hilt of his sheathed sword as he tried to work off tension and anger. "Go on," Ilna said to the soldier who'd spoken.

The man cleared his throat. His hair was a carrot-colored tangle that stuck out to all sides beneath the rim of his simple iron helmet. "The story . . ." he said. "It was my uncle who told me when I was a little boy. They put Romi in a silver coffin."

"He didn't have any friends," volunteered another soldier. "All he had was servants and they were none of them from Third Atara. None of them human, some said."

"Anyway, the coffin got cold as cold could be," the first man continued. "They carried him down in the cave, all the way to the end, and there was a pool of water there. They put the coffin in the pool of water and it started to boil. They all ran back out of the cave, and the steam was coming up after them all the way to the surface again."

"And who told this story that your uncle told you, Digir?" Hosten said in an angry voice. "Was it one of those servants who weren't human, is that it? It's all legend!"

"Did you go down in the cave, Lord Hosten?" said the man who'd talked of Romi's servants. "When you were a boy, I mean; on a dare? *I* did."

Hosten turned to face the others. The afternoon sun shone on him, but his skin looked sallow. "Once. I went to the first bend, where it starts to slant down steeply. My torch went out. I ran back as if the Sister herself was snatching at my heels."

He looked squarely at Ilna. "Don't go in there, mistress," he said. "Maybe there's nothing really down there, but it's the coldest feeling on earth. Don't go."

Ilna shrugged. To the man who'd brought the lantern with him she said, "If you'll light that, I'll take care of my business and the rest of you can go home."

The men looked at their commander. "We'll wait for you, mistress," Hosten said. "We'll wait till the moon sets. Midnight, that is."

The soldier opened a little shutter on the back of the lantern's brass frame. He inserted the glowing punk which he carried in a tube on his belt, then blew gently. Here in the sun it was barely possible to tell that the wick had caught. He handed the lantern to Ilna.

"I'll hope to see you, then," Ilna said as she turned and walked up the three shallow steps to the entrance. One of the soldiers muttered a response—or he might have been talking to his fellows.

Only the first short distance of the cave had been squared by the hand of man. That was as far as light from outside penetrated as well. Though the lantern glowed, it illuminated little except its own horn lenses so far as Ilna was concerned. Her eyes seemed slow adapting to changes in the light; perhaps it was her recent diet.

"Down" was an easy direction, anyway. There were no obstacles except a leather cap lying on the ground twenty paces or so from the entrance. Ilna remembered her escorts' tales of boys daring one another to enter the Elder Romi's tomb. Girls had better sense than that sort of nonsense.

She smiled faintly. Though what was she doing here, unless it was accepting Baron Robilard's dare?

Ilna found she could see better as she proceeded. The walls of the cave were damp. Beneath the moisture was a layer of flow rock, limestone dissolved and redeposited in opalescent layers. Both reflected the lantern light in a bright haze that hid details.

Here and there symbols and perhaps names were carved into the rock. For almost a thousand years the folk of Third Atara had been trying prove that they were braver than a dead man—and proving instead that they were fools and destructive fools besides. Not that this island or any island had a monopoly on fools.

Ilna reached the bend Hosten had mentioned. The cave twisted left. The rock was grubby from the hands of youths gripping it as they peered around the corner and down the steep descent beyond. There were no deliberate markings here, though; visitors hadn't lingered long enough to make them.

Water gurgled in the far distance. Ilna felt a gust from the depths. Did the cave rise again to the open air?

As Hosten had said, it was very cold. Probably because of the damp rock . . . and anyway, Ilna had been cold before. She started down the slope.

Ilna didn't like stone, and stone didn't like her. The path's wet slickness made her feet slip. She caught herself by slapping her left palm against the rounded sidewall.

She smiled again. Dislike—her own or that of others for her—wasn't a new experience. She didn't let it bother her, either way.

The cave kept going down. Ilna wondered how those bearing the Elder Romi's coffin had managed to keep their footing. It wasn't a difficult path apart from the steepness, though.

Ilna was starting to see things in the walls, as though creatures had been entombed in the flow rock. That was nonsense, she knew: discolorations in the underlying rock were further distorted by the lantern light passing through the glistening surfaces of water and translucent stone. She glared at the shapes because she thought that keeping her eyes down on the path might suggest she was afraid.

Ilna laughed. Suggest to who? To the soldiers waiting a lifetime away in the sunlight, perhaps? She patted what would have been the snout of a gaping monster if the shadows hinted the truth.

It felt so cold that the slime on the walls of the cave would have frozen had the sensation been real. Something was toying with Ilna's mind, threatening her with illusions. Her fury when she realized she was being played with warmed her. Prayer might have done the same for someone who had more belief in the Great Gods than Ilna os-Kenset did.

The lantern was growing dimmer. Ilna stopped and examined it. She could feel a sufficiency of oil sloshing in the reservoir. She tried adjusting the wick, first up and then down. She tilted the lantern slightly in case there wasn't a proper length of wick within the tank.

The flame sank to a faint blue glow. Ilna set the lantern near the side of the cave, where a knob would keep it from skidding down on its own. She proceeded without it, touching the left wall with her fingertips.

It grew colder. Ilna's lips pursed in a moue of anger.

Ilna would be the last to deny her responsibility for the two wizards who'd followed her from the Garden, but she knew now that she wasn't doing this for Halphemos or Cerix. She was doing it because Baron Robilard was a boy with more power than judgment. He wasn't evil at heart, but he squeezed his subjects and browbeat his associates because there was no one to stop him from doing it and no desire to stop himself.

He'd just tried to do the same thing to Ilna os-Kenset. When this business was over, Baron Robilard would have learned something. Granted, he might not have long to profit from his lesson.

Ilna heard water plashing ahead of her. She supposed it was a persistent drip from the cave roof, amplified by echoes. She continued downward at a measured pace, guiding herself by the touch of her hand.

She was beginning to see again. The cave walls glowed a blue as pale as starlight. Perhaps the light had always been there and it had taken her eyes this long to adapt to it.

The floor of the cave leveled out. Ahead of her was a pool. Water patted the margins, making the sound Ilna had taken for dripping.

There was no question of going on: the cave ended at the pool.

Ilna walked to the edge and knelt. She was trembling

uncontrollably. The *feeling* of cold was real, though her breath didn't hang in the air before her as it would on a winter morning in Barca's Hamlet.

Ilna bowed as she would have done on being presented to any person of age and respectability. Gazing into the pool, she said, "Master Romi, I am Ilna os-Kenset."

The water was as clear as a diamond. It had the same vague glow as the walls of the cave. Bubbles rose trembling through it and burst with plops when they reached the surface.

"Baron Robilard, who now rules this island," Ilna continued, "has sent me to invite you to dinner tonight in his palace. He claims you as his ancestor."

Laughter filled the domed chamber. Ilna looked up. She couldn't see a source for the sound. A bass voice said, "Ilna os-Kenset, are you afraid?"

Ilna rose to her feet. "I'm afraid of my own will, master," she said truthfully. The chill was passing; her muscles no longer trembled. "I'm afraid of the evil I can do when I'm angry."

"Is there nothing else you fear, woman?" the disembodied voice demanded. It rose to a thunder that echoed and re-echoed within the hollow walls.

Shapes began to form in the air around Ilna. Some were terrible, and some were far worse than that. The light congealed into dead flesh and flesh that had never been alive.

"Nothing else, Master Romi," Ilna said to the lowering darkness. "My own evil is quite enough for anyone to face."

The voice burst into rolling laughter that filled all the world around it. The water in the pool shivered at the spasms of fearful joy.

"Go back to the palace of the man who calls himself my descendant, Mistress Ilna," the voice said. "Tell him that the Elder Romi, who had no descendants of the flesh, will grace his banquet tonight. I look forward to the entertainment."

Ilna bowed again. "I will give him your message, master," she said.

She turned and started up the cave again. Before she reached the point where the floor slanted steeply the voice added, "Tell Baron Robilard that I will come when the moon sets, Ilna. I hope he will be ready for me."

Ilna trudged upward. The return wasn't as difficult as she'd thought during her descent that it might be.

The rippling laughter followed Ilna to the cave entrance. She too smiled, every step of the way.

The slit in the rock wall to Sharina's right showed the white room and the game board, nothing else. The other five windows visible from her frozen vantage displayed the sea. Sunset painted the clouds with rosy light. It reflected like blood onto the water beneath.

The aspects were distant from one another by miles, judging from the swatches of sky overhead. The raft covered with Hairy Men filled all five scenes. In the distance beyond, an island humped in silhouette against the sun.

A fleet of fifty warships was attacking the raft. The vessels were under oars, their sails and mainmasts landed onshore to lighten them for action before they set out. From the ships' jibs floated banners bearing the eagle symbol of the royal house of Ornifal, but crossed with a bend of red fabric.

When Sharina saw the floating forest for the first time from her prison, the Hairy Men had wandered it as they chose. Now phantasms prowled the timber mat and drove the brutish humans with gestures and eyes which smoldered like live coals. Instead of running forward to gibber at the warships or fleeing back in wild panic, a phalanx of Hairy Men hunched with crude weapons just beyond the outer barrier of interlaced branches.

On the narrow decks of the ships, archers stood with nocked arrows. They didn't have any better targets than vague movement that might have been the breeze wobbling shrunken leaves. Some of them loosed anyway. The arrows clipped branches, thudded into tree boles, and occasionally struck one of the Hairy Men. For all the real difference the rare success made, the archers could have emptied their quivers into the sea.

Many of them aimed at the phantasms stalking over the timber in plain sight. The missiles that intersected those demonic figures snapped on through as they would the empty air. If anything, the fiery eyes burned brighter.

The flagship was a massive quinquereme that wobbled because its hull had to be high enough to carry five banks of oars. Signalers around the brazier on its stern platform sent up a plume of purple smoke that all the fleet could see. The triremes that made up the rest of the fleet carried catapults on their bow platforms. Catapult arms slammed forward, sending firepots deep into the mass of floating timber.

Here and there, a splotch of burning oil spread on a tree trunk and struggled to ignite the thick, wet bark. More often the pots splashed into open water and either sank unnoticed or formed a patch of harmless iridescence.

The artillery crews began cranking their lever arms back with small capstans, readying their weapons for another volley. The fleet commander and probably every man abovedecks realized that it would be vain effort. A second smoke plume, this one reddish white, billowed from the signal brazier.

The strokes of a few oarsmen aboard each vessel had enabled the ships to hold their distance from the margins of the raft. At the red signal the vessels began to move forward, their rams toward the mat. Beyond the fringe of branches and yellowing foliage, Hairy Men crouched and phantasms laughed silently.

The fleet could have avoided the raft's slow progress forever, but the island behind them could not. Sharina didn't recognize the dim outline, now hidden in the greater mass of the sea as the sun dropped below the horizon. All that mattered to the entity which commanded the Hairy Men was that the raft would ground on that shore sometime during the night, nothing else appearing; and that the sailors, for their own reasons, didn't dare let that happen.

One after another the warships made contact with the raft. A few approached at ramming speed, a fast walk, and tried to punch their way through the tangled barrier. That was like trying to row through an island.

Most were caught in branches that gave the way a noose flexes when a rabbit runs full-tilt into it. A few were still less fortunate: these collided with the axe-severed trunks of trees that were often thicker than a man was tall. Even bow timbers reinforced for ramming splintered at the impact, crushing enormous holes in the hulls. The sea rushed in, engulfing the oar benches.

The other captains approached with the same caution as they would have done if docking. Their vessels nuzzled the edges of the raft while petty officers shouted nervous commands to the oarsmen. Marine spearmen and archers scrambled onto the floating mass; behind them followed sailors carrying axes and saws.

While the marines faced the bobbing maze of trunks and branches, the sailors tried to cut the raft apart. From Sharina's viewpoint, looking down on an expanse of floating timber miles across, the hopelessness of the attempt was obvious. Even the men working at sea level, unable to judge the full extent of their task, must have doubted they could ever succeed.

Phantasms all across the forward edge of the raft pointed their smoky arms forward. The Hairy Men obeyed, tens of thousands of them scrambling up from cover and falling on the clumps of civilized humans. To Sharina, it was like watching the surf boil over a gravel strand.

Archers loosed one or sometimes two arrows before being crushed down by a club or a stone wielded by a long hairy arm. Spearmen thrust home, then watched their victims crawl up spearshafts to tear their killers' throats out before dying themselves. Often the soldiers toppled from wet trunks into a sea that drank them down, burdened as they were by the weight of armor.

The sailors either tried to defend themselves with their tools or, throwing the equipment aside, to scramble back aboard their vessels. The Hairy Men had three or four gripping hands apiece and in their native jungles had become far more familiar with moving across tangles like this one. They leaped open water and nets of branches, sometimes covering twenty feet in a single bound.

Screaming sailors were borne down by savage enemies. Sometimes they lived long enough to feel two or three of the Hairy Men chewing into their bodies in search of kidneys or other particular delicacies.

Catapults fired into the mass, with no more effect than a few score raindrops would have in extinguishing a grass fire. Captains and petty officers stricken by the suddenness of the disaster shouted conflicting orders to the oarsmen still aboard.

A few of the triremes started to back away, but only a few. Fewer still got far enough clear of the raft that the Hairy Men leaping under the phantasms' command didn't catch railings or the extended oars.

When the Hairy Men swarmed aboard a warship, all was chaos and butchery. The rowers were free men, but they had no weapons except the belt knives every sailor—or rural laborer—carried. They were packed too tightly to fight, and too demoralized by the completeness of the catastrophe even to organize under the command of their officers.

Knives and the officers' swords killed, but stones, clubs, and inch-long canine teeth killed faster and more horribly. Triremes wallowed as slaughter washed across them, filling the bilges with steaming blood.

Sharina felt nothing but mild curiosity as she viewed the slaughter. In her present state she understood everything but cared as little as if she were watching the wind pluck white foam from the tips of rising waves.

Surviving Hairy Men squatted on oarbenches meant for the longer, straighter limbs of civilized humans and grasped the oarlooms. Directed by the phantasms, the new rowers brought those ships that had drifted a distance from the raft back against its ragged margins.

More Hairy Men, young and old of either sex, leaped aboard. The warships had been crowded under their own crews, but this influx of half-men squeezed the narrow hulls the way a sheepfold fills in winter. A phantasm in the stern of each vessel gestured the stroke. Despite the crush, the oars now moved with the precision of wooden cogs engaging to drive a mill wheel.

The captured triremes—forty or so from a fleet of fifty—backed, then swung as one and made for the island lowering in what was now near-total darkness. The raft holding more tens of thousands of Hairy Men drifted along the same course but at the speed that wind and current drove it.

The admiral's flagship and two companion triremes still under the control of civilized humans sped away as fast as oars could drive them. They were visible only because the moon shone on the foaming oarthresh to either side of the hulls. Their destination was not the small island from which they had set out but the greater mass to the north and west of it.

Sharina watched as she might have watched the rain begin to pelt a neighbor's house; knowing that the storm would sweep on to her own dwelling, but unconcerned by what that would mean for her and hers.

"The trouble we'll have in fighting the kind of army a wizard raises," said King Carus, leaning on his forearms with his lean, powerful fingers laced as he watched the battle, "is that they don't care if they're killed."

He turned his head to grin at Garric's dream self and added, "Of course, lots of times they're dead to begin with."

Garric had noticed how the king said "we'll have," a quiet reminder that he and Garric were as close as a man and his shadow now. Garric grinned back. Closer, even: there was no darkness so complete that Garric could be without his ancestor's experience, skill, and steadfast, laughing courage.

On the moonlit field below, Carus' army fought an army of liches. Skeletons of the drowned dead, clothed in translucent slime, threw themselves on the human phalanx with the mindless insistence of rocks rolling downhill. The attackers carried rusty swords and spears whose shafts were barnacle-scaled. Some wore armor or rotted scraps of the garments they had drowned in, but most of the sexless monsters were glisteningly nude.

"You think the queen will send liches against us?" Garric asked. He'd fought the creatures before. They struggled even after they'd been hacked to bits. Only a stroke through the skull or the spine would permanently end a lich's lethal malevolence.

Carus shrugged. "It'll be something that doesn't have a mind of its own," he said. "There's men who'll follow a wizard, but not many and not the sort with the discipline to make good soldiers."

The phalanx was formed in a hollow square so that eight ranks faced in every direction. A younger King Carus stood on a mound of equipment at the center of the formation. Moonlight winked on the blade of Carus' long sword and the circlet of gold binding his hair.

"I wondered what I'd do if they retreated and I had to pursue," the older Carus said, nodding toward the battle. "I needn't have worried: they kept coming as long as there was one left that could crawl. *I* never met a wizard I'd put in command of a company, let alone an army, and I don't guess you will either."

The ground on three sides of the armored square was littered with rotten bones and slick with the noisome ooze into which the liches' flesh dissolved when they died the second time. Rusty weapons lay among the foul debris.

None of the creatures had penetrated the hedge of spears. Though sometimes a lich hacked a pikehead off before another soldier rammed his point through the dead skull or spine, the wall remained unbroken. The jagged end of the pikestaff was still an effective weapon.

"But you've got a different problem, lad," Carus said, turning to look at Garric. "I had an army; you've got a city to defend, and that's going to be a lot harder."

"We're repairing the walls," Garric said. "Pitre's in charge of that, though Tadai's finding the money to pay the laborers. We're getting a loan from a consortium of Serian bankers."

He shook his head. Garric didn't wear the golden diadem when he slept, and thankfully it wasn't part of his dream either. The things that *Prince* Garric had to deal with made his mind spin.

"Wouldn't you think that people would just pitch in without being paid?" Garric said. He watched Carus' grin grow broader. "I mean, it's their lives if the queen comes back. They must know that!"

"They don't know it," the king said, "and if they did, they'd still want to be paid."

He shrugged. "And they still have to feed their families, after all. The folks you've got filling baskets with dirt and carrying stones aren't nobles and rich merchants who could live on their savings for a few days, lad. Most of them'll eat after nightfall when they're paid and dismissed, because they won't have anything to buy food with until then."

Garric squeezed his hands together. Below the battle was nearing its conclusion, though the remnant of the lich army still writhed like a lizard's severed tail.

"This is what being a king is about?" Garric said. "Finding the money to pay laborers, and then finding the money to pay the bankers back? I don't know *how* we're ever going to pay off that loan!"

"It's not much like the epics, is it?" Carus said. He laughed. "You'll manage, lad."

Suddenly grim he added, "Better than I did, at any rate, because I'll see to it that you don't let things slide the way I did."

The younger Carus bent to call an order to the signalers waiting at the base of his vantage point. A trumpeter blew a double call. Company officers turned to see the detailed commands passed by torch because the moonlight was too dim to display flags clearly. Two faces of the square fell in along the flanks of the battalion between them and began to advance in the direction from which the attackers came. The fourth face, the battalion that hadn't really been engaged by the liches, faced about also and followed the main body of the phalanx as a ready reserve. The rear ranks of each company carried a double load of equipment, their own and that of the men ahead of them.

"I didn't like to move by night," Carus said reflectively, "but I didn't want to give the wizard who was rebelling a chance to try again. His name was Abiba. Abiba the Great he called himself, until I hanged him that night. Maybe it was too easy to beat him."

Garric frowned at the battlefield. The victory had been complete and there were few human casualties, that was true; but a less skillful human commander or a less disciplined army could have been lost to a man.

"It didn't look easy to me," Garric said slowly.

"Ah," said Carus. "But it let me think that so long as I had troops who wouldn't panic when they faced wizardry, then I didn't have to fear wizards. The Hooded One sank me *and* my men to the bottom of the Inner Sea because I didn't judge the real risks, just the risks I'd beaten before."

"Ah," said Garric, nodding now that he really understood the king's point. "And what you said before about my job being harder because I have a city to defend instead of an army, you mean because the people *will* panic. A lot of them."

Carus nodded grimly. "It isn't that soldiers are brave and civilians aren't, lad," he said. "They're used to facing spearpoints, the veterans are, that's true; but my men and I had never seen anything like the liches before we tackled Abiba. It's a lot easier to face the unknown when you're standing shoulder to shoulder with people you trust. *That's* the advantage the soldier has."

Garric swallowed. "We'll do what we can," he said. "The walls should help, and I've got Attaper putting together a training scheme for a citizen militia. Even if they don't have much in the way of weapons, I thought people would like to feel they were helping. I thought of evacuating Valles, but I don't know that would make any difference. The queen could attack anywhere, after all."

"There's a satisfaction to hanging a wizard that I never got out of arguing tax policy with the rulers of the separate islands," Carus said, smiling crookedly. "I should've spent more time on the taxes, though, and learned more from the wizards I did hang. Well, you've got my mistakes to look at so you don't have to make them again."

The field was empty now except for grass trampled to mud and the wrack of broken equipment and long-dead corpses. Looking down at the moonlit waste, Garric said, "Sir, I feel like I'm a piece of copper. I'm being hammered out so flat that you could see through me. Everybody has something they want . . . and I'm not sure there's going to be anything left unless they stop hammering."

"They won't stop, lad," Carus said softly. "Not till you're dead, and maybe not then."

The king drew his long sword. The tang and crosshilt were forged all as one piece with the blade; the edges had the sheen of oil trembling on water, smooth and as sharp as was consistent with the strength to shear through armor.

"I didn't have any choice about being king, Garric," Carus said. "The Isles needed a strong hand. My hand, Carilan and his advisors all told me, and I wish they'd been right. I failed in the end because I misjudged a wizard, and the kingdom went down in blood and chaos."

"Nobody could have done better than you," Garric said. He squeezed the coronation medal from King Carus which he wore around his neck. His left hand squeezed it.

"You don't know that!" the king said in a rare flash of anger. His face softened and he smiled, then continued, "But you might be right. Well, what matters now is what you do, Prince Garric. And you don't have any choice either. You'll be King of the Isles because the Isles need you. All the people who live on the Isles need you. That's the part that's important, the people you serve."

Carus raised his sword. Light came from no certain source to illuminate the dream balcony; it ran along the blade like a brook rippling over gray stones.

"This is a fine weapon, a marvel of craftsmanship," he said, speaking to the steel rather than to Garric. "It will do whatever it's asked to do, until the moment it breaks. As I did, Garric."

Carus turned to face the youth who was so nearly the mirror image of his own younger self. "And as you'll do. Because we do the jobs we have to, you and me and the swords in our hands."

The king from ancient times laughed; and as he laughed, he began to fade along with the setting of which he was a part. Garric raised his head from the arms on which he'd pillowed it while dozing on the desk of his private office.

"Garric?" Liane called through the door. "Attaper is here with a report on the militia. Can you see him?"

It was so dark outside that Garric could barely tell the open window from the casement framing it. "Bring him in, Liane," Garric called. He got up, feeling on the desktop for flint and steel to light a candle.

In Garric's dreams, with the strength of King Carus to support him, he could be a frightened boy. It was time to be king again.

Ilna's lantern burned normally when she retrieved it from the floor of the cave, but she was surprised at how little oil remained in the large reservoir. She would have expected it to last all night without being refilled.

She walked up the remaining slope at a brisk pace. She didn't feel as cold as she had while descending, though the air had the chill to be expected from damp stone.

She reached the bend and the floor became level. The cave mouth was only a dim blur. Unless a storm had blown in from the sea, it was much later than Ilna had judged it from the length of time she thought she'd spent below ground.

"Something's coming!" a man said. His nervous voice echoed down the tunnel. Weapons rattled on other equipment and the stones they'd been leaned against.

"*I'm* coming out!" Ilna said. "What's the matter with you?"

She stepped onto the porch. Her escort stood with their backs to one of the huge pillars. Hosten flashed his sword; the four soldiers had their shields raised and held their spears for underhand thrusts.

"Is it really her?" a soldier said.

"Of course it's me!" Ilna said, raising the lantern so that it shone directly on her face instead of lighting her from below. "You knew I was coming."

Hosten sheathed his sword. "We hoped you were coming, Mistress Ilna," he said, correcting her in a quiet voice.

He looked at the sky. The moon was well past zenith; Ilna *had* been in the cave much longer than she'd believed. "We'd best get back to the palace," Hosten said, "or they'll think we don't plan to return. Unless . . . ?"

He looked at Ilna and raised an eyebrow.

"Of course we're going back," Ilna said, though in a milder tone than she might have used. She knew the courtier was trying to do her a service, the sort of act that made the world a better place. It wasn't Hosten's fault that Ilna found kindnesses much harder to accept than insults.

She handed the lantern to one of the soldiers. If it had been Ilna's decision she would have snuffed the flame and returned to the carriage by moonlight alone, but the man kept it lit. The quivering yellow glow was very little use for lighting the broken roadway, but perhaps he found warmth in it.

"How did you find the cave, mistress?" Hosten asked in a tone of deliberate disinterest.

"I did what I went there to do," Ilna said. They were in sight of the carriage. A horse whickered and the driver got up from where he'd been sleeping between the front wheels.

"So the stories are all just fancies after all," Digir said with a half-regretful sigh. "We were just a bunch of kids scaring themselves in the dark."

Ilna looked at him sharply. "No," she said, "it's not. I very much advise you to treat the Elder Romi with the respect due a man who served his community well for a long time."

"That's enough, Digir," Hosten said. "Anything more Mistress Ilna has to say, she should save for Baron Robilard."

"One more thing," Ilna said as they reached the carriage. "Digir, all of you: if a sense of respect isn't enough to keep your children from troubling the Elder Romi, then tell them they should be afraid of him. After tonight, they shouldn't have any difficulty believing you."

The 4th of Partridge

The queen, her eyes as cold as the airless crystal plain, watched Sharina from the room of alabaster. "Come to me, girl," she said. With dizzying suddenness Sharina stood in the white chamber with the game board separating her from her captor.

"I've been occupied with destroying the Royal Fleet, Sharina," the queen said. She smiled with catlike irony. "I let you see so that you could know how useless it is to try to defeat my purpose. Now it's time for you to help me."

Sharina said nothing. She was shivering uncontrollably. She kneaded her thighs with long, strong fingers, trying to work out a stiffness that she knew wasn't physical. Her body was no longer cold, but her soul held the memory of the icy chains which had held it so long.

The queen continued to smile, but her eyes were harder than the tourmaline counters on the game board. Her index finger hovered over one, then withdrew.

"Very well, girl," she said in a mellifluous voice. "I'd hoped you would help me without further demonstration, but I don't require you to be wise. Only obedient, as you will be."

"I'm not going to help you," Sharina said. She knew she sounded petulant in comparison with the queen's mannered sweetness. The contrast made Sharina angry, and the anger warmed her as physical release had not done.

The queen moved her right hand as though wiping the wall, though the alabaster was several paces distant. "Watch, Sharina," she said pleasantly.

"If you could force me against my will to do what you want," Sharina said, her voice rising, "you would've done that. You can't, and I *won't* help you."

"Watch, girl," the queen said. A section of fine-grained stone had opened into a window overlooking a starlit sea.

Two vessels, an oar-driven warship and a tubby merchantman, were underway on opposite courses. From her own travels Sharina knew that during the hours of darkness ships more often anchored on one of the tiny islands dotting the Inner Sea.

The warship's oars moved the way the feathers of a bird's wings do, forward and back together instead of rippling in bunches like a millipede's legs. The merchantman proceeded under a small sail from the slanting foremast and the close-reefed mainsail. The vessels were passing at a bowshot's distance.

Neither hailed the other. The Kingdom of the Isles had too many dangerous rivalries at present for any merchant to want dealings with an armed vessel, even if it wasn't an outright pirate, and the officers of this warship were too intent on their business to trouble themselves with passing strangers.

"Do you see who's aboard the *Arbutus,* girl?" the queen asked playfully. Sharina's viewpoint swooped toward the warship like a diving gull and the scene brightened.

The narrow catwalk serving the bireme as a deck was packed with men. For a horrid instant, Sharina remembered the captured ships she'd seen putting off filled with Hairy Men, but these were crewed by normal humans.

Most of them were normal humans. The queen raised her finger and the viewpoint focused even tighter. On the bireme's sternpost sat an ape. It gripped the curving timber with its hind legs while its fingers combed its belly fur for lice.

Sharina frowned. The ape reminded her of—

The queen's finger ticked down the way a choir director gestured with the rolled-up music. The viewpoint shifted slightly.

"Cashel!" Sharina cried.

Cashel sat on the railing, looking out to sea with his usual placid good humor. He was much the same as when Sharina had last seen him in the flesh, wrestling Zahag in the courtyard of King Folquin's palace. He held his familiar hickory quarterstaff upright between knees so that it wouldn't bump the ship's officers crowded close to him.

The queen's smile was as wide as a seawolf's. The viewpoint surged upward again. The ships were drawing apart. The merchantman's captain shouted a command;

three sailors climbed the stays to let out another reef of the mainsail.

"What will you give to save your Cashel, girl?" the queen asked. "Will you guide me to the Throne of Malkar?"

Sharina looked at the perfect, evil woman. She didn't speak. There was nothing she could say that would make the situation better.

Again the silent anger flashed in the queen's eyes because she'd been balked of the cringing fear she wanted. Her finger pointed to the window onto the nighted sea. "Look," she said in a venomous whisper.

For a moment Sharina continued to watch the wizard instead. But . . . to refuse to look was a child's trick, an attempt to hold back the reality outside by hiding her head under the covers. Sharina os-Reise wasn't a child—or a coward.

She turned her head. *Lady, shelter Cashel in Your arms,* her mind whispered while her lips remained still.

She was viewing the sailing vessel. The warship with Cashel aboard was in the far distance, visible only by the trails of its oarthresh. The sailors had shaken out more sail and dropped to the deck.

The ship shuddered to a halt. The steersman lurched forward against the tiller, and the lookout in the bow would have gone overboard had he not been able to grab the foot of the foresail.

Something thick as an anchor line crawled over the stern railing and wrapped the captain's ankle. He shouted and stamped his foot, trying to shake the touch from his leg. The steersman drew his belt knife and stepped toward the captain.

Two more tentacles gripped the steersman from behind.

Sharina had watched worse horrors from the windowed chamber where the queen had imprisoned her. This one, though, she not only saw with human eyes but understood with a human heart. A wave of dizzying horror gripped her.

Sailors flailed with bare hands or whatever weapons they could snatch up. There were dozens of tentacles, perhaps scores. Railings broke, the standing rigging snapped line by line, and men screaming helplessly vanished overboard.

The ship lurched, throwing its mainmast and sail into the sea to starboard. The deck was tilting under the grip of tentacles questing for prey that might have been missed thus far. They were unsuccessful: the vessel's whole crew had already been snatched into the sea.

The ship tilted further. From the water beside it rose a pearly mass: the shell of an ammonite, but an ammonite the size of an island. One of the mollusk's slitted eyes stared at Sharina while its beak swallowed the sailors its tentacles passed into it one after another.

The ship's hull flexed, then broke under the strain. Shattered timbers swam for a moment, then sank in a boil of foam and cargo.

The moon shone on the monster's opalescent shell. Tentacles groped over the flotsam which was all that remained of the vessel. Finding nothing more that was edible they withdrew. The whole creature sank slowly into the depths from which it had come.

"Which will it be, Sharina?" the queen asked. "Will you do as I ask you, or shall I feed Cashel to the Old Ones also?"

The wall had returned to smooth alabaster. Sharina looked at the monstrous, beautiful figure across the game board from her.

In a voice devoid of outward emotion, Sharina said, "What do you want me to do?"

The guards in front of Robilard's palace stood at attention when Lord Hosten got out of the carriage; their officer stepped from the anteroom and bowed low. Hosten was too preoccupied to acknowledge the honors being paid him.

"This late in the evening . . ." Hosten said. It was past

midnight. "The drinking will have been going on for some hours. It—"

He paused, struggling with the question of how much to say to an outsider. He gave Ilna a twisted smile. "Baron Robilard is a fine young man, but sometimes he's a trifle erratic when he's in his cups. Are you sure you want to see him now?"

"To the degree that I ever wanted to see him," Ilna said. She shrugged. "I owe him a warning. He won't listen, but *I* owe him the warning."

Hosten nodded curtly. "I'll take you through to the banquet hall," he said. He turned to the palace.

"Sir?" said one of the soldiers. "Do we . . . ? I mean, must we . . . ?"

"Send them home," Ilna said before Hosten could answer. "There's no reason they should be involved in it. And I can announce myself to the baron."

"You're dismissed," Hosten said curtly to the escort. The driver took the order as applying to himself as well; the carriage rumbled down the curving drive. The four soldiers trotted quickly after it as though the Sister were on their heels.

Ilna's lips smiled. If she'd read the pattern correctly, that wasn't very far from the truth.

"I'll take you through," Hosten repeated. His smile became even more crooked. "I'm a bor-Horial, mistress. I have no more choice in the matter than you do."

Ilna laughed out loud for the first time in—well, in a long time, certainly. "Let's go, then," she said, falling into step with the proud, straight-backed noble.

Ilna had never understood how people could have pride in their birth instead of their accomplishments. On the other hand, she was clear-sighted enough to know that Ilna os-Kenset, whose father had drunk away his inheritance before he drank himself to death, and whose mother had never been seen by anyone in Barca's Hamlet except—she supposed—Kenset, wasn't an unbiased judge of the matter.

Ilna had never expected to hear a noble claim kinship of a sort with her. And she'd *certainly* never thought that she'd feel vaguely honored when it happened.

The room where she'd met Baron Robilard this morning was empty except for a scurrying servant and the shadows flung by the six lamps, barely enough to light so large a space. Ilna frowned. She'd thought the banquet would be here.

Hosten either saw her face or guessed her question in some other fashion. "The banquet chamber was added at the back of the palace," he said. "That was the baron's first expansion project on coming to the throne."

Ilna sniffed. She could easily understand Ascelei's bitterness at the young ruler's taxes—and the works he spent them on.

They went down a hallway between sets of smaller rooms. From the doorway at the end came music, laughter, and the light of many lamps. A servant carrying out a tall wine jar by one handle—it must have been empty—stepped close to the wall to let them pass.

Long tables were set as three sides of a square with the guests on cushioned seats on the outside. Servants offered food and wine from the inner face, entering from the open side. The only food still being brought out was slices from a salt chine of beef to make the drinkers thirstier.

The hall was so large that not even the present gathering filled it. The floor was covered with bracken rather than the rushes which the better houses in Barca's Hamlet spread to pick up mud and debris dropped at meals; poor folk were more likely to rebuild their huts when the floor rose high enough to make headroom a problem.

The iron cage had been set in the middle of the square of tables. Halphemos sat cross-legged within, waiting with the morose resignation of a hen being carried to market with its legs tied over a pole.

For a moment few of the guests noticed Hosten and Ilna. Some of the courtiers were so drunk that their eyes didn't focus anymore. Baron Robilard wasn't quite that far gone, though his cheeks were flushed and his eyes had a hectic glitter. He sat at the center of the cross-table, with Regowara to his right and his blond wife Cotolina to the left.

Cotolina watched Ilna enter with a gaze as cool as glacial ice. There was a double cradle behind her. A nurse was suckling one of the twins while the other slept.

To Ilna's mild surprise, Lady Tamana was at the banquet also. The surprise vanished when Ilna saw that Tamana was seated at the bottom of the table on Robilard's left, and that the man seated above her was clearly not a noble.

He was dressed with the flashy tastelessness of the clerk who oversaw the villagers' payments following the Tithe Procession in Barca's Hamlet. This man probably served Robilard in similar capacity. The only reason a tax gatherer would be present in this assembly was to make Tamana's disgrace explicit to the dullest intellect.

A harper stood in a back corner plucking an accompaniment. He declaimed, "As Turnus bore the war standard from the citadel of Meriem and the trumpets shrieked their harsh call—"

"My lord!" Hosten interrupted in a voice that everyone in the huge room could hear.

All eyes turned to him. Halphemos grasped the bars, then shook his head in misery.

"—he lashed his fiery horses—" the harper continued.

"Be silent!" Robilard said, raising his hand. "I thought you'd deserted me, Hosten. I think perhaps I should get another military advisor, since you carry out your duties in such a lackadaisical fashion."

Hosten started to speak. Ilna stepped in front of him and crossed her arms.

"Lord Hosten carried out your orders, my lord," she said. Her voice rang like cymbals from the high marble walls. "It took longer than I'd expected, but I've carried out your orders too. The Elder Romi informed me that he would come to your dinner when the moon sets."

Robilard lurched upright and tried to stand. He fell back into his seat at the first attempt. He flung his silver cup to the table and stood with a nervous footman supporting him by either elbow.

Robilard pointed his finger at Ilna. "You're a fool!" he shouted. "And you're a liar!"

"I've often been a fool," Ilna said, each word a whipcrack. "I've never seen the point of lying, though. And I warn you, Baron, I very much doubt that the Elder Romi lies either."

"Put her in the cage with the other one!" Robilard said. "In the morning take them both out and dump them. Let them try their lies on the fish!"

"My lord?" Hosten said desperately. "I really think—"

"Be silent!" Robilard screamed. "Do you want to join them?"

The baron wavered and almost fell on his face. The footmen managed to catch him so that he flopped back on his chair instead.

Ilna turned to Hosten. "Yes, be quiet or I'll silence you myself," she said. She half-smiled. "Besides, I think it's time for you to go."

Hosten shook his head. "I pledged my honor," he said in a stony voice. He led Ilna to the cage and slid the bolt to open it. Ilna curtsied to him, then ducked to enter the tight confines. The door clanged shut behind her.

Conversation resumed but the harper stood uncertain. He played with the tuning pegs, glancing frequently at the back of Robilard's head. The baron's last command had been for silence. He might or might not want the declamation to continue, but the harper wasn't alone in thinking it wasn't a good time to call oneself to Robilard's attention in the absence of a specific command.

Lord Hosten sat in the chair left vacant beside Lady Cotolina. A servant offered a cup of wine. Hosten accepted it, but he didn't drink.

"You shouldn't have come back," Halphemos said in a wretched whisper.

"I don't expect to be here long," Ilna said. "The moon has probably set by now."

The atmosphere of the hall grew colder. Ilna puffed from her open mouth; she couldn't see her breath. "Not very long at all," she said.

The lamps were fading also. Talk stilled; everyone turned toward the doorway. Lady Regowara, able to see down the hall from her position near the center of the cross-table, suddenly screamed and tried to get up.

A figure of blue ice entered the banquet hall. It walked like a man, but it had only a featureless lump for a head. It proceeded around the side of the hall. Behind the first came a line of identical figures, each turning right or left like a parade of footmen taking their places behind the diners.

The harper flung down his instrument and stumbled toward the exit behind him. He snatched the curtain aside, then staggered back bawling in terror. Another of the ice men already stood in the doorway.

Robilard's servants stood transfixed. The intruders directed them toward the main door with deliberate gestures. The servants edged slowly toward the doorway, then broke into a stumbling stampede. Only when they reached the hallway did their terror break in cries of babbling relief.

The ice figure which had blocked the harper's escape stepped aside, then beckoned the man with his finger. The harper stood where he was, gasping like a freshly caught fish.

The ice man gestured again. The harper bolted past him. His screaming terror echoed up the service corridor.

Ilna thought of Garric reading out passages of epic whose majesty escaped her. All Ilna heard was a pattern of words—many of which she didn't know. Even a sniveling coward like the harper shared things with Garric that Ilna, who'd known him all her life, did not.

Ilna's hand touched the loose end of her sash, the pair of the one she'd woven for Liane. Threads go where the weaver places them; and Ilna's life wasn't a pattern of her own weaving.

Across the banquet table, Hosten noticed Ilna and tried to stand. The ice man standing behind him in place of a human servitor put his hand on Hosten's shoulder. The noble shouted, "Let go of me! I'm going to release her!"

For a moment they struggled, the man to rise and the not-man to hold him in his seat. Hosten, gasping and suddenly older than he had seemed before, gave up the attempt.

Halphemos' fingertip drew a circle on the rusty floor of the cage. Though freehand, it was as regular as another person could have managed with a compass. He began to sketch symbols around its margin.

"Cerix taught me to open doors," he whispered to Ilna. "This is iron, but there's so much power around us that I think I can . . ."

An ice figure walked to the cradle beside which the nurse cowered. The creature's limbs moved in fluid curves instead of bending at the joints like a human's. It gestured the nurse toward the doorway, then reached into the cradle.

Cotolina cried out and would have risen. Another ice figure held her in place. The first lifted out the twins. Their shrieks sounded thinner, more distant, than was right for such agony of soul.

The ice man, moving with the deliberation of a storm cloud, handed the infants to their mother. Cotolina hugged them to her flat bosom. She whispered words of empty comfort while her tears dripped on their crying faces.

Halphemos had stripped curling leaves from a bracken stem. Using it as a wand he began to tap the symbols he'd drawn from memory on the iron. With his eyes closed to bring Cerix's training closer in his mind, he said, "*Aeo io ioaeoeu, eeouoai. . . .*"

The tax gatherer squeezed his cup in both hands. Twice

he tried to lift the wine to his lips, but his muscles trembled so badly that the contents spilled as soon as he lifted the base from the table.

An ice man tapped the tax gatherer on the shoulder. The man kept his eyes shut and pretended to be unaware.

The creature lifted him by the shoulder with one cold-fingered hand. The movement was as gently inexorable as that of a mother cat moving her kittens. The other hand plucked the chair away and set it to the side.

The tax gatherer still wouldn't open his eyes. With trembling lips he murmured the same prayer over and over. Everyone in the room but Halphemos was watching the tableau.

The ice figure released the tax gatherer and gave him a little push toward the door. The fellow stumbled, then at last looked around before breaking into a run. Twice his sandals skidded on the bracken; he caught himself on the doorpost, then vanished down the hallway bellowing hoarsely.

"*Ouo ehe damnameneus,*" Halphemos said. Rosy tendrils quivered around the lock. A simple bolt closed the cage but the iron plate and narrow bars prevented a prisoner from reaching the fastener.

Everything else within the huge room glowed blue or was in darkness. The lighted wicks were mere points on the lobes of the lamps, but the ice figures themselves gave off a cold radiance.

Footsteps came up the hallway. They didn't appear heavy, but the echoes persisted as though in a long tunnel.

The Elder Romi, a tall man holding a staff of some pale wood in his right hand, entered the banquet hall.

His robe was black with gold embroidery around the neck, hem, and cuffs. His face was lean though not cadaverous, and his hair the purple-tinged black of a grackle's wing. If Ilna had met him as a stranger, she would have guessed his age at thirty or a trifle less.

Romi's eyes were ancient and ageless.

He glanced at Ilna, gave her a nod and a sardonic smile.

He transferred his attention to Baron Robilard, sitting upright at the head of the table. Lady Regowara had stuffed the knuckles of both hands against her mouth. She was biting so hard that a drop of blood ran down the back of her white wrist.

Cotolina murmured to her infants. Apart from her voice and their wailing, the only one in the hall to speak was Halphemos. The youth was going on with his incantation as if unaware of the ancient wizard's presence.

"I've come at your invitation, Baron," Romi said. "Where shall I be seated?"

The voice was the one Ilna had heard in the cave. It still reverberated, though Ilna had noticed that the acoustics of this great square room were wretchedly bad.

Robilard opened his mouth. He made gagging sounds, then vomited onto the table and his own right arm.

Romi smiled. "I'll just take the empty seat, then," he said pleasantly. He walked over to where the tax gatherer had been. One of the ice men moved the chair into place. Romi sat, still holding the staff upright.

"Io churbureth," Halphemos muttered. *"Beroch tiamos!"*

Spikes of rosy light played across the lock plate the way ghost flames sometimes wrapped tree limbs and the eaves of houses in Barca's Hamlet during cold winter nights. The bolt rasped back. The three staples fixing it to the plate cracked one after the other. With the last, the bolt as well fell clanging to the stone floor.

Halphemos reached for the door. Weakness overcame him. He slumped forward, unable even to sit straight after the exertion of the spell he'd cast. Ilna held the youth, supporting his head with her shoulder. The cage was a good enough place to stay for now.

Ice men silently filled the banqueters' cups. Several of the courtiers drank great slurping drafts; others wept or sat as though nailed to their chairs. Lord Hosten deliberately turned and shook his head at the creature miming an offer to top off a cup already full.

Lady Tamana stared at the wizard beside her. One of her hands was on the table; the other touched the breast of her silken dining chemise. Only the rapid flutter of a vein in her throat proved that Tamana was alive and not a statue like those placed in niches around the hall.

An inhuman servitor mopped the vomit from Baron Robilard's hand and sleeve with a napkin from the neat pile on a serving table. Solicitously, the creature then dabbed the baron's lips and mustache with the cloth. Robilard trembled but did not otherwise move.

The cup at the Elder Romi's place was pewter and without ornamentation. To Ilna's taste it was more attractive than the jewels and florid chasing that decorated the cups the courtiers had been given. Romi lifted the vessel; the wine bubbled into vapor, sizzling more like bacon frying than liquid coming to a boil.

Romi turned the cup over so that all could see it was empty. He set it back on the table. "Is this your hospitality, cousin?" he said in his rolling, laughing voice. "We are cousins, didn't you say?"

"Please," Robilard said, his first words since the beginning of the visitation. "Please, I didn't know."

Romi stood with a terrible grace. An ice man removed the chair more smoothly than a human footman could have managed. All eyes were on the wizard.

"I've accepted your invitation, cousin," Romi said. "Now you and your guests will accept mine."

Around the table, creatures of glowing ice withdrew the chairs of Robilard and the others. Some of the courtiers would have fallen except for the ice men's inexorable support.

Romi pointed his staff to the doorway. His narrow mouth smiled with the detached interest of an adult watching the antics of a group of children. The banqueters walked toward the door like a procession of the dead. Their legs moved stiffly; a few were being carried by the ice men on either side. Lord Hosten kept his back straight, but his eyes stared at the neck of the woman ahead of him.

Lady Cotolina hugged the infants to her. She stumbled because she was blind with tears. Every time an ice man touched her to offer help, she shied away with a cry of despair.

The line of figures, human and inhuman, passed out of the banquet hall. The Elder Romi nodded again to Ilna, then turned and followed the others.

Halphemos had recovered enough to raise his head. Ilna shook his hand out of hers and pushed the cage door open. ''Stay here,'' she said, though it probably didn't matter what the boy did.

She stepped out and stretched her limbs. The cage had been tight, but the tension of what she must do next was worse than stiff muscles. Ilna had acted in anger when she carried out Robilard's bidding; a chasm loomed before her if she failed now to correct her actions.

The lamps in the banquet hall had begun to burn normally again. They illuminated the debris—tableware, spilled wine; bits of clothing dropped and forgotten in the exodus.

Ilna glanced behind her. Halphemos was trying to get out of the cage, though his eyes didn't seem to focus yet. She strode out of the hall and up the empty corridor, walking quickly because Romi and his prisoners had moved faster than she had expected.

The procession had already exited the palace. Romi was walking down the last step from the platform. Ilna, standing on the unfinished porch, called, ''Elder Romi! I have a question for you.''

The ice men stopped. The Elder Romi turned deliberately. ''Ask your question, Ilna os-Kenset,'' he said.

''Sir,'' Ilna said. Her tone was clipped and assured. ''What do you fear?''

Romi laughed, a rumbling sound that the sky gave back as thunder. ''I feared nothing when I was alive,'' he said. ''I fear nothing now!''

"Do you fear your own anger and the evil it allows you to do?" Ilna said.

She stepped down toward the wizard. Most of the halted courtiers watched her, though no few remained hunched over their private desperation.

Ilna waved toward the line. "They're not innocent," she said. "None but the babies, perhaps. But you know that they've done nothing to deserve this. Not even—"

Her eyes and the scorn in her voice identified Robilard.

"—that boy!"

The Elder Romi's face twisted in fury. He struck the butt of his staff on the stone-paved roadway. Lightning blasted upward.

The moonless sky had been clear. At the flash clouds boiled up from the four corners of the horizon. Further lightning stabbed between thunderheads, and a downpour like none Ilna had seen before slashed the ground.

None of the rain fell on the figures in front of Robilard's palace. Ilna crossed her arms and met the Elder Romi's hawk-fierce gaze.

Romi laughed and made an absent gesture with his staff. The clouds vanished. The rain stopped with the suddenness of a lightning stroke, though pools of water stood in every hollow except those among the figures.

The icy servitors dissolved like will-o'-the-wisps caught in a sea breeze. Lady Regowara, no longer supported by the figures at her sides, fell to the ground laughing hysterically.

The Elder Romi began to bow. His form thinned to mist, then empty air. His laughing voice, full and strong, boomed, "When I had flesh, Ilna os-Kenset. When I had flesh!"

The echoes lasted a hundred heartbeats. After that Ilna heard only the last of the rain spewing through the gargoyles on the palace roof, and the sobbing joy of courtiers now alone on the road that would have led them to a tomb before their times.

She staggered with relief. There was a sound behind

her. She looked over her shoulder to see Halphemos coming down the steps. His face was drawn, but he seemed to have made an adequate recovery.

The eastern horizon was lighter. The sun would rise soon.

Lady Cotolina, still holding the infants, threw herself on the pavement before Ilna and tried to kiss her feet. Ilna stepped back in angry embarrassment. "Stop that!" she said.

Baron Robilard came forward with Hosten at his side. Robilard put a hand on his wife's shoulder. She cried out, then looked up and saw that the touch was human. Hosten helped her rise, though she refused to let him take one of the babies from her.

Halphemos tried to step between the baron and Ilna. Ilna gestured him back curtly. The youth hesitated, but her glare finally convinced him. Did he think *she* needed protection?

Baron Robilard knelt. "What do you want?" he said. He'd aged a decade in the past hour. "Anything, *anything*."

Before Ilna could speak—she hadn't thought beyond her confrontation with Romi—Robilard went on, "I'm so sorry. I didn't know. I swear by the Lady, I didn't know!"

"It never crossed my mind that you did know," Ilna said. She gave a sniff of amusement.

Ilna looked around while she gathered her thoughts. A few servants reappeared, one of them the nurse. She paused for a moment, then broke into a bovine gallop toward Cotolina and her charges.

"Stand up," Ilna said to the baron sharply. It was worse being knelt to than facing somebody who thought Ilna os-Kenset should kneel to them. "Do you think I like looking at the top of your head?"

The courtiers all watched her and the baron, though for the most part it was from a safe distance. They seemed as much afraid of Ilna as they'd been of the Elder Romi.

Her smile spread. And perhaps the courtiers had as much reason for fear.

Aloud Ilna said, "My companions and I want to go to Valles, Baron. If you can advance us passage money, I would appreciate it. You needn't worry about being repaid, at least—"

Ilna's smile returned.

"—if I survive."

Robilard stood up as she'd directed him to. Ilna noted with amusement that he winced as his knees came off the pavement; perhaps he'd learned a lesson more general than that he shouldn't invent famous ancestors for himself.

"There's no question of you repaying me anything, mistress," he said. His voice strengthened with every word, and he gave no indication of having spent the night drinking. "I—"

He glanced behind himself to include his courtiers.

"—all of us will be in your debt for as long as we live. I can't offer you passage on a merchant vessel, because none will sail to Valles since the troubles there, but—"

"What troubles?" Ilna said, interrupting before she could catch herself. Sudden fear for Cashel—for Cashel and others—drew the question. She knew she should have waited for the baron to finish what he was saying.

"There've been riots," Hosten explained. He'd remained at the baron's side. Cotolina and the nurse sat on a step where they were still trying to quiet the infants. "There's been wizardry and worse. We have agents on all the islands where we do major business, and those on Ornifal have warned us not to risk cargoes until things settle down."

"But of course that won't matter for you," Robilard resumed briskly. "We'll go aboard one of my warships."

He looked at the man beside him. "The *Erne,* I believe, Hosten?"

The courtier nodded. "Her or the *Cormorant,*" he said. "We don't have crews available for both at the moment, though in a few days I can gather something.''

''I'll accompany you, of course,'' Robilard said non-chalantly. ''Now, when would you like to leave?''

Ilna started to protest, then realized she had no cause to. She had wanted to get to Valles as soon as possible. News of the troubles confirmed her intention—and if Robilard thought he owed her his life . . . well, he was right about that.

''The sooner the better,'' Ilna said. She looked at Hal-phemos. ''When can you be ready?''

''Cerix and I have nothing to ready, mistress,'' he said. ''You're the only reason we have even our lives.''

''We'll leave in an hour, then,'' the baron said crisply. ''That is—can we have the crew ready by then, Hosten?''

''The crew will be ready,'' Hosten said with a grim smile. ''Or else I'll find a better use for the cage than the one you made of it, Baron. And we'll be in Valles before sunset.''

He trotted toward the back of the palace, shouting for grooms and a horse.

Garric bumped the jamb as he tried to follow Royhas through the doorway into the king's private apartments. Liane steadied him. Royhas turned with a look of concern and said, ''Are you all right?'' in a sharper tone than perhaps he intended.

''When this is over,'' Garric said, ''I'm going to sleep for a week.''

He chuckled and added, ''That's assuming we aren't sleeping for all eternity, the lot of us.''

Liane winced. She'd come to recognize Garric's new sense of humor. She didn't fully appreciate it, though.

''The only humor there is on a battlefield, lad, is gal-lows humor,'' Carus' voice whispered. ''*Or on a gibbet, I shouldn't wonder, though there I* haven't *been.*''

The four Blood Eagles in the anteroom remained in front of the inner door when Royhas entered; when Garric appeared behind the chancellor they stepped to either side. The watch commander clenched his fist in salute and said, "He's in with the priests again, sir. He said not to let anyone through."

He nodded Garric toward the door in implicit rejection of the king's orders.

Garric knew the Blood Eagles would without hesitation die to protect Valence. Protecting the king no longer meant obeying him when his orders conflicted with the wishes of the real ruler of Valles. He tapped on the burl panel, then pushed down the latch bar before one of those inside tried to wedge it shut.

Garric smiled. He was indeed ruler of Valles and most of Ornifal; and he had a start on ruling the whole Kingdom of the Isles, at least if he survived the next few days. It made herding sheep—stupid, contrary sheep that kept you out in all weather—seem an idyllic existence.

Valence bleated petulantly, "I said no one—" He fell silent when he realized that Garric was responsible for the intrusion. Instead of court robes or the thin silks a nobleman might wear in private apartments, he wore a horsehair tunic that must be almost as uncomfortable as rolling naked in a bed of nettles.

Garric had already dealt with the two religious figures who were closeted with the king. The Arch Hierophant of Ornifal was a seventy-year-old priestess with skin like ivory and eyes of chilled steel. Before her elevation she had founded a healing order which now maintained nearly a hundred hospices across the island. Her companion was director of the temple of the Shepherd Who Maintains Valles. He was a fat man with a mind that let nothing go—and hands similarly able to keep any wealth that they grasped.

"Your Majesty," Garric said, "we have business to discuss with you."

The priests were already leaving the room. The first time Garric had come for an interview with the king, the priests had expected to stay. They'd learned they were wrong.

Valence shook his head despairingly. "Must you?" he said. "You don't understand how important it is that the Lady forgives me!"

Garric felt his lip twitch, but he suppressed the sneer. In the literal sense, Valence was correct: Garric *didn't* think it was important whether the king received forgiveness from the Great Gods. But what Valence really meant was "You don't understand how much evil I've done." That wasn't true at all.

"The restoration of your government is going as well as we could have hoped, sir," Garric said, ignoring the king's whine. "In the west of the island we're receiving more of the queen's councillors under our warrants than I'd like to, but in most cases these are families who've led their vestries for generations. They'll have to be watched, but there isn't a great deal of choice."

Though Valles had accepted the new government, the rest of the island was a more difficult matter. The fact that Waldron and his fellow northern landowners supported Prince Garric was reason enough for the smallholders of the island's south and east to hang back and even threaten to secede from Valles' authority under their own county councils. Valence's signature on the orders Royhas and Tadai drafted did at least as much to keep Ornifal united as the threat of Waldron's army could.

Liane unfolded the legs of the portable desk in which she transported the latest set of documents. It was an intricate piece of cypress cabinetry with bronze fittings, originally the property of her far-traveling father.

Royhas was present to answer questions about details of the documents, not that in the past days Valence had seemed to care about anything beyond his own afterlife. Royhas was the king's longtime friend, but that didn't matter anymore to Valence either.

Garric had to attend the sessions because the Blood Eagles wouldn't admit anyone else against the king's orders, and because Valence would by and large listen to Garric as to no one else.

Garric heard laughter in his mind. *"It doesn't matter which of us gets the credit so long as the job's done,"* his ancestor murmured down the ages.

"If you'll sign—" Liane said, putting the first of the documents on top of the desk.

Valence brought up the leather quirt he'd been concealing behind him and lashed himself across the back. The thongs popped against the stiff black horsehair. "The Beast will eat us all!" he cried.

Garric grabbed the king's wrist with one hand and the quirt with the other. Valence struggled feebly. "The Beast will take me!" he said.

"Stop that!" Garric shouted, flinging the quirt against the wall. He shook Valence without meaning to; when he realized, he let the king go and stepped back.

"Sir!" Garric said in gasping anger. "You need to be a man. Men have died for you!"

Valence shrank to the floor and began sobbing. The three others looked at one another with a mixture of disgust and discomfort.

Royhas shrugged. "There's nothing that can't wait a day," he said quietly. "I'll have a word with the guards so that they inform me when, ah, the time might be more propitious."

Garric turned the desk over and refolded its legs. "I told Tenoctris that I'd find time to take her to the queen's mansion," he said as his mind wrestled with other things.

Valence had been King of the Isles in name and ruler of Ornifal in all truth. Now . . .

Because Garric was dealing with the portable desk, Liane walked to the corner and picked up the quirt. Valence could get another one, of course. Or he could hang himself with the belt of his horsehair tunic if he wanted to, and then where would they be?

Garric followed his companions into the anteroom, closing the beautiful door softly behind him. *Will the same thing happen to me when the strain gets to be too much?* he thought.

"Not until the sun goes black and all the seas dry up!" thundered the voice in his mind. *"And not even then!"*

"Oh!" Cashel said, tossing his quarterstaff vertically and balancing it for a moment on his upright index finger. When it tilted farther than he could allow for, he let it drop and caught it at the balance in his right hand. "Doesn't it feel good to have some room again, Zahag?"

The ape squatted, scratching his ribs with his right hand while his head rotated farther to either side than a human could have managed. The Pandah bireme that had landed them at Valles' outer harbor was already on its way home.

"Room is fine," Zahag said without enthusiasm. "I don't like the feel of this city, though. I think we ought to go someplace else. Fast."

"Oh, it's all right," Cashel said; though the truth was, he felt a sort of overhanging pressure himself when he let himself think about it. Also, his skin prickled. "Anyway, I'm going to have to find work before we can eat. I thought it'd be easy to get a job loading ships till we learn what's where, but . . ."

Compared to the bustle of Erdin and Divers on Pandah, the harbor of Valles was dead though not quite deserted. Less than half the many slips were occupied, and most of the vessels which *were* present looked unserviceable even to the eyes of a landsman like Cashel. There was no cargo on the quays, and the taverns and stalls which sold rough clothing and the trinkets dear to a sailor's heart were mostly shuttered. The business of the evening should have been just getting under way.

"Well, where are we going, then?" the ape asked in a peevish tone. "We didn't have enough to eat on shipboard to keep my ribs apart, and I'm *not* going to miss another meal."

"Then get it for yourself," Cashel growled. He set off

up the nearest street because he figured it was as good a direction as any. He was hungry, too. Now that the first joy of returning to land had passed, he felt the cramps and stiffness from a day's confinement aboard a ship where there wasn't room to turn around.

A trio of middle-aged women came in the opposite direction, each carrying beer in a leather pail. They'd been talking, but they fell silent and slanted to the other side of the street when they saw Cashel and Zahag approaching. Cashel would have asked them about where he could get meals and a place to sleep—to be paid for in the morning—but their suspicious behavior made him bite his tongue.

Things like that made him wonder if he should've left Barca's Hamlet. Of course he'd had to, because Sharina was leaving; but sometimes he wished *she* hadn't had to go. Cashel had been hungry often enough in Barca's Hamlet, and cold, and tired, and he'd been laughed at for being slow. But he'd never wondered where home was until the day he left it.

"Aria would have given you money," Zahag said bitterly.

"Why should she do that?" Cashel said in surprise. "Anyway, Aria didn't have any money. She was Folquin's guest just like we were."

"Right," the ape said, "and he'd have given you his whole treasury if you'd said you'd stay if he didn't. You're about—"

"Zahag," Cashel said in a hoarse rumble.

"Right, chief," the ape said quickly. "Right, I don't know what I was thinking about to talk that way."

A man wearing two tunics layered to show the gilt embroidery—tatty by now—on the inner one had been standing in a door alcove. He stepped forward and said, "Say, buddy. Did I hear that monkey talk?"

"You may have heard the ape speaking, my good man," Zahag said in a tone he didn't use often in Cashel's hearing. "If you did, you noticed his diction was much better than that of a pimp from the docks district.''

''Hey!'' the man said in delight. ''Say, would you like to sell him?''

Zahag bristled, then looked up at Cashel in frightened surmise. Cashel put a hand on the ape's hairy shoulder. ''No,'' he said, ''but I'd like if you could tell me where I could find work, bed, and a meal, sir.''

''Say, for your trained monkey I can find you a bed and somebody to warm you in it!'' the local said. ''I can find a couple somebodies for a gentleman of your discernment and I'll pay you cash to boot. What sort of price were you—''

''No,'' Cashel said. He didn't raise his voice, but he tapped his staff on the pavement so that the ferrule struck sparks. He'd taken ''pimp'' as just an example of the ape's usual bad temper, but apparently Zahag knew more about these things than Cashel did—or wanted to. ''All I want is a place who'll hire me for work. *Honest* work.''

The pimp grimaced and turned away. ''Go to the palace,'' he threw over his shoulder. ''They're hiring strong backs to haul rocks.''

''Sir?'' said Cashel. He didn't know where the palace was. The pimp kept walking away.

''Sir!'' Cashel repeated at a level that rattled shutters. The pimp stumbled, then faced around again.

''How do I find the palace, please?'' Cashel said in his normal voice. At his feet, Zahag slapped his thighs and cackled enthusiastically.

The pimp managed a professionally bright smile. He pointed in the direction Cashel was already going. ''Three blocks up there's a boulevard with a median and statues on it,'' he said. ''That's Monument Avenue. You turn left and keep going till you hit the palace.''

Cashel looked at his hands, frowning in concentration. Zahag plucked the hem of Cashel's tunic. ''I know which way left is,'' the ape said. ''Let's get going. In Pandah, they feed the king's table scraps to beggars at the gate. Maybe they're civilized here too.''

"It wouldn't kill us to miss a meal," Cashel muttered. Still, the idea of food sounded better and better, maybe because Zahag kept on about it. The sun was getting low, so he lengthened his stride to arrive before the king barred his house for the night.

Zahag fell into a four-legged lope. If his knuckles minded the cobblestones, at least it didn't slow him down.

Cashel chuckled. The ape looked up and said, "What do *you* find so funny?" His voice was sour; likely the hard pavement *did* hurt.

"I was thinking the only time I've moved like this," Cashel explained, "was following an ox team to the water after an afternoon's plowing. Anybody who thinks oxen can't move hasn't seen them when the yoke comes off."

"Don't you know any smart animals?" Zahag grumbled.

Traffic increased as Cashel and the ape got away from the harbor. The problems in Valles seemed to have affected sea trade more than they had ordinary life. Though—they passed a number of buildings on Monument Avenue that had been burned out recently. Smoke, and not just clean woodsmoke, tinged the air around them.

"Umm," Zahag said. "People have been dying here. Can't you smell it?"

"Yeah," Cashel said. "I can."

"I told you we ought to go someplace else," the ape muttered. He was so close to Cashel now that his shoulder brushed the youth's calf at every stride.

A large body of troops filled the half of the avenue Cashel was following. They walked faster than the same number of sheep would have, but . . .

When a narrow cross street joined the avenue at the right angle for a sighting, Cashel cocked an eye at the sun. Unless the palace was closer than he had any reason to believe, the troops weren't moving fast enough for his purposes.

"Let's go over," he said to Zahag. The other side of

the avenue was crowded with traffic mostly moving in the opposite direction, but maybe he and the ape could cross back when they'd gotten around the troops. The median itself was choked with peddlers' stalls where there weren't bronze statues on squared stone bases.

Zahag slid beneath a produce cart while Cashel squeezed between it and a flimsy stall from which a shrill-voiced woman sold fried fish on bamboo skewers. As he and the ape pushed into the crowd on the other pavement, Zahag turned his head to view the troops they'd just skirted.

"Hey, look at their livery," the ape said. "They're not from here. Blue and sea-green are the colors of Third Atara. We worked there a week when I was with the kid and the cripple, but the collections barely amounted to our rations. The baron didn't leave any money loose for other people."

Zahag walked on three limbs while he fed himself a banana with the remaining hand. He ate it skin and all, and Cashel guessed it was too late to ask where the fruit had come from.

"I've never been there," Cashel said, because politeness required a response. He'd never heard of the place until this moment. Between the two divisions of soldiers there was a pair of hired litters. A number of men and women on foot walked beside the rich folk being carried. "Looks like it's some nobles, don't you think?"

"Look!" Zahag shrieked. "Look!"

He stopped in the street and began to jump up and down, gabbling in his own language. Anyway, it wasn't any language Cashel had learned.

"What's the matter?" Cashel said in exasperation. It was bad enough fighting traffic that wanted to go the other way. Having folks bump him because he was standing like a post in the roadway was even worse. Maybe the ape had gotten the last of the banana down the wrong pipe and was choking. He sure hadn't been wasting any time eating it.

"The kid and the cripple!" Zahag shouted. "The kid and the cripple!"

Everyone around Cashel and Zahag was now staring either at the talking monkey or the soldiers on the other side of the median. The soldiers and the civilians in the midst of them turned their heads to see what was causing the commotion on the other side of the street.

A legless man rode in one of the litters. Cashel didn't recognize him, but he was pretty sure the youth in a red robe walking alongside was the wizard from Folquin's court when he and Sharina arrived there originally.

The fellow on the other litter was a nobleman, sure enough. He wore a gilded breastplate which must have been uncomfortable, leaning on the cushion like he had to do, and his matching helmet sat on the litter at his feet. The slim woman walking beside him turned her head.

Cashel hadn't recognized her because it hadn't crossed his mind that she was anywhere within a month's journey. He gaped.

"Good evening, brother," Ilna called across the median in a tone of cheerful satisfaction. "I was hoping I'd find you here."

The 4th of Partridge (Later)

Ilna hugged her brother, feeling a terrible sense of loss. She hadn't realized how much she . . .

Well, she hadn't depended on Cashel because Ilna didn't depend on anyone but herself; but how much she'd grown up *expecting* the presence of Cashel's calm strength. Having him back made her aware of what she'd missed.

Having him back temporarily. Ilna didn't suppose

Cashel's life would lead him to Erdin, where she'd decided her own duties lay.

Halphemos and Cerix were talking to their monkey. The bearers had lowered Cerix's litter to the pavement. Halphemos and the monkey squatted alongside; the monkey scratched his belly with a hind foot. The three displayed the wariness of separated associates who each think the others may have reason to reproach them.

Robilard had gotten out of his litter. At the dock he'd tried to hire a third vehicle for Ilna, but she'd refused it contemptuously. The baron would probably have dismissed his own litter then, except for a justified fear that Ilna would scorn him as indecisive as well as a pampered fop.

She smiled slightly. Robilard wasn't a bad fellow, for a noble. Someday he might grow up to be a man.

Cashel looked at Halphemos. He asked, "Did that wizard tell you how Sharina's doing?"

Ilna shook her head. "They were separated just after you left Pandah," she said. "Now that I've found you, we can look for her. One thing at a time."

She cleared her throat. "I was wondering what you might have heard about Tenoctris and . . . and the others."

"Nothing," Cashel said, shaking his head. "The last I saw, they were being swallowed down by . . ."

He shrugged. "By whatever it was that ate the ship," he went on. "A storm, I thought, but that fellow Halphemos said it was something else."

The troops accompanying Robilard were oarsmen equipped with helmets, javelins, and short, curved swords. They were trained for sea fights, not as heavy infantry, but they still formed a barrier that civilian traffic, no matter how angry, couldn't push aside. For the moment the men waited for their commanders to make up their minds. Judging from their nonchalant demeanor, it wasn't a new experience.

Lord Hosten had marched at the head of the column because he knew Valles. Now he led a middle-aged civilian back through the ranks. "This is Master Talur, our agent for the port and the southern districts, Baron," he said to Robilard.

Talur, whose complexion seemed darker than usual in Valles, bowed to the baron. "I didn't expect to see you, milord," he said. "Ah—things are quite unsettled now, to be frank. I might almost wish you hadn't chosen this moment to visit."

The agent wore layered tunics cinched by a broad silk sash and covered with a short cape embroidered in geometric designs. Ilna knew the garb was in the latest Valles style, but she was sure she heard a touch of a Haft accent in the man's voice. The thought gave her an unexpected twinge.

"A matter of honor brought me here," Robilard said stiffly.

"But we're interested in the local situation so that we can avoid needless danger," Hosten put in. When he saw his young master start to frown, he quickly added, "Consistently with honor, of course. Obviously we want to spare Mistress Ilna from unnecessary risks while she's under our protection."

Ilna felt a smile tug the corners of her mouth. She didn't imagine her opinion of humanity as a whole would ever change, but in the course of her travels she'd met a surprising number of individuals she could respect. Lord Hosten was one of them.

"Yes, of course," Talur said, noticeably relieved. "The riots that expelled the queen are over, but there's rumors of Admiral Nitker invading Valles with the Royal Fleet and also that the queen plans to retake the city by wizardry."

"But these are only rumors?" the baron said. "Certainly I was treated courteously when we docked. Not as a potential enemy."

"Rumors," Talur agreed, "but very credible rumors, both of them. Still, the new government has the city in a posture of defense, and as for wizardry—well, they ousted the queen to begin with.''

He looked around reflexively, then added, ''And not before time. If she hadn't been stopped—''

He turned his hands palms-up.

''Yes, well, none of this changes our plans,'' Robilard said. ''I have to pay my respects to King Valence, of course, and then I'll see if he can help me locate the friends for whom Mistress Ilna here is looking.''

He nodded to introduce Ilna to the agent. Ilna found herself frowning; she knew the baron was trying to help, which rubbed her the wrong way. What prevented Ilna from objecting aloud was her knowledge that Robilard's access to the king might well help locate Tenoctris and Liane . . . and Garric . . . faster than Ilna and her wizard companions could do unaided.

''And we'll want to discuss quartering the crew, sir,'' Hosten added.

''Yes, of course,'' the baron agreed. ''It would scarcely be courteous to march into Valles and put up a hundred armed men in the local inns without informing King Valence.''

''We'll be in sight of the palace when we pass the temple of the Lady of the Boundaries,'' Talur said, nodding agreeably but with a slight frown. ''That's just ahead, as you see.''

He nodded toward the squat, sandstone building with pillars on the sides as well as along the stepped front face. ''But you'll probably be treating with representatives of the new government. Valence remains king, but he's delegated many of the duties of office to his heir presumptive, Prince Garric.''

Ilna didn't speak. She felt the threads of the pattern coming together, but the human part of her couldn't accept what was so much to her desire.

Cashel didn't have any such hesitation. ''Garric?'' he said. ''Garric or-Reise from Barca's Hamlet, is that who you mean?''

Talur turned to look at Cashel for the first time. He said, "Prince Garric was Garric bor-Haft before his elevation. That's what the palace clerks put around, anyway, though I'll admit my concerns were more what his elevation meant in the future than where the gentleman came from."

"Is he with an old lady named Tenoctris?" Cashel continued. "And a girl named Liane os-Benlo? She's near as pretty as Sharina."

Ilna winced at her brother's delight and certainty. Both of Kenset's children saw things in simple patterns, but Ilna could only look from a distance on the sunlit beauty of Cashel's world. She saw clearer than her brother did, of that she was sure; but sometimes Ilna thought it would be a relief occasionally to lose sight of the truth in happy illusions like Cashel's.

"Why yes," Talur said in amazement. "Do you *know* Prince Garric, good sir?"

"We used to," Ilna said decisively. "We were on our way to the palace anyway, and—"

She smiled, half in self-mockery. "—I think we should get on with our business."

"Mannor was Earl of Sandrakkan when Vales the Fifth was King of the Isles . . .," Liane said as she repinned Garric's brown cape closer at the neck than he had. "He used to go out at night in disguise along with his chancellor to learn what his subjects really thought about his rule."

The two of them stood with Tenoctris in a groundskeeper's hut near the main gate of the palace. The compound had a dozen lesser entrances, postern gates as well as spots where the wall had crumbled or been dug away by servants who wanted a quiet route for their own purposes, but so long as Garric was disguised there was no reason not to use the formal one. Tenoctris was too frail to pull herself up a rope to a tree branch, after all.

"That was the story he told for an excuse," said Garric. "I'll bet what he was really doing was hiding so that he could get a meal or a few hours of uninterrupted sleep, which he knew wasn't going to happen so long as there was anybody who knew where to find him."

Liane stepped back and surveyed Garric's appearance, critically but with final approval. She smiled and said, "A young drover from Haft, sightseeing in Valles after bringing a selection of blood stock to Ornifal."

Liane's expression grew more somber. "Are you sure you're up to this, Garric?" she said. "You look awfully tired."

Tenoctris was going through a case of powders: minerals, herbs, and animal products as well, all ground to the finest dust and segregated within copper-mounted containers made from the tips of cattle horns. She looked up and said, "Garric, someone else could—"

"I don't trust someone else!" Garric said. He blushed. He really was close to the edge when he let his temper out that way.

"I'm sorry," he said. "Anyway, that isn't really true about me not trusting a couple Blood Eagles to tend you just as well as I could, Tenoctris. The truth is, I just need to get away and feel that I'm doing something instead of—"

Garric's smile spread. "Instead of talking to people about maybe something being done by somebody, someday," he went on. "Which I know—"

His left hand tapped the coronation medallion on his chest in ironic salute to the king in his mind.

"—is really important and I'm not going to stop doing it. But I'm not going to do *only* that, because I'll start babbling and dance naked in the street. I need to get away from being king once and a while."

"Come back safe," Liane said with a smile that didn't fully conceal the real concern behind it. She'd never argued against Garric and Tenoctris going out unescorted, but she'd wanted to go with them as the three of them had done in the past.

"We'll do that," Garric said. He hung Tenoctris' satchel over his left shoulder and offered her that arm for support. His right hand remained free—just in case.

Things were different in the past. Now someone in the palace had to know where Prince Garric was in case a real crisis occurred. Liane was the only person Garric could trust to summon him from the queen's mansion if it *was* a real crisis, but not to disturb him simply because an envoy from Blaise had arrived or a northern landholder had rolled a royal justiciar in a manure pile before expelling him from his domains.

They walked toward the gate, though Liane let herself fall behind the other two. There was always a bustle at the entrance. The business of government required staff and supplies, including the staff's food and drink. Besides that mundane traffic, more people than Garric could have imagined—though Carus, laughing, had warned him—wanted royal justice or royal monopolies or royal appointments.

At Liane's suggestion, both Tadai and Royhas had provided clerks to screen visitors: the jealousy between the households made it unlikely that a would-be office-seeker would succeed in bribing his way to access. A detachment of Blood Eagles guaranteed that those refused entry took no for an answer.

Besides people trying to enter the palace on business, there were any number of folk who were simply spectators. They in turn attracted small-scale entrepreneurs whose barrows sold everything from meat pies to silver amulets in the shape of the winged monster on which the queen had made her escape (an infallible remedy against violence and defeat in lawsuits, according to the hawker). A woman as lovely as Liane got attention. If Garric was at her side, he was likely to be recognized.

The sun had fallen below the horizon, though the sky still brightly silhouetted the compound's western wall and the tallest of the buildings beyond. The gates were open, as usual; servants had just finished hanging oil lamps from brackets on either door valve so that the entrance clerks had light to work by.

There was more than the usual commotion in the street, though. All twenty Blood Eagles were on their feet. As Garric neared the gate, the officer in command sent a runner back for instructions from higher authorities.

Just outside the gates stood a large body of troops. They'd forced their way through the normal crowd of idlers, but the men in civilian clothes at their head were speaking politely to the commander of the guard detachment. The foreign troops were escorting dignitaries who waited in their litters for the underlings on both sides to reach a conclusion.

"They're from Third Atara," Liane said. When Garric slowed to take in the situation before getting involved in it, she'd come up beside him again. "See the seahorse and the blue borders on their tabards?"

"I saw them," Garric said, "but they didn't mean anything to me."

Reise had given his children an excellent education in the classics, but he hadn't bothered to teach them the details of current precedence and politics. He'd known them, certainly. Reise had been an official in the king's palace and later at the court of the Count and Countess of Haft. Such matters weren't part of a general grounding for life as Reise saw it, and they had no bearing on running an inn in Barca's Hamlet.

The commander of the guard detachment, an undercaptain named Besimon, noticed and recognized Garric standing nearby. The fellow's lips tightened in frustration, but he didn't call out and uncover the incognito prince.

It wasn't fair to leave Besimon in a situation obviously above his rank, however. "I've got to take care of this," Garric muttered as he stepped forward. He wasn't surprised that Tenoctris and Liane followed him, the older woman leaning on the arm of the younger.

"I've asked that the chancellor come to the gate, ah, sir," Besimon said, giving Garric another chance to conceal his identity if he wanted to. The undercaptain was in his early thirties, a younger son from a noble family in the north of Ornifal. "The Baron of Third Atara has arrived with some guests who claim to know Prince Garric."

"Garric!" Cashel boomed. He pushed his way to through the intervening soldiers like an ox plowing under stubble in late fall. "Oh, I thought I'd maybe never see you again!"

Garric hugged his friend, cocking his head sideways so that the quarterstaff in Cashel's hand didn't rap him alongside the ear. It was a measure of Garric's own sturdiness that Cashel's full-hearted delight didn't completely crush out his breath. Cashel knew his own strength, but when he was excited he sometimes overvalued the strength of other people.

"We didn't see you in the Gulf!" Garric said, shouting because of his own joy and the babble of other voices. "I was afraid . . ."

He didn't say what he'd been afraid of. Garric hadn't let himself think about what had happened to Cashel and Sharina until this moment when—

When he knew Cashel wasn't a drowned corpse whose flesh was bloated and whose features had been nibbled away by fish. That was the image that had flashed behind Garric's eyes every time he looked at the sea since the moment he'd awakened on the muddy shore of the Gulf.

Other figures were working their way through the avenue Cashel had cleared. "And Sharina's all right?" Garric said, stepping back and leaning sideways to see past his friend's massive form. He saw a woman's slim form, streaked by the shadows which the high-mounted lanterns threw across it. "Shar—"

Garric's delight stuck in his throat. "Ilna!" he said, trying to recover and seeing Ilna wince at the obvious falseness of his reaction.

He stepped toward her. She flinched away. Garric put his arms around Ilna and picked her up, despite her struggling.

"Ilna, I thought you were safe in Erdin," Garric said. He felt her relax; Garric wasn't as strong as Cashel, but in his father's stables he'd brought refractory horses to their knees with bare hands and a grip on their bridles. "I was worried about Sharina, but I never knew you were in danger yourself."

He set her down. Ilna tilted her face up to look at him. She tried to force a smile.

"Cashel's safe, and you are," she said. She tugged a cord from her sleeve and began knotting it to keep her hands occupied. "We'll find Sharina, Garric. We'll find her."

From somebody else it would have sounded like a pious hope. From Ilna the words were much more.

A young man in travel-stained red brocade wriggled rather than pushed his way to Ilna's side. He stood with his hands behind his back, glaring at Garric. Garric didn't remember ever having seen the fellow before.

Ilna noticed Garric's bemused glance. She turned, saw the youth, and said, "Garric, Master Halphemos here and his friend Master Cerix are wizards. They saved my life and came with me to rescue Cashel at great cost to themselves."

She gave Garric her familiar wry smile. "Cashel didn't need much rescuing, but that doesn't affect the price Halphemos and Cerix have paid."

Garric bowed to the young wizard. He'd have offered to clasp hands, but a glint in Halphemos' eyes suggested he just might have refused. Garric didn't need that kind of awkwardness, especially not right now.

"Anyone who's helped Ilna is a friend of mine," Garric said. He couldn't imagine what Halphemos had against him. Did the fellow think he'd deliberately left Ilna behind?

"Your Majesty?" Liane murmured at Garric's side. He

understood why she thought she should be formal in public, but it was so contrary to the easy relationships of Barca's Hamlet that each "Your Majesty" from a friend felt to Garric like a slap on the cheek. "Another location might . . . ?"

"Yes, of course," said Garric. He'd known that too, but he couldn't find the place to say so when his friends had arrived. He surveyed the milling crowd.

Royhas and a pair of senior aides were coming up the flagstones, preceded by the runner Besimon had sent to summon them. The chancellor was still cinching his cloth-of-gold sash over the beige court robe he'd thrown on when the message arrived.

Outside the gate with the soldiers, a young man with gilded armor waited stiffly in company with the older aide who'd handled the initial discussions with Besimon. His plumed helmet was under his arm. "Ah—" Garric said to the young man.

"Baron Robilard," Liane muttered in his ear. Either she'd known the ruler of Third Atara from when she'd been in school in Valles in past years, or—more likely—she'd memorized the names and stylings of the Isles' potentates as part of her current duties.

"Baron Robilard," Garric said, "my chancellor Royhas bor-Bolliman will see to you and your men."

He nodded toward Royhas. The chancellor was already opening a wax tablet on which to jot orders to stewards and quartering officers. "I hope at some time of greater leisure—"

Garric's smile was disarmingly politic, but it was an honest expression also.

"—which could have been almost any moment of my life before the past week, you'll let me honor you as you deserve for your kindness to my friends."

"Brave beyond doubt," King Carus said in cold assessment. *"Not really stupid either, though that won't keep his kind from acting like fools. He's too hag-ridden by honor to take good advice unless it's honey-glazed."*

The civilian dressed in Valles style leaned close and whispered into Robilard's ear. The baron's eyes widened. He bowed low, bobbling the helmet which he'd almost dropped in his surprise. "Your Majesty!" he said as he straightened. "I had no idea!"

Garric remembered he wore an unadorned cape with a simple, sturdy tunic under it. "Yes, I was off on private business," he said. The Lady knew what Robilard would make of that, but the varied possibilities would prevent him from pursuing the matter. "But if I may suggest, my friends and I will adjourn to my quarters while Chancellor Royhas attends to my honored guests from Third Atara!"

Zahag climbed up Cashel's side, planting his feet on the youth's left hipbone and wrapping a long arm around his shoulders to hold himself in place. "What're you doing?" Cashel said. He didn't mind the burden, but it surprised him.

"I'm not staying here without you, chief," the ape said. "I told you, there's something hanging over this place and I'm not going to face it alone!"

Ilna prodded Cashel in the ribs. "Get Cerix," she said, nodding to the cripple, who'd just loaded himself onto the wheeled chair that had shared the litter with him. The soldiers watched but didn't get involved one way or the other. They didn't have orders to, Cashel supposed.

"My sister told me to help you, Master Cerix," Cashel said politely, transferring the quarterstaff to his left hand. Zahag was holding on for himself, after all.

Cashel bent and reached over the wheeled chair, lifting it and the man together. Cerix snarled "Put me down!" but he didn't struggle. That might have tipped him headfirst onto the pavement.

Waddling a little from the weight of ape and man together, Cashel started through the gate. His sister gave him a look of disgust and said, "You're bragging. You don't have anything to prove to this lot."

"Well . . ." said Cashel. Women—females, better—didn't always see the world the way males did.

"You!" said Ilna, fixing Zahag with her eyes. "Get down immediately. Carry the chair while my brother brings Cerix."

It didn't really surprise Cashel that the ape hopped to the ground and gripped the little vehicle in both hands. Cerix held Cashel's shoulder for a moment while Cashel shifted his arm to support the legless man as a mother would an infant.

The Blood Eagles within the gate closed ranks when Ilna followed Zahag and Cashel into the compound. The fellow Garric had called his chancellor was talking to the baron who'd brought Ilna here.

Garric's chancellor; *Prince* Garric. Cashel shook his head in wonder.

Zahag walked with a rolling gait, holding the chair high over his head. It looked comical, but the ape wasn't putting on a show deliberately. His short legs just didn't work the way a man's did.

Garric and Liane guided the party into what looked from the outside like a flat-roofed windowless building. Within there was a colonnade around an open court where purple and white pansies were planted in the pattern of an eagle. Lamps hung in shades of colored paper.

Cashel looked around. Tenoctris was talking to Halphemos. If she'd seen anything in the young wizard to worry her, she'd have been polite but wouldn't have chatted in such friendly fashion. Halphemos must be all right.

Zahag set the chair on the terrazzo pavement, then caught the gutter with one hand. He swung onto the inward-sloping tile roof. Besides the ape and Ilna's two wizards, it was just Garric and people he'd known in Barca's Hamlet present. None of the soldiers and officials bustling about the grounds had followed them inside.

"I can't get used to all these people being up after sunset," Cashel said, shaking his head. He'd seen the same thing in Erdin but it still felt wrong to him, as if they all sat on the ceiling instead of the floor. "It's not as though they have sheep in the open to watch, after all."

"That's very much what we do have to do, Cashel," Tenoctris said with the familiar quick turn of her head and quick smile. "Or what comes with the darkness will be worse than ever wolves were."

"Sorry," Cashel muttered, feeling silly. He couldn't get his head around the notion that so many people were working on the same thing. Working *together*.

"I don't know how much you've heard about what's happening in Valles," Garric said to the whole group. Cashel noticed that though Garric didn't rest his left hand on the pommel of his sword, he hooked that thumb in familiar fashion over the belt beside the scabbard. "The queen is a wizard and very evil."

"Consciously evil," Tenoctris said. "When the forces increase the way they have in these days, a careless wizard can do harm without meaning to. The queen isn't careless, and she's done a great deal of harm."

"We drove her out of Valles," Garric continued, "but we expect her to come back. And there's another. . . ."

He looked at Tenoctris. "Is he a wizard?" Garric asked. "The Beast, I mean."

"No," said Tenoctris. "The Beast is . . ." She too paused. Very carefully she went on, "The Beast was worshipped as a god in another time and place."

Garric nodded. "Valence—or anyway, the wizard Silyon, who served Valence—summoned the Beast. Tenoctris is trying to find a way to send him, it, back. Before that we have to deal with the queen. She and I were going to the queen's mansion tonight to see if we could get closer to that."

"I know about the Beast," Cashel said. He did, but it still surprised him to be talking about something of that sort here in Valles when he'd just arrived. "I even know about Silyon, I think. At least I met his sister Silya."

"And *she's* not going to be tricking anybody else the way she tried with the chief," Zahag said from the roof.

The ape squatted over the tile pipe that led down into a ceramic pond. Little fish glittered in the lamplight.

"That's right," said Cashel, trying to remember exactly what Silya had said about her brother. "He's got a stone that he stole from her to talk with the Beast."

Tenoctris looked at Cashel sharply. "Does he indeed?" she said. "Is it—"

She turned to Garric with another quick motion. When they'd entered this miniature courtyard, Tenoctris took the satchel of scale-patterned leather that Garric had been carrying, apparently for her. Now it lay on her lap. "Garric?" she said. "Can I talk with Cashel aside? There are things he may know that could help me, but I don't want to take over the discussion when there's so much else to explain."

Garric grimaced. "There's too many things to say and do," he said, "and all at the same time. I don't want to keep you from searching the queen's mansion, but I don't see how I can go with you tonight."

"I'll go with Tenoctris," Cashel said. He caught himself in sudden embarrassment. "Unless it's something that, you know, somebody has to read. If it's just carrying the bag, though, I can do that."

Tenoctris looked from Garric to Cashel. "It's more than just carrying my materials," she said with a growing smile, "but it's nothing you can't do for me, Cashel. If things go in the particular fashion I think they might, I would be very glad of your strength beside me."

Everyone looked at Garric. He blushed, though his deep tan would have made that hard to tell in this light for anybody who didn't know him well. "I don't give orders to Cashel," he said. "I don't give orders to any of you. You're—"

Garric turned his face toward Halphemos. "You're my friends," he said. "All of you, I hope. This is a time that the kingdom needs friends, and I need friends especially."

Halphemos looked at the ground in embarrassment. He nodded fierce agreement.

"We can go now if you like, Tenoctris," Cashel said. He checked the satchel's buckles, then lifted it to his shoulder. It was pretty heavy; too heavy for Tenoctris, certainly.

Zahag dropped to the ground. He didn't speak but he bared his teeth slightly as he looked around, obviously daring anyone to tell him that he couldn't come too. Cashel rubbed the ape's bristly scalp with a knuckle to reassure him.

Liane had been writing with a brush on a thin beechwood board. "I'll tell Maurunus to prepare rooms for our new arrivals," she explained as she stepped to the door.

Liane thrust the door open, her mouth open to call for a runner to take the chit she'd just composed. A group of agitated men led by Royhas stood just outside. The chancellor had already raised his baton of gold-capped ivory to rap on the door panel.

"Your Majesty?" said Royhas, looking past Liane to Garric. "I've summoned Attaper and Waldron, but I'm afraid I have to interrupt you as well."

The group with Royhas included civilians in court robes and four Blood Eagles. The soldiers guarded not the chancellor but a man wearing an ornate jeweled cuirass over a tunic of gold-embroidered silk. His scabbard was decorated like his armor, but the sword had been removed before the guards brought him into Garric's presence.

"Admiral Nitker has arrived with the three surviving ships of the Royal Fleet," Royhas continued. He spoke with a stony lack of inflexion to cover what Cashel suspected was disgust. "The crews are understrength, the officer of the harbor watch informs me. The good admiral appears to have lost half the men on the few ships he saved."

"Do you think you could have done better?" Nitker snarled. He was nearer forty than thirty, though it was hard to tell with nobles. Besides, the terror on his face had aged him considerably. "You couldn't, and you'll learn that quick enough if you try to make a stand here!

The only reason I came to Valles was to give you a chance to get out in the next few hours.''

''If that's the only reason you came here, the oarsmen on your ships don't need to eat or sleep,'' said the stern-faced man in gilded armor who'd just arrived from deeper within the palace compound. The newcomer gave Cashel a look that stiffened the youth slightly; not precisely hostile, but appraising in a fashion that Cashel understood very well. ''It's surprising that such paragons didn't sweep all opposition before them.''

Nitker flushed and groped at his empty scabbard as he turned. Two of the guards grabbed his elbows and bent his arms back.

''Enough!'' Garric said in a crackling voice. ''Lord Attaper, I didn't want to fight the admiral before, and I *certainly* don't think it's a useful occupation now. Can we agree on that?''

The hard-bitten soldier lost all expression for an instant. He bowed. ''I apologize, Your Majesty. I've gotten . . . lax in the past few years.'' He straightened and went on, ''And I apologize to you also, Lord Nitker. We need your information about the threat and your strength to help us meet it.''

Cashel eyed Garric with new interest. He'd always respected his friend, but he'd never guessed Garric could snap a fellow like this Attaper to attention with a command. Break Attaper's head with a quarterstaff, maybe, though that wouldn't be the easiest thing in the world either. Cashel smiled and slid his hand down his own polished hickory.

''You can't meet it, I tell you!'' the admiral blurted. Cashel judged him to be somewhere between tears and a tantrum, utterly undone. ''There's hundreds of thousands of them, all the monkey men on the island of Bight, and they're floating down on Ornifal on a raft. They'll kill everybody in Valles. They'll *eat* everybody in Valles, I tell you!''

''They're not monkeys!'' Zahag said. ''And they're not

apes either; *if* any of you know what either one is.''

Cashel tapped his shoulder, not hard but enough to remind the ape of his manners. ''Ah,'' Zahag said. ''Sorry.''

Garric glanced at Tenoctris and raised an eyebrow. The old wizard nodded. ''That could be,'' she said.

''The Hairy Men of Bight . . . ,'' she went on, focusing for a moment on her memories. ''They've been used for wizardry often enough because they *are* men, but there isn't so much concern about what happens to them as there is when children start disappearing from the neighboring villages.''

She smiled without humor. ''Wizardry of a sort I don't practice, obviously,'' she said. ''To direct large numbers of Hairy Men would require a great deal of power. Even more than raising an army from the undead or the neverliving.''

''Power which the queen has?'' Garric said. He sounded interested but not concerned; the tip of his index finger traced the three rounded tiers of his sword's pommel.

''Yes,'' Tenoctris said. ''It appears that she does.''

Garric shrugged. ''Well, we knew we'd have a fight,'' he said. ''Lord Attaper, get all the details you can from the admiral here. Weapons, numbers—''

He grinned bleakly.

''Which are considerable, I gather. Tactics, command, supplies, the usual things. I'll direct Waldron to put the city militia on alert. Right now, I think, I'd best visit the Arsenal and tell Pior that the Duke of Eshkol—''

He smiled again. The smile came from the Garric Cashel had grown up with, but this talk of armies and tactics was as unlikely as it would be if Garric floated off the ground.

''—has returned with his fleet to the royal service, so it's time for the regular army to do the same.''

Cashel glanced at his friend's feet. They were solidly planted—and his sandals were the sturdy, simple affairs that a youth from Barca's Hamlet wore in the winter or on a long journey. Cashel grinned.

"You're not listening to me!" Nitker said. "You can't fight these beasts! In a few hours or a day at most they'll be landing on the shore of Ornifal and killing everyone they meet. All you can do is run!"

"I've listened to you, Lord Nitker," Garric said in a voice that could have come from the outer dark. "I just don't agree."

He smiled and went on, "We couldn't get all the people of so large a city out in time, and we have the walls and some organization here. That might help."

"You can't run from evil," Ilna said without emotion. She was knotting and unknotting the length of cord, but her eyes rested most often on Liane. "You can't run from yourself."

"Attaper, Admiral?" Garric said. "I think we'd better go to the Arsenal together."

He frowned. "Do you suppose I ought to throw on something that glitters more, or will Pior listen to sense from a brown cloak?"

"If he listens to sense at all, we're luckier than I expect," Attaper said in a grim tone. "I'll rouse a couple regiments of Waldron's men while you change, Your Majesty. It's worth adding a threat to the scales at this point. Since the fool may not believe in the *real* threat."

"Tenoctris?" Cashel said. "Do you still . . . ?"

"More than ever," Tenoctris said, rising from the couch where she'd been sitting during the discussions. "There's so dazzlingly much power layered over the queen's mansion that I'm having difficulty finding the stratum that I need."

Her smile was bright, though her eyes were pinched with concern. "And there's very little time, Cashel. For us, and for the Isles."

* * *

The queen raised her staff of clear crystal. She smiled at Sharina, then said ''*Eidoneia neoieka!*'' and struck it on the floor. Red fire pulsed through the staff. Something unseen shattered.

Sharina stood in a ruby sphere. Beyond the walls was mist in which only her fancy formed images. The queen stood beside her.

The concave surface of the floor tilted them toward each other. Sharina tried to move aside, up the wall's curve.

''Don't move!'' the queen said. She touched the floor again. There was a crackling sound. She walked around Sharina, drawing a circle less than four feet in diameter. The staff's tip left a line across the ruby the way a knife scribes cheese. The wizard was on the other side of the line.

The queen began writing characters in the Old Script around the inner margin of the circle. ''Where are we now?'' Sharina asked.

''Don't speak until I tell you to,'' the queen said coldly.

Sharina laughed. She wasn't so much resigned to what was happening as detached from it. Though her fingers touched the Pewle knife, she knew that she couldn't harm the queen. If the angry queen killed *her,* then Sharina didn't have to worry whether or not helping the wizard was the right decision.

She looked around her but found little of interest. The sphere in which they stood was perhaps twenty feet in diameter, though it was hard to be sure. The luster of the polished ruby walls reflected the figures within it as a myriad of diminishing images.

''Where does the light come from?'' Sharina said. If the ruby itself glowed, there shouldn't be reflections on the walls . . . or so she thought. There was no source of light within the sphere, of that she was sure.

The queen looked at her. Sharina said, ''I told you I'd help. I didn't say I'd be your dog.''

The queen resumed marking the ruby. The rise of the

walls made her movements awkward but she didn't slip on the smooth surface. Sharina couldn't see the queen's feet because the flowing robe concealed them.

Some of the reflected images were of Sharina and a figure that could not have been human, no matter how distorted. Sharina's lips tightened.

The queen had finished writing around the inner circle. Now she resumed the circuit, this time writing outside the line. Each time the staff touched, flashes subtly different in hue from the ruby walls spat within the crystal.

Sharina started to mouth one of the syllables. The queen flicked the staff upward and tapped the girl's chin. A chill greater than what lay at the heart of the Ice Capes froze Sharina's lips and tongue.

"Don't," the queen said. "Not because I care what might happen to you, but because I want to avoid the effort of reanimating your corpse to speak my incantation. But I will do that if I must, girl. Believe me!"

She lowered the staff. Feeling returned to Sharina's mouth. The underside of her chin prickled as though from frostbite.

The queen completed the words of power in the second ring. She looked at Sharina with lips quivering in the semblance of a smile.

Sharina faced the wizard expressionlessly, as Nonnus would have done—had done—in similar crises. The queen could kill her and perhaps could do worse things, unguessibly worse things; but she couldn't make Sharina show fear.

"I will read the words of the outer circuit," the queen said. A catch in her honeyed voice suggested that Sharina's refusal to quail irritated her. "I may have to read them a number of times to reach the result I desire. When I finish, you will read the words within. The scene beyond us will become a vision of an ancestor of yours—"

The queen's smile was terrible, even to Sharina in her present detached state.

"—or mine, at the moment of conception."

The staff in the queen's hand tilted as if moving of its own volition. The tip rapped the wall at eye height. There was no spark within the crystal, nor did the contact mark the ruby surface.

"We will repeat this until we have reached the time of King Lorcan, who founded your line and the Kingdom of the Isles," the queen said. "As though human reigns could matter! Then your task will be complete."

Her cold smile became mincing. "I may well spare you."

"King Lorcan and his wizard ally hid the Throne of Malkar," Sharina said calmly. "You think you'll gain the throne through me."

It was a joy in Sharina's heart to see a flash of bestial fury replace the wizard's sneering smile. "Don't speak of things you don't understand, girl!" the queen said. "Or I'll cut your belly open and force your dead lips to speak the words I desire!"

Sharina crossed her arms as if facing a child. She was fearful, about what the queen might do to Cashel and about what she herself was doing to prevent harm to her friend. Her face was as cold and unmoved as the sharp steel blade of her Pewle knife.

How much did the queen understand? Not as much as she thought she did, of that Sharina was certain. Because the queen had great power, she thought she had great wisdom. The wisdom Sharina had learned from Tenoctris was that there are powers so great that to use them is to destroy oneself. If the queen did reach the Throne of Malkar, the focus of all evil, she doomed herself.

"Ousiri aphi mene phri," the queen said. She paced slowly around the circle, her steps sure despite the slanting, slippery surface. *"Katoi, house . . ."*

Nothing but brief shapes of mist appeared beyond the ruby walls. Sharina looked at her own feet and the words of power she would read when the time came.

"Bachuch bachachuch bazachuch," the queen said,

though the sound seemed to come from the walls themselves. *"Bachazachuch bachaxichuch . . ."*

Sharina tried to think of the Lady, but the rippling tentacles of a great ammonite filled her mind instead. She stood, silent and stern. The fear that filled her heart had no echo on her face.

The 5th of Partridge

Sharina didn't know how much time had passed. Her mental numbness was not far removed from the stasis which had held her after the demon snatched her into the queen's power. The wizard's voice droned like water plashing over black stones. Perhaps it was hypnotizing her.

Because of Sharina's state, her mind didn't process the gradual change in the world outside the ruby walls until well after her eyes had registered the differences. She snapped alert; her skin flickered hot, then cold, and seemed to crawl as though she'd just awakened from a faint.

The walls had vanished, but a red cast like the light thrown off by the queen's staff infused the world on which Sharina looked. Leaves trembled around a clearing in the jungles of Bight. Branches had begun to rise after the heavy rainstorm which had beaten them down.

A figure leaped into sight: a Hairy Man, an adult female whose pelt gleamed with the sheen of good health. She shrieked in mindless terror as she poised to fling herself into the foliage on the other side of the clearing. Startled flies whirled upward from the fruit rotting beneath a giant durian tree.

Her pursuer caught her with the sudden finality of a

praying mantis snatching its victim. The motion was so quick that Sharina saw the hunter only at the instant it struck.

The pursuer was a demon: roughly human in shape, but taller than the tallest man and as thin as the wire armature on which the sculptor shapes the clay of his mold. Steam spouted where the demon's taloned feet stood straddled on the damp soil; hair singed from the victim's arms where fingers like knives gripped them. The female cried out with the despair of one to whom death would be a release from corroding terror.

The demon's lower jaw dropped on a double joint instead of hinging open at the back the way a human's would have. Its teeth were like chipped flint; they slid past one another like shears.

A stream of blue-white flame spewed from the demon's mouth, booming like a waterfall against the base of a dawn redwood. The tree's spongy bark exploded in steam and charred fragments. The victim's cries were lost in the thunder of destruction. The hose of fire ceased when the demon's mouth clamped shut, but the tree continued to crackle and hiss.

The demon's eyes glowed a red brighter than any other light in the jungle's gloom. It shifted its grip on its victim. From a groin which until then had been as sexless as the crotch of a tree the demon's penis extended and entered the female.

She stopped struggling. The rape had frozen her the way a wasp's sting paralyzes the spiders on which her offspring will feed.

The demon stepped back from its huddled victim. Its—*his*—member withdrew completely within the snake-thin abdomen. The demon's jaws opened and loosed another fiery lance of triumph, this time immolating a branch thirty feet in the air. Mosses and epiphytes rooted on the bark blazed in red horror, scattering carbonized leaves and tiny animals killed with painless abruptness.

At no time did the demon make a sound of its own,

though its flame roared deafeningly. Life in the forest went silent, then chittered and squeaked at redoubled volume when the first wisps of smoke rose to the higher levels.

The demon's skin grew dull. The creature began to dissolve: no part clearly before the next, yet not all at once. For a moment the demon's eyes blazed from what might have been the rippling of heated air; then they too had vanished.

The victim lifted herself from the wet soil. Welts were rising on her forearms, and the fur on her haunches still smoldered.

Sharina felt sick. She said nothing, nor did she look toward the queen gloating triumphantly outside the circle.

Limping, the victim turned back the way from which she'd come. Another Hairy Man, then several, entered the clearing. They clucked questioningly at the female but jumped angrily away when she tried to embrace them.

The scene faded slowly.

Instead of resuming her chant or telling Sharina to begin the second portion of the incantation, the queen tapped her staff. From the mist congealed the interior of a spacious room.

Sharina and her captor hung in midair. The room had no windows but both end walls were open, looking out over a city where the eaves swept up like ships' prows. The moonlit roofs were made of palm fronds instead of the grass thatching common on houses in Barca's Hamlet.

Fixed to the walls were long, saw-toothed swords and shields with gold blazons worked into snarling beast heads. Twenty feet above the floor a small windmill bracketed to the central beam turned in the breeze through the long room. On each vane was writing that Sharina recognized as the script local to Sirimat, though she couldn't translate or even pronounce the words.

In a miniature hammock draped with purple silk hung an infant. A nurse, the room's only other occupant, sat cross-legged beside the hammock, swinging it gently by a short cord gripped in the toes of her left foot. She hummed a repetitive tune, pausing frequently to take another bite of leaf-wrapped nut or to spit red juice into the street below.

She turned toward the opening, her lips pursed. The air between her and the sleeping city coalesced like ice forming on the surface of a pond. A demon with a bundle in its arms hunched forward.

The nurse cried out, dropping the remainder of her narcotic. She jumped up. The hammock flailed, rousing shrieks from the baby.

The demon extended its right leg the way a scorpion probes with its pincers. Its hooked hind toe opposed the other three like the talons of a bird. The foot closed over the nurse and squeezed shut. Her scream ended in a startled hiccup of sound as the claws cut her in half at the midriff.

The demon stepped to the hammock with the delicacy of a spider approaching something trapped in its web. It lifted out the infant with one clawed hand, carefully shaking the swaddling clothes from the tiny form. The rich fabrics were soaked with the nurse's blood.

The demon set the child-thing it had brought into the hammock. The human infant in its other hand continued to squeal. The demon's mouth opened. It thrust the infant into its great gape, then closed the jagged teeth around it. The cries stopped.

Men carrying bamboo bows and swords like the ones on the walls ran into the room from the balconies along both sides. The demon grinned at them, then dissolved as it had in the forest of Bight. Sword strokes and black-tipped arrows slashed the air where the creature had been.

The tiny changeling's face was first a demon's, then that of a Hairy Man. When terrified guards bent over the hammock, though, and a man dressed in the feathers of exotic birds rushed in with his aides to see what had happened, the face that looked up at them was that of a perfectly formed human child.

The baby cried for a moment more, then smiled at the men who thought they had rescued her. She was very beautiful.

"My father," the queen said. "The demon Xochial."

She tapped her staff. The scene melted into shadows and swirling mist. "Now, girl," she said, fixing Sharina with her cold eyes. "It's your turn."

Tenoctris finished chanting. She wavered sideways but caught herself before Cashel could. The corkscrew of blue light at the center of the small circle she'd scribed here deep in the cellars of the queen's palace shrank to a point. It vanished, leaving only a memory behind.

" 'Is the sun proud or the moon?' " Zahag muttered. " 'Even a poor man's hut is better than living among the ragged clouds.' "

Cashel's lips tightened. Tenoctris had said the ape was quoting poetry he'd heard in Pandah. It wasn't much for poetry, Cashel thought; and it kept reminding him that the ape was on the edge of breaking down completely. Cashel didn't blame Zahag for being afraid, but he wished the ape had stayed back with Garric if he was going to mumble nonsense.

"Do we move again?" Cashel asked, mostly to make sure that Tenoctris was really awake. She leaned on her outstretched hands, gasping quick, shallow breaths.

" 'Rise early, work hard, and think often of your soul . . . ,' " Zahag said. Cashel's jaw clenched again.

"No, no," the old wizard said. Her smile warmed and brightened both Cashel's mood and the black walls of the cellars. "We're in the right place, and I think I've even found the key. I apologize for wasting so much of my time and yours, though."

"Huh!" Cashel said. "I don't have a better place to be than with you, mistress. And I'm not one myself to rush around doing things fast instead of doing them right."

He cleared his throat. "What is it you need me to do?"

he asked. His duties thus far through the night and morning had been a lot like herding sheep: keeping an eye out while his charges went about their business slowly.

Cashel didn't know what he should be looking out *for,* but he knew there was something close by. His skin prickled, and the unseen eyes watching were hostile beyond reason; hostile to all life, not just to Cashel or-Kenset and his companions.

" 'If you can snatch a jewel from the seawolf's teeth,' " Zahag said. " 'If you can swim the Outer Sea in a tempest—' "

Cashel reached out. The ape cringed, expecting a blow. Cashel rubbed the beast's scalp instead. "It's all right to be scared, Zahag," he said. "But Tenoctris knows what she's doing."

The old wizard grinned. She was so worn that Cashel marveled that the lamplight didn't stream through her like a patch of fog.

"I think I do, yes," she said. "It remains to be seen whether I have the strength to do it, but—"

Her smile broadened. "I have to, don't I?"

Cashel smiled back at her. He liked people who didn't quit. Tenoctris, well; Tenoctris wouldn't quit till she was dead.

Tenoctris took a deep breath and settled herself straighter. "There's a path that leads to the queen," she said. "If the queen can be—dealt with, distracted even, she'll lose control over the Hairy Men. They'll no longer be a threat, even if they do reach Ornifal."

Tenoctris' tone was calm though not nonchalant: she spoke as a master craftsman explaining an apprentice's duties in a fashion that he could understand. "I'll open the path and I hope to keep it open, but you'll have to walk it alone, Cashel."

"Not alone!" Zahag shrieked. "Not alone! Not alone! I'll not be alone in this place!"

Cashel looked at Tenoctris. She nodded. "If Zahag wants to accompany you," she said, "there's no reason he shouldn't. But I don't think he understands—''

''I understand that I'm not going to be alone!'' the ape said. ''Not in this hellpit, not anywhere on this island. Can't you feel it? Don't you know what's waiting out there?''

''Yes,'' said Tenoctris quietly. ''I do.''

Cashel shrugged. ''I'd like to get on with it, then,'' he said. He tried not to sound impatient, but when you knew a fight was coming it was the hardest thing in the world to wait for. He hefted his quarterstaff, giving it a final critical examination by lamplight.

''The caps are iron, aren't they?'' Tenoctris said with a frown. ''That may be useful, if you're strong enough.''

Cashel looked at her. ''Guess we'll learn, won't we?'' he said. His voice was a low growl. ''Let's get on with it!''

''Yes,'' the old wizard said. She took a fresh bamboo skewer from the bundle in her satchel and settled herself before the circle she'd drawn in the dust. ''I will.''

'' 'You still can't change the mind of a born fool,' '' the ape quoted, squeezing tightly against Cashel's bare calf. He was shivering. Cashel rubbed his scalp again.

Poor little monkey . . . But he wasn't giving up either.

''*Ochusoioio nuchie narae, eaeaa . . .*'' Tenoctris said, touching her bamboo wand to a different character with every syllable. Her voice was as calm as a deep pond, but her face writhed with the effort of pronouncing the words of power. ''*Aritho skirbeu!*''

The basalt walls dimmed. Cashel could still see them as shadows at the corners of his eyes, but a bright web of forces filled the vision of his mind. The pattern spread without boundaries. Lines of red and blue light met, sometimes joining but often filling the same apparent space without contact.

Tenoctris continued to chant. The pattern throbbed in unison with the words of power.

What Cashel saw was as beautiful and as terrible as the constellations of the night sky. He stood in awe, but even in his wonder he wished that Ilna could watch it also. What would she make of this pattern that was so far beyond her brother's grasp?

In front of Cashel was a tube of red light, one strand of the infinite web. At a distance the lines of power seemed as thin as spider silk, but the opening here in the palace cellars was the size of the inlet to the ancient tide-powered mill owned now by Cashel's uncle. A man could walk upright into it—if he was a man.

Cashel stepped forward. His hair stood on end and blue fire crackled as his foot touched the insubstantial surface. He laughed deep in his throat and walked on. Zahag, gibbering in terror and refusing to look into the shrinking distance before them, scampered at his side.

From outside the tube had seemed to rise into the distance, but once within Cashel felt only the pressure of the light on him. It was like wading through deep water.

He grinned. He'd done that, carrying a flood-snatched ewe on his back besides.

Cashel couldn't see any end to the passage ahead of them. When curiosity drove him to glance over his shoulder, he couldn't make out Tenoctris stolidly chanting in the cellars either.

"We can't go back now," Zahag muttered in resignation. "It's too late for that."

"I just wondered what it looked like," Cashel said. "I didn't want to go back."

The ape wrinkled his long, solemn-looking face. "No, you wouldn't," he said. "That's why you're the chief. And anyway, we have to go on or there won't be anything left."

Cashel looked at him, but Zahag apparently had nothing to add as he ambled along on all four limbs, looking at the smooth floor of light. Occasionally his lips moved, but he was only mumbling another snatch of verse.

Cashel stretched his arms out to his sides, then bent them back to work other muscles as well. He wondered what they'd find at the end of the passage.

"I guess we'll know soon enough," he repeated aloud.

"Sooner than that, chief," Zahag said, lucid again. "Much too soon for *my* taste."

Ilna supposed you could say that there were more important things for her to be doing than cleaning the rooms the steward had assigned her, but nobody thus far had told her what those things were. She didn't intend to spend another night in a pigsty unless she heard a very good reason for it.

The royal palace was a sprawl of individual buildings, more all told as there were houses in Barca's Hamlet. The women's quarters were in the eastern corner of the compound, separated from the remainder by a wall faced with tiles glazed in a garden scene. For all practical purposes this section had been unoccupied in the years since the queen built her own mansion in the center of Valles.

It irritated Ilna that the steward automatically chose to put her, Liane, and she supposed Tenoctris here simply because of the words "the Women's Quarters." She didn't suppose buildings elsewhere within the palace walls were in better condition than this one, though. The attendant who'd led Ilna to this three-room cottage was a member of Chancellor Royhas' personal household. She'd been drafted to help out because virtually all the royal servants had deserted Valence during the lowering threats of the past year.

Ilna swept briskly, sending the last of the dust and cobwebs out the cottage's open door. It was a good rye-straw broom, not a twig besom like those some folks in Barca's Hamlet used because they were sturdier and lasted longer. Not Ilna, of course.

She'd kept the broom and sent the servant girl on her way. Ilna had never found a servant who worked to Ilna os-Kenset's standards; and besides, she didn't like the feeling of someone else doing her work.

She gave the outer room, a combination of anteroom

and reception area, a final inspection. She'd swept it, beaten dust out of the cushions, and removed the moth-tattered hangings from the walls.

It was a crime what people allowed to happen to skillful craftsmanship! One of the tapestries, an ancient hero setting out from the harbor of Valles, was work that Ilna would have been proud to have woven herself.

Well, it could be repaired. Ilna walked into the bedroom. Moths had been at the cover of the feather bed as well, but that didn't disturb Ilna particularly. The loose feathers would take some hunting down, but for sleeping she much preferred a mattress of woven straw or simply the bare wooden floor where she'd spent the past night.

There was a sound from outside. Ilna turned. Admiral Nitker and half a dozen other men entered through the open front door.

"Yes?" Ilna said, leaning her broom against the wall. A full-length mirror of silvered bronze stood between piers to the side of the door. In it she looked coldly furious.

That was true enough. Ilna didn't know what Nitker thought his business was, but in Barca's Hamlet you didn't enter someone else's dwelling uninvited.

The admiral had changed clothes since Ilna saw him the night before. He no longer wore armor, but there was a sword of simple pattern in his scabbard. Five of the men with him were obvious sailors—tattooed, weather-beaten, and in two cases missing fingers. They also were armed.

That didn't concern Ilna. She wasn't afraid of the weapons or of anything else about the intruders.

The seventh man was a Dalopan: small, swarthy—darker even than Ilna's own Haft complexion—and wearing sheaves of carefully splintered bones through his earlobes. If he'd been an insect, Ilna would have crushed him without a moment's thought.

She reached into the sleeve of her tunic and brought out several short cords. Her fingers began to knot them while her eyes glared at her visitors.

"Mistress Ilna," Nitker said, bowing to her. "Master Silyon—"

He gestured to the Dalopan. The five common sailors had spread out to either side of the doorway, though they weren't for the moment moving toward Ilna.

"—believes you can help us. He was King Valence's wizard until the current troubles transpired and the king turned against him. Silyon came to me because I understood how serious the danger was. Silyon's found the power which alone can defeat the queen. Material weapons are useless, *useless*."

One of the sailors began to shiver. He nodded fiercely when the admiral repeated "useless."

"That's nothing to me," Ilna said in the tone she'd have used to a man propositioning her for sex. "Talk to Garric—*Prince* Garric, that is, to you. And if Valence turned against the dirt that's standing beside you leering, then he wasn't quite the despicable wretch I'd heard he'd become. I've seen wizards' games, and I have no desire to see more."

Silyon cackled merrily. Ilna doubted that the fellow was sane, though she didn't suppose it mattered now. Her fingers wove the cords.

"You don't understand, mistress," Nitker said. His tongue licked his dry lips. The admiral was if anything more frightened than he'd been when Ilna saw him arrive the night before, though at present he held a civilized veneer over the fear. "Prince Garric still thinks swords can—"

"I've never met a man that a sword *couldn't* kill," Ilna said sharply. "Or a monkey either, I daresay. So long as there's a man wielding the sword, that is. Which may be why you failed so miserably."

"Get her," Nitker ordered in a grim voice. The sailors started forward. Ilna threw the knotted cords in the air before them.

The men screamed and fell back, trying to draw the swords they hadn't thought they needed. Ilna stepped to the wall peg where she'd hung her silken noose. She took it down, watching the scene with a bleak smile.

The cords fell to the floor. In the mirror Ilna saw what the men saw: an ammonite whose coiled shell filled the room. Its tentacles writhed about Nitker and his sailors, threatening to draw them into its gaping beak.

Silyon alone ignored the illusion. He edged into a corner to keep from being trampled by the screaming sailors. He was no more willing to close with Ilna herself than the men who'd accompanied him could face the monster they imagined.

"Turn around!" Silyon cried in a high-pitched voice. "Don't look at her!"

Liane walked in the front door. "Ilna?" she said. "Are you—"

"Run, Liane!" Ilna said. In the same shard of time Silyon shrieked, "Take that woman instead. Quickly! The Beast—"

A sailor, already turning to flee the ammonite of his fancy, grabbed Liane by the shoulders. He gasped and doubled up, but two more sailors and the admiral himself had Liane's arms before she could break free.

A sailor twisted the bloody stiletto out of Liane's hand. The girl bit him. Another sailor clouted her across the forehead with the hilt of his cutlass.

Ilna settled her noose over Nitker's neck and pulled hard. The admiral flopped backward, clutching the rope. Ilna braced a foot on Nitker's chest. Her victim's face turned purple.

Four sailors were bundling Liane out the door, wrapped in a long shawl they must have brought for the purpose. The last man was on his knees, weeping in terror as he tried to stuff coils of intestine back through the slit in his belly. The engraved blade of Liane's dagger was no longer than a girl's finger—but that was long enough, and it was as sharp as remorse.

Ilna eyed Silyon, weighing her options. The Dalopan wizard threw a pinch of dust toward the mirror. The metal surface flashed with the silent brilliance of the sun, blinding Ilna.

She lurched backward into a wall; she'd lost her sense of balance with her sight. She closed her eyes—too late! She hadn't expected that attack. Orange and purple blotches danced in her mind.

Ilna heard Silyon and the sailors escaping through the overgrown gardens that separated the structures within the palace compound. The man Liane knifed had collapsed and was wheezing bubbles in his pooling blood. Nitker had ceased to struggle.

Ilna slipped the noose free and stepped forward. She could make out shapes again, though their outlines flip-flopped orange to purple and back every time her heart beat.

"Guards!" she shouted from the doorway. "Guards!"

Figures were running toward her. She ran the noose through her fingers, making sure that neither blood nor vomit had gummed its easy action.

"Mistress?" said a young male voice she didn't recognize. "What's the matter?"

There were three of them, carrying spears. Most of the troops who'd ordinarily be guarding the palace were off training and stiffening the city militias against the threat drifting down on the currents of the Inner Sea.

"Did you see five men run away carrying a woman in a cloth?" Ilna said, furious at her inability to see clearly. She didn't even know which direction the wizard and his minions had gone.

"Mistress?" the guard repeated. The men were still only forms, though Ilna was beginning to contrast the gleam of armor from the duller blur of their faces.

"Take me to Garric at once!" Ilna said. "I can't see, so you'll have to guide me."

A gasp from the cottage reminded her of Nitker. She supposed it was a good thing that he'd survived to explain the attack, though for her own part Ilna wouldn't have lost any sleep if she'd killed the admiral as she'd intended to do.

She gestured behind her. "Take that one, too. Garric will want to question him. And *don't* let him get away!"

Two soldiers entered the cottage while the third took Ilna's hand.

Garric wasn't going to like what Ilna had to tell him. She touched her waist. The sash she'd woven as a twin to Liane's was still in place. Ilna guessed that she'd shortly be able to make up for the unjust hostility she'd shown toward Liane from the beginning.

She smiled. She'd either help Liane escape from the present danger, or she'd die. Either result would cancel the debt Ilna felt she owed the girl.

Garric rested his hand on Ilna's shoulder. He'd put it there to support his friend while a healer applied ointment to her eyes, but now it was Garric himself who needed the contact.

"The Beast is the only one who can defeat the queen's forces," Admiral Nitker said in a rasping whisper. "Silyon said he could raise the Beast through his mirror of art, but the Beast won't help unless . . ."

Nitker subsided, coughing. Ilna's noose had left a bleeding purple welt the full circuit of his neck. The healer had given Nitker a draft of effervescent salts in wine to gargle before the man could speak, but the swelling flesh still threatened to finish the job that the silk had begun.

The healer held a ceramic bowl in which he'd mixed more of his potion. He looked at Garric. Garric shook his head curtly.

"Talk," Garric said, "or there's no reason for you to live further. If you pretend again that you can't go on, I'll kill you with my own hand."

The voice and words were his. King Carus nodded

grimly at the edges of Garric's awareness, but the cold anger Garric felt was a thing of his own.

"The Beast must be fed," Nitker whispered. "Silyon said we should bring the woman Ilna to the Beast's vault, but she raised a monster against us. When the other girl came to the door, I suppose Silyon decided she'd be better than nothing."

"Why?" said Ilna. "Why me?"

Her eyes were red and the sockets glistened with the ointment, but she could see again. Garric wouldn't have wanted Ilna looking at him the way she did the admiral; but then, Garric's own expression was much the same.

Halphemos and the crippled Cerix entered the conference room. The courier Garric had sent for them at Ilna's direction bowed himself out and closed the door.

"I don't know," Nitker said, huddling with his hands clasped in his lap. "And I don't know where the vault was. I'm not a wizard!"

He isn't a man, either, Garric thought with a cold bitterness. Though Nitker must have had courage at one time, or he'd not have claimed the throne when Valence had virtually abdicated.

The door opened for Royhas. To Garric's surprise, King Valence was with the chancellor. The king walked with the small steps of man twice his real age. Two worried-looking attendants followed, ready to catch him if he fell.

"I thought His Majesty should be present," Royhas said. "He's . . . for the most part, he's himself again."

"The Beast is coming," Valence said quietly. Everyone in the room was watching him. "It'll be over soon."

"One way or another, it may," Garric said softly. "Your Majesty, do you know where Silyon would have gone with—"

His tongue wanted to choke on the words, but he forced them out without a pause.

"—the sacrifice?"

"To an underground chamber in the palace of the Tyrants of Valles," Valence said. "Attaper knows the place; most of the Blood Eagles do, I suppose. I took them there often enough."

The king wore a tunic decorated only by simple embroidery at the sleeves and neckline. There were neither food stains nor other signs of his recent degradation. "That's where the Beast will enter our world, Silyon told me."

"Right," said Garric, rising from the seat he'd forced himself to take. He drew his sword a finger's breadth, then let it slide back; just making sure it was free in its sheath. "I'll take a few Blood Eagles and be back as soon as I can."

"He'll already have lowered her to the Beast, Prince Garric," Valence said with the simple clarity of a man who has accepted his end and no longer feels the concerns that rack the living. "Once in the vault, she won't be able to return. Nothing can leave that prison until the Beast itself breaks through the walls that hold it."

Garric clasped his hands. He'd sent for Tenoctris, but he knew it would be at least an hour before she could arrive from the queen's mansion. As great as Garric's need for advice from a wizard he could trust, he knew also that Tenoctris had chosen to deal with the queen first and only then to face the Beast.

Ilna had unbound her sash. She threw it on the floor in the middle of the gathering. To Garric's surprise, the fabric began to unravel. The twisting fibers looked almost like—

"Those are words in the Old Script!" Garric said.

"Cerix," Ilna said in the cold calm of her anger. "Does this mean anything to you?"

The cripple bent closer in his chair. He licked his lips and said, "Mistress, I believe it's the first phrase of the Yellow King's Key, a spell of opening. But . . ."

Ilna balled the fabric in her hands and flung it down again. "And this?" she said as the wool writhed into a different pattern.

"Yes, the next phrase," Cerix said. The pain that twisted his face now was not that of physical agony from his missing legs. "Those two portions are all that remains of the Key. But mistress, even if you can form the whole sequence, there's no wizard alive who can chant it out."

Cerix slammed his fists on the stumps of his legs. He was crying. "I'll fail!" he said. "I'll fail, no matter how much I want to help!"

"If you can write the words for me, Cerix," Halphemos said quietly, "I'll speak them. As we've always done."

"Alos, even for you!" Cerix said in a tone of desperate grief. "No one since the Yellow King could chant this spell, and he was a myth!"

The younger wizard looked at Ilna. "This is what you want, mistress?" he said.

"Yes," Ilna said. "It is."

Halphemos nodded. To Garric he said, "We'll need a carriage for Cerix. I have my athame."

He gestured with the knife of ivory he held in his hand. "Cerix, will I need anything else?"

"More strength than I believe you have, Alos," the cripple said. "I wish I could believe in the Gods."

"Right," said Garric. "Let's—"

"Garric," Royhas said. He didn't raise his voice. "*Prince*. You have an army to command and a country to rule. Leave this business for others."

"I didn't stop being a man when you made me a prince!" Garric said.

Royhas didn't flinch. "You know that I'm right," he said. He stood in front of the door. Garric could push past him—or cut him down!—but the chancellor wasn't going to move of his own volition.

And Garric knew that he wouldn't be so angry if he didn't in his heart agree with Royhas.

"You think I'm letting everything else go because I care about Liane," he said. "All right, I do care about her! But you're all looking at what the queen may do, and

I'll tell you, the Beast Silyon called up is as great a danger. You know *that,* Royhas!''

No one spoke. The image of King Carus, grim as a granite crag, watched from the edges of Garric's mind. This time Carus offered no advice. There were some decisions a king—

With a leap of understanding in his heart, Garric turned to Valence. ''Your Majesty,'' he said, ''your people face a great danger. Go out and lead them. You'll have the best of generals and advisors, but they can't be king.''

Valence looked at Garric with eyes that were a century old. ''Me?'' he said musingly. ''I've never been king, not really.''

''I don't believe that's true,'' Garric said, hearing his tone grow hard though not harsh. ''And even if it were, Your Majesty—this would be a good time to start. Your people *need* you.''

Valence turned to the man at his side. ''Royhas, you'll help me?'' he said. ''I always trusted you, you know.''

''You can still trust me, Your Majesty,'' the chancellor said quietly. ''We'll get you into your regalia. Having you to encourage the troops is better than another ten thousand men on the walls!''

They started from the audience room arm in arm; as friends rather than sick man and attendant. Royhas turned his head and gave Garric a quick nod of appreciation.

He really was the king's friend, Garric realized. A better friend than any toady could have been. Even though at the end Royhas had been willing to replace Valence in order to preserve the kingdom.

Garric looked at the others who waited for him to act. His mouth quirked in a smile. ''Let's go, then,'' he said. ''The sooner we start, the sooner we'll—''

He laughed, checking his sword again by a reflex not originally his own.

''—finish, whatever that means, right?'' Garric said, completing the thought.

In his mind, King Carus joined in Garric's laughter.

* * *

"*Allasan,*" Sharina said. It was the third time she'd spoken the words of the incantation; each iteration grew harder. She felt as though her mouth were full of dry pebbles. "*Eomaltha beth iopa kerbeth. . . .*"

She noticed that the fierce chill was gone and her skin felt warm again. The light changed, shifting from red to blue as though a gossamer screen had dropped and been replaced by one of a different color.

Sharina and the queen watched a moonlit garden, facing the front of a free-standing loggia. At either end of the structure, stone nymphs played in a fountain whose waters spilled into channels among the beds of azaleas.

On the loggia's bench a richly dressed couple made love.

The shadowed figures were anonymous. Cut in the roof molding was a ring on a shield, the coats of arms of the ancient royal line of Haft. Beside it, easily distinguishable because the carving was fresh in decorations otherwise softened by lichen, was the narwhal of the bor-Nallials, an Ornifal noble house.

The couple gasped and moved apart. Both were fully clothed. The woman smoothed the front of her gown while the man laced up the fly of the horseman's breeches he wore with a short jerkin. Embroidery and appliqués of metallic fabrics ornamented the garments of both.

Night-flying insects buzzed among the plantings. Occasionally a bat swooped through them, its staggering flight obviously different from a bird's.

The man turned, looked around cautiously, and walked from the loggia. Sharina recognized him from the miniature portrait she'd long ago found among her mother's belongings: he was Niard bor-Nallial, Count of Haft by his marriage to the Countess Tera. He had been killed eighteen years before in the riots during which Sharina's parents had fled Carcosa.

Niard strode away without looking back. For some time

only the insects and the breeze-ruffled blossoms moved in the night. After a safe interval the woman stepped out of the loggia and walked in the opposite direction.

Sharina's breath caught. The woman was a maid from Countess Tera's household, not the countess herself.

The woman with Count Niard was Sharina's mother, Lora.

The queen was apparently ignorant of the real meaning of what she had just displayed. She smiled at Sharina and flicked her crystal staff, melting the idyllic scene into one of chaos. Sharina's heart was cold.

A midwife wearing the black apron of her profession attended Lora on piled straw in the stableyard of a palace. Men armed with a mixture of weapons and household implements—knives, turning spits, and table legs broken off for clubs—streamed past the open gate. Some carried torches; flames gleamed already in many of the palace windows.

Lora thrust with a great cry. The midwife eased the child halfway through the birth canal. Lora gave a final contraction and slumped back in the straw, gasping as the midwife cut and knotted the umbilical cord.

A mule waited, its eyes bandaged. The animal was harnessed to a two-wheeled cart like those couriers used on the western side of Haft where the roads were better than anything near Barca's Hamlet. Shouting and the smell of smoke made the mule restive despite being blindfolded.

A man came from the palace carrying a bundle wrapped in silk brocade. The midwife bleated in fear, then relaxed when light from the burning building fell across his face.

Sharina recognized the man also, though not so quickly as she had Lora. The intervening years had worn hard on the visage of Reise or-Laver, the man Sharina had always thought was her father.

The midwife had wrapped Lora's child in fine wool. Reise handed the woman his bundle, another newborn infant. He bent and helped the barely conscious Lora first to her feet, then into the cart.

The vehicle had a narrow bench and, behind it, a basket for the courier to place letters and parcels. Now it was filled with straw. Reise took the infants from the midwife and tucked them into the basket one at a time. Lora moaned and clutched herself, swaying on the seat.

Reise handed the midwife a coin; moonlight winked on gold. He walked to the front and tugged awkwardly on the reins to guide the blindfolded mule. It obeyed, though nervously. As the cart passed into the riot-torn street, the infant swaddled in rich damask kicked away its coverings.

The queen's art provided diamond-sharp observation. In the firelight there could be no doubt at all that the child Reise had brought from within the palace was male.

The vision faded into mist. Sharina faced the queen. For a moment the wizard's visage was one of human rage; then it changed and the queen's whole form changed, becoming a demon consumed by demonic fury.

"You're not of the royal line!" the demon cried in a voice like grease burning. "Your brother is the descendant of King Lorcan, not you!"

It was like staring into a lightning bolt. Sharina said nothing, waiting for the anger to blast her to dust.

The queen and the red sphere vanished. Sharina stood in the chamber where she had first been imprisoned. Now she was able to move. Beyond the slitted windows was a landscape of smooth, featureless red.

Sharina tried to squeeze through a window. Her slender body fit between the edges of stone, but a barrier as hard as polished ruby stopped her there. She pushed until her muscles trembled and spots danced in front of her eyes; then she sank back on the floor of her cell.

Somewhere Sharina heard chanting.

The 5th of Partridge (Later)

Besimon, the officer in charge of the guard detachment and Garric's guide to the entrance of the Beast's lair, reined up his horse beside the one remaining pillar of a decorative arch and looked angrily to right and left. "We didn't come in the daylight," he explained apologetically. "I need to . . ."

Two Blood Eagles rode with Garric and Besimon; two more accompanied the carriage thundering close behind with the rest of the party. Garric had decided he neither needed nor wanted more guards.

"*This* way," Besimon decided, pointing his bare blade to the right. He wheeled his horse down a tree-grown avenue. On either side were fallen columns and architraves whose carvings were too weathered for Garric to be quite sure of their subject.

They came out in a court originally surrounded by a circular portico which had collapsed to a line of column bases and fluted stone barrels nestled into the undergrowth. Silyon knelt beside a well curb more ancient than the neighboring ruins. The sailors who'd helped him had fled, perhaps even before they heard horsemen approaching.

A teardrop of green volcanic glass hung from a silver tripod. Silyon wailed to it, "Great Beast, master of this world and all worlds, accept the offering we made you. Strike the queen your enemy—"

Laughter, three-voiced and so loud it seemed to fill the sky, rocked the clearing. The obsidian bead danced to the hellish merriment.

"—and her bestial minions!" Silyon shrieked. He didn't notice the horsemen's arrival.

Garric slipped from his saddle. The small buckler strapped to his back bounced against his kidneys; he should have cinched it tighter. He let his nervous mount scamper off because there was no time to tether it.

Garric grasped Silyon by the shoulder and pulled him to his feet. The tripod fell over on the grass.

"Where's Liane?" Garric shouted, though he already knew. A rope attached to a fallen cornice led to the well curb, where it had been freshly severed.

"Accept our offering!" Silyon cried. Cackling, he toppled backward on the ground. "Accept—"

Besimon ran his sword through Silyon's upper chest, then slashed the wizard's throat to the spine for good measure. "I should have done that a year ago," he muttered as he wiped his blade on Silyon's tunic.

Garric looked over the well curb. He didn't know what he expected to see: rough stonework and darkness, he supposed.

Liane was fifty feet below. At her side was the sash Ilna had woven her, now a tangle of threads. Marks on the well curb showed where ropes had rubbed in the past, but there was no sign below of the burdens they had lowered.

Liane and the stone floor on which she stood were illuminated by pulsing orange-red light. She turned her head as though trying to catch the source of a sound or to focus on motion caught in the corner of her eyes.

"Liane!" Garric called. She didn't look up. Liane's fingers were tented together before her so that she at least appeared composed.

The carriage swung to a crashing stop behind Garric. The iron tire of its right front wheel had powdered a weathered marble transom. Garric turned, Ilna jumped off the vehicle as quickly as the two Blood Eagles. The younger wizard was helping his crippled fellow out of the box while the driver fought the reins of his four horses.

The team was trained for roads rather than overgrown tracks through the forest, but more than that made them nervous. A lowering evil hung over this place.

"Bring the line," Garric said to Besimon. He checked the laces attaching his scabbard to the sword belt, then pulled the end of the shield strap so that the round of iron-bound birch wouldn't flop no matter how he twisted in his descent. "Liane's there, and I'm going down."

A soldier tossed his officer the coil of rope from the carriage. Besimon belayed the free end to a column barrel, then carried the coil to the well. "I'll lead, Your Majesty," he said.

"No," Garric said, "you won't. I'll go down alone while you and your men guard the rope and my friends here while they chant their spell."

He took the line from Besimon and dropped it over the curb. It writhed as though alive, trailing its way down.

"The three of us have to be inside the chamber if we're to open it for you to get out," Cerix said. "Alos, Mistress Ilna, and I."

Halphemos supported Cerix's right arm, a soldier the other. They'd walked Cerix forward with his stumps dangling in the air. The chair's small wheels would have been useless on this overgrown terrain.

"All of you?" Garric said, looking at the assortment doubtfully. "I thought you could—"

He shrugged. "Work out here, the way Silyon did."

Cerix smiled grimly as the men carrying him set him down. "I wonder precisely what we *would* open if we spoke the Yellow King's Key here?" he said musingly. "Not the vault of the Beast, I'm sure; though very likely the result for the world would be equally bad."

A spasm of pain racked Cerix's visage. Garric's eyes narrowed as he considered the cripple's state.

"There's nothing wrong with my arms!" Cerix said sharply.

Ilna toed the dead wizard's face so that she could look at him squarely. She sniffed. "I wonder how many women made this trip before me?'' she asked. ''Well, perhaps I'll be the last.''

''Right,'' Garric said. He raised the line and looped it around his left boot, holding it in place with the toe of the other foot. The leather of his instep would take most of the friction of the descent.

He swung his legs over the well curb and started down. It didn't surprise him that Ilna insisted on coming next.

Garric's sword swung. The shield, though it was now firm against his rib cage, changed Garric's center of balance so that he hung in an almost horizontal posture. Garric's helmet was a simple cup with a camail of iron rings to cover the back of his neck. Halfway down it fell off.

Garric's first thought was a surge of relief that he was rid of the uncomfortable burden; and after he thought about it, he couldn't see much to quarrel with his first reaction. He grinned. King Carus, bare-headed in Garric's mind save for the golden diadem, laughed. *''Sometimes things work out better than common sense'd let them, lad,''* the king from long ago said.

Though Garric didn't hear a clang, the helmet must have hit near Liane. She was staring upward when the sway of Garric's body next let him look toward her. She'd shaded her eyes with a hand but she didn't appear to see him, even though he was no more than twenty feet above her by that time.

The rope didn't reach quite to the floor of the cavern. Garric dangled at arm's length. If escape were merely a matter of climbing a rope, he could toss Liane high enough to grab the dangling end.

He smiled. Yes, and then perhaps the queen would appear and beg forgiveness of her husband King Valence. That would certainly simplify matters, wouldn't it?

Garric let himself drop the last few feet. His boots hit the stone floor. Liane turned with a gasp, seeing Garric for the first time.

And Garric saw their prison.

They were in a domed cavern vaster than anything that

could exist so near to Valles. The walls were of dense igneous rock, not the limestone of surface outcrops in the grounds of the ruined palace. A fiery glow blasted up from a sunken moat here only a few paces from Garric and Liane. In the opposite direction the band of light followed the curve of the walls into the unguessable distance.

Liane threw herself into Garric's arms. "You shouldn't have come!" she said as she hugged him fiercely. Before he could respond, she'd stepped back. "But how . . . ?" she asked, looking beyond Garric.

He raised his eyes, expecting to see the dangling rope. There was nothing but the smooth stone vault, colored by the sullen light from the moat. The air was dry and very hot.

Ilna dropped from nowhere to the floor beside them. In her hands was the noose, her weapon of choice. She gasped from the impact, then stepped aside. "You'll have to catch Cerix," she said. "He's next."

"Right," said Garric. He positioned himself where Ilna had just landed, leaning backward with his arms cupped before him. He couldn't see Cerix or the rope, but presumably the wizard could—

Cerix dropped into his arms. Garric's knees flexed; he stepped back and set Cerix on the ground. Because the legless man was as short as a small child, Garric had subconsciously expected the weight of a small child. Cerix was a solidly muscular fellow, fully as heavy as most men even now.

Halphemos appeared from nowhere. He put a hand down to catch himself safely, but the impact slid the athame from his belt to rattle on the stone. He picked it up, held it to the light, and nodded with satisfaction.

Ilna looped her noose around her waist and took the unraveling sash from her sleeve. She walked toward the moat, stopping a pace from the edge and looking down. Garric uncinched his buckler and, holding it in his left hand, went to Ilna's side.

Orange lava flowed a man's height below the rim of a

channel thirty feet broad. Even at this distance the glowing rock shriveled the fine hairs on Garric's cheeks and right forearm. He touched Ilna's arm and drew her back.

"Let's get on with it," Cerix said in a hoarse voice. He spoke with the resignation of a man who either believes he's already dead or who wishes he were. He'd taken a leaden rod as thick as his little finger from the pouch on his belt.

"Don't we need a circle?" Halphemos said in surprise.

"The Key opens barriers, boy!" the cripple said harshly. He drew the lead across the floor. The metal made a silvery smear, visible as a sheen rather than a color against the black stone. Cerix looked at Ilna and said, "Get on with it!"

Ilna glanced down at him; Garric wouldn't have believed Ilna had the capacity for pity if he hadn't been watching her face at that moment. "Yes, of course," she said mildly and threw the sash on the ground.

The fabric crawled into syllables expressed in the Old Script. Cerix eyed them, then with his lead stylus drew the words in square modern characters. *"Rouche,"* Halphemos said. *"Dropide tarta iao."*

Ilna scooped up the sash and threw it again. Her face was expressionless. The wool fell in a different pattern, equally legible. Cerix wrote quickly, sliding his body back with his left hand so that he had bare stone to write on.

Garric tried to read the Old Script aloud as Halphemos poised to speak his mentor's transliteration. The act was unconscious on Garric's part, though on reflection he knew part of it was juvenile bragging: *"I'm better schooled than you are!"*

And so he was, for Reise had given his children an education that compared favorably to the best available in the academies of Valles and Erdin. But there was more to wizardry than the ability to read the Old Script: Garric's tongue stuck to the roof of his mouth before he could finish pronouncing the initial syllable.

Garric had been involved in wizardry before, aiding

Tenoctris with incantations which required more than one speaker. This was something at another level, as far beyond Garric's strength as it would have been to smash the vault's dense walls with his hand.

Garric felt new respect for Halphemos, and for the first time he had some understanding of the plight in which Cerix found himself. It wasn't just a matter of the cripple needing to get a grip on himself, the way Garric had thought in the arrogance of his own good health. Cerix had lost his legs, and the ability to speak *these* words was as surely a matter of strength as running nonstop from Barca's Hamlet to Carcosa.

"*Abouas sioun serou* . . . ," Halphemos chanted. Ilna picked up the fabric and cast it; Cerix drew the words out, and Halphemos poised to speak them.

Liane stood close to Garric, looking into the distance. Garric checked that his sword was free in its scabbard—again. He was tense, and there was nothing useful to occupy either his mind or his muscles for the moment. It was entirely up to the wizards, the wizards and Ilna.

"*Katebrimo piste agaleision* . . . ," Halphemos said. His face looked fine-etched; sweat beaded his forehead despite the arid atmosphere. His voice didn't falter.

Ilna threw the sash with a sweeping motion of her hand as though she were spreading a cleaned garment on bushes to dry. What did this cost *her*? To look at Ilna's face, the only effort she expended was the slight one of lifting a rag . . . and perhaps that's all it was.

But neither of the wizards could do the thing Ilna os-Kenset was doing; and with Ilna you were never going to learn the real cost. Perhaps the only virtues Ilna had were the virtues of strength; but no one ever could doubt her strength.

Garric took his right hand from the pommel of his sword and rested it lightly on Liane's shoulder.

"*Aelgoso bitto aikisos!*" Halphemos said, his white face painted by the glow of lava.

Garric stiffened. Liane glanced at him. He pointed his

index finger. The chasm nearest the party had narrowed. The solid floor on either side was beginning to arch over the glowing rock.

Liane clutched Garric's wrist. For the first time since she'd been lowered into this vault, she could allow herself to believe in the possibility of escape.

Ilna threw the sash, still-faced. Did she know? Did she even care, so long as *her* task was completed correctly?

"*Opelion ophelime uriskos* . . . ," the young wizard said.

Garric felt the laughter before he heard it, and even what he heard was in his mind rather than through his ears. He'd been watching stone extending like tendrils of waves combing toward one another on a beach. He turned. From the other direction, a thing walked toward them.

Garric shook Liane away without thinking about what he was doing. He drew his sword without haste, just getting ready. The chine of the blade whispered against the scabbard's iron lip, but the keen edges swept clear without rubbing.

King Carus was with Garric, shivering in and out as though the flesh were a garment and the king's spirit a debutante uncertain of her choice of garb. This was Garric's fight; he no longer became the slave of his ancient ancestor when his hand touched a sword hilt or anger rose in him like a hot, crushing tide.

The thing walked on all fours, though occasionally it lifted onto its hind legs like a bear. Not like a man. Not anything like a man.

It had three heads on snaky necks. The heads to either side were reptilian, wedge-shaped like a viper's instead of the narrow, high-combed skulls of the seawolves which occasionally came from the surf to prey on the flocks of Barca's Hamlet. Forked tongues flickered in and out of forests of cone-shaped, finger-long teeth.

The central head might have been a dog's or a baboon's, if ever those beasts had reached the size of this

Beast. It was thirty feet high at the shoulder, and its heads laughed as it came toward the humans.

"I appreciate your efforts on my behalf, Garric or-Reise," the dog-head said. Flaming rock surged in the moat to the rhythm of the words. "You brought me the one who could open my prison."

Over the hissing, barking laughter, Garric heard the timbre of his companions' speech change. He couldn't spare the attention to learn why.

"For your help . . ." the central head said. The snakes continued to laugh like fire in dry leaves. "I will eat you and your friends last of all. Am I not kind, Garric or-Reise?"

"If you come closer," Garric said, "I'll kill you."

"When the Yellow King trapped me here, I was the size of this whole enclosure," the Beast said. Its voice shook the stone, but no real sound came from the dog-fanged maw. "I starved here and shrank . . . but I do not think you will stop me, Garric or-Reise."

"Garric!" Liane called behind him. "The bridge is open! Come back so that Halphemos can close it behind us!"

The Beast laughed thunderously as it came on. Its steps seemed mincing, but each pace covered as much ground as the legs of a cantering horse.

Garric shuffled a half step back, then another. The Beast was close enough that its serpent heads could strike. He felt the lava's heat on the calves of his legs. A hand, Liane's hand, pressed his shoulder lightly to guide him.

"Rouche," said the Beast's central head. *"Dropide tarta iao!"*

Cerix wailed as he understood the Beast's plan. "Write the words!" Ilna shouted. "Your job is to write the words!"

Garric stepped forward, swinging his sword.

* * *

"I see the end!" Zahag said. "We're free now. Come *on*, chief!"

The ape reached for Cashel's wrist to tug him along faster, then changed his mind and scampered ahead by himself. Cashel kept going at his own pace, as he would have done in any event.

"Slow down and we'll get there," Cashel said, loudly enough to be heard over the throb of the air around them. "If there's any *there* to begin with."

Zahag had saved himself the swat he'd likely have gotten if he'd grabbed the youth. Cashel knew his temper was frayed, and he didn't know what was going to happen next. He didn't like uncertainty.

Zahag crouched, then hopped back to Cashel's side. "Don't you see it?" he said. "Just up ahead there?"

He put a long hand on Cashel's waist. The contact was the ape reassuring himself that he wasn't alone rather than him trying to drag Cashel into something Cashel didn't want to do. Cashel didn't object. He had a lot of experience with soothing frightened animals. Zahag had more reason for fear right now than ever a ewe had in a thunderstorm.

"I see something," Cashel said. "When we get there, we'll know better what it is."

The texture of the light farther up the passage had changed, though its dull garnet color had not. Was it brighter?

Cashel shook his head in frustration. He didn't like puzzles. What he wanted was somebody to tell him what to do.

If that involved a fight, so much the better. Cashel didn't fight often, but it was something he understood just fine.

Cashel already knew that he couldn't judge distances within the passage Tenoctris had opened for him. Even so it was a surprise when he and Zahag stepped out onto a vast, bowl-shaped plain before he was aware of it.

Cashel stopped. Zahag, turning his head in nervous

amazement, said, "But where's this? This is as bad as the other!"

"Well, it's different," Cashel said. The first thing he'd checked was that the passage remained open behind them. It did. He examined their new surroundings, shifting the quarterstaff crosswise now that there was room for it.

"It's not *very* different," Zahag muttered in a subdued voice, and Cashel had to admit the ape wasn't far wrong.

The ground, the crater walls, and the spike in the center that was the plain's only feature were all of the same red light as the passage that brought them here. The surface was solid and as smooth as ice, but it wasn't real the way rock is, or a tree.

"It's pretty enough in its way," Cashel said. He shrugged. "I'd like it better if there was a mud wallow or something natural on it. What do you think, Zahag?"

"I think I'd like to be back on Sirimat with the band I was captured from," Zahag said. "None of them were crazy. They were a lot smarter than present company too."

Cashel laughed. "I guess we're in one of those knots we saw in the cellars, where the lines come together," he said. "Let's go see what the thing in the center is."

It wasn't hard to walk. The red light was smooth, all right, but your foot didn't pressure-melt a film of water like when you stepped down on glare ice. All you had to do here was keep your balance. It wasn't any worse than the wet stepping stones when Pattern Creek was in spate.

Zahag had an even easier time: he went down on all fours. Cashel guessed the ape was mumbling tags of poetry again, but it wasn't loud enough for him to tell for sure.

"I didn't like being squeezed in the way that tunnel did," Cashel said. He thought he saw clouds blowing above a layer of red haze, and he was pretty sure he could see real rocks and maybe grass under the surface of stony light on which he walked. "This is a lot better, don't you think?"

Zahag didn't reply. It hadn't really been a question anyway.

He didn't see the queen or anything else alive. Well, maybe in that spike in the center. . . .

Cashel didn't lengthen his stride, but he twirled the quarterstaff just to loosen his shoulder muscles. Lines of blue fire trailed from the iron caps. That surprised him, but not very much. He already knew this was an uncanny place.

"Remember how we got Princess Aria out of the tower?" he said to Zahag.

"I remember," the ape said. He couldn't have sounded more glum if he'd just heard his sister had died.

Cashel thought there was a sun overhead, but its light only marked a spot on the red sky. All the light here came from the shimmering surfaces, just as it had in the tunnel leading to this plain. You couldn't judge distance in the usual way, because there weren't any shadows.

Cashel didn't quite run into the base of the tower of light—but almost. "Whoa!" he said, chuckling at himself.

He'd been in a better mood since they came out of the passage. He was sure he was getting close to a result. A chance to do something, anyhow.

Cashel prodded the column with his left hand. It was straight up and as smooth as the staff in his other hand. The bottom part wasn't any thicker than many of the trees Cashel had felled over the years, but the top spread out into a ball. That was easier to see here, looking up against the paler sky, than it had been when the bowl's glowing wall was the background.

Even Zahag looked interested. He sniffed at the base of the column, running his left fingertips over the surface a little higher as he walked around the curve.

Cashel felt a rhythm. Chanting, he thought. Maybe Tenoctris, keeping the passage open behind them for as long as she could.

Maybe not Tenoctris at all.

"Well, do you think you can climb it?" Cashel said, hefting his staff in both hands. He looked over his shoulder, but he and Zahag were still alone in the bowl of light.

"It's fifty feet," the ape said, looking upward. He saw Cashel glance at his fingers in reflex. "That's ten of your paces, chief, left foot to left foot. Both of your hands in paces."

"Ah," said Cashel. Zahag hadn't sounded peevish or even sneering when he put the distance in terms Cashel could understand. Better than any words could have, that proved how nervous the ape was.

"I can't get onto the top," Zahag said, considering the problem again. "Not the way it flares out. But I could maybe get up the shaft, sure."

"I'd be beholden if you did that," Cashel said, running the hickory staff through his hands. "It looks like there's windows at the top, and maybe inside. . . ."

Of course, even if the queen *was* inside, that didn't bring Cashel any closer to scotching her. He didn't have any better ideas, though; and if Zahag did, he sure wasn't offering them.

A pattern was coming together. Cashel figured it'd be time for him to fit his piece in pretty soon.

The ape hopped upward, grasping the column at Cashel's height above the ground. Cashel could have lifted him higher, using the quarterstaff as a prop, but if Zahag couldn't grip it was better to learn that before he was dangerously high off the ground.

Zahag did grip, though. His arms and his shorter legs spread to their full span, so that the ape looked like a crab spider waiting for prey in a flower's heart. His hands could squeeze against each other on opposite sides of the shaft, and even his hind paws stretched far enough to anchor him for the instant it took to slide his hands higher.

Hunching his body and sliding his limbs, the ape proceeded up the column not much slower than he'd accompanied Cashel across the plain of light. He looked about the same as he had rolling forward on all fours, too.

Cashel could hear him muttering verse again, but he was getting the job done.

"Duzi, help Zahag if you can," Cashel whispered. He eyed the horizon to make sure that nothing was advancing on them unseen. "He's only here to help me, and he doesn't have Gods of his own to pray to."

"I'm there, chief!" Zahag called. "I've gotten there!"

The ape lifted his torso to where the column widened like the sconce on a firedog that takes sticks of lightwood for illumination. In a shriller voice he said, "I see—"

Zahag did something Cashel hadn't thought was possible: holding on to the column with his hind legs alone, he threw his hands up to grip the part of the tower that swelled like an onion about to blossom. To Cashel it was like watching a fly walk on the ceiling.

Zahag weighed about as much as a man did. If he fell that distance—

"I see a woman!" Zahag cried excitedly. "She's a girl! She's blond and she's waving to—"

He went over backward and his hands shot out. The ape's timing was marvelous, so good that if there'd been any kind of a handhold on the shaft for him to grab he would have caught himself.

There wasn't anything, just a smooth surface that not even an ape could cling to when it wasn't just his weight but the speed of his fall he had to overcome. Zahag's hands slapped the column and held just long enough that his body was tumbling when it broke free.

Cashel dropped his quarterstaff, judging the distance. He moved a step to the side and a step out from the shaft. There was a risk to this, but not as great a risk as waking up in the middle of the night and remembering that he hadn't tried to save a friend.

The staff's ferrules spat blue sparks when they hit the ground. Cashel raised his arms, watching between his spread hands. At least in this place he didn't have to worry about the sun blinding him. . . .

Cashel's feet were close under him, but his knees and

the elbows too were bent. He needed to take the shock with his muscles, not his locked joints. *That* would serve to drive him into the ground like a tent peg, and it'd smash the ape up about as bad as if nobody'd caught him.

Zahag bawled, "Ahhhh!" and hit. Cashel's arms gave. He clutched the ape to his chest, rotating away from the shaft. He went down on one knee for an instant before toppling sideways and skidding on the smooth ground.

They fetched up several paces from the shaft. Cashel was still holding the ape. From the way Zahag gibbered in relief, there wasn't anything wrong with him worse than the whack Cashel had taken when the weight of the falling ape drove his own elbows into his stomach.

Cashel got up and walked back to where his quarterstaff lay. The rumble of chanting was louder now. It wasn't coming from anywhere that Cashel could point to; and anyway, he had his own business to tend to. Now he understood what to do.

"Is that the queen?" Zahag asked. He was hopping up and down in sheer joy of being alive, Cashel guessed. "Is it the queen up there, chief, and you're going to get her out?"

"I don't think it's the queen," Cashel said, checking first one, then the other end cap of the quarterstaff. "I'm going to break something now, Zahag. I can't be sure what, so maybe you ought to head for the tunnel to get clear."

Cashel traced his hands over the hickory, making sure there were no cracks that'd appeared since he tossed the staff down in haste. There weren't. It hadn't been likely, but Cashel liked to be sure of things.

He spun the quarterstaff over his head. He kept the revolutions slow as he warmed up, crossing his wrists one over the other at the staff's balance; and again, and again.

Blue fire popped and crackled. It formed rings that hung in the air even after Cashel changed the staff's angle. The sizzle sounded like the laughter of an old man.

Cashel laughed too; and, laughing, stabbed the butt of

the quarterstaff like a battering ram against the column of light. The blow had all the strength of both arms and the weight of his torso behind it.

The universe went white and silent. Even the chanting stopped for several heartbeats.

Roaring blue fire ripped the blankness like a lightning bolt. Cashel fell on his back. He couldn't rise, couldn't even blink for the moment, so great was his exhaustion.

Cracks spread across the shaft of red light. The surface dulled, losing the perfect sheen. A piece the size of a man's fingernail fell off, dissolving like a burned-out spark before it hit the ground.

Everything crumbled. Zahag's mouth opened and closed, but his shouts were lost in the crash of a universe breaking apart.

As the red light of the column rotted away, it left rough stone in its place. Instead of a narrow shaft and a larger sphere atop it, Cashel lay on rock and coarse grass at the base of a plug of volcanic rock that had been fashioned into a rough figure.

Angle and the crude workmanship kept Cashel from telling more about the statue than that it *was* one. Its hand clutched a ball of living rock into which windows had been cut.

Two men ran across the rough ground toward where Cashel lay. One was a huge, rawboned fellow with a big spear; the other was of more ordinary size, holding in his good hand a long knife hooked like a hawk's bill.

The change from ruby wizard-light to natural landscape spread like fire in a dry meadow, not especially fast but as certain as fate. Here and there cracks were appearing in the bowl's sheer walls.

A girl with streaming blond hair leaned from one of the windows in the stone ball the statue held. She climbed out, finding niches for her fingers and bare toes in weathered stone.

"Sharina!" Cashel whispered. His lips formed the

name, but his voice was too weak to be heard even in a quiet room.

A crack ran across the soil. Pieces shook from the carven outcrop, and the ground bucked violently.

In the pause before the next shock, Cashel heard Zahag's voice. "The volcano!" the ape shrieked. "The volcano's about to erupt!"

The 5th of Partridge (Later Still)

Cracks shivered across the wizard-light. For the first time since Sharina's capture, she could see objects in their own colors instead of through a filter of sullen red.

She crawled through the slot in the rock. It was a tight fit, even for her, but she would have squeezed out even if it meant flaying herself on the way.

Sharina understood now what it meant to be free. She'd never imagined restraint as complete as the queen's imprisonment. She'd rather die than undergo that again.

She swung out, clinging to the sides with both hands as her right foot felt for a ledge. She was on the carved outcrop in the center of the crater. A lifetime ago she'd seen it with Hanno and Unarc.

The two hunters were running toward her now. They must have waited on the crater rim instead of looking to their own safety after she was captured. Seeing them, Sharina wondered that she'd ever thought they *might* flee.

Cashel lay on his back at the base of the outcrop; an ape was capering about him. He wasn't moving. "If he's dead . . ." Sharina whispered as her hand tried a knob of rock; it broke off under her weight.

The outcrop was porous and well weathered. Sharina's

toes found a crack that supported her body long enough for her to get her fingers into it as well. She let herself down her body's length, fumbling for another grip.

Sharina laughed. Cashel wasn't dead. He wouldn't leave her that way.

The outcrop shook violently. Sharina flattened herself against the rock face by instinct. Chunks from higher up bounced past her.

The floor of the crater split across. The ground on one side lifted while that on the other sank; the portions twitched at different rhythms. Magma winked in the depths of the crack.

A ledge jutted out a dozen feet beneath her: the knee of the squatting statue. It was a long drop to a hard surface, but there wasn't much time.

Sharina jumped, landing safely on flexed knees. The crater shook again. The ledge slid away, carrying Sharina down with it in a rush and a roar.

She kept her feet, spreading her arms for balance. Dust and pebbles cascaded ahead of her. Hanno and Unarc had lifted Cashel between them. They—a big man and two huge men—lurched farther from the path of the landslide. The ape followed on its hind legs, carrying Cashel's staff in its hands.

The slab finished its thunderous skid to the ground. The choking cloud of the rock's destruction rose over Sharina; fragments from higher up were still falling. Sharina ran out of the snarling chaos, using the rush of her descent to speed her feet.

Chips pelted her. Sharina knew that if she tripped, the scree of sliding rock would bury her at least until the eruption turned the crater into a sea of fire.

She didn't trip. Her face emerged into sunlight before her screaming lungs forced her to breathe dust thicker than a sandstorm.

"Lady, I bless You for Your mercy!" Sharina cried. "Oh, Cashel, I knew you'd come!"

And as she heard herself say the words, Sharina knew that they were true.

Cashel couldn't have stood without Unarc's help, but his eyes were open and he held his head up. Hanno had started back toward the shattered outcrop, but he stopped when he saw Sharina already free.

"This way!" screamed the ape, gesturing toward the crater wall with the quarterstaff. "We can get to the passage before—"

A shock fiercer than those before shook the crater. It threw them all to the ground, even Sharina, who'd ridden a landslide without falling. More cracks ran across the bowl; throbbing, yellow-white lava began to ooze up from below. The queen's wizardry had checked the volcano's anger. Now that wizardry had failed, nature was reasserting itself with a vengeance.

"Let's go!" Hanno said. Unarc sheathed his hooked knife. Hanno tossed his spear to the bald hunter and took over supporting Cashel.

The ape loped toward a ring of ruby light at the base of the crater's wall. He was using three limbs now, dragging the bouncing staff behind him with the remaining hand.

Hanno pulled Cashel's left arm over his shoulders and gripped Cashel's wrist with his own right hand. Linked, the two big men broke into a lumbering trot. Even somebody as strong as Hanno couldn't have carried Cashel for any distance unaided, but Cashel was able to stumble along with the other man's help.

Cashel looked dazed. He smiled when his eyes met Sharina's, though.

She paced the three men. She could have outdistanced them easily, but the last thing she wanted was to be alone. Safety wasn't a place. Safety was friends.

"Is this your friend Nonnus you talked about, missie?" Hanno shouted. His face was set, but he looked as though he could keep running at his present pace until the sun froze.

Sharina's left hand rested on the hilt of the Pewle knife, though the wide belt gripped the sheath tightly enough that it didn't flop when she ran. "No," she said. "He's my friend Cashel."

"You got some right impressive friends, girl!" Hanno said. He bellowed with laughter.

The shimmering ruby had dissolved starting at its center, so now only the top of the crater's rim still shone with unnatural red purity. Even that vestige vanished as the group neared the rock walls. The tunnel mouth was the only remnant of wizardry in the volcano's sunlit bowl.

Instead of simply trembling, the ground rippled like a blanket being shaken out. Hanno stumbled; Cashel touched a hand down to keep them both upright. Cashel and the hunter still clung to each other, but they were more like oxen in yoke than an invalid and a nurse.

The ape reached the mouth of the passage and turned. His eyes looked up and he opened his mouth to shout. An enormous, wet *plopping* noise overwhelmed all other sound. The ground billowed and the crater wall itself split to the sky.

Sharina looked over her shoulder. The central outcrop which the Hairy Men had carved into their own likeness sank into a bubbling pool of lava. Blazing rock spewed high in the air.

Within what had been the idol's head, now bobbling on the lava like a bladder in a millrace, was a sphere of ruby light. There was a figure within.

Sharina saw the queen raise her staff in a desperate attempt to stay the inevitable. Rock fountaining from the depths of the earth flung the ball of wizard-light in a wild career. No one could stand, let alone chant in such a dance.

"Sharina, come!" Cashel cried. He stood at the mouth of the tunnel, holding his free hand toward her. Hanno looked back from his other side with a worried expression.

The ruby sphere sank into the sea of lava. Sharina expected it to bob up again. Instead livid rock sprayed outward in all directions, the way the water of a swamp does when a bubble bursts.

Sharina plunged into the tunnel with her friends.

Cashel and Hanno were directly ahead of her, filling the passage. They clumped forward in a way that transcended human effort.

Sharina had thought the tunnel led down—there was no other way to go from the point in the crater wall where it opened, after all. But the tunnel, like the bowl of light where the queen had made her lair, was separate from the geography of the waking world. She and her companions were climbing, or at any rate they expended the effort they would to climb.

Sharina felt the air compress with a dull thump. She glanced back. The lava that had followed them into the passage blazed behind her. For the moment they were staying well ahead of it.

She didn't say anything to her companions. There was nothing to do except what they were doing, after all.

Anyway, she'd outlived the queen.

Something changed ahead of her. Sharina had glimpsed Unarc and the ape occasionally between the legs of Cashel and Hanno. They disappeared. Hanno shouted; then he and Cashel too were gone, and Sharina sprang out into cool air and lamplight.

Tenoctris was kneeling before a pentacle on a dank stone floor. She swayed, dropping the sliver of wood she'd been using in her art. Sharina caught the old woman before she could hit the stone.

For a moment Sharina saw the end of the tunnel from which she'd just emerged. It glowed, as real as the basalt walls which it interpenetrated but did not touch. The light dissolved into sparkles, then nothing at all.

"I couldn't hold it open any longer," Tenoctris whispered. "Was it long enough? Cashel, is the queen . . . ?"

"No," said Sharina in a tone too grim to be triumphant. "The queen isn't anywhere, Tenoctris. The queen is gone."

"Begging your pardon, missie," Hanno said, "but there was lava coming after us a few steps back. I *don't* think I want to wait here to see if it still is."

Tenoctris smiled, though her eyes were shut and she didn't open them for the moment. "This passage is closed," she said, cradled in Sharina's arms. "If there was anything in it when it closed, well, it won't vanish—it'll find another place to exit. But it won't come out here."

She opened her eyes and glanced with a bemused expression at those with her in the cellars. Sharina grinned back; they were an assorted lot, certainly.

"We should get back to the surface, though," Tenoctris said. "There's still the Beast to deal with."

A low tremor shook the building. Tenoctris started to rise; Cashel and Hanno together lifted the old wizard from Sharina's lap.

"If it isn't too late," Tenoctris said, though her face was calm.

A serpent head on a neck thirty feet long bent toward Garric from his left side. Compared with the creature's huge body, the head looked oddly small—not much larger than that of a horse.

Of course the Beast had three heads to feed with.

The Beast's movement was a feint. Garric turned toward it as if completely fooled, his sword lifted and his buckler out as though to fend off the hissing maw.

The Beast struck very quickly from the other side. Garric jumped back and slashed at the ridged yellow throat scales as the serpent jaws clopped shut on the air where he'd stood a moment before.

The snake heads jerked away, hissing like a pair of mill races. The dog head roared, losing the rhythm of the incantation. Purple blood leaked from the long gash. It looked black in the rock's ruddy glow.

Garric laughed, but he held where he was for the moment. The Beast's necks couldn't be as flexible as the snakes they resembled. They had to hold their own considerable weight and that of the head in the air, while a snake has the ground to support it. Nevertheless the heads could strike from both sides together. Garric didn't want to get so close to the Beast's gigantic body that he couldn't keep all the heads in his vision at the same time.

"If I were that big," thought one—it could have been either—of the personalities in Garric's body, *"I'd stamp a man into the stone instead of worrying about his little sword, but this one isn't me."*

"Bow to me, human!" the dog head said. "I am your god! I am immortal! Look at the way this wound heals!"

The purple blood vanished like water sinking into the sand. The severed scales had bent upward on either side of the wound, drawn by their own resilience. Now they flattened again like lips of heat-softened wax, reforming with only a seam to show the injury—and that smoothed as well.

Immortal the Beast might be, but it wasn't invulnerable and it felt pain. More important, the Beast *feared* pain. By twisting its nose ring, a man can master a vicious boar hog three times his size, though its tusks could tear him in half if they ever closed on his body.

"Come then!" Garric shouted. "If you like the experience so much, let's do it again!"

The serpent heads swayed. It was like watching trees topple. Neither was a serious attack. Garric didn't bother to react.

Laughing he cried, "It doesn't matter if you're a god. To get past me you'll have to prove you're a man!"

"We've crossed the bridge, Garric," Liane called in the clear, dispassionate voice of a noblewoman summoning her carriage across a crowded courtyard.

The head on Garric's left struck hard and fast. He stepped into the attack, slashing. His blade crunched through scales and light bones, cutting half again its own depth in the serpent snout.

That was almost too deep. The shock of the blow

numbed Garric's hand. The Beast snatched back its wounded head with such screaming violence that it nearly pulled the sword from his grip.

The other snake head struck, more in reaction to pain than from calculation. Garric ducked under the blow, swinging his buckler instead of risking a cut before his hand had stopped tingling.

The shield was small but as sturdy as three birch cross-plies and iron reinforcements could make it. The spiked boss bonged against the fanged lower jaw. It felt to Garric as though he'd batted an oak tree, but he heard bones in the snake head break.

The Beast recoiled. If a thunderstorm could be angry, it would sound like the hissing roars of the creature's three heads.

Garric glanced over his shoulder, then skipped backward to the middle of the span. "Chant your spell!" he shouted to the wizards. "Break the bridge!"

"*Betput,*" Halphemos called in a clear voice, "*baiai borbar . . .*"

Heat hammered Garric's body. The bridge had been wider than Garric could reach with outstretched arms when he first glimpsed it. It shrank into itself, narrowing and providing less of a shield against the lava blazing below.

"*Barphor kolchoi tontonon . . . ,*" Halphemos said. He knelt beside Cerix at the far side of the bridge. It must be very nearly as hot for the wizards as it was for Garric at midspan.

Ilna stood with help from the wizards, throwing and retrieving the sash. Liane was beside her, touching the other girl's shoulder with her fingertips. Liane had no need to stay here. Lava lighted a tunnel rising behind her. She might as well have run up it.

"*Phriou rigche alcheine . . . ,*" Halphemos said.

Garric felt his skin crack. His tunic must be singeing; would it burst into flame?

He laughed, both halves of his person again. If only that were all he had to worry about!

"Rouche!" shrilled the serpent heads. *"Dropide tarta iao!"*

The bridge had shrunk to little more than the width of the felled tulip poplar that crossed the gully north of Barca's Hamlet. As the Beast spoke, the span widened again by a finger's breadth.

That was on the track to Seckler the Butcher's yard. . . .

"Before I kill you," boomed the dog head, "I will tear your females apart piece by piece. I will lick up their blood, I will grind their bones between my teeth!"

If the Beast could speak the Yellow King's Key unaided, it wouldn't need to face Garric's sword now. But—

The Beast strode forward thunderously, keeping its three heads high. The attack didn't completely surprise the part of Garric which had survived a hundred battlefields, but the Beast's enormous bulk was as hard to stop as an avalanche.

"Apomche moz—," Halphemos began. One of the serpent heads swung over Garric. The jaws slammed closed on Halphemos.

The Beast's right foreleg swung toward Garric. The foot was a broad pad with five blunt toes, each the size of a human torso. Garric stabbed between two claws, driving the blade into the flesh above the pad of cartilage which supported the monster's weight.

The Beast's cry of triumph changed into a deafening scream. It lurched back on its haunches, jerking Garric forward because he wouldn't release the sword hilt. No human strength could snatch the weapon free when the Beast's injured muscles had spasmed tight on the steel.

Garric held for a moment. Halphemos dangled from the jaws that had struck him; long teeth driven through his skull from both sides had done instantly fatal damage. The other snake head twisted toward the corpse and tore off a mouthful of flesh for itself.

The Beast kicked its injured foot. The weapon remained imbedded in the sensitive flesh, but Garric flew clear. He dropped the buckler and grabbed for the bridge with both hands.

He almost caught himself, but "almost" was the difference between life and death. Garric's fingers brushed the stone but couldn't grip it.

Ilna's noose settled over his outstretched arms and jerked tight. Instead of plunging straight into the blazing lava, his body swung like a pendulum against the far side of the chasm. The shock and the heat knocked him into openmouthed collapse. All Garric saw was concentric circles of red and white glare, expanding to fill the universe.

Garric couldn't use his arms. He felt his torso scrape over the lip of the fiery moat, then hands rolled him away. Merely being sheltered from the lava's radiant heat felt like a plunge into a spring-fed pool. He could see again.

The noose slipped off. Both women bent over him, Ilna with the noose wrapped around her waist to help anchor Garric's weight. She and Liane must still have surprised themselves to have been able to lift him clear.

"Sothaoth agog katochoi!" Cerix shouted. He wept as he spoke the phrases he'd transcribed for his dead friend. *"Kleidia phuschi choroi!"*

A lot of people were surprising themselves this day.

Across the chasm, the Beast started forward again. When the huge right foot touched the bridge, it drove Garric's sword deeper. Screaming from all three mouths, the Beast flinched back.

"Tharona perpo zoile!" the cripple cried.

The span dissolved like dew in the sunlight, leaving the moat clear. Lava slapped and gurgled; droplets of white-hot rock spattered over the edges of the trough. One splashed a finger's length from Garric and quivered as it cooled, giving off a sulphurous stench. The liquid rock was about to overflow its channel.

"Run," Garric said, barely whispering. He tried to

stand; Liane's hands gripped his upper arms. "We've got to get higher."

Cerix weighed more than Ilna did. She lifted him anyway and staggered up the passage. Garric could move his legs, but without Liane he wouldn't even have been able to crawl.

He glanced over his shoulder. Lava flooded from the moat for as far into the distance as Garric could see. The Beast howled words of power as it retreated, but the river of glowing rock continued to widen.

Garric and his companions were out of sight of the domed chamber when the screams began. They were inhuman, penetrating Garric's brain as no sound alone could have done. They went on until the flow of rising lava had filled the passage behind the escaping humans—

And even then, Garric thought he heard the wails of a thing that could not die though all its substance had burned away.

"I'm too heavy for you to carry," Cerix muttered. Ilna wouldn't have heard him except that his lips were so close to her ear. "You can leave me here."

"No," said Ilna, "I can't. Not if I want to sleep nights, at any rate. If you want to do something useful instead of whining, you might clasp your hands around my neck and take some weight off my arms."

The wizard obeyed immediately. That helped, though not as much as Ilna would have liked. Her thigh muscles quivered with the strain and her forearms—her hands were locked under Cerix's buttocks—had gone numb. A pity that Cerix wasn't a midget instead of merely a cripple.

The passage seemed interminable. Since there was no light, Ilna kept her course straight by touching the stone wall occasionally with her elbow. There were no seams. Either the tunnel was lined with enormous slabs, or it had been cut from the living rock.

"Alos did it," Cerix said in a weak whisper. "He killed the Beast."

"He was a brave man," Ilna said. She didn't want to talk about Halphemos, but other people had different ways of dealing with unpleasant situations. "We couldn't have succeeded without him."

Garric stumbled along close behind; on Liane's arm, Ilna supposed. His burns were terrible. Ilna had blisters on the backs of her hands just from leaning over to pull Garric out of the flaming chasm.

"Alos did it!" Cerix said, as close as he could come to shouting. "*He* did it!"

Ilna trudged onward. The wizard began to cry again.

Ilna had started to say, "No, Master Cerix. If there was any one person who killed the Beast, *you* were that person when you closed the bridge over the moat."

But Cerix didn't want praise: he wanted to be forgiven for living when his friend had died. Ilna could understand the feeling very well.

It was odd that people thought it mattered what things cost. A perfectly woven panel was no better or worse whether you bought it for a few coppers or spent a purse of minted gold. Halphemos had done certain things. The things were of the same importance whether they were easy or if they cost him his life.

As they had.

And perhaps there were worse things than lies. "Yes," Ilna said aloud. "Halphemos did kill the Beast."

"Ilna?" Liane called. "There's something ahead of us. I see light."

"Light" was too strong a word, but a square of the blackness in front of them was less absolute than the neighboring portions.

"I see it," said Ilna; and because she *was* Ilna, she added, "Now that you've pointed it out."

"I'll go see what it is," Garric said. His voice rasped like that of a mummy dug from the ancient sands.

"Yes, and maybe Cerix will run alongside to give you

company!'' Ilna snapped; and immediately regretted it. Garric wasn't posturing. There was almost nothing left of him but his duty, so duty had spoken.

There wasn't much left of Ilna either, she supposed. In a mild voice she added, ''I'd rather we stayed together, Garric.''

''I hear voices,'' Liane said quietly.

They were no longer in a tunnel through rock. A forest of pillars supported arches overhead. Ilna had thought the sounds she heard were echoes of their own voices, their own footsteps, but Liane was right.

Ilna smiled tightly. Liane was right again.

A group of people came toward them from the side. Sharina was in the lead, holding a lantern. Behind her were three men—one of them Cashel and another as big as Cashel, which was something Ilna hadn't seen very often.

And the ape Zahag; and Tenoctris.

Somebody else could carry Cerix now. Ilna knelt and lowered her burden carefully to the stone floor. Physical relief washed over her, though the immediate result was that she felt so wrung out that she almost fell over.

Garric supported Ilna's shoulder with the hand that wasn't around Liane. ''Sharina,'' he called, ''I couldn't be happier to see you—all of you. Tenoctris, we've—the Beast is gone.''

Cashel, looking wobbly but not weak—never weak, not him—walked to Ilna, lifted her, and gave her a hug. ''What are you doing in the queen's mansion, Ilna?'' he asked.

''Thinking that we need to get Garric to a healer,'' she said, squeezing her brother hard before she broke away. The parched skin of her face pinched when she smiled. ''And the rest of us too, perhaps.''

''Are we in the queen's mansion?'' said Garric, looking back from where he stood with Tenoctris. Liane was close by, ready to catch him if he fell. ''I've got to join Attaper and Waldron before the Hairy Men attack.''

Tenoctris looked worn, but hearing that the Beast was dead made the old wizard beam like the sun. "The Hairy Men aren't a danger without the queen," she said. "Without her art to rule them, they're just a herd of poor, terrified creatures. They'll starve or drown."

Ilna supposed "dead" was the word for the Beast.

Tenoctris shook her head sadly. "I regret that," she added, "because they were really quite innocent."

"As were the many young girls fed to the Beast over the years," said Garric. "We can't change what's happened; but we can rule the Isles in a fashion that prevents it from happening again."

"Does anybody else want to get out of here?" asked the big man wearing leather. "Because I surely do!"

"Yes," said the youth who was clearly *Prince* Garric. "Tenoctris, will you lead us? Because I'm going to do well if I manage the three flights of stairs by myself, let alone remembering directions. I'm not in good shape."

Cashel lifted Cerix. The wizard was crooning a song of parting, but he'd ceased to blubber.

"Fortunately for me and the Isles," Garric added as they started in the direction Tenoctris indicated, "I don't have to do things by myself."

The 7th of Partridge

Garric, smelling of Mistress Ladra's lanolin ointment and walking stiffly in bandages that made him look as though he had elephantiasis, entered the reception hall that served as headquarters for the defense of Ornifal. There were at least three hundred people present now, twice as many as there'd been when he'd last been here two days past.

"All rise for His Majesty Prince Garric!" bellowed the nomenclator.

An attendant had run ahead to warn Royhas. The chancellor had already gotten out of his chair in the center of a long table and was hobbling to the door as quickly as he could. Garric guessed that Royhas' foot had gone to sleep, though he might just be generally stiff from hours seated during tense discussions.

"It seemed to me," King Carus murmured with his usual chuckle, *"that the only times I wasn't wearing calluses on my butt listening to boring, crucial talk were the times I was in the field. Then I was mostly trying to sleep wrapped in my cloak and not let the rain rust my sword."*

"Your Majesty?" said Royhas over the scrape and murmur of hundreds of people getting to their feet. "Should you be up?"

"Yes," Garric said forcefully. He glared at Liane beside him. She covered a giggle with her hand. "Though I'll admit I seem to be the only one who thinks that."

The reception hall was the largest building in the palace compound. A line of slender pillars down the center of the main room supported a vaulted roof. Clerestory windows lighted the open area, while a portico to either side set off smaller rooms which could be used by officials or for private conferences.

The public entrance on the south side boasted an imposing porch whose pediment displayed the Lady's descent into the Underworld. The private entrance on the north was connected to the royal apartments by a closed passageway. Garric felt a little odd about using the royal suite, but Valence chose to stay in the secluded bungalow to which he'd retired before the crisis.

Besides, though Valence had recovered enough to become a figurehead—Garric *was* King of the Isles, in all but name.

Waldron and Attaper had come out of one of the conference rooms to the side and were walking toward Garric. The commanders themselves were professionally polite;

but the dozen aides in either man's train glared at their rivals in a rage just short of blows.

Garric knew from the visits he'd gotten as he convalesced that there were arguments over how the royal army should be reorganized. He hadn't realized until now quite how serious those arguments were.

"They don't have a million Monkeys from Bight sweeping down on them," murmured Carus in a grimly sympathetic tone. *"So they'll fight each other instead of looking a half-step ahead at the next real problem the kingdom will have to face."*

A moment later—with the usual laughter back—the voice in Garric's mind added, *"Or they would if it weren't for you in charge, lad; but you are."*

Ilna and the baron from Third Atara had been in the group talking to Royhas at the chancellor's table. They'd moved close to Garric, waiting for an opportunity to speak. *What* was the baron's name?

"Baron Robilard," Liane whispered in Garric's ear. Garric almost squeezed her hand in thanks for avoiding the embarrassment.

"Ilna," Garric said, "I haven't seen you since—"

He didn't know how to describe it. The night as a whole was a blur, though he had clear memories of individual moments:

The Beast waddling toward them, huge even while still distant.

The coarse hairs around the monster's claws and the way its skin dimpled as Garric's sword penetrated.

The tears glittering on Cerix's cheek as his mouth shouted phrases that he'd sworn he could not speak. . . .

"I haven't seen you since the other night," Garric concluded awkwardly. Ilna's crooked smile showed that she understood him perfectly. "And Baron Robilard, I still haven't received you as you deserve. I hope the staff has made you comfortable during the past few days?"

"The baron has been scouting the Monkeys with his warship *Erne,*" Ilna said. "He was hoping he might be able to report his findings to you, Prince Garric, though Lord Waldron—"

She turned, transfixing the oncoming noble with eyes as sharp as swordpoints.

"—has made it quite clear that he's in charge of naval matters as well as the army."

Waldron flushed. He'd been treating Robilard as young, foolish, and the ruler of one of the lesser islands. All of that was true, but Waldron might also have remembered that the baron was under the protection of Ilna os-Kenset.

She, never one to neglect kicking an enemy while he was down, added, "Even though as I understand it, the only warship in the Royal Fleet at the moment is the one Baron Robilard commands."

Attaper was far too professional to smirk. In a bland voice he said, "The Military Council thought it was best to integrate the rowers who escaped with the late Admiral Nitker into the city defenses. Though of course you'll want to review that decision and all the other ones we made, now that you're back on your feet, Your Majesty."

What had happened to Admiral Nitker? Not that Garric regretted the swine's passing, but blood feuds and lynch law were no way to run a kingdom.

Garric remembered Liane, standing alone in a flame-lit chamber. His teeth clenched and his hand reached reflexively for the hilt of his sword. The new sword; it should prove thoroughly satisfactory as soon as Garric was healthy enough to put its pattern-welded blade through its paces, but the balance wasn't quite that of the weapon he'd become used to. . . .

Garric laughed, surprising those around him even more than had his stark expression of a moment before. It bothered him that people were always watching him now. He didn't think he'd ever get used to that.

"Nor did I, lad," Carus whispered. *"But thank the Gods, I never came to like the attention either."*

"Blood feud is particularly a bad practice for a king to

indulge in," Garric said aloud. He tried to keep his tone cheerful. "Or even a prince."

He cleared his throat and went on, "I'm going to assume that Lord Nitker died of injuries received when he attacked the palace with a gang of kidnappers . . . but I don't want any more unexplained deaths. Do you all, my friends, understand?"

"Actually, he hanged himself because he was afraid of the queen's victory," Ilna said with a faint smile. She knew that she was the only person in the big room who could say that and be wholeheartedly believed. "Nitker seems to have made a career out of backing losers, himself included."

Garric and the king in his mind bellowed their laughter. Courtiers watched in amazement. This wasn't the sort of decorum expected in the royal court.

"They'll get used to it," Carus chuckled. *"Just as they'll get used to having a real king."*

Garric stepped to Robilard and took his hands. He tried not to wince openly as movement reminded him of his burns.

"Baron," Garric said, "the kingdom is in your debt for providing a naval force at a time we need one badly. Please, tell me the results of your scouting. I've heard only that the Hairy Men were no longer a threat. I'd appreciate the details."

That was true, but there was more in the statement than the words. Robilard swelled with pride, and Ilna's smile of satisfaction was for her a shower of thanks.

In Barca's Hamlet you helped your friends—in small things as well as large ones—because your friends were the ones who would help you. That was a good way to live, for a peasant or a king.

"Let's sit down, *please,*" Liane said. "Mistress Ladra and Tenoctris both said you should keep your legs raised as much as possible."

"If you want privacy, one of the side rooms can be emptied for you at once, Your Majesty," Royhas said.

"In fact—the Military Council was meeting in Room Seven until a few minutes ago, but I see that they've adjourned—"

The chancellor nodded to Attaper, Waldron, and their aides. He smiled innocently. It wasn't only minions of evil like the queen and the Beast who fought among themselves.

But that was going to stop.

"If you don't mind, Lord Royhas," Garric said, "I'll use your table here in the middle of things. I've been cooped up in bed for a day and a half now, and I'd like to have some space."

He gave Royhas precisely the sort of smile the chancellor had offered the soldiers. At the back of Garric's mind, King Carus clapped his hands together in delight.

Garric led the baron toward the table with painful caution. "The Monkeys had captured most of the royal fleet," Robilard said. "They'd apparently been towing the raft—parts of it—with the ships because the currents wouldn't actually push them to harbor, of course. . . ."

Courtiers elbowed servants aside to offer Garric and the baron seats. Garric's face stiffened, though he hoped those watching didn't realize the disgust he felt. "Please!" he called. "I can get my own chair!"

There was nothing wrong with service. Garric's family was among the most prosperous in Barca's Hamlet, and they all had served their neighbors at the inn. Anyone who entered the taproom with a copper in his hand had the right to tell Garric to draw him a jack of ale.

What offended Garric was the way rich folk were using the opportunity to serve Garric as a way of abasing themselves. A freeborn citizen didn't *do* that.

And if these courtiers didn't know what was obvious to any Haft peasant, then by the Lady! that was another thing they were going to learn.

"I thought we'd capture one of the ships and tow it back to Valles," Robilard was saying. "We shot some of the Monkeys aboard one—it was easy, they don't even know how to swim, it seems. But to tell the truth, we didn't have the stomach to finish the job. They just whimpered, and . . ."

Garric nodded as pulled out a chair for himself. It struck him as he sat that Baron Robilard might have more in his favor than had initially been obvious. From the appraising look the image of Carus wore as he listened through Garric's ears, Garric wasn't alone in reassessing his judgment.

Roses of a peach color like none Sharina had seen before covered the pergola. She touched one without plucking it, embarrassed that she and Cashel hadn't thought to step into the open air when the hunters and Zahag came to talk with them. Hanno had to squat in the archway because he was too tall to walk in without stooping.

"Seems like things are pretty well taken care of here, missie," Hanno said. "That's right, ain't it?"

He wasn't carrying his spear here in the palace nor did Unarc have his hooked fighting knife, though both men had their usual assortment of butchering blades thrust under their belts. They probably didn't regard the butcher knives as weapons, and—perhaps because of who the hunters' friends were—Garric's guards hadn't chosen to make a point of it.

Sharina carried the Pewle knife. Nobody said anything about that, either.

"That's right," she agreed. "The problem you and I knew about, the queen, is dead; and so is the other one, Tenoctris says."

Cashel watched Hanno with a respect that the big hunter reciprocated fully. They weren't afraid of each other; Sharina doubted that either man was afraid of anything he could fight. It made Sharina nervous to see them exchanging glances and wondering, even though she *knew* neither man would ever show the other anything but perfect courtesy.

Workmen—gardeners, stonemasons, carpenters, and a dozen other guild specialties—were busy all over the palace compound. Such bustling activity in what had been a wasteland amazed Sharina.

The daughter of Reise the Innkeeper was pleased to see run-down, overgrown structures being cleaned and made right. The innkeeper's daughter also found herself totting up what the work must be costing—at Valles wage-scales, too!

Still, even more than the crowds cheering in the streets, these repairs meant that people believed in the new government.

Sharina remembered where she was. The men and even Zahag were staring at her, though the ape did it while upside down. He hung from a nearby archway commemorating a ruler who'd been lost at sea three centuries past. Unarc saw Sharina look at him directly. He immediately went back to what he'd been doing before: staring fiercely at a stone planter as his big toe probed the acanthus vines carved on the side.

"I was just thinking," Sharina explained in embarrassment. "That people believe in Prince Garric of Haft."

"Huh!" Cashel said. "They'd be fools not to."

He gave her a slow smile, an expression that Hanno echoed unconsciously. "They'd be worse fools," he added, "to let me hear that they didn't."

Four fully equipped Blood Eagles stood politely out of earshot. They kept an eye on the surroundings in general, but particularly on the group at the pergola. Sharina supposed she and her companions were dignitaries being guarded from attacks like the one Admiral Nitker had made, though how could four ordinary humans think they were going to protect men like these?

She giggled. "I'm sorry, Hanno," she said. "I'm still—"

"Recovering" wasn't the right word. "I'm still just so happy to be free that I'm not paying attention to things the way I ought to be."

"I guess you did that all right the times it mattered, missie," the big hunter said. He cleared his throat. "Thing is, me and Unarc don't belong here, though I guess we'll stay for the partying tonight."

The bald hunter nodded violently, though he didn't turn his head toward the others. Now that Sharina was in a palace, she supposed she'd reverted in Unarc's mind to being a woman.

"You're going back to Bight?" she said. "Of course. I'll help you in any way I can, replacing your boat and the rest of your kit certainly. And anything else you'd like. You saved my life, both of you."

Sharina wasn't sure how she went about getting actual money in her present circumstances, but she'd find a way. *That* she was sure of.

Hanno cleared his throat and looked away. He pushed his index finger into the soil for no better reason than why Unarc was polishing stone flowers with his toe.

"To tell the truth, missie," the big hunter said awkwardly, "we figured we'd try someplace different. It's not like either of us liked the Monkeys, you see, but it just didn't seem like Bight would be the same without them. We thought maybe Sirimat instead. There's ivorywood trees there, the ape says."

Zahag dropped from the arch with a grace that belied his size. He joined the group in a four-limbed, sideways shuffle. Hanno stood and moved aside to make room for him.

"In big slabs, ivorywood's worth more than real teeth are," the ape said, looking at the ground also. "That's because the trees eat animals, and they're just as willing to swallow woodcutters as they are baby apes that haven't learned to keep clear."

Zahag parted the hair on his thighs with two fingers of each hand, apparently searching for fleas. "I thought maybe I'd go along with them, chief," he mumbled. "To show them around, you know."

Cashel stood and walked forward to squat in front of

Zahag. ''That's a good idea,'' he said. ''And if you did that, maybe you'd get to see your own band again.''

''I might,'' Zahag said, nodding. He looked worriedly at Cashel. ''It's not that I want to leave *you,* chief. There'll never be another chief like you!''

''Oh, I guess Master Hanno might have another idea about that,'' Cashel said. He chuckled, but Sharina noticed the sudden throatiness that entered the sound. ''And I'd say he might be right, though we'll never know.''

''You got that right,'' Hanno said, looking toward the horizon. ''We'll never know.''

Cashel squeezed the ape on both shoulders. ''Tell your family that Cashel or-Kenset was honored to have you in his band,'' he said. ''And if I ever learn somebody's caught you and means to sell you like a sheep again, well . . .''

Cashel didn't have the imagination or the need to complete the threat in graphic terms. He got up and moved back beside Sharina, though he didn't sit. His fingers caressed the quarterstaff leaning against the latticework frame of the pergola.

One of the iron ferrules had vanished when Cashel broke Sharina's imprisonment, though the flash had only scorched the hickory. The first thing Cashel had done on their return was to have the Blood Eagles' farrier replace the missing cap.

''Well, we'll get on,'' Hanno said. ''My credit with the outfitters is good, but if there's anything they can't handle, maybe we'll come to you, missie.''

He nodded toward two extremely young maids in fringed and colored tunics. They'd appeared while Sharina and her companions were talking. The maids shifted their weight nervously from one sandaled foot to the other, exactly like children in need of a latrine.

''Guess they'd like to speak with you,'' Hanno said. He dipped his head in what was closer to a bow than a nod.

''Honored to have met you, Master Cashel,'' the big

hunter went on. "The missie's got the most impressive friends I ever thought to meet."

"She was lucky to have friends as good as you and Master Unarc when she needed them," Cashel said. His voice was unusually deep and rasping. "And I guess you know that I'll give you any help I can. Ever."

The hunters and Zahag walked away, talking among themselves. Unarc's voice drifted back to the pergola: ". . . but I tell you, what *wouldn't* people pay to see it?"

The maids watched to make sure that the trio wasn't returning. Then they hopped forward, curtsied, and almost in unison began, "Lady Sharina—"

They stopped, looking at each other in horror. They were very nervous.

"You first," Sharina said, pointing to the maid on the right. She didn't like palaces and she particularly didn't like palace protocol.

She grinned. Though it wasn't so long ago that she'd been in places that she liked even less. Her hand found Cashel's and squeezed it.

"There's to be a sacrifice of thanksgiving for Prince Garric's recovery, lady," the maid blurted in a singsong. "He's gotten up and wants to thank the Gods first thing. He'd like you and . . ."

She looked at Cashel and froze.

"Lord *Cashel*!" the other maid hissed. Cashel winced.

"Lord Cashel and all his other friends to join him in the procession," the girl racketed on, "and *we're* the ones who found you!"

Cashel led Sharina from the pergola. "You'd best go with them and put on the kind of clothes they'll want you in," he said. "I'll find Tenoctris—I know where she is. We'll be along."

He touched her hand again. Turning aside, he muttered, "I guess I've got more to thank the Gods for than anybody else."

Cashel walked off, moving faster than he usually did.

"I don't know that you do, my friend," Sharina whispered. To the maids she said, ''Will you lead me to my apartments, then, mistresses?''

Giggling in delight, the girls skipped off down the flagstone walk.

''Excuse me, Mistress Ilna?'' said an attendant with pale skin and hair the texture of raw silk, standing at her elbow. He was one of the clerks who'd been on duty at the palace entrance when Ilna and her party arrived. This afternoon she'd thought he was simply hurrying past.

''Yes?'' she said sharply. She was in a bad mood, but there didn't seem to be much she could do about it.

Robilard and Lord Hosten were talking with Attaper, Waldron, and a score of earnest younger men in one of the side rooms of the hall. Ilna was welcome—there or anywhere else in the palace, Garric had made clear as he went off to have his bandages changed before leading a procession to one of the temples for a sacrifice.

The talk was of no interest to Ilna, and the room was packed like a sheepfold in winter, so she'd stayed in the main hall instead. There was nothing for her to do here either.

''There's a man outside the hall asking you to come out to him, mistress,'' the attendant said. His cautious respect showed that he was experienced at intruding on people who might not be in the best of moods, and who had the power to give their anger concrete expression. ''He says he's not a beggar, and I thought I should pass the message . . .''

''If he wants to see me, why doesn't he—'' Ilna began. She remembered the reception hall's stepped entrance; and realized a number of things at the same time.

''Ah,'' she said. ''No, Master Cerix isn't a beggar. In fact, you owe your life to him, sir.''

Ilna started for the entrance. Over her shoulder she added, ''Which you may think is more valuable than I do!''

That wasn't fair, though perhaps the attendant would be a little slower to assume that a cripple was a beggar. Besides, even when she was in a better mood Ilna had never set much store by fairness.

Cerix was in his chair at the edge of the pavement before the reception hall. The porticoes around it were crowded by hawkers and spectators getting out of the bright sun. Without someone to protect him, the crippled wizard would be repeatedly kicked and buffeted by people who weren't paying attention—which meant most people, in Ilna's experience.

"Thank you, mistress," Cerix said. "I—"

A man with coarsely woven scarves draped over his arm stepped between them. The fabric had been painted—of all things!—with what was supposed to be a picture of Prince Garric.

"Here you go, mistress!" the man said in a voice better suited to shouting across the crowded plaza. "The true likeness of the savior of Valles!"

Ilna's face went rigid. Without speaking, she took three short cords from her sleeve and began knotting them.

"Or perhaps you'd like the Lady Liane, the savior's—" the hawker said. Ilna drew the cords tight in front of him.

"Let's go somewhere with fewer people in it," she said to Cerix. Guards stepped aside as she wheeled the wizard's chair from the public area of the palace into the gardens reserved for residents of the compound. Behind them the hawker stood with glazed eyes, methodically picking his wares into a pile of oakum.

Ilna turned into a semicircular grotto where water fountained from the urns of bronze nymphs. The tendrils of weeping willows formed a screen for those sitting on the stone benches—or in the present case, sitting and squatting respectively beside the stone benches.

"I wanted to say good-bye to you, mistress," Cerix said. He looked drawn, but his clothing didn't smell of the drug he'd used in the past. "There's no reason for me to stay here, so I'm going back to the Garden. Halphemos will be waiting there and, well . . ."

He patted his stumps with a wry smile.

Ilna didn't speak for a moment. "Ah," she said at last. "I can see why you'd want to do that, Master Cerix, but . . ."

She grimaced. "I'm scarcely the person to tell others how to live their lives, am I?" she said. "Is there anything I can do for you before you . . . ?"

"No, no," Cerix said. "Though if you'd tell the others for me I'd appreciate it. I'd tell them myself, but they're busy."

He smiled. "And besides, they wouldn't understand."

Ilna nodded. "I've learned to expect that about most people and most things," she said. She stood. "Can I at least move you somewhere?"

Cerix looked around. "No, this will do very well," he said. "It's particularly fitting, in fact."

"Yes, I can see it might be," Ilna said. "In that case, I'll leave you to your business. Remember me to Halphemos, if you would. Though I suppose he'll have more than enough to occupy him in what he'll think is paradise."

"Halphemos won't have forgotten you, mistress," the wizard said. "Nor will I."

Ilna brushed through the willow fronds. There was soft *plop* behind her. She turned. Cerix's wheeled chair remained in the grotto, but the only thing on it was a peach blossom of remarkable size.

She stared at the bloom for a moment, then picked it up and tucked the twig behind her ear. She smiled. What would the people in Barça's Hamlet think?

An attendant was leading Baron Robilard toward her. "Ah, mistress!" he called. "The procession is about to set out for the temple of the Lady of the Boundaries. We've been invited to join Prince Garric at the high altar. May I escort you?"

"I'll go there with you, but I think I'll watch with the crowd, Baron," Ilna said. She gave him her arm. "I have a great deal of experience at looking down on other people. I like myself better when I'm looking up at them instead."

When Cashel realized that Tenoctris hadn't heard him coming up the path, he tapped one of the wooden pillars. Half a dozen towhees flashed their russet sides as they flew into the bushes.

"What?" said Tenoctris, looking up from the game board. She'd been concentrating so completely that she hadn't seen Cashel standing directly across from her. "Oh, Cashel. Is everything all right?"

Tenoctris had chosen to live in a storage building at one end of a long open shelter used for outdoor parties. A table under the shelter now held the game set she and Cashel had found when they'd returned to the queen's mansion the day before.

"Garric is going to give thanks at the temple just down the road," Cashel said. "I know you don't . . ."

He turned his head. He liked Tenoctris a lot, so he didn't want to say anything that he'd been raised to think was an insult.

"You don't talk much about the Gods," Cashel mumbled. "But I thought maybe you'd like to come. I know Garric would like you there."

Tenoctris got up from her stool and winced. "I've been sitting too long, that's clear," she said.

A ceramic mug and a wide-mouthed jar sat on the table beside her. After draining the mug, Tenoctris dipped a second draft and emptied it almost as greedily.

"I should at least remember to drink when I'm working," she said as she set the mug down.

Her face sobered. She walked around the table to put her hand on Cashel's. "I've seen various powers, Cashel," she said. "I've never seen the Gods. But neither have I ever believed that because I don't see something, it doesn't exist."

"Well, I'm not a priest," Cashel said, still looking at the ground.

"We have a great deal to be thankful for, and I'd regret not showing my appreciation to any power which had helped," the old wizard said decisively. "I'll get ready at once."

Tenoctris grinned. "That is, if I can find my maid. I chose the woman because she doesn't seem disturbed by my work."

She nodded to the game board. Cashel had carried it with great care from the queen's mansion, but the pieces showed no inclination to slide on the slick tourmaline surface. He wondered if they'd have fallen off even if he'd turned the board upside down.

"That seems to be the woman's only virtue, however," Tenoctris went on. "Fortunately I don't put many demands on her."

Birds scratched and chattered on the shelter's roof. Reconstruction plans hadn't gotten to this part of the compound yet. That was another of the reasons Tenoctris had picked it to live in.

Cashel was more comfortable here too. Flowers were all well and good; he *liked* them. But it didn't seem right to grow flowers on a scale larger than any barley field in the borough.

Tenoctris was still staring at the game board. It had caught her again when she glanced in its direction.

"The queen used the board for prediction," Tenoctris said. "I've tried to count the number of pieces, but I can't. The alignments seem to change every time I blink or look away. Several hundred, certainly."

Her index finger dipped toward a counter with a bubbled surface. It had melted onto the square where it rested. "I wonder if the queen realized that she too was a pawn?"

Cashel shrugged. The board had appeared in the queen's private quarters at some time after he and Tenoctris first explored the mansion. Somebody could have evaded the handful of guards to slip the object into the empty room, but Cashel couldn't imagine why anyone would have wanted to do that.

"I think we ought to get moving, Tenoctris," Cashel said apologetically. He should, at least. He wanted to listen to people shout the praises of Garric and Sharina, his friends.

"Yes, of course," Tenoctris said. She pinched a bit of her sleeve and looked at it critically. "Perhaps just a dress tunic over this one rather than a complete ensem—"

She stopped speaking and locked her attention back on the board. Cashel had seen it too, in the corner of his eye: not movement, because none of the counters had moved, but *change*.

Cashel had a good eye for physical relationships. He'd often scanned a woodline or a pasture full of sheep, noticing at once if something wasn't in the place where he expected to find it.

"That piece wasn't there before," he said, extending his finger to point.

"Don't touch it, Cashel!" Tenoctris said.

"No ma'am," he replied. "I wasn't going to."

The counter was a bead of black glass, maybe obsidian. It seemed to shimmer. Cashel cocked his head to look at it from the side. At one angle, the smooth surface flared into dazzling iridescence.

Cashel stepped back, putting both hands on his quarterstaff. "What's it mean, Tenoctris?" he asked.

"I don't know," she said. "This board is a work of great power, but I'm not sure that it's really as informative as the queen probably thought it was. Certainly it didn't help her very much in the end."

The grin she gave Cashel looked a little forced. "Come, help me rummage through the clothespresses that Liane has kindly showered me with and see if we can find something suitable to wear."

She stepped briskly toward her living quarters. Cashel

glanced again at the wickedly gleaming counter. He shrugged, smiled, and followed Tenoctris.

The drums at the head of the procession beat a tattoo, setting the pace for the company of the royal army marching directly behind the band. At every tenth step the trumpets blared as well. The sound never failed to startle Garric but his mount, a big roan gelding, merely flicked its ears at the brassy din.

"A proper warhorse you've got here, lad," whispered King Carus. *"We'll have other use for him shortly, if I'm any judge."*

Gripping a horse with blistered legs was savagely uncomfortable. He tried not to wince at each measured step.

"King Garric!" cried the crowd lining both sides of the street and looking down from the roofs of buildings on the route. "Long live King Garric!"

The highest officials of the government walked before him. The former conspirators, now the chiefs of the Prince's Council, wore their court robes. As a mark of respect they were on foot rather than mounted or in litters.

Garric's friends walked with them. Tenoctris had a robe of splendid silk brocade. She seemed cheerfully able to keep the slow pace, but Cashel was on one side of her and Sharina on the other. They'd make sure Tenoctris was all right, though Garric hated to see her walking.

"It isn't right for any of them to have to walk!" he muttered.

Carus' memories of other processions in a score of other cities cascaded through his mind. Twice Garric recognized a building: a ruin from the Carcosa of his day, and a block of Valles where the present structures rose from the massive foundations of the Old Kingdom.

The cheering crowds were interchangeable.

"King Garric! Long live King Garric!"

"It's part of your duty," whispered King Carus. His visage, a shadow in his descendant's mind, was grim in

a way that it never was during battle and slashing danger. *''Do it for the same reason you sleep in the rain and listen to arguments in inheritance cases that are so complicated your friend Ilna couldn't find the truth in them. Do it because it's your duty.''*

Attaper shouted an order. The detachment of Blood Eagles marching at the end of the procession clashed their spears against their shield bosses and bellowed, ''Hail Garric! Hail Garric!''

''But never,'' the ancient king added in a tone as harsh as an eagle's scream, *''let yourself start to like it!''*

Epilogue

The storm had passed, but the gray sea still churned and a stiff breeze lifted streamers of froth. Gulls riding the waves had their heads tucked tight against their breasts.

A wizard stood in the air, rising and falling with the surge but never touched by the water. He chanted with his arms extended before him. At each syllable, purple lightning crackled from the fingers of one hand to the other.

The sea beneath the wizard humped as though with a slow swell. Instead of settling again, it continued to rise. Gulls lifted in squawking terror, their wings beating heavily for altitude.

An ammonite the size of a small island rose to the surface, its scores of tentacles spreading before it in a vast carpet. From most angles the coiled shell was black, but the touch of the setting sun licked an unearthly radiance from the wet nacre.

The wizard stood on the back of the monster he had called to him. He raised his head, and the heavens echoed with his laughter.

The deeps trembled, shaking a belfry which hadn't moved for a thousand years. Eels with glassy flesh and huge, staring eyes twisted, touched by fear of the power focused on the sunken island. Cold light pulsed across their slender bodies.

A bell rang, sending its note over the sunken city. It had been cast from the bronze rams of warships captured by the first Duke of Yole. A tripod fish lifted its long pelvic fins from the bottom and swam off with stiff sweeps of its tail.

Ammonites, the Great Ones of the Deep, swam slowly toward the sound. They had tentacles like cuttlefish and shells coiled like rams' horns. The largest of them were the size of a ship.

The powers supporting the cosmos shifted, sending shudders through a city which nothing had touched for a millennium. The bell rang a furious tocsin over Yole.

The island was rising.

The Great Ones' tentacles waved like forests of serpents in time with words agitating the sea. In daylight their curled shells would shimmer with all the colors of the sun. Here the only light was the distant shimmer of a viperfish flashing in terror as it fled.

The dead lay in the streets, sprawled as they had fallen. Over them were scattered roof tiles and the rubble of walls which collapsed as the city sank. Onrushing water had choked their screams, and their outstretched arms clutched for a salvation which had eluded them.

The bodies had not decayed: these cold depths were as hostile to the minute agents of corruption as they were to humans. Some corpses had been savaged by great-fanged seawolves which had swept into the city on the crest of the engulfing wave; other victims had been pulled into the beaks of the Great Ones and there devoured. For the most part, though, the corpses were whole except where sluggish, long-legged crabs had picked at them.

Tides of light touched the drowned buildings and gave them color. Faint tinges of blue brightened as the island rose. At last even the rooftiles regained their ruddy tinge.

The Great Ones swam slowly upward, accompanying Yole on its return. The movements of their tentacles twisted the cosmos.

The belfry of the Duke's palace, the highest edifice in Yole, broke surface. Water cascaded from stones darkened by the slime which crawled along the sea's deepest trenches.

Moments later the Great Ones surfaced, their shells a shimmering iridescence in the dawnlight. They swam slowly outward so as not to be trapped by the rising land. The S-shaped pupils of their eyes stared unwinking at the circle of wizards who stood in the air above the rising city.

Three of the wizards wore black robes with high-peaked cowls over their heads. Their faces and bare hands were blackened with a pigment of soot and tallow. Only their teeth showed white as they chanted words of power:

"*Lemos agrule euros* . . ."

Three wizards were in robes of bleached wool, white in shadow and a mixture of rose-pink and magenta where the low sun colored the fabric. They had smeared their skin with white lead so that their eyes were dark pits in the ghastly pallor of their faces.

"*Ptolos xenos gaiea* . . ." the wizards chanted.

The earth rumbled. Torrents thundered from doorways and windows of Yole, spilling in echoing gouts along the broad steets that led to the harbor. Corpses flopped and twisted in the foaming water. Each syllable could be heard over the chaos, though the words came from human throats.

The wizards' leader was black on his left side, white on the right. He chanted the words of power which his fellows echoed, syllable by syllable. From the brazier standing before him, strands of black smoke and white smoke rose, interweaving but remaining discrete.

"*Kata pheinra thenai . . .*"

Facing the leader was a mummified figure whose head the wizards had unbandaged. The mummy's sere brown skin bore the pattern of tiny scales, and the dried lips were thin and reptilian. Its tongue, shrunken to a forked string, flickered as the figure chanted. Words of power came from its dead throat.

The belfry continued to shudder, but the bell's voice was lost in the greater cataclysm. Sea birds wheeled in the air, summoned from afar as the sea thundered away from the newly risen land.

"*Kata, cheiro, iofide . . .*" chanted the wizards.

The ghost of a pierced screen hung in the air beyond the wizards, a filigree of stone that wavered in and out of focus. The screen's reality was that of another time and place, but the incantation had drawn it partway with the wizards.

The soil of Yole touched the wizards' feet. The island gave a further convulsive shudder, then ceased to rise. Waves, shaken away by Yole's reappearance, returned to slap its shore in a fury that slowly beat itself quiescent.

In the harbor the Great Ones floated. Their tentacles waved in a ghastly parody of a dance.

Gulls and frigate birds dived and rose again in shrieking delight. Yole's rise had swept creatures of the deep to the surface faster than their bodies could respond to the changes in pressure. Birds carried away the ruptured carcasses in their beaks.

The six lesser wizards collapsed on the dripping cobblestones of a plaza, gasping in exhaustion from the weight of the spell they had executed. Their leader raised his arms high and shouted, *"Theeto worshe acheleou!"*

Momentary silence smothered the world, stilling the waves and even the screams of the gulls. Sunlight winked on the armor of soldiers and the jewelry of ladies who had arrayed themselves in their finest, not knowing that they were dressing for their own deaths. A child's hand still clutched an ivory rattle; it too gleamed in the sun.

The leading wizard remained standing. His mad peals of laughter rang across the dead city.

The mummy stood also, motionless now and silent. Its sunken eyes were on the wizard, and its reptilian features were twisted into a mask of fury.

Garric's body continued sleeping on the couch in the conference room. His mind got up from it and strolled out of the building. He didn't have any control over his movements, though that didn't concern him at the moment. He supposed he was dreaming.

Garric's legs swung in their usual long stride, but he was moving faster than a walking man and not travelling through space alone. He recognized all the places he passed, but many were in Barca's Hamlet, not Valles, and some were from out of the waking world.

The people Garric met were shadows, but sometimes they spoke to him and he replied. He couldn't hear the exchanges, even the words that came from his own lips.

He was alone for the first time since his father had given him a coronation medal of King Carus. When Garric hung that ancient gold disk against his chest, he and Carus had begun to share an existence closer than twins, closer than spouses. But now—

Garric felt for the medallion. It lay back with his sleeping self. He straightened his shoulders and let the dream carry him where it would.

He reached a bridge and started across. Behind him was Valles; beyond . . . he couldn't be sure. Sometimes Garric saw shining walls; other glimpses were of ruins which might once have been the same buildings. The structure underfoot felt more solid than stone, though to Garric's eyes he was walking on a tracery of blue light, a fairy glow without substance.

Garric reached the far end of the bridge. It was daylight here, though it had been early dusk in Valles when he left his couch. Before him was a city which at the time of its glory must have been magnificent; it was breathtaking even now. He strode toward it.

Modern Valles might be larger; Carcosa in the days of King Carus and the Old Kingdom was far greater yet. In the richness of its fittings, though, nothing Garric knew from his own day or the past could compare with what this place must once have been.

He was walking up an esplanade paved with slabs of red granite, each as wide as Garric was tall and twice as long. The labor of cutting and smoothing such hard stone made him blink.

The blocks were cocked and broken, by time and the roots of trees crawling from the median plantings. The surface should have been as hard to walk on as a seascape frozen in the middle of a lashing storm. In this dream existence, the footing didn't hinder Garric.

Pedestrian porticos flanked the roadway. Some of the arches had collapsed. The core was fitted stones rather than the concrete and rubble of similar constructions in ancient Carcosa.

The buildings to either side were stone also, but originally metal had covered them. Some had worn tin, decayed now to powdery tendrils trailing from the cracks between close-fitting blocks. Others had been clad in sheets of copper and bronze whose blue-green revenants still stained the walls.

Garric frowned. He'd heard of this place, but as a myth of the final days before the fall of the Old Kingdom, a fragment from a discourse of the philosopher Andron, captured in a quirky anonymous compendium entitled *The Dress of All Peoples in All Times*. He couldn't remember the exact words or the claimed location, but he recalled the description of residents wearing striped clothing which reflected variously according to the color of the mirroring walls they passed beside. .

A dream of a myth? *These* ruins had a solid reality.

He walked toward the vast building at the end of the esplanade. The three stages of its façade were supported by pillars of equal height, but those of the middle level were more slender than the massive columns beneath them, while delicate pairs of banded travertine chosen for appearance rather than strength formed the uppermost range. The wooden casements and shutters of the upper-story windows had rotted to dust.

The ground-floor entrance was recessed deeply within a pointed arch, but the door itself was small and so strongly made that it yet survived. Flanking the porch were fountains. Rains had left a stagnant scum in the or-ichalc basins, but the bronze statues from which water had once played were twists of verdigris which gave no hint of their former shapes.

The city was silent save for the wind soughing through the walls.

A broad helical staircase twisted from the ground to the building's roof. The pillared tower was styled to match the main structure, but the two were only connected at the top.

Garric climbed the stairs. Their pitch was shallow, too shallow for his long legs, and should have been uncom-fortable. In his present dream state he only noticed what he had no muscles to feel.

He wondered if King Carus missed Garric's presence as much as Garric did his. Did Carus even realize that Garric was gone?

As Garric mounted the stairs, his view of the city through the columns broadened. The streets were laid out in concentric circles centered on this building, though the docks of what had been a thriving seaport ate an arc out of one edge. The ships were gone, but the quays and stone bollards remained. The port didn't have sloping ramps up which oar-driven warships could be drawn to prevent their light hulls from decaying while not in use.

At the very edge of his vision Garric thought he saw a wall of shimmering light like that which formed the bridge. It was too faint for him to be sure. Though daylight suffused the sky, there was no sun.

Garric stepped onto the roof. It was covered with granite like the boulevard and esplanade, but these slabs were as nearly level as the common table in Reise's inn. The foundations must sink down to the bowels of the earth.

The roof was a vast plaza decorated by a score of stone planters like buttons tucking the horsehair of an upholstered seat. Grass and weeds grew in them now, and from one sprouted a twisted appletree—the progeny many times removed of the tree placed there when the building was new. Roots had burst out the sides of other planters in the distant past, spilling the soil for rains to wash into a film of mud; only the lone apple had been able to reseed itself.

The roof was an audience ground. At the end opposite the staircase was a chamber with a screen of pierced alabaster for its outward-curving front wall. Garric walked toward it, his feet taking him where he would have gone of his own volition.

The translucent alabaster was no more than a finger's thickness. Light both reflected from and refracted through the milky stone, giving the air a soap-bubble sheen. The piercings were not simple holes or even a repetitive pattern. As Garric stepped close he saw a tracery of images, each as subtle and unique as the starlings of a flock wheeling in autumn.

The cut-out shapes had meaning—of that Garric was sure. His conscious mind couldn't grasp what the meaning was, however. Would Tenoctris understand?

The screen permitted citizens to see and hear their ruler close at hand, while still preventing them from touching him—or her, Garric supposed. It was carved from a seamless sheet of alabaster and had no door. A twig with a few dried leaves was caught in one of the small holes.

In ancient Carcosa the King of the Isles addressed the people assembled in the Field of Heroes from a high balcony on the back of the palace. Since the Dukes of Ornifal had become Kings of the Isles, they'd practiced a cooler sort of kinship. The populace had seen Valence III in formal processions and at ceremonies before the great temples, but he'd never addressed them directly. Anything the king had to say to his people came through the mouths of underlings.

That was going to change. It had *already* changed, beginning the day a combination of pragmatism and fear forced Valence to adopt Garric as his son and successor. Garric thought the idea of a podium or high balcony was a better choice than this screen, but the notion was an interesting one.

The screened audience chamber had solid walls on the other three sides. The windows in the sidewalls had screens of electrum filigree, and the door in the back wall had a grate over the viewport.

The room was empty save for dust and a bier of travertine marble. Discolored patches on the floor showed where bronze hardware had decayed. What—

Garric stepped through the alabaster as he had the door of the conference room when he started this journey. He felt momentary surprise, but he was too busy taking in his changed surroundings to marvel at inconsequentials.

Now that Garric was inside, he saw a plump old man in a tasseled tunic on the bier. Over him a serpentine shape waxed and waned, never fully visible but casting a glow like a golden blanket.

The old man's eyes opened. He rose with a cheery smile, pulling with him a tail of the quilted velvet covering the stone. "Good day, sir!" he said, extending his arm to clasp Garric's. "And who would you be?"

The old man paused. His smile slipped into an expression half-wary, half-peevish. "Or have we met? Do I know you? Tell me!"

It was late evening. The sky, visible through the electrum grating, was a sullen red. Crowds were looking up from the streets. Ships packed the quays, moored several deep in some cases, but no vessels were under way in the harbor.

"Sir, I don't think we've met," Garric said. He stepped forward, offering his arm though the old man had jerked his own back as doubt struck him. "I'm Garric or-Reise of Haft."

He swallowed. "But I think I'm dreaming."

The old man's smile returned like the sun flashing after a summer shower. They clasped, hand to elbow so that their forearms joined. The old man's grip was firm; his flesh resilient and vaguely warm.

"Dreaming?" he said to Garric. "Nonsense! You're here, aren't you? How can you be dreaming?"

The room was the same as when Garric viewed it through the alabaster, except that now signs of occupancy littered it. A cushioned pad covered the bier, and wooden bookcases lined all three walls: shelves for codices and pigeonholes for scrolls.

The cases were empty. Here and there a locked screen hung askew, wrenched off as the library was ransacked with brutal haste.

Garric stepped back. The old man looked around him with dawning puzzlement. "Sir, may I ask your name?" Garric said politely.

"What?" said the old man, again with a querulous tone. "I'm Ansalem, of course!"

He'd been looking at the glowing shape rippling in and out of existence above the bier. It seemed to be a serpent with a short, fat body, but sometimes the head appeared to be on one end, sometimes on the other.

Ansalem paused and fingered a wall niche large enough to have held a life-sized statue. It, like the bookcases, was empty. ''I think I am, at least,'' he said. ''But I don't understand. If I'm Ansalem the Wise . . .''

He turned to Garric, his face wrinkling in an expression of concern foreign to it. ''If I am, then where are my books? And where are the baubles I've gathered over the years?''

Ansalem's expression flowed suddenly into something as cold and inhuman as the ice of a pond at midwinter. ''Have you taken them?'' he demanded. ''You must return them at once! They're objects of power. They aren't safe for anyone to have, you see. I know better than to use them, but anyone else might—''

He snapped his pudgy fingers in a sound as sharp as nearby lightning. ''—blast this world to dust! I'm not joking, young man. You must return them at once!''

''Sir,'' Garric said. ''I haven't taken your property or anyone else's. I just arrived, and I don't even know where I am.''

His mouth was dry. Ansalem was as unpredictable as the sky in summer, changing from sun to storm before a shepherd has time to call his flock.

And for all his general good nature, Ansalem was more dangerous than any storm. Garric didn't recognize the name, but he knew that the old man was a wizard. If he'd brought Garric here, he was a wizard of incalculable power.

''Where you are?'' Ansalem said, his sunny disposition reasserting itself. ''Why, you're in Klestis, in my palace. Don't you know?''

He gestured broadly. That made him notice the empty cases again; his face slipped back into a worried frown. ''Where can—''

Ansalem stopped. He fixed Garric with an analytical gaze and took the youth's chin between finger and thumb. He twisted Garric's head from one profile to the other.

Garric accepted the attention, though he felt a surge of anger at being treated like a sheep being sold. Ansalem was an old man and obviously confused.

Ansalem wasn't a bit more confused than Garric, though, if it came to that.

"Are you sure I don't know you?" Ansalem asked, not harshly but with a note of sharp interest. "Surely we've met! Now where, I wonder?"

He turned to the bookcase on his right, obviously reaching for a volume that was no longer there. He froze, his face taking on the terrible icy hardness Garric had seen before.

"Where are my acolytes?" Ansalem demanded. "Have you seen them, Master Garric? Purlio will know what's going on here."

"Sir, I don't know anything," Garric said. "I've never heard of you, and the only Klestis I know of is a fishing village on the south coast of Cordin."

"Fishing village indeed!" Ansalem said in a tone of amazement. He beckoned Garric to the window looking onto the harbor. "Does this look like a fishing village, sir?"

"No sir," Garric said, "but—"

"But what's wrong down there?" Ansalem said, looking himself at the scene and finding it different from whatever he'd meant to show Garric. "Everyone's standing in the streets and staring up . . ."

He spun on Garric with another flash of mercurial temper. "What have you done with my acolytes?" Ansalem said. "Purlio, come here at once!"

"I—" Garric said.

Ansalem stepped to the bier from which Garric had awakened him. He ran his hand through the air, seeming to caress the flickering serpent. "The amphisbaena is here," he said, "but not the other objects. Some of them are too dangerous to use, even for me! Don't you understand?"

Ansalem patted the tall niche, then touched other alcoves and ran his fingers over the top of a marble plinth standing empty beside the door in the back of the chamber. He moved with the quick, jerky motions of a toad hopping, desperate in its terror.

"You must bring them back!" Ansalem said. "They won't do you any good, I assure you. There's nothing there but destruction for whoever uses them!"

The chamber grew foggy as another world began to interpenetrate it. "Bring me . . ." Ansalem cried in a voice as high as a distant gull's.

The words faded. Garric felt his soul rushing back the way it had come. He was a shimmer in existence like the current of a rushing stream.

"Garric?" a voice said. Not Ansalem, but—

Garric opened his eyes. He lay on a bench in the conference room. Liane stood beside him, holding a lamp; the light through the open door was the last red of sunset. His friends were watching him with guarded concern: Cashel and Sharina, Tenoctris and Ilna; and Liane, thank the Lady; Liane, her worry clear in her dark, limpid eyes.

"I was dreaming," Garric said as he sat up cautiously. "And I'm *very* glad to see you all."